Wrestling with Shylock

Shakespeare's *The Merchant of Venice* occupies a unique place in world culture. The fictional, albeit iconic, character of Shylock has been interpreted as exotic outsider, social pariah, melodramatic villain, and tragic victim. The play, which has been performed and read in dozens of languages, has served as a lens for examining ideas and images of the Jew at various historical moments. In the last two hundred years, many of the play's stage interpreters, spectators, readers, and adapters have themselves been Jews, whose responses are often embedded in literary, theatrical, and musical works. This volume examines the ever-expanding body of Jewish responses to one of Shakespeare's most complex and popular plays.

Edna Nahshon is Professor of Theatre and Drama at the Jewish Theological Seminary in New York City and Senior Associate at Oxford's Centre for Hebrew and Jewish Studies.

Michael Shapiro is Emeritus Professor of English at the University of Illinois, where he was a founder and director of the Program in Jewish Culture and Society.

Wrestling with Shylock

Jewish Responses to The Merchant of Venice

Edited by

EDNA NAHSHON

Jewish Theological Seminary

MICHAEL SHAPIRO

University of Illinois

CAMBRIDGE
UNIVERSITY PRESS

CAMBRIDGE
UNIVERSITY PRESS

University Printing House, Cambridge CB2 8BS, United Kingdom
One Liberty Plaza, 20th Floor, New York, NY 10006, USA
477 Williamstown Road, Port Melbourne, VIC 3207, Australia
4843/24, 2nd Floor, Ansari Road, Daryaganj, Delhi – 110002, India
79 Anson Road, #06-04/06, Singapore 079906

Cambridge University Press is part of the University of Cambridge.

It furthers the University's mission by disseminating knowledge in the pursuit of education, learning, and research at the highest international levels of excellence.

www.cambridge.org
Information on this title: www.cambridge.org/9781107010277

10.1017/9780511845789

First published 2017

Printed in the United States of America by Sheridan Books, Inc.

A catalogue record for this publication is available from the British Library.

ISBN 978-1-107-01027-7 Hardback

To our families – past, present, and future

Contents

Illustrations

Figures

Table

Contributors

Susan Chevlowe is Curator and Director of the Derfner Judaica Museum and the art collection at Hebrew Home in Riverdale, New York. She taught Jewish Art and Visual Culture for more than ten years at the Jewish Theological Seminary, where she also served on the Arts Advisory Board. In 2009, she oversaw the completion of the Derfner Judaica Museum and organized its inaugural exhibition, *Tradition and Remembrance: Treasures of the Derfner Judaica Museum*, which explored the intersections of history and memory through objects interpreted in light of how memory shapes both individual and communal identities. As a curator at the Jewish Museum in New York City, she organized such exhibitions as *Painting a Place in America: Jewish Artists in New York* (with Norman L. Kleeblatt); *Common Man, Mythic Vision: The Paintings of Ben Shahn, 1936–1962*; and *The Jewish Identity Project: New American Photography*. Her essay on the internationally acclaimed photographer Adi Nes for the Tel Aviv Museum of Art appeared in 2007.

Judah M. Cohen is the Lou and Sybil Mervis Professor of Jewish Culture and Associate Professor of Musicology at Indiana University. He is the author of *Through the Sands of Time: A History of the Jewish Community of St. Thomas, US Virgin Islands* (2004); *The Making of a Reform Jewish Cantor: Musical Authority, Cultural Investment* (2009); and *Sounding Jewish Tradition: The Music of Central Synagogue* (2011); and the co-editor, with Gregory Barz, of *The Culture of AIDS in Africa* (2011). His current projects explore World War II-era narratives in musical theater, nineteenth-century American synagogue music, and the work of the American-Jewish singer/songwriter/liturgist, Debbie Friedman.

Michelle Ephraim is Associate Professor of English at Worcester Polytechnic Institute, where she teaches courses on Shakespeare, early modern drama, and creative writing. She is the author of *Deborah's Kin: Reading the Jewish Woman on the Elizabethan Stage* (2008) and co-author of *Shakespeare, Not Stirred: Cocktails for Your Everyday Dramas* (2015). She has written on religious conversion, adultery, and other controversial issues in Shakespearean England. She has also published personal essays and humor pieces in *Tikkun, Lilith, The Morning News, Word Riot, Take Magazine, McSweeney's Internet Tendency*, and the *Washington Post.*

Miriam Gilbert is Professor Emerita of English at the University of Iowa, where she taught courses in Shakespeare and drama from 1969 to 2013. She is the author of two studies in performance history, *Shakespeare in Performance: Love's Labour's Lost* (1993) and *Shakespeare at Stratford: The Merchant of Venice* (2002). She is co-editor of *Stages of Drama* (1981 and four subsequent editions) and of *Modern and Contemporary Drama* (1993). As an experienced teacher of Shakespeare through performance, she has led seminars and workshops at annual conferences of the Shakespeare Association of America and eight seminars sponsored by the National Endowment for the Humanities. In the summers of 2005 through 2013, she taught "Shakespeare: Page and Stage" for the Bread Loaf School of English (Lincoln College, Oxford), and she is a lecturer at the Shakespeare Birthplace Trust in Stratford-upon-Avon.

Abigail Gillman is Associate Professor of Hebrew, German, and Comparative Literature at Boston University, where she also serves as interim director of the Elie Wiesel Center for Judaic Studies. Her scholarship focuses on Jewish literature and culture of the German-speaking world. Her first book, *Viennese Jewish Modernism: Freud, Hofmannsthal, Beer-Hofmann, and Schnitzler* (2009), examines a circle of modernist writers and thinkers in Vienna, whose shared obsession with memory led them to write about Jewish memory and identity in creative, experimental ways. Her second book, *A History of German Jewish Bible Translation* (2017), studies the rich tradition of translations into German and Yiddish from the *Haskalah* to the twentieth century, demonstrating that translation in Jewish society was used to promote diverse educational, cultural, and linguistic goals. Her recent essay on "Martin Buber's Message to Postwar Germany" won the Egon Schwarz Prize for an outstanding essay in German-Jewish Studies.

Mark Hodin is Professor of English at Canisius College in Buffalo, New York. His work has appeared in *Prospects*, *Theatre Journal*, *Theatre Survey*, *Contemporary Literature*, and *American Literary History*. His article, "The Disavowal of Ethnicity: Legitimate Theatre and the Social Construction of Literary Value in Turn-of-the-Century America," won the Gerald Kahan prize from the American Society for Theater Research. He recently contributed a chapter on "Late Melodrama" to *The Oxford Handbook of American Drama* (2014).

Gad Kaynar-Kissinger is Associate Professor Emeritus at Tel Aviv University, where he also served as Chair of the Theatre Arts Department. He has been Visiting Professor at the Hebrew University of Jerusalem, Munich LMU, and Venice International University. In 2004 and 2010, he received grants from the Israel Science Foundation. He has published numerous articles on such topics as dramaturgy; Israeli, German, and Scandinavian Drama; Holocaust Theatre; Theatre and Education; and Acting and Directing Theory. Recent publications include: *Another View: Israeli Drama Revisited* with Zahava Caspi (2013); *The Cameri Theatre of Tel Aviv* (2008); *Habima: New Insights on National Theatre*, as co-editor (2016); as well as chapters in *The Routledge Companion to Dramaturgy* (2015) and *New Dramaturgies: International Perspectives* (2014). Kaynar has been editor or co-editor of books on *Sturm und Drang*, Brecht, Ghelderod, and the Cameri Theatre of Tel Aviv; is co-editor of the quarterly *Teatron;* and is Regional Managing Editor for Israel of the *Theatre Times*. He has curated several festivals in Israel and abroad, has worked on Israeli stage, film, and television as dramaturg, actor, and director, and has translated texts from English, German, Norwegian, and Swedish. For his Ibsen translations and research, he was designated in 2009 as "Knight First Class of the Royal Norwegian Order of Merit."

Jeanette R. Malkin is Chair of the Theatre Studies Department at the Hebrew University of Jerusalem. She co-edited the book *Jews and the Making of Modern German Theater* (2010) with Freddie Rokem and is the author of *Memory-Theater and Postmodern Drama* (1999); and *Verbal Violence in Contemporary Drama: From Handke to Shepard* (1992). Her articles on ethnicity and theatre culture; modernist German Theatre; Heiner Müller; Thomas Bernhard; Samuel Beckett; Robert Wilson; and postmodernism have appeared in numerous academic journals and books. She served as a member of the board (Beirat) of the Franz Rosenzweig Research Centre for German-Jewish Literature and Cultural History at Hebrew University from 1998 to 2006. She received grants from the Israel Science Foundation for her research project, "Triangulation: Jewish Cultural Markings in German and American Theatre" (2005–9); and, together with Eckart Voigts, from the German Lower Saxony-Israel Joint Project for their current research project, "Hyphenated Cultures: Contemporary British-Jewish Theatre" (2016–19).

Edna Nahshon is Professor of Jewish Theatre and Drama at the Jewish Theological Seminary in New York, and senior associate of the Centre for Hebrew and Jewish studies at Oxford University. Her primary interest lies in the intersection of Jewishness, performance, and drama. In addition to numerous articles, book chapters, encyclopedia articles, and book reviews, her publications include the following books: *New York's Yiddish Theater: From the Bowery to Broadway* (2016); *Jews and Theater in an Intercultural Context* (2012); *Jewish Theatre: A Global View* (2009); *Jews and Shoes* (2008); *From the Ghetto to the Melting Pot: Israel Zangwill's Jewish Plays* (2005); *Yiddish Proletarian Theatre: The Art and Politics of the Artef, 1925–1940* (1998). Most recently she was the curator of "New York's Yiddish Theater: From the Bowery to Broadway," a major exhibition presented at the Museum of the City of New York (March–August 2016).

Sabine Schülting is Professor of English Literature and Cultural Studies at Freie Universität Berlin. Her research focuses on Shakespeare, early modern cultural encounters, material culture studies, and historical gender studies. Recent book publications include *Dirt in Victorian Literature and Culture: Writing Materiality* (2016) and two co-edited collections of essays: *Shylock nach dem Holocaust: Zur Geschichte einer deutschen Erinnerungsfigur* (2011), and *Early Modern Encounters with the Islamic East: Performing Cultures* (2012). She is also the editor of *Shakespeare Jahrbuch*, published by the German Shakespeare Society. Together with Zeno Ackermann, she is currently working on a monograph on the cultural reception of Shakespeare's *The Merchant of Venice* in Germany after 1945.

Jeffrey Shandler is Professor and Chair of Jewish Studies at Rutgers University. His books include *While America Watches: Televising the Holocaust* (1999); *Adventures in Yiddishland: Postvernacular Language and Culture* (2005), *Jews, God, and Videotape: Religion and Media in America* (2009), and *Shtetl: A Vernacular Intellectual History* (2014). Forthcoming books include *Holocaust Memories in the Digital Age* and *Yiddish: Biography of a Language*. Among other works, Shandler is the editor of *Awakening Lives: Autobiographies of Jewish Youth in Poland before the Holocaust* (2002) and co-editor of *Entertaining America: Jews, Movies, and Broadcasting* (2003) and *Anne Frank Unbound: Media, Imagination, Memory* (2012). His translations of Yiddish literature include Mani-Leyb's children's classic *Yingl Tsingl Khvat* (1986) and *Emil and Karl*, a Holocaust novel for young readers by Yankev Glatshteyn (2006).

Michael Shapiro is Professor Emeritus of English and was founding director of the Program in Jewish Culture and Society at the University of Illinois at Urbana-Champaign. He has been a visiting professor at Cornell, Reading, Tamkang, and Loyola Universities. He is the author of *Children of the Revels* (1977) and *Gender in Play* (1994), as well as articles, notes, and reviews in early modern English literature and drama, and in modern Jewish secular literature. He currently lives in Chicago, where he serves on the Joseph Jefferson Committee, which grants annual awards for excellence in theater arts.

Efraim Sicher is Professor of English and Comparative Literature at Ben-Gurion University of the Negev. His research interests include representation of the "jew"; dystopia; modern Jewish culture; Holocaust memory; second-generation narratives; the city in literature; Charles Dickens; George Eliot; and Isaak Babel. Among his recent books are: (as editor) *Race Color Identity: Discourses about the Jews in the Early Twenty-First Century* (2013); (with Linda Weinhouse) *Under Postcolonial Eyes: The "jew" in Contemporary British Writing* (2012); *Babel in Context: A Study in Cultural Identity* (2012); *The Holocaust Novel* (2005); *Reading Dickens/Reading the City: Representation, the Novel, and Urban Realism* (2003; revised edition, 2015). His new book, *The Jew's Daughter: The Cultural History of a Conversion Narrative*, is forthcoming.

Nina Warnke an independent scholar of Yiddish theater. Until recently she was Assistant Professor of European Studies and Jewish Studies and Assistant Dean of the Ingram Commons at Vanderbilt University. Her research and publications focus on Yiddish theater worldwide, including "Patriotn and Their Stars: Male Youth Culture in the Galleries of the New York Yiddish Theatre, in *Inventing the Modern Yiddish Stage: Essays on Drama, Theatre, and Performance* (eds. Berkowitz and Henry, 2012); and two articles on the New York Yiddish theater for the *Enzyklopädie jüdischer Geschichte und Kultur*, edited by Dan Diner. She is currently working on a study of female Yiddish performers and memoir writing.

Richard H. Weisberg is Floersheimer Professor of Constitutional Law at Cardozo Law School, Yeshiva University. In addition to such pioneering works in the field of Law and Literature as *The Failure of the Word* (1984) and *Poethics* (1992), he has written widely on Shakespeare, from his first scholarly article, "Hamlet and 'Ressentiment'" (in *American Imago*, 1972), to a chapter in his most recent book, *In Praise of Intransigence* (2014). His work on *The Merchant of Venice* has addressed the staging of public performances of scenes of the play which are immediately followed by legal arguments before sitting judges over the merits of Portia's and Antonio's treatment of Shylock in Act 4 (see Elizabeth Widdicombe in the *New Yorker*, December 2008).

Shelly Zer-Zion is a Lecturer in the Theatre Department of the University of Haifa. Her research focuses on the history of twentieth-century Hebrew theatre in Europe and Palestine, and its interconnections with Yiddish and German theatre cultures. In addition to numerous articles on the subject, she has published *Habima in Berlin: the Institutionalization of a Zionist theatre* (2015 [in Hebrew]). A German version, entitled *Habima: Eine hebräische Bühne in der Weimarer Republik*, was recently published by Fink Verlag. She is also the co-editor of the forthcoming volume, *Habima: New Perspectives on National Theatre* (in Hebrew).

Acknowledgments

All books, especially collections of essays, are joint ventures, the end products of multiple intersecting networks. As the editors of this volume, we wish to thank our authors and to express our appreciation to others who helped bring it into being. Our first debt is to the person who, at an annual meeting of the Association for Jewish Studies, introduced us to each other: Barbara Kirshenblatt-Gimblett, Program Director of the Core Exhibition for the Museum of the History of Polish Jews in Warsaw and Professor Emerita of Performance Studies, New York University. We are grateful to Lewis Bateman, acquisitions editor at Cambridge University Press, for his faith in the project and for guiding it to its home, where Claire Sissen, our content manager, deftly shepherded the manuscript through the production process, with the able assistance of Anny Mortada and Phil Clement of Out of House Publishing. We would also like to thank Murray Baumgarten, Distinguished Professor Emeritus of English and Comparative Literature at the University of California at Santa Cruz, for his advice and encouragement. We are beholden to Daniel Belasco, Curator of Exhibitions and Programs at the Samuel Dorsky Museum of Art at the State University of New York at New Paltz, for directing us to Jacob Kramer's work, "Shylock," which appears on the cover of this book. Michael Shapiro is grateful to three friends and former colleagues at the University of Illinois at Urbana-Champaign: the late David Goodman for many conversations about the issues raised by the topic of this book; and Leon Waldoff and David Kay for thoughtful editorial advice. Last but not least, we are obliged to the many archivists, librarians, and curators in the United States, Israel, and Europe who went out of their way to assist us and our contributors in our research and who helped us obtain the many images and illustrations included in this volume. Memory being fallible, we have undoubtedly failed to mention some who were a part of the collective effort that underlies this book; for those omissions we apologize.

On a more personal note, we wish to thank those closest to us. Edna writes: I thank my husband Gad for being there for me, and my son Ken and daughter-in-law Leslie for bringing to the world Zoe Nahshon. Born on December 22, 2015, she has enriched our lives beyond measure and brought us all much happiness and joy. Michael writes: my children, children-in-law, and grandchildren have brought me great joy and have helped me to keep my life in balance by reminding me of what matters most. My wife, Elizabeth, always my first reader, has for over half a century been my beloved and loving companion in so many ways that, in Lorenz Hart's words, "If they asked me I could write a book."

Preface

In 1960, a global wave of anti-Semitic incidents led Orson Welles, known for his daring Shakespeare productions, to cancel his plans to star in *The Merchant of Venice* even though playing Shylock had been his lifelong ambition. He had been thwarted twice, he said. First, "a man called Hitler made it impossible," and now, again, he felt he needed to give up the project as "hate merchants started scribbling swastikas all over the place," referring to the onslaught of synagogue desecrations that had begun on Christmas Day 1959 in Cologne, Germany.[1] Welles stated that though he was "a Christian and not a Jew" yet again he felt that the time for performing Shylock "was out of joint." Making a clear distinction between the written and the performed word, the actor stated: "until all the church walls are clean – and safely clean, too – I think Shylock, with his Jewish gabardine, his golden ducats and his pound of flesh, should be kept on the book-shelves until a safer epoch."[2]

Fast forward to 2013.

A highly favorable review of a production of *The Merchant of Venice* at Canada's prestigious Stratford Festival begins as follows:

> There's a new Shakespeare play premiering on the Stratford Festival's mainstage. It's called The Tragedy of Shylock.
>
> Or rather, it's that old anti-Semitic comedy, *The Merchant of Venice*, skillfully reshaped by Stratford artistic director Antoni Cimolino and actor Scott Wentworth into a melancholy meditation on prejudice and ignorance.

[1] Howard H. Ehrlich, "The Swastika Epidemic of 1959–1960: Anti-Semitism and Community Characteristics," *Social Problems* 9:3 (Winter 1962), 264–72.

[2] Leonard Lyons, "Lyons Den," *Chicago Defender*, January 27, 1960, 11. See also Hedda Hopper, "Looking at Hollywood," *Chicago Daily Tribune*, February 20, 1960. Quoted also in Morris U. Schappes, letter to the editor, *New York Times*, February 4, 1981, A22.

> Even if you don't agree that *Merchant* is anti-Semitic, you still have to concede that it's a comedy about anti-Semites in which the Christians rule the day.[3]

A "re-trial" of Shylock, presided over by Chief Justice Beverley McLachlin of the Supreme Court of Canada, followed soon after the Stratford production. Sheila Block, a "seasoned litigator" who represented Shylock, argued that her client had suffered an injustice at the hands of the justice system, which put him "in the company of other famous cases of people wrongly convicted."[4] The journalist concluded: "Anyone expecting a learned ruling from the judges on an issue that has split theatre-goers and legal scholars for 400 years was out of luck. This is a decision that would take time to work out – perhaps another 400 years."

The character of Shylock and the role of *The Merchant of Venice* in channeling and promoting anti-Semitism have engaged Jewish discourse for over 200 years. The wide range of arguments has been bracketed by two contrary opinions: those who have regarded the play as eliciting anti-Jewish sentiments, and those who have downplayed the anti-Semitism accusation as ethnic hyper-sensitivity. Regardless of one's position in this matter, the historical constancy of the debate demonstrates the issue's relevance and poignancy.

As this book shows, *The Merchant of Venice*, which is inextricable from its extensive baggage of literary and theatrical interpretations, has been a flashpoint that activates the sensitivities, fears, memories, and hopes encompassed in the Jewish experience as a minority group within a larger, primarily Christian society. The Jewish wrestling with Shylock is therefore always reflective of a specific time and place.

The Merchant of Venice has stimulated intense engagement by Jewish writers, directors, actors, and critics. In addition to offshoots, prequels, and sequels in an array of genres, Shylock has also been commented on by means of juxtaposition. In an enlightened Germany the play was twinned with Nathan the Wise (1779), G. E Lessing's play that features an idealized Jew; in New York in 2007 it was shown back to back with Marlowe's *The Jew of Malta*, with the same actor, F. Murray Abraham, starring as both Shylock and Barabas.

[3] Martin Morrow, "The Merchant of Venice's Shylock is Realigned for a Modern Audience," *Globe and Mail*, August 16, 2013, available at www.theglobeandmail.com.

[4] Karin Wells, "Shakespeare in Court: Shylock's Appeal Heard at Stratford," *CBC News*, January 5, 2014, available at www.cbc.ca.

A subversive strand developed in Europe in the 1920s and 1930s when anti-fascist playwrights used the Shylock tale to counter an increasingly anti-Semitic climate. Best known among these is Walter Mehring's *Der Kaufmann von Berlin*. Staged in 1929 by Erwin Piscator, the production played while the SA patrolled in front of the theater building. After the Holocaust the play was reinterpreted and revised perhaps most radically by George Tabori and Peter Zadek to reflect the recent Nazi past. In 2016 the British writer Howard Jacobson, a notable figure in English letters and a Jew, published *Shylock Is My Name*, a novel issued on the occasion of the 400th anniversary of Shakespeare's death. Jacobson explained the impetus for the book:

> For an English novelist, Shakespeare is where it all begins. For an English novelist who also happens to be Jewish, *The Merchant of Venice* is where it all snarls up. "Who is the merchant and who is the Jew?" Portia wanted to know. Four hundred years later, the question needs to be reframed: "Who is the hero of this play and who is the villain?" And if Shylock is the villain, why did Shakespeare choose to make him so?"[5]

A similar sentiment was expressed by American director/playwright Aaron Posner, who in 2016 prepared a radical rewrite of *The Merchant of Venice* for the Folger Theatre in Washington DC. He explained: "If you're a Jewish director of Shakespeare, as I am, it's inevitable that you're going to engage with 'The Merchant of Venice.' "[6] The play, titled *District Merchants*, takes place in Washington circa 1870. It focuses on issues of gender, race, and class, and its characters are primarily Jews and African-Americans.

Numerous books and learned articles have been written about *The Merchant of Venice*, but none has focused exclusively on the responses it elicited from Jews, the people who were most directly affected by it. Not aspiring to compile a reference guide to Jewish responses to the play, the editors of this book chose to focus on a selected number of works created in response to the Jewish aspect of *The Merchant of Venice*. It is our hope that this collection of essays will inspire the study of other works created by Jews who felt compelled to address the Jewish aspect of this play in a variety of styles, genres, and languages.

[5] Kunal Dutta, "Howard Jacobson Takes on 'Anti-Semitism' in Rewrite of Shakespeare's *The Merchant of Venice*," *Independent (London)*, September 9, 2013, available at www.independent.co.uk.

[6] Quoted in Geoffrey Himes, "Coming to the Folger: The Merchant of … D.C.?" *Washington Post*, May 26, 2016, available at www.washingtonpost.com.

Addressing Leah, his deceased wife, Howard Jacobson's latter-day Shylock elucidates his unique position in Jewish life:

> These Jews, Leah, these Jews! They don't know whether to cry for me, disown me or explain me. Just as they don't know whether to explain or disown themselves.[7]

It is this very existential and open-ended discourse this book wishes to address.

Edna Nahshon

[7] Howard Jacobson, *Shylock Is My Name* (New York: Random House, 2016), 191–92.

PART I

INTRODUCTIONS

1

Literary Sources and Theatrical Interpretations of Shylock

Michael Shapiro

There is a long history of Jewish villainy in late medieval English literature, the most prominent example being Chaucer's *Prioress's Tale*, a version of the blood libel, in which Jews are accused of murdering a Christian child and using his blood to prepare *matzah* (unleavened bread). The late medieval English religious drama, *The Croxton Play of the Sacrament*, describes the misguided and unsuccessful efforts of Jews to desecrate the Host by stealing and attempting to destroy communion wafers.[1] After the Reformation, religious drama with its negative depictions of post-biblical Jews waned, as English drama developed along more secular lines during the latter half of the sixteenth century. Although the new, secular drama exhibited pronounced xenophobic tendencies, it showed only occasional interest in Jewish characters.[2]

[1] On Chaucer's tale and *The Croxton Play* see Lisa Lampert-Weissig, *Gender and Jewish Difference from Paul to Shakespeare* (Philadelphia: University of Pennsylvania Press, 2004). See also Stephen Spector, "Anti-Semitism and the English Mystery Plays," *Comparative Drama* 13 (1979–80), 3–16.

[2] Aside from Marlowe's Barabas and Shakespeare's Shylock, Jewish characters are quite rare in early modern English drama. There is evidence of two lost "Jewish" plays: one titled *The Jew* is mentioned in the late 1570s and another, *The Jew of Venice* by Thomas Dekker is of uncertain date (Kenneth Muir, *Shakespeare's Sources* [London: Methuen, 1961 [1957], vol. 1, 47). An extant play, Robert Wilson's *The Three Ladies of London* (1581), has a Jew named Gerontus, who acts with generosity and kindness toward a Christian. See Geoffrey Bullough, *Narrative and Dramatic Sources of Shakespeare* (London: Routledge and Kegan Paul, 1957–75), vol. 1, 445. William Haughton's *Englishmen for My Money* (1598) has a moneylender named Pisaro, who is the comically possessive father of three daughters, each won by a clever English suitor over a foreign rival. Pisaro, like Barabas, is said to have a large bottle-shaped snout, and he is labeled as "Portuguese," a term often used to refer to exiled Iberian Jews. See A. J. Hoenselaars, *Images of Englishmen and Foreigners in the Drama of Shakespeare and His*

The great exception is Christopher Marlowe's *The Jew of Malta* (1592), which preceded *The Merchant of Venice* (1594–96). Most scholars now believe that the Lord Admiral's Men revived *The Jew of Malta* in 1594 to exploit the trial and execution of Roderigo Lopez, a Marrano (new Christian) and Queen Elizabeth's physician, who was accused and convicted of involvement in a Spanish plot to poison the monarch.[3] Most scholars also believe that Shakespeare's company, the Lord Chamberlain's Men, wishing to emulate their rivals and exploit the anti-Jewish sentiment unleashed by the Lopez case, commissioned and staged their own play with a Jewish villain.[4]

Marlowe's play has baffled many readers. Barabas, the leading character – named after the criminal whom "the Jews" asked the Romans to release in preference to Jesus – was evidently presented as a caricature, complete with "bottle-nose."[5] Yet this manipulator and murderer is in fact the least hypocritical character in the play. Because Barabas evokes ambivalent or inconsistent responses, the tone and attitude of the work have seemed so unstable as to defy its classification by genre, and it has been labeled as farce, melodrama, and satire. Most recently, the English

Contemporaries (Rutherford: Fairleigh Dickinson University Press, 1992), 55; Miriam Bodian, *Hebrews of the Portuguese Nation: Conversos and Community in Early Modern Amsterdam* (Bloomington: Indiana University Press, 1997), 13.

[3] On Lopez, see David Katz, *Jews in the History of England* (Oxford: Clarendon Press, 1994), 76–106. On Shakespeare's possible use of Lopez as a model for Shylock, see James Shapiro, *Shakespeare and the Jews* (New York: Columbia University Press, 73–74; and Stephen Greenblatt, *Will in the World: How Shakespeare Became Shakespeare* (New York: Norton, 2004), 270–80.

[4] The Lopez case may have significant bearing on the precise dating of *The Merchant of Venice.* The first performances, by the Lord Chamberlain's Men, are dated sometime between 1594 and 1597. The earlier date makes sense to those who want to connect it to Lopez's trial and execution. Scholarly consensus now seems to favor a slightly later date. The early printing history of the play is well-known. The copy for the text of *The Merchant of Venice* was entered into the Stationer's Register on July 22, 1598, when the printer, James Roberts, recorded his rights to "a booke of the Marchaunt of Venyce or otherwise called the Jewe of Venyce" (Jay Halio, ed. "General Introduction," *The Merchant of Venice* [Oxford: Oxford University Press, 1993], 85), and later that year printed the play in quarto format. Three years after Shakespeare's death, in 1619, a second quarto appeared under a false title page with the date of 1600. In 1623, the play appeared in the First Folio (1623) in a text which closely followed the First Quarto.

[5] Christopher Marlowe, *The Jew of Malta*, ed. Roma Gill, in *The Complete Works of Christopher Marlowe* (Oxford: Clarendon Press, 1995), vol. 4, 3.3.9. Theatrical legends have also maintained that Shylock too was originally played with a false nose as well as a red wig or beard, the supposed color of Judas Iscariot's, as he generally was in productions of the eighteenth and early nineteenth centuries. See Toby Lelyveld, *Shylock on the Stage* (London: Routledge and Kegan Paul, 1961), 7–8; John Gross, *Shylock: A Legend and Its Legacy* (New York: Simon and Schuster, 1992), 128.

barrister and literary critic Anthony Julius has described *The Jew of Malta* as "a parodic dictionary of received ideas about Jews," and has suggested that the beneficent influence of this "anti-anti-Semitic" work, was subverted by *The Merchant of Venice*: "Had Shakespeare not responded to Marlowe, English literary anti-Semitism might well have been laughed into extinction."[6]

Marlowe's Barabas and Shakespeare's Shylock fulfill radically different functions. Barabas is the satiric agent in a play about the fierce competition for power and wealth between Jews, Christians, and Muslims in the eastern Mediterranean, and, like Antonio in *The Merchant of Venice*, he is an international trader. By contrast, Shylock is a usurer, functioning in an economic niche open to Jews because of the Church's prohibition of lending money for interest.[7] Barabas dominates the play until he is killed off at the end. Shylock, as the comic villain in a romantic comedy, appears in only five of the play's nineteen scenes, and his dramatic function is to prevent the union of the lovers. At the play's end, such "blocking" characters are usually either absorbed into or ejected from the new society that forms around the romantic couple(s). At the end of *The Merchant*, Shakespeare has it both ways: Shylock claims to be sick when he begs permission to leave the courtroom but he has just been forcibly re-integrated into the world of the play, on pain of death, if he meets the conditions of his pardon set by the Duke: that he sign a legal document, "the deed of gift" that legitimizes the confiscation and redistribution of his wealth, and that he convert to Christianity.

Despite its traces of the medieval "diabolized Jew,"[8] *The Merchant* suggests that Shakespeare was also alert to newer, more secularized ideas about the status of Jews which arose in the early modern period, such as whether, as James Shapiro puts it, "Jewish identity was understood in terms of nationality and race, as well as religion."[9] *The Merchant*

[6] Anthony Julius, *Trials of the Diaspora: A History of Anti-Semitism in England* (Oxford: Oxford University Press, 2010), 177–78.

[7] By the early modern period, in most European countries the absolute prohibition of charging interest had become obsolete. In Elizabeth's reign, England had legalized the charging of 10 percent interest on loans. See Norman Jones, *God and the Moneylenders: Usury and Law in Early Modern England* (Oxford: Blackwell, 1989), 79.

[8] Several passages in *The Merchant of Venice* refer to Jews as devils: 1.3.94; 2.2.18–19; 2.2.21–22; 3.1.17–19; 3.1.65–66; 4.1.212; 4.1.281–82. The term "diabolized Jew" is borrowed from Frank Felsenstein, *Anti-Semitic Stereotypes: A Paradigm of Otherness in English Popular Culture, 1660–1830* (Baltimore: Johns Hopkins University Press, 1995). Julius, *Trials of the Diaspora*, 179, describes *The Merchant* as "a blood-libel narrative subject to considerable elaboration."

[9] J. Shapiro, *Shakespeare and the Jews*, 6. See also Aaron Kitch, "Shylock's Sacred Nation," *Shakespeare Quarterly* 59 (2008), 131–55.

of Venice thus draws on several conceptions of Jewish identity, so that Shylock's Jewishness may best be described as a superimposition upon medieval stereotypes of various contemporary ideas about Jews – cultural, biological, and theological. Certainly, Shylock's Jewish identity is far more complex than that of the Jew Shakespeare found in his primary narrative source, a tale in *Il Pecorone*, Ser Giovanni Fiorentino's fourteenth-century collection of stories published in Italian in 1558.[10] Whereas Fiorentino's Jewish moneylender is a nameless, isolated, weakly motivated figure, who simply bears the label of "Jew," Shakespeare placed Shylock in a crude but functioning Jewish social matrix, endowed him with a distinctive voice and granted him a smattering of knowledge of the Hebrew Bible and Jewish dietary laws. Drawing on centuries of Christian teaching, he also made Shylock "theologically" Jewish by depicting him as excessively literal-minded. The association of Judaism with such rigid legalism derived from Paul the Apostle's contrast of normative Judaism of the first century with the emerging cult of the resurrected Jesus. In short, Shakespeare transformed the sketchy Jew of his source into a palimpsest – overlaying medieval anti-Judaic notions of Jews with more current ideas of Jews as a nation or people.

Fiorentino's tale shows little interest in any idea of the Jew, whether as diabolized "Other," sinful usurer, or alien presence. What Shakespeare did find in Fiorentino were the basic narrative components of his play: (1) the story of the loan with its collateral of a pound of flesh; (2) the courtship of the lady of Belmont; (3) the tension between male friendship and heterosexual love; (4) the forfeiture of the loan and the trial scene; (5) the heroine in male disguise who saves her husband's friend from the knife of the Jewish moneylender; and (6) the return to Belmont where the hero discovers that his wife was the lawyer who saved his friend's life and to whom he gave the ring he had sworn to keep forever. To these narrative elements, Shakespeare made a number of deft changes, many of which deepen the conflict between heterosexual love and male friendship. He also added Jewish traits to Fiorentino's generic Jewish moneylender. As Kenneth Muir observed, "Shakespeare alone stresses the faith and race of the usurer."[11]

Deepening and enriching source material is a hallmark of Shakespeare's genius as a writer. In his other "Venetian" play, for example, he transformed the nameless Moor of Cinthio's novella into the eponymous

[10] Bullough, *Narrative and Dramatic Sources*, vol. 1, 449; Muir, *Shakespeare's Sources*, vol. 1.

[11] Muir, *Shakespeare's Sources*, vol. 1, 51.

Othello, an eloquent and exotic warrior with a colorful past. In writing *The Merchant*, the playwright's imagination may also have been stimulated by curiosity, or what James Shapiro refers to as the "obsession" with Jews he shared with other Englishmen of his day.[12] What were they to make of this group of people whose biblical forebears were revered, yet who played so lurid a role in the medieval Christian imagination and who now lived scattered and shadowy in many cities and towns in Europe, including Elizabethan London, where, despite the expulsion of Jews from England in 1290, a small colony of Iberian Jews came to reside after the expulsions from Spain in 1492 and from Portugal in 1497.[13]

Whatever his reasons, Shakespeare found many ways to enrich the Jewishness of Fiorentino's nameless Jewish moneylender. He introduced the name, which sounds foreign to our ears but which may have been a family name in Tudor England.[14] In the play's Venetian setting, the name "Shylock" certainly does not sound Italian, and in any case he is more often addressed as "Jew" or referred to as "the Jew."[15] Whereas Fiorentino's creation is an isolated Jew, Shylock is embedded in family and community. He has friends – Tubal, who appears in one scene, and Chus, whom we never see[16] – and he refers at various times to "our sacred nation" (1.3.49), "our tribe" (1.3.106), and "our synagogue" (3.1.107–8).

[12] J. Shapiro, *Shakespeare and the Jews*, 88.

[13] Ibid., 68–77. The best known Jew in England, after Lopez, was Emilia Bassano, the daughter of an Italian-Jewish musician and an English Christian mother. She was married to a court musician and published a book of poems, *Salve Deus Rex Judaeorum*. A.L. Rowse, a historian, believed she was the model for the "dark lady" of Shakespeare's sonnets; see *Shakespeare's Sonnets: The Problem Solved*, 2nd edn. (New York: Harper and Row, 1973), 97–117. Rowse's theory has been challenged by, among others, J. Shapiro, *Shakespeare and the Jews*, 249 n.118; and Roger Prior, "Was Emilia Bassano the Dark Lady of Shakespeare's Sonnets," in *The Bassanos: Venetian Musicians and Instrument Makers in England, 1531–1665*, by David Lasocki (Aldershot: Scolar Press, 1995), 114–39.

[14] "Shylock" turns up as a surname in modern England. A British genealogical website, *Ancestry.com*, names twenty-three English men or women listed in censuses of the latter half of the nineteenth century. An American genealogical web site, *archives.com*, lists official records of 214 Americans with the surname of Shylock.

[15] Derek Cohen, "The Jews and Shylock," *Shakespeare Quarterly* 31 (1980), 54.

[16] The names of Shylock's two friends are those of Noah's grandsons. Tubal is a son of Japeth, and Chus (or Cush, an emendation introduced by the *Oxford Shakespeare*, is a son of Ham, who settled in Africa after the Flood (Genesis 10:2–6). See Stanley Wells and Gary Taylor, *William Shakespeare: A Textual Companion* (New York: Norton, 1997), 326. "Cush"(which came to mean "African" in Hebrew), is the form of the name used in the Hebrew Bible and in the Geneva Bible, but the Bishops' Bible, which Shakespeare seems to have cited with greater frequency in *The Merchant*, reads "Chus," as do the early printed texts of the play (M.M. Mahood, ed. *The Merchant of Venice* [Cambridge: Cambridge University Press, 1987]), 136n. and 197.

He once had a wife, Leah, who gave him a turquoise ring "when I was a bachelor" (3.1.101). His recollection of this gift, prompted by Tubal's news that Jessica has traded it for a monkey, provides the fleeting insight that Shylock was once a young man who loved and was loved in return.

In Shakespeare's hands, Fiorentino's solitary, childless Jew becomes the father of a daughter, Jessica, who, like Barabas's daughter, Abigail, betrays her father by falling in love with a Christian, but Shakespeare may also have found this subplot in Anthony Munday's *Zelauto*, and in a story by Massuccio in *Il Novellini*.[17] By reporting and later dramatizing Shylock's rage over Jessica's elopement, Shakespeare provides him with another motive for collecting the pound of Antonio's flesh that served as collateral for the loan. Indeed, some Shylocks, such as Laurence Olivier's (stage 1970, television 1973), have even dropped the aside in Act 1, Scene 3 where Shylock expresses his hatred of Antonio, preferring to use Shylock's fury over Jessica's elopement to spark the realization that he can now take a Christian's life to avenge the loss of his daughter.

Modern productions, such as Olivier's, often follow Shakespeare's lead and develop Shylock's familial and communal affiliations even further. Whereas Shakespeare provides two "countrymen" for Shylock, Henry Irving (1838–1905), among others, introduced a number of Jews among the spectators in the trial scene.[18] Yet, Shakespeare's enrichment of Shylock's Jewishness has also permitted modern directors to distance Shylock from his Jewish milieu. For example, Tubal, who shares the risk of the loan to Antonio, can be either supportive of his friend, as is the red-cheeked, fur-hatted Hasidic Tubal of the 1980 BBC production (Arnold Diamond), or critical, like the elegant top-hatted Tubal of John Barton's 1979 Royal Shakespeare Company production (Raymond Westwell), who disapproved of Patrick Stewart's grubby, unshaven proletarian Shylock. Similarly, Shylock can be a doting, affectionate father, like Dustin Hoffman, who in Act 2, Scene 5 tenderly caressed Jessica's (Francesca Bulle's) cheek in Peter Hall's 1989–90 London/New York production; or a cruel one, like Stewart, who in the same scene gratuitously slapped Jessica (Avril Carson) across the face. Jessica, in turn, may mock the father from whom she is escaping, as Leslie Udwin did in the 1980 BBC production, or she may display regret, say, by kissing a photograph of her mother, as Gabrielle Jourdan did in Trevor Nunn's 1999 production

[17] Bullough, *Narrative and Dramatic Sources*, vol. 1, 454–57; Muir, *Shakespeare's Sources*, vol. 1, 50–51.

[18] Lelyveld, *Shylock on the Stage*, 90; James Bulman, *The Merchant of Venice*, *Shakespeare in Performance* (Manchester: Manchester University Press, 1991), 45.

at the National Theatre.[19] In similar fashion, when she receives the "deed of gift" at the end of the play, she can either rejoice at her good fortune, or she can seem rueful, like Heather Lind, who, in Daniel Sullivan's 2011 production, sat beside the same pool where her father had been baptized in the previous scene.

Just as Shakespeare augmented Fiorentino by situating his Jewish moneylender within familial and communal networks, so did he link Shylock to selected practices of normative Judaism. For example, he has Shylock initially reject Bassanio's dinner invitation in Act 1, Scene 3, lest he violate the proscription against eating pork, though, having been "bid forth to supper" (2.5.31), he leaves home to attend Bassanio's farewell feast. Shakespeare even made Launcelot Gobbo aware of the Jewish dietary laws, as when he complains to Jessica that "this making of Christians will raise the price of hogs" (3.5.19). Shakespeare also has Shylock swear to take the pound of flesh "by our Holy Sabbath" (4.1.35–36). In short, Shakespeare found opportunities to overlay the bare narrative elements of Fiorentino's tale with textual allusions to details of Jewish familial, communal, and religious life; details which later productions could reshape and amplify. Such was the intention of Herbert Beerbohm Tree (1852–1917), who went to great lengths to present an authentic Jewish ghetto in his 1908 London production. As he wrote in his program notes, he sought the help of "high Jewish authorities" to assist him in presenting "the life of the Jews and the customs and manners of the day."[20]

In other additions to his source, Shakespeare underscored Shylock's Jewishness by showing his familiarity with Hebrew Scripture. He refers to Launcelot Gobbo (inaccurately) as "that fool of Hagar's offspring" (2.5.42), rhetorically addresses "Father Abram" (1.3.156), swears "by Jacob's staff" (2.5.35), and several times in the trial scene (4.1) invokes Daniel the Judge, only to have Gratiano throw the allusion back at him when the tables are turned. His favorite biblical character, however, is Jacob, the third of the Patriarchs, whom he calls "the third possessor" (1.3.70). He seems to admire Jacob as a fellow trickster, as when he retells the story from Genesis (30:25–43) of how Jacob outwitted his uncle Laban in the division of their flocks (1.3.67–86). In Act 2, Scene 2, there is also a subtle reference to Jacob's deception of his blind father, Isaac, where Launcelot Gobbo first denies his real identity to his "sand-blind"

[19] Charles Edelman, ed. *The Merchant of Venice*, Shakespeare in Production (Cambridge: Cambridge University Press, 2002), 147.

[20] Cary Mazer, *Shakespeare Refashioned: Elizabethan Plays on Edwardian Stages* (Ann Arbor: UMI Research Press, 1980), 17.

father (2.2.29) and then tries to persuade the old man who he really is so he can ask him to "give me your blessing" (2.2.68). As John Scott Colley has argued, Old Gobbo's feeling the hairiness of son Launcelot's beard echoes Jacob's and Rebecca's scheme to have Jacob cover his arms with animal fur in order to steal the paternal blessing intended for the first born Esau.[21]

Shakespeare also introduced theological differences between Judaism and Christianity, such as the debate over the relative merits of mercy and justice which runs through the trial scene. This debate begins when the Duke's question, "How shalt thou hope for mercy, rend'ring none?" evokes Shylock's answer, "What judgment shall I dread doing no wrong?" (4.1.187–88). It continues when Portia repeats the Duke's request that Shylock show mercy to Antonio and amplifies it with "the quality of mercy" speech (4.1.179–200) and with the suggestion that Shylock "have by some surgeon ... / To stop his wounds lest he do bleed to death" (4.1.252–53). Shakespeare gives Portia the Christian argument that humans are flawed by Original Sin and would all be damned if not for Christ's redemptive power. Shylock scoffs at the idea of any universal need for mercy, confident that if he does no wrong he need not fear Divine Judgment at his death. To Portia's assertion that "in the course of justice none of us / Should see Salvation" (4.1.194–95), Shylock replies, as he did earlier to the Duke: "My deeds upon my head! I crave the law" (4.1.201). He thus denies Original Sin and the need for redemption through the sacrifice of Jesus. Nowhere in Fiorentino's tale does one find so much as a hint of Paul's supercessionist claim that Judaism, caricatured as the religion of judgment and rigidly legalistic literalism, is inferior to Christianity, the religion of forgiveness, mercy, and compassionate responsiveness to spirit of the Law.

Shakespeare also embodies this theological conflict in the action of the play. Later in the scene, Shakespeare has Portia invoke a second statute,

[21] John Scott Colley, "Launcelot, Jacob and Esau: Old and New Law in *The Merchant of Venice*," *Yearbook of English Studies* 10 (1980), 182–83, reads Jacob's supplanting of Esau in terms of Christian figuration as a foreshadowing of Christianity's superceding of Judaism. Janet Adelman, *Blood Relations: Christian and Jew in "The Merchant of Venice"* (Chicago: University of Chicago Press, 2008), 133, cites this reading as one of many moments where the play struggles to reassert the supremacy and superiority of Christianity over Judaism and finds "*The Merchant* haunted by its own ... fears and guilt about Christianity's relation to the Jews." Susannah Heschel, "From Jesus to Shylock: Christian Supersessionism and *The Merchant of Venice*," *Harvard Theological Review* 99 (2006), 404, sees such moments as parodic or intentionally subversive, "underm[ing] a theology of Christian anti Judaism."

evidently intending to place Shylock himself in the position of needing mercy. In the terms of the law as Portia reads it, Shylock learns that he, as an alien, has committed a crime by threatening the life of a Venetian, and he discovers that his punishment is to have his wealth confiscated and divided between the intended victim and the state, while "his life lie[s] ... in the mercy / Of the Duke only" (4.1.350–51). Portia then orders him to kneel and supplicate: "Down therefore, and beg mercy of the Duke" (4.1.368). The Duke, in turn, responds without being asked, precisely to show Shylock how Christian mercy differs from Jewish judgment: "That thou shalt see the difference of our spirit, I pardon thee thy life before thou ask it" (4.1.364). He also reduces his part of the monetary penalty to an unspecified fine, rather than taking half of the Jew's wealth to which the statute entitles him.

When Portia then asks, "What mercy can *thou* render him, Antonio?" (4.l.373; emphasis added), the result is quite different. Antonio accepts the Duke's right to forgo his half of Shylock's wealth, so long as he himself can keep the other half "in use to render it / Upon his death unto the gentleman that lately stole his daughter" (4.1.378–80). In Fiorentino's tale, there is no second statute and hence no opportunity for Shylock to beg for mercy, no challenge by Portia to the Duke and Antonio to show mercy, and of course no mention of Shylock's agreeing to convert to Christianity, which focuses attention on Shylock's Jewishness by its very attempt to erase it. Many modern productions find ways to indicate Shylock's resistance to conversion, thereby underscoring his commitment to Judaism.

For modern audiences, and perhaps for Elizabethans critical of the Spanish for forcing their colonial subjects in South America to convert to Roman Catholicism, forced conversion is a violation of individual conscience, as well as a forced betrayal of identity and a violation of personal agency. In the light of Jewish historical experience, the threat, let alone the enactment, of conversion can be especially threatening for Jewish spectators. The text calls for Shylock to agree to conversion in principle or at some future date, and actors have often done so with a curt nod. Some directors have amplified the moment by staging a kind of symbolic conversion. In 1972, director Yossi Yzraely startled his Israeli audience by using puppets to create the baptismal scene on stage. In the 1980 BBC production Gratiano (Kenneth Cranham) hung a cross around Shylock's (Warren Mitchell's) neck and forced him to kiss it. Daniel Sullivan inserted a full-scale conversion ceremony in his 2011 New York modern dress production: after the trial scene, two Venetians led Shylock (Al Pacino) to a freshly uncovered baptismal pool and forcibly submerged his head while a priest intoned a Latin benediction. Shylock showed more resistance to conversion in Barbara Gaines's 2005 production, when the actor (Mike Nussbaum) picked his *yarmulke* (skullcap) up off the floor and, as he left the stage, put it back on his head and paused to recite the *Sh'ma*, the Jewish declaration of faith in One God that is repeated several times in any service.[22] The *yarmulke* has been used effectively as a prop by other companies, such as the Theatre of a New City, which performed the play in 2007 with F. Murray Abraham as Shylock; in the last act, taking place in Belmont, Jessica (Melissa Miller) tenderly retrieved her father's skullcap from the floor, where it had fallen during the preceding trial scene, thus displaying an emotional depth not granted to her by the text.

Another way in which Shakespeare deepened the Jewish dimension of the play was to amplify the social tensions between Jews and Christians he found in his source. Although in *The Merchant* there is no mention of a ghetto, which was perhaps the most salient feature of Venetian Jewish life at the time, nor of the requirement that Jews wear distinctive yellow or red hats, Shylock reports that Antonio has railed against him and spits on his "Jewish gaberdine" (1.3.108).[23] The Venetians of the play routinely refer to the Jews as devils, as has been noted, while Jessica, upon arrival in Belmont, is greeted by Gratiano as Lorenzo's "little infidel" (3.2.217). The antagonism is mutual. For example, Shylock not only relates past humiliations but lectures Jessica on the difference between the loose and frivolous behavior of Venetians masquers and the Judaic propriety of "my sober house" (2.5.35), and sneers at the "Christian husbands" (4.1.290) willing to sacrifice their wives in the name of Christian brotherhood.

In modern productions, these social tensions often erupt into stage violence. Antonio's spitting can be shown to us, as in Michael Radford's film (2004), or can turn into a spitting match, as in Bill Alexander's 1987 Royal Shakespeare Company production. Some productions open the play with a physical assault on Shylock, as did the 1998 modern-dress Budapest production directed by Róbert Alföldi, which began with a silent scene: Shylock enters a bar where the young men of Venice hang

[22] Michael Shapiro, "Two *Merchants*: The Glow of the Roaring Twenties and the Shadow of 9/11," in *Chicago Shakespeare Theater: Suiting the Action to the Word*, eds. Regina Buccola and Peter Kanelos (Elgin: Northern Illinois State University Press, 2013), 240.

[23] For an attempt to determine precisely what this garment might have been, see M. Channing Linthicum, "My Jewish Gaberdine," *PMLA* 43 (1929), 757–66.

out at night. As they notice the Jew, the music stops and they turn toward him. Antonio steps ahead and spits on Shylock, who then, humiliated and ridiculed by all present, runs out into the pouring rain.[24]

Whereas Fiorentino's Christians exhibit a vague but mutual dislike of the Jewish moneylender, Shakespeare has imagined a deep-seated and ongoing hostility between Antonio and Shylock. When Fiorentino's merchant forfeits on the loan, the usurer refuses to accept ten times the borrowed sum, insisting on taking his pound of flesh "in order to be able to say that he had put to death the greatest of the Christian merchants."[25] In contrast to this seemingly frivolous wish, Shakespeare's Shylock, in addition to wanting to avenge the loss of Jessica by killing Antonio, bears an "ancient grudge" (1.3.42) against the merchant, which is partly based on religious antagonism; that is, on Antonio's undermining of the moneylender's business by dispensing Christian charity: "I oft delivered from his forfeitures / Many that have at times made moan to me" (3.3.22–23). In a hostile aside, Shylock blends religious and commercial reasons for his hatred:

> I hate him for he is a Christian;
> But more for that in low simplicity
> He lends out money gratis, and brings down
> The rate of usance here with us in Venice. (1.3.37–40)

Shylock sums up the unequal position of Jews in Venice when he asks why Jews should not, like the Christians they resemble in so many obvious physical ways, respond to injuries and insults by seeking revenge, just as Christians do. Whether "hath not a Jew eyes ..." is a specious attempt to rationalize vengeance or a plea for equality, it has no counterpart in Fiorentino, who was as unconcerned with religious antagonisms as he was with Jewish religious practices, Judeo-Christian theological differences, and Jewish familial and communal affiliations.

Shakespeare the artist sought to make his Jewish character into a more complex figure than the usual medieval stereotype and to provide a richer Jewish texture than he found in his primary narrative source. He also endowed the Jew with a voice of his own, a streak of self-justification, and a mordant sense of humor. In enriching the sketchy characterization

[24] Aniko Szucs, "The Relativization of Victim and Perpetrator in the Hungarian Productions of *The Merchant of Venice* and *Mein Kampf*," in *Jews and Theater in an Intercultural Context*, ed. Edna Nahshon (Leiden/Boston: Brill, 2012), 303. See also M. Shapiro, "Two *Merchants*," 238–39; Miriam Gilbert, *The Merchant of Venice, Shakespeare at Stratford* (London: Arden Shakespeare, 2002), 63; Bulman, *The Merchant*, 122–23.

[25] Bullough, vol. 1, 472.

of the Jewish moneylender he found in his source, Shakespeare essentially superimposed more modern conceptions of the Jew on traditional medieval stereotypes, thereby creating a rich and not always consistent matrix of details. Following Shakespeare's lead, modern directors have made artistic choices which further enrich the Jewish texture of the play. If *The Merchant of Venice* has been and continues to be a problem for Jews, one might say it is primarily due to Shakespeare's artistry, that is to say, to his determination to make Shylock a more Jewish figure than he was in Fiorentino's tale. Indeed, "Shylock" might never have become a pejorative synonym for Jew nor might the character have become an archetype if Shakespeare had based his Jewish moneylender solely on medieval anti-Jewish stereotypes still current in his own day or on his primary narrative source.

Changing Stage Images of Shylock: The Rise and Fall of the Victorian Paradigm

Shakespeare's making Shylock more Jewish did not necessarily evoke more sympathy for him in early modern England, if the title page of the First Quarto is any indication.[26] This edition, the first published version of the play, prints a rather lengthy subtitle, which is in effect a highly selective summary, noting that the play includes "the extreame crueltie of *Shylocke* the Jew towards the sayd Merchant, in cutting a just pound of his flesh, and the obtayning of *Portia* by the choyce of three chests."[27] We have no idea whether these are Shakespeare's words or the words of Hayes, the bookseller, or someone in his employ whom we might today call a publicist (Figure 1). Whoever created

[26] The early printing history of the play is summarized in Halio, *The Merchant of Venice*, 85-93. It first appeared in quarto format in 1600. A second quarto appeared in 1619, three years after Shakespeare's death. In 1623, the play was published in the First Folio in a text which closely followed the 1600 quarto and which was thereafter included in all subsequent folios, and the many editions of the collected works which appeared in the seventeenth and eighteenth centuries. There is nothing in the early textual history of *The Merchant of Venice* to suggest that the play was exceptionally popular in its day either in print or on the stage. The printing of only two quartos in the twenty-three years before the publication of the Folio suggests the lack of a market for re-issues and re-editions. The early performance history of *The Merchant* is a bit scanty. The title page of the 1600 quarto claims that the play "hath beene divers times acted by the Lord Chamberlaine his Servants," while court records mention two revivals before King James in 1605 by the same company, known since 1603 as the King's Men. There is no record of what prompted these court performances.

[27] Quoted in Halio, ed. *Merchant of Venice*, 85.

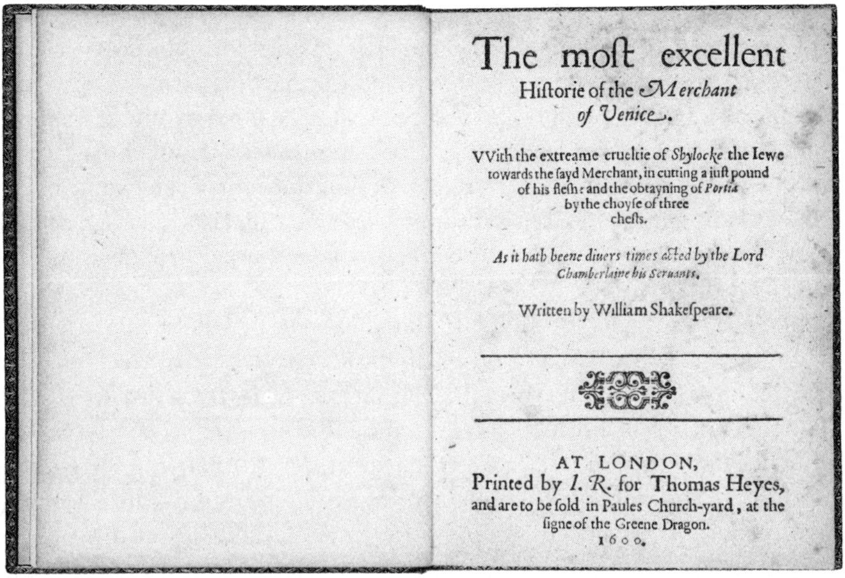

The moſt excellent
Hiſtorie of the *Merchant of Venice.*

VVith the extreame crueltie of *Shylocke* the Iewe towards the ſayd Merchant, in cutting a iuſt pound of his fleſh: and the obtayning of *Portia* by the choyſe of three cheſts.

As it hath beene diuers times acted by the Lord Chamberlaine his Seruants.

Written by William Shakeſpeare.

AT LONDON,
Printed by *I. R.* for Thomas Heyes, and are to be ſold in Paules Church-yard, at the ſigne of the Greene Dragon.
1600.

FIGURE 1 Title page of the First Quarto of Shakespeare's *The Merchant of Venice*, 1600.
Courtesy of the Folger Shakespeare Library, Washington DC.

this blurb assumed that prospective customers might want to buy the book in order to learn more about these sensational happenings. He stresses the love story and the villainy of Shylock. He does not describe the work as a play about a persecuted Jew, who was wronged by his daughter, goaded by anti-Semites, fleeced of his wealth, and compelled to give up his faith, but rather as a story which featured as one of its two highlights the sadistic behavior of a Jew toward a Christian. Whether spectators actually attending performances of the play might have challenged this reading, the first printed version was advertised to potential readers as conforming to popular, if somewhat antiquated, ideas of Jewish villainy.

Over the course of four centuries, the stereotyped villain of the First Quarto's subtitle underwent many transformations onstage, a process that was partly due to the growing number of Jewish immigrants in England, as well to how they were perceived by the larger society, and to their own self-perceptions.

After the closing of the London theaters in 1642, there were no theatrical productions until shortly after the Restoration of Charles II in

1660. Performance rights to *The Merchant* were assigned to Thomas Killegrew, one of the two theater-managers issued royal patents, but the play does not seem to have been revived during this period despite the popularity of other plays with "breeches roles," i.e. roles in which female characters, now played by actresses, assume male attire, which paradoxically afforded spectators a better view of the contours of the female body. Samuel Pepys, an avid Restoration playgoer and diarist, recorded seeing forty-one performances of plays by Shakespeare but fails to mention *The Merchant of Venice*.

In 1701, the story of Shylock and the pound of flesh appeared on stage and in print in George Granville's coarsely comic adaptation, *The Jew of Venice*. By then, the situation of Jews in England had changed. In 1656, both to advance England's mercantile aspirations and to allow Jews to live in every nation prior to their ingathering in the Holy Land for the Second Coming, the Commonwealth government officially permitted a small number of Iberian Jews to reside in England. Jews took advantage of the change, and by 1720 there were between 1,000 and 2,000 Jews in England – a number that continued to rise.[28] Unfortunately, we have no knowledge of whether or how they responded to Shylock during the Restoration period or the first half of the eighteenth century.

Had any of them attended a performance of Granville's *The Jew of Venice*, they would have seen him played by Thomas Doggett, a specialist in low comic roles, one of which was Sancho, a comic Jew in Dryden's *Love Triumphant* (1694). The Prologue described Shylock as a "Stock-jobbing Jew,"[29] a reference to the relatively small number (twelve) of Jews allowed on the stock exchange. Granville's primary focus was on Bassanio's wooing of Portia and his friendship with Antonio, and he inserted a masque to amplify the themes of Love and Friendship. He eliminated half of the characters and half of the scenes including one of the five scenes in which Shylock appears, and shortened most of his speeches. Whether in response to Doggett's virtuosity or his own sense of Shylock's compelling power, Granville also renamed the play to make the moneylender the titular character. He also coarsened the character of Shylock, for example, by having him ask Antonio in the loan-making

28 Todd Endelman, *The Jews of Britain, 1656–2000* (Berkeley: University of California Press, 2002), 410.

29 George Granville, *The Jew of Venice*, in *Five Restoration Adaptations of Shakespeare*, ed. Christopher Spencer (Urbana: University of Illinois Press, 1965), 348.

scene, in a tastelessly macabre jest, to name the part of his body that should serve as collateral:

> Let me see, What think you of your Nose,
> Or of an Eye – or of – a pound of Flesh
> To be cut off, and taken from what Part
> Of your Body – I shall think fit to name.
> Thou art too portly, Christian!
> Too much pamper'd – What say you then
> To such a merry Bond?[30]

Granville also created a toast by Shylock to his Mistress, Money, and added lines to Gratiano's baiting of Shylock in the trial scene. Granville's version supplanted Shakespeare's on the London stage for several decades and was occasionally performed even after Doggett's death in 1721. By 1736, it had appeared in six printed editions, further testimony to its popularity on the stage.[31] In the *Life of Shakespeare* that accompanied his edition of 1709, Nicholas Rowe paid tribute to Doggett's comic interpretation but believed Shakespeare had a darker sense of the role:

> I cannot but think it was design'd Tragically by the Author. There appears in it such a deadly Spirit of Revenge, such a savage Fierceness and Fellness, and such a bloody designation of Cruelty and Mischief, as cannot agree either with the Stile or Characters of Comedy.[32]

Rowe would have approved of Charles Macklin's interpretation, first performed at Drury Lane in 1741. (Figure 2) Using a text much closer to Shakespeare than Granville's adaptation, Macklin replaced Doggett's low-comic Shylock with the "Fierceness and Fellness" of a melodrama villain. In Maria Edgeworth's novel *Harrington* (published in 1817), her eponymous hero is captivated by Macklin's performance as Shylock:

> Shylock appeared – I forgot everything but him. Such a countenance! Such an expression of latent malice and revenge, of everything detestable in human nature! Whether speaking or silent, the Jew fixed and kept possession of my attention. It was an incomparable piece of acting. Much as my expectations had been raised, it far surpassed anything I had conceived; I forgot it was Macklin; I thought only of Shylock.[33]

30 Granville, *The Jew of Venice*, 359.
31 Spencer, ed. *Five Restoration Adaptations*, 29–32.
32 Nicholas Rowe, *Some Account of the Life … of Mr. William Shakespeare* (in Rowe's 1709 edition of Shakespeare). Quoted in Brian Vickers, *Shakespeare: The Critical Heritage* (London: Routledge and Kegan Paul, 1974), vol. 2, 196.
33 Maria Edgeworth, *Harrington* (Peterborough, ON: Broadview Editions, 2004), 136.

FIGURE 2 Charles Macklin as Shylock.
Courtesy of the Folger Shakespeare Library, Washington DC.

At one time Macklin's costume included a red hat, which, based on his reading of Jewish history, he told Alexander Pope, was historically accurate. Evidently convinced of Macklin's fidelity to the author's conception of the role, Pope is said to have written, "This is the Jew / That Shakespeare drew."[34] Macklin is also said to have observed Jewish businessmen in the Exchange and nearby coffee houses. By the mid-eighteenth century, such observations were not difficult: the Jewish population of London had grown to between 7,000 and 8,000.[35]

Later in his career, Macklin wrote a farce called *Love a la Mode*, in which he also played the part of Beau Mordecai, "an unfeeling, wealthy Italian Jew ... described in the play as a reptile, a comic counterpart of his Shylock."[36] But Shylock was his signature role – and his portrayal of Shakespeare's Jewish moneylender defined the role for the second half of the eighteenth century. In the production's first year, 1741, Macklin played Shylock twenty-seven times, and continued to perform the role until his retirement from the stage in 1789.[37] When David Garrick, one of the first of the great actor-managers of England, took over the management of Drury Lane in 1747, his first production was *The Merchant* with Macklin as Shylock, a role he himself never took on. By 1789, Macklin had played Shylock 316 times and defined the role as a melodramatic villain of astonishing ferocity. As Toby Lelyveld puts it, "He was relentless, savage, ominous, venomous" and rendered his character's "malice and vengefulness" with such natural power that many spectators believed he "was some sort of devil."[38]

But changes were afoot. Even while Macklin was still playing Shylock, some theatergoers were prepared to accept sympathetic representations of other figures usually treated as negative stereotype, such as Richard Cumberland's portrayal of an English colonist in *The West Indian* (1771). Some years later, Cumberland wrote a play entitled *The Jew* (1794), whose title character, Sheva, played by a German actor, was a coarsely repellent

34 Lelyveld, *Shylock on the Stage*, 27.

35 Endelman, *Jews of Britain*, 41.

36 Lelyveld, *Shylock on the Stage*, 27.

37 Bulman, *The Merchant*, 25.

38 Lelyveld, *Shylock on the Stage*, 22–23. Macklin's Shylock was almost used as a political lever in 1753, when the Jew Bill, officially known as the Jewish Naturalization Act, was proposed to remove restrictions from foreign-born Jews residing in England. After its passage, opponents of the bill arranged for Drury Lane to revive *The Merchant of Venice*, in an effort to arouse anti-Jewish sentiment for the bill's repeal. Macklin was temporarily sidelined from the role but presumably it was his conception of Shylock which adversaries of the Jew Bill arranged to have produced. The bill was repealed. See J. Shapiro, *Shakespeare and the Jews*, 195–224; Katz, *Jews in the History of England*, 240–53.

and miserly usurer who turns out to have a heart of gold. Cumberland was praised by many for his creation of a Jewish character who displayed such generosity, but not apparently by Jews, an omission he recorded with some bitterness in his memoirs. Sir Walter Scott, creator of Isaac of York, the noble Jewish moneylender of *Ivanhoe* (1814), understood that Jews might resent the portrayal of a Jewish character whose heart of gold beat beneath a repulsive exterior.[39]

The major metamorphosis in the representation of Shylock took place during the nineteenth century as the stage image of the Jewish moneylender deepened and modulated in a series of brilliant portrayals by such actors as Edmund Kean, Edwin Booth, and Henry Irving. James Bulman notes several cultural and historical developments that prepared the ground for this change – "a sense of cultural enlightenment, a fascination with the exotic 'other,' and a public (if not private) disavowal of institutionalized anti-Semitism."[40] On the legitimate stage, a growing emphasis on human subjectivity encouraged actors to find motives for the behavior of "others," and to explore the psychology of characters hitherto treated as caricatures or stereotypes.

These developments coincided with the increasing presence of Jews in England and with their gradual, if uneven, acceptance in the English nation. By the early nineteenth century, the Jewish population of England had risen to between 12,000 and 15,000. By mid-century, the number had swelled to 30,000–37,000.[41] As numbers grew, civil disabilities were removed. Here are some significant landmarks:

In 1831, restrictions on Jewish traders in the City of London were removed.
In 1833, the first Jew was called to the bar.
In 1836, the first Jewish Alderman of the City of London was elected.
In 1841, the first Jewish baronet was created.
In 1847, the first Jew, Lionel Rothschild, was elected to Parliament, but refused to take his seat until the removal of the Christological oath in 1858.
In 1859, a naturalization bill was passed.[42]

[39] Gross, *Shylock: A Legend*, 211–12.

[40] James Bulman, "Shylock, Antonio, and the Politics of Performance," in *Shakespeare in Performance: A Collection of Essays*," ed. Frank Occhiogrosso (Newark: University of Delaware Press, 2003), 30.

[41] Endelman, *Jews of Britain*, 130.

[42] Ibid., 107; Felsenstein, *Anti-Semitic Stereotypes*, 45.

Eventually, large numbers of Jewish immigrants were absorbed and more or less acculturated but framing their experience solely in terms of the removal of civil disabilities overlooks the persistence of social prejudice. Nonetheless, for the nineteenth century, the Anglo-Jewish story, despite ineffectual schemes for mass conversion, ugly backlashes of anti-Semitic rhetoric, and hurtful episodes of social discrimination, is largely one of the increasing numbers and increasing participation in the host culture.[43]

Victorian England, at least at the upper levels of society, had absorbed Enlightenment principles and in general had become a more secular society, so that images of "diabolized Jews," which Hyam Plutzik, in a poem entitled "Portrait" (published in the mid-twentieth century) calls "the older objections," now seemed to many to be throwbacks to less civilized times, "hangdogs, hiding in the privies and alleys of the mind."[44] Anthony Julius cites several Victorian novels which "revert" to fantasies of the blood libel, such as Trollope's *The Way We Live Now* (1875) and *The Prime Minister* (1875–76), although the pre-eminent example was Dickens's *Oliver Twist* (serialized in 1837–39), whose Jewish villain Fagin runs a close second to Shylock as the best-known Jew in English literature.[45] Dickens was stung by some of the reactions to Fagin and tried to make amends. He substituted the name Fagin for "the Jew" in later editions, and he created a sympathetic Jewish character, Riah the Jew, in his final novel, *Our Mutual Friend* (1865), which essentially turns repellent "Jewish" traits like fawning into virtues like courtesy. Other nineteenth-century English novelists followed the philo-Semitic path taken by Cumberland and Edgeworth. Chief among them was George Eliot, whose *Daniel Deronda* (1876) was a powerful challenge to traditional notions of anti-Semitism, based on the author's extensive study of Jews and Judaism and her sensitive portrayal of the complexity of the Jewish world.[46]

Although sympathetic Jewish Shylocks came to be a hallmark of the Victorian period, this paradigmatic shift in the stage portrayal of Shakespeare's Jewish moneylender actually began five years before

43 On organized attempts at conversion, see Michael Ragussis, *Figures of Conversion: "The Jewish Question" & English National Identity* (Durham: Duke University Press, 1995), 15–56. On the persistence of what he calls "minor" anti-Semitism, from Victorian times nearly through the present, see Julius, *Trials of the Diaspora*, 255–83.

44 Hayim Plutzik, "Portrait," in *Apples from Shinar* (Middletown: Wesleyan University Press, 2011 [1959]), 31; Felsenstein, *Anti-Semitic Stereotypes*, 25–26.

45 Julius, *Trials of the Diaspora*, 203–5.

46 Ibid., 205–15. See Edgar Rosenberg, *From Shylock to Svengali: Jewish Stereotypes in English Fiction* (Stanford: Stanford University Press, 1960), passim.

Victoria came to the throne with Edmund Kean's electrifying production of 1814. (Figure 3) Heinrich Heine wrote years later how moved a female English spectator had been by a performance of Kean's in 1827:

> When I saw this piece played in Drury Lane there stood behind me in the box a pale British Beauty who, at the end of the fourth act, wept passionately, and many times cried out, "The poor man is wronged!"[47]

Accounts by many other spectators have testified to Kean's originality and effectiveness. Coleridge compared watching Kean play Shylock to "reading Shakespeare by flashes of lightning,"[48] while William Hazlitt observed that "our sympathies are much oftener with [Kean's Shylock] than with his enemies."[49] Here was a radically different Shylock, neither Doggett's buffoon nor Macklin's monster. Kean's Shylock was passionate, intelligent, energetic, and vibrant, and he played the ending of the trial scene in a way that evoked sympathy and compassion. As Toby Lelyveld put it, "For the first time, the stage-Jew was taking on human form, and for the first time the audience was able to appreciate it"[50]

Other Victorian actors of the period discovered ways to stress Shylock's dignity and humanity. Some actors retitled the play *The Tragedy of The Merchant of Venice*.[51] Edwin Booth, an American actor who developed his Shylock while working in England, wore the costume of an oriental patriarch. He also eliminated the fifth act so that the play ended on a tragic note with Shylock's agonized exit from the court room.[52]

Perhaps the most sympathetic Shylock of the nineteenth century was created by Henry Irving, whose dignified, patrician Shylock graced the

[47] Quoted in Gross, *Shylock*, 258–59. Heine remembered those tears, and the black eyes which shed them, when he was writing a general essay on Shakespeare's plays, in which he included *The Merchant* among the tragedies, despite its many comedic elements. He imagined that Shakespeare came to shape the play as the tragic outcome of centuries of Jewish persecution by Christians:

> Originally, perhaps Shakespeare wanted to please the mob by representing a werewolf at bay … But … it came to pass that in Shylock he presented – despite glaring elements of caricature – the justification of an unfortunate sect which providence, from inscrutable motives, loaded with the hatred of the lower and the higher mob, and which was not invariably inclined to requite this hatred with love. (Gross, *Shylock*, 259)

The tragedy, he argued, arose from "the madly agonized exultation" of a Jew when he had the opportunity to repay a tormentor "with interest for sins inflicted."

[48] Quoted in Lelyveld, *Shylock on the Stage*, 53.

[49] William Hazlitt, *A View of the English Stage* (London: Robert Stodart, 1818), 267.

[50] Lelyveld, *Shylock on the Stage*, 45.

[51] Ibid., 52.

[52] Ibid., 71.

FIGURE 3 Edmund Kean as Shylock.
Courtesy of the Folger Shakespeare Library, Washington DC.

stage from 1879 to 1905. (Figure 4) As he himself put it, "I look on Shylock ... as the type of a persecuted race; almost the only gentleman in the play and the most ill-used,"[53] but his portrayal also depicted Shylock as "a vengeful victim of racial intolerance," his vengefulness increasing over the years he played the role.[54] He made significant cuts in Jessica's lines to represent Shylock as the victim of a cruel and faithless child. In his early productions, he, like Booth, amputated the fifth act.[55] He inserted an episode which he borrowed from Verdi's *Rigoletto*, in which Shylock returns to his empty house after Jessica has eloped; an insertion intended to evoke maximum sympathy for Shylock. After Jessica has eloped, and a group of reveling masquers has left the stage, Shylock appears onstage alone, returning from dinner. He crosses the stage and knocks on the door of his house, only to find the house empty, his daughter gone, and himself the victim of her betrayal.[56] Like Kean and Booth, who had both toured America, Irving's American performances in *The Merchant* helped to establish the tragic approach to the play as the norm in mainstream productions on both sides of the Atlantic.[57]

This Victorian paradigm of Shylock, from Kean to Irving, replaced the comic or melodramatic villain of the eighteenth century, and its legacy of the dignified, sympathetic Shylock persisted well into the twentieth century, as countless actors and directors continued to find ways to humanize the character.

Nevertheless, important counter-currents were also in circulation at the very time the Victorian paradigm of Shylock installed itself in the mainstream theaters of England. In contrast to these stage images of the Jew as oriental patriarch or Victorian gentleman, there coexisted in the popular culture of the day the stereotype of the Jew as a foreign-born rural or urban peddler, perhaps an updated version of the Wandering Jew. The itinerant Jewish peddler of the countryside, who emerged in the eighteenth century, had, by the mid-nineteenth century modulated into an urbanized Jewish street peddler, the Old Clothes Man, a close cousin

[53] Joseph Hatton, *Henry Irving's Impressions of America* (London: Sampson Low, 1884).

[54] Bulman, *The Merchant*, 36.

[55] Linda Rozmovitz, *Shakespeare and the Politics of Culture in Late Victorian England* (Baltimore: Johns Hopkins University Press, 1998), 78.

[56] Irving appears to be the first to create an onstage house, rather than merely a door, for Shylock. See Stephen Cockett, "Serenade in a Gondola: Music and Interpolated Action in Irving's Production of *The Merchant of Venice*," in *Henry Irving: A Re-evaluation of the Pre-eminent Victorian Actor-Manager*, ed. Richard Foulkes (Aldershot: Ashgate, 2008), 99–116.

[57] Bulman, *The Merchant*, 146; Halio, ed. *Merchant of Venice*, 80–81.

FIGURE 4 Henry Irving as Shylock.
Courtesy of the Folger Shakespeare Library, Washington DC.

of Fagin.[58] He appears in drawings in *Punch* with his standard attributes: a long hooked nose and a thick beard, a sack, a black coat, and three hats stacked on his head. Todd Endelman describes the historical reality underlying the stereotyped image of the Jewish Old Clothes Man during the Victorian period:

> The most characteristic Jewish street trade was ... the buying and selling of old clothes ... Jewish old clothes men and dealers cared to the needs of an expanding urban population that could not afford to purchase new clothing. Hundreds of them fanned out each day through the streets and squares of middle-class and aristocratic London to purchase articles now deemed unfashionable or too worn by their owners ... Dealers in second-hand merchandise ... were notorious for purchasing stolen goods.[59]

Under the name of Shylock, a caricatured image of the Jewish dealer in secondhand garments appears in a series of burlesques of *The Merchant of Venice* produced in the mid-nineteenth century, a genre recently discussed at length by Richard Schoch.[60] As Schoch points out, these burlesques regularly parodied Shakespeare by severely cutting and domesticating his plots, representing his characters as familiar English stock figures, and larding the script with music, dancing, and songs (often to familiar arias and airs), as well as with outrageous puns. Written for a young, urban sophisticated audience, the burlesques targeted such icons of Victorian respectability and high culture as opera, melodrama, poetic drama, classical mythology, Arthurian legend, Arabian tales, English history, and of course "the pious pretensions of 'Legitimate' Shakespearean culture," as well as the cult of bardolatry.[61] Of Shakespeare's comedies, only *The Merchant of Venice* was turned into a burlesque, another indication that mainstream versions of the play often presented it in a more solemn mode, often as the tragedy of Shylock. Much of the mockery was in fact directed at mainstream productions of the so-called legitimate theaters, and at some of the great Victorian tragic actors already mentioned

[58] Felsenstein, *Anti-Semitic Stereotypes*, 58–89; Michael Shapiro, "Shylock the Old Clothes Man: Victorian Burlesques of *The Merchant of Venice*," in *Shakespeare's World/World Shakespeares: The Selected Proceedings of the International Shakespeare Association World Congress, Brisbane 2006*, ed. Richard Fotheringham, Christa Jansohn, and R.S. White, (Newark: University of Delaware Press, 2008), 122–24.

[59] Endelman, *Jews of Britain*, 43–44.

[60] Richard Schoch, *Not Shakespeare* (Cambridge: Cambridge University Press, 2002); Richard Schoch, "Shakespeare Mad," in *Victorian Shakespeare*, ed. G. Marshall and A. Poole (London: Palgrave Macmillan, 2003), vol. 1, 73–81.

[61] Schoch, "Shakespeare Mad," vol. 1, 73; M. Shapiro, "Shylock the Old Clothes Man," 124–27.

who were creating a radically new, dignified and sympathetic Shylock. The burlesques, by contrast, presented Shylock as the stereotypical Old Clothes Man, although it is not always clear whether their use of this figure was intended to evoke mockery toward the immigrant Jew, or to ridicule anyone who confused clichés with social reality.

The United States was for a time especially hospitable to this two-tiered arrangement of noble, sympathetic Shylocks in mainstream productions and caricatured Shylocks in more popular venues – what Lawrence Levine has described more generally as "lowbrow/highbrow."[62] Highbrow productions often involved British theater artists like Irving or British companies traveling in America, and home-grown productions also generally opted for the Victorian paradigm of the dignified, sympathetic Shylock.

Lowbrow versions of Shakespeare in a more distinctively American mode were popular throughout the late nineteenth century, even in the western states, where itinerant performers visited frontier towns and mining camps.[63] By the early twentieth century, Levine maintains, lowbrow productions of Shakespeare's plays, straight or parodic, were difficult to find in the United States, so that Shakespeare was known, at least to theater audiences, only through elite or mainstream productions, like David Belasco's in 1922.[64] Consequently, the image of Shylock that emerged in such American venues perpetuated the Victorian

[62] Lawrence Levine, *Highbrow/Lowbrow: The Emergence of Cultural Hierarchy in America* (Cambridge: Harvard University Press, 1988), 56–81. See also Lawrence Levine, "William Shakespeare and the American People: A Study in Cultural Transformation," *American Historical Review* 89 (1984), 34–66.

[63] Comic stereotyped representations of Jews, not necessarily associated with Shylock or Shakespeare, however, flourished in lowbrow venues of entertainment on both sides of the Atlantic. As Edna Nahshon has written, "The Hebrew comic came into vogue in the 1870s and would become a durable fixture in American vaudeville and British music halls and pantomimes" (Nahshon, ed. "Introduction," in *From the Ghetto to the Melting Pot: Israel Zangwill's Jewish Plays* [Detroit: Wayne State University Press, 2006], 49). Harley Erdman has documented stereotyped comic portrayals of Jews in melodrama and musical dramas of the period, as well as the ubiquity of "Hebrew comics" in the less legitimate venues of variety show, vaudeville, and traveling burlesque show (*Staging the Jew: The Performance of an American Identity* [New Brunswick, NJ: Rutgers University Press, 1997], 31–39, 63–92). Eventually, groups like the Anti-Defamation League drove these comic figures from the popular stage and, after a brief success in radio, film, and television, into oblivion. See Paul Distler, "Exit the Racial Comics," *Educational Theatre Journal* 18 (1966), 247–54.

[64] Levine, "William Shakespeare and the American People," 15–16. For a detailed discussion of radio as a venue for popular Shakespeare, see Daniel Yezbick, "Free Will: Orson Welles and the Remediation of American Shakespeare" (unpublished doctoral dissertation, University of Illinois, 2004). On Belasco's production, see Chapter 6 by Mark Hodin.

paradigm – the dignified, tragic Jewish moneylender developed on the English stage by actors from Kean to Irving.

The Victorian paradigm of Shylock outlasted the Victorian period, as new waves of Jewish immigrants, from Eastern rather than Central Europe, arrived in massive numbers in England and the United States from the 1880s until the beginning of World War II. By the outbreak of World War I, the Jews of England numbered 300,000.[65] In the decades after 1880, thousands of Jews left such countries as Russia, Poland, Lithuania, and Romania, many finding their way to the United Kingdom and North America, so that even as earlier Jewish immigrants were assimilating in England and the United States, more recent arrivals repeated the struggles of prior immigrants. Conceptions of Shylock originally forged in the nineteenth century therefore had continued relevance through much of the earlier twentieth century.

The sympathetic, dignified Shylock shows up in non-English twentieth-century adaptations of the play, such as Maurice Schwartz's 1947 Yiddish-language version, set in twentieth-century Italy, and a 1993 New Mexican version set in colonial New Mexico. In both of these adaptations, Shylock actually wins his case but cannot bring himself to cut into the flesh of another human being.[66] Such humane Shylocks outdo their Christian enemies in terms of civility, and so, in a way that Shakespeare did not intend, "better the instruction" they have received from their host culture. In such adaptations, as well as in early twentieth-century productions of the play itself, Shylock asserts his humanity in spite of what he has suffered, even, or sometimes especially, when the play ends in tragic defeat. These adaptations keep the Victorian paradigm of Shylock as, in Ellen Terry's words, a "heroic saint" even as they jettison Shakespeare's text.[67]

As always, there were counter trends. In the name of historical accuracy, William Poel played Shylock in his 1898 production for the Elizabethan Stage Society "as a ludicrous figure in a red wig and big false nose";[68] but it seems to have been regarded as an experiment in historicism and had little immediate influence. During the 1930s and 1940s,

[65] Endelman, *Jews of Britain*, 130.

[66] On Schwartz's production, see Chapter 7 by Edna Nahshon. See also Yael Chaver, "Writing for the Jews, Writing for the Goyim: Twentieth-Century Adaptations of *The Merchant of Venice*," *Jewish Social Studies*, (n.s.) 17:2 (Winter 2011), 28–47; and Elizabeth Klein and Michael Shapiro, "A New Mexican Adaptation of The *Merchant of Venice*," in *World Wide Shakespeares*, ed. Sonia Massai (London: Routledge, 2005), 31–39.

[67] Ellen Terry, *The Story of My Life* (London: Hutchinson, 1908).

[68] William Poel, *Shakespeare in the Theater* (London: Sidgwick and Jackson, 1913).

there was a tendency on the English stage, as John Gielgud put it, "to keep the play from becoming the tragedy of the Jews."[69] Determined to resist topicality that would link the anti-Semitism in the play with that of Nazi Germany and so evoke "excessive" sympathy for Shylock, several productions reverted to the older villainous Shylock, "purging the play of its Irvingesque sentiment" to the dismay and disapproval of most contemporary theater critics, who, for political as well as aesthetic reasons, expressed a preference for the Victorian paradigm.[70] In 1984, a production at the New Jersey Shakespeare Festival repeated Poel's experiment, with disastrous results.[71]

Despite the counter trends noted above, the Shylocks developed by Kean, Booth, Irving, and others in the Victorian era continued to refract the struggles of European Jews to find their places in the modernizing Western countries. English productions of the 1930s and 1940s resisted the Victorian paradigm and often featured quite negative representations of Shylock, whereas during the same period in the United States, the play was rarely produced, perhaps as a result of organized opposition from Jewish leaders, and the rare productions during this time were more or less indebted to the sympathetic Shylock developed in the nineteenth century. Through the twentieth century, however, as the children and

[69] Quoted in Patrick Stewart, "Shylock in *The Merchant of Venice*," in *Players of Shakespeare: Essays in Shakespeare Performance by Twelve Players*, ed. Philip Brockbank (Cambridge: Cambridge University Press, 1985), 18–19.

[70] John O'Connor, *Shakespearean Afterlives* (London: Icon Books, 2003), 123–25.

[71] Harry Keyishian, "The 1984 New Jersey Shakespeare Festival *Merchant* Production and Response: A Case Study," *On Stage Studies* 9 (1985), 11–29, offers an anguished account of a 1984 production of the play at the New Jersey Shakespeare Festival, held annually on the campus of Drew University in northern New Jersey, an area with a sizeable Jewish population. Paul Barry, artistic director of the company and director of *The Merchant*, felt he had to decide whether to "produce the play as Shakespeare 'intended,' or … sentimentalize and soften the characterization of Shylock so as to avoid offending the audience" (p. 15). Framing the issue as he did, Barry felt he would be compromising his integrity unless he produced the play according to the playwright's intentions. Confident that he understood those intentions, Barry directed actor Cal Winn to play Shylock as a comic villain, and to underscore his characters "otherness" by adopting what one observer called a "an eastern European accent, … a shuffling gait [and an] obsequious manner" (p. 17). Many spectators were offended by what they perceived as comic caricature, and said so quite vociferously at post-production discussions. Other spectators wrote letters denouncing the production, which included a Tubal as "quavering comic stereotype" (p. 16), for expressing anti-Semitic attitudes, which some attributed to Barry himself. To each complaining correspondent, Barry sent a form letter restating his conviction that he was being true to the playwright's intent and explaining that the play was a comedy with a comic villain who is cruel and undignified. It has been reported that so many subscribers refused to renew their subscriptions for the following season that Barry resigned as artistic director of the festival.

grandchildren of European immigrants assimilated and as immigration, always subject to the vagaries of war and domestic politics, was slowed to a trickle, the Jewish population of the two major English-speaking countries lost much of its Otherness.

Some recent productions of *The Merchant* have therefore tried to revivify the immigrants' struggle by mapping on to it similar experiences by other ethnic communities. In his 1994 touring production, Peter Sellars devised a scheme of "tribal casting," whereby African-American actors took the roles of the victimized Jews, while Latino actors played macho Venetians and Asian-Americans were cast as the ancestor-venerating women of Belmont. During the trial scene, onstage television monitors displayed footage of police officers beating Rodney King and of African-Americans demonstrating against his assailants' acquittal.[72] In a radical adaptation of the play entitled *The Merchant* **On** *Venice* (emphasis added) and set in a Southeast Asian neighborhood of Los Angeles off Venice Boulevard, Sushir Kurup, an Indo-American playwright, turned the Jewish moneylender and his daughter into Muslims surrounded by hostile Hindus.[73]

Bill Alexander's 1987 Royal Shakespeare Company production, discussed by Miriam Gilbert in Chapter 13 of this volume, avoided the Victorian paradigm by having Anthony Sher play Shylock as "an Eastern Jews closer to his own Semitic roots":

> Sher ... drew his image of Shylock ... from other Semitic peoples, Arabs, Palestinians, Iranians, peoples who are associated in the western mind with frightening and unpredictable extremes of behavior, with Islamic fundamentalism, death threat, and acts of political terrorism.[74]

Determined to avoid any trace of Olivier's attempt to recapture Irving'a Victorian Jewish gentleman in Jonathan Miller's 1970

[72] William Worthen, *Shakespeare and the Authority of Performance* (Cambridge: Cambridge University Press, 1997), 71–86.

[73] Changing Jews to Muslims and Christians to Hindus is a way of finding new subtextual sources of sympathy for Shylock, but it also demonstrates the applicability of the play to other ethno-religious rivalries. Ananda Lal, directing the play at Jadavpur University in Calcutta in 1997, stuck closely to the original text, but had his costume designer dress Shylock in "a black embroidered kaftan with upturned *nagra* footwear, an ethnic Muslim sartorial style which Indians could instantly recognize," in order to suggest the parallels between Christian persecution of Jews and the recent mosque-burning and mob violence directed by Hindus against Muslims. See Ananda Lal, "Re-creating *The Merchant of Venice* on the Indian Stage: A Director's Note," in *India's Shakespeare: Translation, Interpretation, and Performance*, eds. P. Trevedi and D. Bartholomeus (Newark: University of Delaware Press), 223; and Dennis Bartholmeusz, "Shylock's Shoes: The Art of Localization," in Trevedi and Bartholomeusz, eds. *India's Shakespeare*, 231ff.

[74] Bulman, *The Merchant*, 120.

production, Sher made Shylock a Levantine Jew, a figure who aroused sympathy by evoking the historical experience of other victims of ethnic or religious discrimination.

Other twentieth-century versions of *The Merchant*, most of them produced by Jewish theater artists, have aligned Shylock's plight with the pain suffered by Jewish victims in more recent moments in Jewish history. Setting the play in the Holocaust, for example, automatically generates sympathy for its Jewish characters, for however nasty and vengeful Shylock might be, he is the victim of even more vicious genocidal sadists. Such productions have replaced Victorian discriminatory tactics of name-calling and snubs with familiar images of Nazi-style brutality. Similar strategies have been used in Jewish-American fiction for some time, but two novels, Edward Wallant's *The Pawnbroker* (1962), and Saul Bellow's *Mr. Sammler's Planet* (1969), display vestiges of the Victorian paradigm. The protagonists of both books are well-educated Polish Jews who have survived the Nazi terror (as their families have not) and, having seen Absolute Evil, stand out as beacons of decency in a world, represented by Manhattan, where unimaginable luxury and wealth callously rub up against poverty, drugs, crime, and rampant sensuality.

If setting *The Merchant* in the Holocaust guarantees Shylock sympathy, transforming Venetian Christians into fascist murderers also eliminates any shred of romantic love from the production. Some directors have accepted this trade-off, sacrificing romantic love for the assured pathos of a Holocaust setting. Joshua Sobol, an Israeli director and playwright famous for his *Ghetto Trilogy*, set his 2002 production of *The Merchant* at the Illinois Shakespeare Festival (Normal, Illinois) in fascist Italy. Without adding a word to Shakespeare's text, Sobol not only used thickly textured ensemble work to recreate the ambience of Mussolini's last years, but also made it clear that Jessica was about to elope with Lorenzo not out of love but in obedience to her father's implied instructions designed for her to escape deportation. Sobol trashed rather than cut the romantic plot, which he did by farcical gender-bending: opening his shirt to prepare for Shylock's knife, Antonio was revealed to be a woman, "Antonia," Bassanio's lover. Portia not only donned male disguise but turned out to be a man, much to the delight of an evidently bisexual Bassanio.[75]

A few directors, seeking alternatives to the Victorian paradigm, have drawn upon another moment in recent Jewish history, the long and bitter conflict between Jews and Arabs before and after the establishment of the

[75] Michael Shapiro, *The Merchant of Venus* after the Holocaust, or Shakespearean Romantic Comedy Meets Auschwitz," *Cithara* 46:1 (2006), 3–23. See chapters 10 and 11 for other productions using Holocaust settings.

state of Israel in 1948. Charles Marowitz's 1976 adaptation, *Variations on the Merchant Venice*, set in Palestine in 1946, is framed by a radio news report of the bomb attack by a Jewish militant group (on the King David Hotel in Jerusalem), an act which killed and wounded many British army officers billeted there.[76] Marowitz uses huge chunks of Shakespeare's text, reassigns speeches, and adds many lines from Marlowe's *The Jew of Malta*. Indeed, Marowitz's Shylock resembles Marlowe's Barabas in his cynicism and brutality, a far cry from the humane and dignified Victorian Shylocks.[77] Like Sobol, Marowitz also sacrifices romantic love, when he has Shylock command Jessica to use her sexual wiles to extract information from Lorenzo, who, like the other Venetian men of the source-play, is a British officer in the Mandatory Administration. Like Sobol, Marowitz reduces the romantic plot to farce. Bassanio appears to Portia disguised first as Morocco and then as Aragon, so that by the time he appears as himself he knows which casket to choose. Marowitz cuts the fifth act and ends his adaptation when Shylock, along with Chus, recites Barabas's words, defies the Dúke's efforts to sentence him, leads a band of armed Jews in a takeover of the courtroom, and disarms and executes the British. Shylock then recites "Hath not a Jew eyes ...," no longer as an appeal for tolerance, or a plea for mercy, but as a justification for "better[ing] the instruction," that is, outdoing one's enemies in the taking of revenge.

In short, if not for Shakespeare's artistry, Fiorentino's tale about a wicked Jewish moneylender would have probably fallen into oblivion. Shakespeare's play, by contrast, has captured the imaginations of generations of readers, some of them actors and directors whose readings, influenced by their reactions to the times and places in which they lived, as well as by their own personalities, went on to inform their productions. At any given time, the popular image of Shylock therefore derives not only from Shakespeare's text but also from the representation of Shylock on the stage, especially during the nineteenth and twentieth centuries, when he evolved from a stereotypical villain into a more sympathetic figure. In our own day, Shylock continues to evolve, as the productions of *The Merchant of Venice* continue to reflect social and political developments in the world outside the playhouse.

[76] Edelman, ed. *The Merchant*, 91.

[77] Robin Russin's 2010 production of *The Merchant* in Riverside, California, was set in 1920s Venice, California and also imagined Shylock as a "tough" Jew: a former boxer characterized by his "pugnacity and marginalized status." See Robin Russin, "The Triumph of the Golden Fleece: Women, Money, Religion, and Power in Shakespeare's *The Merchant of Venice*," *Shofar* 31:3 (Spring 2013), 129.

2

The Anti-Shylock Campaign in America

Edna Nahshon

> That Shylock was a sheer figment of Shakespeare's imagination, there has never been any doubt. Yet this figment has acquired an objective reality more vital than that of most creatures of flesh and blood. His actions are still a byword, his name is a reproach, and his unfortunate co-religionists actually taxed sometimes with his reputed misdeeds.
>
> *(Cecil Roth, 1933)*[1]

The equation of Jew and Shylock, always derogatory in its implications, was common across diverse registers of discourse in the English-language world of past generations. Examples are numerous. "The Shylocks prefer to be on the navigable streams," grumbled an Ohio merchant in 1849 about his Jewish competitors.[2] In 1855 a *New York Times* story described a Jewish-Italian merchant as "as perfect an embodiment of a Shylock as ever trod the stones of the Rialto," a reference that required no further explanation.[3] In 1917, a South Bend, Indiana newspaper advertisement for a local bank featured the prize-winning essay of a home-grown school boy that began:

> Once there was a nice young fellow. His name was Antonio, and he had a girl whose name was Portia and she was real sweet on him, and he was short on money, so he borrowed some of Mr. Shylock for ninety days. He should have got it at the First National Bank for 6% but he didn't know that and he gave

[1] Cecil Roth, "The Background of Shylock," *Review of English Studies* 9:34 (April, 1933), 148.

[2] Amy Hill Shavitz, *Jewish Communities on the Ohio River* (Lexington, KY: University of Kentucky Press, 2007), 51.

[3] "The Mediterranean Merchants," *New York Times*, November 2, 1855, 2

Mr. Shylock a bond that said if he didn't pay it back on time, Mr. Shylock could cut a pound of meat off him next to his heart."[4]

The snub was similarly invoked in the more rarefied domain of the social elite: Katharine Graham (1917–2001), publisher of *The Washington Post*, described in her 1998 Pulitzer Prize-winning autobiography *Personal History* one of the earliest encounters with her paternal Jewish roots, a taboo subject at home. She was ten or eleven years old, the child of a wealthy family in Washington DC. As roles were being assigned for a class reading of *The Merchant of Venice*, a fellow student suggested that Katharine "should be 'Shylock' " because "she was Jewish."[5]

The term "Shylock," as noun and verb, became fully integrated into the English language. John Gross, author of *Shylock: A Legend and its Legacy*, claims that its use was more prevalent in the United States than in England. There, he writes, it has functioned as a "colorful analogy" that always kept the original dramatic character "in view," whereas in the United States it became more of a "free-floating" word that could also be used in the plural.[6] "Shylock" and "shylocking" as synonyms for loan sharks and their practices have also entered American literary culture, invoked by notable authors, among them Nathaniel Hawthorne, Mark Twain, Frank Norris, and Theodore Dreiser, and more recently by crime fiction writers, including Mickey Spillane, Elmore Leonard, and James Lee Burke. Even when "Shylock" was used for decidedly non-Jewish issues, as when American anti-slavery advocates appropriated Shylock's famous speech and replaced "Jew" with "Negro" so that "Hath not a Jew eyes" became "Hath not a Negro eyes" (and so forth),[7] or when America, trying to collect war debts after World War I was labeled "Uncle Shylock" by irate Europeans, the use of "Shylock," albeit indirectly, Judaized its subject and perpetuated the image of Jew as alien and victim on the one hand, and as excessively greedy and vindictive on the other.[8] Shylock was also incorporated into American political caricature, where he represented improper financial she shennanigans (Figure 5).

[4] Quoted in Hans Adler, "A History of the Anti-Defamation League" (unpublished manuscript, 1941), 133.

[5] Katharine Graham, *Personal History* (New York: Vintage Books, 1998), 52.

[6] John Gross, *Shylock: A Legend and its Legacy* (New York: Simon & Schuster, 1992), 226.

[7] See e.g. "Philadelphia, August 18," *Columbian Herald or the Patriotic Courier of North-America*, September 12, 1785, 3; "Postscript," *Pennsylvania Evening Herald and American*, August 13, 1786, 22; "The Declaration of American Independence," *Liberator*, September 5, 1835, 143.

[8] Benjamin D. Rhodes, "Reassessing 'Uncle Shylock': The United States and the French War Debt, 1917–1929," *Journal of American History* 55:4 (1969), 787–803.

FIGURE 5 "Shylock, We Would Have Moneys and Votes" (1872), *Harper's Weekly*; caricature by Thomas Nast (1840–1902).
Courtesy of the Museum of the City of New York.

In the United States, the use of "Shylock" has been declining in recent decades, sometimes in response to government intervention, as in Florida in April, 2009, when the official use of "Shylock" for predatory financial practices was expunged by then Governor Charlie Christ who signed a bill removing the words "shylock" and "shylocking" from his state's statute books. He did so, he said, out of respect for Florida's Jewish community, and declared: "Harmful terms that communicate hate have no place in our society – and especially not in our laws – and the removal of this language is long overdue."[9] This, however, has not been a universal trend. "Shylock" often appears as a synonym for swindling, rent-racking, usury, and other cut-throat business practices in the English-language press of former British colonies such as India, Pakistan, Swaziland, Nigeria, Zimbabwe, and Kenya. While these countries have practically no Jewish population nor a native history of anti-Semitism, the cultural norms of their educated English-speaking class – to which, one presumes, English-language journalists belong – were shaped by the British educational system and its veneration of Shakespeare.[10] With the globalization of Shakespeare, Shylock has even made his way to China, where he has come to represent both the negative characteristics of the materialistic West, and the victim of the Christians of the "White West."[11]

[9] "Florida to remove 'Shylock' from Loan Sharking Statues," *Orlando Sentinel*, April 27, 2009. In the summer of 2013, the Anti-Defamation League (ADL) asked the (Chicago) Tribune Media Services to apologize for "the use of a racial slur" in a nationally syndicated crossword puzzle, in which "Shylock" was the clue to the three-letter word, "Jew." The author of the puzzle, Victor Barocas, who is himself Jewish, said he intended no offense. He was thinking of Shylock simply as **a** Jew, which is factually correct, just as, say, "Tolstoy" or "Stalin" could hint at the answer "Slav." But the ADL evidently feared that some readers might arrive at the correct answer by assuming that Shylock and Jew were synonymous; in other words, that Shylock was **the** Representative Jew. See Deb Amlen, "Three letters, Starts with a 'J' – and Offends," *Forward*, July 12, 2013, 9.

[10] For recent examples in English see: from India, "Two Arrested in 'Operation Shylock,'" *New Indian Express*, June 19, 2013, available at http://newindianexpress.com; from Pakistan, "IMF: Modern Shylock," *Pakistan Observer*, June 12, 2011, available at http://pakobserver.net; from Swaziland, "Police 'shylock' scheme exposed," *Observer*, July 14, 2012, available at http://www.observer.org.sz; and "Siphasha challenges 'shylock' in court," *Time of Swaziland*, May 31, 2012, available at http://www.times.co.sz; from Nigeria, "Experts Advise Fashola To Build More Houses," *PM News*, June 9, 2013, available at http://pmnewsnigeria.com; and "Where Residents Are Abandoned to Fate," *Saturday Tribune*, January 7, 2012, available at http://www.tribune.com.ng; and from Zimbabwe, "Zimbabwe: Make Tourist Resorts Affordable," *Herald*, January 8, 2012, available at http://allafrica.com. For a scholarly discussion of "shylock" practices in Nigeria, see Toyin Falola, "My Friend the Shylock: Money Lenders and their Clients in South-Western Nigeria," *Journal of African History* 34:03 (November, 1993), 403, 423.

[11] See Fan Shen, "Shakespeare in China: The Merchant of Venice," *Asian Theatre Journal* 5:1 (Spring 1988), 23–37; Alexander Huang. *Chinese Shakespeares: Two Centuries of Cultural Exchange* (Richmond, UK: Curzon Press, 2009); Murray J. Levith, *Shakespeare*

From the nineteenth century on, as Jews were gradually integrating into their host societies, they came to consider the Shylock moniker as not only offensive but also as injurious to their social and economic standing. The prominent British musician Charles Kensington Salaman, a London Jew who successfully straddled both the gentile and Jewish worlds, conveyed in his 1882 treatise, *Jews As They Are*, the deep frustration of the modern Jew with the Shylock stereotype, contending that the character's "purely imaginary, vengeful, inhuman desires unjustly fastened upon the entirely fictitious Hebrew have balefully recoiled upon the whole Jewish race, with an injury to the character of modern Jews which may be regarded as almost irremediable."[12]

Though Anglo-Jewry was clearly invested in the Shylock issue, its major contribution to the controversial topic was primarily confined to scholarly commentary. The more practical efforts to curtail Shylock's ill-effects would mostly take place in the United States, where Jews were not hampered by much of the legal and economic impediments of European Jewry. The struggle against the impact of Shakespeare's fictive Jew, whom the American literary historian Louis Harap defines as the "archetype of the stereotype," began in the 1820s.[13] It commenced in a sparse and sporadic manner, gained momentum in the second half of the century, and in 1913 developed a centralized organizational muscle with the formation of the Anti-Defamation League.

The Jewish-American community during the first quarter of the nineteenth century was miniscule. In 1820 it numbered less than 3,000 people, many of them Sephardim (Spanish-Portuguese Jews) who concentrated in New York, Philadelphia, Charleston, Savannah, Richmond, and Baltimore.[14] Historian Eli Faber writes that they felt secure in their position within American society, enjoying freedom and full citizenry, yet he notes that even this "New Jerusalem" was not entirely free from anti-Semitism with the "Shylock" slur occasionally cropping-up in public discussion.[15] This happened, for example, in the 1784 debate at the Pennsylvania legislature regarding the granting of a charter for the formation of a new bank. The heated discussions included an attack against

in China (London: Bloomsbury Academic, 2004); Xun Zhou, *Chinese Perceptions of the "Jews" and Judaism: A History of the Youtai* (Richmond, UK): Curzon Press, 2000.

[12] Charles Kensington Salaman, *Jews As They Are*, 2nd edn. (London: Simpkin, Marshall & Co., 1885), 217.

[13] Louis Harap, *The Image of the Jew in American Literature*, 2nd edn. (Syracuse, NY: Syracuse University Press, 1978), 6.

[14] Eli Faber, *A Time for Planting: The First Migration, 1654–1820* (Baltimore: Johns Hopkins University Press, 1992), 107–8.

[15] Ibid., 133–34.

Jewish financiers by one member, and the assertion by another that he "could discover worse than a Shylock's temper remaining in the hearts of those despisers of Christianity," – probably a reference to Jewish financier Haym Salomon.[16]

Despite their minority status, it was with a sense of complete confidence in their right to speak up that two noted American-Jewish intellectuals, Isaac Gomez Jr. (1768–1831) of New York and Isaac Harby (1788–1828) of Charleston, South Carolina, critiqued from a manifestly Jewish perspective the truthfulness of *The Merchant of Venice*, a beloved and frequently produced playtext whose plot, mediated by various educational readers, was familiar to practically every school child in America. Gomez and Harby presented scholarly arguments, in both cases based on Gregorio Leti's book *The Life of Pope Sixtus the Fifth*, which was translated into English in the 1750s.[17] (Figure 6) Leti (1630–1701), the illegitimate son of a Milanese nobleman, left Italy due to religious and political resentments, moved to Geneva where he converted to Calvinism, and in the late 1680s lived and wrote briefly in England. In his biography of the Pope, he described in great detail a supposedly real-life Roman "pound of flesh" legal case that took place in the papal court in Rome in 1587 in which it is the rich Christian merchant who demands a pound of flesh from the impoverished Jew.[18] James Shapiro notes that Leti's account was well circulated in literary circles and greatly impressed eighteenth-century English interpreters of *The Merchant of Venice*, and is even mentioned in Maria Edgewater's novel *Harrington* (1817).[19] In the same vein, the *Biographica Dramatica* (1812), a major reference work, fully accepted Leti's report as the source for the play, explaining to the reader that the Shylock story was built on a "real fact," where the intended victim was the Jew and the perpetrator, a Christian. (Figure 7) Yet at the same time the *Biographica Dramatica* fully stood behind Shakespeare's

[16] Elizabeth Nuxoll and Mary Gallagher, eds. *Papers of Robert Morris, 1781–84* (Pittsburgh, PA: University of Pittsburgh Press, 2000), 682.

[17] Sixtus V, a highly controversial figure, served as Pope from 1585–90. He was known for his massive building projects and for his extreme measures in dealing with crooks and criminals.

[18] Leti was the author of eleven books. His book on Pope Sixtus V was published in 1699, enjoyed several editions in subsequent years, and was translated into English by Ellis Farneworth in 1754, a translation reissued in 1799. In a footnote to the pound of flesh story, the translator noted: "The scene betwixt Shylock and Antonio, in Shakespeare's *Merchant of Venice* seems to be borrowed from this story, tho' the poet inverted the persons, and decently enough, alter'd some of the circumstances."

[19] James Shapiro, *Shakespeare and the Jews* (New York: Columbia University Press, 1996), 122.

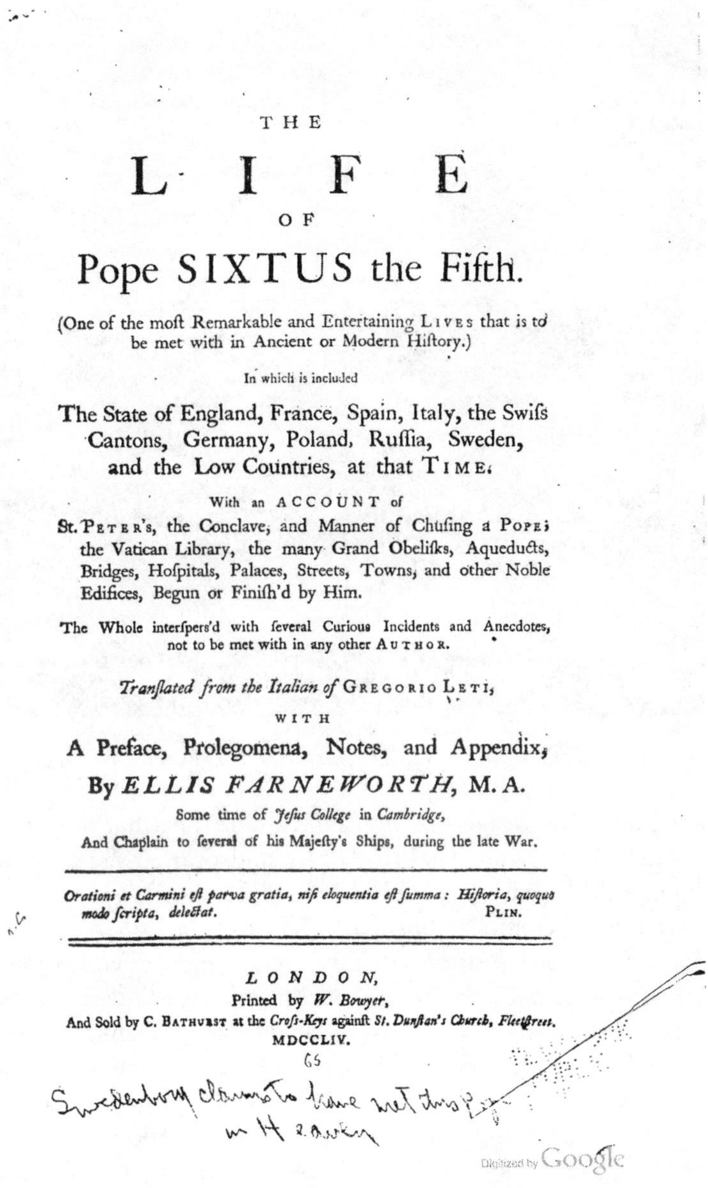

THE

LIFE

OF

Pope SIXTUS the Fifth.

(One of the most Remarkable and Entertaining LIVES that is to be met with in Ancient or Modern History.)

In which is included

The State of England, France, Spain, Italy, the Swiss Cantons, Germany, Poland, Russia, Sweden, and the Low Countries, at that TIME.

With an ACCOUNT of

St. PETER's, the Conclave, and Manner of Chusing a POPE; the Vatican Library, the many Grand Obelisks, Aqueducts, Bridges, Hospitals, Palaces, Streets, Towns, and other Noble Edifices, Begun or Finish'd by Him.

The Whole intersperse'd with several Curious Incidents and Anecdotes, not to be met with in any other AUTHOR.

Translated from the Italian of GREGORIO LETI,

WITH

A Preface, Prolegomena, Notes, and Appendix,

By *ELLIS FARNEWORTH*, M. A.

Some time of *Jesus College* in *Cambridge*,

And Chaplain to several of his Majesty's Ships, during the late War.

Orationi et Carmini est parva gratia, nisi eloquentia est summa: Historia, quoquo modo scripta, delectat. PLIN.

LONDON,

Printed by *W. Bowyer*,

And Sold by C. BATHURST at the *Cross-Keys* against *St. Dunstan's Church, Fleetstreet*.

MDCCLIV.

FIGURE 6 Title page of the English translation of Georgio Leti's *The Life of Pope Sixtus the Fifth*, 1779.

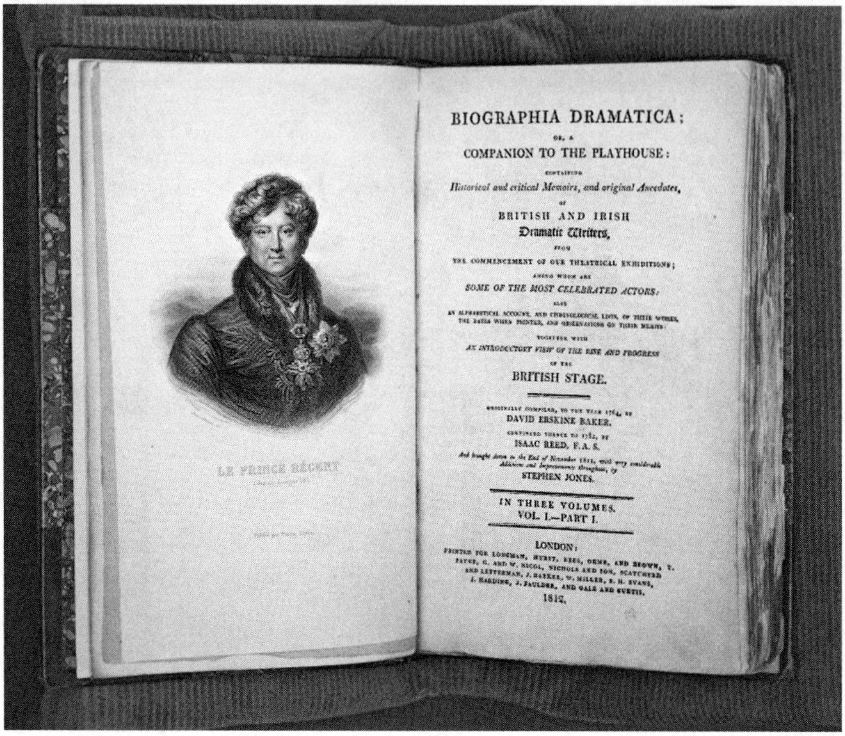

FIGURE 7 Title page of *Biographia Dramatica*, 1812. Public domain.

presumed inversion of facts by breezily commenting that the author was not obliged to adhere to historical facts and praised the dramatist for illuminating the quintessence of the Jew.[20]

In 1820, Isaac Gomez published *Selections of a Father for the Use of His Children*, a compendium intended for the general educational market.[21] (Figure 8) Among the dozens of essays on science, philosophy, and ethics that comprised the multi-subject anthology, Gomez included the full text of Leti's "pound of flesh" story. In his terse introduction he dryly stated: "The following subject shows that Shakespeare altered the character of Shylock, making him to be of the Jewish nation, when in reality he was not."[22] There is little doubt that the inclusion of Leti's account in

[20] Quoted in Isaac Harby, "The Merchant of Venice," in *Selection from the Miscellaneous Writings of the late Isaac Harby, Esq.* (Charleston, NC: Henry L. Pinckney and Abraham Moise, 1829), 29.

[21] Isaac Gomez, Jr., *Selections of a Father for the Use of His Children* (New York: Printed by Southwick and Pelsue, 1820).

[22] Ibid., 326.

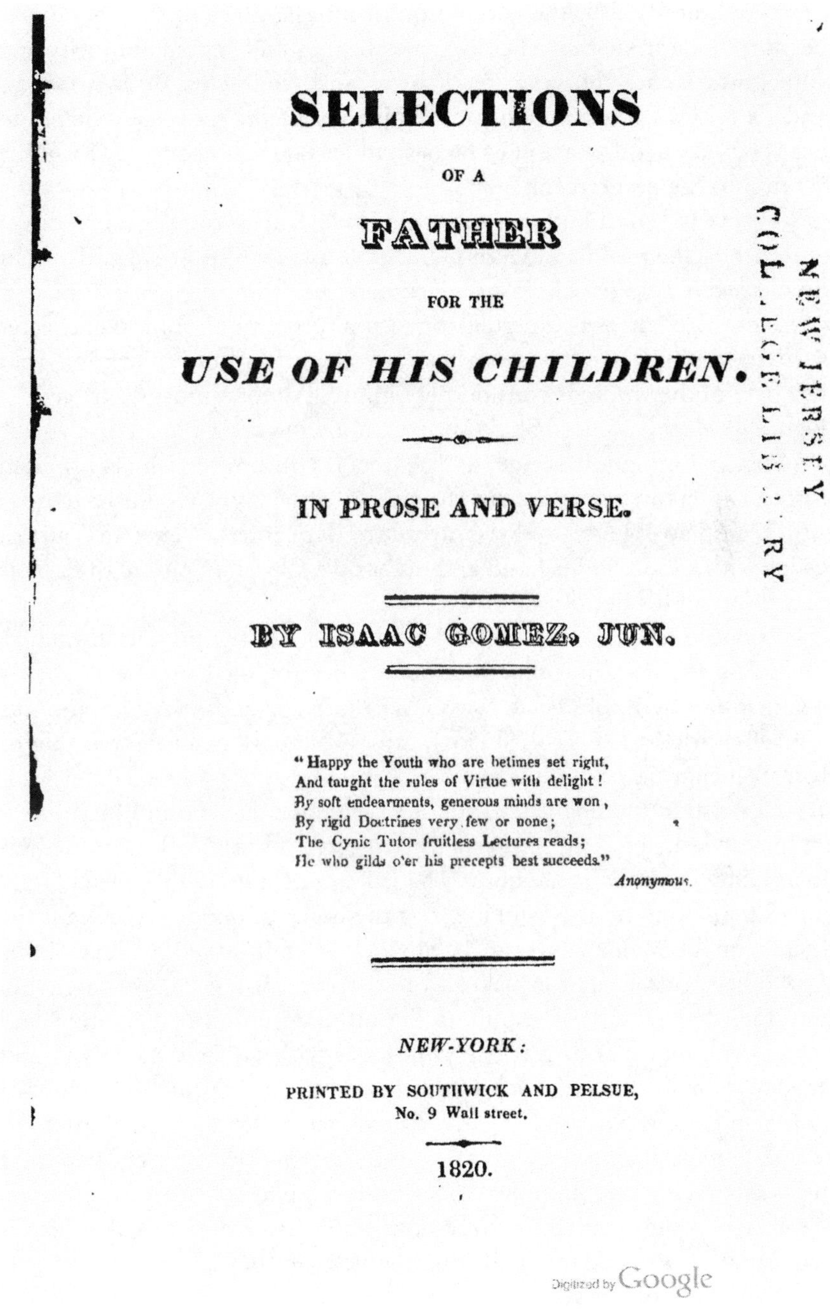

SELECTIONS

OF A

FATHER

FOR THE

USE OF HIS CHILDREN.

IN PROSE AND VERSE.

BY ISAAC GOMEZ, JUN.

"Happy the Youth who are betimes set right,
And taught the rules of Virtue with delight!
By soft endearments, generous minds are won,
By rigid Doctrines very few or none;
The Cynic Tutor fruitless Lectures reads;
He who gilds o'er his precepts best succeeds."
Anonymous.

NEW-YORK:

PRINTED BY SOUTHWICK AND PELSUE,
No. 9 Wall street.

1820.

FIGURE 8 Title page of Isaac Gomez, *Selections of a Father for the Use of His Children*, 1820.

a textbook devoted to the instillation of moral values in the young was meant to undermine the belief in Shakespeare's undisputed authority and to de-authenticate the veracity of his Jewish character. By inviting his reader's critical thinking, Gomez obliquely sent the message that prejudice is based on a distortion of facts so much so that it can transform the victim into the perpetrator.

Seven years later, author and critic Isaac Harby took a more direct approach to the problem in a thoughtful essay in which he suggested that the character of Shylock cast a dark shadow over all of Shakespeare's work, noting: "there is a certain unnatural atrocity about the character of Shylock, which renders disgust so prevalent over our admiration, that the effect of the whole is considerably injured, if not almost destroyed."[23] (Figure 9) Harby accused Shakespeare of bowing his genius to the vulgar prejudices of an ignorant age, and, like many future Jewish critics, used historical facts to argue that at the time of the play it would have been entirely implausible for a Jewish usurer to dare enter a Venetian court of justice with a knife in his hand and insist on a Christian pound of flesh as the penalty of his bond.

Leti's account inspired several Jewish works of fiction and drama. In 1856, *The Israelite*, an influential newspaper founded two years earlier in Cincinnati by Rabbi Isaac Mayer Wise, serialized over several months a novel entitled "The True Shylock Story," a richly embroidered tale of Roman intrigue based on Leti's tale. It told of Antonio Zavella, a lecherous Christian merchant/nobleman who demands a pound of the Jew Shylock's flesh, his extreme cruelty triggered by his failure to seduce Jessica, Shylock's pious daughter. The story concludes with Zavella, knife in hand, insisting on the fulfillment of the bond, announcing "I want the flesh from our Savior's assassin."[24] Shylock is finally saved by Pope Sixtus V, who berates Zavella for his lust for the innocent Jessica, a relationship forbidden by a law that prohibits the intimate union of Christian and Jew under penalty of death. The Pope sides with the Jew. Zavella is executed and Shylock is sent back to the ghetto with a substantial amount of money in compensation. The narrative so enthralled its readers that the newspaper had to explain with the appearance of the last installment that this was actually not the plot of Shakespeare's play.

Leti's account was considered a credible source for Shakespeare's "pound of flesh" narrative through much of the nineteenth century.

[23] Harby, "The Merchant."

[24] "The Shylock Story, (Concluded)," *Israelite*, April 4, 1856, 313.

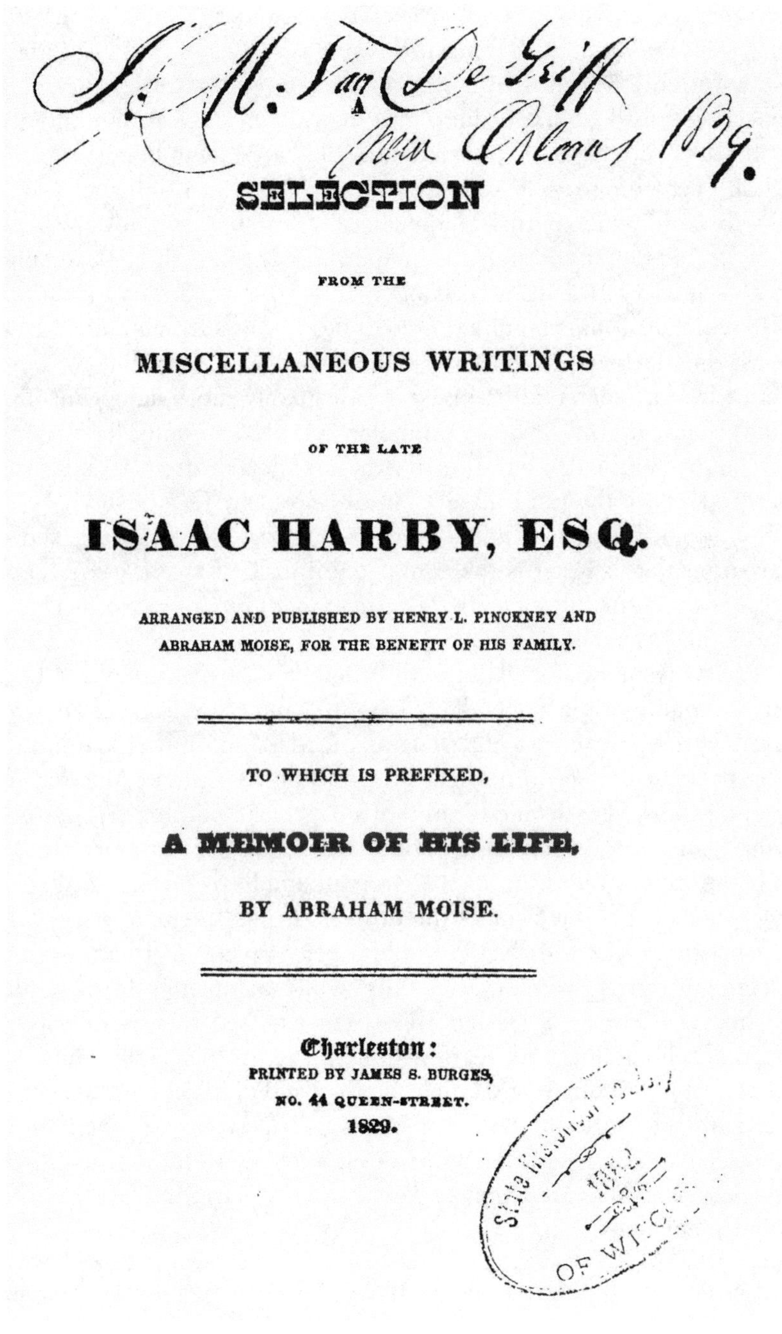

A

SELECTION

FROM THE

MISCELLANEOUS WRITINGS

OF THE LATE

ISAAC HARBY, ESQ.

ARRANGED AND PUBLISHED BY HENRY L. PINCKNEY AND
ABRAHAM MOISE, FOR THE BENEFIT OF HIS FAMILY.

TO WHICH IS PREFIXED,

A MEMOIR OF HIS LIFE,

BY ABRAHAM MOISE.

Charleston:
PRINTED BY JAMES S. BURGES,
NO. 44 QUEEN-STREET.
1829.

FIGURE 9 Title page of collected writings by Isaac Harby, published posthumously.

However, when Baron Joseph Alexander Hubner's book about Pope Sixtus appeared in English translation in 1872, it dismissed Leti's work as filled with more fiction than truth and faulted the author for turning his papal subject into a quixotic hero of romance. Once scholars pointed out that Leti's version actually postdated the Shakespearean text, the "pound of flesh" account soon lost credibility and sunk into oblivion.[25] While Leti's account, which naturally appealed to Jewish sensibilities, was generally discredited, it continued to palpitate in the Jewish cultural sphere and as late as 1922 it inspired Israel Efros's four-act drama *The Bloody Jest* in which Antonio claims a pound of flesh from a Roman Jew.[26] It was the last time Leti was cited as a source in a Jewish text.

In order to understand the next and arguably most significant phase of the American anti-Shylock campaign we need to consider the enormous change in the demography of American Jewry after 1820. Between 1825 and 1880 about 150,000 Central-European Jews, many of them from German-speaking lands, immigrated to the United States, settling in urban centers all across the country. Within half a century America's Jewish population ballooned from a tiny community of 3,000 in 1825 to 240,000 in 1880. The first wave of Central-European Jewish immigrants arrived in their new homeland with little capital or learning and began their occupational life as peddlers, laborers, and storekeepers. They also arrived without a meaningful religious leadership, and it was only in the 1850s that European trained rabbis began to settle in America. The German rabbis were distinctive in terms of their intellectual background, having a first-rate education in both Jewish and secular learning. This combination was the result of the German emphasis on the ideal of *bildung* as an integral element of the process of Jewish emancipation. The German states required that all rabbis speak proper German and hold German university degrees, and, thus, while completely loyal to their Jewishness, German rabbis had also been exposed to rigorous secular academic scholarship with its devotion to classical learning. They were well-versed in the ongoing German literary and cultural discourse of the time, admired Gotthold Ephraim Lessing's milestone play *Nathan the Wise* as a plea for toleration, and were familiar with the learned discussions regarding *The Merchant of Venice*, especially in the larger context of Jewish emancipation.

[25] Joseph Alexander Hubner, *The Life and Times of Sixtus the Fifth* (London: Longmans, Green, and co., 1872), 124. It also became clear that the original 1699 version of Leti's book did not include the "pound of flesh" story and that the account was a late addition.

[26] Israel Efros, *The Bloody Jest* (Boston: Gorham Press, 1922).

The German rabbis' arrival in America provided the local Jewish community with an intellectual elite and boosted the formation of a first-rate English-language Jewish press and other cultural institutions. Moreover, the rabbis' religious position and cultural erudition granted them a respected place in the non-Jewish world where some rabbis collaborated with gentile social reformers and were elected to school boards. Often functioning as cultural intermediaries, they were invited to address general audiences and their lectures and sermons were often reported and even reproduced in full in the local press. Straddling two worlds, these rabbis/intellectuals were acutely sensitive to the image of the Jew in gentile society. "Shylock" became a frequent topic of lectures in which the rabbi offered a close reading and careful analysis of *The Merchant of Venice* from a Jewish perspective and explained the inaccuracies of some elements of the Shylock figure. The great importance the rabbis attached to the Shylock issue was reflected in 1888 in the new academic requirements of Hebrew Union College, the first American seminary for the training of rabbis in Reform Judaism (formed in 1875): it mandated that all incoming rabbinic students take an English writing test based on three major texts: works by Bacon and Milton, and *The Merchant of Venice*.[27]

In the mid-nineteenth century, with the advent of American state-run education, American-Jewish children began to attend public schools, many of which had an overt evangelical curriculum which Jews, at times collaborating with Catholics, strongly opposed. Jewish parents were likewise concerned with the teaching of materials that potentially encouraged anti-Semitic sentiments. Moreover, while Shakespeare was idolized by educators, what American children actually read at school were not full Shakespearean plays but rather extracted and at times rewritten excerpts that appeared in instructional primers such as the extremely popular McGuffey's Readers.[28] *The Merchant of Venice* was one of the anthologists' favorite texts. Jonathan Burton, who analyzed a McGuffey's pedagogic adaptation of the *Merchant of Venice* trial scene, demonstrates how the selection, editing, and follow-up questions of Shakespearean excerpts reflected the anthologist's socio-moral and religious values. The

[27] "The U.A.H.C.," *American Hebrew*, July 13, 1888, 160.

[28] Jonathan Burton notes that the McGuffey readers, which sold 120 million copies between 1836 and 1920 were particularly popular in the Midwest and South and in rural small-town schools. They did not do as well in the big cities and the Northeast. "Lay Off, McGuffey: Excerpting Shakespeare in Nineteenth-Century Schoolbooks," in *Shakespearean Education: Power, Citizenship, and Performance*, Coppelia Kahn, Heather S. Nathans, and Mimi Godfrey, eds. (University of Delaware Press, Newark, 2011), 110, notes 6 and 7.

unit, which first appeared in 1844 in McGuffey's Fourth Reader, cut 312 of the original scene's 452 lines, excised most of the secondary characters, compounded Portia and the Duke into one nameless male judge, and stressed Shylock's status as an alien, a term the reader defined as "one who is not entitled to the privilege of citizen."[29] The unit's study questions further emphasized Shylock's otherness, for example by asking "What does he mean by saying 'my deeds upon my head'?" a question set to remind students of the Crucifixion where, according to the Gospel of Matthew, the Jewish mob preferred to pardon the criminal Barabas rather than Christ and exclaimed, "His blood be upon us and our children" (Matthew 27:25).

In the late nineteenth century a growing number of rabbis and communal leaders, many of them American-born, began to call for the removal of *The Merchant of Venice* from America's elementary and high schools, where the play, or rather selected abridged excerpts of it – was taught. They argued that the text led to the humiliation of Jewish school children and fomented prejudice and ill-will among the young. In 1911 the Central Conference of American Rabbis (Reform) urged that the teaching of the play be confined to colleges and universities, elite venues where it would be studied in a scholarly fashion.[30] Though there was often felt sympathy for the Jewish request on the local level, the main obstacle was the College Entrance Examination Board, formed in 1900. One of the texts students were tested on in depth in the Board's entry exam was *The Merchant of Venice*, thus practically dictating the play's inclusion in high school curricula.[31] In 1914, the newly formed Anti-Defamation League took over the campaign, and succeeded in convincing the College Board to drop the play from its required texts. Some one hundred American cities soon agreed to discontinue teaching the play in their public schools. By the time World War II broke out most American public schools no longer taught *The Merchant of Venice* to their charges.

The oft expressed suggestion that the play be taught at the university level was not a mere rhetorical ploy. It reflected the Jewish enlightenment-inspired belief in the fair-mindedness of the intellectual class and the historically based Jewish fear of the uneducated masses who, it was thought, could be easily swayed by anti-Semitic rhetoric. These sentiments fed for a long time the Jewish anxiety over free performances of *The Merchant*

[29] Ibid., 104.
[30] "Bar 'Merchant of Venice'," *New York Times*, July 5, 1911, 11.
[31] College Entrance Examination Board, *Plan of Organization for the College Entrance Examination Board*, 11. Available at https://archive.org/details/cu31924031758109.

of Venice in large public spaces. In 1955, for example, this led to a last minute cancellation of an open-air performance of *The Merchant* in Philadelphia's Reyburn Park, opposite City Hall. The city authorities explained that the play had a history of controversy and that city policy did not allow for the use of city property for anything of a controversial nature.[32]

Seven years later, a free open-to-the public production of the play at New York's Central Park could not be stopped. In 1962 Joe Papp, son of Jewish East European immigrants and founder of Shakespeare in the Park, planned to open the new 2,300 seat Central Park amphitheater with a production of *The Merchant of Venice* starring George C. Scott as Shylock. The Jewish leadership in New York, both secular and religious, was aghast. A delegation of the New York Board of Rabbis, an organization representing 800 Reform, Conservative, and Orthodox rabbis in the New York area, denounced the enterprise. The rabbis were particularly alarmed by plans to broadcast the production on national television.[33] Rabbi Louis Newman of New York's Reform Temple Rodeph Shalom delivered a searing sermon in which he called the decision to produce the play in a municipal space "hate-provoking" and "obnoxious," and argued that the telecast for a mass audience would enhance anti-Semitism. Papp stood his ground and declared he did not consider the play anti-Semitic. When the play opened, Jewish fears that it would trigger a wave of anti-Jewish sentiments proved highly exaggerated. In fact, Helen Epstein, Papp's biographer, considers the Central Park production of *The Merchant of Venice* as Papp's "official coming out as a Jew."[34]

There may be a measure of truth to Epstein's observation. Papp, the son of Russian immigrants, was a product of a new Jewish community. The mostly Yiddish-speaking 2½ million East European Jews who immigrated to America between 1881 and 1924 were considerably less troubled by Shylock than their Central-European predecessors. Fleeing pogroms and intense state-sponsored anti-Semitism, they were not as sensitive to their public image among the gentiles nor did they desire to "pass" and adopt the style and manners of the Protestant elite. Their left-wing intellectual leadership was entrenched in Russian literature and culture where Shakespeare was respected but not deified. Instead

32 "'Merchant' Canceled: Philadelphia Official Advises Against 'Controversial' Play," *New York Times*, August 17, 1955, 24.

33 "Rabbis Protest Showing of 'Merchant' on TV: Papp May Ask CBS to Limit Taped Preview of Play to Local Stations," *New York Times*, June 15, 1962, 17.

34 Helen Epstein, *Joe Papp, an American Life* (New York: Little, Brown and Co., 1994), 175.

of completely rejecting Shylock they actually appropriated and Judaized him. Beginning in 1901, the thriving Yiddish theatre in New York performed *The Merchant of Venice*, giving it a decidedly Jewish tilt. Some of its most illustrious actors, especially Jacob P. Adler, performed the role to critical acclaim, both on the Yiddish and English-language stage.

Still, the question remains, was Papp right in his assumption that at this day and age the play no longer gives rise to anti-Jewish sentiments? The findings of a relatively recent study conducted by Yael Feiler, a Swedish theater scholar, who compared the reception of three completely different productions of the play, two in Sweden and one in Germany, show that after each performance, regardless of aesthetic style and composition of audience, nearly a quarter of the spectators modified their pre-show viewpoints and were more willing to agree with anti-Semitic statements.[35] Feiler's conclusion, which she admits she did not anticipate at the beginning of her research project, is that as the Shakespeare text was the only common element in the three productions it must be the text itself that swayed spectators toward increased anti-Jewishness. It would be intriguing to examine if a study of British or American audiences would yield the same results.

Presently, American Jews seem to no longer fear the play's repercussions. After years of battle, *The Merchant of Venice* has become an almost "Jewish play," for it is largely Jews who care about it, write on it, talk about it, and are the first to buy tickets for its revivals. Nearly a century ago, Israel Zangwill, Anglo-Jewry's premier writer, commented on the Shylock problem, noting that every age rewrites the old masterpieces as part of a process of an everlasting interpretation and said "It is not important what Shakespeare meant as what he might mean to us."[36]

[35] Yael Feiler, "What Happens When *The Merchant of Venice* is Being Staged?" in *Shakespeares Shylock och antisemitismen*, eds. Yael Feiler and Willmar Sauter (Stockholm: Stiftelsen för utgivning av teatervetenskapliga studier, 2006), 133–63.

[36] Israel Zangwill, "Shylock and Other Stage Jews," in *The Voice of Jerusalem* (New York: Macmillan Company, 1921), 242.

PART II

DISCOURSES

3

Shylock in German-Jewish Historiography

Abigail Gillman

This essay discusses two distinct interpretations of Shylock written by noted German-Jewish intellectuals; one a historian, the other a cultural critic. Both works open a window onto defining moments in modern German-Jewish history and culture. The first work, published in 1880, was composed by the eminent historian, Heinrich Graetz (1817–91), author of the monumental *History of the Jews*, who, at the age of sixty-three, took the unusual step of investigating the historical origins of a fictive literary character in a lengthy essay titled "Shylock in Legend, in Drama, and in History."[1] It first appeared in *Monatsschrift für die Geschichte und Wissenschaft des Judentums*, an important German-Jewish scholarly journal and later appeared in booklet form.[2] Approximately fifty years later, in 1937, living under the oppression of the Nazi regime, Hermann Sinsheimer (1883–1950), a noted theater critic and scholar, devoted an entire book manuscript to Shylock. The book was translated into English in 1943 with the title *Shylock: History of a Character* and was finally published, with an introduction by the English writer John Middleton Murry, in 1947 in London, where Sinsheimer had lived as an immigrant

[1] "Shylock in der Sage, im Drama und in der Geschichte."

[2] *Monatsschrift für die Geschichte und Wissenschaft des Judentums* 29 (September, 1880), 337–54. The journal was published monthly and then bimonthly for almost ninety years (1851–1939), and can be viewed in its entirety at http://compactmemory.de. In this chapter, I quote from the second (independent) edition of Graetz's essay (Krotoschin: Verlag von B.L. Monasch & Co, 1899). All translations are my own. The phrase "faktische Grundlage" appears in Graetz's concluding paragraph.

refugee since 1938.[3] The book was finally published in German by the Ner Tamid Verlag in 1960.

While Graetz and Sinsheimer wrote in a seemingly detached scholarly mode, both conceded that their interest in Shylock was topical, inspired by the resurgence of Jew-hatred they witnessed and endured in their lifetimes. In effect, Shylock served both writers largely as a screen upon which they could project their own experiences of degradation, as they struggled to understand why "The Jews ... are still looked upon as Shylocks, or, rather, Shylock still stands for the Jews."[4] This common premise notwithstanding, Graetz and Sinsheimer came to opposing conclusions about Shylock's usefulness *for* the Jews, and also, about Shakespeare's motives for creating Shylock: Graetz maligns Shakespeare for aiding and abetting Jew-hatred, while Sinsheimer praises him for creating a model of a dignified and sympathetic Jew. In short, in the fifty years separating these two studies by major German-Jewish intellectuals, Shylock was transformed from a stereotyped Stage Jew into a symbol of hope and redemption.

Graetz lays out the goals of his study in a forthright manner: (1) to trace the stages of the legend of the *Fleischverpfändung*, the pledge of a pound of flesh as collateral as is stipulated in the bond; (2) to demonstrate that in sources used by Shakespeare the lender seeking the pound of flesh was not always a Jew; and (3) to explain why it was that Shakespeare so completely Judaized the lender. Graetz argues that the figure of the greedy and bloodthirsty Jewish moneylender has no historical basis, and so no valid connection to Jewish history. Graetz acknowledges that Shylock has been a severe liability for the Jews but finds a deeper injustice in the character's ahistoricity. Shakespeare, he charges, drew opportunistically on current events to create a tendentious play that would appeal to his patrons and to the masses, thus creating the consummate diabolical Jewish villain. Shakespeare's character, says Graetz, is not an artistic achievement; it is a form of libel (*lügenhafte Beschuldigung*), and thus, part of an old story – Christians demonizing Jews – which, in Germany in the 1870s, had just begun a new and lethal chapter:

> The modern *Razzia* against the Jews has taken on a philosophical or ethnophysiological stripe: it is justified through the fatality of race. In order to prove the

[3] I quote from the second English edition, *Shylock: History of a Character*, trans. (New York: Benjamin Blom, Inc., 1960). The original German version was titled *Shylock, Geschichte einer Figur*; the Ner Tamid Press is the Jewish publishing house founded by Hans Lamm in Munich in 1957.

[4] Sinsheimer, *Shylock*, 17.

> inferiority, or the general harmfulness of the Semitic or Jewish race, one turns first to the stock market, next to literature. The bloodthirsty Shylock is the current trump card of those who no longer dare to trot out the accusation of desecrating the host or poisoning well.[5]

In fact, there is much to suggest that Graetz was less interested in educating his readers, most of whom were Jews, than he was in using the topic as a pretext to discredit anti-Semitism as a form of baseless slander.

The opening words of Graetz's essay introduce slander as a central concern. He begins by alluding to the biblical "suffering servant" of God, who is punished for crimes he did not commit: "'for he was cut off out of the land of the living ... And they made his grave with the wicked ... although he had done no violence, neither was any deceit in his mouth.'"[6] A related epitaph from Francis Bacon follows: "*Audacter calumniare, semper aliquid haeret*" – slander boldly, something always sticks. Graetz even uses Shakespeare's own words to make his point: "Be thou as chaste as ice, as pure as snow; thou shalt / not escape calumny."[7] Shylock's literary genealogy, as presented by Graetz, is highly selective; he does not mention Judas Iscariot, the tradition of Jewish moneylending, or any other possible historical influences, nor does he discuss Shakespeare's artistic decisions. The problem is not only, as Susannah Heschel notes, that Graetz has no interest in *The Merchant of Venice* as a work of literature; it is that he approaches the character Shylock as a historian on the defensive, determined to dissociate Shylock from historical Jews and Jewishness.

By contrast, Hermann Sinsheimer's study embraces Shylock as an inspiring character on a par with the heroes of the Hebrew Bible. Sinsheimer's preface introduces the study as a tribute to Shakespeare:

> Shakespeare created the greatest Jewish character since the Bible. Necessarily, he has thus recorded Judaism – that is to say, he has made and written Jewish history.
>
> This book is intended as a tribute to him for this by interpreting Shylock from the Jewish point of view.
>
> In doing so, Shylock has to be treated, not only as a fictitious character, but also as a figure in Jewish history.[8]

Sinsheimer's book begins on a historical note, surveying more than fifty sources on ancient and medieval Jewish history, on the history

[5] Graetz, "Shylock," 2.

[6] Ibid., 1. The source (not mentioned in the essay) is Isaiah 53:9–10.

[7] *Hamlet*, 3.1.

[8] Sinsheimer, *Shylock* , 17.

of Jews in England, and on the place of Jews in German theater. He then – like Graetz – narrows the focus on the medieval motif of the *Fleischverpfändung*. But Sinsheimer emphatically rejects Graetz's conclusion that Shakespeare's approach is continuous with this pernicious tradition. Rather, exonerating Shakespeare, he argues that *The Merchant of Venice* turns the legend on its head: over and against his plentiful sources, historical and legendary, Shakespeare's characterization and plot *refute* the medieval myth of the Jew:

> The old fable yielded the material and the cause. But Shakespeare did the rest – and in so doing he leaves the old fable far behind. No Jewish "problem" is expressly touched. But in some way or other Shylock's arguments, reflecting the fate of the medieval and post-medieval Jew, make up for this. He becomes the spokesman of the bondsmen of medieval Christianity.[9]

In Sinsheimer's eyes, Shakespeare does not perpetuate the myth of the diabolical Jew; rather, he "leaves the old fable far behind," giving "to the European myth of the Jew, as to many another myth and mystery of our earth, "a local habitation and a name."[10] *The Merchant of Venice* becomes the symbolic *Yad Vashem*, the memorial site, of the medieval myth of the Jew. As Sinsheimer concludes, "the anti-Semites must not be allowed to call Shakespeare as a witness for their side."[11]

Whereas Sinsheimer came to the play as a working theater critic, Graetz was a historian and biblical scholar.[12] His interest in Shylock, a literary character, is surely a function of Shakespeare's immense popularity in Germany at that time. Indeed, William Beatty-Kingston (1837–1900), a British writer and dramatic who had lived in Germany for several years, had come to feel that the Germans had a greater appreciation of Shakespeare than did the English: "It is humiliating enough that we should be compelled to admit the greater popularity of Shakespeare's plays in Germany than in England without confessing that we know very little about them and are incapable of appreciating them."[13]

[9] Ibid., 136.
[10] Ibid.,144.
[11] Ibid.
[12] Other articles he published in the same issue of the *Monatsschrift* deal with "An Obscure Passage in the Description of the Erection of the Temple," "The interchanging of אתה and, עתה," and "Ancient Jewish Catacomb Inscriptions in Southern Italy, according to Prof. Ascoli." For a comprehensive discussion of Graetz's career and a bibliography of his works as seen from a contemporary perspective, see I. Abrahams, "H. Graetz, the Jewish Historian," and "The Writings of H. Graetz Chronologically Arranged," *Jewish Quarterly Review*, 4:2 (January, 1892), 165–203.
[13] W. Beatty Kingston, "Shylock in Germany," *The Theatre* (January, 1880), pp. 17–20;86–90.

Consequently, Henry Irving's innovative Shakespearean revivals, first of *Hamlet* and then of *The Merchant of Venice*, which opened at the Lyceum Theatre in London on November 1, 1879 drew tremendous attention in Germany. *The Merchant*, Beatty-Kingston writes, "proved a theatrical event of such extraordinary moment and interest" that the London correspondents of leading German newspapers have discussed at considerable length Irving's interpretation of Shylock, especially as the play "has been an established favourite upon the German stage ever since its first performance at Berlin, nearly a century ago."[14] Graetz seems to have been reacting to the rehabilitation of Shylock, which was the dominant trend of Shylock's stage interpretation in the last quarter of the nineteenth century. Ross Lewin argues that in eighteenth-century Germany the Shylock figure embodied the Jewish threat to German society, whereas in the nineteenth, liberal Jewish intellectuals such as Boerne, Heine, and Gans openly identified with Shylock, reflecting a new phase in the relationship between American-Jewish and German Christians, one framed "in a discourse of civil rights."[15] During this period, the enterprise of "countering Shylock" in Germany also took the form of a debate among legal scholars: Rudolph von Thering's 1877 essay "Der Kampf ums Recht" argued that Portia's judgment is baseless, whereas Josef Kohler and others claimed that the trial was turning point in the history of progressive legal systems, because Antonio is saved through an act of juridical reinterpretation.[16]

Graetz's essay is interesting not only in terms of its conclusions, but also in its over-reliance on the discourse of historical facticity to argue that Shakespeare was one of the first to draw on anti-Semitic traditions in order to present the Jewish moneylender as a villain. The earliest sources Graetz cites in which a person borrows money against a pound of flesh were religiously neutral or "innocent"; the motif appears in a verse novel by the French troubadour Herbers, "Dolopathos or the Seven White Masters of Rome," and in the Latin collection *Gesta Romanorum*. Typically, the borrowers need money to win the love of a beautiful woman who turns up afterwards in male garb, as a judge or lawyer. But these stories did not associate the moneylender with any particular confession, nor was society "poisoned" by Jew hatred. A German medieval poet first introduced a song wherein a young man in need of money pledges his own body to a Jewish lender. When he fails to repay the debt, the two

[14] Ibid.
[15] Ross Lewin, "Shylock in Germany" (dissertation, Stanford University, 2000) p. 7.
[16] Ibid.

men go to Kaiser Karl, who instructs him to remove "*ein Pfund schmers weder minder noch merr*" (a pound of flesh no less no more) at risk of his own life. The Jew then reneges on his suit altogether, forgoes the thousand Gulden and turns over two hundred more to free himself from the agreement. It is hardly a literary masterpiece, Graetz observes, but the characterization of the Jew is favorable for an age in which the Jew was typically cast as a scapegoat in the popular imagination.

In Graetz's account, the "age of innocence" ends with a tale which most scholars believe was Shakespeare's immediate source for the story of the Jewish moneylender and the pound of flesh; it appeared in the collection of novellas, *Il Pecorone* (1378), by the Italian Giovanni Fiorentino. Foreshadowing his argument about Shakespeare, Graetz speculates that "political circumstances" must have led Fiorentino to introduce the *falso Giudeo*, as Fiorentino was writing in the aftermath of the Black Death, when Jews were being blamed for every form of evil.[17] But, as Michael Shapiro has argued in Chapter 1 of this volume, Fiorentino's Jewish moneylender is not depicted as particularly villainous nor as especially Jewish. Yet, over time, with works such as the English ballad "Gernutus, the Jew of Venice, or a New Song Shewing the Cruelties of Gernutus a Jew" from Percy's *Reliques*, the diabolical Jew became a fixture of the legend. While Graetz admits that the type appears also in Persian and other oriental tales, he is convinced that the motif is the product of Christian Europe, where traditional demonizing accusations of host desecration, ritual murder of Christian children, and well-poisoning were far more common than they were in Middle-Eastern cultures.

Although Graetz takes the pains to recount the literary antecedents of the pound of flesh story, he dismisses them as insignificant, maintaining that it was Shakespeare's decision to "place a Jewish Shylock" on stage which was to turn a marginal figure, a "nothing," into a "monster":

> From the aforementioned data, it should be clear as day that in fact there has never been a Jewish Shylock, that this character originally did not even belong to the legend, but rather, only in development, through false imputation (*durch falsche Andichtung*) became Judaized.[18]

Graetz stipulates that even if, as some had claimed, there had been precursors to the play, such as "*The Jew* showne at the Red Bull [Theater]"

[17] Graetz, "Shylock," 12. The fact that the Jew hailed from Mestre rather than Venice suggests to Graetz that Fiorentino didn't want to offend the wealthy Jews of Venice; Shakespeare had no reason to spare them Ibid. 13.

[18] Ibid., 32; my italics.

dated 1579, or in "The Orator" of 1596, Shakespeare alone bears responsibility for vilifying the Jews by creating a "living, breathing" Shylock, a figure that in its inhuman viciousness would become a weapon for countless Jew haters:

> Thus, neither the legend, nor the Ballade, nor the Drama has even the slightest support for the fact that the Jews or a Jew would be so brutal as to do wrong, whether out of Christian-hatred or vengefulness, by demanding a certificate of pledge for a pound of flesh.[19]

Having accused Shakespeare of libeling Shylock, Graetz next questions the playwright's motivation: "How did such an otherwise 'poetically just' dramatic artist commit such a scandalous injustice against this race? How did Shakespeare bring himself to place such a monster onto the stage as a Jew?"[20] Graetz found the answers to these questions in an English-language article, "The Original of Shylock" by Sidney Lee, which appeared in the *Gentleman's Magazine* in February 1880 – half a year before his own essay was published.

Sidney Lee's essay was inspired by Irving's 1879 reinterpretation of Shylock. For Lee, born Solomon Lazarus Levi, the essay was a stepping stone to a much celebrated career in English letters. According to Lee, Shakespeare was inspired by the case of Roderigo Lopez, a descendent of Spanish or Portuguese Jews and physician and advisor to Queen Elizabeth I, who in 1594, was accused of participating in a Spanish plot to kill the Queen.[21] Lopez was hanged in the spring of 1594, and a sign with the phrase *Proditorum finis funis* was attached to his picture on the gallows.[22] Lee believed that Lopez was innocent, a victim of court intrigue

[19] Ibid., 33.

[20] Ibid., 22.

[21] Because of his connections to the Marranoes and his language skills, Lopez became the interpreter and advisor to the recently arrived Antonio Perez, illegitimate son of the King of Portugal, in 1588. In this age of fanatical hatred of Spain and the Spanish King Philip II, Antonio was hailed in England as "King Antonio." The Earl of Essex, the most favored of the Queen, became close to Antonio (who spoke only Portuguese); the Jewish doctor/translator became not only the advisor but also the "alter ego" of Antonio, who was also close with Lord Southampton, one of Shakespeare's supporters (Graetz, "Shylock" 26). Yet Antonio, a "simpleton," soon sought to distance himself from Lopez. The young courtiers sided with Antonio and attacked "Lopez, the Jew." The plot thickened when Lord Essex tried to enlist Lopez to spy against the King of Spain, and Lopez refused and tattled to the Queen, who chastised Essex. Graetz cites Lee's article to the effect that Lopez took an oath to get revenge against Antonio. The intrigue continued and Essex did not rest until Lopez was accused of high treason, with Chief Justice Eduard Coke, the prosecutor, publicly stating that "only a Jew" could contrive such an audacious plot against Antonio and the Queen.

[22] "The rope is the end of traitors."

and anti-Jewish sentiment. From Lee, Graetz pulled isolated facts that he strung together on the thread of his hypothesis. He notes that three plays with hateful Jewish protagonists were performed in England in that same year thanks to the theater entrepreneur impresario Philip Henslowe, who rushed to capitalize on the sensational Lopez affair.[23] In a footnote, he cites the fact that Shakespeare was friendly with Lord Southampton who was close with the Earl of Essex; was it possible, he asks, that in order to please his patron Shakespeare portrayed Shylock as "black and demonic"? According to Graetz, only the story of Lopez can "explain" Antonio's hatred of Jews in *The Merchant*, a trait which otherwise does not suit his benevolent personality; it likewise "explains" why Lorenzo has no scruples about stealing from Shylock and marrying his daughter. And is it only a coincidence, asks Graetz, that the very first actor to play Shylock, Richard Burbage, wore the same beard as did Dr. Roderigo Lopez – the beard that would adorn the face of every Shylock thereafter? These and other facts lead Graetz to conclude that Shylock "is thus not a harmless creation of imagination without factual basis, but rather an intentional caricature, which Shakespeare designed to satisfy his aristocratic patrons and to please the public." In sum:

> Fiorentino gave Shakespeare a "factum," and out of him the poet created a flesh and blood human being, placing in his soul the entire extent of poisonous hatred against Christians – that very hatred which public opinion projected onto the Jew Lopez. To the misfortune of the Jews, Shakespeare preserved this blinded public opinion for all eternity.[24]

Graetz does mitigate his criticism of Shakespeare to some degree. To be sure, Shylock is mistreated, and his Christian antagonists behave immorally. The problem is that he is not innocent enough to be praiseworthy, nor is he guilty enough to be forgotten. Graetz might have forgiven Shakespeare if he had cast Shylock as a "real" criminal, à la Macbeth. The fact that Shylock is *unlike* Lopez fomented the creation of a new type. To Graetz, it is "clear as day" that there never was an original Jewish Shylock, and that Shakespeare "falsely" Judaized him for some ulterior

[23] "For it cannot be merely fortuitous coincidence that caused him in 1594 to produced plays entitled 'The Jews' and 'The Jew of Malta' more frequently than any others within the same lapse of time, and to secure the greatest of his financial successes by these presentations. The entries in his ... diary inform us that 'The Jew' was the subject of no less than twenty presentations between May 1594 and the end of the year. The piece liked best by the populace and therefore most often produced on these occasions was Marlowe's 'Jew of Malta' "; Graetz, "Shylock," 29.

[24] Ibid., 30.

motive. Graetz calls Lee's findings "completely satisfying … conclusive and irrefutable."[25]

Finally, Graetz turns to the sixteenth-century biography of Pope Sixtus by Gregorio Leti, translated from the Latin into English in 1754. Leti's account supplied Graetz with the ultimate counterfactual – a Christian Shylock and a Jewish victim. It is interesting to note that Graetz gives full credence to Leti even though the credibility of his information had already been seriously questioned. Leti offers an account of a Christian named Paolo Maria Secchi who demanded a pound of flesh from a Jewish borrower Sansone [Simson] de Ceneda, against whom he had won a wager.[26] While the Pope initially condemned the two men for their frivolous bet and threatened to kill them, he ultimately fined each of them 2,000 scudi.[27] Whereas Sinsheimer regarded Leti as an untrustworthy historian and speculated that the purpose of the tale was "to glorify the strict, just and wise Pope,"[28] Graetz suspended disbelief, enumerating several reasons why Leti should be trusted. Graetz upheld Leti's tale as evidence that one of the first "Shylocks" was a Christian, and as "proof" that the legend of the pound of flesh was "innocent":

> When Secchi is held up against the Jew from Mestre or Gernutus and Shylock, *one cannot doubt even for a moment where the historical reality lies* … However outrageous it would be to claim, on the basis of the merchant from Rome, that Christians in general are lusting greedily after the flesh or the life of Jews, even more outrageous is to repeat this accusation against the Jews, *in the absence of even a pale shimmer of a factual basis*.[29]

Why was Graetz so determined to de-Judaize Shylock and to prosecute Shakespeare? Why the convoluted strategy of using historical data to invalidate a fictional character? In the first place, such use (or abuse) of history was a standard tactic for a nineteenth-century German-Jewish intellectual, and secondly, Graetz identified with Shylock's plight – the plight of the Jew as victim of libel.

Graetz's Shylock essay acquires further significance when read as a belated contribution to an epoch of political and social emancipation, and religious reform, for German Jewry. In the years 1800–71, as Ashkenazi Jews entered modern society, one of the most important tasks facing rabbis and scholars was to reshape Judaism for the present. Since

[25] Ibid., 32; "*allerbefriedigend … bündig and unwiderleglich*."

[26] Gregorio Leti, *Vita di Sixto Quinto* (Venice, 1587).

[27] In German, "der historische Bericht des Geschichtsschreibers Gregorio Leti."

[28] Sinsheimer, *Shylock*, 76.

[29] Graetz, "Shylock," 36; my emphasis.

German Jewry came of age in the heyday of historicism, when historical scholarship wielded particular authority and influence, any social or religious initiative, any political ideology, drew on earlier chapters in the Jewish past as the ultimate source of legitimacy. Beginning with the circle devoted to *Wissenschaft des Judentums*, Jewish intellectuals in Germany staked everything on their efforts to study and document Jewish history and culture in modern genres and languages that would be accessible to Christians. Debates about reforming Jewish practice, no less than the tendentious controversies between Jewish and Christian scholars, often took the form of seemingly arcane arguments about ancient texts and pre-modern history.

For a conservative scholar such as Heinrich Graetz, it was especially important that "the Jewish present and future be continuous with the essential patterns of the past."[30] Graetz had a traditional Jewish education and acquired secular knowledge through private study. When he obtained his PhD from the University of Jena in 1845, Jewish scholars still were unable to teach at German universities. In the wake of the 1848 revolution, the intellectual and cultural life of German Jewry witnessed a new surge.[31] Efforts were made to unify a community that had already split along denominational lines, and to educate and engage the population at large – efforts in which Graetz played a monumental role. A groundbreaking development was the founding of Jewish seminaries in Berlin, Breslau, and Hungary that would not only produce scholars but also train rabbis and teachers. Graetz was hired as professor of history at the Jewish Theological Seminary in Breslau, founded in 1854 and directed by Zechariah Frankel. Frankel also edited the periodical in which Graetz's Shylock essay would appear, the *Monatsschrift*, which represented a new effort to write Jewish history for a wide, not only academic readership. Another innovation in Jewish popular education was Rabbi Ludwig Philippson's Jewish book-of-the-month club, the "Institute for the Promotion of Israelite Literature,"[32] which published and distributed

[30] Jay Harris, *How Do We Know This? Midrash and the Fragmentation of Modern Judaism* (Albany: SUNY Press, 1995), 175.

[31] See Nils H. Roemer, *Jewish Scholarship and Culture in Nineteenth-Century Germany: Between History and Faith* (Madison: University of Wisconsin Press, 2005), 49–59.

[32] Of all his contemporaries, Graetz was perhaps most comparable to Ludwig Philippson. Both men had German doctorates and roots in the Wissenschaft movement, but they did not value scholarship as an independent discipline; rather they sought to use their knowledge in the service of religion, to tell "stories" (pejoratively used against him) that would inspire a Jewish audience in the present. Many volumes of Graetz' history were published and distributed by Philippson's *Institute*.

Graetz's multivolume *History of the Jews from the Earliest Times to the Present*, a monumental work which is regarded as a partisan history motivated by Jewish nationalism, and which became arguably the most influential work of Jewish history.[33]

Heinrich Graetz emerged out of the *Wissenschaft des Judentums* movement, and he lived long enough to become its first historian. One citation sums up his self-understanding as a modern Jewish historian. He concludes his 1,000 page *Volkstümliche Geschichte der Juden* – a condensed, popular version of the longer *History* – by describing the creation of the three Jewish seminaries. These institutions represent to him the culmination of Jewish civilization as such. The final lines read:

> If they take the exploration of truth seriously, these academies for the *Wissenschaft des Judentums* would have to [take up] the job of the Prophet Elijah to resolve all doubts, and in particular, to respond to the question about the authority, reliability, and boundaries of reform which have divided the minds of Jewry, so as to reconcile in unity the hearts of parents with the hearts of children.[34]

The historian's task, as understood by Graetz, was to sift out truth from lies, but truth was not an end in itself; the scholar is charged with nothing less than preserving Jewish tradition in the modern age, furthering thereby the messianic dream of Jewish unity.

In the 1870s, however, it was not a Jewish religious vision, but political developments in Germany which signaled the beginning of a new era. The unification of Germany in 1871 had brought Jews complete emancipation. But the rise of anti-Semitism in the wake of the economic crisis

33 The first volume to appear was volume 4 (1853), which covered the years 70–500 C.E.; with this material, Graetz entered an especially heated debate about the origins of Rabbinic Judaism among scholars such as Samuel Holdheim, Abraham Geiger, and Nachum Krochmal. When the third volume appeared (1856), Graetz was attacked by his mentor S.R. Hirsch for being too secular, by the Reform scholars for being too reverent, and by the scholars' scholars for being too popular (Roemer, *Jewish Scholarship*, 56). A lawsuit followed, even though Graetz omitted discussion of Christianity at the behest of his publisher! The most controversial proved to be volume 11, which was devoted to the modern period from Mendelssohn through 1848. Graetz was attacked for cricitizing the reformers, while singling out Heinrich Heine as exemplifying the power of Judaism to be "light unto the nations." He sought to strengthen love of the people, "to intensify the attachment to Judaism, whose insitutions and beliefs had been sanctified by the blood of countless martyrs," and he scorned the enemies of the Jews, those who betrayed the Jewish cause, Hellenized Jews, and even his contemporaries. Ismar Schorsch, "Editor's Introduction: Ideology and History in the Age of Emancipation," in Heinrich Graetz, *The Structure of Jewish History*, trans. and ed. Ismar Schorsch (New York: Jewish Theological Seminary of America, 1975), 1–62.

34 Heinrich Graetz, *Volkstümliche Geschichte der Juden*, Bd. II, Lizenzausgabe (Köln: Parkland Verlag, 2000) 1050.

of 1873 brought a new threat – which Graetz called "the modern *Razzia* against the Jews." Just one year prior to the publication of the Shylock essay, Graetz himself experienced this new onslaught in the form of a series of articles written by the national liberal historian Heinrich von Treitschke (1834–96) – essays which attacked the Jews in general and him in particular. What came to be known as the Berlin Anti-Semitism Controversy of 1879–81, as Yehuda Bauer writes, crystallized the transition "from Christian Jew-hatred to modern anti-Semitism," marking the end of the liberal phase of Bismarck's rule, as the German Chancellor turned to ally himself with the Catholic Center Party.[35]

To a certain degree, Treitschke's essay "Unsere Aussichten" (Our Prospects), which appeared in his journal *Preußische Jahrbücher* on November 15, 1879, recapitulated views already in circulation, such as those of the extremist Wilhelm Marr, who was the first to use the term "anti-Semitism" and who founded an "Anti-Semitism League," and of the Christian Socialist Adolf Stoecker, author of the famous slogan "the Jews are our misfortune."[36] Treitschke presents the German *Volk* as a homogenous entity that needed to protect itself from the "Other," that is, the Jew. In the absence of a unified state, the Germans had been defenseless against the infiltration of foreign elements, of which a prime representative is none other than the Jewish nationalist and critic of German culture, Heinrich Graetz. Treitschke singled out the eleventh volume of the *History of the Jews* – the only one which Ludwig Philippson had refused to publish – because of its tendentious treatment of German heroes and antipathy towards Christianity.[37] Treitschke associated inassimilable, international Judaism with the poet Heinrich Heine, who was the hero of Graetz's volume 11. While identifying a few "good Jews," such as Moses Mendelssohn and David Friedländer (whom Graetz had chastised in his *History)*, Treitschke attacked many "third rank" Jewish artists, journalists, and scholars, accusing these

[35] See Yehuda Bauer's essay in *Jahrbuch für Antisemtismusforschung*, vol 1, ed. Wolfgang Benz (Frankfurt/Main, New York: Campus Verlag, 1992); also Gilman and Zipes, "In *Deutschtum and Judentum* Hermann Cohen Applies Neo-Kantian Philosophy to the German Jewish Question," in *The Yale Companion to German Jewish Literature and Culture* (New Haven: Yale University Press), 336.

[36] *Preußische Jahrbücher* 44:6 (1879), 559–76. Treitschke's essays, Graetz's replies, and all other sources pertinent to the controversy are collected in the annotated two-volume work *Der "Berliner Antisemitismusstreit" 1879–1881*, ed. Karsten Krieger, Im Auftrag des Zentrums für Antisemitismusforschung (München: K.G. Saur, 2004). Other racist publications included Marr's "The Talmud Jew" (1871) and "The Jews, Kings of Our Time" by Otto Böckel (1885).

[37] Roemer, *Jewish Scholarship*, 84–85.

"German-speaking Orientals" of incomplete or false acculturation. The goal had to be total assimilation of Jews, lest centuries of Germanness degenerate into a "German-Jewish *Mischkultur*."

Coming as they did from a pen of a highly respected scholar, these ideas acquired new credibility and popularity. Treitschke was an "objective" historian, known for his liberalism and excellent prose style.[38] Virtually every important Jewish intellectual published a response to Treitschke.[39] Heinrich Graetz's "Reply to Herr von Treitschke" appeared in the *Schlesische Presse* on December 7, 1879. Writing "as a historian ... to a historian," Graetz disputed Treitschke's method of using statistics about the Jewish populations of Berlin and some German states and about Polish Jewish immigration and absorption in Germany to construct a Jewish threat. Graetz also defended his *History of the Jews* against the charge that it was anti-Christian and unfairly critical of major figures such as Luther, Goethe, and Fichte – again on the basis of the facts. "Is it *Todhaß* when one recounts the facts of history?" Graetz concluded, "You call me a fanatic. After some deep self-examination, you will discover who the true fanatic is."[40]

One week later, on December 15, 1879, Treitschke published a second essay, "*Herr Graetz und sein Judentum*," which deepened and broadened his attack.[41] He repeated his accusations against the historian, his data, and German Jewry as a whole, in detail. Buried in a long list of charges is the item that is most relevant in our context: "factually speaking, there was no Jewish Shylock, but probably a Christian one."[42] Graetz followed up with a second response, "My Final Word to Professor von Treitschke," also published in the *Schlesische Presse*, on December 28, 1879. He sought once again to disprove the accusation that German Jews constitute a "state within a state," and charged Treitschke above all not to hold all of Jewry responsible for the writings of one man.

[38] In his authoritative work of German national history, *Deutsche Geschichte im neunzehnten Jahrhundert*, Treitschke presented German unification and the founding of the Kaisserreich as the culmination of German history. Roemer, *Jewish Scholarship*, 84.

[39] "Joel's pamphlet 'Offener Brief an Herrn Professor Heinrich von Treitschke' [An open letter to Professor Heinrich von Treitschke] in 1879 quickly went through at least eight editions and sold 20,000 copies, and Heinrich Graetz's initial response sold out three hours after its appearance in Breslau. In addition, special sermons were delivered in various synagogues on the anti-Semitism confrontation." Roemer, *Jewish Scholarship*, 84.

[40] "Reply to Herr von Treitschke," in Krieger, ed. *Der "Berliner Antisemitismusstreit,"* 101.

[41] *Preußisches Jahrbuch* 44:6 (1879), 660–70.

[42] Krieger, ed. *Der "Berliner Antisemitismusstreit,"* 122.

When I said, "factually speaking, no Jew was a Shylock, but a Christian was," *that was true*, and if you doubt me, I will forgive your ignorance. You do not know what Leti recounts in *Vita de Sixto Quinto*. In sixteenth-century Rome there was a wager between a Christian Secchi and a Jew Sansone Coneda. If the Jew lost, he would cut out a pound of flesh … the counteroffer of the Christian was one hundred Scudi. The Christian won the bet and insisted upon his pound of Jewish flesh; the pope banished both men from Rome. *Factually speaking, then, there was a Christian Shylock, and his name was Paolo Maria Secchi.* I am finished. Should you desire to continue to polemicize against me, you may revile and cast aspersions against me to your heart's content. I will not answer you again. I have only one request: if you possess even a spark of conscience, do not hold my brethren in religion and race responsible for what I write. If I am in error, I alone will do penance.[43]

This very personal response reads almost like a first draft of the Shylock article. The slippage from Shylock's innocence to Graetz's own becomes clear, as does his staunch conviction that the innocence and integrity of the Jew can be upheld through recourse to facts and truth. The "factual" reference to Leti's character, Paolo Secchi, the "Christian Shylock," was Graetz's last word in a debate which had a lasting impact on the reception of his work, both in Jewish and Christian circles[44]. Nils Roemer notes that no new editions of the *History* were published between 1879 and 1888. Jewish leaders and historians who dissociated themselves from Graetz were publicly criticized for doing so. Graetz published "Shylock in Legend, in Drama, and in History" in a Jewish periodical only a few months later. Whether or not his theory about Shylock had previously been in circulation (as the dates suggest), it seems likely that this essay, which began "for he was cut off out of the land of the living … And they made his grave with the wicked … although he had done no violence, neither was any deceit in his mouth," was intended as an indirect attack on Graetz's Jewish critics and possibly was also an attempt to win popular sympathy from a Jewish audience.

[43] Ibid., 192; my emphasis.

[44] The debate drew new attention to some of the more controversial aspects of Graetz's *History*, in particular to the "lachrymose conception of Jewish history," and to the controversial treatment of German cultural heroes in the infamous eleventh volume. Writers subsequently adopted a new model of historiography more akin to current cultural studies that emphasized the positive interactions among Jews and Christians. From the 1880s on, the Reform, Conservative, and neo-Orthodox communities joined forces in order to reassess their relationship to the liberal state. "German Jews, therefore, had to defend their civic equality with liberal arguments and reassert their distinctiveness by tacitly reformulating their relationship to the cultural politics of liberalism." Roemer, *Jewish Scholarship*, 82; see also 81–91.

Hermann Sinsheimer differed radically from Graetz in his understanding of literary characters: "Observation and speculation about life and daily experience are not the begetters of the character of Shylock."[45] This comment, found midway through Hermann Sinsheimer's *Shylock: History of a Character*, encapsulates his departure from the Graetzian approach. No doubt he too wrote as an historian, and yet Sinsheimer was not bound up in the binaries that control Graetz's argument: fact or fiction? truth or libel? Jewish or Christian? guilty or innocent? Sinsheimer's Shylock is best described as a mythic figure: a hybrid of history, legend, and the literary imagination. The plot of *Merchant of Venice*

> is as it were embedded in two "tales" taken from literature already current – the tale of the pound of flesh and that of the three caskets. *There was no room for what is called realism.* An appeal, or rather a command, was made to the dramatist and poet to create a subtle fairy-tale character to fit the spirit of the two tales.[46]

To the two tales noted above, Sinsheimer adds a third: he myth of the Jew. "It was from this myth that [Shakespeare] snatched his Shylock. And it was a masterstroke of 'Surrealism' that made him painfully true to that myth."[47] While he concurs that Shylock embodies medieval prejudices against the Jew, Sinsheimer adds an essential caveat: Shylock was never meant to represent a Real Jew. Hence, the first task of this historical study was to teach his readers what Real Jews stand for and how they behave.

Sinsheimer opens with a counter history to the narrative with which Graetz began: a paean to Judaism as a just and humanistic religion. He uses myriad sources to demonstrate Judaism's emphasis on justice, altruism, and "loving thy neighbor." He takes pains to explain that the Hebrew word *rea* (Leviticus 19:18) means "'the other,' without regard to his origin or religion, with the secondary meaning of servant or foreigner eventually accruing."[48] He cites biblical and talmudic sources to show that the prohibition against charging interest has ancient Jewish roots; other voices include Philo and Josephus, Judah Halevi, and the medieval German author of the *Book of the Pious*. Against this backdrop, he argues that the association of Jews with vengeance arose due to the *misreading* of polemical comments against pagans found in Jewish texts, and the misguided notion of a "God of Vengeance." The phrase "eye for

[45] Sinsheimer, *Shylock*, 13.
[46] Ibid., 114; my emphasis.
[47] Ibid.
[48] Ibid., 127.

an eye," never meant literal retaliation, but rather equivalent compensation.[49] In sum: "post-biblical Judaism is in the sharpest possible contrast to the content of Shylock's law-suit and to his sayings and actions, and ... therefore he is nothing else but the product of the medieval myth of the Jew. From the Jewish ethical standpoint, he is no Jew at all."[50] In a somewhat different key, Sinsheimer argues that neither Judaism nor Christianity were of interest to Shakespeare's "humanist and Hellenistic mind," and that this antipathy towards religion likely stemmed from the rise of Calvinist Christianity, which was permeated by the spirit of the Hebrew Bible and which opposed theater and imaginative writing.

Because he takes Shylock seriously as a literary character, Sinsheimer locates his best support for the "ahistorical" interpretation in the play itself, spelling out the character's many non-realistic attributes: an overdetermined relationship to money, property, and possessions ("He is a slave to money, he lives to possess"[51]); an anglicized, un-Venetian name; un-Jewish lack of family (even Jessica's abandonment takes place offstage), romance (the play's "redemptive force"), and music.[52] What dictates the logic of this character is the perception of the Jew in the medieval Christian imagination. Shakespeare's Shylock was intended to embody the spectrum of anti-Jewish images, from the medieval usurer, to Roderigo Lopez, to the Wandering Jew, and to Judas. Intentionally, he is neither a murderer, nor a well-poisoner (like Barrabas of *The Jew of Malta*) nor a political adventurer (like the Jew of Cyprus or Dr. Lopez); he is "surrounded by an atmosphere of murder," evincing "Jewish cruelty and Jewish lust for murder."[53] Much like Joseph K. in Franz Kafka's *The Trial*, the mythic Jew was always guilty a priori.

> As is right and proper for a mythical figure, Shylock is unique and without peers. Shakespeare's realism embraced that of his audience and is conditioned by it. The mythical transformation of the Jew through the medieval centuries and three centuries without any firsthand experience, gave the Elizabethans their picture of Jewishness, or what was left of it: a speaking image, a walking, talking and acting phantom, a legendary creature, thinly existent or even void of reality.[54]

[49] Ibid., 128.
[50] Ibid., 130–31.
[51] Ibid.
[52] Gustav Landauer also makes much of Shylock's lack of intimate relationships. Gustav Landauer, *Shakespeare, dargestellt in Vortragen*, ed. Martin Buber (Frankfurt am Main, Rütten & Loening, 1920). Landauer wrote the Shakespeare lectures in 1916, three years before he was murdered.
[53] Sinsheimer, *Shylock*, 131.
[54] Ibid., 136.

Ultimately, Sinsheimer pays homage to Shylock's character, and to his creator. The genius of the play, in his eyes, lies in Shakespeare's transformation of the mythic Jew, despicable but also comedic, into the "the outsider par excellence," a human being who would not fail to arouse empathy, who "speaks the language of his people, who swings the playgoers to his side."[55] So striking is the trial scene, in Sinsheimer's view, that everyone knows that this "must be the poet speaking," and moreover, that the poet "knew there was something wrong with the treatment of the Jew."[56] As much as Portia is a figure of the future, Shylock is a figure of the past. That the "merciful ending" of the plot involves conversion, the liquidation of Shylock and his fortunes, and the triumph of Portia and Venice, confirms his obsolescence. Sinsheimer concludes that Shakespeare introduced the stage Jew as a comic character and a hated type, but in the course of the play, and in the trial scene above all, he unmasks him as a tragic hero.[57] This reading – the humanistic interpretation – can be summed up by the capsule entry on "Shylock" in the pocket-sized *Jüdisches Lexicon* of 1935:

> Doubtless intended as a grotesque character in the medieval sense, through poetic genius, in the course of the work, felt to be a human being. Though the composition of the comedy is destabilized, it becomes an essential document for the acceptance of the Jew in Europe.[58]

Just as Graetz's approach to Shylock was shaped by biography and by conditions unique to the German-Jewish nineteenth century, so too does Sinsheimer's reading bring important (and often forgotten) facets of German-Jewish life to the fore. There is no doubt that Nazism provoked him to undertake the study. But it was not persecution that shaped Sinsheimer's aesthetics, his humanism and idealism, but rather German culture – a milieu he defines as "paradise." In his memoir *Lived in Paradise*, as in many German-Jewish memoirs of the period, the view of the power of the artist that shapes Sinsheimer's tribute to Shakespeare comes into sharp focus.[59]

55 Ibid., 135, 108.

56 Ibid., 110.

57 G. E. Lessing, author of the drama *Nathan the Wise*, "uses the same trick as Shakespeare, but the other way around. Against a medieval background – Jerusalem at the time of the Crusades – he sets a Jew who is far in advance of his contemporaries" (Sinsheimer, *Shylock*, 143). To emphasize his connection to *Nathan the Wise*, Sinsheimer refers to "Shylock the Unwise."

58 *Philolexicon. Handbuch des jüdischen Wissens* (Berlin: Philo Verlag, 1935), 667.

59 Based on sources from the *Nachlass*, edited by Dr. Gerhard Pallmann, with an introduction by Gustav Waldau and an epilogue by his wife Christobel Sinsheimer. Hermann Sinsheimer, *Gelebt in Paradies. Erinnerungen und Begegnungen* (München: Richard Pflaum Verlag, 1953). The memoir was recently re-issued in its uncensored format, as part of a three-volume edition of Sinsheimer's collected works: Hermann Sinsheimer, *Gelebt im Paradies. Gestalten und Geschichten*, ed. Nadine Englhart (Berlin: Verlag für Berlin-Brandenburg, 2013). All quotations are from the new edition, hereafter referred to as *Gelebt*.

Paradise was, first and foremost, a world in which "to be a good Jew was to be a good German."[60] Coming of age in 1900, Sinsheimer experienced the richness of the 2,000-year-old German-Jewish heritage, in the course of which "Germania or the Franks or Germany was not for even one day without the Jews and their service."[61] Only as an adult would he learn that such a history "did not suffice to insure the Jews their *Heimatsrecht*, their right to call Germany home."[62] Sinsheimer's childhood in a provincial small town was an illusory golden age: "youth was not a duty, but rather a privilege."[63] He speaks of pride of his bourgeois roots, as they entailed a glorious immersion in the humanities. Greek and Latin proved to be more influential than any living mentor: "The two 'dead' languages were more alive to me during my school years than the living ones, French, English and Italian, that I learned in the upper classes. Latin taught me to think, Greek, to rhapsodize ... As I learned the classical languages, I became classical through and through."[64] As a teenager, poetry became his passion: "At fifteen I was ready to die for the belief that Schiller was greater than Goethe," he writes.[65] The ten-cent yellow Reclam volumes put the classics of world literature – above all Shakespeare, who despite his popularity in the German-speaking theater was never read in school – at his fingertips. He describes his *Bildung*, his initiation into the "cult of theater," and into the view, rooted in the German Enlightenment, that theater was a more powerful teacher than morality, law, and religion. Sinsheimer's interpretation of Shylock bears the handprints of the age of Goethe and Schiller – the values of German Idealism and neo-Classicism – which had captivated him as a youth. But no less important was the humanistic modernism of the Weimar years (1919–33), in which he participated as an adult, and his new understanding of the responsibility of the critic after 1945. Each of these epochs adopted the credo that art is neither a mirror of reality, nor an antidote to history, but rather a source of moral authority, counter-reality.

The lived paradise was also the theater in which he immersed himself as a journalist. His memoir is filled with detailed descriptions of theater life in the metropolises of Munich and Berlin and in smaller cities like Würzburg, of his professors, of famous actors and memorable performances. But it is the cosmopolitan, humanistic vision that Sinsheimer singles out.

[60] Gelebt, 60.
[61] Ibid., 71.
[62] Ibid., 71.
[63] Ibid., 56.
[64] Ibid., 52.
[65] Ibid., 58.

> There had never been an age in which, in purely quantitative terms, German literature experienced equal bounty within its borders as from foreign influences. From beyond our borders came – after Ibsen, Strindberg; after Zola – Anatole France and Gide; after Dotoyevsky and Turgenev – Chekov, Tolstoy, Gorky. Bergson cast his first shadow upon Nietzsche. Maeterlink, Verhaeren, Claudel shone brightly on our stages. Walt Whitmann became known though his confession.[66]

Sinsheimer worked as a theater critic in Mannheim and Munich, and from 1923–29 he edited the journal *Simplicissimus*, a literary and artistic journal of a satiric bent. Following that he briefly worked in Berlin, but was fired in 1933, after which he continued to publish anonymously.

Sinsheimer was not raised with the specter of anti-Semitism; in his words, his generation did not see the "snake" that would bring "Eden" down.[67] The earliest intimation came upon reading about the Dreyfus affair in the newspaper, though the main reaction among his school friends and family was that anti-Semitism was a foreign problem.[68] Sinsheimer's "Shylock period" began with the loss of his job, and the ensuing "inner emigration" in the early 1930s. "Outwardly I continued to live in the German air and in the atmosphere of Nazism, but the whole of my inward life was absorbed by Judaism and more particularly Zionism."[69] He spent two years fighting to free an older brother who had been accused of treason and imprisoned. He witnessed starvation, the collapse of Jewish families, death. But he was inspired for the first time to rediscover his Jewish heritage. He became involved in the Berlin Jewish Kulturbund and wrote for the *Jüdischer Rundschau* edited by Robert Weltsch – the first Jewish paper he'd ever seen. Nazism turned Sinsheimer into a Jewish writer, and Shylock, the only conceivable "Jewish topic."[70]

> Meanwhile, I discovered the only Jewish topic which I felt I had the right to discuss competently: Shakespeare's Shylock character. In that character, everything that I had to say based on my lifelong studies and in particular my recent

[66] Ibid., 149.

[67] "The paradise that has been lost to us offered to us so many comforts … that it is difficult to avoid exaggerations and to call up the color of those experiences. One must continually repeat to oneself: this paradise did exist, even if the snake was there too – without the snake, would it even have been paradise? – it should have been strangled by my generation." Ibid., 135.

[68] Ibid., 69.

[69] Sinsheimer, *Shylock*, 19.

[70] In addition to researching the Shylock book in 1936–37, Sinsheimer wrote three historical novels with medieval Jewish protagonists, most famously *Maria Nunnez*, about a Marrano, and also contributed essays to Jewish newspapers, such as the pair of articles "Return to Judaism" and "Loyalty to Judaism" from 1936 (Lisa Lampert, "'O my Daughter!': 'Die schöne Jüdin' and 'Der neue Jude' in Hermann Sinsheimer's Maria Nunnez," *The German Quarterly*, Summer 1998, Vol. 71 (3): 254–70).

research about Shakespeare, the Elizabethan age, Judaism in the Middle Ages and in Modernity, all flowed together. Shylock as the poetic, dramatic configuration of the medieval myth of the Jew, who now again, remote from all reality, had become renewed through Nazi doctrine—that became, for me the topic of all topics, to which I devoted an entire year's work, alongside whatever else I had to do to make a living. [71]

No less than for Graetz was his engagement with Shylock the product of recent persecution coupled with "lifelong studies." The critical difference is that in the former case, Shakespeare became a kind of scapegoat and the essay, a protest; whereas for Sinsheimer, the *History of a Character* became a "road into the open," a *Weg ins Freie*, leading to a new *Heimat*: Jewish humanism.

Some of my friends envied me this "Road into the Open," the road to Jewish humanism that was fully consonant with German and European Humanism. For humanism is one of those words that is not a plural noun but rather a singular noun, and that embodies unity across all nations and above all temporary limitations – with the volatile Isaiah as our roadmap.[72]

In Hitler's Germany (…) the work on this book marked the final station of my road into the open out of the milieu of denunciation, disenfranchisement and mockery…I believe thereby to have fulfilled my obligation as a Jew in the land of Hitler, and also, my last obligation as a German who was forced to stop being a German.[73]

Finally, Sinsheimer's writings offer a rare perspective on the role of the German-Jewish critic in the postwar period. Sinsheimer asserts that the critic of postwar Europe must hold himself to higher standards, and here is where his early work an attorney inculcated him into the deeper meaning of law as "the expression of a balance between self and society."[74] In Nazi Germany, he witnessed an attempt to "transvalue all values" and the "devaluation of all values." The goal of the German critic after the war was to attempt what might be called a second transvaluation of values: to strengthen the common heritage of Germans and Europeans which he experienced in the literary culture of the Weimar Republic; and to restore the values represented by the Age of Goethe and Schiller. This mission too is encoded in the triumphant transformation that Sinsheimer finds in *The Merchant of Venice*; it becomes clear that Shakespeare's "transvaluation" of Shylock becomes a paradigm for the German critic as such.

[71] Sinsheimer, *Gelebt*, 335.
[72] Ibid., 333.
[73] Ibid., 335.
[74] Ibid., 290.

What is a theater critic, after all? The representative of the audience – in an ideal sense – vis à vis the stage, the representative of the stage – in an ideal sense – vis à vis the public. He must be prepared to be a passionate advocate for both, in matters small and large: to hold the small man and the most minor actor in has heart. *Moreover, in the face of both "parties" he must stand up for a third, for the dramatist: and to all these three, be a passionate voice for the idea of the stage.* He stands in many camps or rather in none but his own, which need encompass the entirety of the others.[75]

Graetz the historian, driven by nationalism, takes the side of truth; Sinsheimer the critic, in the spirit of idealism, rises above the fray to represent "the idea of the stage," which must address "the entirety of the others."

Germans have not forgotten Hermann Sinsheimer. Once in England he was able to survive and remarry. British publishers were as little interested in printing German books that required translation as were the British in hiring still more German émigrés. After a stint working as a fact checker for Cambridge University Press, he found his true calling only in 1945, when he began lecturing to German prisoners of war throughout England. The work taxed his health, but restored to him his language and culture – the paradise of his youth. He resumed writing for German newspapers and also translating, and managed to see *Shylock* published in English in 1947. Sinsheimer died in August 1950, having just returned from a visit to Germany during which he had reunited with many friends. In 1983, in honor of his one hundredth birthday, Freinsheim, his hometown, created an annual literary prize in his name. In 2000, the city created a plaque in his memory to be given to writers who bring honor to the literature of the Rhineland-Pfalz; they also named an elementary school after him. But the memorial he erected for himself was the *Shylock* book, which he most aptly called "tragic-comedy of a Jewish refugee from Germany."[76]

The two histories of a character – a minor essay by a major figure, and a major study by a nearly forgotten writer – are cited in secondary literature on *The Merchant* but have not been substantially influential. The two Shylocks – the essays, as much as their authors – form the bookends of "the modern *Razzia* against the Jews," beginning with the resurgence of anti-Semitism following the unification of Germany, and ending with the Holocaust. What can be learned by juxtaposing two studies that deploy identical data to arrive at opposing interpretations – both of whom used history as a point of entry? The key is that the relationship

[75] Ibid., 128–29; my emphasis.
[76] Sinsheimer, *Shylock*, 20.

between Shylock and his history – between fiction and fact – is calibrated very differently in each case. For Sinsheimer, history, understood to mean "the medieval and post-medieval enslavement and calumniation of the Jews," was the problem to which the Shakespearean imagination supplied a solution. "Imagination is still today more potent than fact," he concludes. "Shakespeare's unmatched achievement was to weave the one into the other."[77] Sinsheimer's double-sided image of Shylock as a victim-rebel, a comic figure unveiled as tragic before our eyes, is ultimately a tribute to the power of art to unmask stereotypical figures and reveal them to be human beings. The aesthetic strategy Sinsheimer attributes to Shakespeare was used often by Jewish writers and advocates of the Jews, from G.E. Lessing's plays *The Jews* (1775) and *Nathan the Wise* (1779) to Arthur Schnitzler's *Professor Bernhardi* (1924). This deeply humanistic reading of Shakespeare has a long history in Germany, from Goethe's youthful paean, "Nature! Nature! nowhere so much nature as [in] Shakespeare's human beings!" of 1771, to the famous statement by the socialist revolutionary Gustav Landauer in 1916 that what he finds in Shakespeare can be summed up in one word: "Freiheit!"[78]

In Graetz's essay, history is intended to have the opposite function: it is used to delegitimize the work of art and cast aspersions on the poet himself. Why is Graetz determined to discredit *The Merchant of Venice* as an episode of libel? To argue that Shakespeare libeled the Jews is different than saying that he misrepresented them. To argue the latter is the prerogative of the critic: it is a subjective judgment that opens the door for debate. But to claim the former is to assert one's own authority to distinguish truth from falsehood. To malign is to misrepresent what is true; he who knows the truth can defend it by marshaling the facts – the quintessential tools (or weapons) of the nineteenth-century historian.

Though unpersuasive as a work of literary history, Graetz's defense of Shylock is laudable as a different kind of performance: it was an early effort to deconstruct the premise of the new racial anti-Semitism (and racial politics as such). By "proving" that Shylock's Jewishness is accidental (just as Antonio's Jew-hatred was not thought to be convincing), Graetz sought to reverse the direction of the pound-of-flesh legend – not only to cancel one of the most pernicious images of the Jew, but to

[77] Ibid., 144.

[78] Johann Wolfgang von Goethe, "Zum Schäkespears Tag," in Hans Mayer, ed., Deutscher Literaturkritik Bd. 1. Von Lessing bis Hegel (Frankfurt am Main: Fischer Taschenbuch Verlag, 1985) 390.

de-essentialize it. Unbeknownst to Graetz, the strategy became one of the classic humanist responses to the relentless stereotyping of the Jews. G.E. Lessing's Nathan of *Nathan the Wise* (1783) placed on the German stage an enlightened protagonist who could appeal as a human being precisely because there was almost nothing visibly Jewish about him. When Arthur Schnitzler, writing within the anti-Semitic Viennese milieu after 1900, constructed a Jewish hero for his 1912 drama *Professor Bernhardi*, he invented a noble stage Jew who only "happened to be Jewish" (*zufällig ein Jude*). Sigmund Freud's *Moses and Monotheism* (1932–38), with its improbable argument that the biblical Moses was a composite of an Egyptian Prince and a Midianite prophet, likewise attempted to counter modern nationalism by using historical facts to deconstruct the Jewish identity of the Jews' "favorite son."

4

Yiddish Shylocks in Theater and Literature

Nina Warnke and Jeffrey Shandler

In April, 1934, four months after Alexander Granach (1890–1945) sought refuge from the Nazis in Poland, the Galician-born star of the German stage portrayed Shylock in a literary trial staged by Warsaw's Yiddish-speaking community. In his defense speech, Granach recited Shylock's lines in German and then made a case (presumably in Yiddish) for the complexity of the author and, by implication, the character he embodied. Shakespeare, Granach argued, cannot be merely dismissed as an anti-Semite nor can he be simply regarded as an ingenious writer. "Socially," the actor declared, "Shakespeare was anti-Semitic, but the genius in him defended Jews as they had never been defended before."[1]

In the artistic and intellectual circles of Jewish Warsaw, Granach was well known as an interpreter of Shylock, as a celebrated figure in German avant-garde political theater, and, most recently, as the lead actor in the world premiere of the first anti-Nazi agitprop play, *Professor Mamlock* by Friedrich Wolf (1888–1953), performed in Yiddish as *Di gele late* (The Yellow Patch).[2] At the play's conclusion Granach, as Mamlock, appealed to his subordinates (and by extension, the audience) not to remain passive in light of the political developments since the Nazis came to power.

[1] Letter from Granach to his life companion, Lotte Lieven, from Lodz, dated February, 1935. Alexander Granach, *Du mein liebes Stück Heimat: Briefe an Lotte Lieven aus dem Exil*, eds. Angelika Wittlich and Hilde Recher (Augsburg: Ölbaum Verlag, 2008), 99. For the complete speech, see Alexander Granach, "Dos letste vort funem bashuldiktn – shaylok," *Literarishe bleter*, April 13, 1934, 225–27. All translations from German and Yiddish are by Nina Warnke unless otherwise noted.

[2] According to Nakhman Mayzel, the play was translated by Yitskhok Bashevis-Zinger Nakhman Mayzel, *Geven amol a lebn* (Buenos Aires: Tsentral-Farband fun Poylishe Yidn in Argentine, 1951), 350.

As a committed communist sympathizer (at least until his arrest in the Soviet Union in 1936), Granach used the mock trial of Shylock to suggest the possibility of making this character a mouthpiece for a Jewish reaction to Nazism and to anti-Semitism in general.

At the conclusion of the mock trial (and of his performances of *The Merchant of Venice* that he staged in Yiddish in Poland and the Soviet Union), Granach shared with the audience his vision of Shylock's life after leaving the courtroom – a story the actor repeated, most famously, in his "autobiographical novel," *Da geht ein Mensch*. Shylock, Granach explained, flees from Venice to avoid the baptism and eventually settles in Eastern Europe. There, on the advice of a Hasidic rebbe, Shylock remarries and sires six more children

> who root themselves in the black earth of Russia, Ukraine, and Poland. Some of their descendants are seized again by the eternal "urge to wander" and move West. And some of them become actors and among them are the Dawisons, the Sonnenthals, the Schildkrauts, the Kortners, yes, the Granachs; and we all consciously choose to play Shylock in a partial manner; we side against Shakespeare's social bias and with Shakespeare's genius, and our mission is to perform Shylock – as revolutionary, humane, pugnacious – until the world will change its face. Until Shylock won't need to demand a pound of flesh since no one will spit on him and no one will kick him.[3]

Granach's post-performance speech touched upon some of the core issues Central- and East-European Jews grappled with in relation to the figure of Shylock: the place of Shakespeare within a Jewish, and particularly a Yiddish, literary and theatrical canon; the embrace of Shylock as a Jewish performative polemic against anti-Semitism; and the Jewish embodiment of Shylock as authenticating Shakespeare's creation. Granach's speech also alluded to an internal debate between German-speaking and Yiddish-speaking Jews as to who can offer more authentic renderings of the famous stage Jew.

Because Shylock had been so central to the European image of the Jew since the early nineteenth century, engagements with this character in Yiddish (or with Yiddish in mind) provide a particularly rich opportunity

[3] Granach, *Briefe*, 99. For the version in his autobiography, see the final chapter in Alexander Granach, *Da geht ein Mensch: Roman eines Lebens* (Munich: Weismann Verlag, 1987) or the English translation by Willard Trask, *There Goes an Actor*, recently republished as *From the Shtetl to the Stage: The Odyssey of a Wandering Actor* (New Brunswick, NJ: Transaction Publishers, 2010). Bogumil Dawison (Warsaw 1818–72), Adolf von Sonnenthal (Budapest 1834–1909), Rudolph Schildkraut (Constantinople? 1862–1930), and Felix Kortner (Vienna 1892–1970) were famous East Central-European Jewish interpreters of Shylock on the German stage.

to study the dynamic interactions between Jews and the majority cultures they encountered in Europe and North America, as well as the internal synergy among Yiddish-speaking communities on both sides of the Atlantic and the interplay between German- and Yiddish-speaking Jewish intellectuals and actors. Shylock became a proving ground for European Jews in general, and for Yiddish-speaking Jews in particular, as they strove to find their place in modern European society and argued over their public self-representation within a gentile environment. By interrogating Shylock, both Jews and their neighbors probed larger questions about Jewish relations with the West as these relations were in the midst of a threshold change, in which Yiddish culture played a newly prominent role.

The Merchant of Venice in Yiddish: A Performance Overview

The Merchant of Venice loomed large in modern Yiddish culture during its fullest flourishing from the late nineteenth century through the mid-twentieth century. Yiddish-speaking Jews on both sides of the Atlantic engaged the play, and especially the character of Shylock, in a wide array of cultural works. They include not only Yiddish-language performances of *The Merchant of Venice*, often reworked considerably, but also bilingual performances of the play, in which Yiddish shared the stage with English or German, as well as performances in which actors playing Shylock (and perhaps the play's other Jewish characters) inflected their German or English with what was understood as a "Yiddish accent." Yiddish engagement with *The Merchant of Venice* also entails an extensive discourse, including critical reflections on a particular performance (whether in Yiddish or some other language) or on the play itself, as well as works of memoir and fiction that recount an actor's preparation of the role of Shylock or imagine a counter-history for the character. No other play by Shakespeare, and few other plays by non-Jewish writers, figured so extensively and provocatively in modern Yiddish culture.[4]

Yiddish speakers encountered Shakespeare as part of their rapid entry into the modern practice of theater. Secular Yiddish theater came into being in Eastern Europe in the late 1870s, on the eve of what has been called the "modern Jewish revolution." This period, extending from the

[4] For a detailed analysis of translations of *The Merchant of Venice* into Yiddish, see Dror Abend-David, *"Scorned My Nation": A Comparison of Translations of* The Merchant of Venice *into German, Hebrew, and Yiddish* (New York: Peter Lang, 2003).

last two decades of the nineteenth century through the eve of World War I, is marked by rapid secularization, mass migration, urbanization, and politicization, all of which spurred intense cultural experimentation and creativity. Thus, Yiddish theater evolved as both a product of and a catalyst for the larger social and political changes through which East European Jews lived.

This close interrelation is exemplified by the Russian government's 1883 ban on performances in Yiddish, which hampered the theater's development for decades. As a consequence, Yiddish theater flourished more readily in the international mass dispersion of Yiddish speakers. Among the 2.5 million Jews who left Eastern Europe between the 1880s and the early 1920s were Yiddish actors and playwrights who quickly established Yiddish theaters in all major centers of Jewish immigration. Rather than being disrupted by immigration, Yiddish theater thrived as a result, especially in the United States, where plays could be performed, free of any ban or censor's vetting of scripts, as part of a burgeoning immigrant entertainment industry. By the early 1890s, New York's Lower East Side was the international center of Yiddish theater, boasting quickly professionalizing managements and acting companies as well as a large, dedicated audience. Until the end of World War I, New York remained a magnet for aspiring actors in search of a stable career and was the driving force behind the development of a Yiddish theater repertoire. This repertoire ranged widely, from highbrow works of the so-called "art theater," including classic dramas and modern polemical plays, to lowbrow works of popular entertainment, including vaudeville acts and sentimental melodramas. After 1900, this repertoire was often exported back to Eastern Europe and to other continents; among the many plays to make this journey was *The Merchant of Venice*.[5]

This nascent Yiddish theater had little in the way of an indigenous dramatic repertoire on which to draw. Although Yiddish-speaking Jews had a wealth of established performing traditions as part of their religious life – liturgical music, folksongs and dances, *badkhones* (wedding entertainment), Purim plays – secular Yiddish dramas began to appear only in the late eighteenth century, about a century before the beginnings of Yiddish theater performance. Plays, especially satirical comedies, were an important genre for Yiddish writers during the late eighteenth and

[5] See Nina Warnke, "Going East: The Impact of American Yiddish Plays and Players on the Yiddish Stage in Czarist Russia, 1890–1914," *American Jewish History* 92:1 (March, 2004), 1–29.

early nineteenth centuries, but these texts were written to be read rather than staged.

With the advent of Yiddish theater at the end of the nineteenth century, playwrights – many of whom initially had no experience of writing for the stage – set out to create a body of plays that would appeal to their largely unsophisticated audience. The constant demand for new plays allowed little time for creating full-fledged original works. Most early Yiddish playwrights adapted their scripts from popular European, primarily German, plays. However, adaptation was not simply a matter of default, owing to a dearth of original Yiddish scripts; it was also a strategy for engaging audiences in the new idiom of drama and making it accessible to them on their own terms. More than simply rendering source texts in the audience's vernacular, adaptation was a method of making plays meaningful to Jews. Adaptation entailed an array of possibilities: Judaizing characters' names, changing settings to familiar locales, adding culturally specific plot elements, interpolating Jewish songs or sayings, making references to texts or figures of the Jewish past, and addressing issues of particular relevance to Jewish audiences. This practice was, of course, not unique to the Yiddish theater but was common throughout Europe and the Americas, as stage hits were peddled from country to country.

As Yiddish playwrights and actors searched for scripts that would appeal to their audience, they also sought to establish a repertoire that would help them transcend the constraints of Yiddish theater: its linguistic and cultural isolation, the humble and parochial character of its audience. Actors aspired to roles in which they could measure themselves against the era's great thespians, and critics called for literary plays that would enrich the limited Yiddish repertoire and educate its audience in the canon of Western drama. In the United States, Yiddish theater practitioners quickly discovered both popular and classical English-language repertoires and became especially aware of the cultural capital to be gained from producing Shakespeare. As the pinnacle of classic Western drama, Shakespeare's plays brought wide acclaim to leading performers around the world, including England's Henry Irving (1838–1905), Italy's Tommaso Salvini (1829–1915), and Germany's Ernst Possart (1841–1921). As theater historian Joel Berkowitz has demonstrated, Shakespeare was the playwright that American Yiddish writers and performers turned to most often for inspiration as well as artistic recognition.[6]

[6] Joel Berkowitz, *Shakespeare on the American Yiddish Stage* (Iowa City: University of Iowa Press, 2002).

Within Shakespeare's oeuvre, certain plays had greater appeal for Yiddish audiences than others. As a rule, tragedies – especially *Hamlet* and *King Lear* – proved more popular than the comedies or histories. And, of course, one play stood out as the most provocative for artists and audiences alike. As Yiddish theater critic and historian B. Gorin (1868–1925) observed, "Of all of Shakespeare's works, *The Merchant of Venice* holds the greatest interest for Jews."[7] This interest rested on a question that epitomized the challenge of Western theater: how to engage on one's own terms a play, by Western theater's greatest author, with such a notorious Jewish character?

By the time Yiddish writers and actors began articulating their responses to *The Merchant of Venice*, the play had undergone a sea change in interpretations and performance practices, not only in English (in England and the United States), but also in German, where Shakespeare in translation had come to figure as an essential element in the establishment of a national literary culture.[8] The shift in interpretation centered on rethinking Shylock, who was transformed from a minor character, depicted as comic and evil, to a humanized and even tragic central figure. This transformation resonated with ongoing public debates since the Enlightenment on the place of Jews in Western civilization as fellow citizens and as makers of culture. During the nineteenth century, this new emphasis on Shylock affected the staging of the play as a whole. Productions of *The Merchant of Venice* tended to cut several Belmont scenes, including the fifth act, ending instead with Shylock's exit at the end of the court scene. New approaches to portraying Shylock encouraged various elements of performance that signify his Jewishness, including costume, makeup, gesture, diction, and histrionics. This shift from approaching the play as a comedy, with Shylock as the villain and/or laughing stock, to tragedy did not necessarily entail a more positive portrayal of Shylock. As a tragic figure he could be portrayed, as he was, for example, in the early nineteenth century by Karl Ludwig Costenoble (1769–1837), as a man destroyed by his own greed and evil.

The ongoing rethinking of *The Merchant of Venice* as borne out in its presentation on European and American stages also informed Jews'

[7] B. Gorin, "Shaylok," *Amerikaner*, March 3, 1911, as quoted in Berkowitz, *Shakespeare*, 172.

[8] For a discussion of the Shakespeare myth in Germany, see e.g. Werner Habicht, "Shakespeare and the German Imagination: Cult, Controversy, and Performance," in *Shakespeare – World Views*, eds. Heather Kerr, Robin Eaden, and Madge Mitton (Newark: University of Delaware Press, 1996).

understandings of the play. Two British productions stand out as touchstones for the Yiddish discourse on *The Merchant of Venice*. In his revolutionary portrayal of the first humanized and individualized Shylock, Edmund Kean (1789–1833) abandoned the stock use of a red wig and large nose. Heinrich Heine (1797–1856), who saw Kean's Shylock in London in 1827, was so deeply moved by the portrayal that to him *The Merchant of Venice* belonged among Shakespeare's tragedies, not his comedies. Half a century later, Henry Irving offered his famous portrayal, considered the most sympathetic rendering on the British stage to that date. Irving's interpretation became a benchmark for many East European Jewish actors and their audiences, who first encountered Shylock (and Shakespeare) when they emigrated to England and the United States.[9]

Starting in the mid-1890s, Yiddish theaters in New York boasted translations, adaptations, and re-workings of Shakespeare's oeuvre in their repertoire, including a first unsuccessful staging of *The Merchant of Venice* in 1894. The first significant Yiddish production of the play was spearheaded by Jacob P. Adler (1855–1926) in 1901, who had seen Irving in London and possibly in New York as well. (Figure 10) In 1903 and again in 1905 Adler played Shylock in Yiddish with an otherwise English-speaking cast on Broadway, and Rudolph Schildkraut presented a German-speaking Shylock with a Yiddish-speaking cast in New York in 1911. Among other early efforts to stage *The Merchant of Venice* in Yiddish in the United States was a 1903 performance in Chicago by Elias Glikman (1871–?). Several presentations of the play were given in Yiddish in the 1910s, of which little more than manuscripts remain.[10] In London, Sigmund Feinman (1862–1909) attempted an unrealized production shortly before his death. After the first two decades of the twentieth century, American and British Yiddish theater companies produced fewer plays in translation as their audiences became more acculturated and the repertoire more varied. Thus, other than Schildkraut's guest performance in the Yiddish Art Theatre in 1920 there were no significant new Yiddish productions of *The Merchant of Venice* in England or the United States until the 1946 production of *Der soykher fun venedig* by Abish Mayzels (1893–1959) in London and *Shaylok un zayn tokhter* (Shylock and His Daughter), adapted from Ari Ibn-Zahav's novel and produced by Maurice Schwartz (1889–1960) in New York in 1947.

[9] Harley Erdman, *Staging the Jew: The Performance of an American Ethnicity, 1860–1920* (New Brunswick, NJ: Rutgers University Press, 1997).

[10] The fourteen extant play scripts at YIVO and the New York Public Library do not indicate exact performance dates, venues, or actors.

FIGURE 10 Jacob P. Adler as Shylock in *The Merchant of Venice* (1903). Courtesy of the Museum of the City of New York, Byron Company Collection. 41.420.184.

When the first Yiddish productions of *The Merchant of Venice* were staged at the turn of the last century, it was still a relatively common stage practice in both Europe and the United States to eliminate the last act, so as to highlight Shylock and his struggle. As a rule, the Yiddish stage would continue to insist on deleting Act 5 for decades to come. In contrast, by the turn of the century, the first modernist stagings of *The Merchant of Venice* which restored the last act were produced in Europe and Russia. These include Constantin Stanislavsky's otherwise unremarkable 1897 production and Max Reinhardt's 1905 staging in Berlin. Reinhardt's general re-conceptualization of the play with its emphasis on Venice was path-breaking, and although the role of Shylock was no longer as central as previously, Rudolf Schildkraut's performance of Shylock served as another touchstone for European Yiddish critics and stagings of the play.

Shakespeare's plays began to make inroads into the East European Yiddish repertoire only in 1909, with Sigmund Feinman's guest performance of *Othello*. *The Merchant of Venice* followed in 1912, when the American Yiddish actor Jacob Zilbert (1871–1937) staged the play in several cities of the Polish provinces.[11] The precarious situation of Yiddish theater in Russia before the Bolshevik Revolution accounts at least partially for the relatively late arrival of Shakespeare's plays on the European Yiddish stage. In addition, the literary repertoire focused either on original plays by Jacob Gordin (1853–1909), Sholem Asch (1880–1953), Peretz Hirschbein (1880–1948), and other Yiddish writers, or on translations of contemporary Russian and European drama, to the exclusion of classical European plays.

On the Yiddish stages in Central and Eastern Europe, Shylock became a key role in the careers of a younger generation of Jewish actors and directors – Mikhal Weichert (1890–1967), Aizik Samberg (1889–194?) (Figure 11), Alexander Granach, and Avrom Morevski (1886–1964) – who were at the height of their creativity in the 1920s and 1930s. During this period, Jews in Central and Eastern Europe benefited from new opportunities for ideological and artistic interaction that emerged after World War I. Thus, all four actors and directors were linked, directly or indirectly, to Schildkraut and had extensive ties to German and German-Jewish culture. Unlike the United States, where *The Merchant of Venice* became an infrequent presence on the Yiddish stage during the interwar years, the play was performed more often by European Yiddish companies, in part, no doubt, because of the play's resonance with the rising tide of European anti-Semitism.

Yiddishizing Shylock

As an epitomizing site for Yiddish speakers' encounters with modern Western culture, *The Merchant of Venice* engendered a wide array of engagements, reflecting the fast-paced sprawl of Yiddish culture and the porous boundaries of its complex multilingualism. We have termed these engagements "Yiddishizing Shylock," which is best understood as a series of interrelated discourses taking place both on and offstage, in Yiddish and in other languages, in which the interaction of Yiddish and Shakespeare's most infamous Jewish character provokes a rethinking not only of the play but of larger cultural concerns. These discourses cluster around issues that reach across genres, continents, and generations.

[11] The production included the acclaimed actress Esther-Rokhl Kaminska (1870–1926) as Portia, the only Shakespeare role of her long stage career – a role that curiously none of her biographers mention.

FIGURE 11 Aizyk Samberg as Shylock in Riga.
Courtesy of the YIVO Institute for Jewish Research, New York.

Although Yiddish is central to these discourses, Yiddishizing Shylock extends beyond use of the language per se to include symbolic engagements with Yiddish. For example, Yiddish was obliquely present in some performances of *The Merchant of Venice* as a dialect inflecting the performance of Shylock decades before the play was performed entirely in Yiddish. Therefore in the discourses of Yiddishizing Shylock the language might be thought of as a catalyst interacting with Shylock, thereby provoking an accounting of this character's problematic history of meanings. Just as understandings of Shylock or of *The Merchant of Venice* are not all of a kind, these discourses vary in both substance and approach. We examine these discourses according to approach: "explaining Shylock," "authenticating Shylock," "claiming Shylock," and "fantasizing Shylock."

Explaining Shylock

An ongoing concern for German-Jewish and Yiddish writers and actors was coming to terms with Shylock's characterization. While some dismissed the possibility that *The Merchant of Venice* is anything other than an anti-Jewish play, most, mindful of changing attitudes about Jews in Europe, argued that it offers the possibility of seeing Shylock's suffering as unjust and the character as deserving of empathy. Actors and critics developed a wide range of strategies to make Shylock more acceptable, which entailed rethinking the nature of the character's Jewishness. Whether through critical analyses, counter-narratives, or staging decisions, writers and actors configured Shylock not as a Jewish archetype but as either an emblematic figure of human oppression or an individual personality.

One of the earliest efforts to discern redeeming features in *The Merchant of Venice* and sympathetic qualities in Shylock's character came from Heinrich Heine. In 1839, he wrote that "Shakespeare's genius ... rises above the petty quarrel of two religious parties, and actually his drama shows us neither Jews nor Christians but oppressors and oppressed."[12] Heine characterized the disfranchised Shylock as a tragic hero ruined by the surrounding society. Yet even as he conceptualized the play as a universal allegory, Heine continued to reference the specific religious backgrounds of the characters, implying that Jews stood paradigmatically for the oppressed and Christians for the oppressors. Identifying with Shylock's plight, Heine regarded him as the personification of "justified revenge for unspeakable abuse" and as morally superior to the Venetian

[12] Heinrich Heine, *Works of Prose*, ed. Hermann Kesten (New York: L.B. Fischer, 1943, 185).

Christian men. This reading of *The Merchant of Venice* proved to have an enduring impact on Jewish critics and theater artists, some of whom invoked the poet's words in their own grappling with Shylock.

The early nineteenth century also produced what is, according to theater historian Alyssa Quint, probably the first Yiddish counter-narrative to *The Merchant of Venice*: *Serkele* by Shloyme Ettinger (1803–56). This comedy is a landmark of Yiddish writing during the Haskalah, the West European movement offering a philosophical defense of Jewish modernity in response to the Enlightenment. This movement, whose adherents were called *maskilim*, had its origins in Berlin in the mid-eighteenth century and began to make inroads among East European Jews in the last decades of the century. Though not published until 1861, the play was apparently written, or at least conceived of, during the author's stay in Lemberg (now Lviv) from 1826 to 1829, where he studied German and medicine and became closely associated with local *maskilim*. Ettinger's drama may even have been inspired by a very successful German-language production of *The Merchant of Venice* in Lemberg in 1829.[13] Quint posits that in *Serkele* Ettinger attempted to redress "what he saw as an injustice committed against the Jews by Shakespeare in *The Merchant of Venice*" by creating his own counterpart to Shylock, a "money-grubbing tavern keeper named Shmuelke." Ettinger employs this character to demonstrate that, "despite a typically Jewish and albeit distasteful manner, Shmuelke (like Shylock) is a character of unquestionable integrity with an undeniably salutary effect on his community. While Shakespeare's Jew throws his society into crisis, his Yiddish double, Shmuelke, is the unassuming anchor of his community's economic well-being."[14] Shmuelke – who, like Shylock, is conceived as a minor comic figure – nonetheless embodies an oblique critique not only of Shylock's anti-Semitic characterization but also of the embrace of German culture by Galician *maskilim*. In a most literal form of Yiddishizing, Ettinger associates Shmuelke's use of a Lithuanian-inflected Yiddish with the character's moral integrity, in contrast with the proper German spoken by Dovid Gutherts, the play's "enlightened" hero, and the faulty German of the corrupt Serkele.

Another strategy for rethinking the Jewishness of Shylock emerged in the ongoing discussions of Shakespeare's historical and literary sources for *The Merchant of Venice*, several of which posit that the playwright

[13] See Jerzy Got, *Das österreichische Theater in Lemberg im 18. und 19. Jahrhundert* (Vienna: Verlag der Österreichischen Akademie der Wissenschaften, 1997).

[14] Alyssa P. Quint, "The Currency of Yiddish: Ettinger's *Serkele* and the Reinvention of Shylock," *Prooftexts* 24:1 (Winter 2004), 100.

reversed the situation of a Christian demanding a pound of flesh as collateral from a Jew. As early as 1866, a young *gymnazium* (secondary school) student submitted an essay to the Yiddish weekly *Kol mevaser*, in which he argued that Shakespeare intended to mock Christian superstitions about Jews. The playwright, the student claimed, reversed the situation not because he was anti-Semitic but merely because the situation of a Jew victimized by a Christian was so common that it did not make for good drama.[15] According to another Yiddish reader of the play, writing in the *Yudishes folks-blat* in 1887, the very fact that the author replaced a Jew for a gentile aggressor discredited Shakespeare.[16]

For the Yiddish writer Sholem Aleichem (1859–1916), a creative dialogue with Shylock was out of the question, since, as a gentile representation of a Jewish stereotype, the character was utterly false and thus merely fodder for the anti-Semitic imagination:

> the great figures of world literature ... repeat and keep alive caricatures of us [Jews], which are taken by our enemies as accurate representations. For example, our deluded enemies wish to use even so deeply human a type as Shakespeare's Shylock for their anti-Semitic ends. They hold that all Jews are bloodthirsty, have much money and beautiful daughters. Fools! Don't they know that most Jews are poor and have homely daughters? And our Shylocks will not call for cutting out a piece of your flesh; rather, if you promise not to cut your finger before their eyes, they will gladly forgive your debt entirely, return your signed certificates. So much for Shakespeare.[17]

The contingent variability of opinions regarding Shylock's characterization is exemplified by Sholem Asch. In 1905 he praised Schildkraut's performance as Shylock, but thirty years later the Yiddish writer denied that Shylock had any redeeming qualities and argued that attempts to portray him as heroic or majestic were untrue to the text. Mindful of the Nazis' recent rise to power and Reinhardt's production of *The Merchant*

[15] "Shaylok," *Kol Mevaser* 22, June 9, 1866, 1–2.

[16] *Yudishes folks-blat*, December 10, 1887, 880–81. One of the foundational pieces for this line of argument both among German and Yiddish-speaking Jews was Heinrich Graetz's essay "Shylock in der Sage, im Drama und in der Geschichte," published in *Monatsschrift für Geschichte und Wissenschaft des Judenthums* in 1880. This preoccupation with the sources culminated in a dramatic counter-narrative in German by the Hungarian-born Jewish writer J.E. de Sinoja (Josef Engel de Jánosi, 1851–1939), *Der Kaufmann von Rom oder Shylocks Urgestalt* [The Merchant of Rome or Shylock's Prototype] (Dresden: E. Pierson, 1925).

[17] Letter, December 10, 1910 in *Dos Sholem-Alekhem-bukh*, ed. Y.D. Berkowitz (New York:Sholem-Aleykhem-bukh-komitet, 1926), 234–36, translated by Louis Fridhandler. See "Mendele: Forum for Yiddish Literature and Yiddish Language," vol. 05.239 at http://mendele.commons.yale.edu/wp/.

of Venice at the Venice Biennale in 1934, Asch called on Jews not to stage the play, especially in times of virulent anti-Semitism since it had contributed to the spread of hatred of Jews for centuries.[18]

In the face of failed efforts to suppress *The Merchant of Venice* as a text that promotes rather than condemns anti-Semitism, some Jewish critics offered readings of the play as instructive about the ongoing injustices of Jewish persecution. In a lecture at the Arbeter Ring (Workmen's Circle) in New York, journalist and critic Jacob Milkh (1866–1945) tried to make Shylock palatable to his audience after the New York City board of education decided in 1913, over objections from the Jewish community, to keep *The Merchant of Venice* on the curriculum. Milkh elaborated on Heine's assertion that the play dramatizes the struggle between oppressor and oppressed, arguing that Shylock does not represent a Jewish stereotype but an individual Jew – unlike Antonio, who embodies a Christian type. Shylock, Milkh claimed, does not act according to the Jewish tradition of stoic suffering but is driven by the desire to avenge his people since he can no longer accept the insults that he and the Jewish people have endured. For Milkh, *The Merchant of Venice* is the "tragedy of the Jew Shylock and the tragedy of the Jewish people everywhere and throughout history: persecuted and oppressed, robbed and ridiculed and ... accused of crimes that Jews did not commit but were committed against them."[19]

Similarly, in his review of Zilbert's 1912 performance of Shylock in Warsaw Noyekh Prilutski (1882–1941) felt the need to offer his readers a rationale for Shylock's behavior by arguing that he is not "the personification of the Jewish national character in his inhumane ugliness as anti-Semites often refer to him."[20] Nor is Shylock, as his apologists insist, merely the product of an environment in which gentiles were no better than he. For Prilutski, *The Merchant of Venice* can only have meaning in the realm of the universal, by stripping the characters of any ethnic specificity. Shakespeare, Prilutski posits, did not present Shylock

[18] Sholem Asch, "Venedig," *Haynt*, September 30, 1934. For his 1934 production of *The Merchant in Venice* with an Italian cast, Reinhardt turned the city of Venice, which had been the protagonist of his 1905 production, into the stage by using the square Campo San Trovaso as a performance space. See Erica Fischer-Lichte, "Theatre as Festive Play: Max Reinhardt's Production of *The Merchant of Venice*," in *Venetian Views, Venetian Blinds: English Fantasies of Venice*, eds. Manfred Pfister and Barbara Schaff (Amsterdam, Atlanta: Editions Rodopi B.V., 1999), 176.

[19] Jacob Milkh, "'Der koyfman fun venedig' (Sheylok)," *Di yudishe velt* (Vilna), May, 1914, 244.

[20] Noyekh Prilutski, "Sheylok," in Prilutski, ed. *Yidish teater: 1905–1912*, vol. 2 (Bialystok: Farlag Albek, 1921), 97–103, reprinted from *Moment*, May 10, 1912.

as a representative of his nation, just as he did not depict Hamlet as representing the Danes. Instead, Shakespeare created universal types and explored "the human soul which, as such, is in its core the same all over the world." Prilutski concludes that, "as a representation of our national character the type is false, but as an individual Jewish character he is entirely possible."[21]

Although he repeated Prilutski's argument that Shakespeare's characters, such as Hamlet or Othello, did not represent their respective nations, the Yiddish actor Avrom Morevski did not anchor his reading of *The Merchant of Venice* in universal humanism but in class politics. He claimed that Shakespeare did not attempt to tackle "the Jewish question" but created in Shylock the most "Marxian" of all his characters, who could serve as a role model for the political left, whether Jewish or not.[22] For Morevski, a Marxist who wrote during the rise of Nazism, the play and Shakespeare were meant to serve as weapons in polemics against fascism.

Director Mikhal Weichert elaborated on this need for a universal interpretation of *The Merchant of Venice* in describing his 1929 production of *Sheylok* for the Vilner trupe (Vilna Troupe). He too invoked Heine to stress the play's universality rather than its specific ethnic and religious conflict. Characterizing the play as an allegory of the "eternal struggle of oppressed and oppressors," Weichert asked, "Nations? Races? Classes? What's the difference?"[23] The translation used for his production, now lost, was the collaborative effort of the director, the poet Yisroel Shtern (1894–1942), and Mark Rakovsky (1890–1982), a professional translator, who, unlike Shtern, could read the play in the original.[24] Weichert cut the fifth act, not without regret over the poetic scenes in Belmont. However, he felt that in a time of "mass struggles," the "bloody fight between oppressors and oppressed could not dissolve in music and poetry. The abyss between the two worlds remains till the end of the bloody game ... Love music cannot smooth it over; a moonlit night

[21] Ibid., 97–103.

[22] Abraham Morevski, *Shylock and Shakespeare*, trans. Mirra Ginsburg (St. Louis, MO: Fireside Books, 1985), 6.

[23] Mikhal Weichert, *Zihkroynes*, vol. 2 (Tel Aviv: Farlag Menoyre, 1961), 148. Heinrich Heine, *Works of Prose*, ed. Hermann Kesten (New York: L.B. Fischer, 1943), 185.

[24] "Shtern, Yisroel," in Zalmen Zylbercweig, ed. *Leksikon fun yidishn teater*, vol. 5 (Mexico City: Elisheva Farlag, 1967), 4501.

cannot erase it. During Shakespeare's times – yes. And hundreds of years later as well. But today – no."[25]

Weichert rearranged the order of the play's scenes to highlight the separation between Christian and Jewish spheres, placing the entire first act in Christian Venice, the second in the Jewish ghetto, the third in Belmont, and the fourth in the court. As described by Weichert, the staging tended toward the abstract, highlighting the director's universalist interpretation. Because the stage was too small to show canals and gondolas, he used dances, masquerades, music, and luminous colors to create the carefree atmosphere of playful Venetian society. In the second act, low buildings and narrow streets framed the action in the gloomy ghetto, and in the third act "magical colors" helped suffuse the scene with subtle eroticism. Weichert felt no need to embellish the lives of the Christian Venetians beyond showing their lightheartedness and lack of worries. But to enhance his portrayal of Shylock's world, the director studied literature about ghettos and Jewish-Christian relations in Italy. As he did not want to add text to the second act, Weichert inserted a pantomime that told the story of a young Jew who was forced to convert to Christianity. When he returns to the ghetto, its inhabitants persecute him, until members of the Church and the police lead him out and punish the Jews. Then, carnival revelers pass through the ghetto and mock the Jews, as Lorenzo abducts Jessica. In the trial scene, Weichert had Christians and Jews file into the courtroom, where they were positioned separately from one another and accompanied the trial with their comments. Their presence, Weichert felt, elevated the scene to a struggle between the two peoples rather than between two individuals.[26] Unlike apologetic interpretations of *The Merchant of Venice* that featured a majestic Jewish hero, as Adler had offered thirty years earlier, Weichert presented a modernist reading of the play as a universal struggle. At the same time, his staging was powerfully resonant with contemporary European politics, including the increasingly volatile anti-Semitism in Poland.

Weichert cast the widely admired actor Aizik Samberg as Shylock.[27] In 1925, the actor had discussed his preoccupation with the role in the weekly culture journal *Literarishe bleter*: "Shylock has pursued me for years, and I will have to play him. He gives me no peace ... I have to play the role of a hurt, insulted, oppressed man and Jew. I don't know if my

[25] Weichert, *Zihkroynes*, 150–51.

[26] Weichert, *Zihkroynes*, 152–53.

[27] Miriam Orleska was cast as Portia. Both she and Samberg are best known today for their roles in *The Dybbuk*. Orleska performed Leah in the Vilna troupe's productions in the 1920s and Samberg played the Messenger in the 1937 film version.

concept of Shylock agrees with Shakespeare's."[28] In any event, his concept did not agree with Weichert's, as the director explained:

> To the Warsaw audience, *The Merchant of Venice* meant nothing – it was all about Shylock. It would have been easy for Samberg to have achieved success by playing to the unsophisticated crowd, calling the world to judgment with his deep, emotional voice. But this was the exact opposite of what I wanted. I warned him that he had to forego an easy and certain success for an uncertain but interesting approach. He kept his word and played according to the director's instructions.[29]

Claiming Shylock

Some Jewish theater artists claimed to possess the "true" Shylock, thereby differentiating between Shakespeare's *The Merchant of Venice* and "our" *Shaylok* and even between "their" and "our" Shakespeare. In contrast with those who sought to downplay or qualify Shylock's Jewishness, some actors and directors embraced it and positioned their productions as presenting a properly Jewish Shylock, contrasting their stagings with Shakespeare's hostile or misinformed vision. Even those who, like Weichert, were politically motivated to emphasize a universalizing interpretation, nonetheless embraced Shylock in order to offer a moral corrective to European anti-Semitism. Morevski attempted to rescue not only "our" Shylock but also "our" Shakespeare from the clutches of anti-Semitism and Nazism and presented the play as an antifascist battle cry.

Enacting Jewish "ownership" of *The Merchant of Venice* can also be seen in the practice of changing the play's title. Starting with the 1899 translation by Joseph Bovshover (1873–1915), the play is generally known in Yiddish as *Sheylok* (or *Shaylok*), with such variations as *Sheylok, der koyfman fun Venedig*; *Sheylok der soykher fun Venedig*; or *Shaylok oder der koyfman fun Venedig*. Thus Yiddish theater made Shylock the play's title character, instead of the implied Antonio, and thereby elevated Shylock from usurer to merchant and from a lowly (if wealthy) figure to a respected member of the community.[30] This defiant appropriation eventually extended to Jewish adaptations of the play, such

[28] "Samberg, Yitskhok," *Leksikon fun yidishn teater*, vol. 5, 4645–46.

[29] Ibid., 4647.

[30] The trend in nineteenth-century stagings of *The Merchant of Venice* to shift the center of attention from Antonio to Shylock led to persistent misunderstandings of who, in fact, the merchant is. See e.g. Sammy Gronemann, "Antonio, der Kaufmann von Venedig," *Jahrbuch für jüdische Geschichte und Literatur* 26 (1925), in which the German-Jewish writer sought to rectify the common misconception among his readers that the play's title referred to Shylock, thanks to this longstanding preoccupation with the character.

as Maurice Schwartz's *Shaylok un zayn tokhter* and Arnold Wesker's *The Merchant*, which he subsequently retitled *Shylock*.[31]

One of the first Jewish actors on the German stage to "claim" Shylock in this manner was Bogumil Dawison (1818–72), the Warsaw-born son of a German Jew from Pomerania.[32] Dawison, who grew up speaking both German and Polish, began his career in the Polish theater before turning to the German stage. Opinions of his artistry differed widely: he was described, on one hand, as one of the most formidable German actors of the mid-nineteenth century, an eminently modern performer who challenged theatrical conventions; on the other hand, often with anti-Semitic overtones, as an undisciplined and megalomaniac performer. For example, Heinrich Laube (1806–84), director of the Vienna Burgtheater, who had been his protector and promoter until their falling out, maligned Dawison as a Polish-Jewish arriviste and claimed that his strengths and weaknesses as an actor stemmed from "the peculiarity of the Oriental race."[33] As a Polish Jew, Dawison was doubly alien and endured considerable name-calling and anti-Semitic remarks by critics and colleagues throughout his career.

By mid-century, when Dawison debuted as Shylock, the part had not only evolved into a "serious character role," on a par with Mephisto and Richard III, but had become a virtuoso vehicle in which actors toured to demonstrate their histrionic talents. His performance came in the wake of the 1848 revolution, which, as historian Reinhard Rürup has argued, "set off a transformation in the self-understanding and self-awareness of European Jews, the significance of which cannot be overestimated."[34] Jewish writers, politicians, and actors in Germany and Austria began to engage in the public debate about the place of Jews in society, and took action in the political arena to fight for their cause.

Assessments of Dawison's Shylock either praised or condemned the actor for making him a hero and martyr. Thus, the theater director Julius von Werther (1838–1910) asserted that Dawison had turned *The Merchant of Venice* into a "Tendenzstück" (polemical play) in support of

[31] On Schwartz's production, see Werner Hanak-Lettner and Brigitte Dalinger, eds. *Being Shylock: Ein Experiment am Yiddish Art Theatre New York 1947* (Vienna: Jüdisches Museum, 2009); Arnold Wesker, *Shylock and Other Plays* (London: Penguin Books, 1990).

[32] On Dawison, see Peter Kollek, *Bogumil Dawison: Porträt und Deutung eines genialen Schauspielers* (Kastellaun: A. Henn Verlag, 1978).

[33] Judith Eisermann, *Josef Kainz – Zwischen Tradition und Moderne: Der Weg eines epochalen Schauspielers* (Munich: Herbert Utz Verlag, 2010), 140.

[34] Reinhard Rürup, "Progress and its Limits: The Revolution of 1848 and European Jewry," in *Europe in 1848: Revolution and Reform*, eds. Dieter Dowe, Heinz-Gerhard Haupt, et. al. (New York: Berghahn Books, 2001), 761.

the Jews' ongoing struggle for full emancipation (which they were finally granted in Austria in 1867 and in Germany in 1871). Like other virtuoso actors, Dawison insisted on performing the play without the fifth act, eliminated or altered lines, and demanded, as Werther hyperbolically described, that the "noble Venetians turn into fierce anti-Semites, bristling with intolerance, so that the martyred Hebrew hero could hurl his emancipation theses more effectively at the masses."[35] In keeping with Heine's assertion that Shylock was morally superior to the Venetian Christians, Dawison defied stage conventions by not casting them as positive foils of Shylock.[36] But what Werther decried, the theater critic Karl Frenzel (1827–1914) celebrated: "The artist tore apart the traditional conception of the dirty Jewish usurer like a spider web; in his hands, Shylock turned into a hero of hatred, a martyr to the absolute, to noble custom, and the gruesomely wounded right of beautiful humanity."[37]

Dawison apparently followed convention by performing Shylock with a "Jewish" stage accent – that is, what was often referred to in German as "mauscheln" or "jüdeln." However, according to the actor and director Eduard Genast (1797–1866), Dawison did so with "unmistakable satisfaction."[38] He did not speak with "the quaking voice of anti-Semitic caricature," but with a "full-toned and powerfully demanding" one and presented his Shylock as a defiant figure with a "pronounced sense of Jewish pride."[39] On other occasions Dawison played Shylock without an accent, for example, as during a guest performance in Vienna. He may have done so because the local Jewish audience – which, in fact, had been able to ban *The Merchant of Venice* from the Viennese stage for some years during the first half of the nineteenth century – might have objected to the use of Jewish stage dialect. In an environment where this dialect was primarily employed to stereotype and often to ridicule Jewish characters, Dawison's use of it may not have been interpreted by everyone as a defiant and proud act but as bowing to convention.

Theater historian Simon Williams suggests that "Dawison gave what was possibly the most idealized of all nineteenth-century Shylocks."[40]

[35] Julius von Werther, "Shylock," *Die Zukunft* 54 (1906), 52.

[36] As a rule, the male Christian characters were played by actors whose *Rollenfach* (role type) were "heroic father" (Antonio) and "young lover" (Bassanio, Lorenzo, and Graziano).

[37] Karl Frenzel, *Berliner Dramaturgie* (Hannover, 1877), as quoted in Simon Williams, *Shakespeare on the German Stage, 1586–1914* (Cambridge: Cambridge University Press, 1990), 143.

[38] Genast, as quoted in Kollek, *Bogumil Dawison*, 176.

[39] Kollek, *Bogumil Dawison*, 176, as quoted in Williams, *Shakespeare on the German Stage*, 143.

[40] Williams, *Shakespeare on the German Stage*, 143.

This idealized interpretation included an apologetic streak, meant to elicit sympathy from the audience. At the same time, Dawison's Shylock was also combative and proud. This interpretation may well have been rooted in the actor's response to the actual humiliations he had suffered, thereby using Shylock to re-enact his own combat against anti-Semitism.

Morevski's preoccupation with Shylock began when, still a young actor on the Russian stage, he saw Schildkraut's performance in Berlin. "As Shylock," Morevski recalled, "Schildkraut was tremendous, dramatically convincing, shattering. He portrayed Shylock's pain and anguish."[41] Although he returned to see the performance a dozen times, Morevski felt that the play's premise was wrong. It failed to "shatter the Christian conscience, to remind the people who kneel before the Cross that they are idolaters, that they do not practice that love of their neighbor of which they speak with their lips."[42] Six months later, he wrote the essay "The Role of Shylock: A Handbook for Actors." Although he attempted to play the role several times, to his great regret he was never afforded the opportunity.

Morevski channeled his unrealized performance of Shylock into writing about the role precisely at a time when he felt Shakespeare, "the voice of Europe's conscience," was under attack by Hitler's rise to power in Germany, and the role of Shylock was being abused by anti-Semites.[43] "Aggressive Nazi racism harnessed Shakespeare to its own ends," he wrote in August 1933,

> and made *The Merchant of Venice* dance to the tune of its own bloodthirsty hymns and marches ... The Jews have done their part. They have organized committees, they have written resolutions, and they have not taken a moment's time to stop and reflect that ... "the long night's knife" (the paraphrase is deliberate) should be answered first and foremost with Shakespeare's own *The Merchant of Venice* – as it was truly written, as it expressed the essence and the spirit of Shakespeare's method and philosophy ... Should the state that is home of racial hatred be allowed to enlist Shakespeare in support of its fight against the very concept of "man"? My conscience could not allow this.[44]

[41] Abraham Morevski, *There and Back: Memories and Thoughts of a Jewish Actor* (London: James Clarke & Co., 1967), 181. The multi-volume memoirs were originally published as *Ahin un tsurik: zikhroynes un rayones fun a yidn – an aktyor*. Morevski joined the Yiddish theater in Poland after the Russian Revolution of 1917.

[42] Ibid., 182.

[43] Morevski, *Shylock and Shakespeare*, 25.

[44] The essays were first published in late 1933 in the Yiddish literary journal *Globus*, edited by Arn Tseytlin and Yitskhok Bashevis-Zinger and reprinted in 1937. Morevski, *Shylock and Shakespeare*, x. "The long night's knife" refers to the "Night of the Long Knives," a term most often used for the massacre on St. Bartholomew's Day (August 23, 1572) during the French Wars of Religion when between 5,000 and 30,000 Huguenots were killed. In June, 1934, the phrase would be applied to Hitler's purge of members of the SA to suppress the organization's independence.

Morevski articulated his belief that Shakespeare and Shylock could serve as a weapon against Nazism most clearly and succinctly in his response to Sholem Asch's critique of Reinhardt's production of *The Merchant of Venice* in 1934. He elevated Shylock to a "new Christ-figure, whom Christians crucify because they are not Christians but barbarians." *The Merchant of Venice*, Morevski argued, is a play "from which the world should learn that Shakespeare condemned and derided Hitler three hundred years ago."[45] Although he harnessed the play first and foremost to the Jewish struggle against Nazism, he argued that Shylock had a universal appeal, in particular for the political left, whether Jewish or not. "*The Merchant of Venice* is directly and unequivocally the *song of the masses* ... Shylock is the image, the personification of the *outcast among the powerful* ... The era that lives under the sign of struggle for a classless society – this era can relate to Shakespeare most closely through the figure of Shylock."[46] For Morevski, Shylock could unite members and supporters of the two groups that had been persecuted during the first months of Hitler's reign: Jews and the left.

Authenticating Shylock

Even as some theater artists and critics championed *The Merchant of Venice* as a riposte against a racialized view of Jews, others argued that only a Jewish actor, in particular, one from Eastern Europe, could portray an "authentic" Shylock, there being some innate ethnic sensibility – variously termed "heart," "soul," or "instinct" – that trumps the contrivances of artistry. Thus, Jacob P. Adler contrasted the Shylock of Henry Irving – whom the former hailed as "the greatest actor I have seen" – with his own more sympathetic and more "authentically Jewish" Shylock, whose apparent eagerness to do violence to Antonio was purely for show. "That such a court will interpret the law in his favor, the ironical Jew is not for one instant fatuous enough to suppose ... His whetting the knife on his sole is a hyperbolical menace; his sardonic smile ... is the only sharp edge that shall cut the self-humiliated Merchant."[47]

The Yiddish poet Morris Vintshevski (1856–1932) concurred that Adler's Shylock was a "truly Jewish Jew." Adler's performance, Vintshevski wrote in a review, "will stand forever higher than Irving's, for however great the latter may be, he can never sufficiently understand the

[45] Morevski, "Taynes (vegn shekspir un shaylok)," *Haynt*, October 19, 1934, 7.

[46] Morevski, *Shylock and Shakespeare*, 79.

[47] Henry Tyrrell, "Jacob Adler – The Bowery Garrick," *Theatre Magazine* 2 (November, 1902), 19, as quoted in Berkowitz, *Shakespeare*, 178.

Venetian Jewish merchant's pride ... Adler's heart speaks where Irving's art paints, ... and he does not need a nose that looks like a half-moon ... in order to portray his Shylock, to put flesh and blood and a living soul into Shakespeare's words."[48]

Critics continued to essentialize the authenticity of East European Jewish actors in the role of Shylock even when this ran counter to the production's aesthetic agenda. Thus, despite Weichert's desire to create a more universal characterization of Shylock, the theater historian and Zionist activist Ignats Shiper (1884–194?) saw in Samberg the "authentic" Jew, who brought an instinctual understanding to the role, not an intellectual or studied one. In response to Samberg's 1929 performance, Shiper wrote:

> In Shylock [Samberg] exceeded all my expectations. I have seen many Shylocks, mostly Christian actors, but I could not expect that they would satisfy me. A while back I saw Reinhardt's production of *Shylock* [sic] with a Jew, Felix [sic. Kortner's first name was Fritz] Kortner, in the title role and did not take away a particularly strong impression. Only Samberg's Shylock gives me a clear idea of what the role can be when it falls into the hands of a fundamentally Jewish actor, whose instinct is much deeper and wiser than all the wisdom of the best directors.[49]

Around the same time, Schildkraut came to New York to perform Shylock in both German and Yiddish stagings of *The Merchant of Venice*. Among Yiddish critics, opinions diverged as to whether this Romanian-born Jew presented a "truly Jewish Shylock." To some extent, this debate centered not on the actor's portrayal but on the emblematic value of Schildkraut's performing in the Yiddish theater as a symbolic return to his East European Jewish origins. Some critics delighted in the fact that this great star of the German stage, who, in their words, "relishes everything Jewish," had joined the Yiddish theater – in effect, returning to the East European Jewish fold – and declared that there was "certainly not a more Jewish Shylock than the one Mr. Schildkraut presented."[50] Others, such as Joel Entin (1875–1959), believed that, "when someone has since childhood kept his distance from the Jewish masses, it is difficult to rejoin them" and critiqued Schildkraut's lack of idealization of the moneylender.[51] But even those who did not like his portrayal argued that Schildkraut was truer to Shakespeare's intentions. "The more artistically the artist plays Shylock, the more dark and unsympathetic he seems ...

[48] Morris Vintshevski, "Shaylok, a yidisher yid," *Forverts*, December 28, 1901, as quoted in Berkowitz, *Shakespeare*, 179.

[49] Shiper quoted in "Samberg," in *Leksikon fun yidishn teater*, vol. 5, 4648.

[50] Berkowitz, *Shakespeare*, 185–86.

[51] Joel Entin, as quoted in ibid., 187.

Schildkraut presented the Shylock that Shakespeare created – if not the body, then certainly the soul. The mirror is not at fault for showing an ugly face."[52]

Bilingual productions of *The Merchant of Venice*, in which the actor playing Shylock performed in a different language from the rest of the cast, rendered the innate difference between Shylock and his Christian neighbors in performative terms, doing so in ways Shakespeare could not have imagined. These hybrid performances foregrounded the issue of authenticity precisely by reminding artists and critics of the disparity between Shakespeare's worldview and their own. Adler's bilingual performance of the play in 1903 was vaunted by the actor's champions as a demonstration that his talent could reach beyond the confines of the Yiddish-speaking "ghetto" and prove to be "sufficient to impress itself upon the English speaking audiences despite the fact that they could not understand the language that the actor spoke."[53] However, the *New York Times* critic felt that, despite the fact that "the spacious auditorium was ... crowded with [Adler's] friends, and others who were attracted by his fame," the actor's performance failed, falling "between two stools." The critic attributed this to an inherent clash between the Elizabethan sensibility of Shakespeare and that of Adler, for whom, "more than to another it is needful to represent the Jew in his most sympathetic and most exalted light." Whereas "the audience laughed heartily at national traits and applauded Shylock's outbursts of indignation against the Christians, ... it failed to be swayed with full dramatic force for the simple reason that it was both repelled and mystified." For this critic, the linguistic disparity between Yiddish and English was emblematic of foundational differences between two cultures, which the common ground of theater could not reconcile: "The laughs are in the lines right enough, and no doubt were welcomed by Shakespeare's company; but they are well nigh fatal to any interpretation of the part which can sway the deeper emotions of Mr. Adler's audience."[54]

Quite a different bilingual production proved just as problematic in interwar Poland. There, in 1934, Granach contemplated playing Shylock in German with Yiddish-speaking actors in the other roles. He had recited parts of *The Merchant of Venice* in German at various events, but his plan for a bilingual staging of the play highlighted the complexity of how Granach was identified as an artist. In Germany he often was

[52] Leon Kobrin, "Shildkroyt in Shaylok," *Yidisher kemfer*, April 7, 1911, as quoted in Berkowitz, *Shakespeare*, 188.

[53] "Yiddish Shylock Viewed from Ghetto Standpoint," *New York Times*, May 31, 1903.

[54] "The Yiddish Shylock," *New York Times*, May 26, 1903.

described, and described himself, as a Jewish (and sometimes specifically East European Jewish) actor, but among Yiddish performers in Poland, he was considered a German actor and was resented by many as an alien intruder. Given this quandary, as well as the political climate in Germany, Granach realized that his proposed production of *The Merchant of Venice* was untenable. "I couldn't rehearse Shylock," he wrote, "because it would have looked as if everyone else – Antonio, Graziano, Bassanio, Portia – belonged to one Jewish family, and I, Shylock, was the only gentile. I couldn't do this."[55] Elsewhere he conceded that this strategy would have worked in a cabaret performance, but in a serious production it would have been "ugly."[56]

Bilingual productions of *The Merchant of Venice* were not always deemed problematic. Schildkraut had performed Shylock in German with a Yiddish-speaking cast in New York in 1911, without raising any of the concerns that Granach later faced.[57] German was not yet tainted by its association with Nazism. On the contrary, Schildkraut's performance appealed to a general reverence for German theater then prevalent among Yiddish-speaking immigrants, and the opportunity to appear with a renowned Jewish actor from a prominent European theater burnished the reputation of the Yiddish actors. Moreover, a vestige of *maskilic* Yiddish drama, which employed German or Germanized Yiddish for positive, heroic characters, may have implicitly – and ironically – positioned a German-speaking Shylock as morally superior to the Yiddish-speaking Christians. Schildkraut was not the first actor to perform in German in an otherwise Yiddish-language production of a Shakespeare play. Morris Morrison (1855–1917) – a former member of the Meiningen Court Theater, who first introduced Shakespeare's repertoire to the New York Yiddish stage in the early 1890s – continued to perform his Shakespearean roles in German, supported by a Yiddish-speaking cast, for more than a decade. In a tribute to Morrison after his death in 1917, *Jewish Daily Forward* editor Abraham Cahan (1860–1951) claimed, somewhat cynically, that Morrison "would have lost seventy-five percent of his popularity with us," had he learned to play in Yiddish.[58]

[55] Granach, *Briefe*, 69.

[56] Ibid., 61.

[57] Although Schildkraut learned to perform in Yiddish during his stay in New York, he always spoke the roles of Shylock and King Lear in German. Joseph Schildkraut, *My Father and I* (New York: The Viking Press, 1959), 121.

[58] Berkowitz, *Shakespeare*, 118. For a discussion of the symbolic significance of a German-speaking East European Jewish actor on the Yiddish stage, see ibid., 113–19.

Granach, however, did just that. After abandoning his plan to play Shylock in German with a Yiddish company, he decided to perform his favorite role in Yiddish. In February 1935 he directed and starred in *The Merchant of Venice* with a company of Yiddish actors that he assembled in Lodz. Although Granach had already performed leading roles in Yiddish, including *Professor Mamlock*, *Shvartsbard* by Alter Kacyzne (1885–1941), and *Keytn* (Chains) by H. Leivick (1888–1962), he felt differently about Shylock, explaining that "my entire Shylock experience is in German."[59] Yet, on the eve of his debut as Shylock in Yiddish, Granach was optimistic about what he evidently considered a departure from what was, at least for him, authentically Shakespearean, explaining that, "despite the acrobatics of my tongue (since, as you know, I played Shylock several hundred times in German), much of Shakespeare still remains."[60]

Fantasizing Shylock

Granach's trepidations about performing Shylock in Yiddish are especially curious in light of the actor's complex literary meditation on the character, which blurred the line between fictional characters and actual Jews. His is one of several fantasies about Shylock – which include narratives about a Shylock analog, counter-narratives about Shylock, and imaginings of performing the role – that engage Yiddish culture in some manner. There are a considerable number of works which, as their titles indicate, center on a Shylock analog: the drama *The Russian Shylock* by Michael Zametkin (1859–1939), *Shylock in Berlin*, a play by Walter Mehring (1896–1981), the novella *Der Shylock von Barnow* by Karl Emil Franzos (1848–1904), and the screenplay *Shylock von Krakau* by Felix Salten (1869–1945). Each of these works imagines Shylock anew as an East European Jew, who, by the turn of the twentieth century, had become a provocative exotic figure for Western Europe, Christians and Jews alike. These works evince the extent to which Shylock was on the minds of both Yiddish-speaking Jews and others when thinking about "the Jew" as a type, Jewish–Christian relations, and the place of Jews in the modern world. Transcending the specifics of time, place, language, and genre, Shylock became a paradigm, but a multivalent one – for some he was emblematic of the "Eternal Jew," while for others he invoked *dos pintele yid* – that is, the essential core of Jewishness.

[59] Granach, *Briefe*, 97. He wrote the letter on the day of opening night.
[60] Ibid.

Both Franzos's *Der Shylock von Barnow* (a Yiddish translation of which appeared in the *Lodzher tageblatt* in 1912) and Salten's script for *Der Shylock von Krakau* relate a story that preoccupied Jewish writers, especially Yiddish authors, who gave voice to their audiences' anxiety over the effects of modernity on the patriarchal family structure and arranged marriages, as exemplified by Sholem Aleichem's *Tevye der milkhiker* (Tevye the Dairyman). Numerous Yiddish melodramas and dime novels repeat the tale of a Jewish daughter who, feeling stifled by her father's strict traditional upbringing, rebels and runs off with a gentile. The endings of these works vary according to whether the father rejects or accepts his daughter when she inevitably returns home, having been abandoned by her lover. In both *Der Shylock von Barnow* and *Der Shylock von Krakau* the father cannot break with tradition and does not let his daughter into the house, leaving her to die of hunger on his doorstep. Although in the film (unlike the novella) Shylock is a moneylender and expresses his desire for vengeance after his daughter runs off, in both cases Shylock is portrayed primarily as a father who loses his daughter.

Starring Rudolph Schildkraut, *Der Shylock von Krakau* was shot on location in Kazimierz, the Jewish quarter of Kraków, locating this fantasy within an actual East European Jewish locale. The film opened to excellent reviews in Berlin in 1913 and was soon shown in Poland as well. Berlin film critics agreed that Schildkraut's performance was entirely sympathetic, and the anguish over his daughter's loss was deeply felt by the audience.[61] Literary scholar Manfred Dickel regards the film as a "counterpoint to the assimilationist euphoria" that Salten (best known as the author of *Bambi*) had disavowed in the late 1890s, after which he began to promote national Jewish ideas. Salten's embrace of Shylock was part of a larger rediscovery of Heine's identification with the character among German and Austrian Jews in the 1910s, who wrote sympathetically of their "tragic brother Shylock," to cite the Zionist Ernst Simon.[62]

Other imaginings remain centered on Shylock as he appears in Shakespeare's play and invent the inner life of the actor who portrays (or longs to portray) the character. Such is the case with "Shaylok lakht" (Shylock Laughs), a 1937 sketch written by Moyshe Broderzon

[61] Siegfried Mattl and Werner Michael Schwarz, eds. *Felix Salten: Schriftsteller–Journalist–Exilant* (Vienna: Holzhausen Verlag, 2006), 191. Critics also observed a similarity between the film and Salten's novella, *Olga Frohgemuth*.

[62] Hans Otto Horch, "Brüderkrankheit," *Pardes (Themenheft zum 150. Todestag von Heinrich Heine)*, ed. Nathanael Riemer, issue 12 (2006), 89.

(1890–1956) for Morevski, marking his thirtieth year on stage.[63] Broderzon's script allowed Morevski to personify the first portrayer of a humanized Shylock, Edmund Kean, who imagines Shylock's response to the court while in his dressing room before the fourth act of *The Merchant of Venice*. Kean identifies so completely with the character that the two merge. Kean/Shylock – no longer fettered by Shakespeare's lines, but energized by a sense of righteous indignation – denounces the hypocritical Christian society for what it is. The fantasy ends when Kean/Shylock becomes increasingly frenetic, and laughing hysterically, cuts into the flesh of an imaginary Antonio to prove that the Christian has no heart; then, the actor/character makes the ultimate sacrifice, stabbing himself to prove that he, the Jew, does have a heart. The curtain falls after Kean's dresser finds the actor dead in his room and announces to the audience that he can no longer perform.

Whereas Broderzon's imagined merger of actor and character ends in destruction, a second novel about Shylock by Franzos inspired the creation of yet another fantasy about this character, in which this merger is remarkably productive. In *Der Pojaz*, published posthumously in 1905, Franzos tells the story of Sender Glatteis, a poor young Galician Jew from Barnow, who, even as a child, displays considerable acting talents. The first professional play he sees is a traveling production of *The Merchant of Venice*. Shylock, whom Sender believes is really named Shaye ("After all," he asks, "what non-Jews ever remember Jewish names?"), impresses the young man greatly, and he becomes determined to play this role. The theater company's director, Nadler, who takes a liking to Sender but does not understand his circumstances, advises him to first learn proper German and get enough stage experience before joining his troupe. Years of deprivation as Sender struggles to achieve his goal leave him ill with consumption. When Nadler's troupe returns to Lemberg, the director, made aware of Sender's imminent death, invites him to attend a guest performance by Dawison (playing Shylock) and arranges a meeting with the star. In fact, Nadler had previously spoken to Dawison about Sender's wish to become an actor and Dawison, identifying with Sender's struggles

[63] See Leyzer Ran, "Yidish teater in vilne," in *Yidisher teater in eyrope tsvishn di tsvey velt milkhomes: poyln*, eds. Itsik Manger, Yonas Turkov, and Moyshe Perenson (New York: Congress for Jewish Culture, 1968), 238. "Shaylok lakht" is reprinted in Moyshe Broderzon, *Oysgeklibene shriftn* (Buenos Aires: Joseph Lifshitz Fund, 1959), 163–70. Broderzon wrote a second Shylock-themed sketch, "Tsungenlungen," for a puppet theater. Here Shylock is a vagabond who arrives at the palace of a Spanish princess, Maria. He recognizes her as his daughter Jessica, who had married a Christian prince decades earlier.

as a "ghetto Jew," expressed a keen interest in him. Sender is enraptured by Dawison's performance and his meeting with the star. Convinced that he will soon join Nadler's company, Sender dies peacefully a few days later with his final thoughts on Dawison and Shylock.

Der Pojaz so impressed Granach that he incorporated its plot and central character into *Da geht ein Mensch*, which was published shortly after the actor's death. Granach makes his identification with Sender explicit in this autobiographical novel, explaining that he was born Jessaia (i.e. Isaiah, or Shaye in Yiddish) Gronach and took the stage name Alexander, the Yiddish version of which is Sender.[64] Thus, Shylock/Shaye and Sender/Alexander all merge in Granach. By performing Shylock as his first major role in 1920, Granach fulfills the dream of Franzos's Sender Glatteis. Granach's identification with Sender may also reflect their common origins, growing up poor in small towns in Galicia, as well as the deprivations Granach experienced as he made his way to Berlin to fulfill his dream of a stage career. This dream, the text explains, demanded that Granach master perfect German diction (as Sender had been exhorted to do) as well as having his crooked legs broken and reset in a daring operation, thereby correcting both deformed speech and misshapen body.

After performing for largely gentile audiences in Germany, Granach learned that the expectations of a Jewish audience were entirely different: "To play Shylock before Jews is an entirely new problem. I certainly didn't solve it. Who could? But I tried something new." This "naïve and primitive" audience, he explains, was not interested in the play's merry scenes but was strongly engaged with Shylock's fate.[65]

As mentioned above, Granach concluded each performance of *The Merchant of Venice* in Yiddish with the narrative of Shylock's life after the trial and explained his own identity as one of Shylock's descendants. By claiming Shylock and Sender Glatteis as his progenitors, Granach collapsed the distinction between himself and these two fictional characters. Moreover, he embraced an abject figure of the European imaginary as the source of an imperative for himself both as a theater artist and as a Jew: to perform Shylock as a Jewish riposte to Christian anti-Semitism (including that of Shakespeare), with the ultimate goal of making the play obsolete. As one fellow German exile observed, "The way he elevated

[64] On Sender's reading of Shylock in *Der Pojaz* and Granach's identification with Sender and Shylock, see also Peter W. Marx, *Ein theatralisches Zeitalter: Bürgerliche Selbstinszenierungen um 1900* (Tübingen, Basel: A. Francke Verlag, 2008), 124–29, 165–79.

[65] Granach, *Briefe*, 98.

the lament over the disappearance of … Jessica … to a great accusation against anti-Semitism and cried it out – it was magnificent."[66] At the same time that Granach challenged Shakespeare's "social bias," he also championed his artistic "genius" – which, apparently, entailed writing a play that has long awaited its redemption (and, thereby, its undoing) through the artistry of East European Jewish actors.

Although Yiddishizing Shylock took place when Yiddish served an unprecedented number of Jews as their vernacular, the use or invocation of the language in these performances and texts was always of some symbolic importance. Moreover, in these various phenomena, the symbolic value of Yiddish was inherently provocative. At the same time, its meaning was not fixed but was contingent, defined in relation to other languages: German, Russian, Polish, and above all, English – whether implicitly, as the play's original language, or explicitly, as the language of performers, critics, or audiences whom Yiddish speakers encountered in England or America. The juxtaposition of English and Yiddish in all these examples of Yiddishizing Shylock was emblematic of the new importance of English for Yiddish speakers, as millions of East European Jews emigrated to Anglophone countries.

Yiddishizing Shylock constituted a proving ground for Jews and Christians, each testing its understanding of the other in relation to past archetypes at a time of unprecedented encounters between the two groups. Through *The Merchant of Venice*, Yiddish-speaking Jews scrutinized their new engagements with Western culture in relation to their history of relations with Christians as well as their historical understanding of theater, traditionally regarded as an alien art form. Christian participants in the phenomena of Yiddishizing Shylock tested their understandings of the Yiddish-speaking Jews whom they were encountering, whether through immigration or in relation to new ideas about Jews, including the coining of the term "anti-Semitism" in 1860.

In the course of Yiddishizing Shylock, there were both Christians and Jews who associated the East European Jew and his language with the possibility of realizing an authentic portrait of the character. This notion had, of course, nothing to do with whatever Shakespeare thought Shylock might be like. Shylock is the product of an Elizabethan imagination, as Jews – Venetian or otherwise – were all but unknown in Shakespeare's England. Consequently, the character is open to others' imagination of

[66] Erwin Geschonneck, as quoted in Andrew G. Bonnell, *Shylock in Germany* (London: Tauris Academic Studies, 2007), 123.

his Jewishness. As the phenomena of Yiddishizing Shylock demonstrate, this openness has invited ongoing, wide-ranging innovation, responsive in particular to shifting ideas about Jews in the culture where the play is being performed or discussed. Moreover, this innovation entails a complexly layered process: is it an imagining of a Jew (and if so, based on what resources), or is it an imagining of a Christian's imagining of a Jew?

Yiddishizing Shylock is inherently polemical, even when the polemic is tacit, as in performances of *The Merchant of Venice* entirely in Yiddish. The language's symbolic register implicitly argues for Jewish cultural legitimacy and against anti-Semitism, both as a theme of the play and as a fact of actual life outside the confines of the theater, past or present, nearby or far away. (In this respect, a comparison of Yiddishizing Shylock with Caribbean responses to *The Tempest*, and especially the character of Caliban, seems very apt.)[67]

Other plays that have been performed in Yiddish deal with anti-Semitism, of course, but most are either by Jewish writers or by philo-Semitic non-Jewish writers (e.g. Lessing's *Nathan the Wise*). These plays denounce anti-Semites, employ them to portray unjust Jewish suffering, or do both. In these works, Yiddish writers and performers have some control over anti-Semitism as a dramatic subject that serves to validate Jewish life. But playing *The Merchant of Venice* in Yiddish is unusual, if not unique, in Yiddish theater, as the play portrays anti-Semitic characters and actions from the perspective of a non-Jewish writer whose feelings about Jews were at best ambivalent and whose knowledge of Jews was largely, if not entirely, abstract. The play affords limited sympathy for Shylock, who, lacking Christian grace, is defeated by Christians, who then celebrate his defeat. As a comic figure, his suffering is not ennobled. Some of Shylock's pronouncements and actions do not easily arouse sympathy, obliging apologist critics and performers to rationalize, rewrite, or delete them.

Yiddishizing Shylock emerged from the imperative that Jewish writers and performers reconceptualize *The Merchant of Venice* to suit artistic visions or political agendas that were fundamentally at odds with Shakespeare. The need to do so was precisely because the play is the work of the West's most widely revered playwright. As Yiddish-speaking Jews engaged modern Western culture, exemplified by their forays into theater, they had to come to terms with Shylock. Shakespeare couldn't simply be

[67] See e.g. Jonathan Goldberg, *Tempest in the Caribbean* (Minneapolis: University of Minnesota Press, 2004).

ignored or dismissed, and his portrayal of Jews and Jewishness demanded responses in its own right, even though the problems posed by the play can never be resolved. For this very reason, the many responses of decrying, defending, embracing, emending, translating, and imagining Shylock proved to be a remarkably productive phenomenon of modern Yiddish culture, providing manifold opportunities to make cultural works out of ineluctable discontent.

5

Lawyers and Judges Address Shylock's Case

Richard H. Weisberg

Introduction: Lawyers as Commentators on *The Merchant of Venice*

Beginning in the late nineteenth century in the United States and even more notably in Germany, a distinctive brand of *Merchant of Venice* scholarship emerged. Lawyers entered the critical fray, and they remain there to this day, only in much larger numbers. Divided equally between practitioners and academicians, they have largely taken the side of Shylock, more akin, therefore, to theater directors than to mainstream literary scholars. Lawyers for the most part see not only a victim of Venetian injustice but also a character whose strength derives from his positive values, and not merely his position as an insulted outsider. They discover not so much a "hero" as a figure whose sheer force of verbal directness and uncompromising commitment to his spouse and tribe provide an antidote to the habitual horse-trading and the casual oath-breaking of the insider male characters. They focus on the trial scene, obviously; but their attention is also guided by the play's pervasive legal vocabulary to such scenes as the contract formation among the Jew, the merchant, and Bassanio and Act 5 (at Belmont), which provides a glossary of a half dozen crucial legal terms that must be grasped to figure out the comedy's puzzling and arguably dissatisfying denouement.

Lawyers can occasionally be unbending and righteous, so it is not surprising that they have largely taken the side of Shylock. But lawyers are also careful readers and viewers. So how can they ignore the simple dramatic fact that the character they try to defend seeks a pound of human flesh as an answer to a mere contractual quibble? Are they missing the point? Shouldn't they be reminded that this is a comedy, or at least was so classified by the editors of the First Folio, and that comedies need villains who must in the end be defeated? In fact, they do not lose sight of all the bad things that can be said of Shylock. They simply refuse to go all the way to the other position – that, say, of Harold Bloom and even more recently Anthony Julius (an English lawyer), who contend against all the textual odds that *The Merchant*, "honestly interpreted and responsibly performed is an anti-Semitic masterpiece, unmatched in its kind."[1]

Shylock's Jewish Lawyers: The Germanic Tradition

Rudolf von Ihering: Shylock's Noble Plea for Right vs. Portia's "Miserable Quibble"

Jews constitute a strong sub-set of legally trained critics who empathize even more than their gentile colleagues with the plight of Shylock. We need to keep in mind that the origins of philo-Semitic writings on Shylock are Germanic. Heinrich Heine, the great poet and occasional law student, was particularly influential. His brilliant essay, "Shakespeare's Maidens and Women,"[2] set in motion an increasingly passionate discussion of justice that still constitutes the strongest line of Jewish defenses of the beleaguered moneylender. Rudolf von Ihering, the foremost German jurisprudential thinker of the last half of the nineteenth-century – and a

[1] "To stage the play … now is to attempt what is virtually impossible, since only an audience at ease with its own anti-Semitism could tolerate a responsible and authentic presentation of what Shakespeare actually wrote." Harold Bloom, ed. *Shylock* (New York: Chelsea House, 1991), 7. See also, Harold Bloom, *Shakespeare: The Invention of the Human* (New York: Penguin, 1998), 171; Anthony Julius, *Trials of the Diaspora* (Oxford: Oxford University Press, 2010), 183ff. The thrust of what follows opens the reader to centuries of diametrically opposed thinking.

[2] Heine, "Shakespeare's Maidens and Women," in *Florentine Nights*, trans Charles Godfrey Leland (London: William Heinemann, 1891), originally *Shakespeares Mädchen und Frauen* (1838). See Andrew G. Bonnell, *Shylock in Germany* (London: Tauris, 2008), 32, 102. Heine begins his remarkable study of *The Merchant* by recounting the response of "a pale British beauty who, at the end of the fourth act [of a Drury Lane production he attended], wept passionately and cried out 'The poor man is wronged!' " (Heine, "Shakespeare's Maidens," 377). The awed theatergoer was referring to Shylock, of course. But even without cruel and casual Christian comedic characters, the play's so-called anti-Semitism is diluted down to nothing by the Jew's own positive traits! It does not take a legal specialist to see in Shylock the Jew a whole host of sound ethical qualities. John Dover Wilson also leans heavily on Heine's essay in "*The Merchant of Venice* in 1937," where he compares Shylock's predicament in Venice to that of Jews in Hitler's Europe. Wilson is also acute on the trial scene but claims that the happy ending of Act 5 is inconsistent with the complexities of denouement. See John Dover Wilson, *Shakespeare's Happy Comedies* (Evanston, IL: Northwestern University Press, 1962), 105ff.

Jew – [3] inherits from Heine a keen sense of Shylock's power as the character in the play who stands for ethical and legal *rightness*.[4]

The analytical precision as well as the passion of his pro-Shylock position are palpable in von Ihering's arguments and sustained over many years against several prominent adversaries, notably Professor Josef Kohler.[5] His central idea is that Shylock's "is the language which an injured sense of right always speaks in all times and places; the force, not to be shaken, of the conviction that the law must forever remain the law; the lofty strain and pathos of a man, conscious that he pleads not merely for his own person, but for the enacted law."[6] Von Ihering's consistent vision of justice held that the outsider can rely on nothing but the law. To see in Shylock's insistence on his day in court the excessive tribal narrowness posited by many critics is, for von Ihering, a complete misreading of Shakespeare's meaning. Those with power can bend and break the law, using their flexible interpretive skills to sustain their positions; but those already situated at the periphery of society must seek to enforce the law to the letter when they have it on their side, which occurs infrequently enough. Flexible distortion of law will always work against society's outsider, who legitimately fights it with every ounce of strength available. And private law, for example liberty of contract, often affords the outsider a forum to assert rights that would be otherwise lacking. So the Venetian court might well have taken Shylock at his word: he sought not the pound of flesh but the opportunity to be heard in court as an equal instead of as a despised outsider and "alien." He had no interest at all, they could have realized, in anything but a respectful interpretation of the contract Antonio and he had forged, and he certainly had no interest in killing the merchant in open court, which would have cost him his own

[3] See Rudolf von Ihering's magisterial masterpiece, *Der Kampf ums Recht* [The Struggle for Law], 8th edn. (Vienna, 1886), where under sharp attack for defending Shylock he sustains and enriches his defense over many editions. For the most accessible translation of the passages on Shylock, see the New Variorum edition, Horace Howard Furness, ed. *The Merchant of Venice*, (Philadelphia: J.B. Lippincott, 1888), 410ff. On von Ihering's Jewishness, see Hood Phillips, *Shakespeare and the Lawyers* (London: Methuen 1972), 93.

[4] Contemplating Shakespeare's representation of Shylock, Heine observed generally: "The Jews are a chaste, temperate, I might say an abstract race, and in purity of morals they are nearly allied to the Germanic races," quoted in Bonnell, *Shylock in Germany*, 386. See also Julius Hirschfeld, "Portia's Judgment and German Jurisprudence," *Law Quarterly Review* 118 (1914), 167, where Professor Hirschfeld places von Ihering's sustained defense of Shylock under the sign of Heine's essay.

[5] Von Ihering's primary interlocutors regarding Shylock were Josef Kohler and Anton Pietscher. See e.g. Furness, ed. *The Merchant*, 244ff.

[6] Ibid. In the original *Kampf ums Recht*, 8th edn., this famous passage is on p. 58.

life. "I stand for law" is Shylock's plea, and he begs several times for judgment, not for flesh. Shylock would have been satisfied with any dignified resolution by the court, such as a public account of Antonio's acceptance of the terms of the bond, supplemented by a return of the principal. But all that emerges is Gratiano's hysterical anti-Semitism, Bassanio's self-interested flinging of (Portia's) money in his direction, and Portia's reminder to him of what he knows better than Portia herself: "we are all in need of mercy." Shylock represents, in this tradition of legal analysis, the abused outsider who can count on nothing but an insistence on the court's upholding of the law, because anything besides that will lead to his obliteration as a legal agent, and that of course is exactly what happens when Portia takes the dispute to the level of the Alien Statute, which on its terms destroys the "other" as surely as if he, and not the merchant, were the subject of the trial.

Von Ihering articulates this overview of the scene and brings it down to the level of two technical legal arguments. First, no character in the Venetian courtroom (Act 4) argues that the pound of flesh provision is unenforceable. (Both continental and English law had in fact periodically countenanced such provisions.[7]) So however legitimate the revulsion against the taking of flesh for a debt,[8] that issue simply is not raised by the Duke or anyone else. Second, and more centrally, Portia's reading of the contract is not only absurd but it is a "miserable quibble."[9]

Von Ihering's position has been supported by critics writing in German, as well as by lawyers in England and America, who feel that Portia goes beyond even the self-interested need to save her husband's friend's life and all the way to sophistry or even cruelty. Alfred Polgar, a Jewish Viennese essayist writing in the 1920s, called Portia's contractual argument "rabulistisch" – petty hairsplitting, demagogically vile.[10] Similarly, Daniel Kornstein, a contemporary American lawyer and critic whose fine

[7] See e.g. Theodore Niemayer, "The Judgment against Shylock in *The Merchant of Venice*," *Michigan Law Review* 14 (1915–16), 28, where Niemeyer shows that not only Roman debtor–creditor law but also that of Great Britain had in earlier times countenanced physical penalties on a debtor's very person. See also and more recently on the cutting of a debtor's flesh under Roman law, Edith Z. Friedler, "Shakespeare's Contribution to the Teaching of Comparative Law: Some Reflections on *The Merchant of Venice*," *Louisiana Law Review* 60 (2000), 1091.

[8] But see the next sub-section for a persuasive reading to the effect that Shylock has no intention of cutting!

[9] Furness, ed. *The Merchant*, 411.

[10] See Anton Schuetz's account of the Viennese critical defense of Shylock in "Structural Terror: A Shakespearian Investigation," in *Law, Text, Terror*, eds. Peter Goodrich, Lior Barshack, and Anton Schuetz (New York: Glass House, 2006), 84ff. For more on Polgar's views of Shylock, see e.g. Bonnell, *Shylock in Germany*, 68, 78, 95, 123.

chapter on the play follows von Ihering in this respect, articulates a view common to twenty-first century Jewish commentators:

Liberty of contract is of bedrock importance to Shylock ... [whose] legal stance is far from the harsh caricature often portrayed.[11]

Portia then points out that the contract says a pound of flesh but nowhere mentions blood. Therefore, she rules, Shylock must cut precisely one pound of flesh – no more, no less – and without shedding any of Antonio's blood, an obvious impossibility ... [This] is transparently absurd ... like granting an easement on land without the right to leave footprints.[12]

Portia saves the day, at least from her own highly self-interested perspective.[13] Her rescue of Antonio, whom she already has reason to dislike, reassures the audience that the traditional prohibition of bloodshed on the stage has been respected. Yet her resolution, making Antonio an agent of the law under the Alien Statute, results in the virtual annihilation of Shylock, as either legal or social agent. So the audience ponders the "equity"[14] of the scene's outcome and especially asks whether, indeed, Shylock would ever have cut into Antonio's flesh if his dignity a commercial litigant had been respected rather than flouted.

Anton Schuetz and the Alien Statute Elaborated

Less well known than any other legal commentator mentioned so far in this essay, Anton Schuetz builds brilliantly upon his fellow Jews, Heine and von Ihering, in an essay on the play originally published in 2006. Schuetz understands that Shylock is seeking the court's attention

[11] Daniel Kornstein, *Kill All the Lawyers? Shakespeare's Legal Appeal* (Lincoln, NE: University of Nebraska Press, 2005), 72, 74. See Jacob Rabkin, "A Fresh Look at Shakespeare's *The Merchant of Venice*," *Litigator* 25 (Winter 1999), 69–70: "Portia's interpretation is ... contrary to the intent of the parties ... The ultimate absurdity of Portia's solution lies in the obvious fact that neither Portia nor Shylock wants to have the pound of flesh provision enforced – Portia because it would result in the death of Antonio, Shylock because it would result in his own death for murder ... Portia finds that she has entrapped herself in her own preciosity."

[12] Kornstein, *Kill All the Lawyers?*, 69–70. For Kornstein's arguments not as a scholar but as an advocate (this time for Antonio, but without stressing any legitimacy in Portia's contractual interpretation), see Lizzie Widdicombe, "The Bench/Retrial, *The New Yorker*, Dec. 22/29, 2008, 44-46.

[13] For my own enchantment with Portia – apart from her "rabulistisch" moments – see e.g. Richard Weisberg, *Poethics: And Other Strategies of Law and Literature* (New York: Columbia, 1992), 1000–103; 1031, where I argue that, because of her fierce commitment to the symbolism of the marriage ring, Portia in Act V bonds with Shylock and utterly rejects the intermeddling Antonio.

[14] Are Portia's tactics – clearly not recognizably "legal" – perhaps a move to "equity," the relatively new institution in Shakespeare's England that purported to mitigate the harshness of strict law? For this approach, see e.g. M.E. Andrews, *Law Versus Equity in The Merchant of Venice* (Boulder: University of Colorado Press, 1965).

and respect, and raises the question of whether he truly intended to cut Antonio's flesh:

> The problematic question which comes up, reads: what is really the difference between believing that the Jew Shylock, if he were not stopped, would have killed Antonio, and believing, as did entire urban populations in the earlier Middle Ages, in the narratives – infamous and transparently pogrom-motivating – of Christian babies being the victims of Jewish ritual slaughter? ... What, then, would Shylock have done if he had been allowed to wield his knife? Shakespeare leaves us at a complete loss on this point. Even so, the contention that Shakespeare himself believed Shylock to be a potential killer, is a non-sequitur and an arbitrary reply to an improper question.[15]

We don't know and, on this view, perhaps should not even be asking whether Shylock would have cut. The important element we do know is "the statutory predicament of being a Jew in Venice."[16] Shylock's only chance of gaining respect in Venice – after all he has tried earlier to gain Antonio's friendship and been grotesquely rebuked by that "virtuous, generous Christian"[17] – seems to have been to obtain the court's acknowledgment of his contractual rights. With such a judgment in hand, he would have desisted from an act in violation of his ethical condition as a Jew. And that positive ethic is everywhere available to the average audience member![18]

Poor Shylock, who is his own lawyer during the trial, is unaware that his overt position as an outsider has been inscribed in a Venetian statute! When Portia, having anyway already resolved the problem through her "wretched quibble" pulls the Alien Statute out of the hat, he learns to his amazement that he has no rights that Venice needs to recognize. And this sets up Portia's test of Antonio: whether the Christian merchant can in fact do "mercy" – a test which, as we shall see in the next section, Antonio miserably fails.

For Schuetz, the trial scene is about the progressively dwindling chances of an outsider, perhaps particularly a Jew in a universe hermeneutically

[15] Schuetz, "Structural Terror." On the unlikelihood of any cutting, see Jacob Rabkin's formulations (Rabkin, "A Fresh Look").

[16] Schuetz. "Structural Terror," 79.

[17] The dubious and ironic description is from Harold Bloom, "Operation Roth," *New York Review of Books*, April 22, 1993, and bears no resemblance to the vituperative anti-Christian behavior of Antonio in Act 1, Scene 3.

[18] Anthony Julius seems especially off the mark in (uncharacteristically) assuming rather than trying to prove that the play is unequivocally anti-Semitic; see Julius, *Trials of the Diaspora*, 182 and passim. Oddly, Julius, a friend of mine and a very gifted solicitor, chooses to ignore in his study the entire tradition of legal commentary on the play, opening the door to my chapter here.

controlled by Christian readers, to gain full dignity and perhaps even a measure of legal protection.[19] Until a complete change takes place,[20] Shakespeare shows us, Christian majorities will not accept Jewish interpretations, however plausible they may be.

Antonio's Cruel "Mercy" Unpacked

How Law Aids in Understanding the Trial's Denouement

Why so much interest in the analysis of legally trained readers? And why so much difference among them, so much so that a handful of Jewish lawyers stand foremost in the ranks of readers unsympathetic to Shylock.[21] Like some of his plays, and a few of his Sonnets, *The Merchant* is full of technical legal terminology. Although the argument that the Bard was a lawyer is completely unsubstantiated and represents a speculative exaggeration,[22] there is no doubt that Shakespeare was litigious, attended mootings of legal arguments at the Inns of Court, and generally had great facility with highly technical legal language, which he unflinchingly integrated into the very heart and soul of many a play and poem. Leaving the law out of *The Merchant*, and – worse – disparaging the importance of legal terminology to textual meaning, would be akin to ignoring the narrative sources of Shakespeare's plays.

Consider the single most important "legalistic" speech in *The Merchant*, the one that even an esteemed erudite reader like Harold Bloom gets wrong.[23] Antonio's life has been spared by Portia's contractual "quibble." Probably to test the character of her new husband's friend and mentor, she has gone further by citing the Alien Statute, which places Shylock's life in the hands of the Duke and awards half his present wealth to the

[19] See Kornstein, *Kill All the Lawyers?*, 88ff.

[20] The change would be an overturning of the Christian exegetes' distortions of the Hebrew Bible, evoked, in my view, when Portia so egregiously distorts the meaning of the contract. Harold Bloom startlingly and convincingly prophesies such an overturning in his excellent *Jesus and Yahweh* (London: Penguin, 2005), 37(!); see, in a similar vein, Frank Kermode, *The Genesis of Secrecy* (Cambridge: Harvard University Press, 1979), e.g. 18–20.

[21] See Julius, *Trials of the Diaspora*; Richard A. Posner, e.g. *Law and Literature: A Relation Reargued* (Cambridge: Harvard University Press, 1998).

[22] See Nicholas Knight, *Shakespeare's Hidden Life: Shakespeare at the Law, 1585–1595* (New York: Mason and Lipscomb, 1973).

[23] See Bloom, "Operation Roth": "Antonio suggests that Shylock be compelled to convert to the true faith, or else face execution[!]." This is a surprisingly awkward misreading: Antonio has not the power, which was only in the Duke's hands, to demand Shylock's execution.

state and the other half to his "victim" – Antonio. The Christian merchant now has the chance (as Portia urges) to be merciful to the Jew. After all, the Duke has immediately pardoned Shylock's life and demanded a "fine" in lieu of the state's fifty percent statutory share. No resolution of the play's meanings can take place without fathoming this key speech, yet it has been largely and understandably misconstrued until legally trained readers began recently to parse it:[24]

> PORTIA. What mercy can you render him, Antonio? ...
> ANTONIO. So please my lord the Duke and all the court
> To quit the fine for one half his goods,
> I am content; so he will let me have
> The other half in use, to render it
> Upon his death unto the gentleman
> That lately stole his daughter –
> Two things provided more: that, for this favor,
> He presently become a Christian;
> The other, that he do record a gift
> Here in the court of all he dies possessed
> Unto his son Lorenzo and his daughter. (4.1.373–85)[25]

There are two characteristics of this speech that can be gleaned by everyone. First, it is typically high-toned and exudes the superficial verbal generosity for which Antonio is renowned. Second, despite that appearance of benevolence, it contains a requirement that Shylock be instantly converted, a command that, in the words of a nineteenth-century legal analyst, caused in the Jew "a considerable abatement of his enthusiasm" for the proceedings.[26] But the essence of Antonio's response to Portia's demand for his "mercy" remains hidden to anyone who is not open to legal meanings. Once the rest of the speech is grasped, the superficial graciousness of Antonio's first twenty-two words is revealed to be a sham. Whatever the audience may feel about the demand for religious conversion, knowledgeable viewers throughout the ages would have been strongly critical of the Christian's legalistic cruelty.[27]

[24] See e.g. Richard Weisberg, "Antonio's Legalistic Cruelty," *College Literature* 25 (1998), 12–20.

[25] William Shakespeare, *The Merchant of Venice*, ed. Stephen Greenblatt et al (New York: Norton, 1997). Subsequent quotations in this chapter are from this edition.

[26] "Appeal of the Case of Shylock v Antonio," reported in the *Albany Law Journal* (1872), reprinted in the Furness, ed. *The Merchant*, 407.

[27] See Schuetz, "Shylock as a Politician," in *Shakespeare and the Law*, eds. Paul Raffield and Gary Watt (Oxford: Hart, 2008), 286–87; see to similar effect, Weisberg, "Antonio's Legalistic Cruelty," note 24.

Portia's set-up question, underemphasized in the usual approach to this key moment, indicates that her otherwise unnecessary invocation of the Alien Statute is designed to test Antonio. Alerted to the strange influence the merchant seems to have on her beloved Bassanio, she tests the older man's mettle. Perhaps she has missed something positive in the court room exchange in which Antonio asks Bassanio whether his wife would offer her life to save his and Bassanio replies that he would sacrifice his wife if it would save Antonio's life. Perhaps Antonio will show an inner quality as a Christian that matches his outward reputation as a fine man. Instead, he produces a strange sort of "mercy" – a comment by Shakespeare on Christianity's coercive conversion strategies.[28]

As Heine first observed in connection with *The Merchant of Venice*, when Christians persecute Jews (behavior greatly facilitated by European history's many Alien Statutes), they are likely to be after Jewish wealth![29] Antonio's legalized theft of Shylock's property is a harrowing thing to see, once it is understood.[30] The merchant's first twenty-two words merely reiterate the true mercy shown already by the Duke in forgiving Shylock his life and then driving the state's half of Shylock's property into a "fine" (4.1.363–67).

[28] Forced conversions of Jews were commonplace in the very Venice described by the Bard. How would Shakespeare have imagined the effect of his merchant's bizarre "mercy," whether or not he specifically knew (as a Catholic) of the following contemporary Church practices?: "Rome's house of the Catachumens was founded by Pope Paul III in 1543, and kept under close papal control ... Throughout the seventeenth and eighteenth centuries [it] baptized about ten or a dozen Jews per year, many from Rome but others from lands far and near ... Conversion offered the poor Jew an escape from the poverty of the ghetto, and the chance to enjoy the freedoms that came with being a Christian ... [Still,] the feeling of dread that hung over the ghetto ... produced by the nocturnal visits of the police and the seizure of women and children, continued for as long as did the Papal States." David L. Kertzer, *The Popes against the Jews* (New York: Knopf, 2001), 42f, 59.

[29] As Heine remarks in his brilliant essay on the play: "Only utter hypocrites continue to give their hatred a religious hue and persecute Jews on account of Christ; the great multitude confesses that material interests are really at stake, and will by all possible means make the realization of their industrial capacities impossible to Jews" (Heine, "Shakespeare's Maidens," 391). The legalistic cruelty imposed by Antonio on all of Shylock's wealth is in the service of the merchant's own narrow commercial interests. No stretch of the imagination can find "mercy" in these arrangements, and his own use of the phrase "to the man that lately stole his daughter" makes this palpable to Portia and to us.

[30] Legal commentators have long noted the sheer brutality of the Alien Statute, which separates a class of people out for punitive treatment. Not only is the statute at least as "unconscionable" as the contractual bond it comes to punish, but Shylock really has not even violated its terms "simply by appealing to a court to uphold a mutually agreed upon contract," Furness, ed. *The Merchant*, 408.

Antonio likes to sound all good and noble, and in those first twenty-two words he gets to do so by affirming legal decisions made by the Duke and over which he has no control anyway. Then comes the triple-barreled assault: Shylock must (1) put his present wealth into a trust ("use") controlled by Antonio during Shylock's lifetime, (2) become a Christian, and (3) bequeath any subsequently accumulated wealth to Lorenzo and Jessica. In forcing Shylock to sign over to those same ungrateful children all of the wealth he may earn *from then on and that he still has at his death*, Antonio is clearly going beyond the powers he is given by the Alien Statute.

This "mercy" strikes Shylock as tantamount to physical execution (4.1.369–72) – although Shylock makes his comment, "You take my life ...," *before* Antonio stipulates the terms of his "mercy," perhaps anticipating Antonio's stipulations. These stipulations may have, as I have argued elsewhere,[31] so nauseated Portia that yet another reason is added to her growing, intense distaste for the merchant, whom she goes on barely to greet, when, to her shock and dismay, he follows her beloved new husband back to Belmont. Portia's focus on the entire speech, rather than on its seemingly generous first part exposes Antonio's intent in ratifying the Duke's mercy as prelude to his own legalistic cruelty.

The Participation of Jewish Lawyers and Judges in "Venice-in-America" Mock Trials

American-Jewish lawyers have been in the forefront of testing Antonio's resolution of the Alien Statute against norms of fairness, equality, and due process. We have seen them already joining with von Ihering in wondering about Portia's successful "quibble" with contractual language that really cannot yield her absurd anti-Shylock meaning. Perhaps the most unique contribution they have made to the debates takes the form of "mock trials," in which in one way or another Act 4 and the rest of the play are "litigated" by seasoned trial lawyers in front of appellate "judges" or occasionally a full citizen jury. Other contributions to this volume recount several of these trials. Here, I make note of a fairly celebrated appellate level trial in 2008 called "Shylock vs. Antonio on Appeal" and of a jury trial in 1999 presided over by Justice Ruth Bader Ginsburg.

[31] Richard Weisberg, "Then You Shall be His Surety," in Weisberg, *Poethics*, 94–104, note 13.

Shylock vs. Antonio on Appeal

On December 1, 2008, in the moot court room of the Cardozo Law School in New York City, ten lawyers and judges publicly argued the play's meanings before an audience of several hundred. The event was described in much detail in the *New Yorker* magazine "Talk of the Town" page.[32] After witnessing scenes from the play, the audience watched as a judicial panel (convened by the author of this chapter) decided whether Shylock had been mistreated by the court of Venice. Were there significant legal errors available from a fair scrutiny of the trial scene and the rest of the text that merited a reversal of the Duke's judgment and restoration of at least Shylock's 3,000 ducats? Of the ten legally trained people involved in this "mock appellate court" – Antonio's advocate, Shylock's advocate, seven judges, and I – all but two were Jews. We were joined by two non-Jews – both of whom eventually voted in Shylock's favor: Judge Diane Renwick of the New York State Appellate Division and Bernhard Schlink, a judge, law professor and novelist from Germany.

The judges found in favor of Shylock, by a vote of 5–2. The decision did not break down along religious lines. In fact, the two pro-merchant dissenters, Anthony Julius and Judge Richard A. Posner, thought there had been no significant legal errors in the Venetian court and that Shylock got exactly what he deserved at the hands of the Venetian court. Their votes reflected their prior and subsequent writings (at the time Julius was finishing his *Trials of the Diaspora* book, in which he argues that the play regrettably has, in his view, an anti-Semitic agenda). Their five colleagues that night disagreed and awarded Shylock 3,000 ducats; two of the five would have gone further and granted the Jew 400 years worth of interest, but that view did not command the requisite majority.

A Jury Trial in Washington DC Presided Over by Justice Ruth Bader Ginsburg

Many of the same issues had been raised in 1999, when the Shakespeare Theater Company in Washington DC convened twelve ordinary "jurors" to decide whether Shakespeare intended his play to be anti-Semitic. Three Jews were at the center of the event: Justice Ginsburg, an expert witness named Martin Yaffe,[33] and a superb pro-Shylock lawyer, Freddi Lipstein. The jurors needed to decide whether Shakespeare intended *The Merchant* to be anti-Semitic. Yaffe testified that the "Bard did not intend

[32] Lizzie Widdicombe, "The Bench: Retrial."

[33] Author of *Shylock and the Jewish Question* (Baltimore, MD: Johns Hopkins University Press, 1999).

anti-Semitism" of any kind in the play, while lawyer Lipstein's brilliant cross-examination of the other side's witness undoubtedly brought on the verdict in favor of the play's benign and universal fairness and humanity. The *Washington Jewish Week*'s dispatch put it this way:

> In a 7–5 decision, a 12-person jury, with Justice Ruth Bader Ginsburg presiding, has ruled that while there might be anti-Semitic elements in *The Merchant Of Venice*, William Shakespeare's intent was not to cause harm, ridicule or injury to Jews ... In closing arguments, Freddi Lipstein, senior appellate counsel in the US Dept. of Justice's civil division, said "We should try to understand what Shakespeare is saying: [the play's] ambiguity is its brilliance."[34]

The article ended by quoting Justice Ginsburg's concluding remarks, which underscored the vast difference in legal status between Jews in the United States and Jews in Shakespeare's Venice:

> George Washington [wrote to] the members of the Jewish Synagogue at Newport, R.I. in 1790, borrowing from the prophet Micah: "May the children of the stock of Abraham dwell in this land, continue to merit and enjoy the good will of the other inhabitants: while every one shall sit in safety under his own vine and fig tree, and there shall be none to make him afraid."[35]

[34] Eric Fingerhut, "Extra! Extra! Bard No Longer Villain to Jews!," *Washington Jewish Week*, June, 1999.

[35] Ibid.

PART III

THE STAGE

6

David Belasco's 1922 Production of *The Merchant of Venice*

Mark Hodin

> I am not interested in bonds, or property, or the stock market. But I am interested in the theatre – I eat theatre, and sleep theatre, and dream theatre.
>
> –*David Belasco*[1]

> The divel can cite Scripture for his own purpose.
>
> –*The Merchant of Venice* (1.3.92)

After more than forty years as the highly esteemed theater critic for the *New York Tribune*, William Winter (1836–1917) spent the final years of his life attempting to complete a biography of David Belasco (1853–1931), the director whose stunning theatrical productions had drawn audiences for nearly as many years. In May, 1914 he wrote to Belasco:

> In the course of my work on the "Life" I have had occasion to examine and consider several forms of censure and disparagement which, first and last, have been a good deal circulated about you. One of these is the statement (which I, personally, have heard made by some who ought to have known better) that you have not "produced Shakespeare" because you have been afraid the public would then "find you out."[2]

Though Belasco was known for producing meticulous and emotionally satisfying theater, his reputation suffered from critical complaints that his work was commercial and lacked literary merit. Winter proposed that to disprove this criticism, Belasco produce a trilogy consisting of

[1] John Corbin, "Warfield Warmly Greeted as Shylock," *New York Times*, December 22, 1922, 19.

[2] William Winter, *The Life of David Belasco*, vol. 2 (New York: Moffat, Yard, and Company, 1918), 445.

both parts of *Henry IV*, and *Richard II*. He did not suggest a production of *The Merchant of Venice* for producing it would have seemed to Winter counterproductive, foregrounding Belasco's Jewish identity when the commercialization of American theater had become linked, often in Winter's own writing, with the Theatrical Syndicate, a group of supposedly crass and profit-driven Jewish booking agents and theater managers.[3] In *Shakespeare on the Stage* (1911), Winter called Shylock "the perfect incarnation of hate,"[4] and he would have worried that a Belasco production of *The Merchant* could indulge "a temptation, to which various commentators have succumbed, to provide the Jew with amiable, redeeming human attributes."[5] Such a production would in fact "find [Belasco] out" to be more committed to his Jewish identity than Winter had hoped, and, at the same time, somehow less committed to Shakespeare's art than he had desired.

Winter had already died, when, in the spring of 1922, David Belasco announced that he would produce *The Merchant of Venice* with David Warfield (1866–1951) as Shylock. Following Winter's recommendation, Belasco presented the project as the realization of a career-long ambition: "All my life I have desired and purposed to produce THE PLAYS OF SHAKESPEARE,"[6] he wrote, indicating future plans to feature Warfield in *King Lear* and *Julius Caesar*. However, against Winter's advice, Belasco made explicit that his foray into Shakespeare would enlist the Jewish community, for not only was Warfield considered to be "perhaps the greatest of American Jewish actor[s]," in the words of the critic Alan Dale, but also the role of Jessica was performed by Julia Adler, daughter of the famous Yiddish theater actor Jacob P. Adler, who had performed Shylock twenty years earlier.[7] That Belasco had conceptualized his greatest artistic achievement as the collaborative work of Jewish theater people countered Winter's image of the Jewish theater owner as vulgar and preoccupied with business; however, it also complicated a self-image Belasco had cultivated in public throughout his career as the "Bishop of Broadway."

[3] See Mark Hodin, "The Disavowal of Ethnicity: Legitimate Theater and the Social Construction of Literary Value in Turn-of-the-Century America," *Theatre Journal* 52:2 (2000), 211–26.

[4] William Winter, *Shakespeare on the Stage* (New York: Moffat, Yard, and Company, 1911), 130.

[5] Ibid., 137.

[6] David Belasco, "Preface," in *The Merchant of Venice: A Comedy by William Shakespeare as Arranged for the Contemporary Stage by David Belasco* (New York, 1922), 5.

[7] Alan Dale, "Jewish Stars of the Stage," *American Hebrew & Jewish Messenger*, September 14, 1917, 462.

FIGURE 12 David Belasco, the "Bishop of Broadway." *A souvenir of Shakespeare's The merchant of Venice: as presented by David Belasco at the Lyceum Theatre, New York, December 21, 1922* (1923).
Photo by White Studio © Billy Rose Theatre Division, The New York Public Library for the Performing Arts.

Belasco traced his Jewish ancestry to Portugal, with the family residing in England from the sixteenth century. In 1852, his parents emigrated from London to San Francisco, drawn by gold rush opportunities. Although he expressed pride in his Jewish origins and was active and respected in the Jewish community, Belasco mystified public perception of his identity by dressing in public like a priest and wearing a black suit with a reversed shirt collar. He said that the outfit was meant to honor an early mentor, Father McGuire, a Catholic priest from his boyhood in Victoria, British Columbia. According to the story, McGuire recognized artistic promise in the young Belasco and sponsored him to study at a local monastery over the disapproval of Belasco's father, a trader who practiced Orthodox Judaism. The narrative, repeated numerous times – in one version the father wanted his son to be a rabbi – identifies Belasco's artistic aspirations with the monastery, somehow isolated from the world of commerce and a Jewish heritage.[8] And yet, the decision to produce *The Merchant* appeared to disrupt the carefully crafted biographical story line, breaking down the disparity between theater-art and Jewish identity that seemed to inform Belasco's public persona.

In a profile published in *The American Hebrew*, the premier English-language Jewish newspaper, two months before *The Merchant* opened, Clarence I. Freed narrated the Father McGuire episode but concluded "After all is said, Belasco is a Jew."[9] He continued: "Belasco has all the native shrewdness, the uncommon sense, the infinite capacity for taking pains which characterizes the level-headed Jew. But he combines with it the idealism of the Jew, the optimism and love of the theatre which, in the case of Belasco, amounts to a passion."[10] The formulation expressed, much differently than Winter would have conceived, how *The Merchant of Venice* could in fact culminate Belasco's career, not by signifying an artistic achievement previously unattained but by deconstructing what had appeared to be fundamental oppositions: as a Broadway producer, Belasco was continually torn between art and commerce, but *The Merchant of Venice* not only seemed to shift the supposedly Jewish term in the binary, it also proposed to integrate Belasco's career through a Jewish identity.[11]

[8] The rabbi detail is quoted in Clarence I. Freed, "My Ambitions at 21 and What Became of Them. VII. – David Belasco," *American Hebrew*, September, 1922, 532. After researching the archive in Victoria, British Columbia, Craig Timberlake concludes that the entire Father McGuire story was a fabrication; *The Bishop of Broadway* (New York: Library Publishers, 1954), 12–17.

[9] Freed, "My Ambitions at 21," 541.

[10] Ibid.

[11] This synthesis of art and commerce within a Jewish tradition is actually implied by the Father McGuire narrative itself, for while Humphrey Belasco forbade his son to study at the monastery, Reina Martin Belasco encouraged her son to attend because (in Winter's telling) she "was fond of poetry" (Winter, *The Life of David Belasco*, vol. 1, 6). By rooting his artistic sensibility in the cultural refinement of his mother, Belasco seems to be drawing on a long-standing mythology of Sephardic nobility and sophistication, a pride that was often invoked by Anglo-Jewish Sephardi to disassociate themselves from a supposedly lower class of (Northern European) Ashkenazim. See Todd M. Endelman, "Benjamin Disraeli and the Myth of Sephardi Superiority," *Jewish History* 10:2 (1996), 21–35.

Warfield also spoke of performing Shylock as a career goal.[12] (Figure 13) He had been a highly successful performer of Jewish types in vaudeville when Belasco cast him as Simon Levi in Lee Arthur and Charles Klein's *The Auctioneer* (1901), a drama set primarily in a junk shop in New York City's Lower East Side. Reviewers were struck by how Warfield's performance could absorb audiences in Levi's pathetic situation. In the past, "They have laughed at the shrewdness, the bargaining spirit and queer clothes of the Jew," Warfield explained his take on the so-called Stage Jew, but now "you suddenly want them to feel pity, sympathy and admiration."[13] In *Staging the Jew*, Harley Erdman situates the play's warm reception in terms of broader anxieties about Jewish presence in society and business, explaining how Warfield's performance "reassured [gentiles] as to the non-threatening nature of the Jew."[14] Eventually Warfield would become one of America's most renowned and wealthiest actors by starring as Herr Anton Von Barwig in Charles Klein's *The Music Master* (1904) and Peter Grimm in Belasco's *The Return of Peter Grimm* (1911), roles that evoked pathos in foreign characters albeit not ones marked explicitly Jewish. As Erdman points out, Warfield's acting career thus exemplifies a broader tension in the history of Jewish assimilation in the United States, where the payoff, and cost, of moving from a less legitimate place to a more prestigious one was to become less "Jewish." However, as with Belasco, the decision to appear in *The Merchant* seemed to run against this trajectory. Even as Warfield had made it in the legitimate theater by starring in non-Jewish roles, by becoming the first American-Jewish actor to perform Shylock on Broadway, he was well aware that *The American Hebrew* would proudly include him in its "Who's Who Roster of American Jews" in December, 1923.[15]

The Merchant of Venice may have been the means for Belasco and Warfield to make explicit a Jewish heritage that had been downplayed in the process of assimilating, but the choice was questioned by a number

[12] David Warfield, "My Friends Levi, Barwig, and Peter Grimm," *American Magazine*, December 28, 1913, 100.

[13] "Chat With Dave Warfield," *New York Sun*, November 10, 1901, David Belasco Papers, Series X, Scrapbook 1, Billy Rose Theatre Collection, New York Public Library.

[14] Harley Erdman, *Staging the Jew: The Performance of an American Ethnicity, 1860–1920* (New Brunswick, NJ: Rutgers University Press, 1997), 110.

[15] *American Hebrew*, December 7, 1923, 78. According to Gary D. Cook, Warfield was born "Wohlfeld" in San Francisco to Orthodox Jewish parents who had emigrated from Austria. See Gary Duane Cook, "David Warfield: A Theatrical Biography," (PhD dissertation, University of Nebraska Lincoln, 1975), 312, 350–56, available at http://digitalcommons/unl.edu/dissertations/AA17602014.

FIGURE 13 David Warfield as Shylock. *A souvenir of Shakespeare's The merchant of Venice: as presented by David Belasco at the Lyceum Theatre, New York, December 21, 1922* (1923).
Photo by White Studio © Billy Rose Theatre Division, The New York Public Library for the Performing Arts.

of Jewish theatergoers, many of whom considered legitimate theater patronage as itself a sign of their prosperity and status. As Ted Merwin has shown, the occasion of Belasco's *Merchant* was a moment when Broadway performances often reflected the experiences of American Jews coordinating middle-class identities with the immigrant world of their mothers and fathers.[16] And yet, while plays like Anne Nichols' *Abie's Irish Rose* (1922) and Raphaelson's *The Jazz Singer* (1925) showed audiences that religio-ethnic particularities could harmonize within a marriage between Christians and Jews, and the popular series of dramas featuring Abe Potash and "Mawruss" Permlutter, written by Montague Glass, depicted businessmen who were both humane and specifically Jewish, *The Merchant of Venice* seemed to offer Jewish audiences little reassurance about intermarriage or the acceptance in business.

This tension became particularly evident when, in June, 1922, Barney Bernard, who played the role of Abe Potash, announced that he would follow Warfield's lead and also appear as Shylock. In a letter to the editor of *The New York Times*, one of Bernard's fans wondered why someone "so loyally Jewish, so proud of his racial heritage" and the "delineator of one of the most lovable characters ever presented on the American stage now sully his art with an attempt to put on the most despicable character of the English speaking stage?"[17] A month later, Bernard dropped the role, citing this sort of pressure from the Jewish community. "Now it is Mr. Warfield's turn to publicly announce that he too has given up his plan to act the money-lender in 'The Merchant of Venice,'" wrote Charles H. Joseph, editor of *The Jewish Criterion*, a newspaper serving the Reformed Jewish community of Pittsburgh and eastern Ohio. He explained: "It is ... very well for artists, writers and critics to look upon 'Shylock' as a finely drawn character and to consider him purely from the standpoint of artistic and dramatic consideration. But the average public doesn't do such things; they see a miserable, grasping, usurious Jew demanding his pound of flesh, and they hate him accordingly and are influenced in hating all other Jews."[18] Joseph's reasoning picked up on the argument already articulated in a national campaign of the B'nai B'rith's Anti-Defamation League (ADL) to ban teaching *The Merchant* in public schools. Above all, the ADL had made the issue a problem of reception, for despite the play's potential for philo-Semitic interpretations, *The*

[16] Ted Merwin, *In Their Own Image: New York Jews in Jazz Age Popular Culture* (New Brunswick, NJ: Rutgers University Press, 2006).

[17] Jacob Levitan, "Letters in the Mail Bag," *New York Times*, July 16, 1922, X1.

[18] "Editorial," *Jewish Criterion*, August 4, 1922, 1.

Merchant of Venice "serves to increase misunderstanding of Jews by non-Jews ... because Shylock is erroneously pictured as typical of all Jews ... [and] Shylock has become an unhappy symbol of Jewish vindictiveness, malice, and hatred."[19]

Warfield's response was to "approach the part as if it were absolutely new"[20] and perform Shylock, in the words of *New York Tribune* critic Percy Hammond, as "A Jew rather than The Jew."[21] Through an acting style that was restrained but tense, Warfield traced Shylock's psychological breakdown as he loses Jessica and seeks justice in court, grounding the action in specific personal duress rather than a universal quest for vengeance against Christians. Constantin Stanislavsky, who attended the production when on tour in the United States, called Warfield's naturalistic portrayal, "the best Shylock I have ever seen,"[22] but theater critics who tried to place Warfield's choices within the performance tradition were nonplussed. As I will show, Warfield's modern acting produced a Shylock who was, in Ludwig Lewisohn's words, "flagrantly un-Shakespearean,"[23] unsettling the basis for reading the character as representative of the Jewish people.

If Warfield aspired to "not lean on any other actor's conception or interpretation, no matter how firmly these ideas have taken root,"[24] Belasco insisted that his *Merchant* would prove him to be a "humble, reverent and most earnest student and disciple of Shakespeare."[25] The tension was discernable in the production, especially in places where Belasco wanted to honor a performance tradition that Warfield intended to reject. Although the disagreement was not public, Warfield's biographer, Gary D. Cook, speculates that the rift led to Warfield's sudden retirement from the stage following *The Merchant*, ending a collaboration with Belasco that had lasted more than twenty years.[26] More than simply a disagreement between individual artists, however, it was Belasco's investment in Shakespeare as a Jewish producer that could worry those who were anxious about the broader implications of Jewish assimilation, as if the

[19] Quoted in Neil Baldwin, *Henry Ford and the Jews: The Mass Production of Hate* (New York: Perseus Books, 2003), 7.

[20] Lawrence Hall, "David Warfield: The Actor and the Man," *Arena* 41 (March, 1909), 265.

[21] Quoted in Cook, "David Warfield," 315.

[22] Quoted in Edwin W. Hullinger, "As Stanislavsky Sees Us Americans," *New York Times*, March 11, 1923, SM3.

[23] Ludwig Lewisohn, "Shylock of Venice," *Nation*, January 3, 1923, 21.

[24] Hall, "David Warfield," 265–66.

[25] Belasco, "Preface," 28.

[26] Cook, "David Warfield," 290.

wealthy producer was attempting to buy his way into a more prestigious cultural realm. Following this anxiety as it cuts through reception to Belasco's production helps clarify a key moment in the history of Jewish response to *The Merchant of Venice*. The rising social and economic status of American Jews that made Belasco's *Merchant* production possible also triggered panic about invisible Jewish power, a threat that could be projected on to Shylock's character. While Henry Irving's persecuted and sympathetic Shylock had established a basic expectation for the role, critical responses to the Belasco/Warfield interpretation became focused on Shylock's duplicity. In this way, it was Belasco, the producer of Shylock, who seemed to embody the threat of Shylock himself, a deceiver who uses sympathy as a means of manipulation.[27]

By the time Belasco's *Merchant* opened at the Lyceum Theater in New York City on December 21, 1922, his reputation had already suffered considerably in critical writing about modern theater, especially from proponents of the new European-inspired stagecraft of the postwar era. In such arguments, Belasco epitomized the "old" Broadway establishment and a naturalist style over and against which producers like Gordon Craig and Robert Edmond Jones constructed their "new" expressionistic and symbolic designs. Primarily, the complaint was that Belasco's style continually worked against scenic unity, as the gaze of spectators forever wandered among the hundreds of real-life objects that often crowded his stages. Certainly, Belasco's *Merchant* gave audiences plenty to look at – Stark Young, for example, recommended that theatergoers patronize the production to "see the brocades, the incomparable splendor of the textiles that the actors wear, and to see the reminiscences of Titian, Tintoretto, and Veronese in some of the figures on the stage"[28] – but, as the art critic James Huneker pointed out, Belasco was not merely an "upholsterer" of surfaces but above all a "painter" of "atmospheric effects."[29] In this manner, Belasco's scenic design was not really archeological in the tradition of nineteenth-century producers like Charles Kean and Henry Irving who staged *The Merchant* against the backdrop of recognizable Venetian landmarks. Rather, Belasco's settings in Venice and

[27] See Elmer Edgar Stoll, *Shakespeare Studies: Historical and Comparative Method* (New York: Macmillan Company, 1927), 255–336, for the classic reading of how Shylock supposedly evokes pathos as a "pretense" for revenge.

[28] Stark Young, "The Passionate Pilgrim," in *Immortal Shadows: A Book of Criticism* (New York: Octagon Books, 1973), 43.

[29] James Gibbons Huneker, "David Belasco," *Outlook* 77 (1921), quoted in Alan S. Downer, ed. *American Drama and its Critics* (Chicago: University of Chicago Press, 1965), 35–37.

Belmont gave the impression of authentic places, but the realistic details served to construct an illusion of reality, what Belasco took to be the fictional world of Shakespeare's *The Merchant of Venice*, rather than historical Venice itself.[30]

As Cary Mazer explains in his study of Shakespeare production in England during the same period, the desire to create an authentic picture of Shakespeare's world often stopped at the dramatic text, as the physical demands of massive, three-dimensional sets required that scenes be rearranged. At the same time, however, even major changes to the text were said to honor rather than revise Shakespeare's art. "If Shakespeare was not able to create such a verisimilar world on the stage," writes Mazer, paraphrasing the logic, "this was ... the fault of his theatre, not of his dramatic vision."[31] These assumptions are critical to understanding Belasco's aspiration to present a Shylock who was both tragic and authentically Shakespearean. Borrowing ideas from several previous *Merchant* producers, most notably Henry Irving and Herbert Beerbohm Tree, Belasco rearranged Shakespeare's text significantly. At the same time, he claimed that such changes were what "Shakespeare would have done ... if he were here today."[32]

Regarding *The Merchant*'s representation of Shylock, Belasco's most significant revision was to group Shylock's scenes from the second and third acts of Shakespeare's text into a continuous sequence set in and around Shylock's house: Shylock's scene with Jessica, the scene of her leaving home, Shylock's "Hath not a Jew eyes?" speech, and Shylock's decision to pursue Antonio's bond. (Consequently, Belasco incorporated the Belmont scenes, dropping the Arragon scene, in Act 3.) All together, the Shylock in Venice sequence created the space for Warfield to clearly demonstrate Shylock's lack of premeditated vengeance. "I show [Shylock] to be a very human person in the opening scenes," explained Warfield in the *New York Times*, because "[he] had no idea ... of ever demanding the fulfillment of the bond – he was driven to that state of mind by subsequent events."[33] In this way, Warfield addressed what Irving believed to be the key issue for actors preparing the role – "to try to show when

[30] For an in-depth study of Belasco's innovations in modern stagecraft, including a detailed analysis of his *Merchant* production, see Lise-Lone Marker, *David Belasco: Naturalism in the American Theatre* (Princeton, NJ: Princeton University Press, 1975), 178–202.

[31] Cary M. Mazer, *Shakespeare Refashioned: Elizabethan Plays on Edwardian Stages* (Ann Arbor: UMI Research Press, 1981), 10.

[32] Belasco, "Preface," 27.

[33] Corbin, "Warfield," 19.

Shylock is inspired with the idea of [the] bargain [with Antonio]"[34] – but he answered the question quite differently. Whereas Irving locates Shylock's desire for revenge in Act 1,[35] Warfield emphasizes that Shylock becomes suddenly "insane" when he believes Jessica has been "stolen from him" by Lorenzo.[36]

To accommodate Warfield's interpretation, Belasco staged an expanded version of Irving's famous "return," when Shylock arrives at his house and discovers that Jessica has gone. In Shakespeare's text, Shylock's reaction to Jessica's note is mediated by Solanio, who quotes the words "My daughter, O my ducats, O my daughter" (2.8.15) to foreground Shylock's obsession with money and ridicule his loss. Irving's breakthrough was to adapt a scene from Verdi's *Rigoletto* into a sequence that extended from Jessica's departure through some business of the rowdy masquerade into a quiet pantomime of Shylock approaching the outside of his house. Irving knocked on the door, looked in the window, and the scene ended with a picture of Shylock's utter devastation and isolation. Belasco allowed Warfield to extend this "dumb scene" by dramatizing Shylock's discovery of Jessica's note. Rather than exit from the stage as he opens the door to his home (in the tradition of Irving's performance), Belasco faded the lights as Shylock reaches the threshold and, after a brief interval, showed Shylock enter the interior of his residence: "SHYLOCK *sees a jeweled ring upon the floor; rushes across stage and snatches it up, crying* "Jessica, my girl, Jessica!" *He sees the open chest and utters a piercing cry as he realizes that he has been robbed. Turning, he sees, snatches up and reads, the letter, left by* JESSICA."[37] While the addition reproduces the text's original conflation between a daughter and ducats, it offered Warfield the space to emphasize the trauma experienced from the loss of the former (Figure 12). One reviewer described Warfield's performance this way:

> It is only gradually, as he enters the darkened house with its one lantern emphasizing its loneliness, that the truth dawns upon him. He hurries up the stairs, and then down again; he stumbles over the keys flung into a corner; he treads on a few dropped ducats; he catches sight of some silk protruding from under the lid of a great chest; and then at last his more or less smothered cries rise into a crescendo of misery, a hysterical scream for his daughter.[38]

[34] Henry Irving quoted in Leigh Woods, *On Playing Shakespeare: Advice and Commentary from Actors and Actresses of the Past* (New York: Greenwood Press, 1991), 160.

[35] Ibid., 161.

[36] Corbin, "Warfield," 19.

[37] Belasco, "Preface," 96–97.

[38] "Mr. Warfield's Shylock," *International Interpreter*, January 13, 1923, 1292.

The moment was a crucial place in Warfield's overall performance, for Shylock's anger erupts not into a desire for racial vengeance but into a kind of personal hysteria. Stanislavsky wrote that he was so "seized" by Warfield's performance of Shylock's emotional condition in this scene that "I almost forgot [Warfield] was an actor."[39] In order to keep the audience focused on the process of Shylock's breakdown, Belasco's arrangement followed directly with Shakespeare's Act 3, Scene 1, starting when Solanio relates Shylock's cries of "O my ducats, O my daughter." One scholar has observed that "to have the lines repeated so close to their first utterance must have appeared irritatingly clumsy and awkward,"[40] but the contrast between Warfield's embodied distress and Solanio's mocking account must have also been evident to audiences, underscoring the difference between Shylock's experience and its anti-Semitic reception in Venice. As the scene proceeds, Warfield shows Shylock's increasing agitation – a production photograph shows him wild eyed, with a bare chest and disheveled hair – and through the "Hath not a Jew eyes?" speech and the meeting with Tubal, Warfield dramatizes how Shylock's "insanity" starts to feed a quest for justice and vengeance. This transition marked the fundamental challenge of Warfield's entire performance – to bring a character who had no apparent intention or desire to collect Antonio's bond to a place where such an action could be psychologically believable. Moreover, for such a character study to be dramaturgically powerful, audiences needed to connect the suffering of this particular Jewish father to the broader condition of suffering in the Jewish community.

To this end, Warfield hinted at Shylock's repression, so that the loss of Jessica could appear to unleash a lifetime of resentment and servitude. Reviewers often noted Warfield's restrained affect, his soft voice and subtle hand gestures, but many also remarked the tension evident in that restraint, a "subterranean ferocity,"[41] the "suppression ... [of] hatred [which] has boiled up with hatred as in a steel furnace."[42] As Warfield plays it, the demand for Antonio's bond, observed the critic for *The International Interpreter*, seemed to be "not merely a personal obsession, but a racial impulse, of which Shylock himself does not understand the smallest part."[43] Thus, when Shylock's desire for justice is finally released,

[39] Hullinger, "As Stanislavsky Sees Us Americans," SM3.

[40] Kirk Mallory Reynolds, "A Stage History of The Merchant of Venice, 1596–1982: A Study Based on Selected Promptbooks," (dissertation, University of South Carolina, 1987), 337.

[41] "Mr. Warfield's Shylock," 1292.

[42] "The Theatre," *International Interpreter*, January 13, 1923, 1267.

[43] Ibid., 1268.

Warfield refused to transform him into something like an avenger of the Jews. Rather, Warfield evoked pathos for Shylock as a shattered human being, a "frail and intrepid figure," in the words of Lewisohn, "intense to the point of neurasthenia ... [who has] been rasped until there is no protective covering over his nerves."[44]

Refusing to invoke the tradition of Shylock as a universal Jew, Warfield instead grounded Shylock's Jewish characteristics in the particularities of his behavior. Lewisohn offers a perceptive analysis of Warfield's strategy when Shylock learns from Tubal that Jessica had sold Leah's ring:

> There is a common opinion among Jews, to be accepted for what it is worth, that especially among the older generation acquainted with persecution the bark is worse than the bite and that the "bitter tongue" is merely an explosion of hurt nerves. And thus when this Shylock has cursed his daughter: "Would she were hearsed at my foot, and the ducats in her coffin!" he stops; he recoils from himself; with his frail, old hand he beats his lips. Half of a typical New York audience that has seen this gesture used by its elders at comparable moments a hundred times, knows now that Shylock is the kindest of fathers and was the most domesticated of husbands and that the ducats matter very little in the end. It was only the "evil mouth" that spoke.[45]

By showing that Shylock cared more for Jessica than his ducats, Warfield countered the stereotype of Shylock as an avaricious Jew, but he also refused to universalize Shylock's fatherhood, insisting that he is a Jewish person who loves his daughter. Lewisohn's suggestion that such moves were especially appreciated by Jewish theatergoers is confirmed in a letter Warfield received from Rabbi William Rosenau, then a leader in American Reform Judaism. "You have succeeded in presenting the oft-misunderstood Shakespearean character in the light of Jewish psychology," wrote Rosenau. "Far from being an unwelcome social influence," Rosenau continued, "your 'Shylock' is a means of healthful propaganda."[46] For Warfield, character psychology was a means to humanize Shylock, to root behavior in particular circumstances rather than

44 Lewisohn, "Shylock of Venice," 21.

45 Ibid., 22.

46 Rosenau's letter is quoted in the *Jewish Criterion* by Charles Joseph who had criticized Belasco's *The Merchant* and urged Jewish theatergoers to "forsake" Warfield for the "un-Jewish act" of playing Shylock (August 4, 1922, 1). Joseph's decision to publish the letter, however, framed the issue much differently, now giving readers a way to appreciate Warfield's performance while still insisting upon the ADL boycott of *The Merchant*. "Mr. Warfield is a Jew; let us not forget that," Joseph wrote. "Further, he is a Jew who would not do anything that, in his estimation, would injure his people. He is sincere and honest in the belief that his interpretation of Shylock is ... HELPING rather than hurting his people" (p. 15).

pre-existing motivations; but when this performance becomes also recognized as "Jewish psychology," the ADL's argument against *The Merchant of Venice*, Rosenau suggests, may also need to be reconsidered. If the ADL worried that Shylock's apparently vindictive nature would be seen to represent all Jewish people, then Warfield's grieving Jewish father could appear sympathetic to all parents.[47]

However, Warfield's refusal to invoke the traditional Shylock confounded several of the production's non-Jewish reviewers. "I have seen few things so off, so wrong," wrote Stark Young, "as Mr. Warfield's Shylock in the trial scene, that little, bent, heart-breaking figure of the Jew, with his pious, suffering eyes."[48] Young was responsive to the pathos evoked by Warfield's acting, but he had difficulty accepting the portrayal as Shakespeare's character. Instead, Warfield reminded him of "some old, ragged father on the East Side who stood on the corner peddling … who had in his eyes so much goodness, unapproachable fanaticism, patience, tragic silence and distress."[49] Perhaps Young was thinking of Warfield's Simon Levi in *The Auctioneer* twenty years earlier, but his projection of the particularities of Warfield's performance to a universal conception of the Jew is striking. Not the betrayed Jewish father, Shylock appears to Young as a displaced immigrant, the very embodiment of modernity, utterly lost, and unassimilated. Warfield's Shylock thus "had no dignity, no taste, no style, no health, no beauty, no volume of creative life, he had only pitiful defeat, thwarted mind and purpose, sick wrongs, and dumb profound, unwholesome intensity."[50] In the *New York Times* John Corbin agreed, calling Warfield's Shylock "physically unimpressive in stature and voice."[51] Against the tradition, Warfield portrayed a "diminutive figure … with no touch of the grotesque in his rages, his exultations or his despairs."[52] Corbin did appreciate the "subtle, delicate artistry"[53]

[47] Warfield's low-key Shylock resembled choices made by Rudolf Schildkraut for his 1911 Yiddish theater performance in New York City, a production that Belasco considered one of his favorites. However, in the Yiddish language context, where there was perhaps less anxiety about the production's reception by gentiles, some were disappointed by the resulting weakness of Schildkraut's characterization. See Joel Berkowitz, "'A True Jewish Jew': Three Yiddish Shylocks," *Theatre Survey* 37:1 (May, 1996), 75–98.

[48] Young, "Passionate Pilgrim," 42.

[49] Ibid.

[50] Ibid.

[51] John Corbin, "How Comic was Shylock?," *New York Times*, January 7, 1923, X1

[52] Ibid.

[53] Corbin, "Warfield," 19.

of Warfield's performance, but he stressed nevertheless that the "effect was ... thoroughly un-Shakespearean."[54]

Although Warfield desired the cultural prestige associated with Shakespeare – observing in an earlier interview that "the literary people, the reviewers and critics look upon the man who plays the classics as a big man"[55] – he would have not found Corbin's criticism surprising, given his decision to approach the role of Shylock as if "the play had never before been produced."[56] But such judgments would have certainly troubled Belasco, who aspired to honor the Shakespeare tradition. This tension was marked in Belasco's scenic design, for while his arrangement created the space for Warfield to show subtly the arc of Shylock's particular emotional distress, Belasco's also shaped his production to make that particular experience represent a larger history of Jewish experience and suffering. Most significantly, Belasco staged Act 1, Scene 3, when Shylock and Antonio agree to the bond, in front of a synagogue, in the "late afternoon, fading into a fiery sunset" with the "sounds of chanting by the congregation and cantor ... [and] occasionally, the voice of the rabbi."[57] The choice echoed Herbert Beerbohm Tree's 1908 production which set the play's second act entirely in the Jewish ghetto. But whereas Tree established the subordination of Jews in Venice by contrasting the sound of "men's voices, joining in the Kol Nedrei [*sic*]" from inside a synagogue with "bursts of melody from the revellers [*sic*] without,"[58] and even showed masqueraders actually beating Jewish people on the street,[59] Belasco showed the ghetto to be a place of Jewish power. As Jewish worshipers "hurriedly perfor[m] the ceremony of hand-washing" Bassanio stands just outside the synagogue, unable to enter.[60] He recognizes Tubal, asks him a question, and Tubal points towards Shylock who approaches. Bassanio shouts out Shylock's name, they confer in front of the synagogue door, until Shylock's words, "three thousand ducats, well" become audible and the scene begins.

When Shylock recalls Antonio's insults on the Rialto, the audience at Belasco's production perceives Shylock to now be in a much different territory, and while Antonio does not relent, the affront to Shylock's person,

[54] Corbin, "How Comic was Shylock?," A1.

[55] David Warfield, "My Friends Levi, Barwig, and Peter Grimm," *American Magazine*, December 28, 1913, 28–31, 95–102.

[56] Hall, "David Warfield," 265.

[57] Belasco, *The Merchant of Venice*, 62.

[58] *Daily Telegraph* quoted in Reynolds, "A Stage History," 322.

[59] Mazer, *Shakespeare Refashioned*, 18.

[60] Belasco, *The Merchant of Venice*, 62.

and his "sufferance," is set against the backdrop of an enduring tradition and community. However, if Warfield had intended to propose the "merry bond" without a hint of premeditation, Belasco suggested otherwise, for, as the scene develops, the verisimilar sunset and choral chants appear increasingly figural, symbolic of a looming Jewish resistance. Belasco was known for orchestrating such highly charged emotional moments in the theater, a proto-cinematic style the theater critic and historian Montrose Moses called "the psychology of the switchboard,"[61] and behind Warfield's apparently innocuous behavior appeared something more ominous. Belasco completed the action this way:

(The Scene is darkening into shadows: the Light falling upon SHYLOCK *is a dull, ruddy glow. Sound of Hebrew choir singing within Synagogue. As* ANTONIO and BASSANIO *are off,* SHYLOCK *comes down C., and looking after them, speaks.)*

> Thou call'dst me a dog before thou hadst a cause;
> But, since I am a dog, beware my fangs!
> PICTURE. – CURTAIN.[62]

William Winter credited Edwin Booth for this interpolation of lines from Act 3 (3.3.6–7). By citing Booth, Belasco was honoring one of his favorite actors, but Booth's interpretation of Shylock, enshrined in Horace Henry Furness's New Variorum Edition of *The Merchant of Venice* (1888) as a malicious and essentially inhuman character, completely undermined Warfield's intention. At the same time, however, gestures similar to Booth's were evident in the more sympathetic performances of Irving, who shook his staff and cursed[63] and Tree, who spit back at Antonio.[64] As painful as it must have been for Warfield to inhabit a tradition he sought to defy, the awkward moment clarified the overall purpose of his intention to perform Shylock without vengeance. Warfield seems to have realized that the pursuit of justice could appear very much like a drive for revenge, that Booth's snarl and Tree's spitting could look about the same. For Warfield, the only way to break the cycle was to relinquish Shylock's claim to speak for the Jewish people, for better or worse. From this perspective, it was Belasco's investment in a tradition of Shakespearean performance that was itself the trap, the eruption of Booth's role only an

[61] Montrose Moses, *The American Dramatist* (Boston: Little, Brown, and company, 1917), 230–59.

[62] Belasco, *The Merchant of Venice*, 72.

[63] James C. Bulman, *The Merchant of Venice*, Shakespeare in Performance (Manchester, UK: Manchester University Press, 1991), 35–36.

[64] Mazer, *Shakespeare Refashioned*, 217, note 61.

especially grotesque assertion of the residual anti-Semitism that could haunt even the most sympathetic of Shylocks.

But Belasco's aspiration to honor Shakespeare with his *Merchant* was circular in a more fundamental way, as if the very act of claiming to master the high-cultural discourse on Shakespeare was itself evidence that he was faking it. While the nativist response to the new immigration from Eastern Europe had been confident that Jewish otherness could be detected through signs of racial difference, as successful Jewish Americans like Belasco attempted to enter into previously restricted social spaces and cultural realms, attention shifted from the visible to what may be hidden beneath the surface. "There was always a chance," writes Daniel Itzkovitz, "that the Jew ... would slip by ... that the Jew *trying* to appear white really *does* appear white."[65] This kind of visual uncertainty, coupled with the certainty of Jewish difference, "fed fantasies of dangerous secrets behind the eyes of the suspect Jew," so that "the more 'the same' the Jew was, the more there was to fear."[66]

By the time of Belasco's *Merchant* production, a similar narrative had already shaped critical response to Belasco's theater more generally, as wide admiration for his production technique was tempered by concerns about his own theatricality, sometimes expressed with anxiety that something unsavory was being concealed. This reading was articulated perhaps most influentially by Sheldon Cheney in *The New Movement in the Theatre* (1914), where he defined the mission of modernist theater against "Belascoism."[67] The work of other commercial producers "differs from [Belasco's] simply in that it lacks the disguising gloss, the insinuating semblance of art by which he has led even discerning critics to an acceptance of fundamentally false productions."[68] Moreover, the "disguise" is performed by Belasco himself whose claims of artistry cover up an essentially commercial motivation. "If [Belasco] is content to consider that he is creating mere entertainment ... that belong[s] to the business of amusement rather than to the art of the theatre – one can have no quarrel with him," writes Cheney. "But Mr. Belasco does not admit that he is working outside the boundaries of the legitimate art of the theatre. Indeed, one gathers from his essays that he believes that he is doing a

65 Daniel Itzkovitz, "Secret Temples," in *Jews and Other Differences: The New Jewish Cultural Studies*, ed. Jonathan Boyarin and Daniel Boyarin (Minneapolis, MN: University of Minnesota Press, 1997), 182.

66 Ibid., 185, 178.

67 Sheldon Cheney, *The New Movement in the Theatre* (New York: Mitchell Kennerley, 1914), 156.

68 Ibid., 167.

very important service to American dramatic art."[69] Thus, Belascoism is a "conspiracy of commercialism and bad taste," demonstrating "the way of the business man and the Philistine in the house of art."[70]

A similar distrust of Belasco's sincerity appears in Stark Young's review of *The Merchant of Venice*, for although he praised the costumes and properties for being museum quality, "As for the accuracy of the Venetian atmosphere afforded," he wrote, "the results of laborious days on the spot at great expense et cetera, one may put one's tongue in one's cheek." Belasco's theatricality was remarkable but his "taste [was] ... uncertain to the point of vulgarity," discernable beneath a false front. "Scratch the Shakespeare," he wrote "and you will find Belasco."[71] Indeed, the identical imagery appears in *The Great Gatsby* (1925) where F. Scott Fitzgerald called Gatsby a "regular Belasco" to illustrate the painstaking stagecraft behind his public image. As the story unfolds, however, Gatsby's performance breaks down, revealing to the novel's WASP narrator the "sinister" basis for Gatsby's wealth in a Jewish crime syndicate.[72]

A much more explicit connection between Belasco's theatricality and a Jewish conspiracy appeared in a series of articles published in Henry Ford's *The Dearborn Independent* in January, 1921, two years before *The Merchant* opened on Broadway. After rehashing the standard narrative by which American theater had become "Judiazed," the editors warn that, more recently, Jewish influence has become hidden and devious.[73] In a piece titled, "How Jews Capitalized a Protest Against Jews," the editors claim that Belasco's war against the Theatrical Syndicate was in fact a "pretended protest," a secret plot that "saved [the theater] to Jewish control."[74] The editorial explains:

> Belasco's theatricalism helped to this end. He is an actor off, as well as on the stage. He affects the pose of a benevolent priest, and dresses the part ... he sits in his sanctum with the lights so arranged that his priestly face ... seem[s] to rise out of an encompassing and shadowy mystery. It is very effective – very effective. One woman declared, after being admitted to the presence and gazing on the face that rose out of the shadows into the light – "I have a better understanding of the divine humility of Jesus Christ since I have been privileged to meet Mr. Belasco."[75]

[69] Ibid., 161–62.

[70] Ibid., 152.

[71] Young, "Passionate Pilgrim," 44.

[72] F. Scott Fitzgerald, *The Great Gatsby* (New York: Scribner, 1995), 50.

[73] *Jewish Activities in the United States: Volume II of The International Jew* (Dearborn, MI: Dearborn Publishing Co., 1921), 110.

[74] Ibid., 114.

[75] Ibid., 113.

Antonio jokes that Shylock seems to turn Christian when he charges no interest; for Henry Ford, Belasco shows himself to be a Jew because he pretends to be Christ.[76]

Perhaps nothing revealed the presence of *The Merchant of Venice* in modern America more than how such conspiracy theories essentially followed Antonio's warning that "The divel can cite Scripture for his own purpose" (1.3.92). In this sense, Belasco's promotion of his *Merchant* could signify metatheatrically, as if his claims that money was no object somehow revealed an essentially commercial intention. Needless to say, Belasco's advertising was, on its own terms, inherently conflicted, at once drawing attention to the production's great expense and attempting downplay the possibility of vulgar display. For example, the *New York Times* reported that "rumors" had estimated that $250,000 was spent on the *Merchant* production, but "Questioned as to the sheer financial investment involved, Mr. Belasco … refused to make public any figures … 'It is not important,' was his reply … 'I am telling the simple truth when I say that it does not matter in the least whether the cost of the production is ever recovered, so long as people think it is well done."[77] Like Bassanio, Belasco avowed that all that glisters is not gold, and he ventured all he had for Shakesperean art. But there is a difference between choosing a lead casket and producing casket properties that, according to *Theatre Magazine*, were imported from Italy for $16,000.[78] Deception by ornament was after all the pleasure of Belasco's style.

The problem was that Belasco's attempts to enter into the critical discourse about Shakespeare could also appear to be a "disguising gloss" easily scratched. Throughout his career, Belasco was adept at using public relations to advertise himself as an authority on theater, placing articles in monthly magazines like *Cosmopolitan* and *Munsey's* but, for the production of the *Merchant*, Belasco framed his performance in a way that perhaps he believed more appropriate for the Shakespearean occasion – he published a book, an edition of *The Merchant of Venice*

[76] A much different representation of Jewish threat was evident in Walter Hampden's performance of Shylock in May, 1921 at the Broadhurst Theatre in New York City. Acting against the Irving standard, Hampden showed Shylock to be essentially malicious and threatening – just the "sort of Shylock," wrote Heywood Broun, "which Henry Ford would enjoy" ("Shylock Shows Walter Hampton At His Best," *New York Tribune*, May 14, 1921, 8.). While perhaps Ford would have found Hampden's unsympathetic Shylock entertaining, Belasco's sympathetic production appears more pertinent to Ford's fear of Jewish conspiracy.

[77] Belasco, "Preface," 5.

[78] Quoted in Cook, "David Warfield," 312.

"By William Shakespeare ... as arranged for the contemporary stage by David Belasco." Privately printed for "friends" and released to the press, the volume helped readers reconstruct the production through detailed stage directions. The book also contained an extensive prefatory section, written in a strikingly academic tone and filled with scholarly references and footnotes. This need to swear reverence to Shakespeare while promoting the contemporary value of his *Merchant* cuts through Belasco's writing, sometimes quite awkwardly, as when, for example he explained the value added to Shakespeare by his production using this seemingly crass analogy: "A diamond is always a diamond – but cut, polished, and placed in a suitable and lovely setting it always shows to better advantage than when left, rough and imperfect, embedded in clay."[79] Perhaps most audaciously, Belasco offered that, "[It] is [not] possible for me to doubt that Shakespeare himself would eagerly have employed all the many invaluable accessories of modern stagecraft if they had been available to him."[80]

In his review of *The Merchant* in the *New York Times*, John Corbin quoted these and several other assertions from the Preface, and in a series of articles he took issue with Belasco's claim to honor Shakespeare's intention. "[Belasco] has made Shakespeare's story fit the needs of his scenery, not his scenery fit the needs of Shakespeare's story," wrote Corbin. "Yet he is certain that Shakespeare would smile and approve."[81] Corbin especially homes in on the prefatory section titled "Concerning Shylock," where Belasco explains his decision to portray Shylock sympathetically, as the victim of social prejudice. At the time, such a position was not controversial, but Belasco's claim that Shakespeare did not intend Shylock to be a comic character seemed to Corbin an overreach. "Shylock may even be made a tragic character, as Mr. Belasco declares that he essentially is, and as Henry Irving played him ... But that he could have had any such seeming to the conscious ... mind of Shakespeare, is incomprehensible, impossible."[82] Belasco's transgression was not that he had sympathized with Shylock but rather that he was attempting to sympathize with Shakespeare.

Invoking Shakespeare's intention to de-legitimate modern versions of *The Merchant of Venice* was of course nothing new, but Corbin's concern appears very different from William Poel's 1898 critique of

[79] Belasco, "Preface," 15.
[80] Ibid., 27.
[81] John Corbin, "Slavic Realism and Shakespeare," *New York Times*, January 21, 1923, X1.
[82] Corbin, "How Comic was Shylock?," X1.

Henry Irving's performance. Whereas Poel showed Shylock to be a one-dimensional Elizabethan comic type, his relevant Jewish characteristics knowable simply from a red wig, Corbin wanted to expose the Jewish producer of Shylock as being deceptive and insincere. At the same time, the Shakespeare scholar E.E. Stoll was using similar imagery to describe the character of Shylock himself. In *Shakespeare Studies* (1927) Stoll complains that Shylock sympathizers "rea[d] the lines or pages, not the play," missing Shakespeare's "formal external comic technique" whereby appeals for sympathy are actually traps set by the "trickster" Shylock.[83] The problem is that we buy the act – "such sentimentalists are we!"[84] Anachronism was Stoll's critical aversion, but it is hard to not hear Cheney and Ford in Stoll's argument – the worry that Jews are most threatening when they appear the most sympathetic. Stoll found the reception of Shylock's "Hath not a Jew eyes?" speech especially problematical, "for generations … misread, simply taken, like other supposedly pathetic passages, out of its context, and a meaning superimposed."[85] The distraction from Shakespeare's supposed intention comes at the moment Shylock articulates his oppressed condition as a Jewish person in Venice. "Then and there," Stoll writes, "we, with our humanitarian impulses, jump the track – at once we are, one and all, over on Shylock's side."[86]

For Stoll, and other historicist Shakespeare critics seeking to legitimate their research, contemporary performance derailed academic scholarship. In the case of *The Merchant of Venice*, what gets in the way is a condition of Jewish prosperity and assimilation that assumes a human Shylock. "On the popular stage, to be sure Shylock must be played pretty much as Irving played him," wrote Stoll "but criticism, unlike acting, has to do with truth alone."[87] If Shylock's claims for sympathy are schemes for justifying revenge, then Shakespeare's "modernizers" evoke sympathy for Shylock to disguise what Stoll considers an illegitimate claim to Shakespeare's literary tradition. When Jewish Americans gain the power to represent Shylock, as producers and performers, Shylock ceases to be simply a grotesque object of the dominant culture. At the same time, however, Shylock becomes most threatening as a performer and a producer – a "villain with a smiling cheek" (1.3.94).

[83] Stoll, *Shakespeare Studies*, 333, 303, 328.
[84] Ibid., 328.
[85] Ibid., 325.
[86] Ibid., 326.
[87] Ibid., 341.

7

New York City, 1947: A Season for Shylocks

Edna Nahshon

For Jews, 1947 was a year of complex emotions. The monumentality of the Holocaust had started to sink in, and a long process of grieving and soul-searching had begun; on the other hand, the Zionist dream of a sovereign Jewish state in Palestine seemed to be finally within reach. At the same time, hundreds of thousands of stateless Holocaust survivors were languishing in displaced persons camps in Germany and Austria, trapped in limbo, unable to rebuild their shattered lives as harsh British restrictions on Jewish immigration to Palestine and American immigration quotas kept them stranded in a refugee no man's land.[1] In August 1946 the British authorities began to send to internment camps in Cyprus thousands of Jewish survivors who tried to enter Palestine by sea but were intercepted by British forces.[2] In July, 1947, the vessel SS *Exodus 1947* tried to break the British blockade of Palestine. Its trials and tribulations captivated the attention of the world. Having arrived at the Haifa shore with a human cargo of 4,500 survivors, the *Exodus* was barred by the British authorities from disembarking, and its passengers were forced by the Royal Navy to return to Hamburg, Germany, then in the British occupation zone. The situation in British-controlled Palestine was worsening

[1] In December 1945, President Harry Truman issued a directive that loosened quota restrictions on immigration to the United States for persons displaced by the Nazi regime. This allowed for approximately 28,000 Jewish survivors to immigrate to America. In 1948, the US Congress passed the Displaced Persons Act, which provided approximately 400,000 US immigration visas for displaced persons between January 1, 1949, and December 31, 1952. This facilitated the settlement of an additional 68,000 Jews in the United States. After its establishment in 1948, Israel absorbed 170,000 Holocaust survivors.

[2] The camps, which operated from August, 1946 to January, 1949 held a total of over 50,000 people.

daily, as tensions between Jews, Arabs, and the British approached the boiling point. On February 18, 1947, the British announced their intention to withdraw from the region. On November 29, 1947, the General Assembly of the United Nations voted to recommend the adoption and implementation of a partition plan for Palestine and the establishment of a Jewish state alongside an Arab one. The plan was rejected by the Arab states. An intensifying armed conflict broke out in Palestine between Jews and Arabs and shortly thereafter between Jewish military units and the invading armies of five Arab nations.

In 1947, New York was home to well over two million Jews, marking it as the city with the largest Jewish population in the world. The city's cultural institutions, including the theater, did not insulate themselves from these historical events. On September 4, 1946, the League for a Free Palestine staged with much success *A Flag Is Born*, a Zionist anti-British pageant written by Ben Hecht with music by Kurt Weill, starring Paul Muni, Marlon Brando, and Celia Adler as survivors of the death camps who are attempting to immigrate to Palestine in defiance of British-imposed restrictions. After 120 shows on Broadway, the show went on a national tour. On January 4, 1948, *Skipper Next to God* by Jan De Hartog, a play directed by Lee Strasberg and starring John Garfield, opened on Broadway. Based on the tragic story of the vessel *St. Louis*, whose 937 Jewish refugees were turned away from Cuba and the United States in the spring of 1939 and were forced to return to Europe, the play's relevance could not be missed by its audience.

Given this context, it is clear that the appearance on the New York stage of three distinctly different Shylocks over the period spanning from late winter to early fall 1947 cannot be regarded as merely coincidental. This is not to say that the three productions were coordinated in any way. They were not. They were intended for different audiences, had different agendas, and were distinguished by their use of language. The first spoke the formal elevated English typical of British Shakespearean performance during the late nineteenth and early twentieth centuries; the second was done in Hebrew, a language understood by only a small band of enthusiastic American Hebraists; the third communicated in Yiddish, the mother tongue of most of the immigrant Jewish community. Yet, when considered as a cultural phenomenon and not merely as individual enterprises, the three productions speak of the historical moment. Though each Shylock projected a particular sensibility, together they raised a myriad of questions regarding the connection between topicality and the theater, and more particularly, the impact of the Holocaust on the world of arts and letters.

On the face of it, this Shylock profusion may seem perplexing as *The Merchant of Venice* was still regarded by both Jews and sympathetic gentiles as a premier exemplar of cultural anti-Semitism, a most sensitive issue in the aftermath of the Holocaust. Indeed, in May, 1947, just days before the debut of the second New York production featuring Shylock, the *New York Times* reported that a forthcoming production of *The Merchant of Venice* in Frankfurt, then located in the American occupation zone, had been canceled, the journalist explaining that "the vicious anti-Semitism still pervading Germany makes Shakespeare's play a highly controversial piece."[3] A similar situation arose a year earlier in Naples when the local Jewish community demanded that an Italian production of the play be banned due to its "anti-Semitic character."[4] It was this sort of thinking that must have accounted for the fact that *The Merchant of Venice* had not been seen on the New York stage since 1931, most likely due to the rigorous anti-Shylock campaign conducted by American Jews, who also constituted a significant percentage of New-York's theater-going public. The last notable pre-war production of the play in New York, which starred George Arliss as Shylock, took place in 1928. Two subsequent productions, starring Jewish actors Maurice Moscovitch (1930) and Fritz Leiber (1931) failed to attract the theater-going public and received no more than tepid reviews.[5]

The Donald Wolfit Company

The first Shylock of 1947 made his appearance in February in a production presented by the visiting British actor Donald Wolfit and his company, then touring America and Canada. Though the company's offerings during its New York engagement (February 18, 1947–March 8, 1947) included *King Lear*, *As You Like It*, *Volpone*, and *Hamlet*, it was *The Merchant* that drew the most public attention; its matinee opening

[3] Delbert Clark, "German Theatre in Revival," *New York Times*, May 16, 1947, X3.

[4] "Looking for Trouble," *Manchester Guardian*, February 16, 1946, 4.

[5] The production starring Moscovitch had a run of fifteen performances, Fritz Leiber's, six performances; see http://www.ibdb.com. It's noteworthy that between 1931 and 1947 Hamlet was produced eight times on the New York stage. The *New York Herald Tribune* mentioned a 1932 "brief presentation by the Shakespeare Company." I have not been able to verify or get more information on this particular production. See "News of the Theater," February 22, 1947, 10A.

on Saturday, February 22 was the only one of the Wolfit productions that was completely sold out in advance.[6]

Donald Wolfit (1902–68) (Figure 14) was one of Britain's last actor-managers. He made his professional debut at York's Theatre Royal in 1920 and later honed his skills in productions at the Old Vic and Stratford-upon-Avon. In 1937 he formed his own Shakespearean company and concentrated on touring, visiting London only occasionally. During the Battle of Britain, he gained much approbation for staying in London, where he presented a series of lunchtime Shakespearean performances in defiance of the Blitz. He demonstrated his patriotism as well as his commitment to Shakespeare in 1944 when he took his troupe to army camps in France and Belgium. Wolfit, an actor known for his huge ego, was endowed with a solid physique, a booming voice, and a classic elocution. He was admired by some of his contemporaries as the greatest Lear of his generation while dismissed by others as a ham actor; his productions, wrote J.W. Lambert, one of his critics, lacked taste and a sense of style and their main purpose was to spotlight his own performance.[7]

Wolfit was associated with the histrionic star-centered acting school dating back to the late nineteenth century. A glimpse of his bravura style can be gleaned from a description of his "knife business" in the trial scene of *The Merchant of Venice*: "he sharpened his knife ... and then dropped it point downwards until it stood quivering stabbing the stage."[8] Actor John Gielgud, who disliked Wolfit, dismissed this showmanship as a "terribly vulgar effect."[9] Wolfit was rather impervious to the impact of contemporary events on theatrical interpretation. A 1938 review of his *Merchant of Venice*, presented in London's People's Palace, describes his Shylock as "the kind of Jew whose humiliation an Elizabethan audience would probably have reveled in, the very Jew the bare plot seems to require, one who, as he leaves the court, spits in the face of Antonio."[10] Several reviews of his near-yearly performance of Shylock in Manchester during the 1940s make it clear that the deteriorating situation of European Jewry and even the postwar news of the Holocaust did

[6] The production appealed to a "young crowd," presumably people who had never seen the play staged and included many of school-age youngsters at the matinee performance.

[7] J.W. Lambert, "Wolfit Offers Revival of 'Wandering Jew,'' *Christian Science Monitor*, May 2, 1953, 10.

[8] John Mortimer, *Where There's a Will* (London: Viking, 2005), 142.

[9] Ibid.

[10] *The Times*, October 4, 1938.

FIGURE 14 Donald Wolfit as Shylock. The photo is from Ronald Harwood's *Sir Donald Wolfit. His Life and Work in the Unfashionable Theatre* (London: Secker and Warburg Ltd, 1971).

not affect his portrayal of Shylock, whom he never sentimentalized or interpreted as a subject for pity.[11] His, wrote the *Manchester Guardian* in 1946, was "the Jew sinister rather than the Jew pathetic; he is best when he is most evil."[12] In 1950, when Wolfit performed the role in Dublin, the

[11] "Opera House: Mr. Wolfit's Shylock," *Manchester Guardian*, October 7, 1943, 3.
[12] "The Opera House," *Manchester Guardian*, November 28, 1946, 3.

Irish Times commented that his Shylock was of the sort presented with "complete racial and traditional integrity."[13]

Wolfit's indifference to Nazi genocide, even in the postwar period, needs to be understood within a British context. Unlike the situation in New York, *The Merchant of Venice* was one of the most popular Shakespearean plays on the London stage during the World War II period.[14] Zoltan Markus offers two explanations. One is a commonplace acceptance of anti-Jewish attitudes in Britain's culture of the time.[15] The other is the reluctance to infuse a Shakespearean play with topical relevance, an approach expressed by Harley Granville-Barker when he stated that Shylock "is no more a mere means to exemplifying the semitic problem than is Othello to the raising of the color question."[16] John O'Connor, however, argues against the suggestion that during the war years there may have been a desire "to keep Shakespeare free from the taint of politisation" keeping his texts "pure from temporal issue."[17] He offers as counterexample Laurence Olivier's 1944 film of *Henry V* which was institutionalized into the war effort and was prefaced with a dedication to "the commandoes and airborne forces."[18] He cites theater critic John Gross who in 1938 acknowledged that occasionally theater critics alluded to Jewish persecution when reviewing the play and contrasts it with the British theater's failure to follow suit. In fact, O'Connor makes the case that many of the major productions of the play from the mid-thirties to the late forties presented a repellent Shylock that was practically the reverse of Henry Irving's and Herbert Beerbohm Tree's philo-Semitic interpretations. Mark Dignam's 1935 production was deemed as "purged of its Irvingesque sentiment and Shakespearean humanity" and offered a Shylock as "a dirty, down-at-heel money lender in a bowler had several sizes too big for him ... never more than a grotesque little man in a

[13] "The Merchant of Venice," *Irish Times*, June 13, 1950, 5.

[14] See Zoltan Markus, "Der Merchant von Velence: *The Merchant of Venice* in London, Berlin, and Budapest During World War II," in *Shakespeare and European Politics*, eds. Dirk Delabastita, Jozef de Vos, and Paul Franssen (Cranbury, NJ: Associated University Presses, 2008), 144. Markus, basing himself on J.P. Wearing's *The London Stage, 1940–1949* (London: Scarecrow Press, 1991) notes 213 performances of Hamlet (6 productions), 170 performances of Midsummer Night's Dream (5 productions), and 131 performances of Merchant (7 productions).

[15] Markus, "Der Merchant von Velence."

[16] Quoted in ibid.

[17] John O'Connor, "Shylock in Performance" in *The Merchant of Venice: New Critical Essays*, eds. John W. Mahon and Ellen Maclead Mahon (London: Routledge, 2002), 398.

[18] Ibid.

temper."[19] Three years later John Gielgud's Shylock appeared as "remorseless, toothless – utterly revolting in the remnants of a ginger wig."[20] This heartless interpretation of Shylock as an unappetizing hooked-nosed vulture, writes O'Connor, would last until the new milestone created by Laurence Olivier in 1970.

V.C Janik, who noted the failure of the British theater to re-evaluate the traditional portrayal of Shylock in the wake of the Holocaust, writes that as late as 1953 Shylock was still portrayed as a conventional villain on the British stage. For example, a highly favorable review of the 1953 Old Vic production of *The Merchant* describes Paul Roger's portrayal: "there is a Shylock whose humanity the letter killeth, a fanatical fundamentalist of the lankest, most cringing, oleaginous, and generally poisonous variety ... There is no attempt (not even in the strings of rhetorical questions) to extort an ounce of pity from the audience."[21] A comparable lack of sensitivity was displayed by director David Lean's 1948 film *Oliver Twist*, in which Fagin had been made up to resemble a *Der Stürmer* caricature.[22] This obtuseness was also expressed in the mocking tone directed at Jews, including displaced persons located in Germany, who opposed the theatrical production of *The Merchant* immediately after the war, no less than in a critic's dismissal of Herman Sinsheimer's book *Shylock* (1947) as a publication that "belongs to the literature of the Jew and Weltpolitik rather than to literary or dramatic criticism."[23]

In New York Wolfit would encounter an entirely different sensibility. On February 15, 1947, the *New York Times* reported that Lee Shubert, who controlled the Century Theatre where the Wolfit Company was to perform, made a last-minute request that *The Merchant* be eliminated from the company's New York repertory because "it may prove offensive to Jews of this city."[24] The request was declined, but the news regarding American Jews opposing the production caused ire back home. The

[19] *The Times*, December 3, 1935.

[20] *Daily Express*, April 22, 1938.

[21] *Spectator*, January 6, 1953, 10.

[22] The screening of the film in Munich led to violent demonstrations by Holocaust survivors. In deference to the protests of major Jewish-American organizations the film was banned in the United States for three years and was released only in 1951 after significant cuts in the original were made. John O'Connor, "Shylock: A Performance History with Particular References to London and Stratford-upon-Avon" (PhD dissertation, University of Birmingham, 1999), 92. See also John O'Connor, *Shakespearean Afterlives: The Characters With Lives of Their Own* (Cambridge: Icon Books, 2003), 94–147.

[23] "Books of the Day: Shylock as Symbol," *Manchester Guardian*, June 17, 1947, 3.

[24] "Want Play Dropped," *New York Times*, February 15, 1947, 20.

Irish Times, erroneously reporting that the play was removed from the American stage, published a ferocious counter attack against "racial censorship" in which the Jews who were opposed to the play were compared to Hitler. It concluded with the mocking suggestion that the protesting Jews "may carry the resemblance to the persecutor of their race even further, and to burn in effigy a straw figure of the infamous, scurrilous, scandalous, dangerous, and Aryan William Shakespeare."[25]

The New York critics were not impressed by Wolfit, and most regarded him as a facile barn-stormer who played for surface effects, jumping from one big role to another. Even his Lear, with which he opened his tour, was panned as inferior to that of the home-grown John Barrymore. Reviews of Wolfit's Shylock ranged from civil to negative. Brooks Atkinson, drama critic of the *New York Times*, elegantly wrote off the production by commending Wolfit for servicing the "people who want to supplement their reading knowledge with an acted performance."[26] He criticized Wolfit's Shylock for lack of stature and for his grotesque make-up, and alluded to the recent past by noting that "In the twentieth century perhaps we know better than Shakespeare did how painful a tragedy it is." Louis Kronenberger, writing for the daily *PM*, blasted the production as hammy, accusing Wolfit of "playing Shylock for the groundlings, to get as much pure stage effect and surface sharpness out [of it] ... as he can" rather than probing its depth and significance.[27] He particularly faulted Wolfit for his mode of exiting the trial scene (and the play). Shylock's final lines, he wrote, present us with a man who "with the life crushed out of him must put up with one insult more, then crawl away." Wolfit, however, devised a highly theatrical exit: he spat at Antonio, then drew himself up "to enormous height" and strode out of the room "like some deposed monarch." This, maintained Kronenberger, was "road company theatrics with a vengeance." Kronenberger also contextualized the play in the social environment, noting that "this sort of a performance reminds us that so long as there is a Jewish problem, Shylock must be for many people not just a key figure in a play but a controversial subject in the theater." The bluntest dismissal came from Arthur Bronson of the trade journal *Variety*: "Wolfit would have been well-advised to have listened to the advance plea of the Shuberts and not staged the revival because the message of the play and the damning of the Jew run counter to all

[25] "Shylock Impunged," *Irish Times*, February 19, 1947, 5.

[26] Brooks Atkinson, "The Play," *New York Times*, February 24, 1947, 16.

[27] Louis Kronenberger, "Mr. Wolfit's Shylock Falls Extremely Short," *PM*, n.d. (probably February 24, 1947), 16.

present-day attempts of inter-denominational groups to better relations among races and groups. In a day that sees a rising tide of anti-Semitism everywhere – or before such impressionable audiences as last Saturday ... afternoon school-kids – it's best to let this play rest in spite of obvious dangers of censorship."[28]

Jewish Productions

The subsequent two Shylocks seen in New York in 1947 were presented by Jewish companies and must be considered as reflections of the post-Holocaust, shattered trust of modern European Jews in the superiority and ultimate moral beneficence of Western culture. The belief in the civilizing power of the arts and their innate power to improve humanity crumbled before the chilling reality of mass murderers who also shared a cultivated taste for classical music and poetry: men like Hans Frank, Nazi Governor General of occupied Poland and chief administrator of the "final Solution," who was an avid connoisseur of Bach and Mozart. As George Steiner noted, such barbarism came from the "European heartland" and its "political bestiality" adopted "certain of the conventions, idiom, and external values of high culture."[29] Bitter disappointment with Western culture and its promise of equality and integration into European society was particularly prevalent in the Yiddish-speaking world. In his study of survivors of the Holocaust in occupied Germany, Zeev W. Mankowitz explains that, as the Jews of Eastern Europe had been originally introduced to Western ideas through German mediation, and since Germany was considered the acme of European culture, its "descent into barbarity" stood for the collapse of Western civilization as a whole.[30] He quotes survivor Dr. Shmuel Gringauz, a German-educated attorney and political scientist, who wrote from his Landsberg displaced persons camp one year after liberation:

[28] Arthur Bronson, "Wolfit's Merchant Ill-Advised; British Troupe Opens in N.Y. Rep," *Variety*, February 26, 1947, 60. It would take another six years before another English-speaking Shylock would appear on the New York stage: Luther Adler, bona fide Jew and son of the late Jacob P. Adler, the most revered actor of the Yiddish stage. This 1953 production was panned by the critics.

[29] George Steiner, *In Bluebeard's Castle* (New Haven: Yale University Press, 1971), 63; Max Weinreich, *Hitler's Professors* (New York: YIVO, 1946; New Haven: Yale University Press, 1999).

[30] Zeev W. Mankowitz, *Life Between Memory and Hope* (Cambridge: Cambridge University press, 2002), 83.

> In the hearts of Jews this question will never cease to be asked – how was it possible? How was it possible after two thousand years of Occidental and Christian culture, after Michelangelo, and Leonardo da Vinci, after Molière and Victor Hugo, after William Shakespeare and Lord Byron, after Alexander von Humboldt and Immanuel Kant? How was it possible that professors and writers, priests and philosophers, artists and judges – how was it possible that almost the entire intellectual elite of Germany rapturously cheered on the blood-drunk murderers?[31]

The Merchant of Venice, more than any other work of literature, challenged post-Holocaust Jews to find a way to negotiate the horrendous consequences of anti-Semitism in Western culture, which many were not willing to abandon. The search for a solution to this dilemma was openly articulated in *Shylock '47*, the second Shylock of the year.

Shylock '47

In a complete departure from Wolfit's traditional if not out-dated approach, *Shylock '47* focused on self-interrogation and employed aesthetic reflexivity, its very title a proclamation of its contemporariness. It was presented by the Pargod Theatre, a small New York-based Hebrew-language company, debuting on May 27, 1947, at the Julliard School of Music, with subsequent performances at the Masters Institute Theatre.[32] *Shylock '47*, constructed as a play-within-a-play, used scenes culled from Simon Halkin's Hebrew translation of *The Merchant of Venice* – the same text used eleven years earlier in the Habima production of the play in Tel Aviv – together with transitional scenes, created mostly through improvisation and discussion.

The person who conceptualized and shaped *Shylock '47* was Peter Frye (1914–91), a promising young director born in Montreal to Yiddish-speaking, working-class, left-wing Jewish immigrant parents. In his late teens, Frye came to New York, where he immersed himself in the radical theater scene of the 1930s. (Figure 15) He participated in the Workers' Laboratory Theatre, apprenticed with the Group Theatre and took classes from Harold Clurman, Lee Strasberg, Morris Carnovsky, Elia Kazan, and Roman Bohnen. In 1936 Frye joined the Abraham Lincoln Brigade and fought in Spain for the Republican cause. He returned to

[31] Quoted in ibid., 178.

[32] Julliard was then located on 122nd Street and Broadway, near the Jewish Theological Seminary and Columbia University. The Masters Institute was located on 103 Street and Riverside Drive.

FIGURE 15 Director Peter Frye in his study.
Courtesy of the Israeli Center for the Documentation of the Performing Arts, Tel Aviv University.

New York in 1938 and, disillusioned, left the Communist Party in 1939 in response to the Hitler–Stalin pact. In 1941 Frye began to take classes with Michael Chekhov, and in 1945 he taught acting for the American Theatre Wing, a refresher program for demobilized actors. In 1946 he was appointed to the faculty of Erwin Piscator's Dramatic Workshop (1939–51) based at the New School for Social Research, a program whose students would become major actors in America's theater and film.

At the Workshop, Frye met a colleague named Reiken Ben-Ari, who had been one of the founding members of the Habima in Moscow and was now teaching the Stanislavsky system. Ben-Ari asked Frye to direct a group of actors who wanted to produce a play in Hebrew. The group, consisting of actors with various backgrounds and levels of professional experience, included several former Habima members and a few Holocaust survivors. When they met with Frye they informed him that they wanted to stage *The Merchant of Venice* in Hebrew, a language the prospective director did not know at the time. Frye was astounded by the proposal. "You're crazy!" he responded. "In 1947 you want to play

The Merchant of Venice in Hebrew? A play which is fundamentally anti-Semitic?"[33] Someone retorted, "It isn't anti-Semitic, it depends how you interpret it." After reconsidering, Frye agreed to work with the actors on the condition that they commit to a period of improvisation and discussion, an open-ended creative process more typical of an experimental workshop than a professional production. "We will reason out why we are doing these scenes from *The Merchant of Venice* today in New York in 1947," he declared. What eventually emerged was a script based on Shakespeare's text with added dramatized discussions about the play's meaning and relevance to Jews at that particular moment in history. The discussion sessions explored such issues as suitable performance style, Shakespeare's own attitude toward Jews, the symbolic nature of Shylock, anti-Semitism, the Holocaust, contemporary Jewish identity, and the complexity of self-definition. Frye's papers, located in the theater archive of Tel Aviv University, include a two-page typed transcription of one such session conducted at a cast meeting on Wednesday, February 26, 1947.[34] Many of the sentiments, comments, and recollections voiced by group members survive in the play-text Frye created.

In a draft for what seems like a press release, Frye mentioned in passing some indebtedness to Luigi Pirandello's *Six Characters in Search of an Author*, and to Maxwell Anderson's *Joan of Lorraine* (1946), both metatheatrical plays that focus on the rehearsal process and the formation of meaning rather than on the finished theatrical product. Similarly, *Shylock '47* conveys the offstage relationship between actors and director; the critical and aesthetic strategies they examine, discard, and select; their ongoing dialogue with the Shakespearean text as both actors and Jews; and their rebellion against the final words Shakespeare assigned to Shylock. The play-script, which was never published, consists of three acts. Each act includes scenes from Shakespeare's text and scenes representing actors in discussion. The first act takes place ten days before the opening, the second, two days later, and the third, on the night of the first performance. The Shakespearean text within each act is situated in a different locale and period: Act 1 takes place in sixteenth-century London,

[33] Thelma Ruby and Peter Frye, *Double or Nothing: Two Lives in the Theatre* (London: Janus Publishing Co. 2003 [1997]), 1. The Hebrew Version of the book, Telma U'Peter, *Khayim Ve'te'atron – Ha'masa Ha'kaful*, trans. Tali Nativ-Ironi (Tel Aviv: Zmora-Bitan, 1995), offer some informative tidbits that are not included in the book's English language version.

[34] Private archive, Israeli Center for the Documentation of the Performing Arts, Tel Aviv University, Israel.

Act 2 is situated in post-Reformation Germany, and Act 3, in a Cyprus internment camp for detained Jewish immigrants run by the British.

In the scenes added to the original Shakespeare text, *Shylock '47* tells the story of a group of Hebrew actors who are rehearsing for a production of *The Merchant of Venice*. Their director, Heinrich von Zwick, a Jewish refugee from Germany, presumably modeled after theater artists like Erwin Piscator and Max Reinhardt, has devised an interpretation of the play that aims to ridicule the notion that Shylock is a representative symbol of Jewish life. Von Zwick has moved the action from Venice to London in 1594, the time Shakespeare allegedly wrote the play, and argues that this shift will expose the play as a typical example of Anglo-Saxon prejudice against Jews. Act 1 consists mostly of intra-group disagreements and objections to the director's insistence on comedic acting. The actor playing Shylock vehemently opposes performing his character for comic effect as a "dirty little Jew. A Yiddishlick [sic] from vaudeville." Another cast member, the actor playing Bassanio, challenges the director with equal fury: "Replace me. Go to Yorkvill[e], I'm sure you'll find a Nazi there who'll be glad to learn Hebrew just to appear in this." "Your cartoon," he tells the director, "was printed many times in Julius Streicher's *Der Stürmer* ... What you are creating is the fascist conception of the Jew." The director responds: "No. It is the 'Christian' conception of the Jew. The Nazis printed the cartoon in their public newspapers, but the Christians print it secretly in the minds of their children." And when asked "So why help them? He responds, "To tear it out of people's minds. Anti-Semitism is a mental disease, so we treat it with the most modern, scientific method – what we are doing is a kind of shock-therapy. It's a technique of modern psychology used in the treatment of many neuroses. Well, Shylock is a Christian neurosis."

The actors demand a solemn and dignified Shylock, but the director argues that if Shylock is made human, the group will actually give a new life to a lie. He shares with them a tidbit of his personal history: "I sat in German theatres twenty years ago and I was ashamed to be a Jew. When Shylock cried Revenge! And sharpened his knife ... I was ashamed." One of the younger actors, Yehuda, is particularly forceful in his opposition. "When you ridicule Shylock, you don't demolish him, you don't destroy him – you disown him. You know why. You know why? Because you hate Shylock, because you yourself are an anti-semite ... Yes, there are many like him, Jewish anti-semites!" He concludes his oration with a powerful assertion of identification with Shylock: "We're Jewish Jews! And you can't destroy us. You will only destroy yourself." Finally, the director walks out on the production, leaving the group, at the end of Act 1, to find its own way of interpreting the play.

As Act 2 opens, the group has elected Yehuda, von Zwick's most vocal critic, to take over the direction of the play. He changes sets and costumes to reflect his vision, situating Shylock in an eighteenth-century German ghetto. This modification, he believes, will evoke parallels with the present and will explain the historical circumstances that created Shylock. In the meanwhile, Ruth, the actress playing Portia, has gone on her own to von Zwick to ask him to return. He does, and gradually re-establishes his directorial position without realizing that they need his professional expertise. Von Zwick acknowledges that he decided to rejoin the production for personal reasons, "to find out whether I can be a Jew." He confesses:

> Veintzweig ... the name is Veintzweig. I have spent my whole life running, running. I thought I was chasing them, to get into their world. Then I discovered that all this time they had been chasing me – to push me completely out of this world. Somewhere I have to stop. Can it be here?

As the rehearsal process resumes, we see Acts 2 and 3 of the original Shakespeare text, albeit with some lines deleted, against the background of early modern German nationalist violence and bigotry. At the end of the rehearsal, von Zwick is fully reinstated as the production's director though he admits he has not yet found the right way to present Shylock in 1947. He explains that when one tries to make Shylock sympathetic, "you try to defend him, to justify his demand for revenge." A humanist, he asks rhetorically: "Are we asking for the pound of flesh, the mythical pound of flesh?" "Yes," answers one of the actors, "the symbolic pound of flesh! They took six million lives – how many pounds of flesh is that?!" Von Zwick, who has reverted to his original name, Veintzweig, replies, voicing the views of Peter Frye:

> Don't say "they." I want the play to say "we." We, the people, Jew and Christian and Mohammedan, the sad people of the tragic world. All of us are caught in the nightmare of fear, the same trap of prejudice. Shall we ask for revenge? The Jew has never asked for revenge. Revenge is destruction and self-destruction. Death upon death. We need to free the world from death. We must offer life – that's what the theatre is for.

Act 3 consists of the enactment of Shakespeare's original trial scene, now located in a British military court in Cyprus presided over by the uniformed British camp commander, assisted by an advisor seated next to him and dressed in Arab garb. Shylock is a displaced person now interned by the British, and Portia enters as herself rather than in male disguise. When Tubal objects to her as a witness, the commander cites the privilege of "amicus curae" and allows her to give judgment as a "friend of the court." At the end of the proceedings, after Portia has found the second legal loophole that turns the tables on Shylock, she asks, "Art thou content, Jew? What dost thou say?" Shakespeare's Shylock's resigned reply is "I am content." At this point, Frye has von Zwick, the director, interrupt the Shakespeare text. He turns to the audience and declares, "We cannot accept this judgment, we must change the play." The actors devise a new ending, declaring "We will live as Jews. You cannot change us, you cannot destroy us. Let us be ourselves, that's all we ask – the rest we will do for ourselves. We will live."

Frye's destabilization of *The Merchant of Venice* was enhanced by radical casting decisions that attempted to demonstrate that there was no difference between the noble Antonio and the malicious Jew; they were, in fact, interchangeable. Two male actors played Shylock at different times. One played a "traditional" Shylock, a small, vicious man motivated by vengeance, eager to use the law to kill his enemy, while a second actor played Antonio as a heroic figure. But as the play progressed, the two actors switched roles: the original Shylock played Antonio as a conniving and mean-spirited merchant, while the original Antonio presented a tall, proud Shylock. In the trial scene, when Portia asked "Who is the merchant and who is the Jew?" both actors stood up, breaking the emotional moment with a theatrical gesture that blurred the Manichean division of victim and perpetrator and emphasized Frye's beliefs in the deep-seated camaraderie of humanity.

Despite its use of Hebrew, *Shylock '47*, attracted many spectators, including critics and theater artists. Frye claims to have received several offers to produce the play in Yiddish as well as in English, but hesitated, feeling that the script needed more work and was too much "of the moment." Frye continued to work on it in years to come but it was never produced again. In the final (undated) version, entitled *Shylock*, also located among his papers, the person who plays Shylock in the play, now situated as a university production of *The Merchant*, is a Jew who was hidden in a Catholic monastery during World War II and converted to Christianity, married a gentile wife and has gentile children. Upon learning that his parents perished in the Holocaust, he feels the need to reveal his Jewish identity and say *Kaddish*, the prayer for the dead, in their memory. He asks the actress playing Portia if she knows the prayer. She does, being an Israeli whose two children were killed in a terrorist attack on a school bus. They deliver the *Kaddish* together, marking the end of the play.

Frye's metatheatrical approach was essentially a modernistic Jewish meditation on the moral problems involved in producing *The Merchant* in shadow of the Holocaust. In contrast, Maurice Schwartz, actor and director, rewrote the play in a traditional realistic mode. His Shylock, the third one to be seen in New York in 1947, was presented at the Yiddish Art Theatre. Retitled *Shylock and His Daughter*, it was produced and directed by Schwartz, who also starred as Shylock. The production's target audience consisted primarily of first- and second-generation immigrants, a community with the deepest ties – personal, cultural, and linguistic – to the decimated Jews of Europe.

Shylock and His Daughter

The Yiddish theater, a key institution of the American-Jewish immigrant community, enjoyed a uniquely close bond with its audience and was known to refract the lives of its patrons and address their major concerns. Accordingly, in 1940, Maurice Schwartz (1888–1960) the most prominent figure of the interwar American Yiddish stage, founder, producer, artistic director, and leading actor of the world's premier Yiddish art theatre, advocated the notion of the artist's commitment to relevancy. Great theater and great artists, he wrote, "far from shunning life, both have drawn upon it and made themselves part of it."[35] Ibsen, Gorky, Chekhov, and Eugene O'Neill had helped, he said, "to launch the liberation of the enslaved and to inspire mankind to fight for a better, more attractive world." His company's repertory reflected this commitment. In December, 1943, he presented *The Family Carnovsky*, the first explicitly anti-Nazi play on the Yiddish stage, based on a novel by I.J Singer. The play ran for the entire season. In 1945–46, he produced, directed, and starred in a pro-Zionist play, *Doctor Herzl*, by H.R. Lenz and N. Giloff. In 1947, his *Shylock and His Daughter (Shylock un zein tochter)* (Figure 16) offered an implicit response to the Holocaust by retelling of the story of *The Merchant of Venice* from an entirely Jewish perspective.

Over the years, the most problematic aspect of the Shylock figure was his inhumane stipulation of Antonio's flesh as the collateral for the loan and his diabolical desire for revenge after his daughter's elopement. Even those sympathetic to Shylock's plight found it difficult to justify

[35] Maurice Schwartz, "Theatre in a Democracy," *New York Times*, December 1, 1940, X1.

FIGURE 16 *Shylock and His Daughter* (1947). Handbill.
Courtesy of the Museum of the City of New York. Gift of YIVO Institute for Jewish Research, X2012.7.426.

his unyielding insistence on his right to Antonio's pound of flesh and his wild insistence on revenge. However, after the Holocaust, in the face of the unprecedented amount of suffering and pain, it was understood by Jews and some gentiles that the desire for revenge must be acknowledged. In January, 1945, H. Leivick, a major dramatist and one of the giants of modern Yiddish literature, author of *The Miracle of the Warsaw Ghetto (Der nes fun geto*, 1944), a docudrama about the Warsaw ghetto uprising, published in an Israeli newspaper an essay entitled "The Jewish Blood Avenger."[36] He described an imaginary but very real visitor – the Jewish avenger – who comes to him at night to talk about his frustrations with those who sideline his demand for revenge. Soon, the visitor says, he'll be called a Shylock who claims his pound of flesh. Soon the world will pronounce "Shylock is back! Shylock is yet again demanding the pound of flesh ... What will you say about this Shylock – he actually wants Hitler's death! He wants the entire pound named Hitler! And the entire pound of Goring and of Goebbels!" The visitor continues: "I, Shylock ... I am standing near the open crematoria of Treblinka; near the killing cemeteries of millions; near the border of the murderer's land" and his demand, he says, is that the world should see that justice is done, that it avenge the Jew."

While most of the rhetoric about revenge was no more than fantasy, it is true that Palestinian Jews fighting alongside the British forces in the final stage of the war created NAKAM (vengeance), a group that took upon itself, when briefly stationed in Germany, the actual execution of Nazis hiding in plain sight. Some, like Abba Kovner, World War II partisan and noted Hebrew poet, made wild plans for poisoning German water supplies, a plan that was never carried out. Overall, the myths surrounding the avengers seem far greater than their actual deeds, which are not fully known to this day. This intense desire for revenge, however, was often undermined by a visceral reluctance to exact it even when given the opportunity. This paradox was fully conveyed in *Shylock and His Daughter*, when Shylock, in a radical departure from Shakespeare's play, is given permission by the Duke to cut off a pound of Antonio's flesh. In a state of near collapse, Shylock is unable to do the deed. He groans "To hell – I can't do it – I am a Jew –"

The Yiddish Art Theatre opened *Shylock and His Daughter* (Figure 17) on September 30, 1947 at the Public Theatre in lower Manhattan, with

[36] H. Leivick, "Goel Ha'dam Ha'yehudi," [The Jewish Blood Avenger] *Davar*, January 23, 1945, 2.

FIGURE 17 *Shylock and His Daughter* (1947) at the Yiddish Art Theatre. Courtesy of the Museum of the City of New York. Gift of Wolf (William) Mercur, 65.57.6.

Schwartz as dramatist, producer, director, and leading actor. In addition to Schwartz as Shylock, the large cast included such stars of the Yiddish stage as Charlotte Goldstein as Jessica, Muni Serebrov as Lorenzo, Dina Halpern as Portia, and Isidor Casher in the comic role of Launcelot, Shylock's servant. It was a sumptuous production, enriched by music by Joseph Rumshinsky, and sets by James E. Hotchkis. Hailed by critics and the public, it, played for the entire season, toured major American cities and remained in the company's repertory until 1950.

Schwartz's Yiddish-speaking Shylock was hardly a novelty on the Yiddish-language stage in America. Two of its major dramatic actors – Jacob P. Adler and Joseph Schildkraut – had drawn much praise for their interpretations of the part, and even Maurice Schwartz, though chiefly interested in modern drama, signed up in 1930 with Radio-Keith-Orpheum Circuit in the two-a-day houses to perform Shylock in English. But *Shylock and His Daughter* stands apart from Jewish pre-war productions of the play. It was not intended for Yiddish-speaking immigrants unfamiliar with the Shakespeare play nor was it a Jewish attempt to approve and authenticate the character for general audiences. It was a bold enterprise that unabashedly presented itself as a counter-text to *The Merchant of Venice*, situating its Jewish characters in a credible and historically specific Jewish milieu and interpreting their actions from an entirely Jewish perspective.

Artistic projects of this nature are today usually associated with postcolonial and feminist discourses, where oppositional texts serve to unveil and dismantle the basic assumptions of canonical works by preserving many of their familiar characters and storylines while altering their point of view and thus their structure of power relations. In the theater, this goal is often achieved by use of parody, subversive stage business and body language, metatheatrical devices such as plays within plays, significant deletions and repositioning of sections of the original text, and the addition of prequel- and sequel-like material and other framing techniques. Such devices would be practiced in later years, as the Holocaust became an important factor in the staging of *The Merchant*. However, in 1947, Schwartz's direct literary and embodied challenge to the canonical text was a historic first. His radical and total revision and Frye's workshop experiment pre-dated by nearly two decades the bold reworking of the play by theater path-breakers like Peter Zadek and George Tabori.

For a seasoned theater-artist like Maurice Schwartz, the role of Shylock, if not the problematic historical baggage of the entire play, offered a perfect vehicle for commemorating the recent past and exploring societal issues in which the community was invested, as well as addressing concerns of a more personal nature. In 1947, shortly before he opened the season with *Shylock and His Daughter*, Schwartz had toured the displaced persons camps in Europe and adopted two sibling child-survivors whom he and his wife would raise as their own children. Approaching the age of sixty, he had reached a point in his life where he was thinking of future and legacy in both artistic and personal terms, fully aware that inevitable historic and demographic changes were having a huge impact on the Yiddish theater that had been his life's work. Despite artistic renown and communal valorization, his Yiddish Art Theatre was struggling to survive as the number of Yiddish speakers were decreasing. He had already lamented over this problem two years earlier in the souvenir program of his *The Family Carnovsky*: "the masses have become linguistically assimilated … estranged from our Yiddish language, our literature, and our theatre." Undoubtedly, Schwartz knew that a Jewish take on *The Merchant of Venice* would appeal to these acculturated young Jews whose English-language education had inculcated them with Shakespeare-worship. The subject also attracted him because it would satisfy his love of big themes, emotional oratory, stage pathos, and spectacular costumes and sets. Primarily, though, with *Shylock and His Daughter*, as some newspapers noted, Schwartz was "a man on a mission" to clear the Jewish name and to transmit ethnic values to a new generation of American Jews. It was a project that he regarded as his most ambitious and daring to date.[37] The importance he attached to it was confirmed by his decision to publish the English translation of the play in book form and have it sold in the lobby of the theater. Although New York's Yiddish playbills had always supplied an English-language synopsis, no Yiddish theatrical troupe had ever published a full English translation. Schwartz's decision to do so attests to his realistic assessment of linguistic and cultural changes in the postwar era and of their effect on the future of Yiddish language and culture in America.

Shylock and his Daughter was a dramatization of a Hebrew novel by Ari Ibn-Zahav (1899–1971) entitled *Shylock, the Jew of Venice*, published in Tel Aviv in 1943, serialized in the Yiddish daily, *Morgn Zournal* in 1947, and translated into English in 1948 under the title *Jessica, My Daughter* by Julian Meltzer.[38] Born Leo Goldstein in Poland, the Zionist Ibn-Zahav immigrated to Palestine in 1922 after briefly studying in Germany, and became the first academic secretary of the newly established Hebrew University in Jerusalem, a position he held until 1946, when he arrived in New York to collaborate with Schwartz on the play's production. Ibn-Zahav was a devoted follower of Hebrew University professor Joseph Klausner, an intellectual luminary to whom he dedicated the Shylock novel, and like him was inclined to Revisionist Zionism. Ibn-Zahav's interest in *The Merchant of Venice* may have been piqued by the 1930 publication of Cecil Roth's *History of the Jews of Venice*, by the 1933 publication of the Hebrew translation of Ludwig Lewisohn's *The Last Days of Shylock*, and by the 1936 Habima production of the play. His interest in Italian-Jewish history may also be the result of his association with Hebrew University professor Umberto Cassuto (1883–1951), a native of Italy and a renowned Bible scholar who in his younger years had dedicated some scholarly attention to Italian-Jewish history. Ibn-Zahav had helped Cassuto immigrate to Palestine following the rise of fascism and he may have assisted him in his research at the Vatican library.[39]

[37] Sam Zolotow, "Two Plays Are Due to Arrive Tonight," *New York Times*, September 29, 1947, 16.

[38] Ari Ibn-Zahav, *Jessica My Daughter* (New York: Crown Publishers, 1948).

[39] In 1938, Cassuto moved from his native Italy to the Hebrew University of Jerusalem.

Ibn-Zahav himself attributed his interest in *The Merchant of Venice* to his anguish over the rise of European fascism. In a Hebrew essay entitled "Shylock of Honor, not Shame" written in New York in 1947, he described his state of mind at the time he wrote the *Shylock* novel:

> reports keep arriving from the ghettos and the death camps until your head goes whirling and you despise yourself for not sitting *shiva* day and night, for not tearing your flesh and clothes in mourning, and you wonder how is it that you have not gone mad and are not acting desperately as every bereaved animal would, and you keep mum out of a feeling of helplessness and disgust for anyone who was created in the image of God and sermonizes about freedom and democracy and justice and mercy.[40]

Ibn-Zahav began his Shylock project in 1942, with the publication of a quasi-academic essay in *Tarbitz*, an academic journal emanating from Hebrew University. He pointed at some internal discrepancies in the Shakespearean text and argued that the play as we know it was actually a composite of two previous plays written by different writers, thus suggesting the existence of the "good" authentic Shakespeare who was attuned to Shylock's victimhood and gave him the searing "Hath not a Jew" speech, and a second "bad" author who added the more problematic anti-Jewish material. The essay demonstrates Ibn-Zahav's familiarity with academic literature on *The Merchant of Venice* and his thorough knowledge of Jewish-Italian life and customs of the period. He found Shakespeare deficient in such knowledge and, in somewhat pedantic fashion, corrected Shakespeare's misrepresentations of the everyday life of Venetian Jews, often by the use of footnotes which the English translator wisely omitted. For Ibn-Zahav, the central conflict of the tale was Jessica's inner struggle between Jewish identity, represented by the depressingly prison-like ghetto, and the glamorous freedom offered by gentile Venice.

Ibn-Zahav set the action in Venice in the year 1559, and wove into the storyline such historical events as the auto-da-fé in Ancona, where twenty-five crypto-Jews were burned at the stake. He added historical figures such as Pope Paul IV (1476–1559), whose career as head of the Inquisition (beginning in 1542) and his four-year tenure as Pope (1555–59) were marked by extreme anti-Jewish measures that included the burning of the Talmud in 1553, the closing of synagogues, the segregation of Jews in mandatory ghettos, and the imposition of extreme economic sanctions. Ibn-Zahav worked into the plot such Jewish historical

[40] Ari Ibn-Zahav, "Shaylok shel kavod ve'lo shel kalon," *Hadoar* 37, 1947, p. 1136.

figures as Rabbi Benjamin Nehemiah Ben Elnathan, who, along with five other community members, was arrested in 1559 on the charge of being involved in the conversion of a Catholic priest. Other historical figures in the novel include the physician and scholar Kalonymus Ben Judah and Chief Rabbi Abraham Romano.

Ibn-Zahav eliminated some of Shakespeare's original *dramatis personae* and major "non-Jewish" elements of the plot, such as Portia's suitors, including Bassanio, and the business of the caskets. He transformed Portia and Antonio into a wealthy, religious couple, childless after sixteen years of marriage, who are fond of Jessica and eager for her to join the Church. Shylock was upgraded from usurer to the head of his own banking firm and was now an important community leader, committed to the rescue of Jews hounded or imprisoned by the Inquisition, and active in other welfare projects. Jessica became the Venetian-born daughter of an immigrant father, who, like other girls of her generation, was attracted by the non-Jewish culture of her native city. Ibn-Zahav endowed her with two symbolic suitors: Lorenzo, with whom she elopes in Shakespeare's play, is here an impoverished aristocrat who is the appointed Christian "supervisor" of Shylock's bank; and Samuel Morro, an invention of Ibn-Zahav's, a devout and scholarly young Iberian refugee from Ancona, who finds safety in Shylock's home. Jessica wrestles with the polarities the two young men represent: the elegant Lorenzo offers escape from the ghetto and assimilation into high society, while the quiet Moro offers oppressive ghetto life, sad stories of martyrdom, and devotion to Judaism and Hebrew learning.

The loan of 3,000 ducats comes into the story when Gratiano and Salanio, who guard the gates of the ghetto and who have facilitated Jessica's illicit nocturnal meetings with Lorenzo, become extortionists and threaten to end these escapades unless Lorenzo pays them a bribe of 3,000 ducats. Impoverished, Lorenzo requests help from Antonio, who is keen on seeing Jessica's soul "saved" but is out of cash and thus asks Shylock for a loan, concealing the fact that his money would enable Jessica to elope with Lorenzo and convert to Christianity. To show his disdain for Shylock, Antonio offers a pound of his own flesh as collateral. Meanwhile, Jessica falls ill during one of her romantic outings. When she recovers she feels the need to reaffirm her Jewish identity and so decides to go to Rome to save Rabbi Benjamin and his fellow Jewish prisoners held by the Inquisition. Ironically, she can only do so by using her connections in Christian Venice, obtaining letters of introduction from Antonio and Portia to open doors for her in Rome. In Rome she meets with the tortured Jewish prisoners who look like inmates of Nazi death camps, and helps them out. Yet once she has accomplished her dangerous mission on behalf of her people and returns to Venice, she succumbs to Lorenzo's seduction. Confused and dazed by Venetian opulence, she converts to Catholicism and marries Lorenzo. In the meantime, Antonio has lost his ships and is unable to repay his loan. Shylock, devastated by his daughter's desertion, sets out to avenge his own loss and what he sees as the humiliation of all Jews. He demands the pound of flesh specified as the collateral for the loan, as in Shakespeare's play. Portia's legalistic arguments, which are compelling in the original text, are refuted as childish quibbles by Samuel Moro, who is acting as Shylock's lawyer. The Duke decides the case in Shylock's favor, but the Jews of the ghetto, horrified and frightened by Shylock's mad insistence on collecting his pound of flesh and thereby murdering a Christian, excommunicate him. A few days later, when Shylock goes to collect the pound of flesh, he discovers that, as a Jew, he cannot bring himself to do it. Schwartz concluded the play with the news that Jessica, desperate to return to Judaism, has drowned herself in the canal that separated gentile Venice from the ghetto.[41]

Well-acquainted with his audience and its tastes, Schwartz reworked Ibn-Zahav's novel to conform to the traditional vivaciousness and vigor of the Yiddish stage, where tears and laughter were easily intermingled, where gender-bending roles were popular, and antiquarian accuracy was a low priority. Whereas Ibn-Zahav was in search of realism and veracity, Schwartz was looking for Jewish grandeur. For example, the novel describes Shylock as a practical and impatient father with no appreciation of the magnificent art that surrounds him; Schwartz transformed him into a dignified banker, a highly respected Jew, and a loving, doting father. He also modified details of local color to resonate with the experience of his audiences. For example, while Ibn-Zahav described authentic Jewish-Italian dishes, in one case supplying culinary information in a footnote, Schwartz switched all food allusions to such traditional East European dishes as *kugel* and *latkes*, staged religious rituals and prayers in an Eastern European rather than an Italian style, and added glancing references to current Jewish concerns. The most powerful allusion to the

[41] Ibn-Zahav published two editions of his novel. The first, published in 1947, has an open ending that does not spell out whether Shylock will kill Antonio. A second edition, published in 1969, adopted the ending quoted herein. This ending was authored by Maurice Schwartz for the stage production and was adopted by the novelist.

Holocaust occurs in Shylock's final speech, when he prepares to cut into Antonio's flesh:

For the martyrs put to death by Torquemada, for those buried alive in prison-graves, for those who died in the Inquisition flames, for all the innocent souls who have been tortured, strangled, drowned, slain by the sword, for the theft of our children's soul, for the honor of Israel trampled in the dust by viciousness. The honor of Israel trampled in the dust by viciousness and brutality, I raise my hand in vengeance.[42]

The Jewish audience recognized the reference to the *Yizkor* prayer for the dead that includes the following lines:

May the All-Merciful Father Who dwells in the supernal heights, in His profound compassion, remember with mercy the pious, the upright and the perfect ones, the holy communities who gave their lives for the sanctification of the Divine Name.

They were beloved and pleasant in their lives, and [even] in their death were not parted [from Him]; they were swifter than eagles, stronger than lions to carry out the will of their Maker and the desire of their Creator.

May our God remember them with favor together with the other righteous of the world, and avenge the spilled blood of His servants, as it is written in the Torah of Moses, the man of God: O nations, sing the praises of His people, for He will avenge the blood of His servants, bring retribution upon His foes, and placate His land – His people.

And by Your servants the Prophets it is written as follows: I will cleanse [the nations of their wrongdoings,] but for the [shedding of Jewish] blood I will not cleanse them; the Lord dwells in Zion.

And in the Holy Writings it is said: Why should the nations say, "Where is their God?" Let there be known among the nations, before our eyes, the retribution of the spilled blood of Your servants. And it is said: For the Avenger of bloodshed is mindful of them; He does not forget the cry of the downtrodden. Further it is said: He will render judgment upon the nations, and they will be filled with corpses; He will crush heads over a vast area. He will drink from the stream on the way; therefore [Israel] will hold its head high.

In the introduction to the play that appeared in the playbill, the Holocaust connection was highlighted even further: "All this occurred in Italy during the famed Renaissance period, when art and science prospered as much as in latterday Germany; although of course without the same German thoroughness and technique of the Twentieth Century." It went on to say: "Paul IV's period was a small-scale precursor of Hitler's time, and the Nuremberg laws were practically a copy of Paul's Roman edicts

[42] Maurice Schwartz, *Shylock and His Daughter*, trans. Abraham Regelson (New York: Yiddish Art Theatre, 1947), 144.

against the Jews. A description of the time is almost a replica of the anti-Jewish practices in our own day."[43]

Schwartz used the characters of Shylock and Jessica to address intergenerational tensions between immigrant parents and their American children yearning to move out of the ethnic ghetto and into American mainstream society. While Shylock, standing for the traditional immigrant parent, was largely exonerated, Jessica, the native Venetian, became the representative of the modern hyphenated Jew, in whom the binaries of ghetto and gentile society collided. By making the modern Jew female, Ibn-Zahav and Schwartz gendered the issue of assimilation. When Jessica is most Jewish and embarks on her dangerous mission of rescue, she behaves in a "manly" fashion, but when she succumbs to Lorenzo's seductiveness and to the blandishments of Venice, she falls into the trope of a weak, confused female. Ibn-Zahav and Schwartz overturn the anti-Semitic trope that cast the diaspora male Jew as effeminate, just as they invert the standard view of women as transmitters of Jewish religion and culture. In Schwartz's play, one of the characters comments that all young Venetian Jewesses are hankering for the thrills and worldly pleasures outside the ghetto, defining Jessica's engagement with the Christian world as both gendered and generational. In the playbill introduction Schwartz contemporizes Jessica in the same vein, explaining that she was "a daughter of the Ghetto, longing for the enchanted city of Venice, and capable of falling in love with Lorenzo, like any other Jewish girl of our times might."[44] In this way they accuse young American-Jewish women of cultural and religious disloyalty in yielding to romantic fantasies and material temptations. Shylock derives some comfort from believing that she drowned trying to swim back to the ghetto from Belmont, in a vain effort to return to her Jewish roots. Schwartz granted Shylock an additional measure of parental compensation: in losing a daughter he also gained a son and heir in the person of Samuel Moro, a devoted Jew who will continue his adoptive father's communal work and say *Kaddish* for him when he dies. Even within this Jewish critique of Shakespeare's *The Merchant of Venice*, the only Jewish female character is eliminated, leaving to men the difficult task of maintaining Jewish survival.

Shylock and His Daughter fails to establish a coherent position on the problem of Jewish assimilation in the United States. While Ibn-Zahav's Hebrew novel could posit a Zionist solution to assimilation, what

[43] Ari Ibn Zahav, "Shylock the Jew," in Schwartz, *Shylock and His Daughter*, n.p.

[44] *Shylock and His Daughter*, playbill, Yiddish Art Theatre, New York, 1947.

could Schwartz's play offer to a New York audience undergoing rapid Americanization? Schwartz could not suggest a return to the ghetto of the Lower East Side. All he could offer was a plea for ethnic pride and a call to the young to be tolerant and understanding of their parents even if they considered them vestiges of the Old World who were excessively sectarian and narrow minded. Ibn-Zahav's dream that the play would be produced in Hebrew on the Israeli stage was never realized and his literary oeuvre has been largely forgotten. The Yiddish Art Theatre, unable to sustain itself, disbanded in the early 1950s. In 1960, while working in Israel on a production of *Kiddush Hashem*, Maurice Schwartz died after suffering a massive heart attack.

Shylock after 1947

As for Shylock after 1947, he disappeared from the New York stage for six years. The engagement of Jewish actors and directors with *The Merchant of Venice* was revived in 1953 with Luther Adler, son of Jacob P. Adler, appearing as Shylock. It was the first domestic, New York English-language production of the play since the early 1930s. The reviews were poor and the production closed after sixteen performances. In 1961, an off-Broadway production staged at the Gate Theatre, which happened to be located on Second Avenue, the heartland of New York's Yiddish theater, was directed by and starred Boris Tumarin (1910–79), a Holocaust survivor born in Riga, Latvia.[45] Though reviews were favorable, the Jewish/Yiddish press was decidedly ill at ease with the presentation of yet another English-speaking Shylock on stage. Morris U. Schappes, editor of the left-wing periodical *Jewish Currents* noted that Tumarin "did what he could to make his Shylock 'sympathetic,' but ... no spectator would now go out and use the epithet 'Shylock' as a term of praise."[46] In 1962, Joseph Papp re-drew the map of the Jewish engagement with the play when he chose *The Merchant of Venice* and cast George C. Scott as Shylock in a special production marking the opening of the newly erected open air Delacorte Theater in New York's Central Park built for his Shakespeare Festival. The play's subsequent major revivals consisted of a 1973 production offered by the Repertory Theatre of Lincoln Center, directed by Ellis Rabb in modern dress with Sydney Walker as Shylock;

[45] The production played thiry-seven times. In 1977 Tumarin played the role of Abtalion da Modena, Shylock's tutor, in Arnold Wesker's *The Merchant*, an adaptation of *The Merchant of Venice*.

[46] Morris U. Schappes, "The Editorial Diary," *Jewish Currents* 16: 4 (April, 1962), 25.

a 1989–90 offering by the visiting Peter Hall Company, featuring Dustin Hoffman as Shylock; F. Murray Abraham starred as Shylock in a production for Theatre for a New Audience in 2007; and, most recently, a much hailed 2010 production directed by Daniel Sullivan with Al Pacino as Shylock. The latter, like its 1962 predecessor, was originally staged in Central Park and after enthusiastic reviews and box office success was moved to Broadway.

Looking back at the three New York Shylocks of 1947, one can see them as representatives of disparate ideological and aesthetic approaches to the classics in general and Shakespeare in particular. Wolfit's English-language production chose theatrical isolationism that disregarded its contemporaneous historical matrix by ignoring any possible connection between Shakespeare's play of 1596 and the horrors of the outside world. Peter Frye's modernist metatheatrical version rebutted the notion of the separation of art and life, sharing with its audience the personal and collective struggle involved in engaging with material that is problematic for artists and the community of which they are part. Schwartz, working within a more traditional theatrical framework that spoke to the hearts of his audience, offered a counter-text that presented a usable past in the hope of strengthening Jewish consciousness and providing an antidote to anti-Semitic slights. Whereas some more recent directors have set the play within Victorian England, fascist Italy, or German concentration camps, Schwartz followed Ibn-Zahav in using parallels with an earlier historical period, so that his version might stand alone, or rather stand beside Shakespeare's original version and present itself as a potent critique of its source. There may be other strategies to discover in exploring post-Holocaust productions of the play but these three seem to represent useful paradigms, which might be characterized, respectively, as denial, destabilization, and displacement.

8

The Merchant of Venice in Mandatory Palestine and the State of Israel

Shelly Zer-Zion

In the Zionist imaginary, Shakespeare's Jew has served as a figure who encapsulates what was seen as a dark Jewish diasporic past, representing not only the pre-modern Jewish occupation of moneylending but also the continuing isolation and persecution of the Jew by Christian host societies. Shylock thus embodied an aspect of the Jewish experience that had been rejected by most branches of Zionism, namely an urban capitalist who derived his livelihood from charging interest, a person cordoned off from the genuine productivity of physical labor and from the values of universal humanism. From the perspective of the modern Hebrew stage, both before and after the establishment of the state of Israel in 1948, the mounting of *The Merchant of Venice* exposed a deep cultural conflict: on the one hand Israeli theater artists claimed full rights of access to the western theatrical canon, while on the other hand they felt obliged to challenge its stockpile of anti-Semitic images.

Serious Hebrew engagement with the play began in 1929 when the full text of *The Merchant of Venice* was translated into Hebrew by American-educated poet Simon Halkin (1899–1987). Reflecting more contemporary linguistic norms, the play was retranslated in the early 1970s by Avraham Oz (b. 1944), a native Israeli Shakespeare scholar. A third translation, prepared for a revival of the play by the Habima Theatre in 2012, was produced by musician and professional drama translator, Dori Parnes (b. 1963). To date, the play has been produced in Hebrew six times on mainstream stages:[1]

[1] I refer only to the productions which were put on by Israeli theater troupes in Hebrew. Therefore I will not analyze the Hanan Snir production of *The Merchant of Venice*, which

(1) in 1936, by the Habima Theatre (which became Israel's national theater in 1958), directed by the German-Jewish director Leopold Jessner (Figures 18, 19);
(2) in 1959, by Habima, under the direction of Tyron Guthrie, who had previously directed the play in Stratford, Ontario (Figures 20, 21);
(3) in 1972, by the Cameri Theatre (now the Municipal Theater of the City of Tel Aviv), under the direction of Yossi Yizraeli, the first Israeli-born director to tackle the play (Figure 22);
(4) in 1980, again by Cameri, under the direction of British guest-director Barry Kyle;
(5) in 1994, once more by Cameri, directed by Omri Nitzan, its artistic director and a native Israeli (Figure 23);
(6) in 2012, by Habima, directed by Ilan Ronen, artistic director of the theater, performed first at the Globe in London and subsequently at Habima's theater in Tel Aviv (Figure 24).

The 1936 production, created during the rise of Nazism, was not only a historic first but also a seminal work insofar as it raised fundamental issues which would continue to burden future productions of the play on the Hebrew-language Israeli stage. Directed by Leopold Jessner (1878–1945), one of the premier theater directors in the Weimar Republic, it introduced the *Yishuv* (the Jewish community in Palestine) to the German-Jewish interpretative tradition of *The Merchant of Venice*, (see Chapter 11 in this volume). Jessner's artistic renown notwithstanding, local audiences and critics did not embrace the production or the tradition it represented due to the deep ambivalence felt in Zionist cultural circles towards the character of Shylock and the aspects of Jewish life it represented. While some called for the espousal of Shylock as a Jewish icon and the deliverance of the play from its anti-Semitic baggage, many wished to exclude this embarrassing character from the new Jewish culture which was being created in the land of Israel. This quandary regarding Shylock was expressed in 1957 by David Ben-Gurion, Israel's founding father and first prime minister. In a speech given at an international convention in Jerusalem, Ben-Gurion spoke of the "Shylock condition" in reference to Jewish life in *galut* (diaspora):

> I do not share in the glorification of the *galut* ... the *galut* in which the Jews lived and still live, is, in my eye, a miserable, poor, wretched, dubious experience that one should not take pride in ... I do not disdain Shylock for making a living from

was put on in German by the Weimar Nationaltheater in 1995. This production was a guest performance at the Israel festival in May, 1996. See Chapter 11.

FIGURE 18 Aharon Meskin as Shylock, *The Merchant of Venice*, Habima, 1936. Courtesy of the Habima Theatre and the Israeli Documentation Center for the Performing Arts (ICDPA).

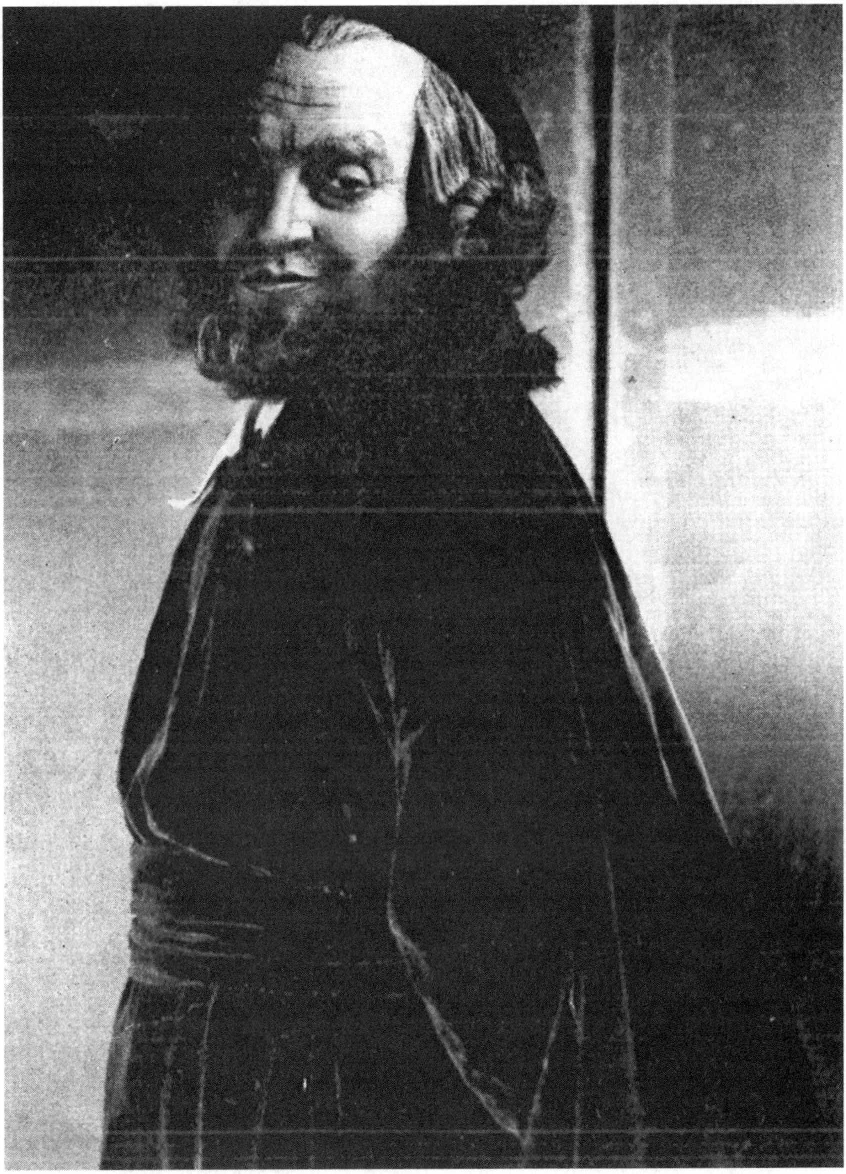

FIGURE 19 Shimon Finkel as Shylock, *The Merchant of Venice*, Habima, 1936. Courtesy of the Habima Theatre and the Israeli Documentation Center for the Performing Arts (ICDPA).

FIGURE 20 Aharon Meskin as Shylock, *The Merchant of Venice*, Habima Theatre, 1959.
Photography: Sam Frank. Courtesy of the Habima Theatre and the Israeli Documentation Center for the Performing Arts (ICDPA).

usury. He had no choice ... and morally speaking, he was better than the exalted nobles who humiliated him. But I will not turn Shylock into an ideal, an exemplary man whom we should strive to emulate.[2]

This ambivalence towards Shylock – grudging acceptance but refusal to idealize – was widely shared by the Jewish community of the *Yishuv* and later of the state of Israel. It helps explain the problematic responses to Jessner's 1936 production and to subsequent productions by the Habima

[2] David Ben-Gurion, "Teshuva la-mitvak'khim," *Hazut* 4 (1958), 167. Quoted in Mark A. Rader, *Nahuman Goldman: Statesman Without a State* (New York: SUNY Press, 2009), 85–86.

FIGURE 21 Shimon Finkel as Shylock, *The Merchant of Venice*, Habima Theatre, 1959.
Photography: Sam Frank. Courtesy of Habima Theatre and the Israeli Documentation Center for the Performing Arts (ICDPA).

and Cameri theaters. It may also explain why none of the play's productions proved particularly successful with local audiences.

Leopold Jessner and Habima

The Habima actors were first introduced to Jessner in 1926, when they were performing in Germany, and during the company's subsequent European tours conducted before 1931. At that time, Jessner was one of Germany's leading theater directors and had gained great prestige for his innovative directorial approach, which combined the wild expressionistic "Schrei" (scream) of the early twentieth century with the political *neue Sachlichkeit* (new objectivity) associated with the Weimar years. His most

FIGURE 22 Avner Hizkiyahu as Shylock, *The Merchant of Venice*, Cameri Theatre, 1972.
Photography: Israel Haramati. Courtesy of the Cameri Theatre and the Israeli Documentation Center for the Performing Arts (ICDPA).

FIGURE 23 Yossi Graber as Shylock, *The Merchant of Venice*, Cameri Theatre, 1994.
Photography: Lihi Lapid. Courtesy of the Cameri Theatre Archive.

FIGURE 24 Yaacov Cohen as Shylock, *The Merchant of Venice*, Habima, 2012. Photography: Gerard Alon. Courtesy of Habima Theatre and the Israeli Documentation Center for the Performing Arts (ICDPA).

notable productions were Schiller's *Wilhelm Tell* (1919), Shakespeare's *Richard III* (1920), and Frank Wedekind's *Marquis von Keith* (1920). Jessner developed a directorial concept which served as a key to the entire performance, and he did not hesitate to make radical textual changes in order to support his concepts. By avoiding naturalistic stage design in favor of abstract and expressionistic sets and by guiding his actors towards a highly stylized mode of acting, he often transformed performance into political statement.

He interpreted the classic repertoire as philosophical collisions of contradictory forces, free from historical specificity. His stage design was abstract, usually consisting of a bare stage with graduated levels and flights of steps that became widely known as *Jessnertreppen;* his *mise en scène* stressed an expressionistic anti-naturalistic manner of acting, especially for leading roles.

Jessner, who was a committed Jew, took great interest in Habima. He was an active and generous member of the Circle of Habima's Friends, and in October 1928 gave a salutary speech at a banquet in Berlin that celebrated the troupe's jubilee.[3] At the time he even stated a wish to stage

[3] "Habimah-Bankett," *Jüdische Rundschau*, October 16, 1928.

a heroic Jewish play at Habima.[4] This materialized in 1936, when the company invited him to direct *The Merchant of Venice*.

By the mid-1930s the fortunes of both the Habima and Jessner had changed greatly. Habima, founded in Moscow in 1917, had left Soviet Russia in 1926 and until 1931, when it settled permanently in Tel Aviv, existed as an international itinerant troupe, performing in European capitals and in the United States. Jessner, a Jew and a socialist, had to escape Nazi Germany in 1933. He had lost his position as the director of the Berlin State Theater, one of the leading theaters of the Weimar Republic, and become an uprooted exile who worked on a freelance basis with various European theater companies. He accepted Habima's invitation with enthusiasm.

Due to the rise of Nazism, a wave of Jewish immigration from Central Europe and Germany reached Palestine in the 1930s. According to estimates by the Jewish Agency, 68,798 German-speaking Jews came to Palestine between 1933 and 1939.[5] The Zionist leadership of the *Yishuv* watched the persecution of Jews by the Nazi regime with much concern, and wished to use the increasingly alarming political situation to encourage large scale immigration of Central-European Jews to Palestine. However, the leadership of the *Yishuv*, dominated by Jews from Eastern Europe, often received the new immigrants with a certain coldness, for while these newcomers were fully assimilated into German culture they were often unfamiliar with Judaism and Jewish tradition. Labeled as "non-Jewish Jews," this new group of immigrants was expected to develop a bona fide Jewish and Zionist consciousness so that they could become active members of the Zionist enterprise. A first step, difficult for many German-speaking immigrants, was to learn Hebrew, whose revival and active usage was a cornerstone of Zionist ideology. The cultural integration of these newcomers was easier in non-linguistic cultural fields such as architecture or the fine arts. However, acceptance was delayed in cultural areas that had already been dominated by the Eastern European Jewish elite, notably politics, Hebrew literature, and theater.[6]

[4] Margot Klausner, *Yoman Habima* (Tel Aviv: Mo'adim, 1971), 92–93.

[5] Yoav Gelber, *Moledet khadasha – aliyat yehudey merkaz eropa ve-klitatam* (Jerusalem: Yad Ben-Zvi and Leo Baeck, 1990), 61.

[6] Ibid., 4: 290–316. Tom Lewy, "Exilanten, Flüchtlinge, Migranten und Einwanderer: Jeckes in palästinischen Theater," in *Zweimal Heimat: Die Jeckes zwischen MitteleurFKlauopa und Nahost*, eds. Moshe Zimmerman and Yotam Hotam (Frankfurt am Main: Beerenverlag, 2005), 153–63. Norith Kenaan-Kedar, "Deutsche Einwanderer und die bildende Kunst in der israelischen Gesellschaft," in *Zweimal Heimat*, eds. Zimmerman and Hotam, 243–54.

Leopold Jessner pinned great expectations on his work with Habima, hoping that the world-renowned company, Jewish and Zionist in its outlook, would become his permanent artistic home. He was also convinced that Habima was the most fitting artistic venue to illuminate the tragedy of Shylock the Jew and to give voice to his own personal protest against the anti-Semitism of the age. However, despite Jessner's intentions, the 1936 production was to reveal an unanticipated conflict between the Habima and its guest director. Their diverging artistic heritages and visions bedeviled the production, as did the history of the play's diverse interpretative traditions.[7] This collision made it impossible to create a single cohesive interpretation; it also highlighted the internal paradox underlying the formation of a Zionist theater culture in Palestine.

Habima was founded in Moscow during the civil war period that immediately followed the Revolution. Previously, Moscow, like other imperial cities, was practically devoid of Jews, but after the Revolution Jews began to flock to the city, its Jewish population increasing rapidly from about 28,000 in 1920, to over 130,000 in 1926. For Jewish theater artists, Moscow, which in 1918 became the capital of the Russian Soviet Federative Socialist Republic (and of the Soviet Union less than five years later) offered previously barely imagined professional opportunities. Nahum Zemach (1887–1939), a native of Bialystock and the founder of Habima, then still a fledgling amateur group, persuaded Constantin Stanislavsky to accept Habima as an external studio that would study and work with personnel of the Moscow Art Theater. Consequently, the troupe attracted young Jewish men and women, mostly from the former Pale of Settlement, who were eager to participate in this new theatrical enterprise.[8]

Habima worked in collaboration with the Moscow Art Theatre from 1918 to 1926, when it left the Soviet Union. Despite the hostility of the Soviet authorities, especially the *Yevsektsia*, the Jewish section of the Soviet Communist Party, and the troupe's often tense relationship with Stanislavsky, those were formative years for the actors of Habima.[9] Especially significant was the troupe's collaboration with the director

[7] Marvin Carlson, *The Haunted Stage: The Theater as a Memory Machine* (Ann Arbor: Michigan University Press, 2001).

[8] Emanuel Levy, *The Habima, Israel's National Ttheater 1917–1977: A Study of Cultural Nationalism*, (New York: Columbia University Press, 1979), 3–45.

[9] Vladislav Ivanov, "Habima and the 'Biblical Theater,'" in *Chagall and the Artists of the Russian Jewish Theater*, ed. Susan Tumarkin Goodman (New Haven: Yale University Press, 2009), 27–48; Zvi Gitelman, "The Political Context of Jewish Theater and Culture in the Soviet Union," in *Chagall and the Artists*, ed. Goodman, 15–26.

Yevgeny Vakhtangov(1883–1922), who worked with them for two years on S. Ansky's play *The Dybbuk*, and in so doing was instrumental in molding the troupe's artistic language.[10]

During its touring period and upon its permanent settlement in Tel Aviv (1931) Habima had transformed from an esoteric avant-garde Russian-Jewish ensemble into a celebrated and exotic Zionist theater company, whose work gained international accolades. Moreover, during its five globe-trotting years, when it toured Europe and the United States, the troupe, which from its outset had been organized as a collective, developed into a small, highly consolidated group of peers who mythologized their working experience with Vakhtangov, canonized him as their only true artistic leader, their "rabbi," and were reluctant to adopt other artistic influences.[11] When the troupe settled in Palestine in 1931, it was celebrated by the literati of the *Yishuv* as the elite Zionist theater company, praised for being steeped in Russian artistic culture and shaped by world-renowned Russian theatrical training.[12]

Leopold Jessner came from a very different world. Raised in an assimilated German-Jewish family in Königsberg, he did not have the intensive Jewish background of most Habima players, or their immersion in the Yiddish-based culture of Eastern European Jewry. Jessner began his professional life as a touring actor in the German theater, but soon turned to directing, serving as director of the Thalia Theater in Hamburg from 1905 to 1915. He associated himself artistically with the German expressionist movement and politically with the socialist movement. When he was appointed in 1919 to the position of director of the Berlin State Theater, it was an unprecedented achievement for someone who was an experimental director, a Jew and a socialist, for during the Wilhelmine Era, this very theater, then called the Berlin Court Theater, had been a fortress of Prussian conservatism and a theatrical institution that was utterly off-limits for Jews. Jessner specialized in staging the classic repertoire, and established an expressonistic performance style which carried his strong imprint as a director. His 1919 production of Friedrich Schiller's

[10] Edna Nahshon, "Jewish, Russian, Hebrew: Habima's production of 'The Dybbuk,'" *Jews in Russia and Eastern Europe* 51:2 (2003), 56–68.

[11] Elena Tartakovsky, "'Habima' beyn studia ke-te'atron: be'ayat he-ader ha-manhigut ha-omanutit," *Mikan* 7 (2006), 29–49.

[12] A good example of that tendency can be seen in an article by Gershon Hanoch about the history of Habima. Hanoch glorified Habima's early days in Moscow. The article contains only two visual images: the pictures of Constantin Stanislavsky and Yevgeny Vakhtangov. Gershon Hanoch, "'Habima be'shnoteyha ha'rishonot," *Bamah*, May, 1933.

Wilhelm Tell set new standards for politically engaged performances during the Weimar years.[13]

Jessner regarded his Jewishness as a private affair and refrained from staging plays which dealt openly with Jewish themes. Although specializing in Shakespearean plays, he never staged *The Merchant of Venice* in Germany. Only in 1930, after quitting his position at the Berlin State Theater in the wake of anti-Semitic attacks, did he stage a "Jewish play" for the first time, Paul Kornfeld's *Jew Suss*.[14]

Privately, Jessner defined himself as a faithful Jew, with a deep religious sensibility, and admitted, for example, that he avoided smoking on the Shabbath.[15] He acknowledged strong sentiments toward the Jewish people, and indeed, he took a special interest in Eastern European Jewish theater artists who came to Berlin, and who seemed to him, as to Martin Buber and Franz Kafka, as the bearers of an "authentic" Jewish culture.[16] For example, in 1924, before he met Habima, he befriended a group of amateur Jewish actors from Palestine who had come to Berlin to study and assisted them in locating acting teachers and providing them with free tickets to his theater.[17] During the 1920s, he was on friendly terms with Shimon Finkel (1905–99), an acting student from Grodno (now in Belarus), who dreamt of becoming an actor on the German stage. Finkel, who would become one of Habima's greatest actors, recalled in his memoirs that it was Jessner who had encouraged him to abandon his German ambitions and join the Hebrew-language Habima.[18]

[13] David Kuhns, *German Expressionist Theater – The Actor and the Stage*. (Cambridge: Cambridge University Press, 1997), 173–217; Hans-Peter Bayerdörfer, "Schrittmacher der Moderne? – Der Beitrag des Judentums zum deutschen Teater zwischen 1848–1933," in *Duetsche Juden und die Moderne*, ed. Shulamit Volkov (Muenchen: Oldenburg, 1994), 39–56.

[14] Anat Feinberg, "The Unknown Leopold Jessner: German Theater and Jewish Identity," in *Jews and the Making of Modern German Theatre*, eds. Jeanette R. Malkin and Freddie Rokem (Iowa City: Iowa University Press, 2010), 232–60.

[15] In numerous publications Jessner defined himself as an Orthodox Jew. He had a strong religious sensibility, yet he did not belong to a specific Jewish congregation. Miriam Bernstein Cohen recalls that he confessed that as a director of the Berlin State Theater he was forced to work on Saturdays, yet he did not smoke on these holy days. He even asked her to read aloud to him from the Bible in Hebrew. According to his wish, he was buried in a Jewish Orthodox cemetery in Los Angeles. See Miriam Bernstein-Cohen, *Ke'tipa ba'yam* (Ramat Gan: Massada, 1971), 110–35; see also Feinberg, "The Unknown Leopold Jessner."

[16] Galili Shahar, *Theatrum judaicum: Denkspiele in deutsch-jüdischen Diskurs der Moderne* (Bielefeld: Aisthesis, 2007), 146–87, 252–93.

[17] Bernstein-Cohen, *Ke'tipa ba'yam*, 110–35.

[18] Shimon Finkel, *Bama u'kla'im* (Tel Aviv: Am Oved, 1968), 115–25.

After Jessner left Germany in 1933, Margot Klausner (1905–75), a German Jew who was Habima's administrative director, invited him to work with the troupe in Tel Aviv. Jessner's arrival in Palestine was heralded as an important intellectual event for Habima, whose respected theatrical journal *Bamah* often reported on his work and other activities.[19] For Jessner, his arrival in Palestine and his connection with Habima represented the apex of his identity as a Jew. He pronounced, "If there should ever be a Congress of Wandering Jews ... – I would credit myself with only two things: that I worked in an alien country as a Jew and in the spirit of Judaism, and that I succeeded in working with Habima."[20]

Jessner took interest in the theatrical culture of the *Yishuv*, especially such indigenous forms as the public pageantry held in Kibbutzim and the Tel Aviv Purim Parade (*Ad'lo'yada*).[21] He even lectured on the potential contribution of the theater to the building of national culture:

> Many immigrate to the land of their dreams: Russian Jews, Poles, Lithuanians, Romanians, Germans and so on. Mutual destiny brought them here, and now these people of many lands should merge into a single political unit. Religion unified these people in the Exile ... Here, in the land of Israel, religion, be it in its orthodox or in its modern form, is no longer the cement which glues them together ... Therefore, the theater should serve as the setting for this emerging unification ... Theater in the Hebrew spirit should participate in this blessed enterprise of nation-building.[22]

Despite his interest in an indigenous Hebrew-language theatrical culture, the two plays Jessner chose to stage at the Habima were completely in line with his previous artistic orientation: *Wilhelm Tell* by Friedrich Schiller, a play which Jessner had repeatedly staged throughout his career, and *The Merchant of Venice*, a play frequently produced on the German-language stage.

Competing Visions of Shylock

Shakespeare's works enjoyed exceptional prestige in German culture as early as the late eighteenth century, when the *Sturm und Drang* writers,

[19] See e.g. Eliezer Lubrani, "Leopold Jessner u'mif'alo ha'te'atroni be'germania," *Bamah*, February, 1936, 59–60; "Mi'sikhot 'khug ha'bima la'no'ar' – Profesor Jessner al khagey ha'ham be'eretz-israel," *Bamah*, May, 1936, 56–58.

[20] "Hatzagat ha'bekhora shel "ha'sokher mi'venetziya" be'habima," *Haaretz*, May 15, 1936.

[21] "Mi'sikhot 'khug ha'bima," 22.

[22] Leopold Jessner, "Al ha'te'atron ha'eretz Isra'eli ve'te'udato," *Bamah*, May 3, 1936, 3.

who regarded Shakespeare as a source of inspiration, introduced them to the German public.[23] After World War I, Shakespearean drama occupied a central place in the cultural struggle to establish an appropriate dramatic canon for German theaters in the new Weimar Republic. Progressive artists and intellectuals wished to reinterpret Shakespearean plays and include them in the body of avant-garde culture, whereas the conservative sectors wished to preserve Shakespeare's iconic status through traditional interpretation.[24] A deep interest in Shakespeare as a prominent, if adopted, contributor of plays to the German canon, also manifested itself in German-Jewish culture, so that his works, alongside those of German classic writers, entered the cultural corpus of German-Jewish culture, known as *Bildung*.[25]

The Merchant of Venice posed a special challenge for German-speaking Jews. Despite the play's popularity with readers and audiences in Germany and Austria,[26] and unlike other plays within the framework of *Bildung*, it served, according to Dietrich Schwanitz, as one of the archetypes that constituted the image of Jews in modern anti-Semitism. Shylock was often understood as a traditional, miserly moneylender, a satanic Jew, who wished to destroy the wholesome body of Christianity.[27]

Towards the end of the 1920s, when Jessner was establishing himself as an important director in the German theater, anti-Semitism was on the rise in the German-speaking world. Shylock served as a key figure in anti-Semitic discourse, and as a lens through which to view the role of Jews in society.[28] On the other hand, the desire to redeem Shylock from his detestable fate, to shed a new and more favorable light on this character, became an obsession within German-Jewish culture, as Chapter 3 and Chapter 11 amply demonstrate. A few examples stand out:

[23] Simon Williams, *Shakespeare on the German Stage 1586–1914*. (Cambridge: Cambridge University Press, 1990), 1–26.

[24] Wilhelm Hortman, *Shakespeare on the German Stage: The Twentieth Century* (Cambridge: Cambridge University Press, 1998), 44–111.

[25] Paul Mendes Flohr, *German Jews: A Dual Identity* (New Haven: Yale University Press, 1999).

[26] Andrew G. Bonnell, *Shylock on Germany: Antisemitism and the German Theater from the Enlightenment to the Nazis* (London: Tauris, 2008), 5–118.

[27] Dietrich Schwanitz, *Das Shylock Syndrom oder die Dramaturdie der Barbarei* (Frankfurt am Main: Eichborn, 1997), 3–45.

[28] Hans-Peter Bayerdörfer, "Shylock in Berlin – Walter Mehring und das Judenportraet im Zeitstueck der Weimarer Republik," *Conditio Judaice* 3 (1993), ed. Hans Otto Horch, 307–23.

(1) Karl Emil Franzos's novel, *Der Pojaz* (The Jester, 1893) tells the story of Sender, a Jew living in a Galician *shtetl*, who dreams of becoming an actor so he can redeem Shylock from being misunderstood.[29]
(2) As if in imitation of Franzos's fictional character, the Galician-born German-Jewish actor, Alexander Granach (1893–1945), confessed that after reading the novel, he was driven by the desire to play Shylock on stage.[30]
(3) Max Reinhardt (1873–1943), the Jewish director and manager of the Deutsches Theater in Berlin, repeatedly staged *The Merchant of Venice*. Theater scholar Erika Fischer-Lichte interprets these multiple stagings as a constant work in progress. While casting different actors of different ethnicities and artistic profiles in the role of Shylock, Reinhardt constantly explored the interrelationship of the Jew and his urban surrounding.[31]

For Jessner, choosing to produce *The Merchant of Venice* meant following the German-Jewish tradition of appropriating anti-Semitic images but trying to cleanse them. Moreover, doing so in Tel Aviv was a way of taking a stand against the international increase of anti-Semitic discourse.[32]

However, his understanding of *The Merchant of Venice* differed from that of the Eastern European Habima actors and their intellectual circle, whose exposure to Shakespeare was mostly based on Yiddish or Hebrew translations derived from authoritative German or Russian translations.[33] While Yiddish productions and adaptations of *The Merchant of Venice* appeared on the Yiddish stage, the play was practically shelved by the post-revolutionary Soviet theater due to its anti-Semitic heritage.[34] Its impact on Jews who had come of age in Russia's post-revolutionary days was marginal. Though there was no scarcity of major Russian writers known for anti-Semitic sentiments, none had produced a literary character that came close to Shylock in terms of importance and canonicity.

Still, *The Merchant of Venice* was high on Habima's list of plays to be used as vehicles for achieving the company's primary goals – to perform

[29] Karl Emil Franzos, *Der Pojaz* (Koenigstein: Athenaeum, 1979 [1905]).
[30] Alexander Granach, *Da geht ein Mensch* (Munich: Piper, 1999), 412–39.
[31] Erika Fischer-Lichte, "Theatre as Festive Play: Max Reinhardt's Productions of *The Merchant of Venice*," in *Jews and the Making of Modern German Theatre*, 219–31.
[32] Jessner, 25: 7.
[33] Joel Berkowitz, *Shakespeare on the American Yiddish Stage* (Iowa City: Iowa University Press, 2002), 1–30.
[34] Ibid., 172–205

classic plays to express inner Jewish experience.[35] The first encounter of Habima with the play apparently took place in its earliest days in Moscow, when Stanislavsky wished to produce it with Habima actors playing the Jews and Russian studio actors playing the Venetians. The project never came to fruition. When Habima actor Moshe Halevi, who was cast as Shylock, asked Stanislavsky for his interpretation of the play, he was told that the actors on both sides needed to persuade him which group was worthier. Eventually, Stanislavsky's posture of neutrality led to intense competition between the two groups, which nearly ended in violence, as Halevi attested:[36]

> sometimes I even had the feeling that in no time the Gentiles were going to conduct a pogrom against us within the "Habima" house itself! It seemed that the exercises exceeded mere "acting" and both groups seemed to be clamoring for blood. Hence, it was necessary to abandon this interesting experiment by this great director.[37]

Halevi's narrative demonstrates the problem *The Merchant of Venice* posed for Eastern European Jews, whose experience had been rife with anti-Jewish discrimination and persecutions. Zionist groups like Habima accepted anti-Semitism as a fact of life and wished to solve the problem by immigration to Palestine and by the establishment of a separate national Jewish entity. In such a context Shylock's claim for justice seemed naïve and irrelevant indeed.

It is interesting to note that the only Shakespearean play produced by Habima prior to *The Merchant of Venice* was *Twelfth Night* (1930), directed by Michael Chekhov, a former member of the Moscow Art Theater. Habima hoped this project, created in Berlin, would notarize its status as a European theatrical company that is capable of performing a classical comedy, regardless of the Jewish identity of its actors. Chekhov, who had his doubts whether the members of this company would be able to portray Shakespeare's Italian Renaissance characters, eventually applauded their success:

> From the first rehearsal on, they worked on "lightness." A part of each working day was dedicated to special exercises. With fanatic enthusiasm and great energy, the Habima people searched for "lightness." And they found it![38]

[35] Freddie Rokem, "From Marginality to Centrality: Jew and Non-Jew in the Hebrew Inter-War Theater (1917–1939)," in *Theatralia Judaice: Emanzipation und Antisemitismus als Momente der Theatergeschichte von der Lessing-Zeit bis zur Shoa*, ed. Hans-Peter Bayerdörfer (Munich: Max Niemeyer, 1992), 264–80.

[36] Moshe Halevi, *Darki aley bimot* (Tel Aviv: Masada, 1955), 70–75.

[37] Ibid., 74.

[38] Michail A. Čechov, *Leben und Begegnungen: Autobiographische Schriften*, trans. Thomas Kleinbub (Stuttgart: Urachhaus, 1992), 286–87.

Perhaps one aspect of "lightness" meant that the actors were able to shed their Jewish body language and, as skilled performers, assumed the "universal" white body of the Renaissance subject, one that is key to classic European culture. Things would prove considerably more complex when they had to tackle *The Merchant of Venice* with its inescapable Jewish content.

Jessner's *The Merchant of Venice*

When Jessner started working with Habima on *The Merchant of Venice* (Figure 25), he saw the interpretative key to the play as the tension between Shylock and the Christian world:

> it was necessary to expose the disgrace of that society, a society of drunkards, borrowers who did not repay, layabouts, boot-lickers to their wealthy friend Antonio. From now on, Shylock vis a vis that society does not appear in terms of his individual fate, but as one of a People that has been oppressed for thousands of years, as an avenger and as a fighter against his abusers, against his torturers![39]

From the start, Jessner intended to undermine the anti-Semitic images imposed on Shylock and to show him in a sympathetic light. To this end, he wanted to sharpen the conflict between Shylock and the radiant Christian worlds of Venice and Belmont. He wanted to paint Venetian society in negative colors, to illuminate its lack of morality and, in this way, to justify Shylock's desire for revenge. Jessner envisaged *The Merchant of Venice* as a remote legend and placed it in an enchanted Renaissance past. The sophisticated, gracious Renaissance atmosphere established on stage was disrupted only by Shylock, a character steeped in tragedy.[40]

The tension between Venetian grace and Jewish tragedy appeared on many levels. In the music written for the production, Italianate harmony was juxtaposed with Jewish cacophony, as the composer, Karl Rathaus (1895–1954) explained:

> In accordance with the wishes of Prof. Jessner, I opened the first scene with a tenor singing in the Italian style … I imagined that the song would be heard as the curtain was raised and that it would sound very "tenorish", very Italian; while the refrain – sung by a choir – gradually turned into that savage "hep-hep" that Prof. Jessner envisaged.[41]

39 Jessner, 25: 6.

40 The description of the dramaturgical adaptation of the play appears in "Ha-mishpat ha-sifruti al Shylock," *Bamah* 4, October, 1936, 23–41.

41 Karl Rathaus, "Al ha-musika le-Shylock," *Bamah* 3, May, 1936, 17.

FIGURE 25 *The Merchant of Venice* at the Habima Theatre, 1936. The trial scene. Photography: Zura Studio. Courtesy of Habima and the Israeli Center for the Documentation of the Performing Arts (ICDPA).

The sound of "hep-hep" that disrupts the pleasant Italianate music evoked the history of Jewish persecution in Germany, and specifically alluded to the "hep-hep" riots of 1819, which were the central trauma of German Jewry's collective memory until the rise of Hitlerism.[42]

The same duality was expressed visually by the designer, Moshe Mokady (1902–75), who created a stage set inspired by the harmonious proportions of Renaissance architecture. A photograph of the set in the trial scene reveals a staircase that enabled a hierarchical representation of the characters in the play. Around the staircase, graceful arcs suggest both a comfortable, somewhat oriental atmosphere and warm Italian architecture. The costumes too reinforced this contrast between Christians and Jews: the Venetians wore bright colors, while Shylock was dressed in a kaftan, or traditional black Jewish robe of Eastern Europe.[43]

[42] Shulamit Volkov, *Germans, Jews and Antisemites: Trials in Emancipation* (Cambridge: Cambridge University Press, 2006), 13–32.

[43] The analysis of the stage design and costumes is based on the photographs from the performance: William Shakespeare, *Ha-sokher mi-venetzia*, directed by Leopold Jessner, Habima, Tel Aviv, May 14, 1936, file no. 221827, Israeli Center for the Documentation of the Performing Arts.

Yet Jessner refused to reduce Shylock to a mere victim. Such a reading, he argued, would be inappropriate for the proud environment of the future Jewish homeland.

> although he (Shylock) falls, defeated by the libelous machinations of his rivals and indeed ends tragically, he ends not as sufferer, but as *tragic hero*.[44]

The interpretation of Shylock as a tragic hero was underscored by Jessner's assigning the role of the Jew to Aharon Meskin (1898–1974) (Figure 18) and Shimon Finkel (1905–99) (Figure 19), who shared the role in rotation. Although each of them shaped the character according to his personality and physical presence, with both actors Shylock emerged as a fighter who demands the revenge that is his due. Both Finkel and Meskin were veteran Habima actors whose public personae were not associated with the Jewish *shtetl*. Meskin, who was a robust tall man with a deep bass voice, had been a soldier in the Red Army prior to joining Habima, and was regarded as the company's "gentile." His prominence was established in 1925 when he played the title role in H. Leivick's *The Golem*, a role that emphasized the actor's physical strength and simple, earthy presence.[45] Indeed, in the eyes of theater critic Yesha'ayahu Klinov, Meskin had created a Shylock of heroic proportions.[46] Shimon Finkel, who had joined the Habima in Berlin, explained his Shylock in similar terms:

> In this play, I tried to highlight a specific character trait of a man who was obsessed with one thing: avenging his insult and the insult to his People.[47]

Unconcerned with Shylock's individuality, Finkel wished to recreate a familiar archetypal figure. He had, in the past, portrayed a series of German-Jewish protagonists who claimed equal rights, avenged insults, yet were eventually deceived by the false promise of emancipation. This was not the first time he had played a noble but failed avenger. Among such roles were the title characters in the dramatizations of Leon Feuchtwanger's novel *Jew Süss* (1933), and Friedrich Wolf's *Professor Mannheim* (1934). Finkel's Shylock bore a resemblance to the other portraits in this gallery. It was a tragic figure of the Jew who dared to stand up for his rights.

[44] Jessner. 25: 6. Emphasized in the original.

[45] Shimon Finkel. *Aharon Meskin ve-agadat ha-golem: perakim le-zikhro* (Tel Aviv: Akad, 1980), 5–27.

[46] Yesha'ayahu Kalinov, "Hasokher mi-venetzia be-habima," *Haaretz*, May 22, 1936.

[47] Shimon Finkel, *Be-mevokh tafkiday: khavayot mi-sadnat ha-bama* (Tel Aviv: Tarbut ve-khinukh, 1971), 33.

Shylock's chief adversary was Portia, who, as the mistress of Belmont, represented a contrast with the corrupt world of Venice. Unlike Venice, Jessner's Belmont was portrayed as a pastoral world which celebrated such pre-capitalist values as compassion, grace, and love.[48] It is Portia who, as the embodiment of Belmont, eventually imposes Belmont's values on Venice when she saves Antonio in the courtroom. Since Habima's entire ensemble was Jewish, the sort of ethnic dichotomy which had often been created in Germany by means of casting a Jewish actor in the role of Shylock against an otherwise gentile Portia was not an option in Tel Aviv. Rather, Portia was played by Hanna Rovina, the leading lady of the theater. In her 1920s roles, especially as Leah in An-sky's *The Dybbuk*, the mother of the baby Messiah in David Pinski's *The Eternal Jew*, and the young Messiah in H. Leivick's *The Golem*, Rovina had established herself as the icon of Zionism and of the Hebrew cultural renaissance.[49] Her public persona evolved further in the mid-1930s, as she became a local celebrity and the object of erotic fantasy, notably when her love affair with the much younger, handsome, and controversial poet Alexander Penn gained publicity.[50] Nonetheless, this "Zionist" Portia, who endowed Belmont, and eventually Venice, with grace and sensual beauty, was also able to represent Shylock's implacable antagonist. Writer Ya'akov Fichman explained:

> Who is the one whose hand burdened Shylock the most? It is the worthiest of his enemies ... Portia (Rovina) ... It is not comfortable for a Jewish actress to shed grace on a world where everything that is to its advantage is to our disadvantage, and her ability to overcome this must undoubtedly be seen as an artistic triumph for Habima. When we see Rovina standing as Doctor of Law, rejoicing on stage over her judicial interventions, each of which strikes a deathblow to miserable Shylock, we sense a supreme dedication to the role.[51]

According to Fichman's observation, Rovina's success as Portia made her a tragic heroine on the metatheatrical level. She, the Jewish actress par excellence, had sacrificed her Jewish self in order to be loyal to the universal, humanistic values to which, as a creative actress, she subscribed. In her performance as Portia, Belmont became a site of emancipation

[48] Terry Eagleton, *William Shakespeare* (Oxford: Basil Blackwell, 1986), 35–63.Jonathan Hall, *Anxious Pleasures: Shakespearean Comedy and the Nation-State* (Madison: Fairleigh Dickinson University Press and Associated University Press, 1995), 53–71.

[49] Carmit Gai, *Ha-malka nas'a va-otobus: Rovina ve-Habima* (Tel Aviv: Am Oved, 1995), 201–14.

[50] Ibid., 166–200.

[51] Yaacov Fichman, "Al ha-te'atron ha-klasi," *Bamah* 4, October, 1936: 3–14, 10.

from Jewishness, an exotic locale associated with eroticism, Renaissance beauty, and universal creativity, a site devoid of Jewish physical presence and blithely unconcerned with Jewish historical fate.

Responses to Jessner's *Merchant*

Theater critics and intellectuals debated whether Habima's *The Merchant of Venice* was a useful or even welcome contribution to the project of building a national Hebrew theater.[52] Habima and its supporters encouraged the controversy, wishing to promote interest in the production which was failing to garner an enthusiastic public response. The youth section of the theater organized a mock trial of Shylock and the Habima production, a popular format in the *Yishuv* period for the discussion of controversial cultural issues. Habima's house organ, *Bamah*, provided the main platform for the controversy and published the proceedings of the trial as well as a series of articles on both the trial and the production.[53]

The "trial" was conducted before a general audience in Tel Aviv at the Ohel-Shem Hall on June 23, 1936.[54] Yehoshu'a Klinov, who served as the prosecutor, accused the following three defendants of complicity in the production of the play: William Shakespeare, for creating an anti-Semitic character; Habima, for choosing to perform a play which was irrelevant to the emerging Zionist life in Palestine; and Leopold Jessner, for staging an incomplete interpretation of Shylock.

The discussion about the play and its relevance to the development of national theater culture focused on two arguments. Those who defended the production argued that it was a complex literary work of "universal" value, and hence was worthy to be performed in the *Yishuv*. Those who opposed the play attacked it for its anti-Semitic nature.[55] The poet Alexander Penn seized the opportunity to deliver a fierce ideological

[52] Lea Goldberg, "Hasokher mi-venetzia be-Habima," *Davar*, May 15, 1936. Kalinov, "Hasokher mi-venetzia be-habima," 50.

[53] "Ha-mishpat ha-sifruti al Shylock," *Davar*, May 15, 1936, 44.

[54] The participants in the trial: Judge Zidkiyau Harkavi presided and the jury consisted of writers and cultural activists – Dr. Haim Harari, Ya'akov Zandberg, Shaul Tchernikovsky, and Fischel Lakhover; Asher Barash and Yaacov Fichman were members of the Presidium. Yeshayahu Kalinov served as prosecutor and Dov-Ber Malkin was attorney for the defense. Simon Halkin, the play's translator, served as expert witness. Writers Avraham Kariv and Alexander Penn were witnesses for the prosecution and the witness for the defense was attorney Dr. Eliyahu Epstein-Halevy.

[55] For a detailed analysis of the literary trial of Shylock see Shelly Zer-Zion, "Shylock ole le-eretz israel: hasokher mi-venetzia le-Shakespeare be-bumuyo shel Leopold Jessner bi-shenat 1936," *Kathedra* 110 (December, 2003), 73–100.

attack on those who were enriching themselves during this period of massive immigration:

> If outwardly, for the world, *The Merchant of Venice* should be an accusation – for us, who have come here to improve our lives spiritually and economically, it should be an urgent warning, a defense against those little Shylocks, the speculators and profiteers who are invading the country.[56]

Penn, a devout Marxist, regarded Shylock a emblematic of the corrupted soul of Jews in the diaspora, where a long history of oppression turned them into vicious unproductive moneylenders. Such corrupt Jews, such Shylocks, he insinuated, immigrated to Palestine out of necessity, but were not committed to the inner spiritual transformation celebrated by Zionist ideology. Thus, he argued, their presence in the *Yishuv* threatened to contaminate the Zionist enterprise.

He explained that Rovina as Portia supported the right of Jews to exist as universal artists and as enlightened Renaissance subjects.[57] The corrupt Shylock, on the other hand, could not make such claim for the existence of Jews in the diaspora had corrupted them to the core. Jews could claim to be included as legitimate members of humanity, he said, only if they cut themselves off from the diaspora and created a new, Zionist identity in Palestine. He argued that there was no reason to perform *The Merchant of Venice* in Palestine, because it relocated and legitimized the Jew's diasporic existence and stood in the way of spiritual transformation.

Eventually, the judge and jury acquitted the three accused – Shakespeare, Habima, and Jessner, and accepted the claim of the defense attorney, theater critic Dov-Ber Malkin, who argued that *The Merchant of Venice* was a complex play and a part of the universal canon of dramatic literature, and as such it deserved to perform in Palestine. Even if the character of Shylock or the interpretation of the play deviated from the Zionist ideology, he argued, the Jewish community in Palestine should be exposed to and take part in the cultural debate regarding the character of Shylock, as well as the intentions of his literary and theatrical creators.

Because of its own intrinsic qualities as well as its reception, Jessner's 1936 production of *The Merchant* became the interpretative framework

[56] "Ha-mishpat ha-sifruti al Shylock," 28.

[57] Rovina was pictured in Penn's critique as the object of desire. It is likely to assume that his involvement with the play was not solely artistic. Penn had an affair with Rovina and he was the father of her daughter, who was born in 1934, two years prior to this production. The relationship between the two was highly intense. See Gai, *Ha-malka nas'a va-otobus*, 166–200.

for subsequent productions and for the reception of Shylock in Hebrew culture as an icon of collective memory, one that encapsulated and condemned Jewish exilic experience.

Israeli (Post-1948) Productions of *The Merchant of Venice*

In 1959 director Tyron Guthrie (1900–71) was invited to stage the play for Habima following the successful *Oedipus Rex* he had directed for the company in 1947. Although Jewish history had been greatly altered since Jessner's production, Guthrie's understanding of Shylock was similar to Jessner's. He was interested in condemning the anti-Semitic images embodied in the play and in presenting the tragedy of Shylock in a sympathetic light. Like Jessner, he cast Shimon Finkel and Aharon Meskin as Shylock, a role they played in rotation. Guthrie gave the role of Portia to Shoshana Ravid, one of the younger generation of actors who joined the theater during the 1940s. She was a talented actress, yet she was not augmented by the symbolic national aura that characterized Rovina's persona and carried over into her performance.

Guthrie situated the play in contemporary Europe, with the actors appearing in modern dress. The trial, now a private anti-Semitic conspiracy rather than a public response to an actual threat posed by Shylock, took place in a dark interrogation room reminiscent of the torture cells of the Gestapo.[58] The play turned into an indictment of Venice as metonym of the European society which had spawned the horrors of Nazism and the Holocaust.

The critical response to the production is puzzling. The critics undermined Guthrie's innovative interpretation of the play. They did not perceive the play as a humanistic cry which deals directly with the Holocaust and the horrors of World War II. Rather, they echoed the public debate of 1936, which questioned whether the play should be put on the Hebrew-Zionist stage, and whether Shakespeare expressed anti-Semitic tendencies in the character of Shylock.[59] Selected paragraphs culled from the proceedings of the 1936 mock trial were even re-published in the playbill for Guthrie's production. Guthrie's contemporizing and re-setting of

[58] William Shakespeare, *Ha-sokher mi-venetzia*, directed by Tyron Guthrie, Habima, Tel Aviv, February 24, 1959, file no. 220851, Israeli Center for the Documentation of the Performing Arts.

[59] See e.g. Shlomo Bin-Nun, "Nos'im bo'arim ve-shaylock nitzkhi," *Davar*, March 6, 1959; R. Kh., "Du Krav al Shylock," *Ma'ariv*, February 27, 1959.

the play in modern Europe was a concept foreign to the Israeli theater critics, who found it intrusive and detrimental to what they considered the poetic beauty of the Shakespearean text. They also failed to perceive the interrogation room setting for the trial scene as a reference to the Holocaust. Critic Emil Feuerstein also argued that the tragic interpretation of Shylock was not innovative.[60] Haim Gamzu, the dean of Israel's theater critics, ignored Meskin's and Finkel's performances and complained about the defective Hebrew diction of the actors in the secondary roles.[61] The production closed after 37 performances, an unimpressive number when compared with other Habima productions of the season, such as Eugene O'Neill's *Desire Under the Elms*, which played 130 times.

In 1972 the Cameri Theatre staged *The Merchant* for a new generation of theatergoers. The production was directed by Yossi Yizraeli, then a thirty-three-year-old rising star of the Israeli theater. Yizraeli, born and bred in Israel, had studied theater directing in London and was inspired by innovative approaches to Shakespeare in contemporary European theaters.[62] Yizraeli did not feel committed to the tragic interpretation of Shylock which had guided Jessner and Guthrie. The play, he argued, was first and foremost a comedy, and the character of Shylock is indeed anti-Semitic. Any attempt to change these facts constitutes a misinterpretation of the play.[63] He cast actor Avner Hizkiyahu (1926–94) in the role of Shylock and directed him to act in a restrained style that differed from the larger-than-life tragic acting style of Finkel and Meskin.

The stage of Yizraeli's *The Merchant of Venice* was bare. He staged the play as an abstract allegory, focusing on the conflict between the Christians and Shylock. All the Christians wore blond wigs and were dressed in white while Shylock and Tubal were dressed in black. Jessica, who eventually crossed over from Jew to Christian, was dressed in a combination of black and white. The anti-Semitic atmosphere was evident

60 Emil Feuerstein, "Hasokher Mivenetzia be-habima", no newspaper name, n.d., in William Shakespeare, *Ha-sokher mi-venetzia*, directed by Tyron Guthrie, file no. 220851, Israeli Center for the Documentation of the Performing Arts..

61 Haim Gamzu, *Dr. Haim Gamzu: Bikorot Te'atron*, ed. Michael Handelsalz (Tel Aviv: Nusewon Tel Aviv le-omanut, 1999), 197–98.

62 William Shakespeare, *Ha-sokher mi-venetzia*, directed by Yossi Yizraeli, The Cameri, Tel Aviv, February 22, 1972, file no. 220852, Israeli Center for the Documentation of the Performing Arts.

63 Immanuel Bar Kadma, "Hayehudi ha-shakhor mul venetzia ha-levana," *Yediot Akharonot*, March 10, 1972, in William Shakespeare, *Ha-sokher mi-venetzia*, directed by Yossi Yizraeli, file no. 220851, Israeli Center for the Documentation of the Performing Arts.

from the very beginning, as the production opened with a parade of Christians dressed in white Ku Klux Klan robes and conical hats. Shylock was persecuted and beaten before uttering his famous monologue. In the trial scene Antonio appeared on the stage as a Jesus-like figure, carrying a large black cross on his back. Haunted by a death wish, he was using Shylock in order to fulfill his desire. Yizraeli also created a metatheatrical commentary on the events that took place onstage by creating a "double," a grotesque marionette, for every character represented by a live actor. The marionettes were placed next to the rear wall and performed acts related to the plot though not necessarily the same as those performed by the live actors. One of the most striking examples was the marionettes' enactment of the baptism and conversion of Shylock after the trial – a scene which is not in the text and did not take place on the main stage. In this manner, the marionettes continuously offered a kind of choric commentary on the story of Shylock.

The critics received the play with apprehension. Most of them did not like Yizraeli's innovative choices. Haim Gamzu argued that his stylistic mannerisms overshadowed the play:

> The director insisted that *The Merchant of Venice* should be performed as a comedy, and he paid a high price for that: he gave up what is tragic in the character of Shylock and stressed only the negative and the ridiculous.[64]

Yizraeli's Shylock evoked in some way the same Zionist critique as Jessner's Shylock: he was not a tragic figure, but rather a grotesque incarnation of years of persecution.

The 1980 production of *The Merchant of Venice* remained on the margins of the Israeli discourse about the play. It was directed by Barry Kyle, a young British director who worked mainly at the Royal Shakespeare Company. Like Yizraeli, he cast Avner Hizkiyahu as Shylock. The interpretative key to the play, wrote theater critic Boaz Evron, was the power of money. All characters of the play were in constant pursuit of wealth. Most of them were blind to any human sentiment other than greed. Shylock was delineated in this production as a satanic character. While some of the Venetian characters, like Antonio or Portia were able to express more noble feelings, Shylock was entirely defined by his greed and could not even mourn the loss of his daughter without grieving over the loss of his money.[65]

[64] Gamzu, Dr. Haim Gamzu, 312.

[65] Boaz Evron, "Ma khadash ba-rialto," *Yediot Akharonot*, August 6, 1980.

Rather than set the play in some version of Renaissance Italy, Kyle imagined it as taking place in an modern, elegant urban space:

> A huge shutter rose at the back of the stage. From time to time, a door opened in it to allow the entrances and exits, or it became half transparent to reveal behind it treetops or glowing candles.[66]

The critics considered the production visually interesting, elegant and well-made, yet cool, detached, and ultimately undecipherable. It evoked some discussion of aesthetic formalism but failed to stir Israeli spectators.[67]

The 1994 Cameri production was directed by Omri Nitzan, the artistic director of the theater. Nitzan understood Shylock as a negative character, corrupted by anti-Semitic persecution. However, unlike Yizraeli, who was interested in the generic framework of the Shakespearean comedy, Nitzan followed Jessner and Guthrie in choosing to highlight the tragedy of Shylock, but did so by staging the Jew as a character who becomes blinded by his own fanaticism. At the beginning, Nitzan's Shylock is a shrewd businessman, suspicious, but not hateful. He lives with Christians, conducts business with them, and even dines with them in order to promote his business, yet he loses this veneer of sophistication when subjected to persecution. The elopement of his daughter is the last straw and it changes his personality from a practical businessman to a crazed avenger who is willing to sacrifice everything for the sake of a single vicious act against his enemy.[68] Nitzan acknowledged that he modeled his Shylock on the Jewish terrorist Baruch Goldstein,[69] who in 1994 massacred twenty-nine Muslims praying at the Cave of the Patriarchs in Hebron. Actor Yossi Garber's portrayal of Shylock was hailed by critics as the apex of his long career. At the beginning of the play Garber's Shylock appeared dressed as a modern Orthodox Jew, but gradually he was transformed into a fanatic settler, wearing a large white yarmulke and toting an Uzi machine gun, a visual code that associated him with the most extremist Israeli settlers on

[66] Ibid.

[67] William Shakespeare, *Ha-sokher mi-venetzia*, directed by Barry Kyle, The Cameri, Tel Aviv, July 22, 1980, file no. 228293, Israeli Center for the Documentation of the Performing Arts.

[68] William Shakespeare, *Ha-sokher mi-venetzia*, directed by Omri Nitzan, The Cameri, Tel Aviv, April 30, 1994, file no. 228324, Israeli Center for the Documentation of the Performing Arts.

[69] Sa'ar Dayan and Tammy Lubich, "Yehudi ra," *Ma'ariv*, April 29, 1994, William Shakespeare, *Ha-sokher mi-venetzia*, directed by Omri Nitzan, file no. 228324, Israeli Center for the Documentation of the Performing Arts.

the West Bank.[70] Despite the abstract set, in which the hedonism of the world of the play was suggested by large deep-red pillows, Nitzan used costumes to link the characters with contemporary Israel and used the character of Shylock to investigate its darker sides.

The 2012 Habima production of *The Merchant of Venice* brought the Hebrew Shylock back to the international/European arena both figuratively and literally. Unlike the first five productions, for which the impetus came from within Israeli, the sixth production was a response to an invitation from the Globe Theatre in London to present the play in the Globe-to-Globe World Shakespeare Festival in the early summer of 2012. The project was an ambitious undertaking that preceded the London Olympic Games. During the six weeks of this international theatrical "Olympiad," thirty-seven companies from around the world each presented a different Shakespeare play in its native language, confirming the Bard's supremacy and England's contribution to world civilization. Habima's participation in the event evoked a loud pro-Palestinian protest, calling for the Globe to disinvite the Israeli company. The objection was not to the play but rather to the company, which had held some performances in Ariel, an Israeli town on the West Bank – an area considered to be illegally occupied by Israel. The Globe Theatre refused to yield to protestors' demands for ostracizing the production. Habima's *The Merchant of Venice* premiered at the Globe on May 28, 2012, where it played for two nights. The theater was picketed by pro- and anti-Israeli groups and there were some disturbances during performances, though they quickly came under control. Upon the company's return to Israel, the production was integrated into Habima's regular repertoire.

In the troupe's home theater, the play was performed in the Bimartef/Bertonov Hall, the smallest and most intimate space of the Habima building, seating less than 200 spectators. This spatial choice was deliberately made by Ilan Ronen, a veteran director (b. 1948) for whom *The Merchant* was his first Shakespearean undertaking. Ronen's choice of performance space was intended to increase physical proximity and facilitate interaction between actors and spectators. His theatrical Venice drew its inspiration from the performative language of *Commedia dell Arte* and the Venetian carnival. The play opened with Shylock's entrance into this playful world. He is a severe and serious presence, who immediately becomes the target of merciless physical abuse by the glamorous revelers. Ronen's casting of

70 William Shakespeare, *Ha-sokher mi-venetzia*, directed by Omri Nitzan, file no. 228324, Israeli Center for the Documentation of the Performing Arts. 68.

the part was unorthodox, to say the least. Shylock was portrayed by actor Yaacov Cohen, a man of small and unimpressive physique and voice, best known as an angry standup comedian. Cohen's Shylock was a sort of everyman, a devoted father and a decent merchant whose sense of responsibility and general decency contrasted with the greediness and deceitfulness of the "beautiful" Venetians. Cohen, the son of a Moroccan family, speaks Hebrew with a very slight "ethnic" accent, thus gently hinting at a difference from the actors playing the Venetians who speak an accentless contemporary Hebrew. It is doubtful whether such bold casting with its suggestion of ethnic overtones would have been possible in earlier times. For example, when the Iraq-born Israeli actor Arieh Elias, an appreciated actor with a noticeable Arabic accent expressed his desire to play Shylock it was made clear to him that he would not be considered appropriate for such a "universal" role as Shylock.

In this 2012 production Belmont is not a magical place, and Christian betrayal is manifest even there with the fair Portia being constantly misled by Bassanio. His wink and glance make it clear that his heart does not fully belong to her, and the audience can easily deduce that he is in love with her money no less than he is in love with her. Though the stage is mostly bare and the set minimalist, the courtroom scene with its ropes and red hooks hanging from the ceiling suggests an aestheticized slaughterhouse. The ropes resemble a spider web, in which Shylock is thrashing around, until he eventually falls prey to Portia, who is watching him standing alone on the stage while she stands behind the audience.

After the production's London premiere, the *Guardian* theater critic, Lyn Gardner, opened her review with an account of the last scene:

> The final image of this production by Israeli company Habima is a stark one. Small and crushed, as if weighed down by history itself, Jacob Cohen's broken Shylock – a man who has lost daughter, fortune and home – is seen, suitcase in hand, walking away from Venice, an eternal wandering Jew. But it was impossible not to think of other displaced people, too, most particularly the Palestinians.[71]

Conclusion

It is noteworthy that the Hebrew playbill of the 2012 Habima production devotes a full page to a summary of the 1936 literary trial occasioned by Jessner's *The Merchant of Venice*. Despite the passage of three-quarters

[71] Lyn Gardner, "The Merchant of Venice – review," *Guardian*, May 29, 2012, available at www.guardian.co.uk.

of a century, a time period that includes World War II, the Holocaust, the establishment of Israel, and armed conflicts with Palestinians and several Arab nations, Jessner's production remains a milestone in the formation of Zionist theatrical culture. This iconic status derives from its willingness to grapple with a deep-seated contradiction between its aspirations to universalism and its commitment to Zionist and Jewish concerns. By the 1930s Habima was the leading theatrical troupe in Palestine, and, as such, claimed equal status with European theater troupes and within the theatrical culture of the world. At the same time, as we have seen, it felt obligated to address burning issues of World Jewry. But while Habima was willing to serve as a theatrical platform for world culture, it also rejected foreign interpretations which did not speak to the concerns of the *Yishuv*, as well as theatrical approaches and practices that differed from its own Russian-based traditions. Thus, the collaboration with Jessner proved problematic on many levels – artistic and cultural, as well as personal. Clearly the masterful German-Jewish director did not fit into the tight-knit Habima collective of Zionist Jewish émigrés from Eastern Europe.

To one degree or another, post-1936 productions of *The Merchant of Venice* in Israel were haunted by the same internal conflict. Yet these productions differed from Jessner's, mainly in their understanding of Shylock: Jessner's Shylock was a heroic figure who was torn between his intense longing to be part of the Venetian world and his furious desire for revenge. Guthie's Shylock was a priori victim of society, and the Shylocks of Yizraeli, Kyle, and Nitzan were essentially villains, victims of their own personalities, who became as evil as their Venetian persecutors. Whereas Jessner drew a contrast between an idealized Belmont and a commercialized Venice, his successors condemned Venice and Belmont alike. Their Belmonts turned from a place which represented Jewish yearning for acceptance, as well as access for Jews to the splendors of Christian Europe, into yet another locus of hedonism, exploitation, and blatant anti-Semitism. Contempt for Shylock as a diasporic victim and for Belmont as essentially corrupt – attitudes affirmed in the 1936 literary trial – became dominant in later Israeli productions of the play. Only in Habima's 2012 Globe production do we encounter a different Shylock, who in some way shares the lot of Jessner's Jew. This Shylock, too, is torn between two worlds. Rooted in his own Jewish world, he tries to claim his place in a global Europe, but it is a Europe that condemns him and what he represents both inside and outside the playhouse.

9

Fritz Kortner and other German-Jewish Shylocks before and after the Holocaust

Jeanette R. Malkin

Ever since its first German-language performance in Hamburg in 1777, *The Merchant of Venice* has been one of Germany's favorite Shakespeare plays, ranking, during some periods, second only to *Hamlet*.[1] The importance of *The Merchant* for German audiences and scholars becomes even more interesting once we place it within its broader local context as the dark cousin of Gotthold Lessing's 1779 play, *Nathan der Weise* (*Nathan the Wise*), written, in part, in reaction to the German *Merchant* of 1777. Lessing's staunchly philo-Semitic play, inspired by the personality of his close friend, the German-Jewish philosopher and emancipator Moses Mendelssohn, was first performed in Berlin in 1783 and nearly non-stop thereafter. Indeed, from the late eighteenth century until today, these two opposed aspects of the stage Jew – Shylock and Nathan – have been dialectically inseparable. Over the last two centuries, many of Germany's most important actors, Jewish and Christian alike, have prided themselves on having played both characters. Fritz Kortner was not one of them. Although repeatedly encouraged by his wife, the actress Johanna Hofer, to play Nathan, Kortner rejected the idea. Marianne Brün-Kortner, his daughter, suggests – convincingly – that "possibly, Nathan was too unambiguous, too good for my father´s taste."[2]

1 Statistics to this effect are cited throughout Andrew G. Bonnell, *Shylock in Germany: Antisemitism and The German Theatre from the Enlightenment to the Nazis* (New York: Tauris Academic Studies, 2008), 18, 41, 63, 93.

2 Cited by Richard D. Critchfield, *From Shakespeare to Frisch: The Provocative Fritz Kortner* (Heidelberg: Synchron Publishers, 2008), 187, from an email he received on January 23, 2002.

I have chosen to present the history of twentieth-century German-Jewish Shylock-actors using the actor Fritz Kortner as our "guide." There are many reasons for emphasizing Kortner (1892–1970). Kortner is considered one of Germany's most important twentieth-century theater figures, actor and director. He appeared in the role of Shylock in three major pre-war productions, between 1923 and 1928, including a Reinhardt revival of his renowned 1905 production. Kortner was one of the actors of the period most identified with Shylock because he played him so often, but also because his own Jewishness could not be ignored: it was carved into his body and sculpted the lines of his face. Square and stocky, with dark eyes, a broad, flat nose, thick lips, and curly dark hair, Kortner had nowhere to hide except, perhaps, in plain sight.[3] His thrusting gestures and trumpeting voice – as critics would testify – fueled his fame as an expressionistic actor and transformed his "too Jewish" physique into a site of power, passion – and rebellion;[4] characteristics well fitting Shylock. In addition, Kortner was the only important Jewish "Shylock-actor" to return to the German stage after 1945. Although he would not play Shylock in front of a live audience in postwar Germany, on principle, he did have two additional Shylock turns in the 1960s: at the age of seventy-four Kortner recreated Shylock's "Hath not a Jew eyes?" monologue in a 1966 private rehearsal filmed by Hans-Jürgen Syberberg, a performance that captures something of the power of Kortner's prewar embodiment of that role; and in 1968 he played the role in a German/Austrian television film, giving an interpretation so severe that it ignited public and media discussion of the question: "May the Jew again be portrayed as evil?"

In each period during his fifty years of Shylock enactments, Kortner's interpretation of Shakespeare's Jew gave contemporary – and contentious – expression to his own hyphenated identity as a German Jew (as well as, originally, a Viennese Jew[5]), revered and recognized by the audience and press, and in equal measure reviled and rejected. Clearly, Kortner

3 See my article: Jeanette R. Malkin, "Transforming in Public: Jewish Actors on the German Expressionist Stage," in *Jews and the Making of Modern German Theatre, eds.* Jeanette R. Malkin and Freddie Rokem (Iowa City: University of Iowa Press, 2010), 151–73.

4 These characteristics were already cited in the context of Kortner's breakthrough Berlin performance as Friedrich in Ernst Toller's 1919 *Die Wandlung* (*Transformation*). See e.g. Julius Bab, *Theater der Gegenwart* (Leipzig: Weber, 1928), 179.

5 Although Kortner was born and raised in Vienna and first came to Berlin in his early twenties, I designate him a "German" in the sense of the German cultural sphere. As with Max Reinhardt, his roots lie in Austria but Germany was the country he considered to be his home and artistic base. After World War II, Kortner returned to Germany, not to Austria.

shared with Shylock the ability to succeed in an often less than loving environment. More significantly, he shared with Shylock an unbending tribal pride and the willingness to court controversy. Shylock in Germany is always first and foremost a political portrait in dialogue with its audience and with the context of the historical moment. As critic Franz Köppen wrote in 1928 about Kortner's recent Shylock, it was certainly not what Shakespeare had in mind; rather, the performance gave voice to "the ethos of our time," a revolutionary revisioning of Shakespeare "for today's audience."[6] Each of Kortner's embodiments of the role, before and after, had a specific nuance. But what all of the portrayals have in common is Kortner's affinity with Shylock's all-encompassing sense of his "Jewishness," deepened through attack, exclusion, and through his indignation at the insult of the Christians toward his people. This affinity was bred in Kortner's biography as a Jew growing up in anti-Semitic Vienna at the turn of the twentieth century.

In his 1959 autobiography *Aller Tage Abend* (The Evening of my Days[7]), Kortner recalls at great length a traumatic incident that occurred in 1908, when he was a sixteen-year-old acting student at the Burgtheater's Academy of Arts in Vienna. It involved his non-Jewish Austrian acting teacher, Julius Meixner, who, despite Kortner's obvious talent and powerful physical instrument, refused to cast him in major roles. When, at one point, Kortner requested that he be allowed to play the blinded and wronged Melchtal in Schiller's *Wilhelm Tell*, Meixner said to him, in front of the entire class: "With that *ponim* you could never play Melchtal; with that *ponim* you shouldn't work in the theater at all. In a bank or a business it wouldn't matter."[8] "*Ponim*," Kortner explains, is the Yiddish version of the Hebrew word for "face" and had, along with many other words, entered into Austrian-Jewish slang. "In the mouth of a non-Jew," he writes, "these words sounded déclassé, mildly

[6] Franz Köppen, "Das Phänomen Fritz Kortner," in *Fritz Kortner*, Die Kunst der Bühne, ed. Heinz Ludwigg, vol. 3 (Berlin: Eigenbrödler-Verlag, 1928), 50.

[7] This is an approximate literal translation of what is an idiomatic expression, here ironically inverted by Kortner. The expression is "es ist nicht aller Tage Abend," which means, roughly, it's not over until it's over. Kortner's removal of "nicht," (not) gives us the inverse meaning which the aging Kortner probably meant. In addition, the literal meaning of the end of the day puts the emphasis on the evening, the time when an actor begins to live. Kortner's memoires were never translated into English or any other language, unlike other equivalent autobiographies from the period, such as Alexander Granach's or Ernst Toller's, despite its great historical interest. All German translations are by me unless otherwise noted.

[8] Fritz Kortner, *Aller Tage Abend: Autobiographie* (Munich: Knaur, 1996 [1959]), 50.

anti-Semitic ... numbingly painful."[9] Used in the context of the teacher's crass public assault, there could be no doubt that for Meixner, as for many in Vienna, Kortner's objectionable face had everything to do with his objectionable race.

Kortner grew up in a religious home in one of the Jewish neighborhoods of Vienna. His father, Yuda Yakob Kohn, was an educated man fluent in Hebrew and deeply invested in the study of the Torah and the Talmud. A watchmaker by profession and the owner of a relatively successful jewelry shop, Kohn stemmed from a small Hungarian village in the county of Pressburg. He came to Vienna in 1891 as a forty-year-old widower with six children.[10] Fritz, born Nathan Fritz Kohn, was the only child by Yuda's second wife, Helene Lunzer, a Viennese Jewess with a special love of the theater. As a youth, Kortner identified strongly with his father's faith and claims to have been "exaltedly religious"[11] and to have seriously considered becoming a rabbi. The attraction to religion may have had something to do with his childhood experience of rejection and abuse as a Jew. The German playwright and political activist Ernst Toller – who grew up in the eastern Prussian city of Posen and in whose play *Transformation* (1919) Kortner had his first great success as an expressionist actor – wrote in his autobiography of "the terrible joy I felt when I passed unrecognized as a Jew,"[12] momentarily invisible as the outsider he knew himself to be. Kortner, with his over-large, unmistakable Semitic facial features, never enjoyed that option. "As a child, I awoke every day with the fear of being mocked as a Jew," Kortner writes and later recalls an incident that occurred when he was five or six years old.[13] Two boys attacked and beat the "Judenbuben," the Jew-boy, who had been sitting, lazily, in front of his father's shop. His father, a burly man, ran after the boys and, in his fury, beat them repeatedly while a crowd gathered around the scene. Fifty years later, Kortner's pride and gratitude toward "the enraged Maccabi, who was my father," the father "who had learned to run and storm as a young soldier" in World War I, the father who emerged bloodied but victorious in his son's defense, is movingly evident.[14] The satisfaction of revenge was a lesson early learned.

[9] Ibid., 49–50.

[10] See Peter Schütze, *Fritz Kortner*, Rororo Series (Hamburg: Rowohlt, 1994), 11ff.

[11] Fritz Kortner, *Letzten Endes. Fragmente*, ed. Johanna Kortner (Munich: Kindler, 1971), 192.

[12] Ernst Toller, *Eine Jugend in Deutschland* (Hamburg: Rowohlt, 1996 [1933]), 161; my translation. The English translation is titled *I Was a German*.

[13] Kortner, *Aller Tage Abend*, 16.

[14] Ibid., 198–99.

The Vienna of Wittgenstein, Mahler, Schnitzler, and Karl Kraus, the Vienna in which the young Fritz Kortner grew to manhood, was also the Vienna of Karl Lueger, legendary mayor of that city from 1897–1910. Lueger, a populist politician and co-founder of the right-wing Christian Social Party, is credited with Vienna's modernization as well as with perfecting crass, instrumental anti-Semitic tactics as a means to achieving his political ends. This policy was perhaps less a reflection of his personal opinions than an indication of popular sentiment, which he exploited, especially among the lower and artisan classes. By 1900, 8.7 percent of the Viennese population was Jewish and a far larger percentage could be counted among the successful entrepreneurs, doctors, lawyers, playwrights, and other cultural agents. One of Lueger's better known speeches – to the Parliament in 1890 – exposes, in rich incantatory tones, the resentment of Viennese society toward this preponderance of cultured Jews. There are in Vienna, Lueger warns:

> as many Jews as there are grains of sand on the seashore; wherever you go, nothing but Jews; if you go to the theater, nothing but Jews; if you take a walk in the Ringstrasse [the central promenade], nothing but Jews; if you enter the Stadtpark, nothing but Jews; if you go to a concert, nothing but Jews; if you go to a ball, nothing but Jews; if you go to the university, nothing but Jews.

The old Christian Austrian Empire, he concludes, is being replaced by "a new Kingdom of Palestine."[15] Yet, despite Vienna's almost official anti-Semitism, Jews prospered there beyond almost any other European city, and the barbs and slings they suffered were not always of the crass variety that ended in beatings and public humiliation. More often, as Kortner repeatedly shows in his autobiography, rejection was felt in the undercurrent of a knowing glance or a casual, cruel remark. As the Austrian-Jewish novelist and playwright Richard Beer-Hofmann wrote in a 1913 letter to Martin Buber:

> Whether we like it or not, whatever we Jews do takes place on a stage … the whole world can sit back in their seats and gape at the Jew. Our expression, voice, posture, hair color, physique – everything must be submitted to hostile judges; and woe to us if we don't walk the stage like demigods.[16]

[15] Quoted in Enzo Traverso, *The Jews and Germany: From the "Judeo-German Symbiosis" to the Memory of Auschwitz* (Lincoln: University of Nebraska Press, 1995), 21.

[16] Letter dated April 3, 1913, reprinted in Alexander Kosenina, "Richard Beer-Hofmanns Briefwechsel mit Martin Buber (1910–1936)," *Modern Austrian Literature* 29:2 (1996), 54–55.

It was in this atmosphere that Kortner grew up with only one ambition: to be an actor. Kortner acquired his two great (and interconnected) sensitivities in Vienna: to anti-Semitism, and to what he would forever consider to be his physical "ugliness." And yet, he seems to have never doubted the appropriateness of exhibiting his Jewish face and form on the stage for all to see; it would, however, be in Berlin and not in Vienna, that he would achieve fame.

Kortner saw his first performance of *The Merchant of Venice* while still a student at the Academy. It was a guest performance of Max Reinhardt's 1905 production featuring Rudolf Schildkraut as Shylock. Reinhardt, an Austrian Jew like Kortner, was the great modernizer of the German theater and Germany's most famous and popular director for the first two decades of the twentieth century.[17] In 1905, the year of Reinhardt's breakthrough production of *A Midsummer Night's Dream*, he directed an equally spectacular *Merchant* on the same revolving stage of his Deutsches Theater, replacing Oberon's enchanted forest with the urban beauty of Venice. Within this charmed fairy-land, with its bridges and gondolas and winding streets, Reinhardt cast the *Ostjude* Schildkraut as Shylock.

Schildkraut, a native of Brăila in Romania and originally an actor in the Yiddish theater, astonished Kortner with his powerful presence. This "levantine *ur*-Jew," Kortner writes, was, despite his short stature, a colossus, a "short-changed giant" whose initial patience erupts into an alarming "desert wildness" when the injustice done to him becomes too much to bear. Kortner's orientalist perception of Schildkraut as an authentic *ur*-Jew in the mold of the biblical forefathers was a commonplace of the period. In his important book *Juden auf der deutschen Bühne* ("Jews on the German Stage," 1928), the writer and cultural critic Arnold Zweig claims, admiringly, that the *Ostjude* Schildkraut was one of the strongest and most moving actors on the German stage precisely because of his unselfconscious and integral Jewishness. His "Shylock smells of onions

[17] This is stated by J.L. Styan, *Max Reinhardt*, Directors in Perspective (Cambridge: Cambridge University Press: 1982), xiii, without source citation, and I have not been able to corroborate this.

and garlic," Zweig writes, "and this is at least as good a taste and smell as slaughtered pigs and goats cooked in their mother's milk."[18] Kortner, who was "shaken to the core"[19] by Schildkraut's performance, surely experienced Schildkraut's Jewish "authenticity" through his own "bifurcated" identity, in Paul Mendes-Flohr's term: an identity split within itself through deracination and self-conscious, incomplete assimilation.[20] "I didn't forget [Schildkraut's Shylock]," Kortner writes, "even when I chose to play the figure very differently."[21] Inevitably, Kortner's Shylock would be far less forgiving from the start.

Reinhardt's Shylocks

In Berlin of the first third of the twentieth century there were four major Shylock actors: Schildkraut, Albert Bassermann, Werner Krauss, and Kortner. Of the four, Schildkraut and Kortner were Jewish, Bassermann, often mistakenly identified as a Jew, was married to a Jewish woman, and Krauss was universally recognized as a great actor whose only ideology was the theater. All four appeared at some point in Max Reinhardt's *The Merchant*, which was the single most important and influential production of the play in pre-World War II Germany. Each of these Shylock's was very different from the others, as I discuss below, and yet all were sanctioned by that most important Jewish theater-person of the first half of the twentieth century, Max Reinhardt. Kortner was the only one among them to resist Reinhardt's interpretation.

Reinhardt's *The Merchant* was performed, with changing casts and at growing intervals, from 1905 until 1930 in Berlin, Vienna, in half a dozen other European cities, and in 1934 in the open air of Venice itself, for a total of 363 performances.[22] In all of its incarnations, the festive joy

[18] Arnold Zweig, *Juden auf der deutschen Bühne* (Berlin: Welt-Verlag, 1928), 179. This is part of a larger historical change of perception. At the end of the nineteenth century, Eastern European Jews, previously viewed by their Westernized brethren as dirty and dangerous threats to their own acceptance as Germans, became objects of veneration, especially among Zionists. Influenced by romantic, nationalist ideals of a rooted, organic community, German Zionists idealized the Eastern European Jews' seemingly unified, holistic identity, rooted, as it was, in community and age-old tradition. See Steven E. Aschheim, *Brothers and Strangers: The East European Jew in German and German Jewish Consciousness, 1800–1923* (Madison: University of Wisconsin Press, 1982).

[19] Kortner, *Aller Tage Abend*, 68.

[20] See Paul Mendes-Flohr, *German Jews: A Dual Identity* (New Haven: Yale University Press, 1999).

[21] Kortner, *Aller Tage Abend*, 68.

[22] Bonnell, *Shylock in Germany*, 52.

Reinhardt invested in Venice took precedence over Shylock's "tragedy," leading Kortner, among others, to complain that Reinhardt – an unabashed Jew – had created an uncritical picture of a society in which everyone was enchanting with the sole "regrettable" exception of Shylock. Today we know better, writes Kortner in a post-Auschwitz aside: "Not one of them is any better than the other ... Their intolerance toward the Jew is what *turns* Shylock into Shylock."[23]

In fact, Reinhardt's staging diverged from the traditional German interpretation of the play. Theater critic Siegfried Jacobsohn commented in 1911 that: "Productions since the German Shakespeare-renaissance up until today have turned the comedy of the royal merchant of Venice into the tragedy of Shylock, who is hounded to death, along with his entire race."[24] Reinhardt, however, chose to emphasize neither comedy nor tragedy but rather enchantment; the magic of an "ever-singing, ever-humming Venice. A city that celebrates its lust of life, its pleasures, joys, and merriment," as Arthur Kahane, Reinhardt's dramaturge, notes in his *Diary of a Dramaturge*. "Hero, heart, focal point and essence of this performance is Venice," he writes, "Not Shylock, but Venice."[25] Or, as Jacobsohn put it, "Venetian joy of life is the dominant tone, with Jewish sorrow only a dissonant note."[26] Erika Fischer-Lichte, in an article on Reinhardt's productions of *The Merchant of Venice*, makes an illuminating distinction between the world of the play and Shylock: "By casting Venice as the protagonist and centre of the performance, Reinhardt found an effective means of reducing and subduing the performance's referentiality, strongly highlighting instead, its performativity." That is, in a perhaps intentional move, Reinhardt chose to stage *the* most popular European play containing a central Jewish character, and to then replace interpretation with theatrical innovation. "Rather than offering an interpretation of the play – whether old or new – Reinhardt presented and created a new concept of theatre," Fischer-Lichte hypothesizes. Contemporary critics of the production seem to confirm this view. Most reacted first and foremost to the theatrical event, the elaborate and stunning sets designed by Emil Orlik and revealed in rotating sequence on Reinhardt's revolving

[23] Kortner, *Aller Tage Abend*, 68–69.

[24] Siegfried Jacobsohn, *Max Reinhardt* (Berlin: Erich Reiss, 1911), 1, my translation. Cited by Erika Fischer-Lichte in a different translation in her article "Theatre as Festive Play: Max Reinhardt's Productions of *The Merchant of Venice*," in *Jews and the Making of Modern German Theatre*, eds. Malkin and Rokem, 220.

[25] Arthur Kahane, *Tagebuch des Dramaturgen* (Berlin: Bruno Cassirer, 1928), 116.

[26] Jacobsohn, *Max Reinhardt*, 1, my translation.

stage; the music by Engelbert Humperdinck; the choreographed crowd scenes and the jubilant, sparkling atmosphere of the production. Fischer-Lichte continues: "Only when describing and evaluating Schildkraut's performance of Shylock, did they deal explicitly with the question of the relationship between text and performance."[27]

That relationship depended, of course, on which actor was performing the role. In Schildkraut's case, critics found that his Shylock evolved, with psychological credibility, from a mild-mannered, if melancholy and quietly suffering figure, "more human than specifically Jewish,"[28] into an enraged, but never demonic, seeker of justice and revenge. Schildkraut, one critic judged, unfolded "the inner development of the character," thus rendering psychologically plausible his need for revenge.[29] His acting neither exaggerated nor caricatured the Jew, and the German critics on the spectrum from left to right were either moved – even finding in his portrayal "a hidden sermon for tolerance and humanity;"[30] or wary, warning that Schildkraut had turned "this malicious, cunning and vengeful swindling Jew into a martyr."[31] Yiddish writer Sholem Asch, who saw the production on a visit to Berlin, was so impressed by Schildkraut's "broad and upright Jew, who stands as firm as a pillar and demands justice," that he wrote his play *Got fun Nekumeh* (*God of Vengeance*) with Schildkraut specifically in mind.[32] The production's popularity can be measured by the impressive number of performances given by Schildkraut: 100 within the first four months, and 206 performances by the time it closed in 1911.

In 1913, Reinhardt revived his *Merchant* as part of a Shakespeare cycle of seven plays he was directing at the Deutsches Theater. This time, Schildkraut alternated with Albert Bassermann, one of the leading and most respected German actors of the time, in the role of Shylock. Bassermann, unlike Schildkraut, was a tall man of athletic build and strong facial features. "On the stage he appeared as a giant with a formidable hooked nose, bristling hair, a wild gray beard, pointed, threatening eyebrows ... amazingly deep eyes and

[27] Fischer-Lichte, "Theatre as Festive Play," 221, 222.

[28] Heinrich Hart, *Der Tag*, November 11, 1905, in Hugo Fetting, ed. *Von der freien Bühne zum Politischen Theater. Drama und Theater im Spiegel der Kritik*, vol. 1: 1889–1918 (Leipzig: Reclam, 1987), 310.

[29] Alfred Klaar, *Vossische Zeitung*, November 10, 1905, in Fetting, ed. *Von der freien Bühne*, 305.

[30] Hart, in Fetting, ed. *Von der freien Bühne*, 310.

[31] Helene Richter, "Berliner Theaterschau," *Shakespeare Jahrbuch* 43 (1907), 338.

[32] Reinhardt accepted this play for production in 1906 and Schildkraut appeared in the main role. Sholem Asch, "Rückblick," in *Von den Vätern* (Berlin: Paul Zsolnay Verlag, 1931), 325.

[produced] noises like a beast of prey," wrote Jacobsohn of Bassermann's Shylock, adding that he was inflexible, iron-cast, throughout.[33] He was a figure taken from mythology, not life, as critic Emil Faktor notes. Faktor – who was Jewish, as were most of the important Berlin theater critics of the time – adds, with the weight of experience, that Bassermann played Shylock "as no actually Jewish actor, inhibited by better knowledge of the psyche of a suffering people, could ever play him."[34] Schildkraut's more human, more suffering Shylock "engenders pity, Bassermann's fear," wrote critic Fritz Engel. Born fully-formed, Bassermann's character doesn't develop, Engel continues and adds: "as certain as I am that Schildkraut's Shylock lends a measure of much-needed refinement to this play that trifles with all manner of cruelty, just as much do I bow before the grandiose picture that Bassermann presents."[35] In the final scene, Jacobsohn writes, where conversion is added to the curse of poverty, "Bassermann draws himself up even taller; Schildkraut mumbles in horror: Shmah Yisroel! [the holiest Hebrew prayer]." Then one of the anti-Semites grabs Schildkraut and beats him – "which could never happen to Bassermann," Jacobsohn continues, "because no one would dare come close to him." Bassermann remains unconquerable; Schildkraut is destroyed.[36]

In 1921, two years after Germany's defeat, in an atmosphere of economic crisis and ideological polarization, Reinhardt presented his *Merchant* in a quite different setting: in his huge circus-shaped Grosses Schauspielhaus, an arena-theater dubbed by Reinhardt as "the theater of the 5000." Rebuilt from an actual circus-top (the Schumann Circus), its immense size and interlinked stage/audience were geared toward spectacle. Reinhardt added musical interludes and intermittent groups of dancers, diluting the original production's poetry and magic.[37] As Shylock he cast Werner Krauss, master of the broad gesture and magnetic stage presence who, a year earlier, had appeared as the sinister Dr. Caligari in Robert Wiener's seminal expressionist film. Krauss played Shylock in a black gabardine, a garish yellow *tallit* (prayer shawl), and a red wig – *de*

33 Originally printed as a review titled "Die Beiden Shylocks," *Die Schaubühne* 9:2 (1913), 1278. An extended version appears in Jacobsohn, *Max Reinhardt*, 6–7.

34 Emil Faktor, "Theater und Musik. Der Kaufmann von Venedig," *Berliner Börsen-Courier*, December 16, 1913; cited in Bonnell, *Shylock in Germany*, 53.

35 Fritz Engel, "Shakespearezyklus IV," *Berliner Tageblatt*, December 16, 1913; cited in Bonnell, *Shylock in Germany*, 53.

36 Jacobsohn, "Die Beiden Shylocks."

37 Taken from Siegfried Jacobsohn's description of the performance in Siegfried Jacobsohn, ed. *Das Jahr der Bühne* 10 (1920–1921), (Charlottenburg: Verlag der Weltbühne, 1921), 120–24.

rigueur in most nineteenth-century portrayals of the Jew, signifying his connection with both the devil and the clown. "With rude, broad steps, sometimes almost hopping, he paces across the stage; more yelling than speaking, wild, grotesque, almost comical in his morbid grief ... Next to this Shylock, all other performances [in this production] must pale," wrote one witness.[38] The reviews all comment on the challenge of the huge space that Krauss managed to fill with his dynamism; they also note the grotesque effect of his comic exaggerations and the demonic intensity with which he invests Shylock. All seemed to agree that he produced a theatrical *frisson* as the bad bogeyman of fairy tales come to life. As Alfred Kerr put it, he was "a strolling horror picture."[39] Interestingly, Krauss gave Shylock dignity in defeat as he remained defiant until the end.

Why Reinhardt would have authorized such a dangerous interpretation at a time of economic stress and growing anti-Semitism is not clear. Perhaps, as Peter Marx suggests, it was his lack of political sensitivity, or his lack of interest in political implications,[40] believing, as he did, that the theater is a sacred and separate space that creates its own reality. Contemporary critic Emil Faktor asked himself this same question, wondering whether Krauss was "a felicitous choice in this present time of racist agitation," since it was hard to miss the demonstrative applause that his Shylock received "from certain quarters." To which he added the caveat, "Werner Krauss's genius raised the figure above and beyond the possibilities of cheap agitation."[41] Hindsight may, however, suggest otherwise, given Krauss's subsequent career in Nazi Germany, especially his famously evil Shylock performed at the Vienna Burgtheater in 1943, preceded by his shameless performance as the Jew Süss in Viet Harlan's violent Nazi propaganda film. Allow me to add, anecdotally, that when Reinhardt left Germany in March, 1933, Goebbels sent Krauss after him with the offer that he return as an "honorary Aryan" and head the theater division of the Third Reich. Needless to say, Reinhardt declined.

I will discuss Reinhardt's 1924 *Merchant*, which featured Kortner as Shylock, below, in the context of Kortner's various incarnations of the

[38] Walther Volback, "Berliner Shakespeare-Vorstellungen," *Shakespeare Jahrbuch* 58 (1921), 146. Cited in Bonnell, *Shylock in Germany*, 73.

[39] Alfred Kerr, "Der Kaufmann von Venedig," *Berliner Tageblatt* (1921), cited in Bonnell, *Shylock in Germany*, 74.

[40] Peter W. Marx, "Die drei Gesichter Shylocks: Zu Max Reinhardts Project eines metropolitanen, liberalen Theaters vor dem Hintergrund seiner jüdischen Herkunft," in *Max Reinhardt und das Deutsche Theater: Texte und Bilder aus Anlass des 100-jährigen Jubiläums seiner Direktion*, eds. Roland Koberg et al. (Berlin: Henschel Verlag, 2005), 57.

[41] Emil Faktor, "Theater, Musik und Kun Monty Jacobs: Shakespeare in Berlin 1922–1924," in *Shakespeare Jahrbuch* 59/60 (1924), 242. Cited in Bonnell, *Shylock in Germany*, 76.

role. But one more version of Reinhardt's production – his last – must be mentioned, although it did not take place in a German theater. In 1934, Reinhardt was invited to stage his *Merchant* in Venice itself, with Italian actors, as part of the first "Festival internazionale del Teatro di Prosa." The play was performed outdoors, on the Campo San Trovaso, a quiet square with a typical small Venetian bridge and winding streets. The story's locations were built into the real landscape, mingling the real and mythic Venice and emphasizing "the theatricality of the performance as well as of the city," as Fischer-Lichte writes.[42] The well-known Italian actor Memo Benassi played Shylock. Fischer-Lichte notes that Reinhardt made no real changes in this production, despite the situation of the Jews in Germany, a year after the Nazis had seized power. Enchantment and theatricality remained his aim, and Shylock's position within the play remained that of the mythic outsider, aside from one detail: in his *Regiebuch* (director's book), Reinhardt writes that when he learns of Jessica's desertion, Shylock "rips the cloth in accordance with an old Jewish mourning custom."[43] The act of tearing one's clothes, the rending of garments, is an ancient and ongoing Jewish mourning custom which would, however, probably only have been understood by Jewish spectators. It was certainly understood by Reinhardt himself and this new gesture may have been the sign of his own mourning inserted, perhaps for himself, into the production.

Kortner's Pre-War Shylocks

During the decade following World War I, Kortner played Shylock in three major productions. The tenor of his interpretations of the role followed the changing fortunes of the Jews in the Weimar Republic. Kortner had first played Shylock, briefly, in 1916 at Vienna's Deutsches Volkstheater, six years after leaving that city to work as an actor in Germany. There had hardly been time for rehearsal and the reviews speak of a lack of "modulation," especially in the exercise of Kortner's always powerful voice. By 1923, when he came to the role well prepared, Kortner was already a famous actor, particularly noted for his interpretation of tyrants such as Richard III or, especially, Gessler in Leopold Jessner's scandalous 1919 production of Schiller's *Wilhelm Tell* at the prominent Berlin State Theater. This production critiqued conservative politics in pre-Weimar Germany

[42] Fischer-Lichte, "Theatre as Festive Play," 227.

[43] Reinhardt's director's book for the play, cited by Fischer-Lichte, "Theatre as Festive Play," 229.

and their potential continuation in the newly formed Republic. Jessner's subversive, anti-nationalistic reading of this most revered of German texts, and Kortner's embodiment of the play's desecration, drew extensive anti-Semitic attacks against them and led the rightist/nationalist press to accuse both men of the *Verjudung* – the Jewification – of the German stage.[44] The scandal lasted for years and was exacerbated by additional joint productions – *Richard III*, *Hamlet* – with similar political aims.

Thus, by the time the thirty-one-year-old Kortner appeared in his first Berlin Shylock, in 1923, the year that Germany's economy had reached hyperinflation causing many theaters to close and leaving many artists without jobs, his fame/infamy preceded him and, inevitably, colored the public's view and expectations. Kortner had left Jessner's State Theater in order to found, together with the German-Jewish writer and director Berthold Viertel, a "fringe" ensemble with literary ambitions and an anti-establishment agenda.[45] They called the new ensemble company Die Truppe, "a troupe of republican autonomous actors," as Alfred Döblin wrote.[46] The first play staged by the group was *The Merchant* with Kortner in the role of Shylock. It was not a great success. Viertel brought two Bauhaus-trained artists to design the sets and costumes and was clearly influenced in his choices by the Russian formalist Alexander Tairov, whose Kamerny Theater had toured Germany earlier that year. Critical consensus held that the production was weak and disunified; indeed, Döblin found it "beyond redemption."[47] Most critics commented on the multi-colored constructivist and cubist costumes and sets, finding them annoying and gratuitous, especially since the acting remained conventional.[48] Kortner, as usual, "directed himself" and stood outside of the production style.[49]

44 Jessner answered this accusation in his article "Das 'verjudete' Theater" (The "Jewified" Theatre), published in the widely circulated *CV-Zeitung*, the publication of the liberal German Jewish establishment (Centralverein); Leopold Jessner, "Das 'verjudete' Theater," *CV-Zeitung* 1/3 (May 18, 1922), 37; reprinted in Leopold Jessner, *Schriften: Theater der zwanziger Jahre*, ed. Hugo Fetting (Berlin: Henschelverlag Kunst und Gesellschaft, 1979), 61–62.

45 Cited in John Warren and Ulrike Zitzlsperger, eds. *Vienna meets Berlin: Cultural Interaction, 1918–1933* (Bern: Peter Lang, 2008 [2005]), 52.

46 Quoted by Bonnell, *Shylock in Germany*, 76.

47 Ibid.

48 Alfred Döblin, *Ein Kerl muss eine Meinung haben. Berichte und Kritiken 1921–1924* (Munich: Deutscher Taschenbuch-Verlag, 1981), 207. Cited in Bonnell, *Shylock in Germany*, 77.

49 The critic Herbert Jhering noted in his article, "Die Truppe," that Kortner's Shylock was "self-directed" and that the production "lacked precisely in the 'unity' that defines a troupe." In Herbert Jhering, *Von Reinhardt bis Brecht. Vier Jahrzehnte Theater und Film*, vol. 1 (Berlin: Aufbau Verlag, 1958), 334 and 337.

As was often the case, Kortner's relationship with his director was tense. He disapproved of most of Viertel's decisions and refused to take direction. The result was that most critics singled Kortner out as the one successful element of the production. Having refused to wear one of the stylized costumes, Kortner immediately "stood out like an island from the swarm of imitators ... a bad bogeyman, wrapped up and bulging in his yellow coat."[50] According to critic Franz Köppen, Kortner alone drew repeated applause from the audience. "Broad and weighty, like a primeval being from the age of sagas," his Shylock, Köppen continues, was "a man of his race, great and forceful in his demanding hatred."[51] This, precisely, was Kortner's aim: to present Shylock as the mythic Jew who was also the culmination of Jewish experience in Europe. First and foremost "a man of his race," he carries the wrongs done to his people in his DNA and his desire for revenge goes beyond the wrong done to him personally. "In the ranks of great Shylock's," Köppen claims, "Kortner is perhaps the simplest, least nuanced, most human (because he is at the same time the most animal and instinctive)."[52] His instincts led him to emphasize two parallel aspects of the character: his specific "Jewishness" – as a believing, traditional Jew; and his unforgiving hatred of those who had harmed and humiliated him and his people. Monty Jacobs tells us that "When he bows in rhythmic prayer, sitting next to Tubal, and racked with torment, he is at his richest."[53] Kortner, who seems to have created a Shylock play almost separate from the troupe's *Merchant*, was accused by critic Herbert Jhering of "insular" acting that undermined the idea of an ensemble.[54] But Kortner's self-centered strategy also functioned to mark Shylock as both the emotional center of the play and as an outsider to a world of warped and weird cubist-attired characters. Kortner left the ensemble he had helped to create after this one production.

A year later, in 1924, Kortner was invited by Reinhardt to play Shylock at the gala inaugural season of his new Theater in der Josefstadt in Vienna (Figure 26). It is unclear why Reinhardt would have offered Kortner a contract – which included subsequent work in Berlin – since Kortner's earlier stint as an actor at Reinhardt's Deutsches Theater

50 Monty Jacobs, "Shakespeare in Berlin 1922–1924," *Shakespeare Jahrbuch* 59/60 (1924), 242. Cited in Bonnell, *Shylock in Germany*, 76.

51 Franz Köppen, "Das Debut der 'Truppe,'" *Berliner Börsen-Zeitung* (September, 1923). Cited in Bonnell, *Shylock in Germany*, 76–77.

52 Ibid.

53 Jacobs, "Shakespeare in Berlin," 76.

54 Jhering, *Von Reinhardt bis Brecht*, 337.

FIGURE 26 Fritz Kortner as Shylock in the 1924 Vienna production, directed by Max Reinhardt Courtesy of IMAGNO, Vienna.

(1911–13) ended with Kortner breaking his contract and walking out. "Perhaps it was my powerful reputation that attracted him," Kortner muses in his memoirs.[55] Indeed, Kortner, who had a history of contentiousness and contract-breaking, would now do so again, after completing the twelve performances slated for *The Merchant* in Vienna. The rehearsals were difficult. Reinhardt wanted a more "humane" Shylock, and Kortner, as always, was unwilling to bend to a direction with which he disagreed. In fact, there could hardly have been two more diametrically opposed concepts of the play than those of Reinhardt and Kortner. Reinhardt, Kortner writes, filled everything with charm and ignored the ugly, money-grubbing underside of the Venetian characters. "There was a lot of delightful dancing in the performance," Kortner reports, "but the dance around the Golden Calf – which is the real subject of the play – was never staged."[56] In the end, Kortner's Shylock was a strained and dissonant element in the play. Viennese critic Alfred Polgar felt that Reinhardt "lets the Shylock tragedy get caught up and carried away by the whirl of the comedy. The tragedy only asserts itself thanks to the demonic element in the actor Kortner." Polgar contrasts Reinhardt's "frothy" staging with Kortner's depiction of Shylock "as an elemental being in search of psychological motivation." In a world of beauty and enchantment (Reinhardt's concept of the play), Kortner's specifically Jewish, primally enraged Shylock could not help but seem "foreign." "Around his wild instincts he builds a superstructure of emotional and rational justifications," Polgar continues in his review; "His Shylock has the truth of nature plus the higher artistic truth of the symbolic." What he lacks, Polgar feels, is "heart."[57] This verdict was sounded by other Viennese critics as well.[58] Kortner's lack of "paternal warmth," or charm – much beloved by the Viennese – was not only at odds with Reinhardt's vision of the play, it was also incompatible, as the Austrian Kortner would have known, with the expectation of his audience – expectations that Kortner, it seems, refused to gratify.

In an unpublished essay on Shylock, Kortner writes of his dissatisfaction with his pre-1927 interpretations of the role. "My performances, in my opinion, didn't express the ethical fervor of the character and the play; the volcanic eruption; the unarticulated *schrei* of rage at not

[55] Kortner, *Aller Tage Abend*, 294.

[56] Ibid., 296.

[57] Alfred Polgar, "Der Kaufmann von Venedig," *Die Weltbühne* 20:2 (1924), 150–51. Cited in Bonnell, *Shylock in Germany*, 78.

[58] Ibid.

being able to make oneself understood."[59] In his continuing search for the essence of the character, Kortner had arrived at the conclusion that Shylock's rage stemmed both from centuries of mistreatment by the Christians, but also from his – and his people's – failure to make themselves "seen" and understood as human by the Christians. This is what he wanted to communicate in his 1927 performance of the role. The fact that the Nazis were already looming on the horizon, he claims, concentrated his focus "and led me to deeply understand that Shylock felt a vehement need, an unspoken *ur*-need to make himself understood to the 'others.' "[60] The result, as is recorded by Hans-Jürgen Syberberg during their 1966 recording session, was more than a theatrical success: "It was a cognitive breakthrough, the eruption of a centuries-old *schrei*."[61]

Kortner's 1927 performance of Shylock took place at Jessner's Berlin State Theater, this time under the direction of Jürgen Fehling. The lovely and popular Elisabeth Bergner played Portia. Once again there were endless and vocal battles between the director and his star actor, "less polite than they had been with Reinhardt," Kortner tells us.[62] The difference in their concepts points to the difference between the two men: Fehling, a Christian – or, as Kortner puts it, "an Aryan with one grandmotherly flaw in his weave" – was eager to soften Shylock's character in order to minimize any anti-Semitic connotations in his production, especially at a time of growing fascist fervor and anti-Jewish propaganda. Goebbels' attacks on the Jews as defilers of German theater had increased during the second half of the 1920s and shortly before the premiere of the play on November 17, 1927, the Nazis had held a large congress in Nuremberg "where the party's racial theories and a call for a general purge of the 'German soul' received national attention."[63] Kortner, on the other hand, demanded that the production, *especially* now, expose Christian duplicity and their hatred of the Jews. He insisted on creating a Shylock who "having been treated inhumanly by the Christian world, deteriorates into inhumanity himself."

[59] The essay can be found at the Kortner Archive of the Akademie der Künste in Berlin. Cited by Critchfield, *From Shakespeare to Frisch*, 47; my translation.

[60] Ibid.

[61] DVD disc *Hans-Jürgen Syberberg, Die Fritz-Kortner-Filme* (Berlin: Alexander Verlag, 1965 and 1966), disc 1, 32:00–33:40.

[62] Kortner's quotes here can all be found in *Aller Tage Abend*, 295–97.

[63] Willam Grange, "Shakespeare in the Weimar Republic," *Theatre Survey* 28:2 (November, 1987), 96–97.

The Shylock that Kortner devised for this production is immediately segregated from the Christian world by his orthodoxy. More than in his previous portrayals, and despite his own secularity, Kortner built a carefully detailed religious Jew who wore side-locks in ringlets, pulled a prayer-shawl over his head when he prayed, murmured in Hebrew, and sang psalms.[64] "His world is one of woe and suffering," wrote Monty Jacobs, "but without self-pity." To Jacobs, Shylock was "a monarch of human suffering."

> He found the way to a majesty of pain, to a dignity of hatred, like scarcely a Shylock before him. At the end, wildness cried out of this Shylock one more time. He flung his phylactery to the ground; his hatred was towering.[65]

Viertel, who had directed Kortner in a *Merchant* production four years earlier, found his enhanced religiosity alarming, even uncanny.[66] Kortner's evocation of Jewish orthodoxy in Berlin of 1927, where most Jews were assimilated and many Germans anti-Semitic, was both a provocation and a refusal to accommodate. Indeed, this choice becomes even more interesting in light of Kortner's own extreme disassociation from Jewish ritual. His daughter, Marianne, remembers learning nothing about Judaism at home and claims that when she once asked her father what, in fact, made her a Jew, "after some thought, he responded by saying, 'Actually, only anti-Semitism.' "[67] Thirty years later, Kortner would write in his memoires that Shakespeare's play has nothing whatsoever to do with religious differences. "The play shows us neither Jews nor Christians, but rather persecutors and persecuted." At the time, religion meant race, and the implied connection between racism and fascism, between the persecuted Jewish race and the growing fascist movement in Germany "electrified both friend and foe." This Shylock, "unsparing and unyielding," in Kortner's own words, "frighteningly contemporary" and a huge success. The *Stürmer* (Julius Streicher's infamous Nazi tabloid), Kortner writes proudly, "spie Gift" – spat poison.[68]

[64] See Ernst Th. Sehrt, "Der Shylock Fritz Kortners," in *Deutsche Shakespeare-Gesellschaft West, Jahrbuch* 1973, 93–94, cited in Bonnell, *Shylock in Germany*, 81.

[65] Monty Jacobs, "Der Kaufmann von Venedig," *Vossische Zeitung*, November 18, 1927. Cited in Bonnell, *Shylock in Germany*, 81.

[66] Ludwigg, ed. *Fritz Kortner*, 40.

[67] Cited by Critchfield, *From Shakespeare to Frisch*, from an email by Marianne Brün-Kortner, September 23, 2003.

[68] Kortner's above quotes are from *Aller Abend Tage*, 296–97.

The liberal critics hailed Kortner's performance as riveting and as the best Shylock of his career. The eminent Walter Kerr wrote, famously, that:

There is in Germany no actor who can speak the lines of that bleeding man, if you prick him, as ravishingly, as simply, as urgently, as deeply lived as this chap [Kortner]. Totally unique – beyond Schildkraut, beyond Krauss, beyond Bassermann, beyond ... I've seen nobody to compare with him.[69]

Postwar Shylocks

Kortner was one of the first prominent German-Jewish exiles to return to Germany after the war. He arrived in Berlin from his Los Angeles refuge at the end of 1947 and would have returned earlier had the US authorities been quicker to approve his request. The exile community in the United States was shocked by Kortner's decision, as he documents in his 1948 semi-autobiographical play/screen-script *Der Ruf* (The Call, or, in its English advertising, *The Great Illusion*). The story of Professor Mauthner, (played by Kortner himself in the 1949 German film) who is "called" by his university to return from state-imposed exile in order to again practice his "calling" in Germany, is analogous to Kortner's inner "call" to return to the Berlin theater he had been forced to abandon and desperately wanted to reclaim. In 1945, Kortner wrote of his "passionate wish, under whatever conditions, to participate in the rebuilding of the German theater,"[70] which he would do as a director, and occasional actor. Kortner would once again become both eminent and controversial; his interpretations of, especially, classical texts would be acclaimed in postwar Germany, while his outspokenness on questions of lingering fascism and anti-Semitism would lead to repeated controversies. *The Merchant* was not among the texts he directed.

The history of postwar German Shylocks is, for obvious reasons, fraught and has been viewed by historians as diagnostic of Germany's attempt to "come to terms" with its National Socialist and, especially, genocidal recent past. Numerous scholarly articles and a number of books have been dedicated exclusively to the history of presentations of

[69] Published in *Berliner Tageblatt*, November 18, 1927, the day after the production's premiere, and reprinted in 1928 as the much publicized "Forward" to the monograph *Fritz Kortner*, a celebratory anthology edited by Heinz Ludwigg and containing 27 essays, 94 photos, and 12 drawings all dedicated to the mega-star.

[70] Letter from Kortner to his German colleagues, cited in Klaus Völker, *Fritz Kortner: Schauspieler und Regisseur* (Berlin: Edition Hentrich, 1987), 138.

Shylock in postwar Germany.[71] These histories often contrast Shylock with the postwar performances of that "other" stage Jew, *Nathan the Wise*, who was in fact the first iconic character recreated on the postwar Berlin stage. On September 7, 1945, four months after the official end of World War II, Berlin's historical Deutsches Theater re-opened with Lessing's play, directed by the well-known pre-war actor and director, Fritz Wisten (born Moritz Weinstein), a Jew who had recently been freed from Sachsenhausen concentration camp. Presented as an orientalist fantasy, with Paul Wegener as the dignified, humanist Jew, the production made no reference at all to the very immediate past.[72]

[71] Here are some of the articles and books published since 1945 about Shylock during the postwar period, arranged in reverse chronology:Zeno Ackermann and Sabine Schülting, eds. *Shylock nach dem Holocaust: Zur Geschichte einer deutschen Erinnerungsfigur*, Conditio Judaica 78 (Berlin: De Gruyter, 2011).Patric Blaser and Brigitte Dalinger, eds. *Shylock gestalten*, themed issue of *Maske und Kothurn: Internationale Beiträge zur Theater-, Film-, und Medienwissenschaft* 56:3 (2010).Sabine Schülting, "Remember Me: *The Merchant of Venice* on the Postwar German Stage," *Shakespeare Survey* 63 (2010), 290–300.Anat Feinberg, "Vom bösen Nathan und edlen Shylock: Überlegungen zur Konstruktion jüdischer Bühnenfiguren in Deutschland nach 1945," in *Literarischer Antisemitismus nach Auschwitz, eds.* Klaus-Michael Bogdal, Klaus Holz and Matthias N. Lorenz (Stuttgart: Metzler, 2007), 263–82.Arthur Horowitz, "Shylock after Auschwitz: The Merchant of Venice on the Post-Holocaust Stage – Subversion, Confrontation, and Provocation," *Journal for Cultural and Religious Theory* 8:3 (Fall, 2007), 7–19.Sabine Schülting, "'I am not bound to please thee with my answers': *The Merchant of Venice* on the Post-War German Stage," in *World-Wide Shakespeares: Local Appropriations in Film and Performance*, ed. Sonia Massai (London: Routledge, 2005), 65–71.Anat Feinberg, "The Janus-Faced Jew: Nathan and Shylock on the Post-War German Stage," in *Unlikely History: The Changing German-Jewish Symbiosis 1945–2000*, eds. Leslie Morris and Jack Zipes (New York: Palgrave, 2002), 233–50.Jörg Monschau, "Der Jude nach der Shoah: Zur Rezeption des *Kaufmann von Venedig* auf dem Theater der Bundesrepublik Deutschland und der Deutschen Demokratischen Republik 1945–1989" (PhD dissertation, Universität Heidelberg, 2002), available at www.ub.uni-heidelberg.de/archiv/3530/.Markus Moninger, "Auschwitz erinnern: *Merchant*-Inszenierungen im Nachkriegsdeutschland," in *Das Theater der Anderen: Alterität und Theater zwischen Antike und Gegenwart*, ed. Christopher Balme (Tübingen: Francke, 2001), 229–48.Wilhelm Hortmann, "Excursus: The Problem of Shylock – Zadek, Tabori and Others," in *Shakespeare on the German Stage: The Twentieth Century* (Cambridge: Cambridge University Press, 1998), 254–62.Hans-Peter Bayerdörfer, "Shylock auf der deutschen Bühne nach der Shoah," in *Shylock: Zinsverbot und Geldverleih in jüdischer und christlicher Tradition* ed. Johannes Heil and Bernd Wacker (Frankfurt am Main: Fink, 1997), 261–80.Dietrich Schwanitz *Der Shylock-Syndrom oder die Dramaturgie der Barbarei* (Frankfurt am Main: Eichborn, 1997).Sigrid Weigel, "Shylocks Wiederkehr: Die Verwandlung von Schuld in Schulden; oder: Zum symbolischen Tausch der Wiedergutmachung," *Zeitschrift für Deutsche Philologie* (special issue) 114 (1995), 3–22.Dietrich Schwanitz. *Shylock: Von Shakespeare bis zum Nürnberger Prozess* (Hamburg: Krämer, 1989).Maria Verch, "The Merchant of Venice on the German stage since 1945," *Theatre History Studies* 5 (1985), 84–93.

[72] See Feinberg, "The Janus-Faced Jew," 234.

Few important Shylocks can be noted on the German stage until the 1960s and none made an explosive impression until Kortner's appearance in a television version of the play in 1968. In his historical study of Shakespeare on the German stage, Wilhelm Hortmann notes that in the fifties and early sixties, "there was a predominance of noble Shylocks, half-brothers of Gotthold Ephraim Lessing's *Nathan the Wise*, near-innocent victims, more sinned against than sinning." Two examples of such Shylocks were Erich Ponto (in Stuttgart, 1955) and Ernst Deutsch (in Düsseldorf, 1957) whose profoundly good Shylocks, driven to extremes by their inhumane treatment at the hand of the Christians, came to be called "expiation Shylocks," who, arguably, offered their German audiences moral comfort and spiritual balm before any accounting of their crimes had actually taken place. Ernst Deutsch, originally from Prague, who began his career with Kortner in Hamburg, was a particularly handsome German Jew famous in the Weimar theater for his noble Nathans; in postwar Germany he was most closely associated with the new apologetic Shylocks. He repeated his Düsseldorf performance six years later, in 1963, for Erwin Piscator at the Freie Volksbühne in Berlin. There, "Shylock's nobility and control, but also his Old Testament sternness when demanding his revenge," writes Hortmann, "so impressed themselves on the public mind that it became difficult to think of the figure in any other terms."[73]

The unwritten taboo against performing Shylock "in any other terms" remained virtually unbroken in Germany until 1968, when Kortner appeared in the Austro-German television production, directed by Otto Schenk, as a distinctly unpleasant Shylock: bitter, insular, speaking in sing-song Yiddish intonations and with the expressive body gestures of an *Ostjude* (Figure 27). Kortner had appeared in dozens of films during his career and had often written and directed for the screen.[74] Thus, the seventy-six-year-old Kortner knew well how the camera recorded facial expression, gesture, and tone, and he used this knowledge to create a highly detailed outsider, scornful and wary of the Christians, deeply attached to his religion and his family, remorseless in his quest for revenge. Shylock's behavior, considered shocking at the time, became increasingly manic and deadly as his losses mounted and he treated his right to revenge as religiously sanctioned.[75] As a television film, this

[73] Wilhelm Hortmann, *Shakespeare on the German Stage: The Twentieth Century* (Cambridge: Cambridge University Press, 1998), 254–55.

[74] A filmography for Fritz Kortner can be found at www.imdb.com/name/nm0466776/.

[75] See Verch, "*The Merchant of Venice*," 88.

FIGURE 27 Fritz Kortner as Shylock in the trial scene of the 1968 Austro-German television version of *The Merchant of Venice*. Courtesy of IMAGNO, Vienna.

production reached a huge audience both in Austria and Germany and it provoked an extensive inner-German debate on whether "the Jew may again be [presented as] evil," – *Darf der Jude wieder böse sein?* This was the title of a television panel-discussion aired in 1969 in the wake of Kortner's upsetting performance. The panelists included author Günter Grass, philosopher Hartmut von Hentig, Rabbi Dr. Schereschewsky, and the theater director Peter Stein. The debate about the legitimate limits of Jewish representation in postwar Germany was probed for months by newspapers, radio, and television.

The astonishing impact of Schenk's production had more to do with its timing and context than with its intrinsic value. As a result of the televised trial of Eichmann in Jerusalem in 1961, followed by the extensively publicized 1963–65 Frankfurt Auschwitz trials, Auschwitz and the murder of Europe's Jews had become a topic of public discussion and education in Germany. The Frankfurt trials lasted for almost two years during which they received daily media coverage, which provided West Germans with their first comprehensive picture of the extermination machinery at Auschwitz. This coverage played an important role in politicizing West German youth. In 1965, Peter Weiss turned the Auschwitz trial's transcript into a powerful play/oratorio entitled *Die Ermittlung* (*The Investigation*). On October 19, 1965, in a nationally commemorative event, the play was simultaneously staged, or read aloud, in fifteen West and East German theaters, as well as at the Aldwych Theatre, London, where Peter Brook conducted a public reading. This was the mental landscape within which Kortner agreed to once again portray Shylock – a post-Shoah Shylock who refused to be sensitive to his audience. Kortner's Shylock came to be considered as the first "anti-Semitic" theatrical portrayal in postwar Germany; but far more offensive Shylocks were to follow. The compensatory mechanism of the "good" Shylock, at once acknowledging and assuaging guilt, would be further shattered by two young Jewish directors, Peter Zadek and George Tabori, who created grotesque Jewish caricatures and taunted their audiences by claiming to reflect in their work the suppressed, but still potent, German image of the Jew.

Zadek, a German Jew who, as a child, had escaped to England with his parents and who returned as an adult in 1958, directed a *Merchant* in 1972 in Stuttgart which presented the Jews as vile, malignant, and unscrupulous to the point of grotesquerie; a nightmare that seemed to emanate from the collective German subconscious. Zadek's Jew, as played by Hans Mahnke, was kin to the devil, shockingly similar to the hook-nosed, knife-wielding, grubby, grasping *Stürmer* caricature featured on the outsize poster that hung over the theater's main entrance. As Hortmann writes, Zadek's aim was to recreate the Shylock played by Werner Krauss for Reinhardt in 1921; but this time, the discomfort was meant to be felt by the Germans, not the Jews:

> Hans Mahnke as Shylock skipped, shuffled and slurched; rubbed hands, spread arms and raised shoulders in the typical manner associated with a bartering Eastern Jew, he glared and grimaced, leered and fawned, switched in a trice from submissive self-abasement to snarling anger and triumphant hooting: Zadek was certainly forcing actor and audience through embarrassing paces and emotions.[76]

The reaction to the production was outrage; the press was hostile and only a few critics saw the point of Zadek's "cryptic catharsis."[77] Zadek responded that his Jewishness entitled him to adopt such a tactic and, in any case, that he (like Kortner) found German philo-Semitism unbearable.

[76] Hortmann, *Shakespeare on the German Stage*, 257.
[77] Ibid.

It is interesting to note that eleven years earlier, in 1961, Zadek had already directed an outrageous *Merchant* in Ulm, with all the taboo-breaking distortions that later became his trademark. At the time, however, there was little reaction, perhaps because Ulm is smaller than Stuttgart. But I suspect that another force was at work: before 1965, "expiation Shylocks" – Shylock as punishment – did not strike a chord with the audience or press. The concept was seemingly out of context. After 1965, after the watershed of the two-year Auschwitz trials, it became possible to exhibit outrage by violating taboos, or, as critic Volker Canaris put it, "to provoke the public into examining its repressed prejudices."[78] In 1988 Zadek produced a third major *Merchant*, this time at the Vienna Burgtheater, and with very different tactics. Zadek presented Shylock – via actor Gerd Voss – as the image of a well-dressed Wall Street businessman, a tall, blond, and Aryan Jew physically indistinguishable from the other businessmen. As Sabine Schülting describes it:

> His defeat at the end of the play was the failure of a businessman, who accepted his bankruptcy without batting an eyelid. When at the end of the trial scene, Shylock dropped to his knees, this was not an act of submission. Rather than asking for mercy, he just bowed down in order to sign the cheque for Antonio ... In Zadek's interpretation, Christian society cannot ward off the "foreigners", since the boundary between the self and its others has become blurred. Shylock remains; he is a member of a society which has to come to terms with its prejudices.[79]

A second spectacular Shylock scandal was directed by a taboo-breaking Hungarian-born Jew whose father was murdered in Auschwitz, whose mother's escape from a similar fate was immortalized in his play *My Mother's Courage*, who worked for years in England and the United States, and who spent the last forty years of his life as a famous *provocateur* in the German and Austrian theater: George Tabori. Tabori's outrageous *Merchant* was staged in 1978 in a small room in the cellar of the Munich Kammerspiele. Despite Kortner, despite Zadek, Tabori's *Shylock Improvisations*, fully titled *I Would My Daughter Were Dead at My Foot, and the Jewels in her Ear (Ich wollte, meine Tochter läge tot zu meinen Füssen und hätte die Juwelen in den Ohren)* – took his audience by surprise. Like most Tabori plays, this is an ironic performance piece devised as a play-within-a-play. Ostensibly, it takes place in a concentration camp where a group of Jewish prisoners are forced to perform Shakespeare's *The Merchant* for the amusement of the guards. The acting

78 Volker Canaris, "Style and the Director," in *The German Theatre, ed.* Ronald Hayman, (London: Oswald Wolff, 1975), 273.

79 Schülting, "'I am not bound,'" 69.

was openly theatrical with beards and costumes added onstage. At one point the actors dispersed into the audience wearing false beards and crooked noses straight out of *Jud Süss*, openly taunting the spectators' sense of propriety. Puppets representing Jews were grotesquely mutilated onstage and when Shylock is baptized at the end of the play, he is made to stand in a pool of blood while his hair is spray-painted blond. The impact was traumatic: "Spectators wept (and had to be consoled)," writes Anat Feinberg, "expressing anguish and consternation."[80] This deviation from the canonical text is a great distance from Kortner's view of theater; but the fearless goading and taunting as a means to emotional purgation was very much in Kortner's spirit.

I end with Hans-Jürgen Syberberg's 1966 film *Fritz Kortner Records Monologues*, made before Schenk's television film but which became available on video, and then DVD, only some years later. The original goal of the meeting between the two men was to record Kortner reading monologues from his more famous 1920s' roles: Shylock, Richard III, Faust. Syberberg set the stage for these readings on the actual stage of the Munich Kammerspiele, where Kortner had directed many plays since the 1950s. The stage was now equipped with a table and chairs, facing an empty auditorium. Syberberg filmed sixteen hours of the onstage session and edited it down to two hours for the finished film. Included are a few attempts by Kortner to actually "play" the roles, and not merely read them.[81]

The importance of this project is the retrospective light it sheds on our understanding of Kortner's pre-1933 power as an actor; but it also teaches us the impossibility of "returning" to an older interpretation within a new context. The Kortner of this film is not the Kortner of legend or of the autobiography. He's old, tires easily, is agitated by the prospect of playing Shylock in light of his failing memory and depleted strength. Yet, after a few failed attempts, Kortner gets up and slips into Shylock's "Hath not a Jew eyes?" monologue, working his way into the

80 Feinberg, "The Janus-Faced Jew," 240.

81 This recording/film was part of a larger documentary project meant to memorialize the "traces" of performance artists (a film on Brecht and one on actress Romy Schneider were also made). The DVD, *Die Fritz-Kortner-Filme*, available through the Alexander Verlag, Berlin, includes two discs. The second shows Kortner directing a scene from Schiller's *Kabala und Liebe* (*Intrigue and Love*), also at the Munich Kammerspiele.

memory of performing the role forty years earlier. He builds slowly up to the turning point of the speech:

> and if you wrong us, shall we not
> revenge? If we are like you in the rest, we will
> resemble you in that. If a Jew wrong a Christian,
> what is his humility? Revenge. If a Christian
> wrong a Jew, what should his sufferance be by
> Christian example? Why, revenge. (3.1.52–56)

Kortner grows increasingly agitated by the logic of Shylock's argument. By the time he asks Salarino "If a Christian wrong a Jew, what should his sufferance be by Christian example?" Kortner, body bent, face thrust forward, has turned into that elemental, animalistic creature described in the reviews of the 1920s. "Nu," he growls at Solorino, waiting for an answer, "nuuu," he demands, cupping his ear, stooped, swaying dangerously, waving a fist, "*nuuuuuuu*?!" He answers the question himself in a heart-stopping wail: "*Rache!*" (revenge). Voice raising and cracking with emotion, Kortner repeats the cry – *Raaaaacheee!* – and suddenly we see not Shylock but the post-Holocaust Jew demanding impossible revenge. Some judge this return-with-a-difference to be Kortner's most shattering performance (it can be watched online).[82]

[82] The "Hath not a Jew eyes" section is available on YouTube, titled "Fritz Kortner spielt *Shylock*."

10

Evoking the Holocaust in George Tabori's Productions of *The Merchant of Venice*

Sabine Schülting

In his 1979 essay on his Munich adaptation of *The Merchant of Venice*, George Tabori addresses the complex issue of Holocaust remembrance. What is being remembered? What is – consciously or unconsciously – forgotten? How does the past haunt our imagination? Whereas memorial sites exhort us "never to forget," Tabori writes, the theater teaches us that "true remembrance" can only be sensual: "It is impossible to cope with the past without reliving it again with one's skin, nose, tongue, buttocks, feet and belly." Paradoxically, "we can only forget what we have truly remembered." He was eager to forget the murders, he admits – but without success, as he describes with a drastic metaphor that establishes an uncanny parallel between Shakespeare's *The Merchant of Venice* and the genocide of the Holocaust: once in a decade he felt "naked pounds of flesh" "burp up."[1]

George Tabori was born as György Tábori in Budapest in 1914 as the second son of the Jewish journalist Cornelius Tábori and his wife Elsa, née Ziffer.[2] The boys grew up as Catholics in the bilingual and cosmopolitan Tabori household (with Hungarian and German being spoken at home) and it was only at the age of seven that George became aware of his Jewish background.[3] Tabori writes that he only gradually acknowledged this heritage: "Fascism in Germany and Hungary prodded me to

1 George Tabori, "Es geht schon wieder los," in *Unterammergau oder Die guten Deutschen* (Frankfurt/Main: Suhrkamp, 1981), 200, 202, 201; my translation.

2 The biographical information on Tabori is largely based on the first chapter ("A Biographical Introduction") of Anat Feinberg's seminal monograph on Tabori: *Embodied Memory: The Theatre of George Tabori* (Iowa City: University of Iowa Press, 1999), 1–51

3 See ibid., 14.

realize that I am a Jew. At some point I accepted this role."[4] According to Anat Feinberg, it was particularly Tabori's "nearly twenty-year stay in Germany" from 1971 onwards that "did much to build his Jewish identity," although Tabori "resisted official affiliation" with Jewish communities.[5] After finishing school, he was sent to Germany where he spent eighteen months working as a trainee in hotels in Berlin and Dresden. In 1935 he returned to Budapest, but in the following year he joined his brother Paul in London. It was here that Tabori, who had grown up with Hungarian and German, learned English, the language in which he would write all of his works, including novels, plays, and essays. When the war began Tabori worked as a journalist for the United Press, the BBC, and the British Secret Service in Sofia, Istanbul, Jerusalem, and Cairo. He did not succeed in convincing his parents to leave Budapest and emigrate. His father was arrested for the first time in 1941; three years later, he was deported to Auschwitz where he was killed.[6] His mother was also arrested but amazingly managed to escape from Auschwitz by telling the guards that she possessed a pass issued by the Swedish Red Cross – the story on which Tabori based his *My Mother's Courage*. Tabori went back to London in 1943 as a journalist and writer, and was granted British citizenship in 1947. A literary agent brought him to the United States in 1947, where he first worked as a scriptwriter for MGM and Warner Brothers. He met Thomas Mann and Bertolt Brecht, to whose popularity in the United States he contributed with the production *Brecht on Brecht* (1961). It was allegedly when he helped Charles Laughton translate Brecht's *Galileo* into English that he eventually detected his fascination for the theater. Encounters with Elia Kazan and Lee Strasberg considerably influenced his work as a playwright and director. In 1966 he founded his first troupe, the Strolling Players; several more were to follow: the Theaterlabor in Bremen (1975–78), a group of young actors in Munich, and Der Kreis (1987–90) in Vienna. His return to Germany was initiated by an invitation in 1969 to stage his *The Cannibals* at the Schiller Theater in Berlin. He worked with various German troupes in the 1980s before moving to Vienna in 1986 where he enjoyed the peak of his career at the Burgtheater under the artistic management of Claus Peymann. Here he directed his much-acclaimed production of Shakespeare's *Othello* (1990) as well as his own plays, with *Mein Kampf* (1987) marking his greatest

[4] Tabori in an interview, quoted in ibid., 14.

[5] Ibid., 15.

[6] Many other family members, including uncles, aunts, and cousins, were murdered in the Holocaust.

success. In 1999 he moved to the Berliner Ensemble where he was to remain until his death on July 23, 2007.

George Tabori stressed that "to write about Auschwitz 'is an imperative.' "[7] In addition to his so-called Holocaust plays,[8] it was in particular Shakespeare's *The Merchant of Venice* that opened up a way of addressing the 'undigested' past through this precarious trope: "Historians speak of six million murders – a statement that is meaningless like rubbish. However, if one considers that it was six million times one murder, one returns to Shylock's pound of flesh."[9] Shylock's pound of flesh, which for Tabori metaphorically and metonymically evokes both the Holocaust and the long tradition of European anti-Semitic stereotypes, did indeed 'burp up' regularly in his works. Between the mid-1960s and 1989 he adapted Shakespeare's contentious comedy three times. His first production, *The Merchant of Venice (As Performed in Theresienstadt)* was shown at the Berkshire Theater Festival in Stockbridge, Massachusetts, in 1966. His next venture was his Munich adaptation of 1978, whose title quoted Shylock's lines in Act 3, Scene 1: *Ich wollte, meine Tochter läge tot zu meinen Füßen und hätte die Juwelen in den Ohren: Improvisationen über Shakespeares Shylock* (I would my daughter were dead at my foot and the jewels in her ear: Improvisations on Shakespeare's Shylock). Eleven years later, he returned to the play for the last time when he included a scene based on *The Merchant* in his *Verliebte und Verrückte* (Lovers and Lunatics, 1989) in Vienna. All three productions constituted radical deviations from the Shakespearean original. They placed Shylock at the center of attention and explored this problematic figure who for the last one hundred years has been realized alternately – and sometimes even in one and the same production – as an important Shakespearean character, as a stock figure of the stage, as an anti-Semitic stereotype, as a Jewish individual, and as a figure of memory.[10]

[7] Quoted in Feinberg, *Embodied Memory*, 199.

[8] The term refers to Tabori's *Variations on Shylock*, *The Cannibals*, *My Mother's Courage*, *Jubilee*, and *Mein Kampf*; see Feinberg, *Embodied Memory*, 195–262.

[9] Tabori, "Es geht schon wieder los," 204. My translation.

[10] Jan Assmann has coined the term "figure of memory" (*Gedächtnisfigur*) in order to describe the ways in which a society remembers or, rather, (re)constructs its history. Figures of memory are "sensualized ideas." These ideas can be represented by events, places, or persons, which are invested with a particular meaning and become part of the group's historical narrative. The term 'figure' stresses the specific conflation of image (or iconic form), concept (or meaning), and narrative form. Cf. Jan Assmann, *Das kulturelle Gedächtnis: Schrift, Erinnerung und politische Identität in frühen Hochkulturen* (Munich: C.H. Beck, 2002), 37–38.

Tabori's interventions did not merely address Shylock's problematical stage history, but first and foremost posed the question as to whether and how Shakespeare's Jewish moneylender can be realized on the post-Holocaust stage. They explored the tension between actor and role, as well as between stage and audience, stressing the difficulties in performing Shylock and seeing him being performed. In turn, they established a complex connection between Shylock, the story around the pound of flesh, and the Holocaust, so that the productions turned into exercises in cultural remembrance that thoroughly disconcerted audiences.

The Merchant of Venice (As Performed in Theresienstadt) (1966)

George Tabori's 1966 *Merchant* was one of five plays produced for the Berkshire Theater Festival at Stockbridge, Massachusetts, in 1966.[11] Tabori developed the unconfirmed story of Shakespeare's *The Merchant* being performed by prisoners in a concentration camp, presumably Auschwitz or Theresienstadt.[12] In his unpublished writings on the production, Tabori notes:

> I dont [sic] to this day know for certain if the play was ever done, or where, or by whom, and how, but the legends persists [sic], unconfirmed and hauntingas [sic] legends are. I've come across it for years. This spring, a Hungarian magaxine [sic] carried an item, suggesting that the play had been presented – at the command of the nazis – in Theresin, already famous for its performance of Verdi's Requiem. On the other hand, a Stockbridge artist has recently sent word that he knew the man who directed it in Auschwitz. Perhaps, there were several productions.[13]

The stage, which was completely bare except for a huge portrait of Hitler, represented a concentration camp where *The Merchant* was given for a Nazi audience. The idea was that the Jewish prisoner-actors had created their props and costumes with material available in the camp: dirty

[11] The other plays were Robinson Jeffers's *The Cretan Woman*; Murray Schisgal's *Fragments*; Thornton Wilder's *The Skin of our Teeth*; and Samuel Beckett's *Waiting for Godot*, see the festival website at: www.berkshiretheatregroup.org/about/history/history-of-btf.

[12] This idea was taken up in Tibor Egervari's adaptation, influenced by the writings of Primo Levi, *Le Marchand de Venise de Shakespeare à Auschwitz/The Merchant of Venice in Auschwitz* (1977–99; see www.canadianshakespeares.ca/a_auschwitz.cfm); and in Hanan Snir's 1995 production of *The Merchant* at the Weimar National Theater.

[13] George Tabori, "For B.H." (typescript), George Tabori-Archive, no. 3079, Akademie der Künste, Berlin, n.p.

blankets for the curtain, prisoners' garb, rags, paper, and twisted wire. This frame for Shakespeare's comedy provided the rationale for the maxim of purism and utmost concentration on the actor, which Tabori had adopted from Jerzy Grotowski's concept of the "poor theater."[14] The setting of the concentration camp furthermore contributed to the denaturalization of the characters on stage. Tabori writes that "according to photos, the prisoners often looked as if they were made-up, with very white faces, huge dark eyes, etc. The actors as they come in as prisoners should have an 'unnatural' look, a 'theatrical look.' "[15]

The Berkshire *Merchant* was obviously influenced by Peter Weiss's *Marat/Sade* (1963), "which had played in New York in the mid-1960s," as Michael Shapiro notes.[16] Like in Weiss's play, there was a constant shift between the two theatrical levels, between the frame story and the play-within-the-play, where the realization of Shakespeare's characters was thoroughly shaped by the identities of the prisoner-actors. And comparable to the inmates of the lunatic asylum in *Marat/Sade*, who manage to deviate from the director's production plans, the actors in Tabori's play also sought to make use of the limited leeway available to them. In particular, they were faced with the problem of how to perform a *Merchant* that would allow them to keep their dignity (or even defy the authority of their guards) while at the same time satisfying the Nazis. The group of prisoners was heterogeneous, consisting of "finks" and potential rebels.[17] The prisoner playing Portia (Viveca Lindfors, Tabori's second wife) appeared as the "victim of unspeakable sexual abuse within the camp" and spoke her lines "as if in a daze."[18] Some resisted their roles and the anti-Semitic lines they were supposed to speak so that, repeatedly, monologues and dialogues erupted into passion. Consequently there was always the danger of the production of the play-within-the-play going out of hand.[19] After all, the guards, who were constantly present on stage, wanted to see "their" interpretation of *The Merchant of Venice*, i.e., an

[14] Jerzy Grotowski, *Towards a Poor Theater* (New York: Simon & Schuster, 1968).

[15] George Tabori, "Notes on *The Merchant of Venice (as performed in Theresienstadt)*," George Tabori Archive, no. 3079, Akademie der Künste, Berlin, 2.

[16] Michael Shapiro, "*The Merchant of Venice* after the Holocaust, or Shakespearean Romantic Comedy Meets Auschwitz," *Cithara* 46 (2006), 15.

[17] George Tabori, "Programm Notes" (typescript), George Tabori-Archive, no. 3065, Akademie der Künste, Berlin, n.p.

[18] Arthur Horowitz, "Shylock after Auschwitz: *The Merchant of Venice* on the Post-Holocaust Stage – Subversion, Confrontation, and Provocation," *Journal for Cultural and Religious Theory* 8:3 (Fall 2007), 16.

[19] Tabori, "Programm Notes," n.p.

anti-Semitic play by a playwright whom the Germans had adopted as one of their classical authors: "Unser Shakespeare."[20]

With this interlacing of fictional levels, Tabori moved away from more conventional approaches to *The Merchant* that have been used to interpret Shakespeare's play as *either* anti-Semitic or critical of anti-Semitism. The metadramatic dimensions of Tabori's version not merely revealed the contradictions in Shakespeare's play and showed it to be principally open to both interpretations, but it also stressed that one and the same production, even one single line, can work on various levels, for the actors and for different audiences. In addition, in a move that was unprecedented in the United States of the 1960s, Tabori forced his audience to see Shakespeare's romantic comedy with the horror – through the prism of the Holocaust.[21] This was made shockingly clear from the opening scene, which "opened on a bare, raked stage, bare except for the body of a thin, naked dead man, lying stage center," as Viveca Lindfors recalls in her autobiography. "While a military orchestra joyfully plays 'Lili Marlene,' two men in prison clothes carry him out."[22] It was only after this frame was completed with the portrait of Hitler hung up in the background and the officers taking their seats that the play-within-the-play, Shakespeare's *The Merchant of Venice*, began. Tabori wanted spectators to imagine

> those stinking skeletons creating Venetian splendor out of what bloody rags and twisted wire; studying the text in the dead og night [sic], hesitating between the need to defy, to offend, to submit, to survive, and thus duscivering [sic] the key of the Janus-headed enigma. The paly [sic] seems to alternate between low farce and high tragedy between the mask and the real face, the world as it is and the illusion it would create of itself.[23]

The costumes, the actors with their 'shaved heads,' and also the *mise en scène* continuously reminded the audience of the frame that affected (and infected) both the grandeur of Venice and the fairy-tale world of Belmont. The bond was signed in a room resembling a steam-bath in a fitness studio, a "frightening reminder of the camp itself, and the unseen shower

[20] Ibid.

[21] See also Michael Shapiro, "Shylock, the Jew on Stage: Past and Present". *Shofar* 4:2 (1986), 1–11. Horowitz has even called Tabori's adaptation the "first Post-Holocaust conceptualization of *The Merchant of Venice*" (Horowitz, "Shylock after Auschwitz," 15) – not quite correctly, I would argue, since this ignores Ernst Deutsch's interpretation of the role of Shylock at Düsseldorf in 1957.

[22] Viveca Lindfors, *Viveka … Viveca: An Actress … A Woman* (New York: Everest House, 1981), 251. Lindfors incorrectly gives the title of the play as *The Merchant of Venice as Performed in Auschwitz*.

[23] Tabori, "For B.H.," n.p.

rooms somewhere outside, where people were being slaughtered,"[24] as an unidentified critic noted whose (unpublished) account of the production is among the material at the Berlin Tabori Archive.

So, in the Berkshire *Merchant* the audience were not allowed to sit back and reflect on what happened on stage.[25] They were drawn into the action and transformed into the Nazi audience for whom *The Merchant of Venice* was being staged by the prisoners. In this way Tabori tested the limits of what an audience was prepared to accept – while the very same problem was simultaneously being enacted on stage. The anonymous commentator stressed: "One could not choose not to be. A mere laugh became an act of oppression; an anti-semitic portrayal was of your doing; sympathy or tears was hypocritical."[26] In his comments on the play, the same critic interpreted the inclusion of the audience into the action as "revolutionary" for the time: by involving them into the event, their response could no longer be "a question of agreeing or disagreeing with an interpretation of the world." Instead, they were kept "literally in the theater."[27] The experiment seems to have been exceptionally effective – despite the conventional proscenium stage with which Tabori worked. The show "provoked violent reactions in the audience; some walked out, some talked out loud, some demanded their money back, great numbers seemed deeply moved."[28]

An even more radical conflation of actor and character and a more thorough dissolution of the boundary between stage and auditorium would characterize Tabori's Munich *Improvisations on Shakespeare's Shylock*. The 1966 production, however, was unique in that it revolved around the problem of how to direct and play Shylock's story as a Jew in

[24] Anon., typescript of an untitled and presumably unpublished article on Tabori's Berkshire *Merchant*, George Tabori-Archive, no. 3079, Akademie der Künste, Berlin, 13. In a note, the author refers to himself as "an outsider" (p. 25) who had interviewed Viveca Lindfors. Actually, there are close parallels between this article and the respective passages in Lindfors's autobiography (*Viveca ... Viveka*, 251–52), so that I assume that Lindfors used the article when she was writing the passage on the Berkshire *Merchant*.

[25] Despite his involvement in translations and productions of Bertolt Brecht's plays in the United States (see Feinberg, *Embodied Memory*, 22–25), Tabori never adopted Brecht's didactic approach to the theater but was rather influenced by Jerzy Grotowski's experimental theater. Iwona Ubermann discusses in detail the influences of Grotowski, Artaud, Brecht, and Strasberg on Tabori, focusing in particular on his Holocaust plays. See Iwona Ubermann, *Auschwitz im Theater der "Peinlichkeit": George Taboris Holocaust-Stücke im Rahmen der Theatergeschichte seit dem Ende der 60er Jahre* (Munich: Dissertationsverlag NG Kopierladen, 1995), 19–26.

[26] Anon., 8.

[27] Ibid., 3, 2.

[28] Ibid., 5.

a gentile society. And even more than Tabori's later responses to Shylock, the Berkshire *Merchant* sought to explore the possibilities Shakespeare's play offered for Jewish opposition to Nazism and anti-Semitism. In his notes, Tabori tied the legend of a *Merchant* production in a Nazi concentration camp to the experience of his father, who was among the group of artists and intellectuals arrested by the Nazis in Budapest in 1943 and "moved from camp to camp, from Szaboloczucca to Csepel to Kistarcsa and finally to Auschwitz."[29] For Tabori the idea that they might have rehearsed and staged a production of Shakespeare's *Merchant* suggested the possibility of resistance, even if the production was mandated by the Nazis. In his notes, he summarizes the concept behind the production as "defiance."[30] Yet these brief moments of defiance were shown to simultaneously evoke unimaginable suffering and invite further abuse, not least because of the onstage presence of the armed guards. In the scene entitled "The Marriage of Portia and Bassanio," it was suggested that the actors playing Shakespeare's romantic couple were indeed married "in real life." Any gesture of love or concern for each other was impossible in the daily life of the camp and would have been considered an act of resistance. So it was paradoxically the coercion to participate in the performance of *The Merchant of Venice* that "afforded them the opportunity to be together again and at the same time shames them because they are in front of hundreds of people." This was not just because of the public display of their love in front of the Nazis, but also because "the prisoner Portia has been raped by all the Nazi guards and everyone knows it."[31]

Comedy, farce, and tragedy were inextricably intertwined. Every scene was introduced by the clown Launcelot Gobbo, played by a black actor, who functioned as a stage manager of sorts and constructed an uncanny tension between distancing laughter and the inescapable horror of the action. Morocco was played as an imitation of Cassius Clay (aka Muhammad Ali), the famous African-American boxer, whereas another 'actor' decided "to play Aragon as a ranting and raving Hitler figure."[32] According to the reviews, Alan Epstein as Shylock was extremely funny, playing the moneylender as a "deliberately gross, slimy, and caricatured role." However, the audience's involuntary laughter was not innocent

[29] Tabori, "For B.H.," n.p. In his "Programm Notes" (p. 1) Tabori writes "The Historical Context: C.T. at Csepel."

[30] Tabori, "Programm Notes," 1.

[31] Anon., 18.

[32] Tabori, "Notes on *The Merchant*," 7.

and reminded them of their complicity in perpetuating this anti-Semitic cliché: "You see, he seemed to say, we Jews really are funny. But don't forget, you made us this way, we're doing it for you, so don't think you're superior to Antonio."[33]

The overlap of the two dramatic levels eventually led to a catastrophe in the plot when, in the trial scene, the prisoner-actor who had been forced to play Shylock with a long false nose and a pathetic wig made of red yarn was no longer willing to go along with the degrading show. He took off his wig and nose and ceased to speak in the "horrendous Yiddish accent" of the previous scenes. In his normal voice, he asked "What judgment shall I dread, doing no wrong?,"[34] thus using Shylock's very words to stand up to the Nazi terror although he knew that his resistance would lead to his certain death. While the other 'actors' tried to play down the 'revolt' and convince 'Shylock' to play along, he suddenly attacked the Nazi guard with the moneylender's knife. But before he could act out his revenge, he was shot. The play closed with the prisoner-actors silently carrying his corpse away.

Originally, Tabori had envisioned a different ending but, due to various problems during rehearsals, Arthur Penn took over the direction a few days before the premiere and changed the end.[35] He obviously preferred the melodramatic conclusion to the more radical perspective intended by Tabori, "in which the entire cast would perform a collective revolt, starting of course with Shylock's resistance, then followed by Portia … and finally spreading to most of the cast, crawling on their knees downstage towards the audience, kissing the floor."[36] According to Tabori's own notes on the play, this tableau would then have been

> a sort of farewell as if they knew they would all be arrested. Curtain calls: 1, the entire company with Shylock missing. 2, Shylock allowed to join them, all his teeth have been knocked out. 3, No actors, neat piles of clothes on the floor.[37]

[33] Anon., 14.

[34] Ibid., 13, 22.

[35] Ibid., 24, footnote.

[36] Ibid.

[37] Tabori, "Notes on *The Merchant*," 11. In her autobiographical memoir, Lindfors seems to recall only the original version. In her account, a German officer asks "the Jew, to … ask forgiveness." After a moment of excruciating tension, the prisoner-actor playing Shylock gets on his knees, but so do all the other inmates. "We slowly start to crawl toward the front, as did the inmates in the opening of the play. As we reach the edge of the stage there is a sudden blackout. When the lights slowly come up again, left on the stage are only piles of or clothes." (Lindfors, *Viveka … Viveca*, 252)

Improvisations on Shakespeare's Shylock (1978)

It took Tabori more than ten years to stage what he had intended to be the last image of the Berkshire *Merchant*: a pile of clothes on the floor, evoking the shocking pictures that were taken after the liberation of Auschwitz. In 1978 Tabori's *Improvisations on Shakespeare's Shylock*[38] were staged in a rehearsal room of the Kammerspiele in Munich, which offered seating for one hundred spectators. The performance began with the "Ballad of Shylock," a song based on a seventeenth-century text by Samuel Pepys, during which the actors, with their long false noses resembling caricatured Jews in the tradition of the Nazi weekly *Der Stürmer*, prowled through the audience. This scene was followed by a dumb show, in which puppets, wearing shabby clothes, each displaying a yellow star, and carrying suitcases, were violently 'tortured' and then destroyed, several of them with an electric drill. The broken parts – puppet arms, heads, or feet – were distributed as 'gifts' among the audience. The remaining pieces, together with the puppets' clothes, were thrown in a pile under the piano at the centre of the room, where a pool of blood was slowly spreading across the floor.

Tabori had returned to Germany in 1969 with a production of *The Cannibals* in Berlin – to great critical acclaim. "Ever since this return," Feinberg writes, "Tabori sought to approximate [the] enigma" of German-Jewish relations.[39] This is also true for *Improvisations*, which in addition showed clear influences from Tabori's years in Bremen between 1975 and 1978, where he had worked as the director of the Theaterlabor (theater laboratory) at the municipal theater. This phase of intense experimentations came to an end in 1978, when the new director of the theater, together with Bremen's senator of culture, disapproved of the unconventional character of the project. Public money was withdrawn and the work contracts of the actors not renewed. Tabori decided to move to Munich where the Kammerspiele offered him and six members of the old troupe a new home.[40]

Returning to Shakespeare's *The Merchant*, Tabori had originally intended to repeat the concept of his Berkshire production and include a

[38] I have already discussed Tabori's *Improvisations* elsewhere. See Sabine Schülting, "'I am not bound to please thee with my answers': *The Merchant of Venice* on the Post-War German Stage," in *World-Wide Shakespeares: Local Appropriations in Film and Performance*, ed. Sonia Massai (London: Routledge, 2005), 65–71; Sabine Schülting, "'Remember Me': Shylock on the Postwar German Stage," *Shakespeare Survey* 63 (2010), 290–300.

[39] Feinberg, *Embodied Memory*, 214.

[40] See ibid., 84–85.

play-within-the-play in which inmates of a concentration camp worked on a performance of Shakespeare's comedy. The whole event was meant to support this idea and Tabori had made arrangements to include the audience into this story. Anat Feinberg summarises the plan as follows:

> Spectators and actors would be bused from the theater to the railway station in Munich, escorted to the Venice-bound train by a Bavarian band. The journey – overtly paralleling the journey that ended in the gas chamber – would be disrupted when SS storm troopers took the passengers (actors included) by surprise, shoved them into groups, and stitched a yellow star on their coats. ... In Dachau [the site of a former concentration camp, close to Munich] trucks would transport the audience from the railway station to the camp site. The actors were to perform the play in the barracks under the permanently menacing presence of the guards. The audience would be taken back to Munich by buses, leaving behind the dim site and the lonely Shylock, only just baptized.[41]

A slightly revised plan envisaged Acts 1–3 to be played in the theater, and only the trial scene – after a bus ride that would have been interrupted by actors in Nazi costume abusing the passengers – to be staged in Dachau. However, the permission to perform in Dachau was declined, so the concept of the production had to be reconsidered. It was only then that Tabori decided to turn this *Merchant* into a series of improvisations on the figure of Shakespeare's Jewish moneylender, "an exhaustive investigation of Shylock, of 'Shylockism.'"[42] This decision implied the interweaving of the different temporal layers – early modern England, Nazi Germany, and late 1970s Germany – into an investigation of 500 years of Christian anti-Semitism. Despite this broad historical perspective, the performative exploration of the possibilities (or rather difficulties) of playing Shylock after the Holocaust was placed at the center of attention. In an interview published in the daily *Süddeutsche Zeitung* on November 17, 1978, two days before the premiere, Tabori explained that they did not want to offer "an interpretation in the sense of Kortner or Olivier," but something more radical:

> We almost exclusively have only young actors, and there is no Jew among them. So it was crucial how one can play a Jew; how one can play a Jewish girl (... because in this production, just as in Shakespeare's times, there are only male actors, also because men and women were separated in Dachau); and how one can play the experience of the concentration camp.[43]

[41] Ibid., 216–17.

[42] Ibid., 218.

[43] George Tabori, "Das Einmalige wiederholen: Gespräch mit George Tabori über sein Münchner Shylock-Projekt", *Süddeutsche Zeitung*, November 17, 1978. My translation.

Tabori had already addressed similar problems in his 1966 *Merchant*, but the perspective had shifted. While in 1966 the primary question was "How can a Jew play and direct Shylock?," the 1978 production asked "How can a gentile play Shylock and Jessica?" What links the two productions is their systematic metadramatic design, their focus on the actor, and their stress on the tension rather than the identification between actor and role. In 1966, Tabori had already sought to break with realistic acting through experiments with masks. He explains: "Their function would be to: (a) make a visual comment on the 'Jewish nose' and the non-Jewish nose; (b) create the effect at times of a uniform mass of people; (c) be used for the purposes of doubling, so that some actors can move from one character to another simply by changing noses."[44] The Munich *Merchant* radicalized this exploration of the Shylock figure and the particular interest in the actor playing Shylock.

The extensive documentation of the production, edited by Andrea Welker and Tina Berger, provides ample insight into the rehearsal period, which for the actors took the form of continuous approximations towards the role. Tabori is quoted as having said that he very much liked the German word for rehearsal, that is, *Probe*, based on the verb *(aus)probieren* (to try out). "The French term is '*répétition*,' that is, the repetition of something that has once been set."[45] Repetition and improvisation, as in jazz music, were two of the central ideas of the production. The scene (2.5) where Shylock takes his leave from Jessica, exhorting her to lock the doors and keep an eye on the house, was entitled "Four Father Scene."[46] It featured four Shylocks, all products of Jessica's fantasy: "a Jewish patriarch, a benevolent, a mythical and a poetical [father]."[47] During the rehearsals, the actors experimented with different versions of the scene. One version had Jessica lying under the piano with the four Shylocks running around her and speaking their lines to the piano accompaniment of Stanley Walden, who hammered out "torture music" with thimbles and a knife on the strings of the instrument.[48] Eventually Jessica cried "no" and attacked one of her "fathers." In a revision of the scene Tabori suggested that the four Shylocks either cry the name "Jessica" for one minute or

[44] Tabori, "Notes on *The Merchant*," 2.

[45] George Tabori, *Ich wollte meine Tochter läge tot zu meinen Füßen und hätte die Juwelen in den Ohren. Improvisationen über Shakespeare's Shylock*, eds. Andrea Welker and Tina Berger (München: Carl Hanser, 1979), 39 (my translation).

[46] Feinberg comments that "Jewish folk tradition refers to three biblical patriarchs and four matriarchs"; *Embodied Memory*, 221.

[47] Tabori, *Ich wollte ...*, 49.

[48] Ibid.

speak Shylock's text not in unison but with staggered entrances, as in a canon.[49] Another scene (3.1, which Tabori entitled "Tannhäuser Szene") was multiplied even more often and "best exemplif[ied] the jazz-like quality of the performance."[50] Shylock's outrage at Jessica's elopement was played thirteen times, by all thirteen actors in their individual interpretation, which transformed the scene alternately into slapstick, burlesque, tragedy, and so on. One actor expressed his grief in a low and subdued voice. Another maintained that Shylock's lamentation must have been louder so that he ran over the stage screaming and howling. A third actor was convinced that Shylock had spoken in dialect; a fourth imitated Fritz Kortner playing Shylock; a fifth transformed the scene into a musical.[51] By staging a variety of re-enactments rather than giving a single coherent interpretation of either scene or role, Tabori underscored the bewildering array of possibilities that Shakespeare's Shylock has represented for every actor and director since the Holocaust.

In this way, Tabori's *Improvisations on Shakespeare's Shylock* managed to avoid the pitfalls that have characterized quite a number of twentieth and twenty-first century interpretations of Shylock, including: attempts to read Shylock as *either* stereotype *or* psychologically coherent character; the short-circuiting from dramatic character not merely to 'real' human beings but also to whole ethnic groups; and the practice of cultural self-reflection through either identifying with or 'othering' Shylock. *Improvisations* instead can be said to have replaced the interest in the *figure* of Shylock through an exploration of the processes (and limits) of *figuration*. In this way, Tabori's experiments paralleled and even surpassed the iconoclastic approaches to Shylock and *The Merchant of Venice* of Peter Zadek, in whose 1972 Bochum production Shylock was played as an exaggeration of the anti-Semitic stereotype of the money-grabbing Jew, whereas he appeared as a businessman who was indistinguishable from his 'Christian' counterparts in Zadek's Vienna production (1988).

In recent years, the term 'figuration' has gained prominence in a number of disciplines, including literary, theater, and film studies; art history; and media studies. On the basis of, among others, Erich Auerbach's and Norbert Elias's understanding of the term,[52] figuration has been redefined

[49] Ibid., 49.

[50] Feinberg, *Embodied Memory*, 222.

[51] Georg Hensel, "Shakespeare, Jazz und Judenhaß: George Taboris Shylock-Improvisationen", *Frankfurter Allgemeine Zeitung*, November 23, 1978.

[52] See Erich Auerbach, "Figura," in *Scenes from the Drama of European Literature* (New York: Meridian, 1959), 29–53; Erich Auerbach, *Mimesis: The Representation of*

against the backdrop of poststructuralist challenges to a Cartesian understanding of the subject, taking into account the displacements of character in postmodern theater or performance art as well as current theories of performativity.[53] Figuration thus encompasses both the conditions and the processes of performing and receiving dramatic characters. It addresses such topics as the actor's bodily performance, the director's 'script,' audience expectations, theatrical conventions, and cultural discourses (e.g. of identity). In Tabori's *Improvisations*, the multiple figurations of Shylock included the reflection of the changing historical conditions of (de)constructing Shakespeare's Jewish moneylender and the demarcation of the *space of possibility*, in which this character can be actualized through the actor's bodily performance. This space is delineated by the director's 'script,' audience expectations, theatrical conventions, and, last but not least, cultural discourses, including the long tradition of anti-Semitism as well as forms of cultural remembrance (or forgetting) of the Holocaust. In *Improvisations*, the result resembled a cubist picture; a simultaneous deconstruction and multiplication of Shylock, who – in stark contrast to nearly all previous approaches to the character – was not played as a coherent, autonomous subject.

This multiplication of Shylocks was reinforced by the disjunction of linear time. In the eighteen scenes, the setting or frame of reference changed continuously. Some scenes, such as "Antonio ist traurig" (Antonio is sad), "Bassanio braucht Geld" (Bassanio needs money), or "Shylock macht ein Angebot" (Shylock makes an offer) were closely linked to the Shakespearean original which was played in the classical translation of Schlegel and Tieck. Other scenes, such as "KZ-Erzählung" (Concentration camp narrative) or "Kristallnacht" (Night of broken glass), used Shakespeare's characters or lines in order to evoke Nazi pogroms and genocide. Jessica's romantic elopement was transformed into the violence and aggression of *Kristallnacht*. In "Concentration camp narrative," Jessica (played by Siemen Rühaak) was transformed into a male homosexual prisoner in a concentration camp who described

Reality in Western Literature, trans. Willard R. Trask (Princeton, NJ: Princeton University Press, 1953); Norbert Elias, "Figuration," in *Grundbegriffe der Soziologie*, ed. Bernhard Schäfers (Stuttgart: Leske+Budrich, 2003), 88–91.

53 See e.g. Gottfried Boehm et al., eds. *Figur und Figuration: Studien zu Wahrnehmung und Wissen* (Munich: Fink, 2007); Atsuko Onuki and Thomas Petkar, eds. *Figuration – Defiguration: Beiträge zur transkulturellen Forschung* (Munich: Iudicium, 2006); Gabriele Brandstetter and Sibylle Peters, eds. *De figura: Rhetorik – Bewegung – Gestalt* (München: Fink, 2002); Bettina Brandl-Risi et al., eds. *Figuration: Beiträge zum Wandel der Betrachtung ästhetischer Gefüge* (Munich: Epodium-Verlag, 2000).

in detail the abuse and torture he had gone through. At no point, however, did the performance suggest historical realism. Rühaak's narrative was interrupted by the musician Stanley Walden, who addressed the audience with the question: "Do you believe this? It was well acted, but it is not true – he is an actor. Perhaps it used to be true, once, but how can we know? Who was in a concentration camp – probably none of us. Was anybody taking part? I'm grateful that I wasn't there either."[54]

Can a production of *Merchant* ever give truthful testimony to the dead? Tabori's *Improvisations* did not answer this question, but problematized the process of remembrance of the Holocaust via Shakespeare's Shylock as contradictory and inevitably inadequate. Rather than establishing a linear or causal relationship between the past and the present, *Improvisations* disrupted the present and offered uncanny glimpses of the past – from the anti-Semitism of Elizabethan England to the Holocaust. The perspective was always on the "maltreated, down-trodden, and persecuted victim ... with no trace of the bittersweet or black humor permeating so many of Tabori's so-called Holocaust plays,"[55] including his Berkshire *Merchant*. Not surprisingly, the Belmont plot was altogether abandoned.

In his approach to history and remembrance, Tabori's *Improvisations* can be compared to the philosophy of history that Walter Benjamin outlined in his essay, "Angelus Novus."[56] Benjamin's "Angel of History" represents an approach to history that is strictly differentiated from nineteenth-century historicism. The angel's "face is turned toward the past," where "he sees one single catastrophe which keeps piling wreckage and hurls it in front of his feet." He would like to stay and "make whole" what has been destroyed. But the storm of progress, blowing from Paradise, "irresistibly propels him into the future to which his back is turned, while the pile of debris before him grows skyward."[57] Like Benjamin's Angel, but lacking his Messianic vision, Tabori's adaptation forced the audience to look back and confront the catastrophe, albeit without hope for either redemption or hope. The juxtaposition of historical fragments could not be reconstructed into a coherent picture of the past, nor did it become meaningful as a teleological sequence. *Improvisations* only offered shocking recognitions, in which past and present coalesced.

[54] Tabori, *Ich wollte ...*, 52.
[55] Feinberg, *Embodied Memory*, 215.
[56] See also Schülting, "'Remember Me,'" 297.
[57] Walter Benjamin, "Theses on the Philosophy of History," in *Illuminations*, ed. Hannah Arendt, trans. Harry Zohn (New York: Schocken Books, 1969), 257–58.

In the words of Benjamin: "The true picture of the past flits by. The past can be seized only as an image which flashes up at the instant when it can be recognized and is never seen again."[58]

Improvisations, even more than Tabori's earlier project, sought to turn remembrance into a sensual and affective experience. During the rehearsals, Tabori once brought a pound of raw meat, which was meant to represent Shylock's bond, and asked the actors to touch it in order to 'feel' its materiality. Nor was the audience spared such disturbing experiences. Rather than offering them a play that triggered emotions like pity or sympathy[59] or demanded an intellectual response (as in Brechtian drama), Tabori made spectators experience the production corporeally by asking them to touch the puppets, assaulting them with anti-Semitic jokes as well as attacking their eardrums with the noise of drills, loud cries, and other cacophonous sounds, and assailing their eyes with images of debris and blood. Many spectators who had expected to see a sentimentalized *Merchant* rejected the production as "tasteless." In particular, they were put off when they were handed the savaged puppets. One theater critic saw them as metaphorical representations of the historical rupture caused by the Holocaust, that is, the literal cracks which in Tabori's *Improvisations* were no longer "papered over" but staged as a "menetekel"(as writing on the wall).[60]

In a comment on his production, Tabori called his multi-faceted Shylock a "*Peinlichkeit*," an embarrassment, since he confront(s) spectators with events they would rather forget. Tabori's "Theater der Peinlichkeit"[61] (theater of embarrassment) explored the relation between torture, physical pain, and embarrassment which is suggested by the German adjective *peinlich*. In an older (and now obsolete) sense *peinlich* (from *Pein* = pain) meant not so much 'embarrassing' as 'painful and agonizing,' in particular referring to the pain caused by torture and corporeal punishment, as well as the humiliation and the sense of personal violation. The term *peinlich* thus establishes a link between historical

[58] Ibid., 255.

[59] Brian Massumi in his introductory notes on *A Thousand Plateaus* differentiates between impersonal affects and emotions, the latter of which presuppose a subjectivity "having" them ("Notes on the Translation," in Gilles Deleuze and Félix Guattari, *A Thousand Plateaus: Capitalism and Schizophrenia*, trans. Brian Massumi (Minneapolis and London: University of Minnesota Press, 1987, xvi)).

[60] Michael Krüger, "Menschen-Spiele: Anmerkungen zum Münchner Shylock," *Theater heute* 2 (1979), 4. My translation.

[61] This term is borrowed from the title of Iwona Ubermann's study of Tabori's Holocaust plays: *Auschwitz im Theater der "Peinlichkeit."*

anti-Semitic violence (as well as the violence of both Shakespeare's play and Tabori's adaptation), the painful quality of remembering the past, and the affective impact of Tabori's production on its audience.

Lovers and Lunatics (1989)

In an article on *Lovers and Lunatics*, published in the Austrian daily *Der Standard* a day prior to the premiere on March 14, 1989 in the Theater in der Porzellangasse, Tabori was quoted with a remark on his *The Cannibals*: "Shakespeare explains the past, but he doesn't master it."[62] This motto aptly characterizes all of Tabori's responses to *The Merchant of Venice*, every one of them addressing the past, the problem of cultural and individual remembrance, and the role of the theater in this process, without eventually offering a coherent historical narrative.

Such purposeful incoherence is certainly evident in his six-hour collage of scenes from Shakespeare, *Lovers and Lunatics*, where the scene between Shylock and Portia represented Tabori's most radical reworking of material from Shakespeare's original text of *The Merchant of Venice*. He cut everything except for the trial scene and Shylock's "Hath not a Jew eyes" speech, and he refashioned Portia and Shylock, played, respectively, by Hildegard Schmahl (who was already in her late forties) and Tabori himself (aged seventy-five). Both partners and antagonists at the same time, they stood out in the series of lovers that were shown, among them Richard, the Duke of Gloucester, and Anne; Silvius, Phoebe, and Rosalind; Orsino and Viola/Cesario; Macbeth and Lady Macbeth; Troilus and Cressida; Petruchio and Katherine: "Portia and Shylock are two aging partners, worn out by the endless disputes and unable to resolve the differences between them. While she still hopes he will for once reveal his feelings and display a touch of human warmth, he maintains a cool aloofness and, no less embittered than she is, feels that 'she does not really listen to me.'"[63]

On an almost bare stage, which was surrounded by a U-shaped wooden platform in front of a brick wall, *Lovers and Lunatics* explored "the art of the impossible," as Tabori described the contradictions of love: its dreams, disenchantments, and cruelties.[64] The scene from *Merchant* was

[62] "Utopisches Illyrien und Pandämonium der Liebe: George Tabori über seine Entdeckungsreise durch Shakespeares Leidenschaften, Kulturpolitik und experimentelles Theater," *Der Standard*, March 13, 1989. My translation.

[63] Feinberg, *Embodied Memory*, 170; (Feinberg quotes Tabori here).

[64] George Tabori, "Betrachtungen über das Feigenblatt: Eine Expedition in den unergründlichen Kontinent Shakespeare," *Die Zeit* 22 (May 25, 1990). My translation.

the penultimate one in the collage, appearing between episodes from *Antony and Cleopatra* and *Romeo and Juliet.* When Shylock, at the end of the previous scene, entered the stage with a bloody dressing covering his left eye, the actors/characters on stage started to cough and make gestures as if to shoo away flies or disperse a bad smell. Only two actors remained on stage, sitting down next to each other: Shylock and 'Cleopatra,' who turned into 'Portia.' The scene started with Portia asking Solanio's question introducing Act 3, Scene 1: "Now, what news on the Rialto?" When Shylock reached the line in his famous monologue, "And if you wrong us, shall we not revenge?" (3.1.56), he drew out a pocket-knife but had to ask Portia to help him open it. Collaboration and mutual affection did not eliminate the tension between the two. Indeed, Portia visibly became more and more impatient, while Shylock remained obstinate, insisting on his bond, even when Portia drew down her dress and put Shylock's hand on her breast.

As in Tabori's previous approaches to Shylock, in this production actor and role also began to merge. During one rehearsal, for example, Tabori as Shylock suddenly exclaimed: "For the umpteenth time, Hildegard, how often do I have to tell you that I insist on my bond." That moment was singled out for comment by the critic for *Der Standard*: "Nobody who has survived Auschwitz can be tolerant; no, he won't listen to her questions, he won't react – and this is the worst one can do to someone."[65] Again the relation between perpetrators, bystanders, and survivors of the Holocaust, or between Germany and its Jewish population, surfaced. After Portia had spoken Shakespeare's lines indicting Shylock as an alien who intended to kill a Venetian, Shylock took off his hat and crumpled it in his hands, while suddenly experiencing a fit of coughing. He choked and collapsed on the stairs at the back of the stage – a drastic proof that he was, indeed, not well. When he sat up again, he had transformed into Romeo, who then spoke – first in English, then in German – the lines from Act 2, Scene 2 ("But soft, what light through yonder window breaks"). However, any hopes for innocent love were immediately dashed. In this production, Romeo and Juliet were not Shakespeare's young lovers but aging actors who, "senescent and disillusioned, [were] only play-acting the juvenile lovers, rehearsing the passionate heroes they [could] never really *be*."[66] Their Shakespearean love scene was overshadowed by the lack of communication, the violence, and the despair of the preceding

[65] "Utopisches Illyrien." My translation.
[66] Feinberg, *Embodied Memory*, 171.

episode from *The Merchant of Venice*, just as the cloth Romeo cried into was the same one Shylock had just used to polish his knife.

"What is the connection between *The Merchant of Venice* and *Romeo and Juliet?*," Tabori asked in an interview with Ursula Voss in 1989. "At first, everyone would say: nothing. But today, when we read it, the word 'hate' kept turning up, in both *Romeo and Juliet* and *The Merchant of Venice*. It is exciting to follow connections like this one and to unlock them."[67] For Tabori, the collage "opened up doors" to reveal new perspectives on Shakespeare and on the painful topics he dealt with in his plays. *Lovers and Lunatics* also addressed the question that had run through all of Tabori's responses to *The Merchant of Venice*, namely, the absolute indeterminacy of the character of Shylock: "in the crucial moment Shylock says that he doesn't want to explain why he demands the pound of flesh."[68] Tabori's improvisations on Shakespeare's *Merchant* did not supply an ultimate answer to Shylock's secret, nor did they provide a coherent interpretation of the play, of its most contentious character, or of the symbolic meaning of the uncanny pound of flesh. What they did offer were multiple and contradictory perspectives on the Shylock figure, and, most importantly, metadramatic reflections both on the task of playing Shylock and on the ways Shakespeare's play can evoke the memory of the Holocaust.

Throughout his work, Shakespeare exhibited an amazing ability to turn the most cruel things into fairy tales, Tabori stressed. He readily acknowledged such metamorphoses but insisted on seeing both ends, rather than settling for one: "I think it is wrong to see Shakespeare without the fairytale, but also to see Shakespeare without the horror."[69]

[67] Tabori in an interview with Ursula Voss, in *William Shakespeare: Verliebte und Verrückte – Eine Collage. Vienna: Theater Der Kreis*, 1989. 248.

[68] Ibid., 247.

[69] Ibid., 249.

11

The Merchant of Venice on the German Stage and the 1995 "Buchenwald" Production in Weimar

Gad Kaynar-Kissinger

Shylock as a Touchstone: *The Merchant of Venice* on the German Stage

From the Enlightenment to our own day, German-language productions of *The Merchant of Venice* have reflected the always problematic state of German-Jewish relations.[1] All German-language productions of *The Merchant of Venice*, along with their reception by German critics, reaffirm Elmar Goerden's contention that "Shylock ist ein Lakmustest für den Status deutsch-jüdischen Miteinanders" (Shylock is a touchstone for the state of German-Jewish coexistence).[2] This observation is profoundly and poignantly applicable to the Israeli director Hanan Snir's production of *The Merchant of Venice* at the Weimar National Theater (April, 1995), a hallucinatory and transgressive theatrical event for both spectators and participants, in which I served as one of the two Israeli dramaturges. The different motivations on the part of both the German theater and the Israeli team for mounting this production were, as we shall see, deeply influenced by the intricate critical reception history of *The Merchant of Venice* in the German theater.

A more recent German-language production of the play by Israeli director Avishai Milstein at the Theater Freiburg (March, 2011) sustains this problematic approach to *The Merchant of Venice*. Milstein's reading

[1] This research was supported by the Israel Science Foundation (grant no. 435/10).

[2] Elmar Goerden, "Der Andere: Fragmente einer Bühnengeschichte Shylocks im deutschen und englischen Theater des 18. und 19. Jahrhunderts," in *Theatrlaia Judaica*, vol. 7, ed. Hans-Peter Bayerdörfer (Tübingen: Niemeyer, 1992), 130. Unless otherwise indicated all the translations from German are mine.

seems to be in accord with our own globalized, capitalist, value-eroding *Zeitgeist*:

The spirits at the stock market of Venice are rather high. The merchants in their grey suits carry attaché cases, pig heads under their arms and a joyful "Morning!" on their lips. ... Shylock [Israeli actor Doron Tavori] stands out among these bored Venetians as a stranger, the Other. The fatal idea of Antonio's pound of flesh is nothing but a brilliant joke of Shylock's, invented on the spur of the moment. Otherness, the essential name of the game in this stage interpretation, is communicated linguistically. German is not the only language spoken on stage; Shylock speaks English, the international business language, and at times uses Hebrew and even Yiddish.[3]

But in spite of the director's contemporary multicultural concept, in which everyone on stage, not only the Jew, is a stranger and acts his part as one, the weight of history proves inescapable. Indeed, the production is permeated by recent history. "History in this constellation is also something like a pledge," asserts Annette Hoffmann,[4] a contemporary German theater critic, who notes the symbolic nature of a theatrical enterprise in which *The Merchant of Venice* is staged by an Israeli director in a German city with a cast that is quite atypical for such a theater. This symbolism, she argues, "overburdens the action on stage from the very beginning, and overshadows any other interpretive option that Milstein's rather conventional reading might have offered."[5]

The play's reception history on the German-speaking stage needs to be grounded in two general premises that profoundly affect the manner in which *The Merchant* has been interpreted, staged, and perceived in the German-speaking world. The elevated and "naturalized" position of Shakespeare in Germany goes back to the early eighteenth century when Germans became acquainted with his plays through English touring companies. The popularity of Shakespeare reached such heights that Gotthold Ephraim Lessing in his seventeenth *Literaturbrief* to Goethe, Herder, and Schiller, compared Shakespeare to German folk literature. Like Herder and Schiller, Goethe celebrated Shakespeare as a dramatist who deviated from oppressive Aristotelian and neo-Classicist rules, thus formally sustaining the politically activist agenda of the young writers who strove to liberate their nation from the oppression of the feudal

[3] Peter Michalzik, *Frankfurter Rundschau*, February 23, 2008.

[4] Annette Hoffman, www.nachtkritik.de/index.php?option=com_content&view=article&id=5412:der-kaufmann-von-venedig-navishai-milstein&catid=211:theater-freiburg, March 19, 2011.

[5] Ibid.

regime and puritanical middle-class morals. In 1771, Goethe organized a Shakespeare jubilee in Frankfurt and modeled his own *Götz From Berlichingen* on Shakespeare's use of structural fragmentation and multi-plots. Schiller took this practice a step further by combining the plot of *King Lear* with what he considered to be the unfettered and stormy spirit of Shakespeare for his own youthful and revolutionary play *Die Räuber* (The Robbers), which inspired the entire group of the *Sturm und Drang* (Storm and Stress) and early Romantic writers. Romantic criticism hailed Shakespeare for breaking artistic boundaries, and for revealing a chaotic, contradictory world as a counterpoint to the orderly, stable world of the bourgeoisie. Yet Shakespeare soon became more than a rallying point for a small, oppositional group of subversive writers. First translated into German in the late eighteenth century, Shakespeare's plays gradually began to be seen as expressing the German national *Geist* (spirit), even to the point of raising the question whether William Shakespeare was not truly *Wilhelm* Shakespeare. It was even suggested that Shakespeare possessed some sort of innate Germanness after the appearance, in the early nineteenth century, of the Shakespeare translations of Tieck and Schlegel, which were considered by many as surpassing the English originals in quality and clarity. In fact, the world's earliest Shakespeare Society is the German *Deutsche Shakespeare-Gesellschaft*, founded on the occasion of the Bard's 300th birthday in 1864, its headquarters located in Weimar, the symbolic cradle of German literary and dramatic culture. (As will be seen later, Snir's production of *The Merchant of Venice* in that town took on a special significance.)

Shakespeare retained his iconic status even during the Third Reich. The Nazis, who had their reservations about the humanist German classics, glorified Shakespeare as "Aryan," and shortly after Hitler's ascent to power in 1933, an official publication was issued with the title *Shakespeare – a German Writer*. Hitler himself had lifted the ban on Shakespeare's works, even as the rest of English drama was condemned by the Nazis after the outbreak of the war. Today, apart from being the most popular and most often produced foreign classical author in Germany, Shakespeare is celebrated in festivals such as the *Shakespeare's Tage* in Bochum, Neuss, and Weimar.

The reception history of *The Merchant of Venice* in Germany can be divided into two periods. In the first, which lasted until the end of the nineteenth century, the figure of Shylock was seen primarily through the lens of the star-actors who played the part, and the fact that some of them were Jewish became a central issue for predominantly Christian audiences. The second period, which persists albeit with modifications until today, is marked by the supremacy of the director's vision. It is characterized by a process that began with Max Reinhardt at the turn of the century and was particularly energized by the *Regietheater* (director's theater) tradition inaugurated by such brilliant directors as Peter Stein, Peter Zadek, Jürgen Flimm, and Hans-Michael Grüber in the 1970s. This period is also distinguished by the socio-political *Weltanschauung* of particular directors as well as by their theatrical aesthetics.

It is a history that started with the period of philo-Semitic Enlightenment and Jewish acculturation that began in the mid-eighteenth century with the Jewish emancipation (whose paragon was the philosopher Moses Mendelssohn ([1729–86]) and can be traced through the constantly shifting attitudes toward Jews in the nineteenth century, up to the anti-Semitic hostility at the turn of the twentieth century and the resentment toward the alleged Jewish cultural hegemony during the Weimar period. It also encompasses the persecution and annihilation of Jews during the Holocaust, as well as the positive portrayal of Shylock's figure on the German stages immediately after it, as will be henceforth shown.

In light of this layered history, the first part of this essay offers a re-examination of several key moments in the reception history of *The Merchant of Venice* in the German-speaking world.

Part I

Austria of the nineteenth century offers an excellent example for the reciprocal relations between the social position of Jews and the interpretation of Shylock on the German-speaking stage. Most historians maintain that there was an improvement in the condition of Jews under the rule of Emperor Josef II. After the 1848 revolution, however, there was an increase in anti-Semitic sentiment, especially at the end of the century, under the influence of Georg von Schönerer, an ardent German nationalist, and Karl Lueger (1844–1910), the notoriously anti-Semitic mayor of Vienna.[6] Consequently, in the first half of the nineteenth century Jews were generally presented on the Viennese stage in a positive

[6] Johann Hüttner, "Ich spiele 'König Philippe', 'Belisare', 'Shylöcke', 'alte Mööre': *Der Kaufmann von Venedig* im Wiener Theater des 19. Jahrhunderts," in Patric Blaser and Brigitte Dalinger, eds. *Shylock gestalten*, themed issue of *Maske und Kothurn: Internationale Beiträge zur Theater-, Film-, und Medienwissenschaft* 56:3 (2010), 103. See Chapter 9 in this volume.

light, despite undercurrents of "latent anti-Semitism" which would later become explicit.

In Germany, as in Austria, the popularity of Shylock must also be seen in relation to that of Lessing's Jew, the idealized *Nathan der Weise* (Nathan the Wise), who stands for tolerance and humanism, and for the fundamental commonality of all humanity and monotheistic religions. Theater scholar Hans-Peter Bayerdörfer contends that "*Nathan* became the master narrative of German Jewry with regard to its basic standards of acculturation and its cultural and religious aims," while "*Shylock* became the master narrative with regard to the history of Jewish exile in Europe before acculturation."[7] In other words, whereas Nathan *der Weise* (also: the one who acts wisely) accords with the Enlightenment's ideal of *Vernunft* (reason, rationality), Shylock is the paradigm of the zealous, separatist, and unflinching Jew of the late Middle Ages and early Renaissance, who proclaims his religio-ethnic uniqueness even if it is at the expense of intensifying his host-society's anti-Semitic sentiments.

Yet Bayerdörfer's acute observation concerning Nathan and Shylock as master-narratives requires some modification. For instance, during the Enlightenment period, from about the second half of the eighteenth to the middle of the nineteenth century, theatrical representation of Shylock could reflect the period's benevolent view of Jews, so long as the stage at large also offered a contrary pejorative viewpoint. Thus, we read that Friedrich Ludwig Schröder's (1744–1816) impersonation of Shylock in Hamburg in 1777 "was ... intended to challenge the traditional image of the ridiculous stage Jew of the German pre-Enlightenment wandering troupes,"[8] and was notably free of "any inkling of the collective Jewish dialect";[9] and that Johan Friedrich Fleck (1712–86), Berlin's first Shylock (National Theater, August, 1778), maintained "a dignified and aristocratic style" through the contrast with the "haggling-Jew Tubal."[10] At the same time, August Wilhelm Iffland (1759–1814) offered a comic interpretation of Shylock (Mannheim, 1783).[11] Iffland's approach, which made Shylock the typical blocking character of a romantic comedy, drew

[7] Hans-Peter Bayerdörfer, "Bringing Together Shylock and Nathan, or: Lessing's Dream," in *Jewish Theatre: Tradition in Transition and Intercultural Vistas*, ed. Ahuva Belkin (Tel Aviv: Assaph Book Series, 2008), 174.

[8] Ibid., 173.

[9] C.T. Costenoble, quoted in Goerden, "Der Andere," 134.

[10] Ibid., 135.

[11] Peter Kollek, *Bogumil Dawison. Ein deutscher Schauspieler: Ein Beitrag zurPhänomonologie und Typologie* (Kastellaun: Henn, 1978), 129, describes a similar strategy employed by Dawison, which was severely criticized.

on the tradition of the Wandering Jew figure, with his grotesque Jewish gestures, broadly comic Jewish jargon, and "typically Jewish" tricks of deception. Iffland thus emphasized the character's ludicrous, rather than evil, traits.[12] In his book, Iffland explains the motivation for this approach:

> The actor, who in his performance retains the repugnant character of his part … interests us as an artist if he clearly highlights the reason that incites the anger, the hatred, the paranoid obsession, the revenge in the performed persona. The spectator must at least be able to apprehend, why he, who appears before him as a villain, is so bad … Nobody exerts evil only in order to be evil. The first question of an actor, allotted the part of a vile person, is therefore – in what way – through what tendency, through what loss, grief, insult – did the character reach the point at which he acts thus and not otherwise.[13]

Schröder's and Fleck's tragic and dignified personification of Shylock on the one hand, and Iffland's and Dawison's low-comic portrayal on the other, constitute the two polar approaches to the role during the relatively philo-Semitic climate of the early nineteenth century, when, as Hüttner informs us, "Shylock belonged to the repertoire of almost all great character actors."[14] Audiences evidently admired the virtuoso aspects of performance, irrespective of the actor's interpretation, possibly because at the time Shylock did not yet evoke the grave thematic and ideological questions later associated with the character. Paradoxically, however, it was precisely this congenial atmosphere of acculturation and seeming indifference toward problems of anti-Semitism that in fact permitted actors to use stereotypical Jewish traits in representing Shylock as a bloodthirsty character dissociated from actual living Jews. Indeed, the Viennese Jewish community, embarrassed by such a blatantly theatricalized representation sought to prohibit productions of *The Merchant of Venice*.[15]

Alongside the comic representations of Shylock, the stage history of *The Merchant* during the first half of the nineteenth century includes several attempts to render the character more dignified, if not outright sympathetic. The most potent inspiration in this direction was Edmund Kean's historic 1814 interpretation of Shylock at the Drury Lane Theater,

[12] Ibid.

[13] A.W. Iffland, "Über Darstellung boshafter und intriganter Charactere auf der Bühne," in *Theorie der Schauspielkunst für ausübende Künstler und Kunstfreunde*, vol. 1 (Berlin: Neue Societäts-Verlags-Buchhandlung, 1815), 52–54.

[14] Hüttner, "Ich spiele," 100.

[15] Ibid., 101–2.

which was hailed for its tragic grandeur. Kean's performance had a deep impact on Heinrich Heine – the greatest German poet of the nineteenth century, of Jewish origins, who converted for utilitarian reasons, but never really gave up his Jewish identity, as reflected in his work – who felt that the actor had promoted Shylock to the rank of "tragic hero."[16] In his publication *Shakespeares Mädchen und Frauen* (1838) Heine described Shylock as a personification of "substantiated retaliation for unspeakable humiliation."[17]

In 1814, the same year Kean premiered as Shylock in London, Ludwig Devrient (1784–1832), Iffland's heir at the Royal Theater in Berlin, devised his own Shylock: he did not resort to Iffland's comic devices, nor did he lend the figure the tragic grandeur of Kean. Devrient played the part as a deeply wronged old man. Gershon Gershoni – one of the first Israeli theater historians, explains:

> Iffland emphasized the idiosyncratic Jewish nature, whereas Devrient embodied a specific and definite character within this framework of Jewish nature. The poignant and brilliant humor of the figure was entertaining in Iffland's presentation, but striking and annihilating according to Devrient. When Shylock-Iffland said: "I stand here on my bond", one could even smile, whereas Devrient, as he uttered these words, was frightful and shocking.[18]

In 1827, Carl Ludwig Costenoble (1769–1837), using a completely different register, played the character of Shylock as demonic, the epitome of pure Evil. In his diary, however, Costenoble insists that: "*Shylock ist mir Ausnahme der Regel*" (for me Shylock is an exception to the rule).[19] That is, through Shylock's viciousness he sought to indicate, *via negativa*, the virtuous, non-fiendish nature of actual Jews, explaining that, "the worst Jew in our times would at the most aspire to appropriate the money of his Christian most deadly adversary, but never to mangle his flesh."[20]

The second half of the nineteenth century was marked by rising anti-Semitism. In response, the role of Shylock, according to Goerden, took

[16] Heinrich Heine, "Kean als Shylock," in *Historisch-Kritische Gesamtausgabe*, vol. 12, part 1, ed. Manfred Windfuhr (Hamburg: Hoffmann und Campe, 1980), 487.

[17] Ibid., 117.

[18] Gershon K. Gershoni, *The World of the Theater: Great Actors and Their Creation* (Tel Aviv: Yavne, 1963), 43. Bayerdörfer furthermore maintains that "the dignified stage appearance created by Edmund Kean and his German followers endowed Shylock with the significance of the eternal victim, symbolizing the fate of European Jewry in the Diaspora." Bayerdörfer, "Bringing Together Shylock and Nathan," 174.

[19] Carl Ludwig Costenoble, *Tagebücher* (January 11, 1820) (Vienna: Collection of the National Library), quoted by Goerden, "Der Andere," 151.

[20] Ibid.

on "an increasing performative value that elevated it above the realm of a characteristic Jewish part," supposedly to avoid arousing further anti-Semitic sentiments. The part thus turned into a comic, melodramatic, or tragic tour de force, a challenge for outstanding actors, so that "the antagonists of Shylock are merely the other Shylocks [Bogumil Dawison, Carl Seydelmann, or Friedrich Mitterwurzer]"; and "humanization or demonization are as a matter of fact nothing more than two variants of the same aesthetic process."[21] Rendering Shylock a "star-vehicle" within the prevailing "actor-manager" system of theatrical organization resulted quite often in the cutting of Act 5, where the romantic plot lines are resolved when the lovers return to Belmont.

Shylock's exit at the conclusion of the trial scene of Act 4 provided the production with "a lively end" in Eugen Kilian's formulation;[22] and perhaps, from a Jewish perspective, deprived the gentiles of the final word. The 1874 guest performance in Berlin of *The Merchant of Venice* by Duke Georg II's Meiningen Troupe distanced itself from the anti-Semitic sentiments of the period by stressing the historical accuracy of costumes and sets. Hans-Peter Bayerdörfer pointedly critiqued the deliberately apolitical nature of such theatrically self-contained and self-referential strategies adopted by mainstream German-language theaters at the time of expanding anti-Semitism in the late nineteenth century as a way of avoiding a contentious political issue.

In the twentieth century, the tension between theatrical conceptualizations of *The Merchant of Venice* and relations between Jews and Germans came to a head. One reason for this tension can be attributed to the overwhelming prevalence of Jews in the German-speaking theater. Moreover, the boundary between the world of the play and the world of the playhouse became blurred when Shylock's part was performed, indeed, *incarnated*, by such Jewish actors as Rudolph Schildkraut, Alexander Granach, Fritz Kortner, or Ernst Deutsch. The "ghosting" effect of the actor's personal Jewish identity raises questions about the performer's body language – Shylock's "Gestus," to use a concept developed by Bertolt Brecht that refers to a physical gesture and epic delivery mode that usually reveals a socio-political attitude towards the dramatic character or situation. That is, one wonders whether the representation of Shylock by a Jewish actor is socio-typological, stereotyped, or individualized. Although directors are offstage and therefore unseen by spectators, similar questions about

[21] Goerden, "Der Andere," 155, 157.

[22] Eugen Kilian, "Nekrolog: Ernst Possart," *Shakespeare Jahrbuch* (1921), 85.

representations of the part are raised when the play is staged by a Jewish director such as Max Reinhardt, Fritz Kortner, Leopold Jessner, Peter Zadek, or George Tabori (who staged his own written adaptations of the play). In the case of both actors and directors, there is often a question of whether one is dealing with artists whose lives have been impacted by the impending, actual, or retrospective experience of the Holocaust.

In 1905 and again in 1913, Rudolph Schildkraut alternated in the part of Shylock with Albert Bassermann in Max Reinhardt's productions of the play (Figures 28 and 29). Whereas the gentile Bassermann accentuated the grotesque aspects of the character, Schildkraut, a Romanian Jew who belonged to the stratum of the *Ostjuden* (Eastern European Jews) who were looked down upon by both gentiles and German-Austrian Jews, portrayed a tortured Jew "who rises from his suffering to become a giant fit to execute that terrible revenge."[23] "Schildkraut's Shylock was the most Jewish Shylock of all," wrote one of the leading German critics of the early twentieth century, Julius Bab, himself a Jew. "He and his Shylock are entrenched in the deepest and simplest layer of Jewish life … As Portia [in the Court scene] reproaches him … he looks at this bunch of Venetian noblemen who betrayed him, and it is obvious that in his innermost being he re-experiences all the shame and disgrace, all the humiliation and degradation that they made him suffer … and he nods his head, this typically Jewish nod like no other, that means: And all these base types I have to treat humanely?"[24]

In the 1920s, Fritz Kortner acted Shylock in a production staged by Leopold Jessner, then in the vanguard of modern directing; Kortner employed a similar approach to Schildkraut's, albeit with a greater intellectual and oratorical flair, as reported by the critic Alfred Kerr. Notably, Jessner, Kortner, and Kerr (as well as Schildkraut) were all Jewish. "Kortner as Shylock," in Kerr's description, "is the hero of an eternal tragedy. [He is] an old man, initially more burdened with worries than with anger. Only in the depths of his consciousness lies concealed the insurmountable feeling of enraging injustice to which he has been relentlessly subjected … In the German theater there is no other actor who can express as he does those words about the man who bleeds when he is pricked."[25]

Schildkraut and Kortner dispensed not only with the comic and burlesque elements in Shylock but also with the tradition of motivating his revenge through national and personal suffering. They, along with

[23] Gershoni, *The World of the Theater*, 162.
[24] Julius Bab, quoted in ibid., 163–64.
[25] Alfred Kerr, quoted in ibid., 246.

FIGURE 28 Rudolf Schildkraut as Shylock in a production directed by Max Reinhardt, 1905.
Courtesy of the Theater Collection of the University of Cologne, Germany.

FIGURE 29 Albert Basserman as Shylock.
Courtesy of the Theater Collection of the University of Cologne, Germany.

Alexander Granach, influenced the interpretations of German-Jewish actors throughout the twentieth century. Granach, who acted what he called his "dream part" three times (Munich 1920, Berlin 1925, Kiev 1936), chose to end his autobiography, *Da geht Ein Mensch* (*There Goes an Actor* is the English title), published in 1945, with a paradoxical Nathan-like apology for Shylock's conception as "a victim and prosecutor of that society that spits on and persecutes him."[26]

> And one has to continue to act him thus until the artificial differences between us fall and disappear, and Man will recognize his fellow human being as his brother, and will love the other like himself and will do unto him nothing that he himself would not like to suffer.[27]

The recognition that seeing Shylock as a brother, according to Granach, was anathema to the Third Reich, might be a partial and insufficient explanation as to why so few productions of *The Merchant of Venice* were staged in Nazi Germany. As Wilhelm Hortmann contends: "*The Merchant of Venice* had always been a popular comedy. During the Nazi period there was a sharp drop in the number of performances. Whereas previously it had averaged twenty to thirty productions every year with about two hundred performances, after 1933 the average dropped to less than a third."[28] In fact the only production of the play in a major repertory theater was by Lothar Müthel, the director of the Viennese Burgtheater's (the national Austrian theater) production that premiered on May 15, 1944; namely, as late as almost precisely one year before the end of World War II.[29] This viciously anti-Semitic production had been initiated by Baldour von Schirach, the Nazi governor of Vienna, to celebrate the fact that the city was now "Judenrein."[30] Shylock's part was played by one of the stars of the Third Reich, Werner Krauss, who four years before acted one of the major parts in Veit Harlan's infamous propaganda movie *Jud Süss*, about a crooked, corrupt, and lecherous eighteenth-century Jewish financier of a prince, whose dire financial situation is exploited by Süss for opportunist gains. Despite the fact that

26 Alexander Granach, *Da geht ein Mensch: Roman eines Lebens* (München-Zürich: Piper, 1990), 417.

27 Ibid.

28 Wilhelm Hortmann, *Shakespeare on the German Stage* (Cambridge: Cambridge University Press, 1998), 134.

29 Ibid., 135.

30 Although it might very well be that this assertion has been generated by the claim of Müthel and Werner Krauss, who acted Shylock – as an attempt to purge themselves of the blame of serving the prevailing anti-Semitic ideology – that they acted under direct order from von Schirach. See ibid.

Krauss acted a rather "retrograde" part from an anti-Semitic viewpoint – that of the aged Rabbi Loew who reproaches Süss for his haughty behavior and opulent lifestyle, and warns that it could be his downfall, the affinity between the depth structures of the plots of *Jud Süss* and *The Merchant of Venice* – that is, the anti-Semitic pattern of a vile and vicious Jew, who becomes a victim of his own schemes – might explain why the popular Krauss was invited from Berlin to Vienna to act a part that he had already played several times before (quite apart from the enormous success of *Jud Süss* that made the association with *The Merchant of Venice* an excellent marketing booster). In one of the pre-war productions of the play, Krauss even acted the part under the Jewish mega-star director, Max Reinhardt, a fact that he used after the war to explain his willingness to participate in Müthel's outright racist production.

However, we are still faced with the major question: why was the Burgtheater's production the only "all-German," trans-regional attempt during the Third Reich to mount this distinctly anti-Semitic play – from the Nazi perspective anyway – on a Central-German stage (and even then – not in the capital of the Reich, Berlin!), despite its propagandistic exploitation, according to Bogusław Drewniak, on provincial stages and on the radio?[31] Was it because – as Hortmann suggests – "a sense of shame stopped most theatre managements from adding insult to injury,"[32] or because of the reluctance of directors to devise Shylock's part as a typical revolting caricature of a Jew in the style of the anti-Semitic weekly, *Der Stürmer*, thus suppressing the tragic, contemporaneous implications of Shylock's famous philo-Semitic and anti-racial monologues, since to interpret the part in this humane spirit might have endangered the lives of everybody involved in the production?[33] But then, why did an avowed Nazi like Baldur von Schirach, who had allegedly initiated the production, take it off after only thirty-two performances? Was it because the *Reichsdramaturg* office had problems with the match between Shylock's Jewish daughter, Jessica, and a Christian, which was considered a *Blutschande* (a race-defiling act) – a problem that had been "resolved" through a dramaturgical device, to the dissatisfaction of most German theater managers and artistic directors?[34] Was it because "Werner Krauss's lolloping and wildly gesticulating Shylock ... was not so much a fiend in human form as a pantomime

[31] Bogusław Drewniak, *Das Theater im NS-Staat: Szenarium deutscher Zeitgeschichte 1933–1945* (Düsseldorf: Droste Verlag, 1983), 251.

[32] Hortmann, *Shakespeare on the German* Stage, 134.

[33] Ibid., 135.

[34] Gerwin Strobl, *The Swastika and the Stage: German Theatre and Society, 1933–1945* (Cambridge: Cambridge University Press, 2007), 130.

villain," making the audience laugh instead of shudder?[35] Could it possibly be that the (in)famous Nazi star would risk his career and life in a sophisticated attempt, under the cover of the play's generic demarcation, to subvert the ideological tenets of the prestigious propaganda production? This seemingly far-fetched hypothesis is sustained by an anecdote recounted by Erwin Strobl: "Werner Krauss … starred in *Jud Süß* and gave a notoriously nasty interpretation of Shylock … Yet the same man had over several critical days escorted his [half-Jewish] friend Carl Zuckmayer around Berlin to protect him from misadventure; and when it became obvious that Zuckmayer was indeed in imminent danger of arrest by the Gestapo, Krauss insisted on accompanying him to the train to safety in Prague."[36] If my speculation is correct then we have here an even more extreme case than that of the famous Gründgens, who had his reservations about Nazi ideology, and even claimed that he saved Jews, yet collaborated with the regime for opportunist reasons.

The influence of Schildkraut, Kortner, and Granach was evident in postwar productions. In the 1950s and 1960s, Ernst Deutsch appeared as Shylock in Düsseldorf (1957, directed by Karlheinz Stroux) and Berlin (1963, directed by Erwin Piscator), putting an end to the controversy as to whether it was still proper to play *The Merchant* in Germany (Figure 30). According to Bayerdörfer, Deutsch was among the advocates of restaging "the traditional dual constellation of Nathan and Shylock."[37] In this regard, what Granach had decreed and partly realized Deutsch developed more fully, although with important differences inasmuch as between their interpretations lay the abyss of the Holocaust. Critic Georg Zivier commented on Deutsch's 1957 Shylock:

> Ernst Deutsch finally discarded all the Shylock images that I have seen on stage … He eliminated the comic elements of the play. Now he walks, burdened with all the suffering of his people, yet without self-pity, without resignation, unbroken in his obstinate hardness.[38]

These traits reappeared in Piscator's 1963 Berlin Volksbühne production: Zivier claimed that Deutsch's Shylock "towers above [his rival] even in his humiliation,"[39] thus rendering Act 5 superfluous. Overall, the outstanding feature in these descriptions seems to be their repudiation of the

[35] Ibid., 183.
[36] Ibid., 120.
[37] Bayerdörfer, "Bringing Together Shylock and Nathan," 178.
[38] Georg Zivier, *Ernst Deutsch und das deutsche Theater* (Berlin: Haude & Spenersche Verlagsbuchhandlung, n.d.), 106.
[39] Ibid., 107.

FIGURE 30 Ernst Deutch as Shylock, 1957.
Courtesy of the Theater Collection of the University of Cologne, Germany.

anti-Semitic physical and mental characteristics ascribed to the Jew in Nazi propaganda, to which audiences of the 1950s and 1960s had been exposed only one or two decades earlier.

Part II

Since the 1970s, such interpretive decisions have been discussed as the province not of the actor but rather of the director. Now, under the reign of the concept of *Regietheater*, plays are seen as raw materials to be ordered and shaped by the director according to his or her own creative vision. It has therefore become incumbent on the theater scholar to attend to the underlying conception of the production *in toto* rather than to such individual figures as Shylock. Accordingly, we must no longer detach the character of Shylock from its aesthetic context and we cannot analyze it as if it existed in a vacuum, but must articulate the director's vision of the play in its entirety.

An earlier strong director like Max Reinhardt seems in retrospect to have been reluctant to impose a definitive and comprehensive concept on the play, at least one that reflected his response to Shylock and his relation to Jewish historical and social reality. In his five productions of the play between 1905 and 1934, as noted by Erika Fischer-Lichte and Peter Marx, Reinhardt reduced Shylock's stature in favor of an overall opulent, synesthetic spectacle.[40] This self-imposed limitation may have reflected Reinhardt's sense of himself as an assimilated Jew in the pre-Nazi years. It is ironic that even in 1934, when Reinhardt, now a persecuted Jew, had to move his production to Venice, he still refrained from imposing a political concept on the production.

The pressure of history as well as the expanded role of the director were manifest in the 1972 Bochum production of *The Merchant of Venice* by the Jewish director Peter Zadek (1926–2009), one of the leading figures in the *Regietheater* movement, who together with Peter Stein revolutionized the stultified postwar German theater, and gained renown for his unconventionally conceptualized productions of Shakespeare, Chekhov, and Ibsen. His Bochum *Merchant* (one of the four productions of the play directed by Zadek) was informed by his vision of a highly intense and emotionally charged interaction between the Jewish moneylender and the

[40] Erika Fischer-Lichte, "Sinne und Sensationen. Wie Max Reinhardt Theater neu erfand," in *Max Reinhardt und das Deutsche Theater, eds.* Roland Koberg et al. (Berlin: Deutsches Theater, Henschel Verlag & authors, 2005), 21. Peter W. Mark, "Die drei Gesichter Shylocks. Zu Max Reinhardts Theater vor dem Hintergrund seiner jüdischen Herkunft," in *Max Reinhardt*, eds. Koberg et al., 51–59.

Venetians who surround him, or as one critic put it, between "the Jew Shylock and the prejudices that he triggers by serving them."[41] The gentiles were depicted as participants in a Venetian carnival, in which "the joyful masks relentlessly converted into grimaces of racist prejudice."[42] This approach was aimed, according to Bayerdörfer, at "what was at that time called a lenient and convenient philo-Semitism on the German side, including easy self-exculpation and *Bewältigung* [coping], a common post-Holocaust German term for the manner in which German society dealt with its Nazi past."[43]

George Tabori's collaborative adaptation *Improvisations on Shakespeare's Shylock* (1978) may define if not actually cross the line dividing high-concept direction and adaptation.[44] Tabori reduced the entire text of *The Merchant of Venice* to "Shylock's plot" and divided the roles in the Shylock scenes among the entire cast, instructing the actors to find their own Venetians and their own Shylocks, since, as Tabori explained, "we show what each of us has inside himself, we are the hangmen and the victims."[45] This dispersal of the Shylock figure – reincarnated collectively through the actors' bodies – coincided with Tabori's constant preoccupation with the processing of the Holocaust experience. The production was initially designed to be performed in a Dachau barrack, and the various performers in these Shylock scenes were instructed "to recall situations and memories of the concentration camp experiences and to bring these as close as possible to the audience."[46]

Tabori's version raises major questions regarding the representation of the gentile Venetians, Shylock's persecutors, and their relation to the implied spectators.[47] Are the actual German post-Holocaust spectators

[41] Volker Canaris, *Peter Zadek: Der Theatermann und Filmmacher* (München: Hanser, 1972), 174.

[42] Ibid., 51.

[43] Bayerdörfer, "Bringing Together Shylock and Nathan," 178–79.

[44] See Georg-Michael Schulz, "George Tabori und die Shoah," in *Theatralia Judaica (II): Nach der Shoah. Israelisch-deutsche Theaterbeziehungen seit 1949*, ed. Hans-Peter Bayerdörfer (Tübingen: Max Niemeyer Verlag, 1996), 161–62. See also, Chapter 10 in this volume by Sabine Schülting.

[45] Tabori, quoted in ibid., 162.

[46] Bayerdörfer, "Bringing Together Shylock and Nathan," 179.

[47] See Kenneth Gross, *Shylock is Shakespeare* (Chicago: University of Chicago Press, 2006), 1; Gad Kaynar, "The Actor as Performer of the Implied Spectator's Role," *Theatre Research International* 22:1 (Spring 1997), 49–62. The "implied spectator" denotes "the processed image … of the performance's addressee" which emerges from the rhetorical system of the theatrical text and expresses the attitude of the text towards the audience. This image is imposed through the dramatic and theatrical affective stimuli on the real individual spectator who comes to the performance and feels compelled to play the part of the implied spectator by reacting in accordance to these stimuli.

to be defined against their will as Shylock's enemies, and consequently as the counterparts of the anti-Semitic stage Venetians simply because of their recent historical heritage? Should not one draw a clear distinction between such an imposed spectator role and the spectators of the 1943 notorious Burgtheater Nazi production directed by Lothar Müthel, in which Werner Krauss as Shylock was jeered both by the audience and by the "Aryan" Venetians?

Indeed, Tabori's insistence that his implied spectators use the occasion of the play to examine their individual and collective roles in German-Jewish relations before, during, and after the Holocaust, makes this work a major precursor of Snir's 1995 Weimar production, the subject of the next section of this chapter. In the interest of full disclosure, the reader should be aware that I, an Israeli-Jew, served as one of the production's dramaturges.

The Merchant of Venice in Buchenwald: The Conception and the Concept

The rhetorical aim of Snir's Weimar production of 1995 was to extend the conflict that occurs within the world of the play to a conflict between the stage and its implied spectators. These spectators were rather naively defined by Snir and his Israeli production team as the offspring of German perpetrators, members of a generation now suffering from guilty consciences. The Israeli team regarded itself as avenging the Nazis' victims and believed that they were entitled to manipulate the German actors for their own purposes. While the production may have failed to achieve its rhetorical aim, it ranks high among adaptations of *The Merchant of Venice* for its bold use of the play as a vehicle for exploring one of the darkest chapters in Jewish and German history and its lingering social dynamics.

The theatrical project began sometime in 1994 when I received a telephone call from a friend, Günther Beelitz, a leading West German theater-manager who had emerged in the 1980s as an ardently philo-Semitic and pro-Israeli artist. Beelitz was the former *Intendant*, or General Manager, of the State Theater of Darmstadt, the Düsseldorf Playhouse, and the Bavarian State Theater in Munich. In the mid-1990s, after German unification, he had been "exiled" to the provincial, impoverished, and dysfunctional National Theater in Weimar in former East Germany. At the time, the dismal state of this theater was an anomaly in Germany's theater world. The country's decentralized and economically stable theatrical system boasts more than 700 state, municipal, and independent theaters (*Staatstheater*, *Stadttheater, Freie Gruppen*) across Germany, reflecting a law that entitles every township with a population of more than 50,000 inhabitants to a repertory theater, 90 percent of whose budget is supplied by the government. However, despite its depressed state, the Weimar theater was one of the most symbolically charged national emblems of Germany: it is located in the town of Goethe, Schiller, Wieland, and Herder, the cradle of humanist German Classicism, the birthplace of the Weimar Republic, and is the town where, because of its very national prestige, the Nazis had chosen to hold mass ceremonies. Weimar's status, which had been preserved throughout the communist regime, explains the attempt, ascribed to Beelitz by Bayerdörfer, to encourage Weimar and its theater to alter the attitude toward the Holocaust inculcated by the East German communist state, which paid more attention to the Nazis' murder of communists and socialists than to the annihilation of European Jews.[48]

Beelitz asked me to suggest an Israeli director to stage *The Merchant of Venice* in conjunction with the April 9, 1995 commemoration of the fiftieth anniversary of the liberation of the Buchenwald concentration camp, and invited me to serve as dramaturg for the production. The project was especially important and timely, he emphasized, because of the resurgence of xenophobic and anti-Semitic sentiments in German, especially East German, society. Unaware of this socio-political background and having at the time only a sketchy knowledge of the reception history of *The Merchant of Venice* in Germany, I thought Beelitz's request a bit strange. It also seemed an absurd proposition to several prominent Israeli directors I approached, some of whom considered it a cynical joke made in rather bad taste.

The proposal began to make sense only after Hanan Snir (b. 1943), a prominent Israeli director, agreed to take on the challenge. Trained at the Royal Shakespeare Company, Snir returned to Israel in the mid-1970s and directed plays at the Municipal Theater in Beer-Sheba, and at the Cameri Theatre and Habima, Israel's National Theater, both located in Tel Aviv. Among his productions were plays by Chekhov, Brecht, Pinter, and Strindberg, as well as plays by Israel's leading dramatists. Snir became one of the foremost Israeli stage directors primarily due to his

[48] Hans-Peter Bayerdörfer and Gad Kaynar, "'Jedem das Seine' oder Buchenwald in Weimar: Eine israelische Inszenierung des *Kaufmann von Venedig* zum fünfzigsten Jahrtag der Befreiung des Konzentrationslagers Buchenwald," in Blaser and Dalinger, *Shylock gestalten*, 37.

profound and hybrid reading of the classics, as well as because of his quite paradoxical approach of intermingling epic strategies such as withdrawal of the illusion-evoking "fourth wall," leaving the entire cast on stage throughout the performance as witnesses to scenes in which they do not participate, and psychodramatic techniques aimed at magnifying psychological credibility (Snir is a certified psychodramatic therapist, who pursues this profession alongside his theatrical career). Snir and I realized that producing *The Merchant of Venice* in Weimar, only six kilometers from the Buchenwald concentration camp, could force the German spectators, in Snir's words, "to re-encounter their suppressed guilt and hostility toward foreigners."[49] Weimar's close proximity to Buchenwald refutes the oft-repeated claim made by local inhabitants that they knew nothing of what was going on in the camp. Snir and I sought a way to somehow link Buchenwald with *The Merchant of Venice* in order to magnify what we believed was the inherent anti-Semitism of the play.[50] "Even if Shakespeare did not intend the play to be anti-Semitic," maintained Snir, "this does not alter the fact that today the play is racist and anti-Semitic."[51] We did not ponder this assumption any further, nor did we seriously question the conventional, structural, and generically conditioned interpretation of the play as a comedy, or the hypothetical reception modes of the real spectators. In short, we focused exclusively on our own rhetorical intentions, which were based, as far as Snir was concerned, on historically modified assumptions regarding the post-Holocaust German implied spectator.

We consequently opted for a metatheatrical framework which involved several planes of reality, namely a play-within-a-play within present-day German reality, set in the Officers' Club of the Buchenwald concentration camp, a locus that one might define as the perfect realization of Foucault's "Heterotopias of Deviation, namely those [places] in which individuals whose behavior is deviant in relation to the required mean or norm are placed."[52] Roni Toren, our Israeli set designer, reproduced this space naturalistically with all its grotesque details, including the cynical motto, originally inscribed on the camp's gate, *Jedem das Seine* (Everyone gets his due share). Shakespeare's play, set in Venice, the legendary European capital of

[49] Hanan Snir, *Program Notes on "The Merchant of Venice"* (Jerusalem: Israel Festival, 1996).

[50] Hermann Sinsheimer, *Shylock – The History of a Character* (New York: Citadel Press, 1964), 6.

[51] Snir, *Program Notes*.

[52] Michel Foucault, *Of Other Spaces*, available at http://foucault.info/documents/hetero Topia/foucault.heteroTopia.en.html.

commerce, art, and pleasure, and in the never-never land of Belmont, was now meant to intersect with the personal biographies of the actors and the implied spectators, primarily those of the older generation of Weimar's residents. Our *Merchant of Venice* was conceived as a play-within-a-play, a sort of amateur entertainment staged by the SS officers in honor of the birthday of the camp's commander, a ruthless victimizer who ironically would play the role of Antonio, Shylock's intended victim. The other "Aryan" Venetian roles would be played by a deliberately kinky all-male cast in order to foreground the prohibited latent homosexual inclinations of the SS. Jewish camp inmates were to play the roles of Shylock, Jessica, and Tubal.

Snir's approach resolved the endless controversy over whether the play is a romantic comedy, with the Jew as the blocking agent, or a tragedy, with a Jew as its tragic hero. By conceptualizing Shakespeare's *The Merchant of Venice* as performed by Nazi officers in a concentration camp, Snir transformed it into a deliberately simplistic melodrama in which the Venetians embodied by the SS brutes were the ultimate "bad" villains and the Jewish inmates the ultimate "good" victims. To answer the question that Kenneth Gross puts to Shylock: "What could you have been thinking? Given what you know of Venetian society, polity, and law, and of the Venetians' very particular malice toward you, what made you suppose that you would be allowed to take the life of a Christian merchant on open court?"[53] – one might answer that, indeed, as the "real" Jew, Shylock would not have stood a chance in a Venetian court. Yet in Snir's Manichean world, the fictionalized Shylock character, a Buchenwald inmate and thus the ultimate victim, would have obtained the implied spectator's approval in his demand to carry out to the letter the sanction against Antonio as stipulated in the contract for it would assert the "poetic justice" principle implicit in melodrama. This transformation to melodrama was most evident and enraging during the "Hath not a Jew eyes?" speech, in which, while Shylock presents his motives for his monstrous revenge scheme and asserts his likeness to Christians, Snir had him ridiculed, physically and verbally abused by the burlesque team of Salarino and Solanio, who hurled Shylock from one to the other, beat him up violently, threw him to the floor, trampled on his fallen skullcap, and then used it to play catch. Antonio's past harassment of Shylock, merely reported earlier in the play, is visually and experientially concretized, leaving the guilt-ridden German spectator no other choice but to

[53] Gross, *Shylock is Shakespeare*, p. 1.

support Shylock's planned revenge in keeping with the production's melodramatic spirit.

Snir further aggravated this painful situation for the implied spectator through the employment of his customary epic technique of keeping the temporarily non-participating actors seated on stage as witnesses, that is to say, as histrionic agents of the spectators who are now forced to assume the morally condemnable position of bystanders. Whereas the onstage "spectators," Nazi officers relishing the comic abuse of a Jewish villain, react according to the comic stylistic code, their counterparts in the auditorium, the real spectators, are compelled, perhaps in spite of themselves, to condemn their *Doppelgänger* on the stage and resist the aesthetic conventions of comedy.[54] The audience's moral plight was still further aggravated by Karl Merkatz's performance as a repulsive, stereotyped Shylock, a Shylock who greedily *jüdels* (makes stereotypical Jewish gestures with his fingers), and who, as Rüdiger Schap, the theater critic of the influential *Süddeutsche Zeitung*, keenly observed, appears exactly "as his murderers would like to see him: disheveled, abject, beastly, a mean, unchangeable skinflint."[55] This dual reception pattern was sustained throughout the show, through the simultaneous presence of the Venetian setting of Shakespeare's script and the Buchenwald camp's historical reality, such as when articles of Italian Renaissance clothing appeared draped over the SS club's furniture.

Dramaturgy and Performance

To heighten the audience's sense of disjunction, we decided to use Schlegel-Tieck's classical translation, a reminder of the romantic and humanist German culture that stood in eerie contrast to the barbaric environment of the production's reproduction of Buchenwald. The Buchenwald master-narrative began with the appearance of the melancholic camp commander as Antonio at the decadent party in his honor. The evening's entertainment would include erotic horseplay and a drag performance that included a transvestite parody by an SS officer of Zara Leander, the diva of the Third Reich, singing her most popular song *Die Nacht ist nicht allein zum schlafen da* (The night is not only for sleeping). This sarcastic and bawdy performance was a de-romanticizing counterbalance to *The Merchant*'s famous lyrical duet, "In such a night," and

[54] See e.g. Northrop Frye, "The Mythos of Spring: Comedy," in *Anatomy of Criticism: Four Essays* (Princeton: Princeton University Press, 1973), 163–86.

[55] Rüdiger Schap, "Der Kaufmann von Buchenwald," *Süddeutsche Zeitung*, April 11, 1995.

a cruel antithesis to the children's song that the inmates would soon be forced to sing. The framework of the Buchenwald master-narrative was further developed when the Jewish prisoners were brutally dragged up from the cellar through the stage's trap door, a sardonic allusion to the Elizabethan stage, where ghosts and devils, and other ungodly elements emerged from below. Once onstage, the Jews were ordered to undress and were threatened with a mock execution. They were then forced at gunpoint to perform their parts, whereupon the old actor, the "real" father of the inmate who plays Jessica and who had been designated to perform Shylock, now refused to do so. As he stood center stage, his eloquent, demeaning, and frail nakedness aroused an *a priori* and irreversible pathos-laden identification with the real and imaginary performer, and hence with Shylock as well (Figures 31 and 32). At his refusal to comply with the command to perform, the commandant threatened to shoot him, a threat that brought forth his daughter's pitiful (Yiddishized) outcry: "*Spiel, Tate, spiel!*" (Play, father, play!). Only then did he sing ... the Jewish *credo* anthem, "Ani ma'amin" (I believe). The jarring clash between this heart-rending interlude and the perversely entertaining drag show illustrates how Snir mixed seemingly arbitrarily and irreconcilable stylistic elements in order to make his audience squirm. Whereas the earlier German-speaking productions described generally followed simpler generic or stylistic guidelines, imaging Shylock either as low comic villain or tragic hero, Snir boldly conflated such alternatives, hoping that the resulting dissonance would make his spectators morally uncomfortable.

These metatheatrical devices were intended to underscore Nazi-Venetian malice and thereby to vindicate Shylock's original desire for revenge, which was seen as pre-dating his daughter's elopement. Many of these devices were used in later scenes originally conceived to illustrate the Jew's villainy, such as the moment in Act 1, Scene 3 when Shylock and Antonio agree on the terms of the loan. Here, Snir had Shylock driven onto the stage, blindfolded, and ruthlessly turned in a circle by Bassanio, in an obvious reference to the blindfolded figure of *Synagoga* in medieval anti-Jewish iconography. The moment is echoed in the scene in which Launcelot, characterized as a Nazified Shakespearean fool, misleads and torments his own blindfolded old father, thus turning both comic interludes into pseudo-Brechtian *Lehrstücke* (instructional pieces), as demonstrations of German moral depravity, just as Brecht's *The Measures Taken* and *He Who Said Yes; He Who Said No* were intended to teach Marxist lessons. When Shylock offered Antonio a friendly loan free of interest, the merchant/SS Commander responded by spitting into the Jew's extended

FIGURE 31 *The Merchant of Venice* at the Weimar National Theater, 1995. Courtesy of Hanan Snir.

FIGURE 32 *The Merchant of Venice* at the Weimar National Theater, 1995. Courtesy of Hanan Snir.

palm. By keeping his palm open for the rest of the scene, Shylock elicited the audience's mute approval for the terms of the bond, despite the inhumane stipulation that the collateral be a pound of Antonio's flesh.

In order to amplify the hatred and harassment of the Jews, we occasionally took liberties with Shakespeare's text. For instance, we decided that Jessica would be the victim of rape, an assault directed against both Shakespeare's Jewish character and the Jewish actress in the play-within-the-play, thereby blurring the boundaries between the dramatic and the historical spheres, and consequently between the world of the play and the world of the playhouse. We began the rape sequence by showing the virginal Jessica singing a Yiddish lullaby while seated in the attic of her father's house, represented by two tables set atop one another. When she eloped with her Christian beloved, Jessica disguised herself not in "the lovely garnish of a boy" (2.6.45), as Shakespeare puts it, but in a male SS uniform. Once she fled her home, she descended from the highest point on the stage to the lowest, crawling on all fours towards Lorenzo, as an expression of repugnant animalist passion, only to be violated by his friends, who are masked as werewolves. After her rape, the humiliated Jessica feigned a defensive madness in retaliation, cleaning the floor with a toothbrush in evocation of an early SA technique for humiliating Jews.

From this devastated and degraded state, she rose again to choose a martyr's death, provoking the Nazi director of the play-within-the-play to shoot her; she reappeared again, in the last act, as a specter who threatened to spoil a party celebrated by the ex-Nazi brutes, now recast as postwar Germans in bright civilian clothing of the 1960s.

A similar metatheatrical or intertextual linkage of Venice and Buchenwald was created for the Belmont scenes (Figure 33). This legendary, romantic locale seemed at first to be detached from the hate-filled cruelty of Venice. Snir confined the Belmont scenes to the inner stage of the Officers' Club, where the grace and charm associated with Shakespeare's Belmont was undercut by the sordid, campy play-within-a-play of a 1940s-style Nazi drag show. Amateurish and primitively designed, this ludicrous entertainment evoked artificial hilarity for the participants, while the actual spectators, aware of the wretched situation of the Jewish "actors," also took note of the saccharine, excessively romantic pseudo-feminine body language of the female figures, Portia's blond wig, Nerissa's *völkisch* (ethnic) braids, and the maid's *Heimat* (native land) dress. Nazi "Aryan" racism manifested itself in the casket scenes through racist parodies of the colonial African Morocco and the

FIGURE 33 *The Merchant of Venice* at the Weimar National Theater, 1995. Courtesy of Hanan Snir.

Far Eastern Aragon. Shakespeare's romantic Belmont seemed perverse and inappropriate in this murderous context.

In the fifth act, the Nazi era gave way to the "new" postwar Germany. Once again there is a birthday party for the commander, this one taking place some twenty years later. All the Nazi paraphernalia have disappeared. The space now reminded the 1995 spectators of a 1960s West German environment, though they might merely have been familiar with it as a phenomenological cultural image of a foregone era. Nevertheless, the stage still represented the Officers' Club in Buchenwald, and as such the undeletable presence of the past (both the Nazi past and the 1960s past) in the present of the fictional stage representation and the 1995 theatrical event. The birthday celebration also marked the birth of the "new," "other" Germany, ostensibly cleansed of its past sins. The representatives of this Germany were costumed in dazzling white outfits typical of the sixties symbolizing the attempt to *whitewash* their past crimes. Antonio was now a rich Venetian, no longer a concentration camp commander. Then memory intruded, as the past was reincarnated through the dead Shylock and Jessica, who at first went unnoticed. Jessica found her toothbrush, a metonymical proof of anti-Jewish atrocities, at the very same moment that Antonio received the letter which informed him that his ships had returned, teeming with merchandise. All the Venetians assembled on the inner stage, where the Belmont scenes had previously been performed, and which had now been transformed into a ship's upper deck, and the "ship" sailed away. The fictive play-within-a-play-within-a-play was finished, the back wall of the stage – namely, the *real* theater with the set parts that leaned against it – was exposed, and seemed to signify that we were back again in the "real", present world. Yet this real world was ironically nothing but the illusory world of the theater, thus signifying the imaginary, non-existent world of the "other" Germany.

Even in this situation, Antonio still emerged as the big winner, and the Jew appeared on stage, with his back to the audience, crouching, wearing the poor clothing of the dreary past. The power relations were clear: Antonio, on a high podium, towered over Shylock, still superior to the Jew. Shylock took off his hat, revealing a skullcap, a gesture that was both deferential to Antonio and insistent on his own Jewish identity. The theater general-manager, Günther Beelitz, had suggested that at this moment both would shake hands; Snir absolutely rejected the idea. In his view, there is no real reconciliation. In his ending, Shylock and Antonio stood frozen in the tableau of the towering Aryan and the abased Jew, glaring at each other, while the stage gradually went dark. The meaning was simple and unequivocal: Germany had indeed regained its position as a leading nation with economic power and diplomatic influence, but it was haunted by the spirits of the dead Jews, who symbolize the lurking bad conscience from which Germany cannot escape.

The Production Process

The tensions present in Shakespeare's *The Merchant of Venice* as well as in Snir's Buchenwald master-narrative were matched by the tense relations between the Israeli-Jewish production team and the cast of mostly young and uninformed East German actors. I personally felt such tension when I, as the dramaturge, tried to obtain information from the older actors about the SS hierarchy and military ranks, its uniforms and insignias. I also felt these tensions when I tried to cope with the actors' complaints that "our," namely, the Israelis', obsession with anti-Semitism was annoying them, or when they protested that the "villainous" Nazi figures were too flat and one-dimensional to permit audience identification. My job also included the curious task of lecturing to young communist-raised Germans about their own "brown" past, since what they knew about Jews boiled down to the ambiguous and ambivalent admonition that "a Jew is somebody you have to be nice to." Another extra-textual factor we had to confront was the need to redirect the economic bitterness of our poorly paid (and in many cases mediocre) actors toward its "correct" address – namely, the imaginary Jewish inmates – and away from us, "the others," now seen as the victims turned into victimizers. In the minds of our German actors, and perhaps some of our German spectators, we did not stage Shylock, we *were* Shylocks who used our economic and moral advantage to punish modern-day Germans for the sins of their fathers.

Thus, a dense web of updated experiences, analogous to German-Jewish relations during the Nazi regime infiltrated the theatrical project, and so supplied subtexts where our performers might find the motivations of their characters. The actors' hostility toward us as foreigners, as intercultural appropriators, as privileged Jews, and as theatrical authorities, who had arrived as avengers to demand from them personally, and through them from the audience, a pound of their flesh in recompense for their historical guilt, eventually manifested itself as the actual meaning of the production, as German reviewers did not fail to observe.[56] In its mildest form, this resentment was expressed through the easiest escape-hatch

[56] Cf. ibid.

for the German conscience, the question raised by the reviewer for *Die Welt*: "Why do we even try to discuss our problems through a problematic Shakespearean play?"[57]

Reception and Conclusion: The World of the Play, the World of the Playhouse, and the World beyond the Playhouse

One may conclude that the contaminated memory patterns of the Holocaust featured, mostly unintentionally, as the real protagonist of the double-edged stage allegory and theatrical event directed by Snir. The ghost of Shylock, drowned in our production by the Venetian Nazis during his baptism rite, only to reappear in the fifth act, was actually our own ghost. Memory was the pivotal element of the two correlative performances: the performance of a racist dramatic metaphor on the fictional theatrical stage; and the inverted personal enunciation of the Holocaust memory on the rehearsal stage.

An unforeseen result of our deliberate attempts to juggle the world of play, the theatrical production, and the surrounding culture was that the production and reception contexts almost completely overshadowed the dramatic script throughout the pre-production and rehearsal stages, and eventually made it too difficult for the Germans to digest. Yet, wasn't this the reception that we had hoped for? Whatever the case, the final product could have been regarded as the "colonization" of a Shakespearean text by producers attempting its theatrical realization as well as by implied spectators still in recovery from a historical nightmare.

There is a short but edifying epilogue to the story of *The Merchant of Venice* in Buchenwald/Weimar. In spring 1996 the production was invited to the Israel Festival in Jerusalem. There, to our surprise, our work received a chilly reception. One reason may be Holocaust-overload. For many Israeli spectators, the experience of the play evaporated into a sense of *déjà vu*, their sensibilities having been blunted by an excess of Holocaust commemoration and Holocaust theater. Another reason for the chilly reaction by Israeli spectators was their inability to decode a self-referential framework which relied so heavily on German history. Moreover, as Israelis and not Germans, they were unable to generate the receptive resistance which was built into the design of the production.

[57] L. Schmidt-Mühlich, "Wie der Jude bei der Taufe ertränkt wird." *Die Welt*, April 10, 1995.

Whereas German audiences resisted our efforts to make them confront their own guilt, Israeli audiences were simply baffled by the work's rhetorical aims, as well as its metatheatrical complexity. Still, despite its problematic reception, the 1995 Weimar production was undoubtedly a significant contribution to the body of work which represents a Jewish critique of Shakespeare's vexed and vexing text.

12

Recasting Shakespeare's Jew in Wesker's *Shylock*

Efraim Sicher

Postcolonial Shylocks

There have been a number of attempts by both gentiles and Jews to reclaim Shylock as the moral standard-bearer of Shakespeare's *The Merchant of Venice*, a noble figure who exposes the decadence, corruption, and hypocrisy of the Christians and the evil of capitalism. It is to Shylock that German Jews looked when their rights as human beings were being challenged by the Nuremberg laws which sought to return them to the pariah status of medieval society. We recall the essay of Heinrich Heine, himself an expert in jurisprudence, in which he reports overhearing an English lady at Kean's performance of Shylock cry out, "the poor man is wronged!"[1] The German legal expert Josef Kohler even made out a case for moral victory in Shylock's mockery of the law.[2] After Auschwitz, however, the fate of real Jews in the gas chambers made a mythical treatment of Shylock unacceptable since Nazi propaganda used the stereotype of the Jew to prepare for genocide, as the Hungarian-born director George Tabori reminded us when in 1966 he reimagined a performance of *The Merchant of Venice* ordered by the Nazis at Theresienstadt, an anti-Semitic production in which the real-life victim of the Nazis is killed in a Pirandello confusion of the play with its performance.[3] In Roman

[1] *The Works of Heinrich Heine*, trans. Charles G. Leland (London: Heinemann, 1906), 384–86.

[2] *Shakespeare vor dem Forum der Jurisprudenz* (Würzburg: Stahel, 1883).

[3] Tabori, whose father was murdered at Auschwitz, used another version of his rewriting of Shakespeare to break through the repression of memory of the Holocaust and taunt German audiences with the racial stereotypes used by the Nazis to conscript Hitler's "willing executioners." In 1978, this time in Munich, near the concentration camp of

Polanski's 2002 movie version of Władysław Szpilman's autobiography, *The Pianist* (1998), adapted by British dramatist Ronald Harwood, Shylock's lines about the humanity of the Jew ("Hath not a Jew ...") sound more like an accusation when declaimed, while waiting deportation to a concentration camp, on the Umschlagplatz in Nazi-occupied Warsaw.

Before looking at one Jewish post-Holocaust response to Shylock, by British playwright Arnold Wesker (1932–2016), we must first understand the background of postcolonial performances of Shakespeare's play in the United Kingdom. In this context, Wesker's response introduces a subaltern "writing back" to Shakespeare. Recent approaches to performance of *The Merchant of Venice* have appropriated Shakespeare for postcolonial agendas – and when, we might ask, is drama production not appropriation and interpretation? If Jan Kott recognized Shakespeare as "our contemporary," we might ask whether the canonic Shakespeare, handed down as fossilized cultural artifact to the television generation, might, indeed, not be our contemporary only. It is high time we recognized "foreign" readings of Shakespeare as equally legitimate.[4] In another sense, Shakespeare can be reread, along with other classics of the English cultural canon, in a postcolonial, transnational, multiethnic culture as an author only too aware that national identities were in flux as people of color – strangers and aliens – landed on English shores.[5]

Homi Bhabha's contention that reading from the margins deconstructs the Great Tradition and shows cultural difference and racial discrimination at the center of a racialized discourse (which determines received definitions of "culture") has been taken up by Bryan Cheyette to argue that the "jew" is at the center of constructions of national identity in English

Dachau, Tabori had thirteen inmates play Shylock in a collective acting out of Germany's guilt for anti-Semitism. In *The Cannibals* (1967) Tabori also underscored the potential for barbarism in Shakespeare by citing *King Lear* and *The Merchant of Venice* as referents when he posed the moral question of cutting and eating human flesh in order to survive in a concentration camp. See Chapter 10 in this volume and Jack Zipes, "George Tabori and the Jewish Question," *Theater* 29:2 (1999), 98–107.

4 For "foreign" readings of Shakespeare see Dennis Kennedy, ed. *Foreign Shakespeare: Contemporary Performance* (Cambridge: Cambridge University Press, 1993). Although the book touches on deconstruction of African types in *The Tempest*, its focus is fundamentally Eurocentric; the one chapter on non-European productions – in Japan – makes the salient point that Shakespeare was for a long time an agent of Westernization and cultural colonization in that country before being appropriated to local traditions and political discourse.

5 See e.g. Ania Loomba, *Shakespeare, Race, and Colonialism* (Oxford: Oxford University Press, 2002).

literature, not its margins.[6] The "jew" remained part and parcel of theological and literary discourses for nine hundred years, and "Shylock" passed into common usage in the English language as a pejorative term for a mean loan-shark, often an underworld figure ruthlessly demanding his pound of flesh (most recently in allegations of organ-trafficking). Far more sinister than Scrooge, Shylock was incorporated in a series of demonic stock types, such as that other merry old gentleman, Fagin, and remains inseparable from the cluster of hostile stereotypes that stick to the Jews in popular culture and the media. But what of real Jewish readers and audiences who might fail to recognize themselves in Shylock and are confronted with an offensive, defamatory image? To perform *The Merchant of Venice* in front of a Jewish audience one has to resist their taking offence at a racist stereotype, a difficulty American director Mark Lamos tackled by exploring judgmental valuation and portraying Shylock as a tragic figure who has lost his daughter and who is bound in an inhuman bond, just as Portia is bound by her father's will. Indeed, Portia fails to see the irony of her judgment of Shylock or of her words of dismissal to Morocco, an irony underscored by Nerissa who was cast as a black. Shylock's indictment rings true here: "You have among you many a purchased slave."[7] In *Cultural Politics – Queer Reading*, Alan Sinfield theorizes the Jewish reader as analogical to other "subordinated" minorities who read "queerly" and thus resist the social constructions of the Other by "hijacking" the text.[8] This is not entirely to the point, or at least not to mine, since hijacking is legitimized only in as much as it suits the ideology of the cultural critic for whom it inexplicably remains a metaphor despite the daily risk of violence that is opposed to all literary and humane value (vide the Rushdie sentence, IRA bombing, the attack on the World Trade Center, 7/7 in London, or the suicide bombers of the *Jihad islami)*. Terrorism is a term that has, in fact, been applied to the violence with which Shylock threatens the body of the Christian, yet it also challenges the normalcy and morality of official discourse.[9] It works as a performance of a real threat: in the Elizabethan context the danger could be imagined in the Lopez affair.

[6] Bryan Cheyette, *Constructions of "The Jew" in English Literature and Society: Racial Representations, 1875–1943* (Cambridge: Cambridge University Press, 1993), 3–4.

[7] Robert L. King, "Shylock after Auschwitz," *Chicago Review* 40:4 (1994), 59–67. For a discussion of Jewish Shylocks and Jewish directors on the English stage see Chapter 13 in this volume.

[8] Alan Sinfield, *Cultural Politics – Queer Reading* (London: Routledge, 1994), 1–12.

[9] Avraham Oz, *The Yoke of Love: Prophetic Riddles in The Merchant of Venice* (Newark: University of Delaware Press, 1995), 121–33.

However, directors of the play do not always, unfortunately, feel constrained to ward off criticism by toning down the anti-Semitism in the portrayal of Shylock, and some productions have used an anti-Semitic portrayal of Shylock to deliver a postcolonial message, as well as to externalize the audience's own latent prejudices. British director Bill Alexander's controversial production of *The Merchant of Venice* at the Royal Shakespeare Company in 1987, for example, presented Shylock as a projection of the Venetians' alienation and of their sexual, religious, and economic anxieties in order to work thorough the audience's own prejudiced responses. Unfortunately, the by now conventional use of Shylock to expose racism may work so well that the audience responds with credulity to the real possibility that the Jew is capable of drawing the knife and cutting Antonio's flesh, a dramatic realization of what remained for centuries a mythic fear and what today (in ignorance of real Judaism) can still be credited with belief. After Portia had announced her verdict, Antonio was readied for his crucifixion with the necessary surgical preparations for a ritual blood-letting, a ritual which would have been identified in the minds of Shakespeare's contemporaries with the Jew, although such an outrage is contrary to the spirit and law of Judaism.[10] To make the identification explicit, Shylock donned a prayer-shawl and started chanting actual Hebrew prayers, in fact part of the Passover service which was associated for centuries with an Easter-time blood libel. In James Bulman's account in his most excellent history of productions of *The Merchant of Venice*: "Like one possessed, he circled behind Antonio, cupped one hand around his victim's neck, and in the other raised a dagger above his head. The crowd screamed. Suddenly, as if by a miracle Portia cried 'Tarry a little' (4.1)." Antony Sher, a South African Jew who played Shylock in this production and who has been accused of self-hatred for his performance of a despicable, villainous concentration camp survivor in Peter Flannery's *Singer* (1989), described the experience as like being at a Nazi rally.[11] Unfortunately, the intention to

[10] For a *halakhic* ruling on the non-permissibility of contracting a loan on collateral of a pound of human flesh see Rabbi Shlomo Yosef Zevin, "Mishpat shaylok lefi hehalakha" [Shylock's trial according to Jewish law], in his *Leor hekhalakha: ba'iot vebiurim* [In light of Jewish law: Issues and clarifications] (Jerusalem: Bet Hillel, n.d.), 710–35.

[11] James Bulman, *The Merchant of Venice* (Shakespeare in Performance) (Manchester: Manchester University Press, 1991), 118–19. For two opposing responses to this production by Israeli scholars see Eli Rozik, "Aparteid bevenetsiya" [Apartheid in Venice], *Bamah* 111 (1988), 74–86, and Oz, *The Yoke of Love*, 194–96. Hebrew prayer and Jewish dress are not, however, an innovation in the play's stage history, but the almost compulsive spectatorship by members of the Jewish community and the compulsory performance by the Royal Shakespeare Company make the experience all the more a strange ritual reenactment of a myth.

goad audiences into realizing their own complicity in racism, particularly in apartheid and intolerance of Third World immigrants, highlighted the power behind the myth of the Other, not just the power behind racial, gender, and sexual constructions. In his survey of the Shylock legend, the critic John Gross spares few kind words for what he sees as a misguided attempt in this production to expose racist stereotypes and mutual violence, expressed most distastefully in a punk orgy of spitting at the Jew.[12] The Merchant of the play's title, Antonio, can be vindicated at the end and read legitimately both in Shakespearean and postmodern terms as a foil of Venetian patriarchal society, as well as (in a queer reading) an antipode for the underwriting of heterosexual binding in Belmont. However, the Jew is left no sympathy in either site of valuation, whether universalized as society's necessary scapegoat or as an allegorical reflection of Puritan or patriarchal attitudes (such as Shylock's wish to shut his house's ears to the carnival).

By translating the play's themes into Third World issues, Sher claimed it was not "about anti-Semitism only, but about racism more generally" – which had "applications to South Africa and the Middle East today."[13] Yet Sher's condemnation of the fanatic extremism of Shylock when pushed by the barbarism of Venice borders dangerously on vindication of the persecution it attacks. The way in which persecution has made Shylock intransigent and violent has made him a moral type that is identified with the stereotype of the Israeli aggressor, unwilling to turn the other cheek, demanding the pound of flesh, as seen in Charles Marowitz's *Variations on The Merchant of Venice* (1977), which conflates Shakespeare's play and Marlowe's *Jew of Malta* and portrays Shylock as an underground Jewish terrorist fighting the British Mandate in Palestine.[14] The play opens with Shylock's vengeful brooding over the terrorist attacks on British headquarters at the King David Hotel in Jerusalem, vowing, in the words of Barabas, to deal as treacherously with the Christians as they themselves do, entrusting his daughter Jessica (in the role of Abigail) with the seduction of Lorenzo. Only then do we pass on to Antonio, compromised by British policies, and to Bassanio, a cynical spendthrift, who represents

[12] John Gross, *Shylock: Four Hundred Years in the Life of a Legend* (London: Vintage, 1994), 306–7. The book was first published as *Shylock: A Legend and its Legacy* (New York: Simon & Schuster, 1992).

[13] Cited in Gross, *Shylock*, 307.

[14] Charles Marowitz, *The Marowitz Shakespeare* (London: Marion Boyars, 1978), 226–83. For a discussion of Marowitz's adaptation, see James C. Bulman, "On Being Unfaithful to Shakespeare: Miller, Marowitz, and Wesker," *Haifa University Studies in Jewish Theatre and Drama* 2 (1996), 64–68; Gross, *Shylock*, 309.

British hypocrisy and anti-Semitic prejudice. Marowitz stages a Brechtian presentation of a cultural materialist critique of the institutionalization of power, in which Antonio plays Ernest Bevin against Shylock the vindictive (and in some ways vindicated) Zionist who actually does carry out Sinfield's terrorist act. Shylock's speech, "Hath not a Jew eyes ...," closes the play by turning the trial on its head as the Jew has his revenge on his persecutors in a terrorist attack on the British.

Such appropriation of Shylock for a political agenda has become commonplace, since, as Marowitz puts it, Shakespeare is merely the "sperm bank" that can spawn modern productions which update the ideology in the director's image – and the director is free to rewrite the play in a new interpretation, just as Shakespeare was pillaging and "raping" his sources.[15] Marowitz explains that anyone has squatter's rights to Shakespeare's plays and they are ripe for reconstruction according to contemporary needs, though he distinguishes between adaptations and autonomous cinematic or dramatic re-workings of themes taken out of Shakespeare's plays in new contexts, which nevertheless relate to the original text, such as Edward Bond's *Lear*, or Tom Stoppard's *Rosencrantz and Guildenstern Are Dead*.[16] Only academic purists, he reasons, have any interest in defending Shakespeare against adaptation and reinterpretation. To divorce Shakespeare's play from a contemporary audience's consciousness of Jewish history – the Holocaust and the Arab–Israel conflict – is to reduce it to fairy tale, just as Othello cannot be perceived without American slavery or Sharpeville, even though Shakespeare could have had no knowledge of these events. Marowitz's own intrusion into the text through collage produces, however, a variation, not an adaptation. Marowitz was determined to undo the injustice done to Shylock in the trial scene in his humiliation, forcible conversion, disenfranchisement, and stripping of his property. He therefore had to devise a situation in which the moral positions of Shylock and Antonio were reversed and the Jew could emerge as victorious over British imperialism and racism.[17]

[15] Marowitz quoted in Bulman, "On Being Unfaithful to Shakespeare," 60; Charles Marowitz, *Recycling Shakespeare* (New York and Houndmills: Macmillan, 1991), 14–15.

[16] Marowitz, *Recycling Shakespeare*, 9. See Ruby Cohn's eclectic summary of leftist critiques of English society through Shakespeare adaptations which includes discussion of Wesker, "Shakespeare Left," *Theatre Journal* 40 (1988), 48–60; Michael Scott, *Shakespeare and the Modern Dramatist: Contemporary Interpretations of Shakespeare* (London: Macmillan, 1989); Alan Sinfield, "Making Space: Appropriation and Confrontation in Recent British Plays," in *The Shakespeare Myth*, ed. Graham Holderness (Manchester: Manchester University Press, 1988), 128–44.

[17] Marowitz, *Recycling Shakespeare*, 24–27.

Moreover, if the theological interpretation of the play as a debate between Christianity and Judaism is admitted, Shylock's symbolic crucifixion of the Christian can legitimately be reworked into an eye-for-an-eye castration of the Jew's persecutor.[18]

The question of "what to do with Shylock" is one with which Philip Roth's *Operation Shylock* (1993) consciously plays mischief, though the novel comes, I believe, to no serious conclusions beyond a postmodern playing with self-invention and cultural constructions. Casting John Ivan Demjanjuk in the role of the crucified Jew on trial by Shylock is not a helpful way to solve the Diaspora Jew's split loyalty, divided not between Israel and America, but between his identification with Israel and his concern for Israel's treatment of Palestinian Arabs, between his self-hatred as a Jew and his defiance of his stereotyped identity as Shylock, a villainy which he plays out, "and it shall go hard but I will better the instruction" (3.1). And yet, though he accepts (albeit unwillingly) the 3,000 ducats from the Mossad for spying on Arafat, he resists playing out Shylock's vengefulness.

"Writing Back" to Shakespeare

What to do with Shylock poses an insoluble dilemma for producers, many of whom sidestep the difficulty by staging *The Merchant of Venice* as a comedy or neutralize the Jew's role in the play, but for British authors who are Jewish and claim Shakespeare's heritage as their own it is a particularly difficult barrier, and any corrective must of necessity be also a claim for cultural identity by the Jewish artist stamped with the image of Shylock. Arnold Wesker is not satisfied by attempts to whitewash Shakespeare, to posit Shylock as a product of less enlightened times, or to concentrate on other themes of the play. His blood boiled at Jonathan Miller's 1970 production at London's National Theatre, in which Laurence Olivier played Shylock as a Victorian Rothschild, a banker whose revenge was not motivated by hatred of Christians, but by his daughter's defection to intermarriage, which Shylock avenges by inflicting on Antonio the lessons of prejudice and intolerance. Wesker protested not just because the rendering of Venice in terms of Victorian capitalism showed the Jew to be pitiless and sadistic in his money-making, and not just because the portrayal of the Jew was a lie. The very idea that Shylock ever *could* cut another man's flesh was a libel that threatened the Jew's

[18] Ibid., 28–29.

humanity. Worse, the depth and potential tragedy of Shylock's character, despite (or even because of) Shakespeare's poetic genius and the play's dramatic power, provides the audience with conscience-salving extenuating circumstances for anti-Jewish prejudice whose basis is confirmed, rather than denied. Anti-Semitism, it is often said, may be deplorable, but Jews bear the blame for their behavior. Wesker explained:

> The portrayal of Shylock offends for being a lie about the Jewish character. I seek no pound of flesh but, like Shylock, I'm unforgiving, unforgiving of the play's contribution to the world's astigmatic view and murderous hatred of the Jew.[19]

The Jewish playwright cannot but see in the degradation of Shakespeare's villain the despair of the concentration camp victim, especially when, as if by willful irony, the actor playing Shylock happens to be himself of Jewish descent, as was David Suchet in John Barton's 1980 production for the Royal Shakespeare Company:

> When Portia asks "... which is the merchant here and which the Jew?" the difference is so obvious – Antonio a tall upright Aryan, Shylock stooped, dark and diminutive – that Suchet releases a huge, mischievous laugh at the crassness of the question. And at the end, forced to confront the oppressiveness of the state and his self-inflicted humiliation, Suchet's face reveals a despair which has more to do with concentration camps than anything we've seen till now. In fact, his eyes betray the play.[20]

As someone who grew up in the Jewish immigrant experience of London's East End, Wesker is upset just as much by attempts to introduce into the portrayal of Jessica an East European *shmaltzy* sentimentality reminiscent of *Fiddler on the Roof*.[21] This too falsifies the truth about the Jews.

Wesker's play *Shylock* (1977) was first performed as *The Merchant* and later renamed, evidently to reflect the focus on the Jew, not the Merchant. Wesker went back to Shakespeare's sources and rewrote the story as one of a ghetto Jew called Shylock Kolner who befriends a Venetian merchant called Antonio.[22] It was an attempt by Wesker to

[19] Arnold Wesker, "Why I Fleshed Out Shylock," *Guardian*, August 29, 1981; reprinted in Arnold Wesker, *Plays*, vol. 4, *Shylock and Other Plays* (London: Penguin Books, 1990), 178.

[20] Ibid., 181

[21] Ibid., 180.

[22] *Shylock*, in Wesker, *Plays*, vol. 4, 171–261. This version of the play is Wesker's ninth, based on a workshop production at the Riverside Studio in London in 1989. All references will be to this edition of the play and will be given in parentheses. For the earlier version of the play see *The Merchant*, with commentary and notes by Glenda Leeming (London: Methuen, 1983). Wesker's play premiered in Stockholm in 1976, aired on BBC

FIGURE 34 Joseph Leon (1918–2001) took over the role of Shylock after Zero Mostel's death during *The Merchant* previews (1977).
Courtesy of the Museum of the City of New York, F2013.41.4553.

establish himself as a major dramatist on the English stage, after a career which he began at the end of the fifties as a successful Angry Young Man, but which was dogged by ill luck and lack of popularity (with the exception of *Chips With Everything*, about a raw recruit's confrontation with authority). It was written after the Yom Kippur War, when Israel and world Jewry faced growing isolation and boycotting. However, the play's success seemed doomed from the start, with the death of Zero Mostel (Figure 34), the designated leading role in the short-lived production on Broadway in 1977. It has, in fact, never been produced on London's West End stage, although John Dexter, the theater director whose name is most often associated with the new wave of drama that began with *Look Back in Anger* and with Wesker's early plays, flew over to New York to produce the play, in which he made savage cuts.[23]

radio, and toured several countries; in 2005 Wesker prepared a tenth draft incorporating the cuts and changes made for the radio version and performances around the world.

[23] Arnold Wesker, *The Birth of Shylock and the Death of Zero Mostel* (New York: Fromm International, 1999). This account of the writing, rewriting, and rehearsals of the play is an attempt to vindicate the twenty years which Wesker invested in this play, but also

Wesker's *Shylock* goes beyond the use of Jewish milieu or Jewish immigrant experience familiar from *The Wesker Trilogy* and addresses from a Jewish point of view the situation of the Jew in history and – through the interplay with Shakespeare – in literature (the Jewish writer is represented in the play by the sixteenth-century Portuguese playwright and translator of Petrach, Salomón Usque). Unlike Marowitz's adaptation of Shakespeare, Wesker does not so much reinterpret Shakespeare as answer him.[24] Wesker fleshes out Shylock Kolner, a German Jew, with the East End exuberance of his former idealists in *Chicken Soup with Barley* and *I'm Talking About Jerusalem* (in *The Wesker Trilogy)*, as well as the warmth of Nathan the Wise, another anti-archetypal Jew who breathes tolerance, good will, and the spirit of his author's ideals. Dave Simmonds and Ronnie Kahn in *The Wesker Trilogy* enthused about their ideals because they had grown up in a community that cared about each and every individual and was ready to fight for a cause. They failed to realize their ideals because, while they understood why society was in need of reform, they forgot that the utopian New Jerusalem had not yet been built. They believed in bringing socialism into being through living it, rather than transforming society, a belief that may seem even more romantically idealistic in a postmodern age than it did then. Wesker's Shylock similarly fails because he forgets that he lives in a reality not built for his idealism. The idealist makes mistakes and fails, but that does not necessarily invalidate the ideal. However, whereas Ronnie and Dave in *The Trilogy* were solely responsible for their failures and self-delusions, Wesker's Shylock bears responsibility towards the Jewish community, a reflection, perhaps, after a lifetime's involvement in workers' solidarity movements, that all power structures and legal systems are corrupt and that, despite the stand against the fascists in 1936 in Spain and in the East End (described in *Chicken Soup with Barley*, the first play of *The Trilogy*), the Jews were abandoned in the Holocaust and now are threatened by the encroaching new anti-Semitism. If acting

provides a painful day-by-day, blow-by-blow record of the hostility of English theater directors (including London's National Theatre) to Wesker's dense, wordy presentation of so many contemporary issues, and, the most painful of all issues, that of anti-Semitism, as well as their lack of sympathy for his failures, misfortunes, and disasters.

[24] For a comparison of the two plays see Michael Scott, "Demythologizing Shylock: Arnold Wesker, *The Merchant*; Charles Marowitz, *Variations on the Merchant of Venice*," in Scott, *Shakespeare and the Modern Dramatist*, 44–57; John M. Picker, "Shakespeare Divided: Revision and Transformation in Marowitz's *Variations on the Merchant of Venice* and Wesker's *Shylock*," *Haifa University Studies in Jewish Theatre and Drama* 2 (1996), 75–91; Bulman, "On Being Unfaithful to Shakespeare," 59–73.

for Wesker and other *engagé* writers of the sixties meant social action through acting out their ideas, the Wesker of *Shylock* is less angry than embittered after years of disappointment and failure to make his ideals work.[25]

Wesker insists on a detailed and more or less accurate historical setting as he places Shylock inside the Jewish ghetto of Venice in the year 1563. The ghetto is teeming with Portuguese *anusim* (forced converts to Christianity) fleeing the Inquisition. Printed Hebrew books (but not the Talmud) have just been allowed out of the closet. This is the heyday of Jewish intellectual life in Venice, and the play presents Jewishness as something alive and lived, a wonderful cultural heritage of a moral stature equal, if not superior, to Christianity. However, the Jew's lot is that of a despised minority restricted to the ghetto walls and to moneylending, bled dry by the Venetian tax-collector and compelled to purchase their residence rights by a contract whose renewal is uncertain. It is into this Jewish situation that Antonio becomes intrigued (in more than one sense) when Shylock adopts him as a kind of Righteous Gentile with whom he can share intellectual discussion and friendship. Shylock, who is not recognized as a brother by Christian law, claims the Christian as brother.

Like Dave Simmonds in *The Wesker Trilogy*, Wesker's Shylock is fired by enthusiasm for an ideal, in his case his vision of the Jews' moral mission, in which they are bound by covenant to God: "to bear witness to what is beautiful in Creation, and just" (*Shylock*, 195). Wesker imagines his Shylock to be a "free spirit," who embodies what he regards as the essence of Judaism and who arrogantly challenges the supremacy of the state's authority, its oppressive laws, and the established conventions of a power hierarchy based on sycophancy and hypocrisy.[26] Shylock Kolner wins Antonio over with his ecumenical vision, converting him in a sort of circumcision of the heart to his humanist vision of a love of scholarship and intellectual debate. The two friends, however, make the same mistake as Dave Simmonds and forget that reality has not caught up with their ideals. They mock barbaric laws which prevent Shylock from lending the money at no interest to his friend and

[25] See Arnold Wesker, *As Much as I Dare: An Autobiography (1932–1959)* (London: Century, 1994). For his ideas on the ideal society see Wesker, *Fears of Fragmentation* (London: Jonathan Cape, 1970).

[26] "The Two Roots of Judaism" (unpublished paper, Rockefeller Foundation conference, Bellagio, Italy, 1982), quoted in Glenda Leeming, "Commentary," in Wesker, *The Merchant*, xxxv–xxxvi.

"brother," to whom charging interest is prohibited by biblical law, and they make a nonsense bond to mock the cruel inhumanity of the laws of Venice which require a contract in all dealings with Jews. Their bond, remarks Sinfield, "is their protest against the oppressive laws of Venice, and, beyond that, against the whole, well-attested history of persecution of Jews."[27]

Antonio's melancholy at the beginning of Shakespeare's play (which has plausibly been explained as preparation for Christ-like sorrows prior to his crucifixion) here becomes a world-weariness in recognition of the hypocrisy and vanity of Venetian society and the killing boredom of public life (another Wesker theme). The Jew claims his heart – out of love – poisoning him with intellect.

> ANTONIO: You've poisoned me, old Shylock, with
> restlessness and discontent, and at so late a time.
> *(Shylock, 191; Act 1, Scene 2)*

Wesker belies the alleged duplicity of Shakespeare's Jew:

> I would be friends with you and have your love,
> Forget the shames that you have stained me with,
> Supply your wants, and take no doit
> Of usance for my moneys, and you'll not hear me.
> This is kind I offer. *(Merchant of Venice, 1.3)*

Wesker inverts the sinister overtones of the "merry sport" of this devilish Jew, when his Shylock would freely lend the money for Antonio's godson, Bassanio, a young patrician on the make in Venetian society and with an eye on Portia's caskets, out of love for his friend Antonio. It is gentile law which demands a bond that demeans the friendship of Antonio and Shylock. Such an ecumenical interpretation of the biblical commandment *veahavta le-re'akha kemokha* ("you shall love your brother as yourself" [Levitcus 19:18]), which, according to the midrash, Rabbi Aqiva declared to be the fundamental principle of the Torah, deflects the threat of conversion in Shakespeare's play and turns the mythical poisoner and anti-Christ into a catalyst of Christian society.

Shylock has made Antonio aware that his trade is a dead thing from which he is alienated, reminding us of another theme of *The Trilogy* – the estrangement of modern urban life which divides home and job; he has infected him with thirst for travel, for life. The Jew makes money

[27] Sinfield, "Making Space," 137–38; see Bulman, "On Being Unfaithful to Shakespeare," 69.

not the "barren" breed of usury, but rather something which works and makes life worth living. Excess is no gold lust; it is a boon to the world. Lorenzo articulates the Aristotelian and Christian position (challenged by Calvinism) that "Money is a dead thing, with no seed, it's not fit to engender" (*Shylock*, 214). For Lorenzo the trial is about Jewish money. Usury is allegedly a plot to hold Venice in thrall to the Jews – the very opposite of the truth, that Jews are held ransom by the state's restrictive and oppressive laws. Shylock's Judaic response is to offer the dull young patricians his knife after the trial to sharpen their wits. They have no appreciation of the need for intellect, for art and craft, no recognition of the value of the Jew, whom they condemn, in conformity to Christian teaching, as a doomed unchosen race.

When Antonio's fortunes are shipwrecked, Shylock must face the tragic consequences of his foolishness. His sister Rivka reminds Shylock of the fundamental error of the idealist who mistakes ideal for reality:

> you *can't* pretend you're educated, just as you can't pretend you're not an alien or that this Ghetto has no walls. Pretend, pretend, pretend! All your life! Wanting to be what you're not. Imagining the world as you want. (*Shylock*, 238; Act 2, Scene 3)

Or as Antonio warns him, when a tipsy Shylock bursts with enthusiasm for the glories of Venice during a dinner party,

> Venice is distorted through your gratitude, Shylock, you've forgotten your yellow hat.(*Shylock*, 224; Act 1, Scene 7)

Shylock, however, is not to be deterred from his "grand scheme of things," his compulsive obsession with the purposeful pattern of history, with the preservation of classical learning as an explanation of the prosperity and raison d'être of the Venetian republic.

So carried away is he at the end of Act 1 that he forgets it is not *his* Renaissance until Antonio reminds him that it is time to return to the ghetto as the bells ring for curfew: he must don his yellow hat, that shameful "badge of sufferance," which seems to refute all he has been saying, but fails to dampen his enthusiasm (*Shylock*, 229). The tolerance of the mythical Venice imagined by Shakespeare cannot conceal the real system of apartheid below the surface of Renaissance humanism (in its discriminatory laws and segregation in the Venice ghetto), or the acrimonious contempt for the Jew of Lorenzo and Graziano, who are quite deaf to Shylock's admonition that Judaism is Christianity's parent religion, that Jews and Christians belong to the same family and must be friends, whether they wish it or not.

> The Jew is the Christian's parent. Difficult, I know. Parent–children relationships, always difficult, and even worse when murder is involved within the family. But what can we do? It is the family! Not only *would* I be your friend but I *have* to be your friend. (*Shylock*, 225; Act 1, Scene 7)

The existentialist argument of Shylock's ecumenicism falls on deaf ears, for his message of universal love has no place in Christian theology and Venetian politics, in which the Jew serves as an object of contempt and hatred. Lorenzo cannot wait for the day when the young patricians will take over and put an end to the sin of usury.

Worse, Shylock's intellectual arrogance blinds him to Jessica's willful straining at the leash of his suffocating care and affection that give her no freedom from her father's regime of instruction and studying. Like the American-Jewish daughters of comfortable, wealthy, assimilated homes in the late twentieth century, she wishes to be free from patriarchal codes and stringent rules of behavior which prevent her tasting love and enjoying the freedom of a gentile world where one can come and go as one pleases.[28] No wonder she is attracted to the poet Lorenzo whose scathing critique of the elderly Councilors of Venice speaks for a generational revolt. In her rebellion, Jessica is a natural ally of Portia, who, in Wesker's version of the story, is a "new woman," a figure of great intellect with a thirst for knowledge, but also a victim of a father's philosophical lunacy (the theme of parents' oppression of their children and the repression of women are additional topical issues that weigh down Wesker's play). Portia's obedience to her father's test does not make her one bit less determined to think for herself and forge her own independent way in the world. In some ways she is the daughter Shylock Kolner would have wished to have.

The Jew's Bond/The Bonded Jew

Although in Wesker's play the gentile has as much as the Jew to learn from the Jew's moral and historical message, it is Shylock, not Antonio, who must confront his inescapable fate, dictated by the economic and psychological conditions of anti-Semitism in a burgeoning proto-capitalist society, as well as the fate written by Shakespeare and his sources. Wesker's Shylock does, nevertheless, have a choice. He can forgo the bond or

[28] See Chapter 15 in this volume.

advance Antonio more money once his ships are wrecked. But this would endanger the credibility of the Jewish community and undermine the Venetian economic system, for the Jews are forced to depend on usury and without the Jews the economy cannot function. As Rivka reminds him, it's not just Shylock's problem now, it's the community's, since only sticking to the law can assure their survival if law is to be respected, as Antonio himself had earlier urged. Moreover, some in the community would not agree to bend the law:

RIVKA: Having bent the law for us, they'll say, how often will the Venetians bend it for themselves, and then we'll live in even greater uncertainties than before. They'll be divided, as you are, my clever brother. Who to save – your poor people or your poor friend?

Racked by anguish over the loss of his daughter, which he cannot understand, Shylock at first shrugs off the problem, but then chooses loyalty to his community and insists on the bond whose price is his friend's life. The friends pledge silence, for no explanation will be understood, and Shylock certainly does not want to be seen as a martyr for the Jews.

Unlike Shakespeare's Shylock, he chooses a Jewish destiny, the bond of community, a bond which identifies him as an "authentic" Jew in Sartre's sense. It is a valedictory Ladino song that sets the tone as the embittered old man sets off for Jerusalem, despairing of books and men. The ideal was, after all, like Ronnie Kahn's, too big, too arrogant. The Jerusalem of *The Trilogy* has faded from the utopian dream of building socialism in a green and pleasant land and shrunk to the traditional place for old men to die. Portia's intellect has saved Antonio's life, but she exposes the sham of the law's claim to justice. She will marry according to her father's will an opportunist who is interested in bedding her, not in her mind, while Jessica will not convert or marry Lorenzo now that she has seen the depth of his contempt for her religion and her people, his male vanity and shallowness, now that she realizes the virility of hatred in men's hearts. It is Nerissa who has the last word, closing the play (in contrast to the harmony of Belmont in Shakespeare's final act) by dispelling the jovial picnicking and Bassanio's triumphant mood. She taunts the vain, self-seeking young men who have set themselves up as the heroes of the piece: "True Heroes, heroes indeed. Heroes!" (*Shylock*, 261; Act 2, Scene 6).

After Hitler it is not easy to believe Jew and Christian can live together as if nothing had happened. Antonio, an exceptional Venetian, is Shylock's friend and his defense of Shylock at the trial indicts Venice's treatment of the Jew which he holds responsible for the predicament of the bond:

> The usurer's a Jew, and the Jew the people's favourite villain. Convenient! Easy! But the Jew pursues what he hates to pursue in order to relieve *us* of the sin. But usury *must* exist in our city. We have many poor and our economy can't turn without it ... Do we condemn the Jew for doing what our system has required him to do? (*Shylock*, 253; Act 2, Scene 6)

As in our own day, the anti-Semite replies that his charge against the Jew is not anti-Semitic. It is because he grants the Jew an equal share of humanity that the Jew's plot against the Christian is monstrous (just as Bill Alexander seems to subscribe in his production of Shakespeare's play to a postmodern discourse in showing this monstrosity to be only too human). The Jew stands trial for the principle of usury, not for being a Jew, even though special laws apply to him as an alien in Venice. The plea of Shakespeare's revengeful Jew, "Hath not a Jew eyes?" (3.1), passes therefore to Lorenzo, where it becomes an accusation of the Jew's ungrateful perfidy in return for the Christian's tolerance. This the Jew will not accept.

> SHYLOCK: No, no, NO! I will not have it. *[Outraged but controlled]* I do not want apologies for my humanity. Plead for me no special pleas. I will not have my humanity mocked and apologised for. If I am unexceptionally like any man then I need no exceptional portraiture. I merit no special pleas, no special cautions, no special gratitudes. My humanity is my right, not your bestowed and gracious privilege. (*Shylock*, 255; Act 2, Scene 6)

Wesker's Shylock speaks directly to the sycophants and demagogues of the contemporary progressive liberal intelligentsia who similarly speak in the name of the people, because he is fed up with being society's scapegoat, with being automatically guilty and blamed for everything that goes wrong in public and private life. He knows that whatever he says, he will be misrepresented and condemned. Shylock has been burdened with responsibility for centuries for the anti-Semitism of which he is the victim, but now he bursts with indignation at Lorenzo's cynical use of a humanist argument in pleading for his humanity, which should be taken, after all, for granted. Wesker is undermining the humanist discourse which critics have ascribed to Shakespeare and he condemns the uses to which *The Merchant of Venice* have been put that have furthered anti-Semitic prejudice. In so doing, Wesker "both acknowledges and unsettles Shakespeare's cultural authority."[29]

[29] Bulman, "On Being Unfaithful to Shakespeare," 70.

Shylock after Auschwitz

Far from confirming Jewish blood-lust Wesker's Shylock sighs with relief when relieved of having to shed Antonio's blood. There still remains the logical flaw, which Sinsheimer and others see in Shakespeare's play, that an audience could believe only an inhuman monster capable of ever contemplating cutting into another human being's flesh.[30] There is also the snag that the nonsense bond would have to be witnessed and properly registered with the authorities, who would surely look askance at such a contract, unless the play depended on pure fable.[31] Wesker is aware of the risk, and had to answer criticism during the American rehearsals that Shylock should overcome his "racial" loyalties and be merciful, a criticism that reaffirmed Wesker's sense of Shakespeare's injustice in accusing the Jew for being ungenerous and cruel. Nevertheless, audiences would have to believe that Shylock was capable of drawing his knife and killing his friend Antonio, but Wesker notes in his diary that his play is not about this irresolvable dilemma:

> My play is about "barbaric laws – barbaric bonds," simply that. That's all I want to explore ... I didn't think about it this way when I was writing, but now see that I instinctively avoided what I felt I could not honestly handle ... I use Shakespeare's device and bring in Portia.[32]

Shylock's resorting to barbaric bonds in response to barbaric laws makes him a victim of the cruel system which turns the Jew into an unwilling accomplice of his own destruction, an insight characteristic of a post-Holocaust understanding of how anti-Semitism works.

The post-Holocaust perspective makes Wesker's "rewriting" of Shakespeare different in focus and motivation from previous modernizers of the Shylock myth, such as Tristan Bernard, whose *Juif de Venise* (1936) is apologetic of Shylock's injurious stance, or Ellis Rabb, who dignified Shylock in a modern-dress production in New York in 1973 and contrasted him with the corrupt jet-setters and homosexuals of trendy Belmont. Wesker's Shylock is a destereotyped, unstereotypable individual

30 Hermann Sinsheimer, *Shylock, the History of a Character, or the Myth of the Jew* (London: Gollancz, 1947), 95–98.

31 Wesker, *The Birth of Shylock*, 127–28.

32 Ibid., 141; a rabbi later wrote in to point out that Judaism forbids raising one's hand to kill another person (ibid., 329). In Howard Jacobson's novel, *Shylock is My Name* (London: Vintage, 2016), Shylock is not so sure and refuses to answer the question what he would have done had Portia not intervened at the trial.

who indicts Christian, not Jewish, iniquity. The author of a monograph on the Jew in drama, Ellen Schiff, has declared that

> Wesker has thoroughly inverted the myth, negating its negativity by returning wickedness to its proper source, and giving Shylock not only hands, organs and passions, but fingerprints.[33]

Wesker seems to be arguing that the Shylock of the post-Holocaust period must accept the relentless cycle of Jewish destiny if he is to be human and a Jew; the Christian must accept him as he is and not as the myth will have him. Even if he does not surmount the logical obstacle between myth and reality, Wesker is addressing a modern audience as one whose people has been gassed in concentration camps and weighed up into bars of soap like so many pounds of flesh. And yet, as Leslie Fiedler once remarked, "the myth of Shylock ... cannot be killed"; to try to kill it is to "risk unleashing a counterhysteria in others, of which we would ourselves be victims."[34] After the Holocaust, the Jew has to resist the role constructed for him. However, in order to do this, Wesker is telling us, he must assert his Jewishness as his humanity, not just his humanity as a Jew.

[33] Ellen Schiff, *From Stereotype to Metaphor: The Jew in Contemporary Drama* (Albany: State University of New York Press, 1982), 94. See Konrad Gross, "Arnold Wesker, *The Merchant*," in *Anglo-Amerikanische Shakespeare-Bearbeitungen des 20. Jahrhunderts*, ed. Horst Priessnitz (Darmstadt: Wissenschaftliche Buchgesellschaft, 1980), 100–13; Meinhard Winkgens, "Historisierung und Aktualisierung in Arnold Weskers Shakespeare-Bearbeitung *The Merchant*," *Literatur in Wissenschaft und Unterricht* 19 (1986), 301–22; Meinhard Winkgens, "Die Widerlegung des negativen Judenstereotyps: Arnold Weskers Neukonzeption der Shylock-Figur in seiner Shakeseare-Bearbeitung *The Merchant*," in *Jüdisches Leben und Leiden im Spiegel der englischen und amerikanischen Literatur*, ed. Franz Link (Paderborn: Ferdinand Schšningh, 1987), 146–63; Eckhard Auberlen, "Reimagining Shylock: Shakespeare, Lessing, Wesker," *Archiv für das Studium der neueren Sprachen und Literaturen* 227:2 (1990), 235–41. Iska Alter has given a general thematic and structural treatment of the play in "'Barbaric Laws, Barbaric Bonds': Arnold Wesker's *The Merchant*," *Modern Drama*, 31:3–4 (1988), 536–47. See also Bulman, *The Merchant*, 148–51; Gross, *Shylock*, 309–10.

[34] Leslie A. Fiedler, *Fiedler on the Roof: Essays on Literature and Jewish Identity* (Boston: Godine, 1992), 27. See also Leslie A. Fiedler, "What Can We Do About Fagin?: The Jew-Villain in Western Tradition," *Commentary* (May, 1949): 411–18.

13

Jewish Directors and Jewish Shylocks in Twentieth-Century England

Miriam Gilbert

Let Patrick Stewart (b. 1940) and David Suchet (b. 1946) – distinguished English actors – set up a major question. Both actors played Shylock for the Royal Shakespeare Company, Stewart in 1978 in the company's flexible space, The Other Place, Suchet in 1981 on the main stage. Both productions were directed by John Barton, so when Barton created *Playing Shakespeare* in 1984, a Channel 4 television series, the participation of both Stewart and Suchet offered Barton the chance to explore not simply moments from many different plays, but to take an in-depth look at a single character. In that program, Barton and the actors talked about Shylock and played parts of four different scenes, with Stewart and Suchet recreating the Shylocks they had previously acted. Barton opened with a sincere, if provocative comment, about what he thought "Shakespeare means us to feel about the character. We believe that he shows Shylock as a bad Jew and a bad human being, but that this in itself does not make the play anti-Semitic."[1] Stewart seemed to agree, pointing out that "to concentrate on Jewishness can lead to missing the great potential in the character which is its universality … Shylock is essentially an alien, an outsider. I think if you see him as a Jew, first and foremost, then he's in danger of becoming only a symbol. Shylock is an outsider who happens to be a Jew."[2] Suchet's reply was immediate: "I would challenge that. I would say that as Shylock I'm not an outsider who *happens* to be a Jew, but *because* I'm a Jew."[3] It's not an accident that Suchet was a Jew (he

[1] John Barton, *Playing Shakespeare* (London: Methuen, 1984), 169.
[2] Ibid., 171.
[3] Ibid.

has since converted to Christianity) and that Stewart was not. And their disagreement raises a central question: what difference does the religious background of either director or actor make to the interpretation of this perennially challenging play?

Asking such a question naturally raises larger concerns, both theoretical and historical. The audience's awareness of the actor is difficult to assess, although, as Marvin Carlson argues in *The Haunted Stage*, "Every well-known actor brings to the mind of the theatregoing public memories of certain productions or types of production, sometimes even of a specific dramatist or dramatic school."[4] Beyond the purely theatrical memories that a given actor carries onstage, what about the more personal details? And how much do such details matter? For years, white actors played Othello, in various shades of brown or black makeup; gay actors have always played heterosexual roles; and gender-switching is nothing new (male actors playing Lady Bracknell, for instance). So does being Jewish affect the playing of *The Merchant of Venice*, and of Shylock?

The brief answer might be that in England, being Jewish has not been crucial, in part because there have been relatively few Jewish actors who played Shylock in major professional productions,[5] in part because Jews in England are not only a minority, but, at times, an almost invisible minority. Todd M. Endelman's *The Jews of Britain, 1656 to 2000* traces the complex history of English Jews, noting the paradox that toleration and even social acceptance (especially in the nineteenth and twentieth centuries) might, in some measure, have contributed to "pressure to become more 'English,' pressure that was no less powerful because it was subtle and diffuse."[6] Endelman's penultimate chapter is titled "The Fracturing of Anglo-Jewy (1945–2000)," presenting both the success of Anglo-Jewry (upward mobility, affluence, greater presence in universities, waning of anti-Semitism) and yet the concomitant suppression of

[4] Marvin Carlson, *The Haunted Stage: The Theatre as Memory Machine* (Ann Arbor: University of Michigan Press, 2001), 69.

[5] The work of John Gross and Toby Lelyveld reveals only four Jewish actors (most of them not born in England) who played Shylock in English in a major professional production before World War II: Sherenbeck (Covent Garden, 1917), Maurice Moscovitch (London, 1919, after working in New York's Yiddish theater), Ernest Milton (London, 1932), and Frederick Valk (Old Vic, 1943); John Gross, *Shylock: A Legend and Its Legacy* (New York: Simon & Schuster, 1992); Toby Lelyveld, *Shylock on the Stage* (Cleveland: Press of Western Reserve University, 1960). George Arliss, playing the role in New York, 1928, and associated with Jewish roles because of his success as Disraeli, was not Jewish, according to Gross, *Shylock*, 189. Productions in Yiddish did take place.

[6] Todd M. Endelman, *The Jews of Britain, 1656 to 2000* (Berkeley: University of California Press, 2002), 200.

Jewishness through what Endelman calls "genteel intolerance" which, he argues, "encouraged [Jews] to mute their Jewishness, rather than accept it naturally or even revel in it."[7]

Such contradictions are particularly interesting when considering the performance history of *The Merchant of Venice*. Five major productions in England in the late twentieth century both inform and are informed by the contradictions Endelman charts so fully. All come from major national companies – the Royal National Theatre, the Royal Shakespeare Company, and the BBC (in its Shakespeare series). In these productions, Jewish directors – Jonathan Miller at the National in 1970 and Jack Gold for the BBC in 1981 – and Jewish actors – David Suchet at the Royal Shakespeare Company in 1981, Warren Mitchell for the BBC, Antony Sher at the Royal Shakespeare Company in 1987, and Henry Goodman at the National in 1999 – have created interpretations that surround Shylock with different historical contexts, offer different explanations for his behavior, and focus insistently on the problem of whether the Jew, in a Christian world, can camouflage his otherness, or display it proudly.

From Fagin to Disraeli

The 1970 production of *The Merchant of Venice* at the National Theatre, directed by Jonathan Miller, with Laurence Olivier as Shylock, marks a significant turning point in twentieth-century productions of the play, in part because of Olivier's presence, but even more because Shylock appeared not as an outsider but as a would-be insider. By creating such a Shylock, Olivier was deliberately choosing between contradictory images of the Jew, one fictional, one historical: "My Shylock owed more to Benjamin Disraeli than to Fagin, physically and mentally. There was to be no stropping of knives on the soles of shoes, no fingering the sharpness of the blade, no splitting hairs with the curved edge, no spitting oaths on to the courtroom floor, no rolling eyes to the deaf gods. I was determined to maintain dignity and not stoop physically and mentally to Victorian villainy. Not for me the long matted hair, invariably red, the hooked nose and the bent back."[8] Olivier's images are primarily visual; his Fagin grows out of George Cruikshank's caricature as much as from Dickens's text, his Disraeli is filtered through a Hollywood film: "I had seen George Arliss play Disraeli in a 1929 movie, and it suggested shades

[7] Ibid., 247.

[8] Lawrence Olivier, *On Acting* (London: Weidenfeld & Nicolson, 1986), 119.

of the Shylock that I wanted to give."[9] That performance won George Arliss the Academy Award for Best Actor, and grew out of his noted stage performance as well as a silent film. What images motivated Olivier? The opening sequences of the film set up Disraeli as outsider: a speaker at a rally at Hyde Park Corner reminds his listeners that Disraeli is a Jew and his grandparents were foreigners; the head of the Bank of England, seen at the Liberal Club, calls him a dangerous dreamer with "greedy hands"; and in the House of Commons, his Liberal opponent Gladstone attacks with a series of phrases each beginning with "unworthy." But when we first see Disraeli, in the Commons, he seems to snooze through Gladstone's attack; he's a small man with a large head dominated by the extraordinary curling ringlet down his forehead, but this slightly stooping figure commands the screen with quiet humor. And though he is attacked as an outsider, he dresses as a wealthy nineteenth-century gentleman and lives in an elegant country house.

Looking back at Olivier's choices, the director, Jonathan Miller, described the actor's intentions: "He began with the idea of being a grotesque, ornamentally Jewish figure and bought himself very expensive dentures, a big hook nose and ringlets. I think he had a George Arliss view of himself, but gradually he realized the possible advantage of making himself look much more like everyone else, as it is this crucial question of difference that lies at the heart of the play."[10] The contradictions are teasing – no "hooked nose," insists Olivier, while Miller specifies the "big hook nose" as something that had to go. Certainly the final result – visible both in photographs of the 1970 production, and in the 1973 television version based on that production – show a Shylock much less exotic than Arliss's Disraeli. The long black ringlet dominating Arliss's forehead became, in 1970, a very short grey half-curl in Olivier's wig, and by 1973 not even that curl is visible. Olivier's Shylock dressed like his counterpart, Antonio, in frock coat, striped trousers, and elegant top hat (Figure 35). Underneath that hat was a small yarmulke, and the door to Shylock's house (at least in the television version) had a small mezuzah that Shylock automatically touched as he went in. But these reminders of his Jewishness were small ones and the dominant impression was of an almost completely assimilated Jew, who spoke with a posh accent, casually dropping his final "g's."

[9] Ibid., 122.

[10] Jonathan Miller, *Subsequent Performances* (London: Faber, 1986), 107.

FIGURE 35 Laurence Olivier as Shylock and Anthony Nicholls as Antonio. National Theatre Archive/ Anthony Crickmay (1970).
Photograph by Anthony Crickmay © Victoria & Albert Museum, London.

If Olivier thought of Disraeli and Arliss,[11] what, if anything, does the presentation of Shylock as potential insider rather than exotic outsider owe to the presence of a Jewish director? Jonathan Miller openly stressed his personal background in a 1970 interview, just before the production opened: "I have a particular interest in the character of Shylock as I'm Jewish myself and am concerned about the way the Jew has been portrayed on the stage."[12] But what Miller means by "Jewish" is less clear. As Ansorge reminds his reader, immediately after Miller's assertion,

[11] Olivier seems not to have known – or at least does not mention – the fact that Arliss played Shylock in 1928.

[12] Peter Ansorge, "Director in Interview: Jonathan Miller," *Plays and Players* (March, 1970), 53.

Miller had, as a performer-writer in the comic revue, *Beyond the Fringe* (1960), replied to the "awful situation" that would obtain if one were both "working class *and* a Jew" by saying "In fact, I'm not really a *Jew*. Just Jew – ish. Not the whole hog, you know."[13] Miller's essay, "Among Chickens," delineates his Jewishness in terms of guilt, describing his father as "an embarrassed and guilty [Jew]. He was guilty because he had sprung away from his traditional orthodox ghetto background in the East End of London";[14] the father's solution was to try to turn his children into observant Jews:

> My father would create these Friday-night suppers with candles and an instant décor of Judaism. I had no interest in this whatsoever. I was told constantly by my father that I owed it to my people to identify with them. I didn't know how to, and didn't want to. I could feel Jewish only for anti-Semites, not for Jews. As a child I resented being Jewish: it seemed designed just to prevent me having fun. I spent the early part of my life dreaming, not of a white Christmas, but of a White Anglo-Saxon Protestant Christmas.[15]

So the idea of presenting Shylock as a Jew who wants to be like the Christians – of being essentially an assimilated Jew – makes sense in terms of Miller's own background.

Miller's concept established Olivier's Shylock as a figure of considerable commercial power, first visible sitting behind a desk, signing papers while listening to the nervous pleas of Bassanio. When he donned a top hat and gloves he looked almost indistinguishable from the Antonio of Antony Nicholls, another white-haired gentleman wearing a frock coat, striped trousers, gloves, and top hat, even carrying a cane (like Shylock). The visual similarity initially underscored politeness as a social façade; men dressed so formally, and looking so much alike, treat each other as equals. But the tenuousness of that façade soon becomes evident, when Shylock turns first to a mildly sarcastic tone, "Well, then, it now appears you need my help," and then pounces on the word "You" as if assaulting Antonio: "You (pointing his cane), that did void your rheum upon my beard" (1.3.106, 109).[16] Not only the visual likeness but the use of particular props (Shylock carries an Italian newspaper which he opens and

[13] Alan Bennett, et al., *The Complete Beyond the Fringe* (London: Methuen, 2003), 83.

[14] Jonathan Miller, "Among Chickens," *Granta* 23 (Spring 1998), 145.

[15] Ibid., 146.

[16] William Shakespeare, *The Merchant of Venice*, ed. M.M. Mahood (Cambridge: Cambridge University Press, 1987). All quotations from the play are from this edition and are identified parenthetically in the text.

reads while pretending not to be listening) emphasizes the social world that both men seem to inhabit.

And, of course, "seem" is the operative word here. Portia's question, "Which is the merchant here and which the Jew?" (4.1.170), becomes tellingly apt in this setting, and with a Shylock who is excluded not because he is obviously an outsider, but because he is inwardly so. Rich descriptions of this production – in James C. Bulman's chapter and in Marion D. Perret's article – already exist.[17] But I will stress two moments, drawn from the television production, one primarily created by the actor, the other by the director, which seem to me to have especially long reverberations in later productions. The first is the moment in Act 3, Scene 1 *before* Shylock's great speech, when Olivier's Shylock, isolated on a bridge over a small canal, hears a bell tolling, and slowly turns to face the camera; his shocked expression and his hand coming slowly to his mouth signal his thought process. As Bulman puts it, "Here it occurs to him *for the first time* that the bond may serve as a vehicle for retribution: an Antonio for a Jessica."[18] I would add that the triple repetition, "Let him look to his bond" (3.1.37, 38, 39) becomes a way to chart the thinking; as he speaks the line the first time, he is getting the idea; the second time, the line gets no special emphasis, but he moves forward, towards Salerio and Solanio, no longer trying to get away from them, but about to challenge them; and the third time, he spaces out the words so that they become a clear threat. By yoking his resentment of Antonio to his pain over Jessica's defection, Olivier's Shylock thus creates a highly plausible motivation for his future actions. The long pause before he first says "Let him look to his bond," the slow-motion turn, and the evolution of his purpose through the thrice-repeated phrase, make the moment inescapably powerful and force the audience to link Jessica's elopement with Shylock's determination to attack Antonio.[19]

And the production's final moments return us to Shylock, even though he does not physically appear. Here, in spite of Miller's comments about finding the Jewish texts he saw in the synagogue "peculiar,"[20] the director

[17] See James C. Bulman, "Aesthetes in a Rugger Club: Jonathan Miller and Laurence Olivier," in *The Merchant of Venice*, Shakespeare in Performance (Manchester: Manchester University Press, 1991); Marion D. Perret, "Shakespeare and Anti-Semitism: Two Television Versions of 'The Merchant of Venice'," in *Shakespeare on Television*, ed. J.C. Bulman and H.R. Coursen, (Hanover, NH: University Press of New England, 1988), 156–68.

[18] Bulman, *The Merchant*, 89.

[19] Of course, Olivier and Miller also eliminated Shylock's earlier line, "If I can catch him once upon the hip," (1.3.38), thus making the Act 3, Scene 1 moment the crucial one.

[20] Miller, "Among Chickens," 146.

clearly recognizes the symbolic and evocative power of the chanted Kaddish, and the way in which the chant will tell us of Jessica's thoughts. The document she reads gives Shylock's money to her and to Lorenzo, but at the cost of Shylock's loss, and, the prayer implies, his death. At that moment, Jessica's physical isolation – she has moved away from Lorenzo, and from Antonio's tentative gesture of reconciliation and support – takes her out of the Christian community she wanted so desperately to join. The insistence on Jessica's Jewish identity at the end of the play echoes the production's most visible emphasis on Shylock's Jewishness, something we've seen only in passing. When Olivier's Shylock hears about Antonio's misfortunes from Tubal, he takes out a *tallit*, kisses it, and then drapes it over his head, saying "At our synagogue, good Tubal" (3.1.103); the combination of words and action might suggest that Shylock is about to pray for revenge on Antonio. But the grief-stricken look on Shylock's face, and the resemblance between the *tallit* and a shroud, suggests that he is actually in mourning. Earlier in the scene, with Tubal present, he smashes the framed photograph of Jessica to the floor, violently breaking the glass, and wishing for her death; now, as the scene ends, he is grieving for the lost daughter, just as the Kaddish at the end of the play completes the circle with the chant and Jessica's sad isolation in mourning her lost father.

Hand-Rolled Cigarettes or a Cigar?

Miller's moving of the play into the late nineteenth century was echoed in both of John Barton's productions (1978 and 1981), in which Patrick Stewart and David Suchet took different approaches to dealing with the insider/outsider question. Indeed, though Patrick Stewart comments in *Playing Shakespeare* that he wanted to "avoid the easily recognisable elements of Jewishness, the ringlets, the gown, the nose and so on", he admits "I should add, though, that I had a very large bushy beard and a lot of long, dirty, tangly hair. I wore a shabby, dirty broken-down frock-coat ... because I thought that if he was obsessed with money he would not waste it on how he appeared. So I made an attempt to make my Shylock very shabby and down-at-heel."[21] The connection with the visual stereotype of Fagin – the one Olivier wanted to avoid – seems clear.[22]

[21] Barton, *Playing Shakespeare*, 171–72.

[22] In 2011, playing Shylock in a production directed by Rupert Goold for the Royal Shakespeare Company, Stewart first appeared as an elegantly dressed casino owner (the production was set in Las Vegas) but by the trial scene he was wearing not only a

Stewart emphasized the shabbiness with his smoking of small hand-rolled cigarettes, beginning in his first scene; after he finished the cigarette, he then thriftily put the remaining fragments of tobacco back into a silver case, for further use. Although Stewart saw Shylock as a foreigner, he also felt that Shylock (and here he shares the Olivier approach) was trying to assimilate, and so his accent was, in Stewart's words, "more cultured, more refined and more native than the natives."[23]

David Suchet's Shylock also was both "insider" and "outsider," although he insisted on looking wealthy, wearing at first a long overcoat with a large heavy fur collar, and later, in his home office, and with Tubal, smoked a cigar (Figure 36). He too saw Shylock as foreign, but rather than hiding that otherness, he chose to emphasize it vocally, with a slight accent: "I just wanted to make it foreign because his language was somehow foreign. I felt that was important. I also never wanted anybody to forget that I was an outsider."[24] The choice grows out of the actor's thinking about Shylock: "I felt that Shylock would not have tried to alter his accent because he, or rather I, my Shylock, was very proud of his Jewishness. Why should he hide it? Why not exploit it if necessary?"[25]

Thus, being a Jew really was key to Suchet's reading of the role, and when I spoke with him in January, 2011, I asked him directly about Barton's characterization of Shylock as a "bad Jew." He quickly replied, "I never did buy that," and moved immediately to talk about *The Merchant of Venice* as a reply to *The Jew of Malta*, titles that he hears as echoing/reversing each other. Indeed, the connections to Marlowe's play (whether of difference or similarity) turn up repeatedly in Suchet's thinking, whether one listens to him talking to Barton (seeing Shylock as "pretty mild" compared to Barabbas) or writing about his Shylock in 1986 and noting a series of similarities between Shylock and Barabbas ("both have only daughters, both are very wealthy, both hate and do their best to catch out their Christian victims, and both are in the end thwarted in their aims"[26]). Speaking with me in January 2011, Suchet made the point

yarmulke (skullcap) but also a *tallit katan* (small prayer-shawl), with the fringes visible underneath his jacket; he later put on the *tallit gadol* (large prayer-shawl) as he prayed.

[23] Barton, *Playing Shakespeare*, 172. Stewart extends the discussion of accent in "Shylock in *The Merchant of Venice*," in *Players of Shakespeare: Essays in Shakespeare Performance by Twelve Players*, ed. Philip Brockbank (Cambridge: Cambridge University Press, 1985), 14–15.

[24] Barton, *Playing Shakespeare*, 172.

[25] Ibid.

[26] David Suchet, "Talking about Shylock – A Personal Essay," in *The Merchant of Venice*, ed. Gãmini Salgãdo and Fenella Salgãdo (Burnt Mill, Essex: Longman, 1986), xii.

FIGURE 36 David Suchet as Shylock in the trial scene, watched by Gratiano (Arthur Kohn) and Bassanio (Jonathan Hyde). Royal Shakespeare Company production (1981).
Joe Cocks Studio Collection © Shakespeare Birthplace Trust.

that Shylock at least has "motivation for his evil desires," and suggested that Shakespeare couldn't portray a Jew as a good person, but could, "bravely," create motivation. For Suchet (and here one looks back to Olivier), Jessica's elopement is crucial; until then, he may be a persecuted alien, but he has learned how to play the role of "the cowed, smiling, subservient man," whose real feelings come out only in the soliloquy in Act 1, Scene 3. But Jessica's elopement "shatters" his domestic life. Suchet noted Shylock's mention of Barabbas in the trial scene ("Would any of the stock of Barabbas / Had been her husband, rather than a Christian," 4.1.292–93), both in his essay and in his conversation with me; the line is, for him, a reference to Marlowe's Jew, perhaps a "final joke."

But more important than this historical context as a way of shaping Suchet's notions about Shylock is his commitment to the text. When we talked together about the trial scene, he spoke in detail about how clearly the rhythm of the text led him into Shylock's thinking. Thus, Portia's appeal, "bid me tear the bond" (4.1.30), runs into the reversed foot opening his reply, "*When* it is paid" (italics mine), the change from the iambic pentameter signaling his assurance; and the hard "t" of "teno[u]r," as he completes his answer, "according to the teno[u]r" (4.1.231) seemed, to Suchet, almost a moment of exasperation. Or when Portia suggests a surgeon, Shylock's choice of the word "nominated" ("Is it so nominated in the bond" – the long word in an otherwise monosyllabic line, 4.1.255) – indicates how sure he is that he's right. When Portia traps him, explains what he's lost, and asks "Why doth the Jew pause?" (4.1.331), Shylock *knows*, says Suchet, that his world has collapsed. Still, the language offers him a way to survive. While Portia's question, "Art thou contented, Jew?" (4.1.389) shows (for Suchet) that she still thinks of him as "other" even though he's just been forced to convert, Shylock's answer, "I am content" (4.1.390) becomes his way of fighting back, "is that what you want me to say?" And when he leaves, Suchet finds that the monosyllables offer him – and Shylock – time: "I pray you give me leave to go from hence. / I am not well" (4.1.392–93). The exit then becomes a moment of dignity in defeat; Shylock leaves, but on his own terms, as Julie Hankey's description suggests:

> He kneels for mercy with a wearily smiling sense of habit, as though it were an old game, this, of bearing the ancient curse. He stumbles a little getting up, but with a quick self-deprecating laugh, refuses Portia's hand. Then he removes his skull-cap and simply takes himself off.[27]

The refusal to ask for pity – as emphasized by Suchet's calm demeanor – becomes a moment when Shylock garners both respect and sympathy. David Nathan saw the exit as one of an "undefeated" Shylock: "When he walks out of the court, it is not to wail and rend his clothing, but to see if there is a boat in the harbour that will take him to Amsterdam, or Hamburg, or one of the Baltic ports. He is, in short, a survivor."[28] Unlike Olivier's crumpled Shylock, with his unnerving and chilling offstage scream, Suchet's Shylock is still a powerful force as he leaves the stage.

Yet along with the respect that Suchet's Shylock evoked from reviewers, one also reads the frequent references to Shylock as someone who

[27] Julie Hankey, "The Merchant of Venice," *Times Literary Supplement*, May 21, 1981.

[28] David Nathan, "Suchet's Shylock Masterstroke," *Jewish Chronicle*, May 1, 1981.

has learned to play the game. Hankey's comments, above, find an echo in Rosalind Carne's description of this Shylock as "a self-dramatising comedian," in Michael Coveney's appraisal of Suchet as "a true Jew, unpatronisingly conceived, operating with a Gentile system," and in Irving Wardle's suggestion that Suchet's Shylock "is the genial Jew: a mask he has long since perfected – and his personal tragedy is that for once he is tempted into dropping it."[29] For Wardle, Suchet's exit underscores that mask: "'I am content,' he says quietly, still smiling. He has learnt the old lesson once again."

The reading that Shylock is unalterably a Jew but a Jew who can – and does – act as Christians wish to see him takes me back to Suchet's own complicated religious background. Born into a Jewish family (with roots in the Pale of Settlement), his father gave up his Jewish faith when he emigrated from South Africa, and wrote "Church of England" when asked for his religious affiliation. Suchet grew up essentially in a non-religious home, yet he also identified himself as Jewish, most notably in the *Playing Shakespeare* series where he talked about Shylock and anti-Semitism in light of "being Jewish myself."[30] Suchet is now a baptised Christian, after a profound conversion in the mid-80s, and describes himself (in our conversation) "as Christian by faith, believing in Christ who was a Jew." So I ask how he, now, sees his playing of Shylock in relation to his religious beliefs? And his immediate answer is to remind me that he was probably the youngest professional actor to have played Shylock in England, not for the Royal Shakespeare Company, but at the Gateway Theatre in Chester, in January, 1970, when he was just twenty-four.[31] That experience made him think about his Jewishness, about his roots, even though he would not finally have a full sense of those roots until the BBC program, "Who Do You Think You Are?" (Fall, 2008) enabled him to discover the small town where his great-grandfather had lived and from which he escaped possible attacks and pogroms. So playing Shylock might embody both his sense of being born into a Jewish family while living very much as a Christian *and* an experience that made him aware of being Jewish.

29 Rosalind Carne, "The Merchant of Venice," *Financial Times*, July 20, 1981; Michael Coveney, "The Merchant of Venice," *Financial Times*, April 22, 1981; Irving Wardle, "Shylock as a Barely Tolerated Alien," *The Times*, April 22, 1981.

30 Barton, *Playing Shakespeare*, 170.

31 John Elsom, *Theatre Outside London* (London: Macmillan, 1971), 180.

"The villainy you teach me, I will execute"

If Olivier and Suchet showed audiences a Shylock who could – at least visually – belong to Venetian and Christian society, other major productions have stressed Shylock as alien, a foreignness growing out of his religion. Certainly the BBC production of 1980, part of the much-publicized and circulated series of thirty-six plays, makes that choice, and, as reviewers and scholars have noted, both the director (Jack Gold) and the actor playing Shylock (Warren Mitchell) are Jewish, with Jonathan Miller serving as overall producer. I will not repeat the fine analyses of Marion Perret and James C. Bulman, but I would suggest that the choice to portray a clearly alien Shylock, in dress and accent, also seems inextricably connected with choices that make the Venetian Christians look appallingly callous and finally vicious. The chief "villains" here are not the major characters, Antonio and Bassanio, but rather Salerio and Solanio, and, of course, the verbally abusive Gratiano. Warren Mitchell's small stature immediately sets him apart from the Venetians who always seem to tower over him; in his first entrance, he's a dark silhouette, framed by a dark archway, and underscored by sinister-sounding chords. His strategy for dealing with Bassanio is to move close to him, uncomfortably close as Bassanio's (John Nettles) body language suggests. While filming a play for television may well encourage the number of shots that crowd characters into the same frame, Gold's choices constantly show us first how Shylock gets "in the face" of the Venetians, and then how the Venetians treat him similarly, but more brutally. John Rhys-Davies, who plays Salerio, is a big, burly actor, and together he and Solanio (Alan David), surround Shylock both visually and with extra-textual sounds. When Shylock appears in Act 3, Scene 1, he again enters through the same dark archway, his hurried walk showing him so focused on his inner pain that he actually bumps into Salerio and Solano. From that moment on, they are in the front of the frame, with Shylock crowded into the middle. And they respond to everything he says, not only with their lines but with gestures (including grabbing for his genitals when Shylock laments, "My own flesh and blood to rebel," 3.1.28) and constant "ums" and "ahs," building to a shared loud "Ah" after "I am a Jew," as if Shylock has just made a tremendously funny joke. The more Shylock speaks, the more Salerio and Solanio continue to respond, either in mock agreement ("ah") or with laughter. Marion Perret calls the scene "almost unbearable"[32] and certainly for anyone who knows the text, the fact that Shylock fights to be

[32] Perret, "Shakespeare and Anti-Semitism," 156.

heard as he delivers what is one of the play's two most famous speeches, makes an audience member uncomfortable, even on the level of just trying to hear the words, let alone absorb their content.

Yet the very lack of attention and respect that Salerio and Solanio give to Shylock's insistence on his humanity leads to the powerful moment when Shylock asks "And if you wrong us, shall we not revenge?" (3.1.52) and Salerio and Solanio fall silent. Their silence not only allows – but forces – us to hear Shylock, and what's more, given what he (and we) have just experienced in the last few minutes, to feel the justice of his words. There is no way, physically, for this small man to overcome two larger men, but he can, finally, make them pay attention to him. The moment resists sentimentalizing, and leads us to fight back, with Shylock, against the ugly attacks of the Christians.

So too does the moment of Shylock's exit from the courtroom, a moment I recall with great clarity from my first viewing, as I watched the BBC production in 1981 with a group of freshman students. I remember the students making approving noises when Portia stopped Shylock by forbidding even a "jot of blood" – they sounded both delighted and surprised. And then, as the trial scene continued, their background chatter died down. The final moments where Shylock is stripped of his money and his religion focus almost obsessively on Shylock himself, kneeling on the ground, the camera angle looking down on him, as do the Christians standing in a semi-circle behind him. Unlike the visual crowding of the frame in Act 3, Scene 1, here Shylock's is the only face we see, except for several long shots that show the others looking at him, as if he's an unsightly piece of trash. And unlike the constant barrage of laughter and sound that underscored "Hath not a Jew eyes?," here the silences between Shylock's few words are what we hear. We also see hands – Gratiano's hands removing Shylock's skull-cap, and then Salerio's hands draping a long chain with a crucifix on it over Shylock's shoulders, and pushing the crucifix against Shylock's lips. My students gasped, as did I – the viciousness catching us unprepared. What this production presents – and perhaps the fact that there were three Jews centrally involved is relevant – is not the façade of polite tolerance masking hatred, but the hatred itself. And yet, at the same time, the portrayal of Shylock also embodies clichés of representing the Jew: the Eastern European accent, the long beard and hair, the gestures, even the ingratiating self-deprecation. Do those clichés lead us to see Mitchell's performance as supporting an anti-Semitic view? My contention is that the two sets of choices fit together, namely that the more alien a Shylock we see, the more likely a production is to attack that Shylock with open, even violent, disdain and hatred. In part, the Renaissance setting that seems associated with Shylock-as-foreigner licenses the extreme behavior; we assume, or perhaps expect, that "back then," people were willing to behave in more obviously ugly ways (the era of public executions, etc.). By contrast, the Victorian and Edwardian periods lend themselves to stereotypes of polite behavior where people repress or hide extreme feelings). So the "assimilated" Shylock of Olivier, or the wealthy businessman played by Suchet is unlikely to meet with the overt rudeness and physical abuse that Warren Mitchell faced.

And certainly the 1987 Royal Shakespeare Company production of *The Merchant of Venice*, directed by Bill Alexander, with Antony Sher as Shylock, took that violence even further (Figure 37). In a Renaissance setting (at least in terms of costumes) Sher's Shylock – a Levantine Jew, with long beard and hair, a guttural accent (Sher describes it as Turkish), long caftan, and striped turban – was clearly the victim of prejudice, but also a fiercely vengeful person himself. The opening moments of the production established the motifs that forced the audience to think of the play in terms of religious prejudice: the set was a series of wooden platforms, suggesting walkways over the canals of Venice, but one's eyes went immediately to the back brick wall, half-plastered, with a Byzantine gold-leaf icon of the Madonna stage right, and a hand-scrawled yellow

FIGURE 37 Shylock (Antony Sher) is attacked by Salerio (Michael Cadman) and Solanio (Gregory Doran). Royal Shakespeare Company production (1987). Joe Cocks Studio Collection © Shakespeare Birthplace Trust.

Star of David stage left. Downstage, Antonio stares moodily out into space, while upstage, a figure with a yellow Star of David on his shoulder stands on the bridge (the promptbook says Tubal, but the audience can't know that yet). As Salerio and Solanio saunter by him, he leaves, and one of them spits on him. That unprovoked spitting immediately tells us about the world we're in, a world of casual nastiness, part offense, part defense. We see the defensiveness when Bassanio (Nicholas Farrell) goes to Shylock, who lounges barefooted on cushions, fingering his worry beads – and Bassanio's anxious look around immediately conveys discomfort.[33] Antonio's actions are much more direct; he grabs the abacus on which Shylock is calculating (or pretending to calculate) the "rate" and flings it on the floor as he asks, "Well, Shylock shall we be beholding to you?" (1.3.97). At first Shylock seems taken aback, scurrying across the stage, bending over; but when he replies to Antonio, he imitates the deep tones of John Carlisle, the actor playing Antonio, so that "Shylock, we would have moneys" (1.3.108) sounds extremely sarcastic. In fact, Antonio grabs Shylock, shakes him, lets him go, giving real point to Shylock's "Why look you, how you storm" (1.3.130). The amount of physical contact is surprising – and alarming. No one spits on Shylock – yet – and there is a slightly comic moment when, to seal the bargain, Shylock spits on his hand, offers it, then wipes it off, "if not adieu." But no one would actually shake his hand – and, as Shylock leaves, Bassanio spits after him.

Not only do major characters indicate their contempt for Shylock in this production, but three street urchins, who at first seem to exist only as set decoration and set-changers, become increasingly noticeable as anti-Shylock figures. When Shylock comes in to talk with Jessica, he's followed by these street figures (wearing carnival masks); and Launcelot Gobbo also wears a mask, his representing Shylock, beard and all. By the beginning of Act 3, Scene 1, the street urchins are actively pursuing Shylock, chasing him in, throwing rocks at him; since his forehead is bleeding, one has already struck home. The urchins spit at him, Solanio pushes him to the ground, then catches him under the chin with a stick, and shoves him towards Salerio (Figure 37). As Salerio and Solanio leave and Tubal enters, they spit on him, then exit upstage shouting "Jew, Jew." Shylock's greeting to Tubal, "How now, Tubal," is accompanied by a gentle gesture, wiping the spit off Tubal's face and gown – the first time that Shylock

[33] Farrell, talking to a group of Fulbright exchange teachers, said that "Bassanio doesn't like having to deal with this smelly foreign man."

ever seems to acknowledge the ugly behavior. And in the trial scene, the street urchins are still around, upstage on the bridge, and from time to time, they chant "Jew, Jew, Jew" – their presence and intermittent voices reminding us that Shylock is a hated figure – and just why he is hated.

But what made this production both memorable and controversial was the extent to which Shylock fought back – and insisted on his Jewishness. Not only did Sher's Shylock look and sound like a foreigner, a Jewish foreigner, but the production added to the text an invented ritual as Shylock prepared to take his pound of flesh in court. What's more, that ritual included a Hebrew prayer, "Sh'fokh," from the opening verb, "Pour out Thy wrath." So extreme, and extraordinary, was this sequence that James Bulman starts his chapter on this production with a description of this invented ritual. My own description reads as follows:

> The production had emphasized Christian anti-Semitism but now, frighteningly, those prejudices seemed almost justified with a Shylock who put on the *tallis* [*sic*] (prayer-shawl), chanted a Hebrew prayer imploring God, "Pour out Thy wrath upon the nations that know Thee not," a prayer taken from the Passover Haggadah, and poured some drops of blood on to a white cloth (another echo of the Passover Seder, where drops of wine signify the plagues that afflicted the Egyptians); meanwhile the Duke became the icon of Christian religiosity, kneeling and intoning the "Salve, Regina" prayer. Shylock seemed possessed, a whirling dervish whipping himself up into a murderous frenzy; he tore off Antonio's shirt, and was about to slit his throat when Portia yelled "Tarry a little."[34]

"Pour out Thy wrath" is a later addition to the Haggadah; it first appeared in eleventh–twelfth century France, probably after the First Crusade in 1095.[35] What makes the use of this prayer – seemingly so foreign to the celebratory spirit of the Seder – particularly ironic in the context of *The Merchant of Venice* is the long and shameful history of blood libels in medieval times, that is to say, the accusation that Jews murdered Christian children in order to use the blood in the preparation of Passover matzah. So, while one can understand Jews wishing to ask for vengeance as they were themselves being persecuted, the creation of a ritual for shedding blood that includes this prayer seems almost perverse. Or, maybe not, if one remembers Shylock's earlier line: "The villainy you teach me, I will execute, and it shall go hard but I will better the instruction" (3.1.56–57).

34 Miriam Gilbert, *The Merchant of Venice*, Shakespeare at Stratford (London: Arden Shakespeare, 2002), 135–36.

35 Rabbi Lawrence A. Hoffman and David Arnow, eds. *My People's Passover Haggadah*, vols. 1–2, (Woodstock, VT: Jewish Lights Publishing, 2008), 150.

That notion of vengeance rebounding from the victim to the persecutor also may grow out of Antony Sher's own background, not only as a Jew but as a South African. Speaking to Carol Muskoron of the *Jewish Herald*, Sher insisted that being Jewish wasn't central to his understanding of Shylock: "First of all, I'm not a practising Jew. The part means more to me as an ex-South African than as an ex-Jew."[36] And Sher goes on to point out: "the underdog isn't necessarily a better person. My grandparents fled Jewish persecution in Lithuania at the turn of the century and became part of a system supporting apartheid. Just as Jewish people fled to Israel and support the current treatment of the Palestinians. Again and again people who have suffered go on to persecute others. The Merchant of Venice seems to me to be about that." Such a comment makes the invented blood ritual seem more understandable. And in his autobiography, published in 2001, Sher expands the point, this time in terms of black persecution rather than Jewish:

> So the more Bill [Alexander, the director of the production] and I talked about *Merchant* the more I heard myself using the word racism rather than anti-Semitism. I found this more inspiring as an explanation for who Shylock is, why he behaves the way he does – "racism" – this rang bells in my head, quickened the blood, brought back sense memories. Grown men grinning and nodding like children, their status nil, eager to please, nervous, fawning, harmless. Yet they're suffering inside, they're profoundly insulted. When their anger breaks out it's ugly, brutal, unreasonable, unstoppable; their eyes are bloodshot, they're not seeing where they're going, not seeing clearly at all. This was on display in every news bulletin coming from South Africa in 1987, as well as in the harrowing documentary which Michael Buerk assembled about his time as BBC correspondent there. What the Soweto children had started the adults were continuing, with adult violence, sometimes in the craziest way imaginable: black on black. When they gained real status, real power, these hurt, furious people – what would they be capable of then?
>
> I've just described Shylock's journey. The Christians go to him for help because, although they need his skills as a usurer, he's essentially powerless. But then the tables turn and a terrible force is unleashed. The intended violence is nonsensical – a pound of flesh? – but the instigator is unreasonable, unstoppable.[37]

While Sher's words here stress racism rather than religious prejudice, a careful reader of his autobiography would conclude that racism is only part of the background shaping his Shylock. Indeed Sher speaks frankly

[36] Carol Muskoron, "What the Shy Mr. Sher Feels about Shylock," *Jewish Herald*, June, 1987.

[37] Antony Sher, *Beside Myself: An Autobiography* (London: Hutchinson, 2001), 190.

of being an outsider: his sense that, as a young gay man, he didn't "fit in"; his inability to sing ("I'm tone-deaf, seriously tone-deaf") and thus "one of the worst experiences of my childhood" was trying to learn to chant the Torah portion for his bar mitzvah;[38] and his experience as a conscript in the South African Defence Force where, in an all-white group, he nonetheless saw a hierarchy:

> Afrikaans-speaking Christians
> English-speaking Christians
> Jews
> Poor whites[39]

Here he couldn't escape his Jewishness:

> I was at first shocked by being routinely referred to as that fokkin *Jood* – the word is uncomfortably close to the German and these blunt-featured Afrikaners with close-cropped blond hair conjured up further associations – but you quickly learn to stop hearing it.[40]

Though Sher claims that he stopped hearing the insult, the "further associations" may have lingered. Indeed, as Sher describes his childhood "in paradise," listening to his Uncle Nat advise him to "bask" in the South African sunshine, he reflects on his own family's blindness:

> Whenever I talk about this, I hear myself sounding like the citizens of the towns of Dachau or Auschwitz – "We didn't know, we didn't know!" In fact, I'm saying something worse – not that we didn't know, but that we didn't see. Robben Island was there, right there, clearly visible from the pretty white beaches of Sea Point, yet we didn't see it.[41]

Here Sher brings to the fore the shadow that audiences and readers of *The Merchant of Venice*, from the middle of the twentieth century on, must remember, namely the Holocaust. So too did the production and its reviewers, with the chanting of "Jew! Jew! Jew!" evoking "street-corner Nazis" for the *Mail on Sunday*'s Kenneth Hurren or leading the *Observer*'s Mary Harron to connect the set's Mogen David with "the yellow star Antony Sher wears as Shylock in the trial-scene. We are not allowed to forget the Holocaust in this production."[42]

[38] Ibid., 13, 17.
[39] Ibid., 29.
[40] Ibid., 30.
[41] Ibid., 9, 10.
[42] Quotations from these reviews come from *Theatre Record* 7:9 (1987), 557–59.

"I am a Jew"

How then does *The Merchant of Venice* look when the Holocaust is even more specifically implied, as in the National Theatre's 1999 production, directed by Trevor Nunn, with Henry Goodman as Shylock? Reviewers identified the setting variously as "Twenties Italy" (Nicholas de Jongh, *Evening Standard*) or "Venice in the early 1930s" (Michael Coveney, *Daily Mail*), but almost all of them felt, on some level, that the look was, as Robert Butler put it, "closer to Isherwood's Berlin than Shakespeare's Venice."[43] And although the casting at the National did not insist on Teutonic types for the Venetians, the louche atmosphere of the nightclub where Salerio, Solanio, Gratiano, and Lorenzo gather to plan Lorenzo's elopement with Jessica, and where Bassanio and Antonio have gathered to meet Shylock certainly evokes memories of *Cabaret*. There are two singers in black-and-white striped dresses, sporting frizzy hair and lots of black eyeliner; as they end "Everything I have is yours," they raise their skirts and thrust their crotches forward at the cheering audience. What makes the scene almost unbearable, however, is the insertion into the scene of Launcelot Gobbo's soliloquy (from 2.2) debating whether or not he should leave Shylock, here performed as if he's a stand-up comedian. Offering an exaggerated mimicking of "the Jew" – ostentatiously counting out money coin by coin, then rubbing his hands – Launcelot encourages the audience to join in on "Budge" while he adopts a high squeaky voice for the conscience on "Budge not." The speech is trimmed and reshaped, so that just after "'Budge not,' says my conscience," he returns to the phrase, "The Jew my master" and again starts the mimicry. At that very moment Shylock, scrutinizing a piece of paper as if looking for directions wanders in and is caught in the spotlight with Launcelot; he can't quite understand – or believe – what he's hearing and seeing, and, mercifully, Bassanio hurries up to him and escorts him out of the light and into a side hall. But for a moment, the black actor playing Gobbo, resembling a performer in a minstrel show, and Shylock, in his long black overcoat and black hat, are trapped together, a shockingly mismatched pair. Gobbo pauses slightly, embarrassed, but after Shylock is hustled out, continues his act. Such a moment stamps this society as casually callous, verging on decadent.

And the scene stands in sharp contrast to the one that precedes it, Act 2 Scene 5, where we see Shylock at home. In Shakespeare's text, our

[43] Butler's review appeared in the *Independent on Sunday*; that quotation and others are found in *Theatre Record* 19:12 (1999), 769, 771.

first view of that home comes with Jessica in Act 2, Scene 3, but Nunn inserts into Act 2, Scene 3 an entrance for Shylock, followed by Jessica who is carrying a copper pot and a towel; he chastises her in Yiddish, pointing to a spot she hasn't cleaned, and then leaves, giving her enough reason to complain to Gobbo, "Our house is hell." In Act 2, Scene 5, the father–daughter relationship becomes much more complicated. We see a small table with two candles for the Sabbath, and also on that table a small framed photograph. Shylock doesn't want to leave, and as he looks at his daughter, he gently reaches out and strokes her hair on "Jessica, my girl" – the tone is both loving and possessive (Figure 38). And then, with an occasional gentle touch of her head, as if blessing her, he sings "Eshet Chayil," the lines from Proverbs that begin, "A woman of valor, who can find? / For her price is far above rubies." The chant is part of the home celebration of the Sabbath, traditionally sung to the wife, but since Shylock has no wife alive, he sings to his daughter, and she responds, first singing a verse by herself, and then the two joining in a duet.

If the interpolation of a Hebrew passage in the Alexander/Sher production underlined the power, as well as the irony, of Shylock's desire for vengeance, in Nunn's production a very different interpolated Hebrew

FIGURE 38 Henry Goodman as Shylock and Gabrielle Jourdan as Jessica. National Theatre production (1999).
John Haynes/Lebrecht Music & Arts.

passage speaks to the world Shylock wishes he still had, a world with a loving family tradition. The text, of course, does not show us this Shylock, except by implication – in the line spoken in Act 3, Scene 1, when he hears that Jessica has traded her late mother's ring for a monkey. There, as every Shylock discovers, the inner man reveals himself, however briefly: "it was my turquoise, I had it of Leah when I was a bachelor. I would not have given it for a wilderness of monkeys" (3.1.95–97). But this production brings that world onstage, in the song Shylock would have sung to his wife, in the framed photograph that he gazes at so lovingly before he leaves the stage (a moment that also allows Jessica to speak privately to Gobbo and to hand him a letter for Lorenzo with lines taken from 2.3), and in the tenderness he shows to Jessica.

Yet, this revelation of Shylock's love for Jessica is immediately counterbalanced by a reminder that his love can turn both ugly and possessive. No sooner does Gobbo mention masques than Shylock becomes the protective father overlaid with a highly suspicious alien; his mention of the "wry-necked fife" (2.5.29) implies that he's heard it far too often, and when he warns, "Nor thrust your head into the public streets," (2.5.31) he slaps Jessica's face, as if he's had to give this warning before. He calms down, and uses the explanation of "my house's ears – I mean my casements" (2.5.33) as a kind of embarrassed apology. Taken aback with his own behavior, he looks ashamed, covers his face briefly, then hugs her. All of the embraces and touches in this scene start with Shylock, never with Jessica. The final over-protective moment comes as he leaves, then reappears to call out "Fast bind" and to hear her reply "Fast find" (2.5.52), as if they have a parting ritual. But the damage has been done and the motivation for "I have a father, you a daughter lost" (2.5.55) is clear.

Where did this interpolated scene come from? In a 2007 interview with Rivka Jacobson, given while he was playing Tevye in *Fiddler on the Roof* at the Savoy Theatre, Goodman talked about his Jewish background directly, and especially about the connections he felt to Shylock and to Tevye, both, of course, fathers with a daughter who marries "out." Goodman was born into a Jewish family, lived in the East End, watched his mother light candles on the Sabbath, and was bar mitzvah; yet, as he explained to Jacobson, his name was Henry (and his brothers were named Stephen and Gerald), his parents spoke only English although they clearly knew Yiddish, and their synagogue attendance seemed primarily confined to holidays. After his bar mitzvah, Goodman did get up early some mornings for a minyan (the required quorum of ten for prayer) at the synagogue, but he did so in order to make "a few shillings." According to Goodman, the Hebrew in this production seems to have come from him:

Goodman explains that he and Nunn discovered things together. There is no Hebrew in the play but he put in Hebrew songs because "I thought this guy is ... he does not have to be, but if you assume he is ... an Orthodox Jew looking after his daughter. The mother is not there and therefore he has to perform the mother's functions. He has to keep the Sabbath table, he has to light the candles, and he would know all that."[44]

Speaking to John O'Connor, Goodman explained the backstory he had created: "Leah had died within the past year."[45] That decision lies behind the insertion of the Hebrew text:

Trevor would say "What are the Hebrew prayers, who would teach the daughter what to do?" and I'd explain the background. I would bring in Hebrew songs and prayers and he would say "We can use a bit of that."[46]

And the conflicting moods visible in the short scene with Jessica grow out of Goodman's sense of Shylock as a Jew in a Christian world: "The great thing about Shylock is that he tries to joke with you and maintain a convivial relationship with Christian merchants. Even though he has hatred and bitterness in him, he tries to convey warmth, not irony and cynicism. But the two pull against each other and if you push him a little, the underlying bitterness comes out."[47] Goodman's understanding of Shylock – and certainly the playing of both warmth and hatred – in no way sentimentalizes the character, and he was emphatic about seeing the character clearly:

Shylock has been so brutalised and traumatised that if you push him too hard he becomes an animal. I felt very strongly that we don't want to be too nice and sympathetic to him. We must believe that he could kill someone. He is actually not a nice guy. He is a scheming, dangerous man. And if you try and make him a nice guy because he is Jewish, and I am Jewish, then you throw away the play. You don't feel sorry for him. You become weary of him.[48]

44 Rivka Jacobson, "On Jewishness, Shylock and Tevya," www.britishtheatreguide.info/otherresources/interviews/HenryGoodman.htm.

45 John O'Connor, "Shylock in Performance," in *The Merchant of Venice: New Critical Essays*, ed. John W. Mahon and Ellen Macleod Mahon (New York: Routledge, 2002), footnote 45.

46 Judi Herman, "Shylock Revisited – Playwrights Julia Pascal and Arnold Wesker and Actor Henry Goodman Talk to Judi Herman," *Jewish Renaissance*, October, 2007.

47 Jacobson, "On Jewishness."

48 Ibid.

In such a statement, Goodman echoes Sher talking about the way in which Shylock's violence must be acknowledged. And indeed, when Sher wrote about preparing the role that he "didn't feel haunted by Olivier's performance as I had before [when he played Richard III in 1984]," he added a graceful parenthesis: "though I'm glad I hadn't yet seen Henry Goodman's Shylock, quite simply the best."[49]

Though Alexander's and Nunn's productions made such different choices in terms of setting – and the level of expression of prejudice, both towards Jews and towards Christians – they are also clearly similar. Both Shylocks are foreigners, Sher exuberantly so, Goodman a more sober, tailored, genial figure, closer perhaps to Suchet's Shylock; all have foreign accents. While the hatred for Sher's Shylock – and his for the Christians – is overt, it's more hidden in Nunn's production. But, in a chilling way, the willingness to mock *anyone* who is different shows us a society that is destroying itself. Thus, while Lancelot Gobbo's ugly parody of Shylock becomes entertainment for a smoke-filled room of men who drink too much, the production shows us that these same men, notably Salerio and Solanio, also scorn Antonio. David Bamber's Antonio looks vaguely like T.S. Eliot, with slicked back hair and nerdy glasses; his accent is faintly regional and it is this regional accent that Salerio and Solanio use when they report how Bassanio left town and what Antonio said to him. Clearly Salerio and Solanio see Antonio's homosexual attraction to the younger, more handsome Bassanio, and they're sniggering about it, like schoolboys. But the fact is that they're not schoolboys; what's more, they, like Bassanio, take advantage of Antonio (always expecting him to pay the bill), and so their mimicry isn't funny, but nasty.

Yet this production balances the casual nastiness of the Christians (and the stupid nastiness of Gobbo) with moments that imply the society's ability to glimpse, and perhaps move away from, its own prejudices. Salerio, for instance, played by Peter de Jersey, is no longer mocking but serious when he brings Antonio's letter to Bassanio in Belmont, and, in the trial scene, he is the one who pulls the frantic Gratiano away from Shylock (Charles Spencer saw him as "visibly appalled"[50]), although, unaccountably, Salerio is completely absent from the televised version. Portia, in the trial scene, is shocked when the Duke starts to exert his authority; first, he speaks her lines as she gives the judgment – "The court awards it, and the law doth give it"; "The law allows it, and the court awards it"(4.1.296, 299); then she is taken aback by his threat of

[49] Sher, *Beside Myself*, 190.
[50] Charles Spencer, "The Merchant of Venice," *Daily Telegraph*, June 6, 1999.

recanting the pardon if Shylock doesn't convert. So her line, "Art thou contented, Jew?" becomes almost a kind of apology, as she kneels in front of Shylock and asks the question in a tender voice. And, most noticeably, Nunn reshapes the ending of the play to stress the uncertainty of the happiness, moving Portia's line, "'tis a day / Such as the day is when the sun is hid" (5.1.125–26) from her conversation with Lorenzo earlier in the scene to the very end. Even more strikingly, Nunn gives the silent (in the text) Jessica a tearful reprise of the Hebrew song she sang with Shylock; the lines she starts with praise the woman's faithfulness, "She doeth him good and not evil / All the days of her life," and her anguished face and voice reflect her awareness of the song's irony, and the loss she has both created and now feels.

Just as the production gives these characters some awareness of the implications of their actions, it also makes of Shylock a man who is able, throughout the play, but especially in the trial scene, to see what he is doing and to choose his actions. Thus he listens attentively to Portia's appeal for mercy, in part because she draws up a chair and speaks conversationally to him, in part because her words seems to resonate with him, so much so that he takes a long pause after she finishes, buries his face in his hands, and then, with a deep breath, says "My deeds upon my head" (4.1.202), as if he's struggled and finally come to his decision. He's a man whose feelings are always visible, whether in the tears that seem to come unbidden as he says "The pound of flesh which I demand of him / Is dearly bought" (4.1.99–100), clearly choking on the memory of Jessica's elopement, or with the shocked look on his face when Tubal leaves the courtroom after hearing Portia announce, "You must prepare your bosom for his knife" (4.1.241). That silent reproach stuns Shylock, but does not stop him. He is, however, almost unable to take the pound of flesh, approaching the bare-chested Antonio, then backing away, then nerving himself for the blow by tucking a towel into his belt; that gesture is the moment at which Portia suddenly thinks of the blood, perhaps by seeing him as a butcher.

The two moments of awareness that most vividly define Goodman's Shylock come after Portia stops his attack and motions him to sit in the very chair where previously Antonio sat, squirming in fear. Shylock listens as Portia reads "If it be proved against an alien" (4.1.345ff) and his face reflects his reproachful consciousness that he has always known about this law, so much so that he can almost speak the line with her; on stage, he mouthed the words, and in the televised version, we hear those words. He's angry with himself for having been so stupid as to forget what he must have known. And as he leaves the courtroom, he faces the implacable face of Antonio. Suddenly he discards his jacket, takes off his *tallit*, pointedly rips his *yarmulke* from his head, and then, wadding up the *tallit* and the *yarmulke,* drops the bundle into the scales he had brought with him. The pound of flesh is indeed dearly bought, and Shylock's gesture makes clear to all that he recognizes the price he's forced to pay. Quiet defiance, but utterly pointed as well.

"The likeness of a Jew"

As must be clear, I think that John Barton was wrong when he called Shylock "a bad Jew and a bad human being." The very different Shylocks I've discussed here all display the complex nature of the character, and the ways in which his behavior – both in its viciousness and in its moments of pathos – stems not only from his marginalized role as "the Jew" in a Christian society, but from his own perception of what being a Jew means. What emerges from the last forty years of performance is the inescapability of otherness rather than the suppression of one's religious affliation and practice. Even actors who are not Jewish, such as David Calder (in 1993, with the Royal Shakespeare Company) and Patrick Stewart (in the 2011 Royal Shakespeare Company production) have created Shylocks who at the play's beginning see themselves as "insiders" but who come to realize that they are not. Over thirty years ago, Patrick Stewart could claim that Shylock "is an outsider who happens to be a Jew," but as he prepared to play Shylock in 2011, he not only talked with one of England's most prominent rabbis, Lionel Blue, but visited Jerusalem and Tel Aviv. Moreover, like Henry Goodman, he blessed Jessica in Hebrew, using the Sabbath prayer, "May God make you like Sarah, Rebecca, Rachel and Leah."

Thus, to borrow Marvin Carlson's helpful term, the "ghosts" of past Shylocks both haunt and transform today's Shylocks. Victorian theatergoers saw Henry Irving perform – over the course of his entire career – two contrasting but related signature roles, Burgomaster Mathias in *The Bells* (first produced in 1871), the man who murders a Polish Jew, and Shylock (first produced in 1879); did Mathias's guilt find expiation in Shylock's pain and dignity? From Irving, England's first theatrical knight, to Laurence Olivier, England's first theatrical peer, the haunting power of a Shylock who reminds us that he is an abandoned father as well as a vengeful moneylender still remains. Since Olivier, Jewish actors and directors have, through their own complicated negotiations with their Jewishness, found in Shylock an expressive mirror of those dilemmas.

PART IV

LITERATURE, ART, AND MUSIC

14

Zionism in Ludwig Lewisohn's novel, *The Last Days of Shylock* (1931)

Michael Shapiro

In an essay on George Eliot's *Daniel Deronda*, John Picker proposes that the many sequels to that novel attempt "to honor the power of the original ... and to recapture and further extend that power."[1] One can readily recall other sequels, however, which draw on the cultural capital of their sources but present subtle or trenchant critiques, if not outright parodies. One example of the critical sequel is John Fletcher's extension of Shakespeare's *Taming of the Shrew*, which he entitled *The Woman's Prize, or The Tamer Tamed.* (Interestingly, it is dated 1611 and was probably written and performed around the time Fletcher succeeded Shakespeare as the chief poet of the King's Men.) In Fletcher's sequel, Petruchio, the man who tamed the shrew in Shakespeare's play, is now a widower and has just married his late wife's cousin, Maria. Maria, however, not only refuses to be tamed, but, supported by the other women in the play, defies her husband's authority and wins the upper hand only relinquishes it once Petruchio agrees to a marriage based on mutual respect. Like Fletcher's play, Lewisohn's novel is less of a testimonial to Shakespeare than a corrective.

Along with many of the works discussed in this volume, Lewisohn's *The Last Days of Shylock* is a corrective, perhaps even a reproach to *The Merchant of Venice*, from a Jewish perspective, and might therefore be listed, somewhat playfully, under the rubric of "Shylockian midrash." Like true midrash, that is, narratives based on rabbinic responses to the Hebrew Bible, the adaptations of Shakespeare's *The Merchant of*

[1] John Picker, "George Eliot and the Sequel Question," *New Literary History* 37 (2006), 363.

Venice by Lewisohn and others raise and answer questions about their source-text, discover and fill gaps, and find and tie up loose ends. In doing so, these adaptations establish a dialogue with Shakespeare and tacitly suggest other ways he might have handled the plot and characters, elements which he himself usually adapted from pre-existing literary works. Moreover, many of these adaptations introduce new issues, often using the Shakespearean text as a platform for exploring matters of current interest. Lewisohn's novel reframes the original play and extends the life of his protagonist well beyond its Shakespearean confines. He uses flashbacks to describe Shylock's early life, including the establishment of the ghetto and his marriage to Leah, and moves forward from the trial scene to describe his conversion to Christianity, his escape from Venice to Turkey, his return to Judaism and participation in Jewish life, and his reunion with Jessica. Lewisohn's invented material not only reduces the events of the play to a handful of snapshots in the photo album of Shylock's rich, full life, but also addresses such current concerns as the plight of assimilated Jews in Western societies and the fate of the Jewish settlement in Palestine.

Who was Ludwig Lewisohn? There was a time when his name was a household word among American Jews. He was a prolific writer, translator, and editor, and traveled tirelessly throughout North America as a lecturer on Jewish topics. The major events of the middle of his life, his rediscovery of Judaism and his marital and romantic difficulties, were the topics of several autobiographical works, such as *Mid-Channel: An American Chronicle* (1929), as well as of his fictionalized autobiographies, *Don Juan* (1923), *The Case of Mr. Crump* (1926), and *The Island Within* (1928). He lived in Europe from 1924 to 1934, but upon his return to the United States, until his death in 1955, he was probably the best-known Jewish public intellectual in North America. Lewisohn's life has been exhaustively chronicled in a two-volume study by Ralph Melnick published in 1998, a work I cite often, and has been revaluated more recently in an essay by Julian Levinson in *Exiles on Main Street* (2008).[2]

Lewisohn was born in Berlin in 1882. When he was seven, his parents brought him to South Carolina and soon thereafter settled in Charleston, where he attended local schools and the College of Charleston. He was a brilliant student of English literature, but felt socially stigmatized for being a Jew.[3] Although Lewisohn did graduate work at Columbia

[2] Ralph Melnick, *The Life and Work of Ludwig Lewisohn*, 2 vols. (Detroit: Wayne State University Press, 1998); Julian Levinson, *Exiles on Main Street: Jewish Writers and American Literary Culture* (Bloomington: Indiana University Press, 2008), 56–75.

[3] Melnick, *Life and Work of Ludwig Lewisohn*, vol. 1, 53–61.

University in English literature, his native fluency in German allowed him to immerse himself in modern German literature and to develop a great admiration for German culture. When the chair of the Columbia English Department informed Lewisohn that a teaching position for a Jew was an unlikely possibility, he essentially abandoned his graduate studies and found occasional work as a literary journalist.[4] Gordon Hutner sees this moment as seminal for Lewisohn's career:

> [he] spent most of the next fifty years examining the role of the alien in a gentile country, the Jew in America. He transformed the hatred and shame he suffered into a writing career, of some forty-three volumes, remarkable for its productivity, variety, frankness, and occasional distinction.[5]

He did not totally abandon the academy. Because of his knowledge of German and German literature, he found a teaching position in the German department at the University of Wisconsin in 1910. The following year he moved to the German department at Ohio State University, but left in 1917, after America's entry into World War I, in the face of hostility caused by his outspoken pacifism and by his opposition to wartime "patriotic" condemnations of German culture.[6] He moved back to New York City, where he became drama critic and then associate editor of *The Nation*,[7] aligning himself with social critics like Dreiser, Mencken, and Sinclair Lewis against what they perceived as the smugly complacent patriotism and Christian piety celebrated by mainstream American culture. In 1924, he abandoned his blossoming career as a New York literary journalist and began what was to be a ten-year European exile.

His decision to leave the country was the result of the collapse of his first marriage, the impossibility of divorce, and his relationship with the woman who would become his second wife. In 1906, Lewisohn had married Mary Childs (b. 1861), a non-Jewish playwright more than twenty years his senior. To her, he represented escape from a miserable marriage and domestic life; to him, she offered escape from loneliness and sexual frustration.[8] But after sixteen years, this unlikely and unhappy marriage started to come apart at the seams, when, in 1922, Lewisohn, aged forty-two, met and fell madly in love with the nineteen-year-old Thelma Spear (b. 1903), a half-Jewish woman from Burlington, Vermont, who wrote

[4] Ibid., 104.

[5] Gordon Hutner, "The Dynamics of Erasure: Anti-Semitism and the Example of Ludwig Lewisohn," *Prospects: An Annual of America Cultural Studies* 16 (1991), 391.

[6] Melnick, *Life and Work of Ludwig Lewisohn*, vol. 1, 210.

[7] Ibid., 241.

[8] Ibid., 109–10, 117–19.

poetry and had come to New York to pursue a career as a singer. Mary refused to give Lewisohn a divorce and indeed fought tenaciously to preserve the marriage and, failing that, to secure what she considered appropriate financial support.

By 1924, Lewisohn could see no recourse but to leave the country, with Thelma at his side, to evade the legal and emotional webs he felt Mary had woven to ensnare him. He had come to believe that the divorce laws of the United States were irrationally perverse, the product of a Christian culture that idealized wedlock as a sacrament and consequently held naïve notions about marriage.[9] In Lewisohn's mind, Mary became the symbol of much that was wrong with that Christian culture, and he began to articulate a growing interest in his Jewish roots and Jewish identity, an interest which would soon cohere into a strongly anti-assimilationist set of attitudes. His most famous novel, *The Island Within* (1928; originally published as *The Defeated* in 1927), chronicles the return to Judaism on the part of a highly assimilated Jew who "abandons his comfortable middle-class American life and gentile wife."[10]

Lewisohn had first articulated his anti-assimilationist position in an address to the Menorah Society at Harvard in 1923. Drawing on his knowledge of psychoanalysis, he argued that Jews could never really be fully themselves in the United States or anywhere else in Christendom and that the effort to assimilate was spiritually destructive and mentally debilitating.[11] The speech made a strong impression on Kurt Blumenfeld, a German Zionist leader, who introduced Lewisohn to Chaim Weizmann, head of the World Zionist Organization.[12] It was subsequently suggested that Lewisohn would quietly conduct a fact-finding mission to Poland, Austria, Italy, Egypt, and Palestine, reporting privately to Weizmann on the state of Jews in those countries.[13] After a second meeting, it was agreed that Weizmann's office would pay Lewisohn a stipend and cover expenses for a short trip to Poland, a four-week tour of Palestine, and a short stay in Austria.[14] Lewisohn would write articles for *The Nation*

[9] Ibid., 351.
[10] Ibid., 459.
[11] Levinson, *Exiles on Main Street*, 67.
[12] Melnick, *Life and Work of Ludwig Lewisohn*, vol. 1, 331–32.
[13] Ibid., 350.
[14] Ibid., 386–87. Further research may reveal the extent to which the World Zionist Organization or other Zionist agencies subsidized trips to Palestine by well-known writers who would agree to publish their observations and impressions, an idea anticipated by Theodore Herzl. Some of those invited to make such visits were prominent Jewish writers, who, like Lewisohn, had not been identified with the Zionist cause. One was Abraham Cahan, the editor of the socialist daily, *The Forward*, who was personally

and *New Palestine* (the official organ of the World Zionist Organization) and presumably a book. Meir Weisgal, editor of *New Palestine* and a close associate of Weizmann, had attended the second meeting between Lewisohn and Weizmann and recalled with pride the recruitment of this well-known writer to the Zionist cause:

> At that time, the early twenties, Lewisohn was at the height of his career. He was the literary editor of *The Nation* and famous for a number of books ... He was, however, remote from the Zionist ideology. *I sent him to Palestine for a series of impressionistic articles*, and he returned with a song of Zion on his lips. Like all converts he burned with a bright new flame ... and as a writer he brought to us not only his distinguished name but as felicitous a style as was known in America.[15]

The arrangement with Weizmann would provide him with an escape route from both Mary and the United States, and supply enough money to allow him to establish himself in Europe as a freelance writer. His immediate plan was to make brief sojourns in Germany and Austria, to travel to Poland, and then to spend four weeks in Palestine.

Lewisohn did indeed publish articles in *The Nation*, *Menorah Journal*, and *Harper's*, articles which then served as the core of a book.[16] In that volume, *Israel* (1925), he argued that the Jewish settlement of Palestine offered Jews a far better chance to be their most authentic selves than

invited by Weizmann to spend four weeks in the summer of 1925 in Palestine, where he met with labor leaders and visited kibbutzim. Preceded by much hype, his illustrated account of his visit ran in *The Forward* from October 4 to December 15 (Moses Rischin, "*The Promised Land in 1925: America, Palestine, and Abraham Cahan*," in *YIVO Annual* 22, ed. Deborah Dash Moore [Evanston: Northwestern University Press and YIVO Institute for Jewish Research, 1995], 88). He expressed admiration for "the moral beauty of the halutzim" and declared that there was no conflict between "Zionism (a Jewish question) ... [and] Socialism, a world question" (Quoted in ibid., 97). Another visitor to Palestine in 1925 was the German-Jewish writer, Ernst Toller, part of Lewisohn's social circle in Paris (Melnick, *Life and Work of Ludwig Lewisohn*, vol. 1, 413). Toller published a few short sketches but failed to write a comprehensive account of his trip, explaining that he had lost his notes. Essentially unsympathetic with the Zionist project, he advised the Zionists to ally themselves with the Arabs, rather than the European nations. He recognized but dismissed the opposition of the local Arab population, but feared its power when it was supported abroad by anti-imperialist sentiment ("Ernst Toller Discusses Palestine," *American Hebrew*, June 2, 1927, 178). In 1927, Weizmann also tried to recruit Waldo Frank "to become a spokesman for Zionism," inviting him to travel in Eastern Europe and Israel. Frank's book-length account of his travels in *Israel, Bridgehead: The Drama of Israel*, did not appear until 1957 (Levinson, *Exiles on Main Street*, 76, 84). Levinson (ibid., 67) credits Blumenthal with enlisting Albert Einstein and Hannah Arendt in the Zionist cause.

[15] Melnick, *Life and Work of Ludwig Lewisohn*, vol. 1, 350; emphasis added.

[16] Ibid., 390.

did the various Western nation-states, which insisted, gently or forcefully, on a high degree of assimilation. After the tour of Palestine, he settled in Paris, where he supported himself through royalties and freelance writing, began to collect Jewish antiquities, and immersed himself in the study of Jewish history, Hebrew language, and Judaic literature. His own writing during this period increasingly speaks to his interest in Jewish issues, particularly the futility of assimilation. Most of what he wrote during his Parisian exile drew on Jewish historical material or offered a Jewish perspective on other literary or cultural topics.

The Last Days of Shylock reflects his return to Judaism, including a reckoning of the costs, for himself as for Jessica, of marrying out of the faith. Melnick describes it as "a visionary novel of Jewish revival in the face of anti-Semitism's dominance."[17] It was received with great interest in both Jewish and non-Jewish circles. For Jews, it was an important restatement of Lewisohn's anti-assimilationist platform, important enough for the *New York Times* to report that local rabbis would give sermons based on the novel.[18] Melnick summarizes the American reviews, which appeared over several months: "some were negative, some mixed, more were positive than not."[19] Two common themes were "the delicate balance of art and propaganda" and the recognition of Shylock as "a much-abused Zionist."[20] Granville Hicks, writing in Lewisohn's former periodical, *The Nation*, praised Lewisohn for telling "a story that in a remarkable and tragic way, parallels certain events in the recent history of Palestine," but complained that the author "cannot believe in Shakespeare's Shylock [but] ... created a different person of that name,"[21] Gerald Sykes dismissed the book as "learnedly and capably written but without imagination."[22]

In 1934, three years after the publication of *The Last Days of Shylock*, Lewisohn returned to the United States. During his exile he had secured a dubious rabbinic divorce from Mary in Poland, married Thelma, and fathered their child, James. Mary continued to cause legal and financial difficulties for him, but he finally secured a Mexican divorce.[23] Once back in the United States with his domestic life in order, he threw himself into

[17] Ibid., 521.
[18] *New York Times*, January 12, 1933, 19; and February 9, 1933, 17.
[19] Melnick, *Life and Work of Ludwig Lewisohn*, vol. 1, 543.
[20] *Form and Century* 35:2 (1931), xv. See also *New York Times*, January 11, 1931, 65, 81; and *Christian Science Monitor*, July 31, 1931, 12.
[21] Granville Hicks, "A Daniel for Shylock," *Nation*, February 18, 188.
[22] Gerald Sykes, *Bookman* 73:1, 1931, 8.
[23] Melnick, *Life and Work of Ludwig Lewisohn*, vol. 2, 46.

Jewish and Zionist affairs. He began to write more and more frequently for *New Palestine*, the organ of the Zionist Organization of America, and assumed its editorship in 1943.[24] By the 1940s, he had completely transformed himself from an American man of letters into (1) an unofficial spokesperson for the Jewish community, especially noted for his early, virulent, and unrelenting attacks on the Nazis; and (2) an official representative of the Zionist movement, fully in accord with its maximalist goal of an independent Jewish nation-state in all of Mandatory Palestine.

The Last Days of Shylock catches Lewisohn in transition from cosmopolitan New York literary journalist to Jewish public intellectual. He uses the novel to articulate his disenchantment with assimilation and to confront issues he had skirted or failed to notice in his earlier reflections on the Zionist project in Palestine. Lewisohn first began to think about a novel based on *The Merchant of Venice* as early as 1929, five years after his tour of Palestine. As he wrote in October of that year to Cass Canfield, his editor at Harper and Brothers, his version of Shylock would be the first to tell the story "in connection with actual facts of his time."[25] Like many adapters of *The Merchant of Venice*, he proposed to correct the defects in the source-text caused by its author's unfamiliarity with Jewish history. This supplementary material adds details to Shylock's life both anterior and subsequent to the events of the play, as if to suggest that Shakespeare's depiction of the Jewish moneylender is merely an interlude in a far more complex life history.

Despite its polemical sub-text, the life-history Lewisohn invents for Shylock is presented in the flowery, anachronistic style of a historical novel. Drawing on wide reading, Lewisohn imagines the life of a typical Italian Jew in the early part of the sixteenth century, limning an imaginary portrait of a man of great intellect; a man deeply bound to his people, their traditions, and their current troubles; a man skilled in managing financial and administrative affairs; a man with a sharp and sardonic wit. Lewisohn fleshed out these somewhat generalized traits with details drawn from the history of Sephardic Jews.

He freely invents a life for Shylock before the opening of Shakespeare's play. When Shylock was a young boy, Jews could live anywhere in Venice until the edict of 1516, the result of a rising tide of anti-Semitism, required that they confine themselves to the ghetto.[26] On the day his family moved

[24] Ibid., 292.

[25] Ibid., vol. 1, 507.

[26] Ludwig Lewisohn, *The Last Days of Shylock* (New York: Harper and Brothers, 1931). Lewisohn's description of the herding of Venetian Jews into the ghetto conflicts with

into the ghetto, Lewisohn presents an ugly incident of anti-Semitic teasing, in which some adolescent louts torment young Shylock by hurling fresh pig meat at him and "dab[bing] him with swine's blood."[27] Shylock comes of age in the ghetto, where he studies diligently in the yeshiva until the age of seventeen, when his father dies and he must find a way to support himself and his mother. He accepts an offer from Tubal to teach him the trade of moneylending and finds he is good at it. Embittered by the suffering of his fellow Venetian Jews, as well as that of fugitive Iberian Jews, he savors the discomfort of his Christian borrowers, drives hard bargains, and eventually prospers. Much of his wealth goes to ransom Jewish refugees held as slaves or prisoners. He witnesses the burning of Jewish books in Venice and the burning of twenty-five Jews in an *auto-da-fé* in Ancona, as well as the visit of the false messiah David Ha-Reuveni. He enters into an arranged marriage with Leah, the beautiful daughter of a prominent rabbi and, while the marriage is a happy one, Leah dies young, leaving Shylock to raise their daughter, Jessica. As in the play, Lewisohn's Jessica elopes with Lorenzo, her Christian beloved, stealing some of her father's money and jewels. She lives with Lorenzo for a time in Belmont, a world which Lewisohn drains of its Shakespearean moonlit charm and presents as the epitome of pseudo-sophisticated, decadent frivolity.

In addition to creating a life for Shylock before the play opens, he also modifies some of the work's major events and carries them forward to a point well beyond the play. For example, he makes Jessica pay heavily for betraying her father, her community, and her religion. She has three sons by Lorenzo, who turns out to be a completely irresponsible husband and father. Leaving Belmont, they wander Italy together with no visible means of support, until he finally deserts her and the children, whom she supports by "the meanest labour and beggary."[28] Destitute, starving, clothed in rags, she and her sons eventually turn up on a boat full of Jewish refugees in Cyprus, where she is reunited with her father. Although she is truly penitent, he does not greet her with unalloyed rapture. His immediate response to meeting his grandsons is to order them circumcised and to rename them Abraham, Isaac, and Jacob, but little by little he softens

more recent historical accounts, which describe the formation of the ghetto in 1516 as a contractual arrangement between the government of Venice, which hitherto forbade Jews to reside permanently in Venice, and Jewish moneylenders from the mainland, whose services were now considered vital to the Venetian economy; see Riccardo Calimani, *The Ghetto of Venice* , trans. K.S. Wolfthal (Milan: Oscar Mondadori, 1995), 28–40.

[27] Lewisohn, *Last Days of Shylock*, 22.

[28] Ibid., 211.

toward Jessica, who becomes a dutiful Jewish daughter and takes good care of him in his old age, as shown in one of the illustrations made by Arthur Szyk for Harper's deluxe edition of the novel (Figure 39).

Jessica tells him the story of her marriage and its sad aftermath, but Shylock's childhood, marriage, and the elopement of Jessica are all presented as flashbacks recalled through his memory. Events and characters from Shakespeare's play are similarly presented from Shylock's point of view. He recalls Antonio as a vicious anti-Semite, "the instigator of the burning of the sacred books,"[29] from which he profits first by collecting an informer's fee and later when the same works are to be republished by a firm in which he has an interest.[30] With bitterness Shylock remembers Portia, that "young effeminate advocate from Rome" who tricked the court into denying the legality of his contract on spurious grounds.[31] The Duke, another hypocritical anti-Semite, "had tightened every Jewish restriction and deepened every Jewish shame."[32] As for the pound of flesh, it was never more than a grim joke, but he had been careless of the circumstances, as he puts it, and fell into a trap designed to fleece him of his wealth and property. He never intended to kill Antonio, for "his knife would not have gone very deep into the bosom of his adversary."[33] In short, in Lewisohn's re-presentation of the trial through Shylock's memory, he is not the agent of cruelty but the victim in part of his own naiveté, but more of Venetian cunning, hypocrisy, and greed.

What happens to Shylock after the trial, all of it invented by Lewisohn, is narrated as it unfolds. Antonio and his friends bring him under guard to the Church of San Marco, where he is to receive baptism. Lewisohn describes the conversion ceremony in elaborate and painful detail, making clear that Shylock is going through with it only to save his life and still feels himself a Jew. But as a crypto-Jew, he is vulnerable to the charge of Judaizing, that is, lapsing into Jewish belief or practice, and therefore knows it is only a matter of time before he is denounced to the Inquisition, arrested, tortured, and executed. He needs to leave Venice, and in contriving for him to do so, Lewisohn lifts him completely out of Shakespeare's Venetian framework and inserts him into an actual historical event, a Turkish-sponsored Jewish attempt to establish a colony in Ottoman-controlled Palestine. Lewisohn accomplishes this insertion by connecting

[29] Ibid., 5.
[30] Ibid., 24, 65.
[31] Ibid., 4.
[32] Ibid.
[33] Ibid.

FIGURE 39 Arthur Szyk illustration of Shylock in bed, attended by his daughter Jessica and her three sons.
Reproduced with the cooperation of the Arthur Szyk Society, Burlingame, CA; www.szyk.org.

Shylock with real historical figures, the wealthy and powerful Mendes family, Dona Gracia and her nephew and son-in-law Joseph Nasi, for whom he once did some work in Venice (Figure 40).[34] Originally Iberian, the Mendes family amassed great wealth in Europe and are now based in Turkey, where they enjoy the Sultan's favor. Lewisohn imagines that they have arranged for Shylock to escape to Constantinople immediately after his conversion and to become part of their entourage there as Joseph's "almoner," that is, his director of charitable projects. Before long, Joseph involves him in their project to establish a Jewish colony in Palestine in the decayed city of Tiberias on the shores of the Sea of Galilee.

Shylock's experience in Tiberias is much darker than Lewisohn's depiction of Palestine in 1924, as reported in *Israel*. Optimistic and idealistic, that work is essentially a Zionist travelogue; it emphasizes the necessity for a Jewish homeland, the natural beauty of Palestine, the improvements Jews have made to the land (e.g. the draining of swamps), their scientific and collectivized approach to agriculture. It mentions the Arab problem as "our most serious one" but touches on it lightly and infrequently. From our postcolonial vantage point, his view of the Arab problem sounds condescendingly idealistic. Despite their neglect of the land, he argues, their ignorance and poverty, their resistance to progress, and their understandable distrust of the growing Jewish presence, "Their rights and our duties remain the same."[35] For him, those rights and duties preclude Jewish political domination: "We desire to possess the land creatively and not in terms of power and force and dominance. A constitution will be drafted in time. Under it we expect equal rights with Arab and Christian. No more. For all that we bring to the land we ask no more than equality with the people of continuous residence in it."[36] Lewisohn seems to be advocating a bi-national state (an idea advocated at this time by such Zionist thinkers as Martin Buber and Judah Magnes). But in a later passage, he suggests that the Jews, who have seen the danger of the nation-state, do not even want a bi-national state let alone a nation-state of their own, but are content "to abstain from the exercise of political power, from the ambition for it, and rather suffer temporary ills and disappointments than question the right and supremacy of the British Mandatory."[37] Such a settlement "that abstains from power ... shall ... be a light unto the

[34] For a historical account of this illustrious family, see Cecil Roth, *The House of Nasi: The Duke of Naxos* (Philadelphia: Jewish Publication Society, 1948).

[35] Ludwig Lewisohn, *Israel* (New York: Albert and Charles Boni, 1925), 238.

[36] Ibid., 209.

[37] Ibid., 236.

FIGURE 40 Arthur Szyk illustration of Dona Garcia and Joseph Nasi. Reproduced with the cooperation of the Arthur Szyk Society, Burlingame, CA; www.szyk.org.

Gentiles", and will be the realization of the deep-seated pacifist strain he traces in Judaic thought through a flurry of Biblical quotations.[38]

Lewisohn's views were in accord with official Zionist statements on the Arab problem. Indeed, in 1922, his own journal, *The Nation*, published a statement from the Jewish National Council of Palestine, which sought to reassure the Arabs that Zionism was not a threat to the indigenous population: "We come not to dominate you, as our traducers allege against us, nor yet to encroach on your own perfect and sacred rights." Instead of domination, "[we seek] to bring a sheaf of blessings on all the toilers in this land; and above everything, not to encroach on anybody's rights and privileges."[39]

In *Israel*, Lewisohn's remarks on the Arab problem reflect the benevolent statements of the Zionist leadership. Not wishing to present the Arab problem "in colors unduly dark," he acknowledges "the breath of a sullen hostility" in "purely Arab towns and villages," but hastens to observe that "in many other parts of the country ... the relations between Jewish and Arab workers are excellent."[40] Any existing tension results from "the anti-Jewish influences of Europe."[41] The prosperity that the Jews have brought to Palestine, as well as the availability of new Jewish-built hospitals and clinics and the advantages of sanitary engineering, have not only benefited Palestinian Arabs but have attracted Arabs from neighboring lands. What is totally absent from the book is any sense of the depth of resentment or hostility on the part of the Arabs and thus a lack of awareness of the need for self-defense on the part of the Jewish settlers.[42]

Lewisohn's failure to mention the issue of self-defense in *Israel* is puzzling. Even before the Balfour Declaration (1917), Jewish settlers responded to theft and armed robbery against Jewish settlements and

[38] Ibid., 254–55, 276.

[39] Jewish Manifesto, 674, quoted in June Sochen, "Views of 1920s Palestine," *Judaism* 53 (2004), 73.

[40] Lewisohn, *Israel*, 239.

[41] Ibid.

[42] Lewisohn's account of his visit makes the *Yishuv* of 1924 resemble in certain respects the Jewish settlement of Palestine as imagined by Theodore Herzl in *Old-New Land* (n.p.: Filiquarian, n.d. [1902]). In Herzl's imagination, the Jewish community of Palestine in the 1920s would be a quasi-socialist utopia under Turkish political control. It has no army (ibid., 94) because there is no need for one. The local Arab population is grateful to the Zionists for bringing prosperity to the land, along with the draining of swamps and the introduction of modern sanitation and medicine (ibid., 141–45). Herzl also describes a public relations project whereby the leaders of the *Yishuv* chartered a cruise ship, "The Futuro," so that a group of specially invited international intellectuals could visit Palestine and write about their impressions (ibid., 247–50). I am grateful to Rhona Seidelman for pointing out these parallels.

individuals by organizing armed militias, such as *Bar Giora*, formed in 1907, and *Ha'shomer*, formed in 1909. Widely celebrated in the Zionist movement, and sometimes romanticized, the members of these groups wore colorful Arab or Circassian garments, as shown in photographs of their units, spoke Arabic, became expert horsemen, and mastered the use of weapons. Arab militancy in 1920 and 1921 led to an even more serious measure of self-defense: the formation of the Haganah, the clandestine self-defense militia of the *Yishuv*, the Jewish settlement in Palestine.[43] It is hard to believe that Lewisohn, an intelligent and well-informed man, was unaware of Arab militancy and Jewish self-defense and one suspects that he viewed Israel in 1924 in the light of his belief in Judaism as a religion of pacifism, and perhaps in a light that would please his Zionist patrons.

Like *Israel*, Lewisohn's fictionalized account in *The Last Days of Shylock* of the proto-Zionist colony in Tiberias describes no measures for self-defense but differs from the earlier work in acknowledging the need for them. As we have seen, in a bold addition to the Shylock story, Chapters 8 and 9 of Lewisohn's novel inject Shylock into Jewish history, into the lone effort to resettle Jews in Palestine several hundred years before young Jews from Russia created the first modern settlements at the end of the nineteenth century. The historical rebuilding and resettlement of Tiberias were sponsored, with the approval of the Ottoman Empire, by Joseph Nasi, who had become a close advisor of Emperor Suleiman the Magnificent of Turkey (1520–66). In 1561 or 1562, following up promises made to his aunt and mother-in-law, Dona Gracia, Suleiman leased to Joseph the right to restore the ruined city of Tiberias and the control of seven adjacent villages. The real Joseph Nasi himself never traveled to Palestine, but appointed his agent, Joseph ben Ardit, as his on-site manager. The actual plan was to encourage Jews from Italy (probably Iberian refugees) to emigrate to Tiberias, rebuild the fallen walls of the city, establish Tiberias as a center for the weaving of wool and silk, and build a yeshiva. The historical colony was apparently disbanded in the early seventeenth century. In Lewisohn's imagined Tiberias, recast as a major player in Levantine Jewish history, Shylock becomes co-manager of the colony, a colony which has important similarities to and differences from the *Yishuv* under the British Mandate as he observed it in 1924.

Like the actual *Yishuv*, Lewisohn's Tiberias is to be a haven for Jews of Europe (more so than from elsewhere in the Levant). Nasi's actual

[43] Howard Sachar, *A History of Israel: From the Rise of Zionism to Our Time*, 3rd edn. (New York: Knopf, 2010), 80–81, 171, 213–14.

historical plan to bring Italian Jews to Tiberias becomes, in the novel, a Zionist exodus from all over Europe. Lewisohn has Nasi issue "a proclamation in the harbours of Europe that the oppressed of Israel were to arise and make themselves ready to return to the land of the fathers under his protection."[44] In describing the response to this proclamation, Lewisohn rhapsodizes about Jews streaming toward the ports of Europe "from Lithuanian bogs, from Volhynian plains, from the immemorial congregations of Rhineland cities, from the towns of the Vosges Mountains and from the fair towers of France."[45]

The political situation of Lewisohn's Tiberias colony resembles the *Yishuv* under British administration as seen from a Zionist perspective, with Turkey playing the role of Great Britain. Although the colony of the novel has the blessings of the Sultan, some of the officers he sends to accompany Shylock are less than enthusiastic about their mission to assist in the development of a Jewish colony. One of them seems to be in collusion with hostile Bedouin leaders. At one point, Shylock wonders how they will be able to protect their people and receives the following reply from his co-manager, astonishing in its naiveté: "If need be there will be signal fires burned by the holy rabbanim of Safed and these will be answered and lit from hill to hill, even to Yerushalaim where dwells the governor of the Sultan, an honourable man and one who is indebted to our master."[46] Unlike the leadership of the *Yishuv*, they make no other plan for self-defense, with the exception of rebuilding the walls of the city. Shylock daydreams about "a great, free Jewish folk, which would armour itself with strength and with valour and, if need were, with the sword ... and defend its right to be avenged upon its foes," but realizes that "for more than thirteen centuries ... Israel had not touched a sword" and that "there was not a word in Talmud or liturgy ... that bade the people rebel or fight or even defend themselves."[47]

In its relationship with the indigenous neighbors, Lewisohn's Tiberias colony also suggests parallels with the *Yishuv*. While artisans of the seven surrounding villages are eager to have the work of rebuilding the walls, others in the area are strongly opposed to the settlement of Jews from abroad in what they regard as their traditional territory. Bedouins set up encampments all over the new town in order to reassert what they claim is their ancient right to graze their cattle on the shores of the Sea of

[44] Lewisohn, *Last Days of Shylock*, 134.
[45] Ibid., 135.
[46] Ibid., 139.
[47] Ibid., 160–61.

Galilee. Lewisohn interprets the situation in terms of friendly neighbors (Arabs) and hostile agitators (Bedouins), a binary formulation often used by early Zionists: "the poor villagers desired to partake of these gifts [work, grain, healing and peace], but the wild men of the desert would not let them."[48] Lewisohn gives Arab hostility a more religious cast than was usually presented in Zionist accounts. Shylock's co-manager fears that opponents of the settlement will claim that the presence of Jews discourages pilgrimage and so weakens the Islamic faith: "They will lie and steal, if no worse, and believe that they are defending the honour of their Prophet."[49] Still later on, a holy Muslim elder cites an ancient parchment cursing anyone who rebuilds the walls of Tiberias.[50]

As Jews in Mandatory Palestine would often claim, inter-ethnic tensions led to hostility which led to violence. In Lewisohn's Tiberias, when four Jews are found murdered on a construction site, Shylock and ben Ardit seek justice from the Pasha of Safed, a Turkish official appointed by Suleiman, but are appalled by his severity. Here the parallel with Mandatory Palestine breaks down. Whereas Jews of the *Yishuv* perceived the British response to Arab rioting in Palestine as lenient, the Pasha summarily orders the beheading of the three men accused of the crime along with the chiefs of their villages, and further orders that their heads be affixed to poles set up around Tiberias as a warning to those who would harm Jews against the Sultan's wishes. Appalled by the Pasha's brutality, Shylock and ben Ardit agree that more trouble is likely to follow: "now are our hands no longer clean, and we are made strife unto our neighbours."[51] They return to Tiberias to find that both the Jews and friendly Arab artisans have stopped work on the rebuilding of the fortifications of the colony, and that the Jews are in a demoralized and disillusioned state: "They had come with a great hope; they had sent their midwives to help the Arab women in labour and their leeches to heal the sick and had worked beside the Arabs and called them brethren, remembering the words of the Torah that the sojourner in the land of Israel was to be entreated even as the homeborn."[52]

Nor does the novel endow the Jewish colonists with the resiliency to persist, as did the settlers in the *Yishuv*, in the face of Arab resentment and even violence. When an expected shipload of supplies and new settlers

48 Ibid., 153.
49 Ibid., 155.
50 Ibid., 165.
51 Ibid., 171.
52 Ibid., 174.

fails to reach Palestine, Shylock decides to return to Constantinople to investigate. Once back at court, he discovers that the Sultan's affections for Joseph Nasi have cooled. Shylock is able to help him regain the Sultan's favor, but Suleiman is now preoccupied with other matters, to which the novel turns its attention, and although the actual colony lasted for several more decades, as the novel tells us no more about it, it has, from the narrative point of view, withered away.

Taken as his veiled account of the *Yishuv's* relationship with the British colonial administration and its Arab neighbors, Lewisohn's narrative of the Tiberias project and its problems is far more candid and pessimistic than the observations about the Jewish settlement in Palestine he published in 1925. While Shylock may articulate Lewisohn's belief in a pacifist Judaism, he cannot ignore intense local opposition to Jewish settlement in Palestine. By the summer of 1929, no one could ignore such opposition, as newspapers throughout the world reported the outbreak of violence that August, supplying graphic accounts of atrocities committed against Jews and the relatively high number of casualties and fatalities on both sides. In a letter to Cass Canfield, dated October 12, 1929, around the time he first began thinking about his adaptation of *The Merchant of Venice*, he referred to "the tragic events in Palestine."[53] In short, writing during his Parisian exile, no longer a guest of and not yet a spokesman for the Zionist movement, newly aware of unprecedented violence in Palestine, Lewisohn evidently felt he had the freedom and the opportunity to address the conflicts between Jewish settlers and Arab residents with greater candor than he had earlier. In subsequent years, in response to the rise of Nazism, the horrors of the Holocaust, and the perils of the *Yishuv* in the years after the war, Lewisohn would abandon the pacifism of his earlier days. He not only supported measures of self-defense in principle but even played an active role in smuggling weapons to Jewish fighters in Palestine, who were in active conflict with local Arabs and later with armies of neighboring states, as well as with the British civil and military authorities.[54]

Stanley Chyet, who has traced the evolution of Lewisohn's Zionist thought, misses the importance of *The Last Days of Shylock*, ascribing its author's shift from a pacifist to a more aggressive and maximalist Zionism to the rise of Hitler and the Holocaust.[55] But *The Last Days*

[53] Melnick, *Life and Work of Ludwig Lewisohn*, vol. 1, 506.

[54] Ibid., vol. 2, 347–48.

[55] Stanley Chyet, "Lewisohn, a Zionist," in *Rafael Mahler Jubilee Volume*, ed. S. Yeiven (Tel Aviv: Vered Press, 1973), 103–36.

of Shylock seems to me to indicate that such a transition was already under way as early as 1929–30, and that in reworking Shakespeare's treatment of Shylock and extending it, especially through the Tiberias episodes, Lewisohn was able to assess more clearly than he had in 1924 the depth of Arab resentment and the need for Jews to defend themselves.

Nonetheless, he apparently still felt the need to distance himself from these issues and so in the novel addresses them through a veil of Sephardic history, a choice which makes his Shylock into far more of an Iberian Jew than he was in *The Merchant of Venice*. In so doing Lewisohn seems to be following the lead of many German-Jewish authors of historical romances, a school indebted to Walter Scott's *Ivanhoe* (1819), published in German in 1820. Influenced by Scott's portrayal of Rebecca, daughter of Isaac of York, works in this sub-genre often featured alluring Sephardic Jewesses at the center of romantic narratives through which these writers addressed such problems as assimilation and intermarriage.[56] In *The Last Days of Shylock*, Lewisohn used the Sephardic father–daughter dyad not only to correct what he saw as Shakespeare's anti-Semitic caricature, but also as a vehicle for his own concerns – the false lure of assimilation and the deepening problems of the Zionist project in Palestine, concerns which continue to resonate powerfully in the minds of Jews throughout the world.

[56] Jonathan Hess, *Middlebrow Literature and the Making of German-Jewish Identity* (Stanford: Stanford University Press, 2010), 27–28, 33. Herman Sinsheimer, whose work on *The Merchant of Venice* is discussed in Chapter 3, contributed *Maria Nunez* (1934) to this tradition, Lewisohn was soon to begin another novel, *Renegade* (1942), set in France, in which his Sephardic hero would embrace not the political ideals of the French revolution but "the spiritual promises embodied in Jewish tradition" (Melnick, *Life and Work of Ludwig Lewisohn*, vol. 1, 163).

15

Jessica's Jewish Identity in Contemporary Feminist Novels

Michelle Ephraim

> Alack, what heinous sin is it in me
> To be ashamed to be my father's child!
> But though I am a daughter to his blood,
> I am not to his manners. O Lorenzo,
> If thou keep promise, I shall end this strife,
> Become a Christian and thy loving wife.
> *Jessica, The Merchant of Venice* (2.3.15–20)[1]

Beginning with Erica Jong's erotic romance *Serenissima*,[2] adaptations of *The Merchant of Venice* by women novelists start to appear contemporaneously with the rise of "third-wave feminism" in the 1980s. As the feminist movement broadened to embrace diverse issues of race, religion, and ethnicity, Jewish novelists were drawn to Shylock's daughter, Jessica, in whom Shakespeare constructs female autonomy and Jewish identity as a rigid binary opposition. Of Shakespeare's rebellious literary daughters, Jessica is unique in that her marriage to a Christian man is both a rejection of her father and of her religious/racial identity (Figure 41).[3] Jessica was

[1] William Shakespeare, *The Merchant of Venice*, ed. M. Lindsay Kaplan (Boston: Bedford/St. Martin's, 2002). All quotations from the play are from this edition and are identified parenthetically in the text.

[2] Erica Jong, *Serenissima* (Boston: Houghton Mifflin, 1987).

[3] As Jessica's statement above about her shared blood with Shylock suggests, her religious conversion, problematic in itself, also does not resolve the issue of her racial identity as a Jew. Scholarship on *The Merchant* over the last two decades has shown that the text complicates Jessica's Christian conversion in its suggestion of blood-based or racial ties between Jewish father and daughter. On the play's ambiguity about Jessica, see Mary Janell

FIGURE 41 Shylock gives Jessica the keys to his house, Act 2, Scene 3. Engraving, c. 1830s, anonymous.
Courtesy of the Folger Shakespeare Library, Washington DC.

once hailed by feminist critics for her independent spirit and escape from an oppressive father.[4] But the five adaptations I discuss in this chapter represent Shylock as a compassionate humanitarian for the purpose of what I contend is their main objective: to rehabilitate Jessica as a loyal daughter who feels no "strife" about embracing her Jewish identity. Mirjam Pressler's *Shylock's Daughter* (1999), Grace Tiffany's *The Turquoise Ring* (2005), Erica Jong's *Serenissima* (1987), Faye Kellerman's *The Quality of Mercy* (1989), and Paula Marantz Cohen's *Much Ado about Jessie Kaplan* (2004) span a range of traditional "women's lit" genres – historical fiction, romance novel, and chick lit – but each of their adaptations of *The Merchant* similarly refuses Shakespeare's representation of Jessica as a contented Christian wife unmoved by the persecution of her father.[5]

It will be my central contention in this chapter that feminist writers seize onto the opportunity of the textual gaps surrounding Jessica's character in *The Merchant of Venice*. By filling in these gaps through their revisions and amendments to her story, these authors turn Shakespeare's Jewish daughter into a site of reconciliation between female sexual/emotional independence and traditional, patriarchal Judaism. Ultimately, their novels are deeply invested in the idea that Jewish faith, culture, law, and ritual are fundamental to the Jewish woman's most satisfying conceptions of selfhood.

Despite her theft of her father's gold and her marriage to Lorenzo, *The Merchant* is ultimately ambiguous about Jessica's familial and marital attachments. In Act 5, she taunts Lorenzo for "Stealing her soul with many vows of faith, / And ne'er a true one" (5.1.18–19) and looks on silently as Lorenzo celebrates the news that Shylock's death will make

Metzger, "Now by My Hood, a Gentle and No Jew": Jessica, *The Merchant of Venice* and the Discourse of Early Modern English Identity," *PMLA* 113:1 (1998), 52–63; M. Lindsay Kaplan, "Jessica's Mother": Medieval Constructions of Jewish Race and Gender in *The Merchant of Venice*," *Shakespeare Quarterly* 58:1 (2007), 1–30; Janet Adelman, *Blood Relations: Christian and Jew in The Merchant of Venice* (Chicago: University of Chicago Press, 2008).

4 Like other Shakespearean daughters, of course, Jessica struggles against a father unwilling to let her grow up; Camille Slights, "In Defense of Jessica: The Runaway Daughter in *The Merchant of Venice*," *Shakespeare Quarterly* 31:3 (1980), 357–68.

5 Mirjam Pressler, *Shylock's Daughter*, ed. and trans. Brian Murdoch (New York: Phyllis Fogelman, 2001); Grace Tiffany, *The Turquoise Ring* (New York: Berkley Books, 2005); Jong, *Serenissima*; Faye Kellerman, *The Quality of Mercy*, (New York: William Morrow, 1989); Paula Marantz Cohen, *Much Ado about Jessie Kaplan* (New York: St. Martin's, 2004). While Tiffany herself is not Jewish, I would argue that her novel, like the adaptations of *The Merchant* by Jewish feminist authors I discuss in this essay, is similarly invested in restoring Jessica's Jewish identity.

him a rich man.[6] In fact, for the last 250 lines of the play, as the Christians announce that Shylock has been charged with attempted murder, and punished with poverty and forced conversion, Jessica is onstage but does not speak a word. Is she relieved? Remorseful? In imagining and articulating Jessica's desires for both autonomy and Jewish identity, the adaptations I discuss perform *The Merchant* as a type of feminist midrash (scriptural commentary), evoking the integrative work that female theologians have done in their re-readings of rabbinical texts. As these feminist novels offer us different endings for Jessica, they also enact symbolically an interpretive control over the male, Christian authorship of the play. While *The Merchant* is frustratingly inconclusive on the matter of Jessica's emotional life, her silence, I would argue, becomes a lacuna of opportunity in the feminist novel.

As I will show, the novels offer two models of a revised Jessica: the tragic daughter and the feminist heroine. I first discuss the tragic daughter figure in Pressler's and Tiffany's historical novels, *Shylock's Daughter* and *The Turquoise Ring*. They are, like *The Merchant*, set in sixteenth-century Venice, and both follow the basic plot of Shakespeare's play: Jewish daughter trades oppressive usurer father and their depressing Venetian ghetto for a Christian man and his ostensibly charmed life. But through their elaborations on Jessica's character, Pressler and Tiffany revise *The Merchant* as the tragedy of the Jewish daughter; her fate is not freedom but, instead, heartbreak and remorse. Most significantly, both authors depict Jessica's lament for her family and her faith as also a yearning for a specifically female Jewish community. Tiffany, notably, constructs the back story of Jessica's mother, Leah, to offer what is for Jessica (and the reader of *The Merchant*) an elusive model of Jewish, female identity that reconciles religious devotion and personal desire.

This fantasy of Leah anticipates the second model of Jessica I discuss: the feminist heroine who emerges in Erica Jong's *Serenissima* and Faye Kellerman's *The Quality of Mercy*. Jong and Kellerman liberate Jessica from the ghetto, imagining her instead as a privileged American or British beauty who travels extensively (even, in Jong's case, through time itself). Their romance novels construct an original plot for Shylock's daughter and, as I will show, appropriate the nineteenth-century literary

[6] Jessica's provocative exchange with Lorenzo on the subject of filial and marital infidelity and her final line, "I am never merry when I hear sweet music" (5.1.67), perhaps suggest Jessica's remorse. In response to Portia's announcement that Lorenzo and Jessica will receive "From the rich Jew, a special deed of gift,/After his death, of all he dies possessed of," Lorenzo effuses "you drop manna in the way/Of starved people" (5.1.290–93).

prototype of the *Belle Juive* (beautiful Jewess) as a post-feminist, sexually liberated heroine.[7] Their precocious Jewish daughters – the aging starlet Jessica Pruitt and the cross-dressing heiress Rebecca Lopez – reconcile the rigid binaries of *The Merchant*. Both protagonists are able to occupy simultaneously the roles of independent, sexually empowered adult and devoted Jewish daughter. As I will show, in both Kellerman's and Jong's novels the Jewish daughter's sexual control over the fictional character of Shakespeare is symbolic of the interpretive agency of the Jewish, female author who rewrites and rehabilitates Shakespeare's Jessica.

This sexual and metatextual conceit emerges too in Paula Marantz Cohen's "chick lit" novel, *Much Ado about Jessie Kaplan*, with which I conclude this chapter. In Cohen's novel, the elderly widow Jessie insists that she was once the paramour of the "real" Shakespeare; *The Merchant*, she explains, is merely Shakespeare's bitter reaction to their break-up. My reading of *Much Ado* serves as a type of coda to this chapter; through her story, too, Cohen imagines an interpretive mastery over Shakespeare, but the Shakespeare in her novel has come full circle. Cohen's Shakespeare is not a formidable Christian author who suppresses the Jewish daughter, but a sympathetic lonely-heart in need of Jessie Kaplan's benevolent attention.

The trope of Shakespeare's passion for a "real-life" Jessica is not a sexual fantasy so much as the writerly fantasy that inspires all of these novels. In their imaginative retellings, *The Merchant* is rewritten as a story focused on the Jewish daughter, and Shakespeare is conceived as an author obsessed with her as a lover and as a subject, intimately familiar with her complex emotional life, her sexual and religious desires, and the Jewish identity to which she is committed.

The Merchant as Feminist Midrash

In the most traditional reading of *The Merchant*, the disobedient daughter Jessica serves as foil to Portia, who is able to fulfill her romantic desires while adhering to her father's posthumous stipulation that she marry the man who solves the riddle of the three caskets. But it is Portia's

[7] On the *Belle Juive*, see Harley Erdman, *Staging the Jew* (New Brunswick, NJ: Rutgers University Press, 1997), 40–57; Florian Krobb, "La Belle Juive: Cunning in the Men and Beauty in the Women," *Images in Literature* (1992), 5–11. Bergman-Carton notes the "wide and varied" traits of this literary figure (p. 55); Janis Bergman-Carton, "Negotiating the Categories: Sarah Bernhardt and the Possibilities of Jewishness," *Art Journal* 55:2 (1996), 55–64.

persona as a clever interpreter of texts that is most illuminating to the feminist revisions of Jessica that I discuss in this chapter.[8] In her magisterial disguise during the trial in which Shylock seeks Antonio's "payment" of a pound of flesh, Portia demonstrates her interpretive mastery over Shylock, ascertaining the flesh-but-not-blood loophole in the bond's language that thus enables the Christians to prevail in the trial.

In the feminist adaptations of *The Merchant* that are the subject of this chapter, however, this interpretative mastery is associated instead with Jessica who, I contend, also serves as a figure of the feminist author who revises and appropriates *The Merchant* as her own. As I will ultimately argue in my discussion of the three novels that represent Jessica's romance with Shakespeare himself, the Jewish daughter's dominating role in this relationship, her power over his physical body, becomes also a symbolic wresting of control over Shakespeare's Christian, male text.

I would contend, too, that the authors' deployment of this conceit takes inspiration from the work that feminist theologians have done over the last four decades to identify and validate the female, Jewish subject in Jewish *halakhah* (the interpretation of Jewish law in the Talmud). The feminist versions of *The Merchant* I discuss below subvert Shakespeare's authorial power by embracing the reconciliation of patriarchal Judaism and female autonomy that feminist theologians have argued for in their re-readings of traditional rabbinic commentaries on Jewish law.

Scholars such as Rachel Adler have shown that Jewish law can be read as supporting women's rights, whether the freedom to divorce or the pursuit of sexual pleasure. Adler, while addressing the restrictions of *halakhic* marriage law, notes also how the traditional Jewish marriage contract, the *Ketubah*, includes stipulations that a married woman has a right to a share of her husband's property and to sexual satisfaction.[9] Rabbi Danya Ruttenberg, for example, argues that the Talmudic interpretation of *niddah*, the law prohibiting sexual intercourse during menstruation, can be understood through a feminist lens. Discussions of the ritual, she notes,

[8] In literary adaptations and popular culture, Portia connotes a clever rhetorician, trailblazing lawyer, and feminist advocate. Edith G. Gelles takes the title of her biography on Abigail Adams, first lady and champion of women's rights, from Adams's Shakespearean pen-name: *Portia: The World of Abigail Adams* (Bloomington: Indiana University Press, 1991). The Portia School of Law (later, the coed New England School of Law), the first law school for women, was founded in 1908. See also Claude Pearson's law-partner protagonist in his novels *Portia, a Lawyer for All Seasons* (2006) and *Portia Rising* (2009).

[9] Rachel Adler, "The Jew Who Wasn't There: *Halakhah* and the Jewish Woman," in *On Being a Jewish Feminist*, ed. Susannah Heschel (New York: Schocken, 1983), 16. See also Rachel Adler, *Engendering Judaism* (Boston: Beacon Press, 1998), 135.

have "a long textual history in which women are depicted as evil and polluting," but *niddah* can also be interpretively reclaimed in feminist exegeses "as a way of sanctifying intimate relationships, of instilling a sense of a sacred cycle into our partnerships."[10] Indeed, the general purpose of these reconsiderations of *halakhah* is to show how Jewish law supports the "sanctifying [of] intimate relationships" rather than the oppression or silencing of women.

Claire Satlof contends that such acts of interpretation are a tool for implementing feminist voices and thus a defining practice of Jewish feminism.[11] Similarly, I believe, feminist writers embrace *The Merchant* as an opportunity to collapse Shakespeare's dichotomy of oppressive Jewish father/miserable Jewish daughter and to explore how the play can generate the interpretive possibility of a daughter who ultimately values her Jewish identity as fundamental to her conception of selfhood.

As I will show in my discussions of the adaptations by Erica Jong, Faye Kellerman, and Paula Marantz Cohen in the second half of this chapter, Jessica's rejection of her Christian lover, Shakespeare, and embrace of her benevolent Jewish father, Shylock, is a revision that rehabilitates the desperate-for-Christian-husband Jessica of *The Merchant* as a young woman who embraces both her female autonomy and Jewish identity.

The Tragic Daughter: Jessica in *Shylock's Daughter* and *The Turquoise Ring*

As in *The Merchant*, Jessica in both Mirjam Pressler's *Shylock's Daughter* and Grace Tiffany's *The Turquoise Ring* is desperate to leave her father and marry the Christian Lorenzo. Pressler's and Tiffany's Jessica truly feels what is in *The Merchant* only a brief suggestion of filial guilt; in *Shylock's Daughter*, Jessica must suppress her "fierce love" for her father to go through with her escape from the Venetian ghetto.[12] The character of Jessica in these feminist novels, however, still shares Shylock's daughter's sentiments in *The Merchant*: "O Lorenzo, / If thou keep promise, I shall end this strife, / Become a Christian and thy loving wife" (2.3.18–20). Like her Shakespearean prototype, this Jessica also is desperate to fulfill

[10] Rabbi Danya Ruttenberg, "The Hermeneutics of Curiosity," in *New Jewish Feminism: Probing the Past, Forging the Future*, ed. Rabbi Elyse Goldstein (Woodstock, VT: Jewish Lights Publishing, 2008), 60.

[11] Claire Satlof, "History, Fiction, and the Tradition: Creating a Jewish Feminist Poetic," in *On Being a Jewish Feminist*, ed. Heschel, 186–206.

[12] Pressler, *Shylock's Daughter*, 44.

her romantic desires for a marriage that is also a means of escape from the confines of the ghetto: "[Lorenzo] really has to marry me, or else I'm lost. If he doesn't marry me, I'll kill myself."[13] Like Shakespeare's Jessica, too, who declares "Our house is hell" (2.3.2), she resents what she perceives as her father's bitter, dour world: the dress restrictions, dietary laws, and anything else that prohibits a lavish, carefree life. Outside of the ghetto, the freedoms and pleasures of the Christian world tantalize her. Amidst the palazzi of Venice "She felt ... that she was going into another world, a wonderful, beautiful, happy world – one that suited her far more than the Ghetto – a world where she really belonged."[14] In *Shylock's Daughter*, Jessica tells her adopted sister, the homely Delilah: "It's only an accident that I was born a Jew's daughter – a mistake of nature, yes, just like you sometimes get a white mouse in a litter of gray ones."[15] She indulges in a fantasy of racial, religious, and familial dissociation: through sheer bad luck of being born Jewish, she believes, she's been deprived of the social opportunity and material indulgence her beauty would otherwise afford.

As Pressler and Tiffany imagine Act 5 and beyond of Shakespeare' story, Jessica's dreams of life as an Italian noblewoman quickly shift to the reality of domestic disaster. She turns a blind eye to Lorenzo's stupidity and convinces herself that a small portion of her father's money would suffice to get him out of debt and allow him to establish a new business in foreign trade.[16] Lorenzo's debts are astronomical, however, and he himself is reckless, perpetually inebriated, and only interested in his wife as a cash resource. When Portia callously announces Shylock's fate and Lorenzo and Jessica's subsequent financial windfall, "Jessica stiffened and her face turned white. Not noticing, Lorenzo picked her up and whirled her in the air, crowing."[17] The Christians' relentless greed and materialism, notably, is a clever inversion of their accusations that Shylock equates "daughter" and "ducats" in *The Merchant*.

The Jessica constructed by Pressler and Tiffany experiences alienation in both the domestic and religious experience of Christian marital life. In both novels, Jessica discovers a vulgar Christian world that is a more insidious form of entrapment than the Jewish ghetto. Indeed, she "did

[13] Ibid., 106. In *The Merchant*, Jessica states that she is "much ashamed of her exchange" (2.6.36) as she elopes with Lorenzo, which may refer to her cross-dressed disguise or her secret "exchange" of father for husband.

[14] Pressler, *Shylock's Daughter*, 3.

[15] Ibid., 18.

[16] Tiffany, *The Turquiose Ring*, 130.

[17] Ibid., 342.

not speculate on the cost of changing faiths."[18] In this depraved Christian community, Jessica starts to view the Church as a place filled with graven images and, in Pressler, the surly priest who baptizes her appears "diabolical ... like an evil spirit."[19] As her new Christian companions attempt to instill in her a love of the material, hedonistic life, she becomes more pained by her choice to leave her Jewish home.

For the character of Jessica in these feminist novels, the experience of loss includes also that of female identity. In this Christian world, women are expected to be vapid, social creatures, always ready to oblige their adulterous, boozing husbands. Jessica resigns herself to the lewd behavior of Lorenzo's cohorts (a stark contrast to Jewish modesty, she observes), and to life as an objectified puppet: "her lips now formed themselves into a gracious smile, she inclined her head prettily to one side when a man paid her a compliment, and answered him with a pleasantry."[20] In becoming Christian, she has forsaken not just her Jewish identity, but her entire sense of self. In *Shylock's Daughter*, where Jessica rejects her father as well as her fellow women in the ghetto, including her adopted sister and her loyal, elderly caretaker, her most devastating loss is that of this female Jewish community whose gendered bonds are reinforced by their shared religious rituals. Jessica ultimately laments how her conversion has severed her ties with the protective female world of the ghetto:

> Never again would she stand in the [synagogue] gallery with all the other women, never again would she breathe in that familiar smell from the people around her, never again say the prayers in a Hebrew that she could barely understand. And she would no longer have the feeling when she was with other Jews of being one of them, one with the people of Israel, one with their God.[21]

Whereas at the beginning of the novel, Jessica feared being "lost" if Lorenzo were to reject her, ultimately her most devastating loss is that of the female Jewish community.

Tiffany's novel, *The Turquoise Ring*, takes its name from Jessica's mother's ring, which in *The Merchant* she insolently barters for a monkey. Tiffany's novel is striking for her addition of Shylock's deceased wife as the Jewish daughter's alter-ego and, I would argue, as an elusive Jewish, female role model for Jessica. Leah is mentioned exactly once in *The Merchant of Venice* – in Shylock's brief, mournful allusion after

[18] Ibid., 131.
[19] Pressler, *Shylock's Daughter*, 146.
[20] Ibid., 182–83.
[21] Ibid., 146–47.

he learns of Jessica's frivolous trade: "it was my turquoise; I had it of Leah when I was a bachelor: I would not have given it for a wilderness of monkeys" (3.1). But Tiffany creates an extraordinary back story for Leah – her romance with Shylock in their home village of Toledo, Spain and her tragic death at the hands of her Christian persecutors during childbirth – and integrates this storyline into the main plot. Leah's murder provokes Shylock's decision to leave Toledo and to seek refuge with the infant Jessica in Venice.

Tiffany's novel even goes so far as to explicate Jessica's attraction to Christianity as a transference of her desire for the maternal figure she has lost in Leah. Ironically, it is this yearning for a Jewish mother – for the devout Jewess Leah who, in Tiffany's novel, embodies what I describe at the beginning of this chapter as "a reconciliation between female sexual/emotional independence and traditional, patriarchal Judaism" – that motivates Jessica to run hastily toward Christian marriage. Jessica visits the local church to gaze a longing eye on artistic representations of the Virgin Mary; she also addresses the "painted Magdalen" as "sister" and "friend."[22] Without her mother and ignorant of the circumstances of her death (Shylock insists on sparing his daughter knowledge of this), Jessica's story becomes the tragedy of an impressionable, vulnerable girl suffering for the lack of a female role model.

In *The Turquoise Ring*, the noble and devout Leah becomes the vehicle through which Tiffany ironically reworks Salerio's slander, in *The Merchant*, of Shylock's Jewish blood as a corrupt "jet" to the Christians' "ivory" (3.1.30) into a young woman's proud claim of both her mother's Jewish ancestry and her devotion to Shylock. Leah, whom Tiffany constructs as the daughter of an adulterous, abusive Christian nobleman and a converted Marrano Jew, berates her father: "There is more difference between [Shylock's] blood and yours than there is between fine red wine and muscatel."[23] Most strikingly, Leah's passion for Shylock – she "dreamed of [Shylock's] laugh, tossing on the sheets of her bed"[24] – transforms the emasculated Jewish father in *The Merchant*, mocked for missing his two "stones," into the testosterone-charged hero of the Jewish resistance in Toledo, and the eroticized object of female desire.[25] With Shylock, Leah experiences a simultaneous ecstasy of religious and sexual

[22] Tiffany, *The Turquoise Ring*, 109.

[23] Ibid., 53.

[24] Ibid., 45.

[25] See also Salerio's taunting "misunderstanding" of Shylock's dismay at Jessica's rebellion ("my flesh and blood to rebel," 3.1.26) as frustrated sexual desire.

awakening that in turn offers us a counter-image to Shakespeare's Jessica, the Jewish daughter who perceives her family's faith as an obstacle to love and desire. This counter-image is developed to full effect in the novels I discuss below.

Daddy's Girl and Feminist Heroine: Jessica in *Serenissima* and *The Quality of Mercy*

In Tiffany's adaptation of *The Merchant*, the figure of Leah, the Jewish woman who maintains her independence and her faith, is the woman whom Jessica fails to become. But other feminist novels imagine such a reconciliation of sexual desire and religious faith, familial approbation and romantic love in their unique versions of Jessica's own story. Shakespeare's Jessica is the prototype of the *Belle Juive* or "beautiful Jewess," the erotic, and often dangerously exotic, beauty who later pervades the nineteenth-century novel. Because in her most deviant form the *Belle Juive* poses the threat of racial and religious contagion, this character often gets altered or marginalized in the course of a narrative. Jessica's conversion in *The Merchant* is a case in point. As Janis Bergman-Carton notes, the *Belle Juive* is often made "contained and palatable" by abandoning her Judaism – either through conversion or assimilation.[26] Jong's and Kellerman's versions of Jessica draw from this literary type, but they appropriate the *Belle Juive* for their own feminist ends.[27] In my discussion of *Serenissima* and *The Quality of Mercy* below, I hope to show how the Jewish daughter embraces the benevolent, patriarchal world of her Jewish father, while acting as a sexually and emotionally independent

[26] Bergman-Carton, "Negotiating the Categories," 56.

[27] As Erdman notes, the complex character of the *Belle Juive* "becomes the object of gentile male longing, an exotic and sometimes dangerous creature whose end is pathos and whose effect is frustrated desire" (Erdman, *Staging the Jew*, 40). Although there are different variations of this literary type, she is always irresistible to Christian men, and often saved by a Christian paramour from an oppressive father (e.g. Walter Scott's Rebecca in *Ivanhoe* and George Eliot's Mirah in *Daniel Deronda*, ed. Terence Cave [London: Penguin, 1995]). She may be associated with sexual treachery as well as moral fortitude. In a number of contemporary fictional versions of *The Merchant*, authors deploy the Jewish daughter as a moral compass, and a device through which to make a pointed statement about the depravity of her Christian counterparts. In Simon Hawke's mystery *The Merchant of Vengeance* (New York: Forge Books, 2003) a middle-aged version of Jessica, the dignified, beautiful Rachel Locke (wife of "Shy" Locke) is portrayed in stark contrast to the jealous, vindictive Christian woman who murders her son. Similarly, the innocent Jessica in Jules Tasca's play *Shylock's Daughter and Other Small Chips* (New York: Samuel French, 2007) is juxtaposed against the mercenary priest who robs her of her father's money.

adult. As such, I argue, these versions of Shylock's daughter rescind what is, for many readers, Jessica's troubling rejection of her Jewish identity in *The Merchant of Venice*, without sacrificing her independence.

Of the *Belle Juive* figures in the nineteenth-century novel, the character of Berenice in Maria Edgeworth's novel *Harrington* (1817)[28] provides an important point of contrast against which we can understand Jong's and Kellerman's particular feminist innovations to their versions of Shylock's daughter. While in Edgeworth's novel the female Jew serves to affirm male sexuality, the contemporary authors I discuss here are concerned with the sexual empowerment of their Jewish heroines. Jong and Kellerman both invoke the type of *Belle Juive* that we see in the character of Berenice, but their version of Jessica is not a marginalized figure whose foreign sensuality – and Jewish identity – is suppressed. Instead, they position the Jewish daughter, and her own sexual, familial, and religious desires, as primary subject.

In Edgeworth's novel, the young English gentleman, the eponymous character Harrington, still retains his childhood fear of Jews. But his phobic belief in Jewish malevolence is ultimately cured through his chance meeting of the noble Jewess, Berenice, the very paradigm of virtue and kindness. Significantly, Harrington first encounters Berenice during a performance of *The Merchant*. As he observes first the character of Jessica onstage, and then Berenice's horrified reaction to Jessica, the scene becomes a metatheatrical moment of recuperative transference: as Harrington's gaze shifts, the disloyal Jessica is replaced by the devoted daughter Berenice. But the blurring of the two Jewish daughters suggests also how Berenice converges with the alluring *Belle Juive* Jessica and with the figure of the actress, both of whom were associated with erotic spectacle.[29]

The hyper-sexuality of the *Belle Juive* can emasculate or sexually fortify: *The Merchant* contrasts the Jewish daughter's attractiveness with the withered sexuality of her father; *Harrington* uses the Jewish daughter to affirm her Christian lover's normative, heterosexual manhood.[30] Berenice, I would argue, is significant in the novel as an antidote for Harrington's

[28] Maria Edgeworth, *Harrington*, ed. Susan Manly (Toronto: Broadview, 2004).

[29] See Erdman, *Staging the Jew*, 46. On the association of *Belle Juive* and actress, see also Bergman-Carton, "Negotiating the Categories."

[30] In Solanio's account of Shylock's cry – "My daughter! O, my ducats! … A sealed bag, two sealed bags of ducats, / Of double ducats, stol'n from me by my daughter! / And jewels, two stones, two rich and precious stones, / Stol'n by my daughter!" (2.8.15, 18–21) – he loses his daughter and his testicles simultaneously.

traumatic identification with Jewish men, one colored with cultural association of male Jews and emasculation. Berenice's most important role is to establish Harrington's normative sexual potency and thus enable him to break away from his psychological identification with his mother – from whom he inherits his "hysterical" constitution.[31] Ultimately, the threatening aspects of the *Belle Juive* are contained, as Berenice is discovered to be of Christian parentage on her mother's side. The revelation of Berenice's Christian mother not only reassures that Berenice is less racially or religiously "Other" but rids her of the hyper-sexuality associated with the *Belle Juive*.

Unlike Edgeworth's novel, Jong's and Kellerman's erotic romances draw on the *Belle Juive* tradition to foreground the Jewish and sexual identity of their rehabilitated Jewish daughters. In the first model of *The Merchant* adaptations I discussed in this chapter, the character of Jessica starts to occupy a resistant subject position that counters her role of silent Christian wife in Shakespeare's play. This flicker of Jewish, feminist consciousness – her disgust with the treatment of women in Christian Venice, her remorse at giving up her Jewish faith – escalates in Jong's and Kellerman's novels, in which the Jewish daughter protagonist starts to become aggressive towards the figure of Shakespeare himself. Their versions of Shylock's daughter are culturally empowered; no longer entrapped in the Jewish ghetto, she is an affluent American citizen or British subject, interacting with the world as a privileged tourist.

Serenissima is in some sense an attempt to resolve Erica Jong's own ambivalence about religious identity that she describes in her 1995 memoir, *Fear of Fifty*. She describes Judaism as a fundamentally misogynistic institution that causes a double self hatred in Jewish woman as both Jews and members of the inferior sex. Yet she also expresses regret for falling away from Jewish ritual and practice, especially her failure to pass along these traditions to her own children. It is possible, I believe, to read *Serenissima* as Jong's attempt to represent Jewish identity as a journey of self-empowerment in concord with her feminist sensibilities.

In *Serenissima*, the Jewish novelist Jong constructs in her protagonist an alternate self who is not Jewish – the Park Avenue-bred, forty-three-year-old starlet Jessica Pruitt who, in a feverish delirium while in Venice,

[31] His mother "lament[s] that her dear Harrington, her only son, should so much resemble her in this exquisite sensibility of the nervous system," her amateurish medical explanation of which invites her husband's scorn and abuse: he "laughed at the whole *female* doctrine, as he called it" and beats Harrington because his wife has made "a Miss Molly of his boy" (Edgeworth, *Harrington*, 74–75, 80–81).

awakens in the sixteenth century as Shylock's daughter. The time-travel episode involves a series of kinky liaisons between Jessica-Pruitt-as-Shylock's-daughter and a very effete Shakespeare. Ultimately, this Jessica beds Shakespeare not just for sexual pleasure, but as a symbolic, metatextual gesture that points to Jong's revision of *The Merchant* itself.

At the beginning of *Serenissima*, Jessica Pruitt arrives in Venice to judge the annual film festival and to start shooting a "filmic fantasy" of *The Merchant of Venice*, in which she is to play her namesake.[32] For Pruitt, Venice signifies the provenance of her sexual identity: she recollects her first visit during her adolescence, when her diary was filled with "crypto-sexual longings."[33] Venice thus also foreshadows her adult "promiscuous lifestyle" that resulted in the loss of custody of her daughter.[34]

Soon after being magically transported to Shakespeare's time, Jessica Pruitt-as-Shylock's-daughter encounters Shakespeare himself, a bisexual thespian on the public stage who, at the will of his patron, "Lord S," participates in all variations of erotic deviance. As her sixteenth-century self, the daughter of Shalach (Shylock), Jessica Pruitt indulges in her real-life fantasies about sex with Shakespeare as well as her real-life fantasy of a loving family life. Compared to Pruitt's sterile Upper East Side childhood full of numerous delinquent step-fathers, Shalach's possessiveness is immensely desirable. As the sixteenth-century Jessica, she describes Shalach tenderly as a man who prioritizes his family over all else: "Bitter as he is toward all the world, under his grumbling exterior he is sweet to his daughter ... 'What are ducats compared to a daughter?' he likes to say. 'A Jew must oft have money to save his life, but what use is that life to him if he hath no family?' "[35]

Shakespeare's sexual relationship with Shalach's daughter begins with a scene of hedonistic, cross-dressed consummation and ends with a sadistic orgy that takes place in the synagogue. Along the way, they manage to save an abandoned infant boy, who will later figure prominently for both Jessicas – past and present – as they emerge as maternal figures. Shakespeare becomes increasingly disempowered and feminized as the sixteenth-century Jessica's determination to return home (to both Shalach and Judaism) becomes more intense. During the orgiastic frenzy at the synagogue, in a twist on *The Merchant*'s plot, rioters demand Shakespeare's flesh – as if to rape or castrate him. But Shalach's

[32] Jong, *Serenissima*, 6. In 1995, the novel was released as *Shylock's Daughter*.
[33] Ibid., 4.
[34] Ibid., 98.
[35] Ibid., 151.

daughter ultimately saves Shakespeare by way of a magic ring, a sly symbol, I would argue, of the sexual power she wields over him.

Ultimately, Shalach's daughter rejects the role of Shakespeare's lover for the role of Jewish mother and Jewish daughter, that is, for the benevolent patriarchy of Judah Shalach and his namesake, her adopted infant son, Judah: "all of history is held in abeyance as I play my greatest role. A son! We fall in love with our daughters, but we adore our sons. If women have any weakness on this earth, it is that they put their sons before themselves!"[36] She imagines Shalach "melted by grandfatherhood ... neglecting his counting house."[37] When she finally awakens from this dream-fantasy, Jessica Pruitt is forever altered, and she, too, decides to embrace the traditional roles of mother and daughter. This foray into the past inspires Jessica Pruitt to reclaim her daughter and ducats in the real world: her daughter from her ex-husband and her trust fund money from her estranged father. But Pruitt, moved by Shalach's relationship with his daughter, is also motivated to rekindle her own filial bond.

Importantly, Jong's adaptation of *The Merchant* allows for the Jewish daughter to be both erotic *Belle Juive* and devoted daughter/mother. As I argue above, the purpose of Berenice's sexual appeal is to affirm Harrington's own male, heterosexual identity; her sensual and exotic persona, linked to her Jewish identity, is repressed with the discovery of her Christian parentage. Jong allows her heroine to achieve both sexual autonomy and filial devotion, establishing her roles as mother and daughter as a conscious, independent choice. Ultimately, Jong's romance novel offers an alternative to the traditional romance: instead of choosing her lover William Shakespeare, Jessica chooses her role as single mother. As Jessica Pruitt at the beginning of the novel, she compares herself negatively to the feminist icon Queen Elizabeth I: "Tough as any man, tender as any woman, she was fast becoming my heroine. The more I read of Elizabethan England, the more I submerged the present into Shakespeare's past, the more I realized that all the last four hundred years had been a falling away from the feminism that Elizabeth herself embodied."[38] By way of her interlude as *The Merchant*'s Jessica, she is ultimately able to access this persona within herself.

Jong's narrative also places Shakespeare's fate, and that of all his writing, in Jessica's hands. Jessica's wish upon her magic ring in the final

[36] Ibid., 213.
[37] Ibid., 212.
[38] Ibid., 39.

scenes – "Let Will Shakespeare live to write!"[39] – establishes her as a type of author figure, co-opting Shakespeare's role as author of her own story. Like Jong, two other female authors, Faye Kellerman and Paula Marantz Cohen (whom I discuss in the final section of this chapter), cast Shakespeare as the means through which the Jewish daughter may enact a literal and symbolic type of control over the text of *The Merchant*. Through their portrayal of a romance between Jessica and the character of Shakespeare, these feminist adaptations of *The Merchant* enact an authorial fantasy about negating the male, Christian narrative of the play and giving voice instead to *The Merchant*'s silent and suppressed Jewish daughter.

In *The Quality of Mercy*, Faye Kellerman swaps *The Merchant*'s Venetian ghetto for an exclusive London estate, the angry moneylender Jew for the humanitarian Dr. Lopez, and self-hating Jessica for the righteous Rebecca Lopez. And Kellerman imagines a heroic motive for the real-life Lopez's ostensible communication with King Philip of Spain, a charge that led to accusations of treason. In Kellerman's story, Lopez bribes the king in exchange for the safe passage of Iberian Jews into England.[40] Most significantly, *The Quality of Mercy*, like Jong's *Serenissisma*, depicts the character of Shylock's daughter exerting sexual and authorial control over Shakespeare. In Kellerman's version of this relationship, the Jewish daughter is both a sexual partner to Shakespeare and also in possession of a type of aggressive phallic power that undermines him as both lover and author.

In *The Quality of Mercy*, the Jewish daughter Rebecca Lopez also plays the role of favorite son; Rebecca's bravery, intelligence, and swordsmanship far supersedes that of her brother. But Rebecca's most important quality is her exquisite beauty, which renders men helpless – and sometimes violent – in her presence. From a young age, Rebecca experiences how her physical attributes make her more vulnerable to men, but she also learns how to use her sexual appeal to her advantage, a strategy that defines her character – and ultimately her relationship with Shakespeare. Rebecca's sexual initiation begins in childhood, courtesy of her cousin, the dashing Dunstan, who, like every man, lies in her thrall, devastated by her every rejection. As a young girl, Rebecca parlays his lust into opportunity for advancement: Dunstan becomes her sexual as well as her

[39] Ibid., 185.

[40] See Greenblatt's discussion of the charges against Lopez. In the accounts, Lopez is accused of taking money from the King of Spain in exchange for treason against Elizabeth; Stephen Greenblatt, *Will in the World* (New York: Norton, 2004), 273–87.

academic mentor, providing her the classical education usually available only to men in exchange for full access to her body.[41] Even her rape at age twelve by the elderly Lord Marlburn she turns to her advantage. Wracked with guilt, terrified that he'd impregnated her, and foolishly believing that he'd taken her virginity, Lord Marlburn regards her with fear and lavishes gifts upon her.[42]

For Rebecca, sexual experience, in addition to being greatly pleasurable when it is of her own choosing, provides an education and a viable way of life. She can capitalize on her sexual wiles, using them for personal and political advantage – even in her efforts to rescue persecuted Jews on the continent. In this sense, Rebecca regards herself as the antithesis of her own mother, whom she sees as entrapped in a domestic space, living only to serve her husband and children and suppressing her own desires. Rebecca views her mother as enacting destruction of the female self: "her mother had confided her reveries as a young girl – how one day she'd live in the clouds made of spun sugar, fly upon the back of a golden eagle and touch the sun. Where did those dreams go? Her mother – her heart in the sky, her muscles saddled with duty."[43] Marriage terrifies Rebecca because she associates it with sexual disempowerment:

> Unlike most of the girls her age, it had never been her dream to marry, to become the perfect English gentlewoman. All she could see was young girls turning older than their years, weighted down by pregnancy that turned into obesity. Fat and saggy, disgusting in the eyes of husbands who leered and groped after smooth, supple bodies.[44]

Rebecca's concern is not vanity, however. To prematurely lose this "smooth, supple" body would rob her of her most important means of independence.

Rebecca embraces her true self when she cross-dresses and can indulge in the pleasures afforded to men such as the public theater and sword-fighting.[45] Nowhere are these attributes more significant than in the context of her relationship with Shakespeare, a romance and a power struggle in which Rebecca prevails. At the beginning of the novel, her swordfight with Shakespeare in her male disguise anticipates the man's part she plays in their sexual relationship as well: the phallic implications of the sword she thrusts (and allows to be thrust at her) reflect Rebecca's

[41] Kellerman, *The Quality of Mercy*.
[42] Ibid., 41.
[43] Ibid., 66.
[44] Ibid., 39.
[45] Ibid., 137.

sexual aggression in the bedroom as well as her forceful intervention into political matters. As a type of Jewish feminist, Rebecca is able to embrace simultaneously her carnal and spiritual desires. In symbolic terms, Rebecca's entanglement with Shakespeare – and matching his skill in fencing and in wit – plays out a metatextual fantasy of authorial control over the writer of *The Merchant of Venice*.

Seduced by Rebecca's exotic sensuality – her physical beauty and her Jewishness – Shakespeare abandons his own search for his friend's murderer to aid Rebecca in her quest to help the Spanish Jews:

> Dear Becca. His Jewess, an enchanting Levantine beauty, forbidden to him as a Christian. To his absolute surprise, that now excited him rather than repelled him. But it wasn't the only reason he'd come along. Something about what these Jews were doing felt righteous. Though Shakespeare would never understand the mulish will of the unbaptized, neither could he fathom the cruelty of the Inquisition.[46]

Despite their passionate affair, and her temporary rebellion against her father, Shakespeare becomes secondary to what Rebecca values most: her family and her Jewish faith. In response to Shakespeare's echo of Lorenzo's promise to Jessica in *The Merchant* – to make her Christian in marriage – Rebecca rejects both the institutions of Christianity and marriage: "I don't want a Christian husband. I want no husband at all!"[47] Although Rebecca does ultimately consent to marriage, it is with the man of Rodrigo Lopez's choosing – the secretly homosexual Miguel, with whom Rebecca has an unbreakable, Jewish bond: they share a commitment to the alliance of their families and to the mission of saving Jews overseas. Her marriage is based neither on romantic love or lust but rather a shared fidelity to family and religion.

Like Jong's Jessica Pruitt, Rebecca's decisions are ultimately dictated by paternal attachment. Ultimately Rebecca and her father are noble martyrs, and their tireless commitment to life-saving surgery is a redemptive reversal of Shylock's threat to perform a fatal surgical procedure on Antonio. After her father is released from his first imprisonment, Rebecca devotes herself to assisting him:

> As hard as she worked, her father's labors were even more stressful – his hands washed as often in blood as in water. Death was a constant companion, life as fragile as spider's silk. Yet despite the raw and demanding days, her father's tongue lashings and an occasional slap, a tacit understanding grew between them, and with it came a stronger bond of love.[48]

[46] Ibid., 359.
[47] Ibid., 426.
[48] Ibid., 458.

When her father is arrested, done in by Lord Essex's accusations of a collusion with King Philip, Rodrigo's final words while being dragged out of the house are a pledge of love to his daughter.[49] At the end of the novel, Rebecca saves her father's life and reflects appreciatively on his parenting: "more than anyone, it had been he who had noticed her achievements, who had bestowed upon her lavish praise when she had accomplished something of value."[50] Her dedication to her father, her acquiescence to his will regarding the issue of marriage, is also what she has chosen for herself.

Rebecca's rejection of Shakespeare is not merely a reversal of Jessica's desire to escape her father and marry a Christian; Kellerman's protagonist also fulfills what I've described as a fantasy of reconciliation on the part of the Jewish female novelist. The novel ends with Rebecca accepting the roles of wife and mother on her own terms. The decision ultimately also becomes a metatextual commentary on the author's own reconciliation of female autonomy and Jewish faith. Rebecca's role as wife and mother is meant to sustain the Jewish community; her political work accomplishes the same. But her character also enacts a rewriting of *The Merchant* from a Jewish, feminist perspective. Almost as a type of author herself, Rebecca dictates Shakespeare's actions in the novel, including his "quality of mercy" speech, which she requests that he write for her to use in an appeal for her father's life.[51] Instead of Portia's speech that condemns Shylock's adherence to the law in *The Merchant*, Kellerman imagines the speech as a means to liberate the Jewish father from persecution. Rebecca, like Kellerman, takes control of the "the quality of mercy" speech and makes it the Jewish daughter's own. Rebecca sacrifices her own desires for the greater good, but her character also makes the choice independently. She controls her own life as well as the literary iteration of her life, playing out symbolically the Jewish feminist novelist's co-opting of Shakespeare's authorial, phallic pen.

In a letter to Shakespeare, Rebecca promises to name her first child "William," but the birth of a girl ensures that he will bear no mark on Rebecca's bloodline. Instead, the baby carries her grandmother's name, the matrilineal tradition emphasizing how Shakespeare is doubly removed as a man and a Christian. At Rebecca's request, though, Shakespeare will be the conduit of her own story. Most significantly, when Miguel notifies Shakespeare about his wife's death, he conveys

[49] Ibid., 493.
[50] Ibid., 399.
[51] Ibid., 533.

her deathbed wish: for Shakespeare to "pen a work that will pay homage to her dishonored father. A book about a man hated and spat upon, a man wronged because he was a Jew."[52] In Kellerman's version of the Jewish daughter's story, it is the faithful daughter's own passion for the Jewish identity of her father and herself that brings Shakespeare's *The Merchant of Venice* into being.

Jessica in America

In some sense the chick lit genre, a combination of female self-empowerment and an affirmation of the traditional value of marriage, is the ideal vehicle for the rehabilitation of Jessica as a Jewish feminist. The chick lit novel acknowledges the traditional yearnings of its female reader, while also championing a woman's autonomy and independent spirit in both professional and romantic matters. I conclude with Paula Marantz Cohen's *Much Ado about Jessie Kaplan*, a novel that transforms Jessica's story into chick lit that is a distinctly American story about gender and Jewish identity. In the protagonist Jessie Kaplan, Cohen creates a Jessica who brings traditional values into Jewish women's lives and in doing so suggests that Jewish faith, culture, law, and ritual are indeed fundamental to the Jewish woman's most satisfying conceptions of selfhood. Instead of the aggressive, erotic entanglement with Shakespeare we see in Jong's and Kellerman' versions of the *Belle Juive*, Cohen depicts Shylock's daughter's benign relationship with a sympathetic Shakespeare – a victim of heartbreak, and, in his modern incarnation as a soft-spoken schoolteacher, a man for whom Jessica can serve as matchmaker. In Cohen's novel, the point is not to screw or supplant Shakespeare; it's to invite him over for Shabbat dinner.

In *Much Ado about Jessie Kaplan*, the elderly widow Jessie shocks her family by declaring herself Shakespeare's former lover – and the true model of both the Dark Lady of his sonnets and his deceptive Jewish "infidel" Jessica in *The Merchant*. The characters of Shylock and Jessica, she claims, were Shakespeare's attempt at vengeance after she ended their relationship. Jessie confides to her granddaughter's English teacher, Hal Pearson, a man she believes to be a reincarnation of Shakespeare, that she ended the romance after finding out about Anne Hathaway, via a letter from Hathaway that accused her of being a "Hebrew Harridan."[53] As

[52] Ibid., 604–5.
[53] Cohen, *Much Ado about Jessie Kaplan*, 147.

Jessie explains to Hal, "That's when he wrote the play smearing Poppa and me."[54]

The comic dumping of Shakespeare, the inspiration for his "smearing" of Jessica and Shylock, is symbolic too of the change in Jessie's Jewish identity. In her altered state as Shylock's daughter and Shakespeare's former lover, Jessie becomes, for the first time, an observant Jew. To her family's complete shock, Jessie invites Hal over for an elaborate Shabbat dinner, and performs the Sabbath prayers and rituals. Cohen's farcical version of *The Merchant*, as a woman's delusion in the midst of a clichéd tableau of bourgeois Jewish-American life (complete with high-end bat mitzvah planning and trips to a psychiatrist), transforms Jessie into the matriarch of a newly invigorated Jewish community and an antidote to its suburban malaise. What begins as a parody of American-Jewish stereotypes – the JAP bat mitzvah girl, the neurotic mother – are all recuperated as Jewish pride by the figure of Jessica.

In *Much Ado*, the story of Jessica's rejection of Jewish family life in *The Merchant* is rewritten as a reuniting of Jessie with the lost love of her youth, the Jewish Saul Millman, the man she favored over Shakespeare. Her Shakespearean delusions, however ridiculous to her family, have facilitated this meaningful partnership, as well as a relationship between her glamorous, status-conscious unmarried daughter and the humble schoolteacher Hal. At the end of the novel, all couples are united on the occasion of Jessie's granddaughter's bat mitzvah, an event that has, through Jessie's invocation of Shylock's daughter, been transformed from just another token of affluent American-Jewish consumerism to the rite of passage meaningful to all as a triumph of Jewish life. The previously cynical bat mitzvah girl, Stephanie, becomes invested in her family, thus suggesting that she will not go the way of Shakespeare's Jessica and reject her family history. Cohen's conclusion rewrites *The Merchant* as a celebration of Jewish marriage, ritual, and history.

The women in Cohen's novel have achieved true romance and an affirmation of Jewish identity through the agency of Shylock's Jessica. In a setting dictated by generations of women (Jessica, Jessie, her daughters, and granddaughter), Cohen imagines a reconciliation of female desire and familial obligation, the dichotomy that troubles *The Merchant* and inspires the Jewish feminist adaptations I have discussed in this chapter. Pressler, Tiffany, Jong, Kellerman, and Cohen are very conscious of Jessica as a Shakespearean construct that can be manipulated. As their

[54] Ibid., 147.

adaptations make clear, the textual gaps in *The Merchant* offer the feminist novelist opportunities to script alternative, provocative narratives about the Jewish daughter that convey the complexity of her personal and familial conflicts.

In exploring how *The Merchant* raises questions – and possibilities – about the Jewish daughter, these authors perform what Satlof calls, in reference to feminist reinterpretations of *halakhah*, "the wresting of linguistic control from men."[55] In this sense, they take over Shakespeare's role as author, as well as that of his proxy Portia, whose interpretive prowess reigns supreme and insures the Christians defeat of Shylock. In the context of *The Merchant*, these feminist novels reclaim this linguistic control from both the Christian man and the Christian woman who assumes a male guise and whose skillful manipulation of words and meaning originally banished Jewish identity from Shakespeare's play.

[55] Satlof, "History, Fiction and the Tradition," 192.

16

Christian Iconography and Jewish Accommodation in Maurycy Gottlieb's Painting, *Shylock and Jessica*

Susan Chevlowe

Maurycy Gottlieb's painting *Shylock and Jessica* is the best-known work by a Jewish visual artist on the theme of *The Merchant of Venice* (Figure 42). Gottlieb (1856–79) created this work in 1876 at the age of twenty, when he was a student at the Academy of Fine Arts in Munich. Gottlieb's painting has been reproduced widely in both print and electronic media, even though the original, life-size work was lost during World War II.[1] At first glance, the viewer sees in this painting a depiction of the warm embrace between father and daughter, yet a closer reading reveals that Gottlieb subtly reinterprets the Jewish father–daughter theme

[1] The lost painting has been published online at a website maintained by Poland's Ministry of Culture and National Heritage at the Division for Looted Art of the Department of Cultural Heritage http://dzielautracone.gov.pl. A colored reproduction of the work was included in a portfolio of twenty-six plates, bound in an edition of one hundred copies, entitled *Meisterwerke von Maurycy Gottlieb* (Vienna: Christoph Reiser, 1923). An example was recently acquired by Yale University Library from the auction house Kestenbaum & Company. See http://web.library.yale.edu/international/judaica-collection. Gottlieb's brother Marcin (1867–1936) also created a copy of the painting in 1887, which has occasionally been on view at the Synagogue Museum in Kraków, leading to some confusion about which of the versions is the original by the elder brother. This information was confirmed by Eugeniusz Duda, Curator, Historical Museum of the City of Kraków, Jewish Department, in an email to the author, September 29, 2007. It is not known why Marcin created a copy of the work, but perhaps it was to improve his own skills as a painter. Copying was and remains a standard tool of artistic training. In the mid-2000s, Marcin's version of the painting was frequently misattributed to Maurycy. For example, the Norton Critical Edition of *The Merchant of Venice* published in 2006 mistakenly used the Marcin version of the painting on its cover, crediting it to Maurycy Gottlieb. There is an undated postcard that is extremely rare and shows a different color palette for the dress, which is dominated by gold. An original of the postcard was acquired by the author on ebay.

FIGURE 42 Maurycy Gottlieb, *Shylock and Jessica*, 1876, oil on canvas, 150 × 115 cm, lost painting.
Photo courtesy of the National Museum in Warsaw. Public domain.

to make it particularly relevant in the context of the political, social, and cultural worlds he inhabited in late nineteenth-century Europe. While the potential reconciliation of conflicting national identities is a pervasive theme in his oeuvre, it is less often recognized in *Shylock and Jessica* to the extent that it has been in his other works.

In Gottlieb's time, some Polish Jews who craved acceptance into both a national and wider European culture reached their goal by converting to the religion of their host society. Shylock and Jessica serve as perfect vehicles for representing this assimilation/conversion dilemma, for Shakespeare presents us with a daughter ready and easily able to renounce her Jewishness and a father who faces the choice of conversion or death. For his painting, Gottlieb must have studied various available visual prototypes. However, any precedents that he may have encountered as a young artist studying in several European capitals would have offered the anti-Semitic stereotype of Shylock as a vile moneylender whose hatred of Christians and Christianity fully justified his punishment (that he "become a Christian," 4.1.398). In Munich, too, he would have become familiar with Wilhelm Kaulbach's anti-Semitic painting *Destruction of Jerusalem* (1846). This monumental work by Kaulbach, who became the head of the Munich Academy just three years after it was completed, prominently features a depiction of the "Wandering Jew," a figure of medieval fabrication allegedly cursed to wander the earth for all eternity as punishment for taunting Jesus on his way to Golgotha. This stereotype was ubiquitous in depicting Jews as rootless aliens. Gottlieb may also have known some of the many English prints illustrating Shakespeare's Jew, such as an engraving after a work, published between 1873–1876 by Sir John Gilbert (British, 1817–1897), *Shylock after the Trial* which draws on the iconography of the "Wandering Jew."[2] The pervasiveness of the stereotype in the nineteenth century is further demonstrated by the work of the French artist Gustave Doré (1832–1883), who represented the figure in a series of 12 woodcuts, entitled *The Legend of the Wandering Jew*, first published in 1856.

Since artists training in the fine art academies of Western Europe in the late nineteenth century were taught to base their compositions on established visual models that reinforced dearly held cultural and nationalistic values and norms, their works could be highly polemical. Inevitably, for a Jew, the process of becoming an artist in nineteenth-century Europe was a process of accommodation to non-Jewish tropes as well as to latent or overt anti-Semitic ones.[3] As a Jew, Gottlieb was from the outset

[2] The title of Gilbert's painting is a misidentification as Emory University's website, "Shakespeare Illustrated," points out. After the trial (4.1), Shylock leaves the stage and does not appear again. Gilbert instead illustrates Act 2, Scene 7, after Shylock learns Jessica has eloped with Lorenzo and much of his fortune. See http://shakespeare.emory.edu.

[3] Larry Silver, "Jewish Identity in Art and History: Maurycy Gottlieb as Early Jewish Artist," in *Jewish Identity in Modern Art History*, ed. Catherine Soussloff (Berkeley: University of California Press, 1999), 87–88. Among the iconographic and compositional conventions that Silver suggests as having influenced Gottlieb's is "the ill-matched pair,"

challenged in his efforts to become a professional artist by virtue of being defined as alien. Art historian Larry Silver has noted that Gottlieb's choice of a literary historical subject was influenced by his teacher in Munich, Karl von Piloty (German, 1826-1886).[4] According to A. Ryszkiewicz and J. Dabrowski, all students at the Academy "were encouraged to paint 'A scene from *The Merchant of Venice*,'" a text that had a prominent place in German letters, and which carried added relevance following the increasing anti-Semitism triggered by the 1873 financial crisis.[5]

At the same time, Gottlieb's choice to paint Shylock and Jessica in this particular scene (2.5) was seized by him as a platform for expressing his complex feelings about how "The Jew" should be represented. Gottlieb's project was ambitious given the nature of academic history painting in the late nineteenth century. History painting depicted important actions by heroic figures from ancient history, religious history, or myth.[6] The genre conveyed moral lessons for a contemporary audience and allowed artists to demonstrate their technical skills as well as knowledge of both visual and textual traditions, derived from such sources as the Bible, Greco-Roman mythology, or in this case, from

that is, depictions of a lecherous old man with a greedy young woman. Silver cites, in particular, an example from the first quarter of the sixteenth century, Quinten Massys's *Ill-Matched Lovers* (c. 1520/1525, National Gallery of Art, Washington, DC). He also mentions the possibility of Rembrandt's *Jewish Bride* in the Rijksmuseum, Amsterdam, as a prototype though it is also a painting Gottlieb could have known only in reproduction. See also Lawrence Silver, "The *Ill-Matched Pair* by Quinten [sic] Massys," *Studies in the History of Art, vol. 6* (Washington, DC: National Gallery of Art, 1974), 4–23; Alison Stewart, *Unequal Lovers* (New York: Abaris, 1977). Nehama Guralnik, *In the Flower of Youth: Maurycy Gottlieb 1865–1879* (Tel Aviv: Tel Aviv Museum of Art, 1991), 53–54, reproduces Jan Matejko's *Zygmunt August and Barbara in Radziwill's Court* (1867, National Museum in Warsaw), which shows a pair of lovers in a warm embrace, adjacent to *Shylock and Jessica*, suggesting Gottlieb also was inspired by the work of his teacher in Kraków during his brief time at the Academy there in 1874.

[4] Silver, "Jewish Identity in Art and History: Maurycy Gottlieb as Early Jewish Artist," 92–93.

[5] A. Ryszkiewicz and J. Dabrowski, *Szekspir w plastyce polskiej* [Shakespeare in Polish Arts] (Wroclaw, Warszawa, Kraków: Zaklad Narodowy imienia Ossolinskich – Wydawnictwo, 1965). This Polish work is a source of information about the depiction of Shakespearean themes in Polish art in the nineteenth century. "The first great painters who took up the Shakespearean themes in their works were Aleksander Gierymski (1850–1901). Władyslaw Czachorski (1850–1911), and Maurycy Gottlieb (1856–1879). Their fascination with Shakespeare started in Munich where, as students in the Academy of Fine Arts, they were encouraged to paint 'A Scene from ***The Merchant of Venice***'"; Krystyna Kujawinska Courtney, "Shakespeare in Poland," Internet Shakespeare Editions, University of Victoria, 13; available at http://ise.uvic.ca/Library/Criticism. See also Ezra Mendelsohn, *Painting a People: Maurycy Gottlieb and Jewish Art* (Hanover, NH: University Press of New England, 2002), 124, and fig. 76, p. 125 for an illustration of Gierymski's *Trial Scene from The Merchant of Venice* (1872).

[6] Silver, "Jewish Identity," 87.

Shakespeare.[7] Gottlieb's depiction of Shylock within the genre of academic history painting would thus present a convincing challenge to the anti-Semitic representations that pervaded his culture. As Silver has observed, in Gottlieb's most ambitious works, painted after *Shylock and Jessica* – *Christ Preaching at Capernaum* (1878–79, National Museum, Warsaw) and *Christ before His Judges* (1877–79, The Israel Museum, Jerusalem) – the artist attempted to create what he terms "a new hybrid Jewish history painting," in which both sacred scriptures and Jewish identity could be simultaneously represented to a broad – not exclusively Jewish – viewing public."[8] By taking on traditional subjects of Western Christian art, in these two episodes from the life of Jesus that emphasize his identity as a Jew, Gottlieb was able to assert his own Jewish identity within the Christian art world and evade assimilation into that world. At the same time he sought to avoid marginalization as a Jewish artist.[9]

The double portrait of *Shylock and Jessica* demonstrates a similar hybridity. This is in large part because of affinities it shares with representations of the iconographic trope of the Judas kiss, typically included in visual representations of scenes from the life of Jesus. As we shall see, Gottlieb deliberately recast the meeting of father and daughter in this critical scene, in ways that set it apart from works by other non-Jewish artists by evoking sympathy for Shylock and focusing on Jessica's moral ambiguity. Gottlieb's unique approach allowed for a nuanced exploration of the internal conflict he experienced as an artist and Galician Jew, including his search for artistic and national belonging. Indeed, his painting reflects anxieties regarding his own physiognomy and his ability to fully assimilate into the Christian art world, as well as into the Polish nation. The resulting image approaches iconic standing in its own right as one that counters stereotypical and racist representations of the Jew and reflects Jewish efforts during his own time to reach accommodation with Christian society.

Gottlieb was born in 1856 into a wealthy, observant Jewish family in Drohobycz, Galicia, then part of the Austro-Hungarian Empire (today in Western Ukraine). A talented youth, he went on to train in three different European art centers – Vienna, Kraków, and Munich. It was not uncommon for aspiring artists of means from all over Europe as well as from the United States to make their way to such academies. Although Jews were admitted into these schools, it was still difficult for them to be accepted as artists; this was a result of anti-Semitism both in the academies and

[7] Ibid.

[8] Ibid.

[9] Ibid.

in the discipline of art history itself, which was structured around decidedly nationalist and ethnocentric paradigms. This basis for defining art and artists through a predetermined set of highly constructed national characteristics was an obvious problem for Jews, who were neither a nation unto themselves nor fully accepted into the nations in which they resided. Therefore their lack of a secure national identity led to their exclusion from the national canons that defined art history.[10] At the same time as he sought to develop as an artist, Gottlieb struggled to acquire a Polish national identity for himself. He lived during the time when Polish Galicia had been given home rule within the Austro-Hungarian Empire (1867), a development that led to increased Polonization of the region, and encouraged Jewish families like Gottlieb's to move toward modernization, including secular education. Typically, Jews in Galicia combined their adherence to Judaism with a belief in acculturation and integration. They liberalized the synagogues, becoming progressive and building grand new edifices, maintaining male choirs, and modeling changes in religious practice on Jewish communities elsewhere in the German-speaking world, such as having sermons given in the vernacular, though stopping short of adopting reform Judaism. Politically, the question of whether Jews could fully integrate into Polish society and the Polish nation was debated inside and outside the Jewish community.[11]

Scholars have noted how such issues of national identity are often mirrored in Gottlieb's self-portraits. In his romantic-realist style *Self-Portrait*, dated 1878 (Collection Weizmann Institute of Science, Rehovot, Israel), produced when the artist was twenty-two years old, Gottlieb painted himself as distinctly "other." Ezra Mendelsohn, author of a comprehensive study of the artist, commented that Gottlieb has a look of melancholy and has painted himself "in the attire of the Central European intellectual or professional man."[12] It is a role that he inhabits with some discomfort. As Mendelsohn notes, Gottlieb was obsessed with his own appearance and quite aware of its negative implications: "His physiognomy meant, among other things, that he could never hope to pass as a non-Jew, as was recognized by many of his acquaintances, both Jews and Poles."[13] This inescapable awareness of his Jewishness co-existed with a high degree of acculturation: Gottlieb spoke German and had even attended a monastery school and a public high school.

[10] Margaret Olin, *Nation Without Art: Examining Modern Discourses on Jewish Art* (Lincoln, Nebraska: University of Nebraska Press, 2001).

[11] Mendelsohn, *Painting a People*, 13–17.

[12] Ibid., 103.

[13] Ibid., 107.

After some art training in Lvov, and then at the Academy in Vienna (1872–74) while still in his teens, Gottlieb moved on to the Academy in Kraków in 1874, where the Polish history painter Jan Matejko (Polish 1838–1893) became a model for the young artist's burgeoning Polish nationalist aspirations. Yet, the anti-Semitism of his fellow students in Kraków compelled Gottlieb to move again, this time briefly back to Vienna in 1875, before continuing on to Munich where he arrived in 1876.[14]

In *Shylock and Jessica* Gottlieb represents a moment from Act 2, Scene 5 in which Shylock gives Jessica his keys to lock up the house before leaving for dinner at Antonio's. In the painting we see an old, yet dignified Shylock – upright, tall, and broad. His long arms provide Jessica with a sheltering embrace as he presses the key to his house to her chest, symbolically even to her heart, in a gesture of trust. Jessica touches her father's arm with her left hand, returning his embrace, and she is about to grasp hold of the keys with her right hand. She is dressed demurely, in rich and heavy fabrics, certainly of silk and velvet, and her head is modestly covered. While Shylock looks only at his daughter, she looks out toward the viewer with slightly downcast eyes and an expression that suggests both something of deceit and of sadness. We do not know whether the coloring in either the copy of the work by Gottlieb's younger brother Marcin (1867–1936) or in the reproduction from the 1923 portfolio *Meisterwerke von Maurycy Gottlieb* published in Vienna, is completely true to the original. Marcin shows Jessica wearing a dress with a blue skirt and gold trim and a gold bodice and a white blouse with red velvet on the forearm and above the elbow on the sleeves. Color is less varied in Shylock's costume. He wears traditional Eastern European clothes, including a fur-trimmed hat and heavy black outer cloak trimmed with the same brown fur, what Shylock famously refers to as "my Jewish gaberdine" (1.3.110). The distinctively Jewish elements of Shylock's costume in Gottlieb's painting mark his Otherness at the same time as they transport him to the artist's own time, appropriate as Gottlieb wishes to address the struggles of Jews in his present. Aspects of his dress are particularly associated with Polish Jews; most strikingly, the fur-trimmed *spodik*, a tall hat typically worn by Hassidic Jews in Russian Poland.[15] Jewish men in Venice in Shakespeare's time, by contrast, wore the flat beret, or Jewish barette, much like the Yiddish-speaking merchant from nearby Padua depicted in an engraving dated 1594.[16] Though

[14] Silver, "Jewish Identity," 89. Extensive biographical information is also found in Mendelsohn, *Painting a People*; Guralnik, *In the Flower of Youth*.

[15] A similar example of the *spodik* may be found in Alfred Rubens, *The History of Jewish Costume* (New York: Crown Publishers, 1973), fig. 146, p. 109.

[16] Ibid., fig. 191, p. 137. The Jewish barette was also worn elsewhere in Europe.

Gottlieb was schooled in historical accuracy, the purposeful anachronism and geographical misplacement in the costumes subsumes the story of *The Merchant of Venice* into a metanarrative of Jewish integration in Poland. The same holds true of Jessica's costume as well.

Though Jessica's dress appears to have some historically accurate elements, when comparing it to an illustration from a Venetian book of Jewish customs that dates from 1601, it is evident that her head covering represents a departure from the Italian style.[17] Her head covering is that traditionally worn by married Jewish women in Galicia, the same one in fact that Gottlieb had used in his painting *Uriel Da Costa and Judith Van Straaten* (1877, Private Collection) and for one of the women in his famous painting, *Jews Praying in the Synagogue on the Day of Atonement* (1878, Tel Aviv Museum of Art).[18] This irony makes the depiction more complex as Gottlieb depicts Jessica as an already married woman – although at this point in the play she is as yet to be married, and ultimately it will be to a Christian for whom she is assumed to convert – wearing the costume of a traditional Jewish wife.

Did Gottlieb intend for us to understand that she would not convert and thus represent her counter to prevailing literary stereotypes of the redeemable Jewish woman? In typical representations of the same subject by such Christian artists as H.C. Selous, Heinrich Hofmann, Sir Samuel Luke Fildes, J.M.W. Turner, and others, it may be argued that Jessica is represented as a Christian Jew. Gottlieb, on the other hand, represents both Shylock and Jessica as Polish Jews, that is, "'Judaic' Jews." Even Jessica, the "latent Christian," remains a Jew, as indicated by her attire.[19] It is possible that Gottlieb's depiction belies interpretations by Polish Zionists, who, after his death, embraced his work as a vehicle for their own ideology. For example, Galician Zionist Benjamin Spira wrote in

[17] *Lighting the Lights, Eve of Yom Kippur*, woodcut, from *Minhagim* (Venice, 1601), Bodleian Library; reproduced in Rubens, *The History of Jewish Costume*, fig. 196, p. 138.

[18] Shylock may even be wearing the same fur-collared cloak as the woman. Both works are reproduced in Guralnik, *In the Flower of Youth*.

[19] Even those who will betray their Jewish roots, perhaps Gottlieb suggests, are still Jews. Mendelsohn understands Gottlieb as privileging universalist and integrationist views. However, he points out that since his portraits and some other works emphasize Jews' otherness, Eastern origins, strangeness, and difference, "[a] paradox lies at the heart of Maurycy Gottlieb's Jewish art project" – a contradiction that "accurately expresses the dual nature of Judaism"; Mendelsohn, *Painting a People*, 149. See also Mary Janell Metzger, "Now by My Hood, a Gentle and No Jew": Jessica, *The Merchant of Venice*, and the Discourse of Early Modern English Identity," *PMLA* 113:1 (1998), 52–63, who writes of how "representations of Jessica, unlike those of other characters in the play, turn on alternating characterizations of her as a latent Christian and as a racialized and thus unintegrable Jew" (p. 52).

1892: "How great is the distance between Shylock the Jew and his rebellious daughter, as great as the difference between east and west, between a Jewish assimilationist and a true national Jew."[20] Similarly, in 1932, Gottlieb was cast as an artist whose "national instinct" led him to represent Shylock "as a suffering hero" and "Jessica as the prototype of the wicked assimilationist."[21]

But Gottlieb's reading of this scene may be far more nuanced and ambivalent than these assertions. Jessica's conversion and Shylock's attitude toward it, especially when viewed from the perspective of nineteenth-century Galician Poland, evoked thorny questions of national, racial, and religious identity. The attention given to Jewishness in relation both to Shylock and Jessica, to say nothing of Jesus, would have reflected and stirred anxieties among both Christians and Jews. As Susannah Heschel aptly phrased it: "The conversion of Shylock and Jessica does not resolve the unease but points to the unresolved question: Is Jesus a Jew or a Christian?"[22]

Gottlieb was probably aware of some recent German-language productions of *The Merchant* as well as some of the critical discourse in German about the play, written by both Christians and Jews during the nineteenth century (see Chapter 3 and Chapter 11 in this volume).[23] For example, the German-Jewish historian Heinrich Graetz (1817–91), author of the monumental eleven-volume *Geschichte der Juden von den ältesten Zeiten bis auf die Gegenwart*, was among those who contributed to this revisionism. Graetz addressed the play very briefly in *History of the Jews* and at greater length in "Shylock in der Sage, im Drama und in der Geschichte," an essay which appeared in 1880, a year after Gottlieb's death.[24]

For most modern critics, Gottlieb's painting focuses on a single aspect of Shylock's suffering: his betrayal by his daughter, Jessica. For

[20] Binyamin Spira, *Matsevet zikaron: Toldot hatsayar moshe david ben yitshak hamek–huneh moritz gottlieb zikhrono livracha* (Kraków, 1893), 9. Cited in Mendelsohn, *Painting a People*, 172.

[21] Mendelsohn, *Painting a People*, 182, referring to the views of Oziasz (Yehoshua) Thon, a Zionist rabbi.

[22] Susannah Heschel, "From Jesus to Shylock: Christian Supersessionism and *The Merchant of Venice*," *Harvard Theological Review* 99:4 (2006), 427.

[23] Mendelsohn, *Painting a People*, 124.

[24] Graetz included a long quotation from Heine's *Shakespeares Mädchen und Frauen* in *History of the Jews*, vol. 5, 553. A section on Jessica and Portia from the same essay is excerpted in *The Merchant of Venice: Authoritative Text, Sources and Contexts, Criticism, Rewritings and Appropriations*, ed. Leah S. Marcus (New York and London, W.W. Norton and Company, 2006), 145–52. It is taken from "Shakespeare's Maidens and Women" (originally published in 1838), Heinrich Heine, *The Works of Heinrich Heine*, 12 vols., trans. Charles Godfrey Leland (London: William Heinemann, 1906), 377–400.

Mendelsohn, the "main point" of *Shylock and Jessica* is "to rehabilitate Shylock as a loving father, about to be betrayed by his faithless, conniving daughter."[25] In this, he follows Nehama Guralnik, the curator who organized the first major retrospective of Gottlieb's work for the Tel Aviv Museum of Art in 1991, who, like many, regards the Jessica of the play as "avaricious and scheming."[26] The scene in which she sees her father for the last time before she elopes, ends, after all, with Jessica's "Farewell, and if my fortune be not crossed, I have a father, you a daughter, lost" (2.5.57). Guralnik and Mendelsohn suggest that Gottlieb's sympathetic interpretation of Shylock may have had some connection to the artist's affection and esteem for his own father, Isaac Gottlieb, who ran an oil refinery business; indeed, the painting seems to represent the Venetian moneylender as a protective and loving parent, and as one who wishes "to remain loyal to his Jewish heritage and to earn an honest living among the gentile elite of Venice." Mendelsohn sees Gottlieb's Shylock through the lens of the Enlightenment, attempting to "be a Jew at home, and a man outside."[27] Perhaps the artist meant to imply this concept by posing the characters on the threshold of their home.

At the same time, the core Christian narrative of Judas Iscariot's betrayal of Jesus is also implicit in *Shylock and Jessica*. The association of Shylock with Judas had already been made visual in the early performances of the play, when Shylock was presented wearing a red wig, traditionally the color of Judas's hair in Christian iconography especially prior to Edmund Kean's stage reinterpretation of the character in 1814.[28] This underlying narrative of the betrayal of Jesus is made manifest in *Shylock and Jessica* through the

[25] Mendelsohn, *Painting a People*, 125.

[26] Guralnik, *In the Flower of Youth*, 52.

[27] Mendelsohn, *Painting a People*, 125, writes that "Isaac, like Shylock, was engaged in a 'Jewish business' that exposed him to charges of exploiting Christians." Guralnik also cites Aurelja Gottlieb, wife of the artist's brother Leopold, who was an art historian and who wrote about the connection between Gottlieb's subject of Shylock and the artist's relationship to his own father in "M. Gottlieb's Life and Work," *Miesięcznik Żydowski* 2:3, 1932 208–24; Guralnik, *In the Flower of Youth*, 53.

[28] Hermann Sinsheimer, *Shylock: The History of a Character* (London: Gollancz, 1947), 116. Macklin, beginning in the 1740s, portrayed Shylock as less a comic than a tragic villain. He wore "a red beard, conventional for stage Jews; the 'Jewish gabardine,' the rough wool robe that sets [sic] him off from the high fashion of his Venetian clients" and "a cloak covering unfashionably wide black trousers." Kean's Shylock was more sympathetic, "essentially a martyr to Christian intolerance," and the actor was the first to dispense with the red wig. See Stephen Orgel, *Imagining Shakespeare: A History of Texts and Visions* (New York: Palgrave, 2003), 146. See also Toby Lelyveld, excerpt on Edmund Kean as Shylock, in William Shakespeare, *The Merchant of Venice: Authoritative Text, Sources and Contexts, Criticism, Rewritings and Appropriations*, ed. Leah S. Marcus (New York: W.W. Norton and Company, 2006), 219–25.

iconography and composition of typical representations of this persistent theme from Christian art. Gottlieb's composition, in which a pair of figures embrace, and one (Shylock) bestows a kiss upon the other (Jessica), echoes the betrayal by Judas as found in art history. It was likely influenced directly by such masterworks as Giotto's *The Arrest of Christ (Kiss of Judas)* from the Arena Chapel (Padua, 1306) or Doré's overtly anti-Semitic *The Judas Kiss* created over 500 years later, in 1865 (Figure 43). Gottlieb used the iconography of the embrace and kiss associated with the gospel of Mark to suggest that the conflict between love and betrayal in the relationship of Judas and Jesus parallels the conflict between fatherly devotion and filial betrayal in the relationship of Shylock and Jessica.

The compositional resonances of Christian works and their meaning may also be understood in the context of Gottlieb's familiarity with then current Jewish attitudes toward Christianity. As a Polish-Jewish artist of Galician-Polish origin living under Imperial Austro-Hungarian rule and struggling for acceptance in the mainstream, inherently Christian art world, Gottlieb was deeply concerned about the role of the Jew and, especially, the Jewish artist, in Poland and in Europe. While he could not resolve such historical struggles, he did not vilify one side or the other, Christian or Jew, assimilationist or Jewish nationalist.

Gottlieb's contemporaries, on the other hand, included Polish-Jewish intellectuals, such as Wilhelm Feldman (1868–1919), Aleksander Kraushar (1843–1931), and Salomon Lewental (1841–1902), who were familiar with his work. All three were assimilationists or integrationists, whose struggles to reconcile their Polish national identities led them to convert to Christianity.[29] Mendelsohn has noted that in the second half of the nineteenth century there were two competing options for most enlightened Polish Jews: nascent Jewish nationalism or total assimilation. *Shylock and Jessica* played into the discourse around these choices. Gottlieb himself had wrestled with this dilemma. In 1878, a year before his death, he wrote to a friend: "How deeply I wish to eradicate all the prejudices against my people! How avidly I desire to uproot the hatred enveloping the oppressed and tormented nation and to bring peace between the Poles and the Jews, for the history of both people is a chronicle of grief and anguish."[30] Gottlieb's

[29] Mendelsohn, *Painting a People*, 137. Mendelsohn discusses Feldman, Kraushar, and Lewental in his sections on Gottlieb's representations of Jesus.

[30] Letter written by Gottlieb in Rome, December 14, 1878, cited in Guralnik, *In the Flower of Youth*, 51; originally published in M. Narkiss, "Introduction," *Maurycy Gottlieb 1856–1879 Commemorative Exhibition on the Occasion of the Centennial of his Birth* (Jerusalem: Bezalel National Museum, 1956), 55–56. Also cited by Silver, "Jewish Identity," 105. Ezra Mendelsohn publishes a somewhat different translation of the letter,

THE JUDAS KISS.

FIGURE 43 Gustave Doré, *The Judas Kiss*, 1865, from the Holy Bible; originally published in London, 1866.
Wikimedia Commons. Public domain.

longing for reconciliation provides a rich context for understanding *Shylock and Jessica*. He represents the characters, neither condemning nor justifying the actions of either, and, perhaps, leaving the door open for empathy for the difficult choices that both made in order to assuage their personal grief and anguish.

As we have seen, after completing *Shylock and Jessica*, Gottlieb created two monumental works dealing explicitly with the life of Christ – *Christ before His Judges* and *Christ Preaching at Capernaum*. His last major paintings, these works have been read and interpreted in the context of mid-nineteenth century efforts to reclaim Jesus as a Jew, one strand within a larger project of Jewish integration and accommodation to European society.[31] These works may have been influenced by the writings of the contemporary Jewish scholars Abraham Geiger and Graetz, who emphasized that Jesus remained true to Judaism and never intended to invent a new faith.[32] Gottlieb was not alone among Jewish artists who sought to affirm Jesus's Jewishness in their works. They were often motivated by a desire to counter the anti-Semitism they and their brethren faced and to reconcile Jewish–Christian relations.[33] Both the historical Jesus and the fictional Shylock and Jessica were compelling subjects for an artist concerned with the ways in which one could negotiate and maintain one's Jewish identity within the framework of citizenship in the modern European nation.

This larger, public negotiation of Jewish identity was mirrored in Gottlieb's private dilemma and explored both in other works preceding *Shylock and Jessica* and in the romantic-realist self-portrait from 1878 discussed above, especially in other self-portraits. In 1874, while a student at the Academy in Kraków, Gottlieb had expressed his Polish nationalist longings in the now lost painting, *Self-Portrait as a Polish Nobleman*, in which he represented himself as an eighteenth-century Polish Catholic aristocrat. He wears the indigenous "gilt embroidered girdle known as a 'Słuck sash,' a sword, a lush fur around his shoulders and a four-cornered hat (traditional garb of the Cracow [sic] region adopted by Polish warriors in the 1784 rebellion)."[34] But the self-portrait also references more recent events: both the costume and pose were favored for photographs of the leaders of the Polish uprising of 1863 directed against control

and cites the original source, "Auszug aus einem Briefe Moritz Gottliebs," *Der Israelit*, 1879, 6; Mendelsohn, *Painting a People*, 40.

31 See, for example, Silver's discussion, in "Jewish Identity," esp. 100–6. Also Mendelsohn, *Painting a People*, 129–38.

32 Mendelsohn, *Painting a People*, 129. Both of these works also include self-portraits. In both cases, Gottlieb has inserted himself among the crowd of spectators.

33 See especially, Ziva Amishai-Maisels, "Origins of the Jewish Jesus," in *Complex Identities: Jewish Consciousness and Modern Art*, eds. Matthew Baigell and Milly Heyd (New Brunswick, NJ: Rutgers University Press, 2001), 51–86.

34 Guralnik, *In the Flower of Youth*, 29.

by the Russian Empire.[35] As Silver comments, Gottlieb's costumed self-representations chart his aspirations as well as his adherence to particular political and religious beliefs at different times during his career.[36]

Two years after the *Self-Portrait as a Polish Nobleman*, in 1876, Gottlieb painted himself as Ahasaver, conflating the "Wandering Jew" with Ahasuerus, the Persian King who saved the Jews in the story of Esther. In this darkly lit, Rembrandtesque work, Gottlieb's head is dramatically tilted to one side and his clothing is draped so that his tunic hangs off one, hunched shoulder. The artist depicts himself with a jeweled diadem atop his tightly curled hair. He has thick lips, a large nose, heavy-lidded eyes, and a swarthy complexion, features that emphasize his semitic origins. In 1878–79, Gottlieb used the same self-portrait image to cast himself among the crowd in *Christ Preaching at Capernaum*, in a way that suggests he intentionally chose to identify himself with Judas. This conflation of identities, conveyed by the title and by the particular iconography associated with Judas, is apparent when the self-portrait is compared to Doré's *The Judas Kiss*. Doré's orientalized Judas also wears a tunic and a large hoop earring, and, in line with the stereotypical physiognomic features of the Jews, also has curly hair, a beard, an exaggerated hooked nose, and a hunched posture. But by crowning his "Wandering Jew," Gottlieb gives his self-portrait a more complex, nuanced meaning that denies a fixed identification of the image with any one of these characters, whether the Persian King, Jesus, Judas, or the artist himself (Figure 44).[37] Such a complex of overlapping and competing cultural and religious identities also surrounds the images of Shylock and Jessica in

[35] Ibid., 30. Also noted by Silver, "Jewish Identity," fn. 15, p. 109; Mendelsohn, *Painting a People*, 110.

[36] Silver, "Jewish Identity," 89.

[37] Arguing that Gottlieb's self-portrait, Ahasver, was painted in reaction to Kaulbach's *Destruction of Jerusalem*, Avraham Ronen observes: "The diadem on Gottlieb's head thus transforms the defeated Wandering Jew into a triumphant royal figure." Avraham Ronen, "Kaulbach's Wandering Jew: An Anti–Jewish Allegory and Two Jewish Responses," *Assaph* 3 (1998), 251. See also Jerzy Malinowski, "Maurycy Gottlieb: A Polish Perspective," in Guralnik, *In the Flower of Youth*, 98. For a recent consideration of the iconography of the Wandering Jew, see Richard I. Cohen, "'The Wandering Jew' from Medieval Legend to Modern Metaphor," in *The Art of Being Jewish in Modern Times*, eds. Barbara Kirshenblatt-Gimblett and Jonathan Karp (Philadelphia: University of Pennsylvania Press, 2008), 147–75. Cohen states that the association of the name Ahasuerus with the Wandering Jew appears in a German chapbook, *Kurtze Beschreibung und Erzehlung von einem Juden mit Namen Ahasverus*, published in 1602 (p. 148).

FIGURE 44 Maurycy Gottlieb, *Ahasaver*, 1876, oil on canvas, 63 x 53 cm, Laboratory Stock National Museum in Kraków (Laboratory Stock National Museum in Kraków).

the painting of that name, where visual allusions to the kiss of Judas, echoing the theme of betrayal in both the painting and the play, intimate the problematics of Jewish identity for Gottieb and other Polish Jews living at this moment in the Austro-Hungarian Empire. As we have seen, it is not unusual for Gottlieb to represent identity as complex and layered, nuanced and ambivalent.

In contrast to earlier visual representations of the same scene, in *Shylock and Jessica* Gottlieb pares down the distracting narrative elements, and provides a less literal, more iconic representation in which meaning is derived from the emotional pairing of father and daughter. It is instructive to examine a few of Gottlieb's deviations from the choices made by other artists' representations of the same scene. For example, a late eighteenth-century engraving by Jean Pierre Simon (British, c. 1750–1810), after a painting by Robert Smirke (British, 1752–1845), is more theatrical (Figure 45).[38] Setting the scene in an opulent interior, Smirke presents an agitated Shylock, caught just as he is about to turn and exit through the door that Launcelot holds open, possibly representing a moment at the end of the scene. In his right hand Shylock clutches a walking stick. In the Gottlieb painting, on the contrary, the scene takes place on the threshold to the house – itself a charged locale if it is understood to symbolically refer to Jewish Emancipation. Gottlieb also leaves out the conspicuous walking stick associated with the character (an allusion to the "Wandering Jew"), while including a mezuzah on the doorframe. Also, having left out the clown Launcelot, the focus is on father and daughter at the moment of betrayal, even if the precise circumstances of betrayal are unclear.

Smirke avoids ambiguity. His Shylock is in mid-stride in a grand foyer. He is clearly agitated, having already felt some "ill a-brewing" (2.5.18) a visceral response exacerbated by the cryptic words of his former servant Launcelot, alluding, though in a comic and intentionally obscure way, to the dangers from revelers outside, as well as to Jessica's scheme. Shylock is intensely shadowed, and even at this time the racial implications of the contrast with Jessica's virginal "whiteness" would have been understood.[39] It is as if the artist is entirely unconcerned with Jessica's plan to rob her father and elope with Lorenzo. Shylock is stooped and Jessica is upright, her moral purity evoked by her construction as a white, latently Christian woman. Clearly, the visual vocabulary of anti-Semitism, much of which Gottlieb avoids, and which was increasingly tied to physiognomy and racial science by the late nineteenth century, is germinating in Smirke's late eighteenth-century representation.[40]

[38] It was published in 1795 for John Boydell's popular "Shakespeare Gallery."

[39] The racialized differences between Shylock and Jessica in this work are noted in Metzger, "Now by My Hood," 52–63, especially 58.

[40] Nevertheless, certain visual conventions underlay Smirke's depiction. For hundreds of years before Emancipation Jews could be identified by their hats. The association here may arise from the idea suggested by Orgel that "one way to play Shylock 'authentically' would be as one of the Puritan moneylenders of Shakespeare's London." And as

FIGURE 45 Jean Pierre Simon, after Robert Smirke, *The Merchant of Venice, Act Two, Scene Five*, 1795, engraving, published in John Boydell and Josiah Boydell's *Collection of Prints, from Pictures Painted for the Purpose of Illustrating the Dramatic Works of Shakespeare, by the Artists of Great-Britain* (London, 1803).

Gottlieb, by contrast, in avoiding so theatrical a representation, retains the ambiguity of the moment, especially in his portrayal of Jessica. On the one hand, many regard Jessica as immoral and selfish, as evidenced, for example, by the trading of her late mother's stolen ring for a monkey.[41] On the other hand, as John Gross notes, Jessica also may be seen as "the ogre's beautiful daughter, who makes her escape from his castle, and it is the clearest proof of her goodness that she is as different from him as possible; she is 'a gentle, and no Jew.' "[42] Jessica's iconographic and metaphorical significance has traditionally been connected to the idea that the physical beauty of the (virginal) Jewish woman, a reflection of moral virtue, allows for her to symbolize a kind of reconciliation of a theological paradox: while Jesus was born of a Jewish woman and the Jews were God's chosen people, Jews were also the evil murderers of the son of God. Women, who do not wear the mark of Judaism on their flesh, and who had not been directly responsible for Christ's death, were seen as a mediating presence whose conversion to Christianity would pave the way for the redemption of the Jews.

Among the most direct sources for Gottlieb's composition is *Shylock and Jessica* by Henry Courtney Selous (1811–90), c. 1830, and published in London between 1864 and 1868 in Charles and Mary Cowden Clarke's *The Plays of William Shakespeare* (Figure 46). Selous's illustrations were done after the originals of a number of different artists. They were also used in the first full edition of Shakespeare's works in Polish translation (1875–77), though as we know Gottlieb was less than fluent in Polish.[43] Nonetheless, this translation is nearly exactly contemporaneous with his painting. In Selous's illustration, as in Gottlieb's painting, the characters are set just outside Shylock's house at the moment that Shylock gives the keys to Jessica to lock it, though in Selous's version, unlike Gottlieb's, and

we see in the Smirke, Shylock is depicted wearing what appears to be a Puritan style hat, surely not part of the required costume for sixteenth-century Venetian Jews (which instead was at various times a yellow or red cap or scarf tied to a hat), but a convention of the time. See the illustration "Jewish merchant of Padua," Ferdinand Bertelli, *Ominum fere gentium nostrae aetats habitus nunquam antehac aediti*, 1563, reproduced in M. Channing Linthicum, "My Jewish Gaberdine," *PMLA* 43:3 (September, 1928), 757–66. Rubens reproduces the same engraving, dated 1594, which shows a Yiddish-speaking Jewish merchant from Padua. Other Italian-Jewish costumes from the fifteenth to the eighteenth centuries are illustrated through paintings and prints; Rubens, *The History of Jewish Costume*, 137, 138–41.

41 Heschel, "From Jesus to Shylock," 429.

42 John Gross, *Shylock: A Legend and Its Legacy* (New York: Touchstone, 1992), 69.

43 There is a link to an image of the cover to the Polish edition at Courtney, "Shakespeare in Poland," 13.

FIGURE 46 H.C. Selous, *Shylock and Jessica*, c. 1830, engraving, published in Charles and Mary Cowden Clarke, *The Plays of William Shakespeare* (London, c. 1864–68).
Public domain.

closely following the text, Launcelot looks on. In Selous's illustration, an angry-looking, heavily bearded Shylock, dressed in a fur-trimmed cloak, with walking stick, money bag, and skullcap seems to be admonishing Jessica to stay inside, away from the window and out of site of carnival revelers. The chief difference in Gottlieb's painting is the absence once again of any allusion to the "Wandering Jew" and the tenderness he portrays between the two figures.

A comparison of Gottlieb's painting with another, compositionally closer contemporary print of the same scene, engraved by Georg Goldberg (German 1830–94), after a painting by Heinrich Hofmann (German, 1824–1911), underscores the rich ambiguity of Gottlieb's interpretation, as well as its potential for misinterpretation (Figure 47). It is evident

FIGURE 47 Georg Goldberg, after Heinrich Hofmann, *Der kaufmann von Venedig – The Merchant of Venice* (Act 2, Scene 5), 1876, engraving, published in Friedrich Pecht, *Shakespeare-Galerie*, (Leipzig: F.A. Brockhaus, 1876). Courtesy of the Folger Shakespeare Library, Washington D.C.

from the composition that Hofmann, too, was equally influenced by Selous's illustration. Hofmann, a professor at the Dresden Academy, was best known for his depictions of the life of Christ. Given the overt anti-Semitism of Hofmann's work as engraved by Goldberg and the fact that the print was published in 1876,[44] it is likely Gottlieb's *Shylock and Jessica* was a direct response to it. (The same print later appeared in Seymour Eaton's *Shakespeare: Rare Print Collection* [London, 1900]). Hofmann's and Gottlieb's works are very similar, but there are important differences in their interpretations of both figures.[45] Hofmann's is a lecherous Shylock, with hooked nose and unkempt beard, wearing a pointed cap that resembles the medieval Jew's hat. His spidery fingers seem about to grab the keys out of Jessica's hands rather than having just released them to her. He holds a walking stick, a clear allusion to the "Wandering Jew," and wears a very large money bag on his belt. In contrast to Selous's work, Jessica makes direct eye contact with the presumed gentile viewer, as if to seek sympathy for having such a father and approval for her elopement. In Gottlieb's painting, as Jessica looks out to the viewer, she has more a look of guilt or possibly regret for what she is about to do than of arrogance.[46] Gottlieb's Jessica is less sure of herself, her dress more modest than Hofmann's bare-armed Jessica. Hofmann plays up the comic interpretation of the moment by having a laughing Launcelot, who appears to confirm that the joke is on Shylock. Perhaps the greatest difference is the lack of an embrace, the tenderness that Gottlieb's Shylock shows for his daughter. Compared to many other interpretations of the scene, Gottlieb's Shylock is clearly less anxious and less angered. Instead, he is a warm, loving, and, above all, trusting father.[47] If indeed Gottlieb was responding to

[44] In Friedrich Pecht, *Shakespeare-Galerie* (Leipzig: F.A. Brockhaus, 1876).

[45] In fact the Goldberg print has been used on an anti-Semitic website. Goldberg, a copper and steel engraver arrived in Munich from Nuremburg in 1856 and spent the rest of his life there, creating most of his work. His connection to the Munich Academy at the time Gottlieb was there is not known.

[46] Remarkably, while some sources say that Jessica, like other of Gottlieb's female protagonists, was modeled on his former fiancée Laura Henschel Rosenfeld, who was pictured in a similar head covering in his famous painting *Jews Praying in the Synagogue on Yom Kippur* (Tel Aviv Museum of Art), Mendelsohn, states that they did not meet each other until 1877; Mendelsohn, *Painting a People*.

[47] Judaism as an ancient and enduring religion is commonly embodied in a positive way through the image of patriarchal figures. Here Shylock is depicted as an elderly Jewish man, much older in fact than he needs to be to have a daughter the apparent age of Jessica. Gottlieb's use of this stereotypical figure does not necessarily indicate that Judaism is the old religion, or signal Christian supersession as typical contrasts of a youthful Jessica and an old Shylock might otherwise suggest. On supersession in general see Heschel, "From Jesus to Shylock," 407–31.

the work of Selous and Hofmann, he did so by increasing the pathos of the father and stressing the moral quandary of the daughter.

The various uncertainties evoked by Gottlieb's painting boil down to a significant overarching question about the figures in it: Where is Judas in this picture? Gottlieb's painting may offer some insight. Shylock's head is lit by a bright background like a halo. He becomes almost Christlike, as he kisses and, in a sense, forgives his daughter for what she is about to do. In Gottlieb's rendering, Shakespeare's Jew provided a vehicle for the rich exploration of pressing questions about conversion, integration, and anti-Semitism through the iconography of the Judas kiss. To learn that the original owner of the work was an apostate Jew also adds another layer to the complex meaning of this work and, indeed, to an understanding of the changing ways that this painting speaks to each generation. One imagines that the owner, like many viewers of the painting, recognized in the work a mirror of their own struggle.[48]

[48] The gentile ownership of the work was the claim and lament of the Polish artist Leopold Pilichowsky, "Moritz Gottlieb," *Renasans* 2:1 (January, 1920), 36, cited in Mendelsohn, *Painting a People*, 99, and fn. 24, 239.

17

Shylock in Opera, 1871–2014

Judah M. Cohen

Overture

On July 18, 2013, the Bregenz music festival in west Austria staged the world premiere of Polish-born Jewish pianist/composer André Tchaikowsky's *The Merchant of Venice* (Opus 7), his only opera. Born Robert Andrej Krauthammer, the Jewish Tchaikowsky (1935–82) had his name changed to hide his identity shortly after escaping from the Warsaw ghetto. After the war he received musical training in Poland and France, eventually settling in London in 1960. He began to write his opera in the late 1960s, during a period when he wrote smaller pieces for other Shakespeare works. After forging an initial three-act-plus-epilogue English-language libretto with writer John O'Brien, Tchaikowsky set the text one act at a time during breaks in his concert schedule from the early 1970s through to his death: first Act 2 (in Belmont, with the coffin scene), then Act 1, the Epilogue, and finally Act 3 in 1980–81.[1] Different musical atmospheres distinguished Venice (cosmopolitan, materialistic, hard-edged) and Belmont (dreamy, fantastic, incorporating "early" instruments) in the opera through an eclectic assemblage of stylistic and compositional techniques. Yet the center of the opera continued to reflect the conflict that the play had come to symbolize: between Shylock the Jew, composed as a baritone, and the high-voiced countertenor Antonio (a voice type used only rarely in modern opera until then).

[1] For a fuller account of the opera's creation and reception, see Anastasia Beline-Johnson, ed. *A Musician Divided: André Tchaikowsky in His Own Words* (London: Toccata Press, 2013), 384–400.

Shylock is taunted during the carnival celebrations in Act 1 – emphasized in the 2013 production by passing bands of revelers dressed as Hitler Youth, hooded Klansmen, and large-nosed Hasidic Jews – but the conflict plays out in full in the trial, where the two battling figures square off in a world that marginalizes them both. The dispute hints at the composer's own search for identity in a Europe from which he felt doubly estranged. Bregenz Festival organizer David Pountney described Antonio's voice in the scene as effeminate, reflecting "a very personal and sensitive self-portrait of André himself – a depressive homosexual ... who is left alone once everyone has happily paired off beneath the idyllic night-sky of Belmont."[2] The Shylock at the trial, meanwhile, appeared to reflect the composer's sharply divided views on Jewish identity, which he expressed during his first trip to Jerusalem in 1980 and his subsequent reunion with his father in Paris. Tchaikowsky declared comfort with his Jewishness for the first time in Jerusalem, and kinship with Israelis' brashness. Reversing earlier negative attitudes toward Jews as resulting from encounters with "hateful, claustrophobic, paranoic" diaspora Jewish populations, he provocatively described Israel as "the best place to get away from them" – a utopian "final solution."[3] His return to Europe to see his weakened father appeared to confirm that dualism. In composing his musical setting of the trial scene – enhanced by what he saw as the play's increased "unreality" after several centuries – he thus created unflattering, insecure characters on both sides of the conflict.[4] Tchaikowsky intentionally ramps up Shylock's fury in his music causing him to "thunder" from the start of the trial; while Antonio seems meek and aloof.[5] In the end, after Portia humiliates Shylock, the Jewish character appears to unite vocally with Antonio: shooting up "to the same Jewish beggar's whine that he'd parodied to Antonio in Act 1, except that now it's no longer a parody."[6] While Shylock leaves the room, defeated and destroyed, Antonio's victory is only temporary, as he too eventually finds himself estranged, alone, and staring at the moon.

Premiered thirty-one years after Tchaikowsky's death, in a full production co-produced by the Bregenz Festival, the Polish Adam Mickiewicz Institute, and the Grand Theatre in Warsaw, *The Merchant of Venice* (in English, with German supertitles) received broad international acclaim,

[2] "David Pountney's Blog – May 3, 2012," http://andretchaikowsky.com/composer/blog.htm.

[3] Beline-Johnson, ed. *A Musician Divided*, 271.

[4] Ibid., 219.

[5] Ibid., 298.

[6] Ibid., 300.

including the 2014 International Opera Award for the best world premiere, heralding a major resurgence of attention for its nearly forgotten composer.[7] Ultimately, the production served as a stop on a tour that began with a reading at the English National Opera in 2012. The 2013 production included a research symposium about the composer's life and a new set of scholarly publications, and led to the creation of a documentary and DVD/Blu-Ray issue of the production itself on the EuroArts label. And the following year, the production received four additional performances at Warsaw's Grand Theater, symbolically bringing the opera back to the composer's "home" and adding a new layer of alienation by featuring African-American baritone Lester Lynch as Shylock.[8] Promoted internationally by both press and producers as a hidden masterpiece, particularly in light of the Bregenz Festival's 2010 "rediscovery" of Mieczysław Weinberg's 1968 opera *The Passenger*, the opera's fascination no doubt hinged on its challenging material, its eclectic music, and the biography of its composer, whose own struggles with anti-Semitism and Jewish identity seemed to inform the work deeply. At the same time, this opera served as the latest musical incursion into the fraught landscape created by Shakespeare's text and innumerable productions, presenting a new meditation on the problematic and ever marginalized position of Shylock in European society.

A Musical Voice for Shylock

Music holds an integral place in Shakespearean theater. Shakespeare's regular inclusion of songs and background music in many of his plays ensured that musicians would have a collaborative role in both contemporary and future productions.[9] Participating composers and

[7] André Tchaikowsky, *Die tâgliche Mühe ein Mensch zu sein* (Hofheim: Wolke, 2013).

[8] See e.g. Papageno, "'The Merchant of Venice' in Warsaw," (in Polish) on the blog "Opera czyli boski idiotyzm," October 29, 2014; http://operaczyliboskiidiotyzm.blogspot.com. See also the page dedicated to the Warsaw staging on André Tchaikowsky's memorial website, including publicity photos of the production: http://andretchaikowsky.com/composer/merchant_of_venice.htm. Several reviewers of *The Merchant*'s Warsaw production openly discussed this new layer to the story, assessing the success of Shylock's new voice while debating the feasibility of combining Jewish and African-American alienation.

[9] Among the many books that have explored Shakespeare's use of music, see Alfred Roffe, *The Handbook of Shakespeare Music* (London: Chatto & Windus, 1878); Edward W. Naylor, *Shakespeare and Music* (London: J.M. Dent, 1896); Louis C. Elson, *Shakespeare in Music* (Boston: L.C. Page, 1921); Christopher R. Wilson and Michela Calore, *Music in Shakespeare: A Dictionary* (New York: Continuum, 2005); David Lindley, *Shakespeare and Music* (London: Thompson Learning, 2006).

instrumentalists consequently sought musical strategies that supported the action on stage and pleased their audiences. They interpolated familiar tunes, composed in "period" styles that spoke to spectators' cultural and educational backgrounds, and used sounds and instruments that evoked abstract ideas such as love, fear, and war.

The role of music did not end, however, with staged productions of Shakespeare's original texts. Musicians, like writers and visual artists, have imported Shakespearean characters and plots into musical works in a broad array of musical forms ranging from popular songs, operas, and ballets to avant-garde musical compositions, and from symphonic works to film soundtracks.[10] Crafting their own sonic interpretations of key roles and narrative moments, and using a reduced or absent text, they provided Shakespeare's works with a nuanced and strikingly different sensory balance that greatly expanded their international cultural appeal.

The Merchant of Venice, because of its Jewish content, holds an intriguing place among these musical adaptations. The play has inspired notable incidental music, from Gabriel Fauré's contributions to the performance of Edmond Haraucourt's 1889 French translation (later adapted into Fauré's "Shylock Suite," Opus 57) to Jocelyn Pook's soundtrack for Michael Radford's 2004 film (released by Decca in 2005 as a stand-alone album); and interpolated songs in other productions have characterized the world of the play, sometimes providing and in some cases provided a provocative counterpoint to Lorenzo's claim that Shylock "hath no music in himself."[11]

In this essay, I focus on three operatic adaptations, chosen from at least fourteen *Merchant of Venice*-based operas produced since the nineteenth century (see Table 1): Ciro Pinsuti's *Il Mercante de Venezia* (Italian, Bologna, 1873), Reynaldo Hahn's *Le Marchand de Venise* (French, Paris, 1935), and Mario Castelnuovo-Tedesco's *Il Mercante di Venezia/The Merchant of Venice* (Italian/English, 1956; first performed Florence, 1961). These operas recast the play to accommodate the expanded role of music in the storytelling, while adding their own layers of commentary on

[10] Among others, see Julie Sanders, *Shakespeare in Music: Afterlives and Borrowings* (Malden, MA: Polity Press, 2007); Adam Hansen, *Shakespeare and Popular Music* (New York: Continuum, 2010); Irene G. Dash, *Shakespeare and the American Musical* (Bloomington: Indiana University Press, 2010).

[11] Ruth HaCohen, *The Music Libel Against the Jews* (New Haven: Yale University Press, 2011), 58–66. In June, 2015, the American Sephardi Federation similarly staged an adaptation of *The Merchant* that interpolated "Jewish Ladino music of the era" ("David Serero to Star in The Merchant of Venice at the Center for Jewish History this June," www.broadwayworld.com, April 7, 2015).

TABLE 1 *Opera Adaptations of The Merchant of Venice*

Year	Premiere (Theater)	Title	Composer	Librettist	Acts	Comments
1873 (November 3)	Bologna (Teatro Comunale)	Il Mercante di Venezia	Ciro Pinsuti	George Thomas Cimino	4	Italian.
c. 1891	(Performed?)	La Fille de Shylock	Pierre Louis Deffès	Adenis?	3	Possible 3-act version of the 1898 iteration. French.
1898 (March 25)	Toulouse (Capitole)	Jessica (also "La Fille de Shylock," and "Le Marchand de Venise")	Pierre Louis Deffès	Jules Adenis & H. Boisseaux	5	5-act version. Student of Halévy. French.
1905 (April 16)	Prague (Národny Divadlo)	Jessika	Joseph P. Foerster	Jaroslav Vrchlicky	3	German trans.: R. Batka. 7 performances in 1920–21.
1907	Paris (Comédie Musicale)	Le Marchand de Venise	Henri de Saussine	De Saussine	4	Op. 14. French.
1913 (November 22)	Antwerp	Shylock	Flor Alpaerts	Herbert Melis	3	
1916	Frankfurt	Porzia	Otto Taubmann	R. Wilde	3	
1922 (September)	Brighton (Grand Theatre)	The Merchant of Venice	Adrian Beecham	Shakespeare (adapted by Beecham)		Also Duke of York's Theatre, November 20.
1930	Chicago	Shylock	Wesley La Violette	Shakespeare (adapted by La Violette)		Won David Bispham Memorial Medal Award.

(*continued*)

TABLE 1 (*Continued*)

Year	Premiere (Theater)	Title	Composer	Librettist	Acts	Comments
1933 (January 30)	Brussels (Theatre de la Monnaie)	Le Marchand de Venise	F. Brumagne	P. Spaak	5	Revived in first half of 1940.
1935	Paris	Le Marchand de Venise	Reynaldo Hahn	Miguel Zamacoïs	3	
1937	Not performed	Shylock	Aldo Finzi	Arthur Rossato	4	Only first act set to music. Shylock set as a tenor.
1955	Derby (Hippodrome)	The Gay Venetians	Tom Chatburn	Tom Chatburn		
1956	Florence (Teatro Comunale di Firenze) May 1961	The Merchant of Venice/Il Mercante de Venezia	Mario Castelnuovo-Tedesco	Adapted by Castelnuovo-Tedesco	3	Op. 181. Written in both English and Italian. Premiered in LA on April 13, 1966 (English).
1982	Bregenz, Austria (Bregenz Festival) July 2013	The Merchant of Venice	André Tchaikowsky	John O'Brien	3+ep.	Composer worked on it from 1968; completed by another just after composer's death.
1984	Not performed	Shylock	John Thomas Magee	Magee	2	

A verified and expanded update of the following tables: Winton Dean, "Shakespeare in the Opera House" (1965), reprinted in *The Cambridge Shakespeare Library*, vol. 3., eds. Catherine M.S. Alexander and Peter Holland (Cambridge: Cambridge University Press, 2003), 151; Christopher R. Wilson, "Shakespeare, William," in *The New Grove Dictionary of Opera*, ed. Stanley Sadie, Oxford Music Online; http://www.oxfordmusiconline.com/subscriber/article/grove/music/O008793. (NB: this list includes only European and American productions; there have been several additional productions by Beijing opera companies. For the purpose of focus, I also exclude incidental music and musical theater works from this table.)

Shylock, and by extension, on Jews' roles in the broader European social structure. By employing specific vocal qualities to represent Shylock's character, reinforcing, discarding, or blunting specific traits through textual consolidation and musical explication, and skillfully weaving symbolic musical themes through the work, composers complemented scenery and staging design to produce meaningful contemporary performances, particularly beyond the English-language stage.[12] Perhaps even more intriguing, and less frequently recognized outside of opera scholarship, composers regularly used their prerogative as artists to reinterpret, complicate, and in many cases radically alter the libretti they received – actively exerting control the production as a whole. The rich confluence of music and Judaism in *Merchant* operas consequently presents an often overlooked dimension of Shylock's legacy, expanding the play's reach, and offering considerable interest when, as in two of the three cases here, the composers themselves were of Jewish ancestry.

The Emergence of *The Merchant of Venice* as Opera

In his seminal discussion of Shakespeare in opera, Winton Dean traces operatic adaptations of Shakespeare's plays up to the late eighteenth century, linking them to the general rise in Shakespeare's literary and theatrical popularity in various European countries.[13] These early operas, as per contemporary convention, often shared little more than their titles with their dramatic sources. Many eighteenth- and early nineteenth-century Shakespeare-based operas in Germany, for example, appear to have retained only the barest traces of Shakespearean plot elements and characters.[14] In such freewheeling adaptations, it was unclear whether the operas' creators were at all familiar with the dramatic source, especially in such lighter fare derived from *The Merry Wives of Windsor* or *The Tempest*.[15]

[12] My argument here parallels that of Christoph Clausen in his discussion of Verdi's Shakespeare-based operas; Christoph Clausen, *Macbeth Multiplied: Negotiating Historical and Medial Difference Between Shakespeare and Verdi* (New York: Rodopi, 2005), 12–13.

[13] Winton Dean, "Shakespeare and Opera," in *Shakespeare in Music*, ed. Phyllis Hartnoll (New York: St. Martin's Press, 1964), 89–176.

[14] Guido Bimberg, "William in Slippers: German Operas after Shakespeare," in *The Opera and Shakespeare*, ed. Holger Klein and Christopher Smith, Shakespeare Yearbook, vol. 4 (Lewiston: Edwin Mellen Press, 1994), 269–94.

[15] See also Michael Burden, "Shakespeare and Opera," in *Shakespeare in the Eighteenth Century*, eds. Fiona Ritchie and Peter Sabor (Cambridge: Cambridge University Press, 2012), 204–23. Burden points out how the issues of nationalism played into the choice and production of opera subjects in this era as well.

More problematic plays such as *The Merchant of Venice* received minimal attention in operatic circles until the mid-nineteenth century, when operas began to introduce more complex plots and to adhere more closely to their literary sources. As the availability and quality of Shakespeare translations improved, composers began to see the plays as an increasingly viable source for darker and more serious projects.[16] *The Merchant* in particular may have benefited from the changing perceptions of Venice during the nineteenth century, which historian James H. Johnson describes as moving "from tyranny and deviance [as seen in Mercadante's 1839 *Il Bravo*] to personal liberation [such as Strauss's 1883 *Ein Nacht in Venedig*, which features Carnaval and masque]."[17] Containing both qualities in generous measure, *The Merchant* proved well-suited for this period of transition.

Adapting Shakespeare proved no easy feat, however. Opera's elaborate formal practices and musical conventions imposed severe demands on the original narrative material, in part because of opera's reliance on elaborate atmospheric ensemble numbers and solos that expressed and prolonged a single thought or narrative moment. The libretto itself had to be severely reduced and simplified in order to conform to a stream of connected musical forms: recitatives (sung dialogue), solos, and passages written for multiple singers. The rhythm of Shakespeare's text, challenging to achieve even when translated into other languages' literary/poetic idioms, proved especially difficult to reproduce through musical conventions. And the characters themselves needed to conform to such operatic vocal conventions as the heroine's soprano or the villain's bass in order to be comprehensible to an opera audience. Composers compensated for the changes they introduced by giving the music its own internal logic. Many composers organized the plot around a series of themes and textures, which they varied and repeated strategically in order to create a unified sonic world, to evoke emotional moments, and to allude to specific characters. Operatic treatments of *The Merchant of Venice* in particular tended to build these meanings around the music given to

[16] Agostino Lombardo points out that Shakespeare had been coming onto the Italian stage around this time: Carlo Rusconi had completed a prose translation of Shakespeare's works into Italian in 1858, and Giulio Carcano began publishing a complete verse translation of Shakespeare in 1874 (Agostino Lombardo, "Shakespeare in Italy," *Proceedings of the American Philosophical Society* 141:4 [December 1997], 458).

[17] James H. Johnson, "The Myth of Venice in Nineteenth-Century Opera," *Journal of Interdisciplinary Studies* 36:3 (Winter 2006), 553.

Shylock, establishing for him a musical space of his own from which he could respond to the surrounding Christian/Venetian world.

The creation of a *Merchant of Venice* opera consequently had to find musical solutions to three problems related to its Jewish characters. First, composers had to create music that characterized Shylock and the other Jewish characters as outsiders to Venetian society, using minor modes, exotic-sounding intervals, and idiomatic musical ornaments to convey separateness. Second, they had to distinguish that music from the music of the play's other "exotics" – the princes of Morocco and Arragon, whose "Orientalized" characterizations presented far less complexity.[18] Finally, adaptors needed musical strategies for depicting the relationship between Shylock and Jessica. As with other Jewish father/daughter pairs in opera (including Eléazar/Rachel in *La Juive* and Isaac the Jew/Rebecca in Arthur Sullivan's 1891 operatic adaptation of *Ivanhoe*),[19] Jessica lived in closer proximity to the Christian world, so her musical characterization needed to traverse the sonic spectrum to reflect the social gap between Shylock and the other Venetians. The solutions to each of these problems collectively created a sonic framework of Jewishness within each opera and thereby connected the composer's fantastical world on the stage with audience preconceptions of "Jewish" qualities.

Ciro Pinsuti, *Il Mercante di Venezia* (1873)

In the closing scene of *Il Mercante di Venezia*, which premiered at Bologna's *Teatro Comunale* on November 3, 1873, composer Ciro Pinsuti set two competing choruses against each other.[20] As the lovers, in Belmont, resolve their misunderstanding over the rings, an offstage prayer interrupts their celebration. Reprising a modal, ancient-sounding melody that Jewish characters had sung twice before in earlier acts, the same group (as Israelites/Israeliti) now

[18] I draw these designations through studies on musical exoticism such as Ralph Locke's *Musical Exoticism: Images and Reflections* (Cambridge: Cambridge University Press, 2009), esp. 106–212.

[19] See Jeff S. Dailey, *Sir Arthur Sullivan's Grand Opera Ivanhoe and its Musical Precursors* (Lewiston, NY: Edwin Mellen Press, 2008).

[20] Winton Dean, "Shakespeare and Opera," in *Shakespeare in Music*, ed. Phyllis Hartnoll (London: Macmillan & Company, 1964), 102.

sings in defeat: "O God of Abraham, from our hearts we beseech your counsel and pardon / That in this supreme hour you do not impose your just wrath upon us."[21] The onstage assemblage, annoyed at being interrupted, sees Shylock and the Israelites on "a boat traversing the sea in the distance." Transforming in the published score from "People" [*Popolo*] to "Christians" [*Christiani*] they curse the "unholy tribe, who go into exile never to return!" Antonio, however, chides them: "Using anger against them is useless! Let us pray for those miserable people going away."[22] A study in contrasts follows: the Israelites, accompanied by a harmonium (a portable reed organ, often associated with pre-modern religiosity), sing in a modally modified minor tonality, mostly in unison, using a triple meter. At the front of the stage, Jessica, Lorenzo, the other lovers, and the chorus of Christians commence a prayer in lush, multi-part harmony featuring harp accompaniment, a major key, and duple meter: "Father of us all, gentle Lord," they pray, "guide the exiles and have mercy on them."[23] The *Israeliti* become progressively softer, their prayers increasingly distant until their voices sound like an echo; they move offstage, exiled and silent. The *Christiani* complete the opera in triumph, their prayers reaching a climax and then fading to four quiet calls for "mercy" ("pietà") over the Israelites. As "the curtain slowly falls," the orchestra swells to a fortissimo climax in the same key and time signature as the Christians, affirming their final victory.[24]

The juxtaposition of these two choruses, each with its own distinctive sound, may have encouraged audiences to reflect on the great changes taking place in Italian society in the years after unification (which began in Bologna with the expulsion of papal government in 1859). Looking outward rather than inward during a period of "intellectual crisis" in Italy, the municipally supported Teatro Comunale largely jettisoned the more mainstream operas of Giuseppe Verdi in the 1860s and 1870s, and instead introduced Italian audiences to premieres of Halévy (*La Juive*, 1868), Meyerbeer (*L'Africaine*, 1868), and Richard Wagner (*Lohengrin*, 1871; *Tannhäuser*, 1872) among others.[25] While

[21] "O Dio d'Abramo! / Dall'imo petto – A te chiediamo / Consiglio e venia – O Dio d'Abramo, / Ed in quest'ora – Per noi suprema / L'ira tua giusta – Su noi non prema." Unless noted otherwise, all descriptions of the opera refer to the published score: Ciro Pinsuti and G.T. Cimino, *Il Mercante di Venezia: Melodramma en Quattro Atti da Shakespeare* (Milan: Ricordi, 1875); translations are mine.

[22] "Incrudelire – Contr'essi è vano! / Preghiam pei miseri – Che van lontano."

[23] "Padre di tutti – Mite Signor, / Sii guida agli esuli … – Pietà di lor!"

[24] See also Christopher Wilson, *Shakespeare and Music* (New York: Da Capo Press, 1977), 75.

[25] Axel Körner, *Politics of Culture in Liberal Italy: From Unification to Fascism* (New York: Routledge, 2009), 221–62.

these choices proved locally controversial, stoking tensions between the *anciên regime* that continued to dominate theater box ownership through the 1880s and the emerging progressive bourgeois class that consumed a growing portion of ticket sales, they also established Bologna as "the Italian capital of Wagnerism with a major influence on Italy's musical life as a whole."[26] Historian Axel Körner argues that this kind of opera programming allowed the Bolognese to fashion their own aesthetic sense of modernity based (in the case of Wagner, at least) on "the narrative and on selected melodic and romantic passages which corresponded to their own expectations of lyric theatre."[27] In this vein, *The Merchant of Venice* offered another coherent example: an Italy-situated story adapted by a playwright of international renown, and turned into an opera by an Italian-born, cosmopolitanized creative team with extensive international experience. In this context, the music, libretto, and proposed staging of Pinsuti's finale may have alluded to a number of sensitive topics facing contemporary audiences: from the specific tensions between Jews, the Catholic Church, and the municipal government, to more general questions about social heterogeneity on the one hand and nation-building on the other. Shakespeare's play, in other words, contributed the musical groundwork for a treatise on societal reform.

With the possible exception of a 1787 opera by Johann-August Just,[28] *The Merchant of Venice* seems to have held little interest as a topic for opera adaptation until the collaboration of Pinsuti (1829–88) and dramatist Giorgio Tomaso Cimino (1823–1905) (Figure 48). The Siena-born Pinsuti, who had lived in Bologna for a short time between his musical training in England (c. 1840–45) and a long-term appointment at London's Royal Academy of Music (1848–72), appears to have been approached by Cimino in the mid-1860s with the idea of setting Shakespeare's play to music. Cimino, who had used the Venetian setting in a previous musical drama (*Orio Soranzo*, 1869/70)[29] would later promote the opera by claiming that he chose *The Merchant* to present a new operatic paradigm – a story "full of honest and generous emotions" that trumped the "torments of daggers and gallows, of suicides and wife

[26] Ibid., 249.

[27] Ibid., 261.

[28] This opera is mentioned in Félix Clément and Pierre Larousse, *Dictionaire Lyrique, ou L'Histoire des Opéras* (Paris: Grand Dictionaire Universel, 1881), 428. Notably, recent publications such as Michael Burden's discussion of Shakespeare-based opera in the eighteenth century currently affirm this assertion through exclusion (Burden, "Shakespeare and Opera").

[29] Music by Gustavo Ruiz; performed during the carnival season at Venice's La Fenice.

killings, poisonings, conspiracies, and other such frights" common on the Italian opera stage at the time.[30] The adaptation of a complex play like *The Merchant*, such comments suggest, allowed the creators to bring more nuanced characters and situations to a genre that they had critiqued as excessively focused on melodramatic spectacle.

Pinsuti apparently completed a draft of the opera in 1866 while still in London and would not see its premiere until after he moved back to Italy in 1872.[31] The Comunale, while suffering from a major cut in municipal funding the previous year, saw the opera as worthy enough to give it a widely praised production. At the same time, the work most likely gave its audience a chance to think about major social issues facing the nascent Italian state; and among the Bolognese especially, the opera might have connected with the famous case of Edgardo Mortara, a continuing topic of concern among the area's Jews.

Fifteen years earlier, Bologna had become the center of an international scandal that pitted Jews against the Catholic Church. In 1858, six-year-old Edgardo Mortara, child of a Jewish Bolognese family, was removed from his home by the papal police after a servant claimed that she had secretly baptized him four years earlier. The Church brought Mortara to Rome and successfully resisted a prolonged international outcry for the boy's return, as well as several entreaties from prominent Jews who met with Pope Pius IX. Tensions continued through the period of Italian unification. In 1870, however, the now-grown Mortara chose to remain in the Church despite a final plea by his family and later entered the Augustine order, adopting the name Pius to acknowledge his papal mentor.[32] Pinsuti's opera, which featured Jessica's flight from her father's house into the arms of a Christian suitor, probably raised some recollection of the Mortara case, while also making the point that the overthrow of papal rule in Bologna shortly afterward, in 1859, continued to resound in the region's political memory.

Pinsuti's provocative musical gloss on *The Merchant of Venice* provided a way into this reading by characterizing Shylock as a desperate father, determined to use all his resources to bring back the daughter he

[30] G.M. Cimino, "Argomento," in *Il Mercante di Venezia* [libretto] (Bologna: Società Tipografica dei Compositori, 1873), n.p. Cited in Biancamaria Brumana and Gina E. Pagano, "*Il Mercante de Venezia* di Ciro Pinsuti (Bologna, 1873)," in *Esercizi: Musica e Spettacolo* 20, n.s. 11 (2006–7), 92.

[31] There is evidence that Pinsuti finished at least a draft of his opera in 1866 ("Musical and Dramatic Gossip," *Athenaeum* 2035 [October 27, 1866], 539, col. 2). For more on the history and reception of this opera, see Brumana and Pagano, "*Il Mercante de Venezia.*"

[32] David Kertzer, *The Kidnapping of Edgardo Mortara* (New York: Knopf, 1997).

FIGURE 48 Ciro Pinsuti, *Il Mercante di Venezia* title page from the published score (G. Ricordi, 1875).[33]

[33] I am grateful to Andrew Wilson and the Eda Kuhn Loeb Music Library for their assistance in obtaining this image.

feels has been abducted by a Christian suitor, yet finding himself forced to negotiate with a Christian-dominated legal system already stacked against him. Cimino had already opened the opera to this interpretation by moving Jessica's flight earlier in the plot, giving Shylock a darker motivation for his deal with Antonio; and Cimino's decision to invoke Jessica only as an offstage character may have heightened the opera's parallels to the sequestered Mortara.

Pinsuti's musical realization of Shylock imbued the character with qualities that later composers would replicate, knowingly or not. He began by writing Shylock as a "1st Bass," a low voice (but not the lowest voice) used most frequently with patrician and/or aged characters. His designation as a first bass suggested that Shylock was not inherently villainous, nor would he exhibit the moral profundity of the Duke or Priest (described in the score as a "Bass" and "2nd [lower] Bass" respectively), the social respectability of Antonio (baritone) or the heroic nature of Bassanio (tenor). Rather, Shylock's sonic portrayal showed a character buffeted by circumstance, negotiating a difficult situation imposed by the society around him, and nursing but ultimately not acting upon dreams of revenge.

Shylock did not appear in person until Act 1, Scene 4; yet Pinsuti insinuated his presence from the start. A few measures into the opera's overture – an instrumental prelude featuring several of the key musical motifs present in the rest of the work – Pinsuti introduced a "kernel" of four sixteenth notes that established a specific, rhythm, contour, and character. After opening the opera with a set of slow introductory chords, Pinsuti rapidly repeated this kernel eight times in sequence, starting quietly and then repeating each repetition at a higher pitch and volume, rocketing frantically upward; then he repeated the sequence on a contrasting chord (the dominant). Pinsuti used this familiar technique to introduce a short snippet of sound that he would later modify for dramatic effect.

The kernel lay in abeyance during the first five scenes: Bassanio wooed Portia to different musical themes; and even when Shylock first came onstage, harassed by the local rabble, Pinsuti held back. Once Shylock entered his home in Act 1, Scene 6, however, the composer revealed the four-note kernel to be a reflection of Shylock's inner thoughts. Pinsuti referenced it in several different, related forms to illustrate Shylock's rapid emotional shifts in his extended solo aria: introducing the aria using an elaborated version of the original rising sequence to establish Shylock's already agitated state; marking the moment when Shylock discovers his daughter's disappearance through a series of short variations on the sequence; illustrating Shylock's fury by restating the original sequence after he reads her note stating that she has left his household to become a Christian's wife; accompanying his subsequent rage; underscoring Shylock's rhetorical challenge to his daughter's abductor; and concluding Shylock's prayer for revenge, now fully transformed into a cascading series of arpeggiated notes.

The richly varied development of material in this scene, all based on the same musical idea, gives Shylock a flexible musical foundation and an idiosyncratic sound. This music might not mark "Jewishness" outright – in truth no music does. Yet Shylock's musical qualities resonate with what Ruth HaCohen has depicted as centuries-long practices of Jewish "noise" in opera, oratorio, and other forms of Western vocal music.[34] Pinsuti's use of these same musical conventions, denoting darkness and constant agitation, remain with Shylock throughout, attaching a series of negative stereotypes to his character's Jewish identity through the rest of the score.

Pinsuti also used music to connect Shylock's personal motivations with the communal voices of Venice's Israelites. In the same aria from Act 1, Scene 6, while Shylock reacts to his daughter's loss, he suddenly stops and asks for divine intervention "in an act of prayer." This significant intervention on Pinsuti's part goes unmentioned in the published libretto. Pinsuti's musical accompaniment changes at this moment to a slow, hymn-like series of chords as Shylock sings: "God of Jacob, return her to me; to come to the pardon of Jehova and of a father who is dying of grief." This musical texture establishes a "sound" of Jewish prayer that recurs twice – with different words – at important moments of the opera. At the start of Act 3, just before the trial scene, Shylock returns to his prayer as the Israelites gather, with Pinsuti once again reinterpreting Cimino's text. Using a similar sonic arrangement, Shylock's personal supplications begin to overlap with his co-religionists' prayers for divine assistance. Starting in unison with an organ accompaniment, the assemblage develops the earlier theme into modal-sounding four-part harmony that recalls pre-modern tonalities – now a fully realized indicator of Jewish difference that simultaneously marks Shylock's community and indicates his social inferiority. By the end of the opera, this same musical texture becomes the Israelites' theme. Together with Shylock, they sing the prayer while traveling into exile together. The musical richness of Shylock's role thus works in concert with his increased presence in the

34 HaCohen, *Music Libel*, esp. 1–16.

libretto to create a carefully constructed Jewish musical identity, linking both his religion and his fate to that of his entire community.

Reviews of the production provide little comment on the narrative and musical heightening of Shylock's role, or on the place of Jews in the world of the opera. Music critics commented generally on the quality of the production and its individual performances, rather than on the story and its musical characterizations. Its successful premiere in Bologna, however, led to subsequent performances in 1878 in Florence, Reggio Emilia, and Siena, each producing similarly positive notices. In retrospect, we can see that Pinsuti's decisions created a model for the opera-based Shylock through the choice of voice parts, the use of characteristic motifs, specific questions of Jewish musical representation, and the incorporation of additional Jewish characters and choruses to amplify Shylock's voice. As the first effort to set *The Merchant of Venice* to music, moreover, Pinsuti's opera brought sounds of Jews and Judaism deeply into the play's narrative, contributing to ongoing debates in Italy about the role of culture at the meeting point of nationalism, history, and religious pluralism.

Reynaldo Hahn, *Le Marchand de Venise* (1935)

German-language interest in *The Merchant* increased in the first decades of the twentieth century – exemplified by Prague-based stagings of Czech composer J.B. Foerster's opera *Jessika* in 1905 and 1935, and Max Reinhardt's high profile theater productions of the Shakespearean text in Berlin, Vienna, and Venice. In parallel, the resurgence of interest in operatic and theatrical representations of Jewish characters in France brought the play to prominence during key debates about "la question Juive." Four French-language operatic versions of *The Merchant of Venice* were staged between 1898 and 1940, closely coincident with the period of the Alfred Dreyfus trial (1894–1906) or with the rise of Nazi Germany: Pierre-Louis Deffès' *Jessica* (Tolouse, 1898), Henri de Saussine's *Le Marchand de Venise* (Paris, 1907; restaged Monaco, 1933), Fernand Brumagne's *Le Marchand de Venise* (Brussels, 1933; restaged 1940), and Reynaldo Hahn's *Le Marchand de Venise* (Paris, 1935; restaged 1938).[35]

[35] It appears that Deffès' opera was supposed to have been staged in 1889–90, but the producer reneged on the agreement, delaying the premiere until 1898 (*Gazette Artistique de Nantes* 6:167 [October 8, 1890], 6; *Le Ménestrel* 49:4 [December 24, 1882], 29 [re. Deffès' almost-completed opera in 1882]). On Saussine's 1933 performance, see *Le Ménestrel* 95:47 (November 24, 1933), 459. On Brumagne, see *Le Ménestrel* 102:8–9 (February 23, 1940), 38. On Foerster's 1935 performance, see *Le Ménestrel* 97:33–34 (August 16, 1935), 270.

The performance history of *La Juive*, one of the most frequently produced operas of the nineteenth century (which also included the Jewish father–daughter dyad made popular throughout Europe by Walter Scott's 1820 novel *Ivanhoe*) reinforces this pattern: it fell out of the Parisian repertoire after 1893, as a new round of debates about Jewish identity and character played themselves out on the French stage, only to return to Paris in 1933, around the same time as other French-language *Merchant of Venice* operas appeared in Monaco (de Saussine), Brussels (Brumagne), and Paris (Hahn).[36] A remarkable coincidence despite the number of official opera venues in the region, these revivals and programming choices occurred as tens of thousands of German-Jewish refugees fled to France, generating a public debate over immigration, specifically over the admission of Jewish immigrants.[37]

Within this context, Reynaldo Hahn's adaptation of *Le Marchand de Venise* – with libretto by French poet and playwright Miguel Zamacoïs – seemed particularly well-received. Hahn, known most favorably for his *Belle Epoque chansons*, was born in 1874 in Caracas to a Venezuelan-Catholic mother and a German-Jewish father (who later converted to Catholicism).[38] Hahn moved with his parents to Paris when he was three years old; there he studied piano and composition at the Paris Conservatoire, and eventually found his way into the salon circles of the intelligentsia. By 1898, he had become a celebrated musician and composer. Hahn's musical output comprised a large number of vocal works, including operettas and operas, and he became a sought-after conductor. His literary career included a turn as chief music critic of *Le Figaro* starting in 1934, in addition to the publication of several volumes of criticism and memoirs. Although he seemed to have had no direct relationship with Jewish cultural circles of the post-Dreyfus period, in 1940 Hahn left German-occupied Paris for Toulon and then Monaco; he did not return to Paris until 1945, though some of his own works were staged there,

36 For more on Jewish stage representations in France during this period, see Chantal Meyer-Plantureaux, *Les Enfants do Shylock ou l'Antisémitisme sur Scène* (Paris: Éditions Complexe, 2005).

37 See Vicki Caron, *Uneasy Asylum: France and the Jewish Refugee Crisis, 1933–1942* (Palo Alto, CA: Stanford University Press, 2002), 1–116.

38 For more on Hahn's life, see Bernard Gavoty, *Reynaldo Hahn: Le Musicien de la Belle Époque* (Paris: Editions Buchet/Chastel, 1976); Jacques Depaulis, "Un Compositeur Français Sous-Estimé: Reynaldo Hahn." *Fontes Artis Musicae* 53:4 (2006), 263–308; Philippe Bley, "Reynaldo Hahn." MGG Personentheil v. 8, cols. 402–6; Mario Milanca Guzman, *Reynaldo Hahn: Caraqueño* (Caracas: Biblioteca de la Academia Nacional de la Historia, 1989); Thea Sikora Engelson, "The *Mélodies* of Reynaldo Hahn" (PhD dissertation, University of Iowa, 2006), esp. 11–41.

Photo G.-L. Manuel Frères.

M. ANDRÉ PERNET
(rôle de Shylock).

FIGURE 49 André Pernet as Shylock, in Hahn's *Le Marchand de Venise* (*Le Ménestrel*, March 29, 1935, 3).
Courtesy of the Bibliotheque National de France.

seemingly against his will, in the 1942–43 season.[39] There is no evidence that he was ever persecuted for either his Jewish background or his homosexuality, and his personal ethno-religious identity remains ambiguous. Nonetheless, though baptized and raised as a Catholic, the racial norms imposed by the Nazis and their French collaborators forced him to experience some awareness of his Jewish background during a significant part of his professional life – at the very least in his concern for other members of his family.[40] How much that awareness influenced the characterization of Shylock in *Le Marchand de Venise* is a matter of conjecture.

According to biographer Bernard Gavoty, Hahn first developed his idea for an opera based on *The Merchant of Venice* in about 1917, while he was a soldier on active duty during World War I.[41] Concentrated work on the opera, however, did not appear to take place until about 1933, the year Hitler came to power in Germany, and when *La Juive* returned to the Parisian opera stage. The resulting musical piece – the product of a mature composer – was relatively conservative by contemporary compositional standards, but received acclaim by both audiences and critics for its classical Mozartean format and its adherence to French *chanson* traditions.

The Parisian opera tradition, for which Hahn wrote *Le Marchand de Venise*, carries with it a number of conventions; the emphasis on music and the opulence of the sets leave little space for complex plot development, numerous scene changes, involved dialogue, and frequent entrances and exits. Zamacoïs, writing his first opera libretto, described these restrictions with bemusement:

> The task [of writing the libretto] isn't made easier by situating in the four fixed sets of the theater [as per opera convention] multiple scenes that pass, return, disappear again, like the turning pages of a picture book. Fortunately, the musical part allows for great boldness and casual ingenuity, and one is in good sacrilegious company in the repertoire of opera and comic opera, including *Faust*, *Carmen*, and *Manon Lescaut*, to name but three famous adaptations among many others.[42]

39 Engelson "*Mélodies* of Reynaldo Hahn," 38–39.

40 Ibid., 38.

41 Gavoty, *Reynaldo Hahn*, 233.

42 Miguel Zamacoïs, *Pinceaux et Stylos* (Paris: Librarie Arthème Fayard, 1948), 382; "La Tâche n'est pas aisée de situer dans les quatre décors fixes d'un théâtre ces multiple tableaux qui passent, reviennent, disparaissent encore, comme les pages tournées d'un album d'images. Heureusement, la pièce musicale autorise les grandes audaces et l'ingéniosité désinvolte, et l'on est en bonne compagnie sacrilège dans le répertoire de l'Opéra et de l'Opéra-comique, à côté des *Faust*, des *Carmen* et des *Manon Lescaut*, pour ne citer que trois adaptations fameuses parmi tant d'autres." My translation.

Consequently, Zamacoïs simplified plot and locations. The resulting adaptation, comprising five scenes over three extended acts, eliminated several minor characters (including the Gobbos, Salanio, and Salarino). Like Pinsuti, however, Zamacoïs emphasized the role of Shylock, and largely preserved the climactic trial scene. Act 1 focused on Shylock's loan to Antonio, followed by Jessica's flight and Shylock's enraged reaction to it. Act 2, set in Belmont, contained most of the play's other subplots, including all of the casket scenes, Bassanio's successful suit of Portia, and the news of Antonio's impending trial. Act 3 trial, the opera transitioned into a final reunion scene with the lovers.

This radical consolidation brought Shylock's story to the foreground, giving him significant latitude to comment on the action around him. Virtually eliminating the Venetian ghetto, Hahn placed Shylock's house midstage (on a "main thoroughfare") in order to centralize Shylock and Jessica's several entrances and exits. Zamacoïs, moreover, accentuated Shylock's prominence and power by giving him two substantial soliloquies that Hahn would transform into "rage arias." In one he railed against Christians just after he made the contract with Antonio in Act 1; in the other, he lamented his ruined state after the trial scene in Act 3.

Hahn's musical treatment of the libretto enhanced the importance of Shylock and the other Jewish characters in the opera, including Tubal, Jessica, and Shylock's supporters at the trial. Like Pinsuti, Hahn shaped Shylock's arias by composing music that marked his difference from the Christian population. Rather than orientalizing Shylock musically, as, for example, Halévy did by giving Eléazar augmented second intervals in *La Juive*, Hahn kept Shylock within the margins of Western harmonic language, reserving augmented seconds for the princes of Morocco and Arragon.[43] In so doing, Hahn reinforced Shylock's presence as an "internal exotic," an integral, if intrinsically marginal, part of Venetian (*qua* European) society.

A comparison between the 1935 published score and the separately published libretto suggests that Hahn also used his prerogative as composer to blunt some of his librettist's more anti-Jewish representations.[44]

[43] It is tempting to speculate that Hahn's geographical schema of musical exoticism emerged around 1911, when he was inspired by "the music of the muezzin and the exotic dances" during a trip to Algeria (Engelson, "*Mélodies* of Reynaldo Hahn," 27).

[44] All references to the opera's music come from the work's piano/vocal score (Reynaldo Hahn, *Le Marchand de Venise: Opera* [Paris: Heugel, 1935]); and references to the published libretto come from Miguel Zamacoïs, *Le Marchand de Venise* (Paris: Heugel, 1935). Zamacoïs, at least in hindsight, knew that his words would be changed to fit the composer's musical ideas, though he felt Hahn more reasonable on this front than other

In the first scene of Act 1, for example, Zamacoïs' libretto has Gratiano describe Shylock as "the Devil's masterpiece"; in the musical score, however, Hahn reduced the phrase to simply "a masterpiece," and then set the words to an ironic, higher-pitched "off-rhythm" duplet figure – thus blunting both the phrase and its delivery. Changes of this sort, peppered throughout the opera, illustrated the composer's ability to alter meaning through editorial control and musical commentary.

Hahn made the most extensive textual changes to Zamacoïs' libretto in his setting of the trial scene in Act 3. In theatrical productions, according to Charles Edelman, Shylock did not regularly appear at the trial in the company of other Jews until the early part of the twentieth century.[45] Pinsuti and Cimino's 1873 opera included a chorus of Jews who serenaded Shylock immediately before the trial scene, and then reappeared after the trial; but Shylock remained alone during the trial itself. Notably, Josef Foerster, in Prague, took an interesting middle ground in his 1905 opera by having Shylock sing alone during the trial, silently supported by some "friends" (*Freunden*), according to a reference in the score. Zamacoïs apparently responded to the recent trend in theatrical staging by adding a trio of singing Jews to the trial scene, who heckled the Christians constantly throughout the proceedings.

Hahn's musical setting of this text and his approach to vocal characterization led to further transformations that emphasized the presence of Shylock's co-religionists in the trial scene and represented them more favorably than in the libretto. He wrote the three Jews as two basses and (perhaps for some vocal contrast) a tenor, but in order to produce a more balanced sound he also added higher voices – a pair of Venetians, who sang tenor. With the change in personnel came a change in tone and character. Whereas the Jews had nearly all the heckling lines in the published libretto, in the opera score Jews and Venetians exchanged barbs equally. Hahn, in fact, preceded the first barbs by the Jews with a line from a Venetian that did not appear in the published libretto: "Before anything else, I'd hang the plaintiff!"[46] These vocal and rhetorical tensions remained intact as six more Jewish basses and six more Venetian tenors joined in the exchange by the middle of the scene, leading to a sizeable

composers (Zamacoïs, *Pinceaux et Stylos*, 382–83). Hahn's minor adjustments probably represented the last stage of editing before the score was readied for performance and/or publication.

45 Charles Edelman, ed. *The Merchant of Venice*, Shakespeare in Production (Cambridge: Cambridge University Press, 2002), 212.

46 Hahn, *Le Marchand de Venise*, 300; "Avant toute chose je pendrais le plaignant!"

divided chorus that commented contentiously on the unfolding events. Hahn, in adding Venetian hecklers, not only provided a much more even distribution of vocal parts, but also placed the Jews in a more sympathetic light. While Zamacoïs depicted the Jews as bloodthirsty aggressors, Hahn put Jews and Venetians on the same rhetorical level, exchanging insults with each other as the trial progressed.

Like Pinsuti and Foerster, Hahn designated Shylock as a higher bass. Indeed, Hahn seemed to regard the bass register as specifically Jewish, for he set Shylock, his companion Tubal, and all but one of the nine other Jews called for in the trial scene as basses. Only three other characters in Hahn's opera were written as basses – Antonio (as a patrician character), the Duke (as royalty), and the Prince of Morocco (as exotic royalty). Hahn's decision to designate all of the Jewish male characters but one as bass parts reinforced a seemingly familial set of Jewish musical traits, thus providing a pointed commentary on the Jews' status as Others, musically ghettoized within the Venice of the opera, and by extension within contemporary Paris.

Hahn also followed the practice of giving each major character musical "themes" that further illustrated his or her qualities by means of Western music conventions. These themes, marking the character's presence and inner thoughts throughout the narrative, changed over time according to the character's actions and interactions. In Shylock's theme, Hahn used musical indications of tension and otherness that usually accompany villains, such as rapidly ascending chromatic runs, diminished and dissonant intervals, and frequent shifts to the minor mode whenever the character is mentioned.[47] Shylock's particular theme is first heard a full two scenes before he appears on stage, when Bassanio and Antonio resolve to approach Shylock for a loan, and knock at his door only to have his daughter Jessica answer. Later, when Shylock enters, the musical reference repeats, joining the music to its subject.

Le Marchand de Venise also uses Shylock's theme in his two "rage" arias, which further humanize the character by providing deep insight into his motivations. The first aria, "Je le hais" ("I hate him"), takes place just after Shylock's deal with Antonio, and catalogues in detail the abuses perpetrated by Christendom on him and the Jews:

[47] Ruth HaCohen has argued that this same set of musical ideas is also associated with Jews in nineteenth-century European art music, where they are used to suggest a "sophisticated but distorted and degenerate kind of noise" (Ruth HaCohen, "Between Noise and Harmony: The Oratorical Moment in the Musical Entanglements of Jews and Christians," *Critical Inquiry* 32 [Winter 2006], 258).

I hate him for the hatred that his people have toward mine!
I hate him for the invisible chain that we carry,
And I hate him for it is impossible to pardon those ancient insults!
I hate him for his happy race,
For his generous nature which always rivals my roughness!
I hate him for the promised lands that we never attain
And for those [lands] they've conquered and will leave to their descendants.
For our mass exoduses from state to state for thousands of years
For our births and deaths, scattered over so many foreign lands!
For the new days awaited in vain!
For the false prophesies that keep our arms ever extended toward elusive homelands.
I hate him for walking about joyfully without ever having pity for the sad fate of millions of Hebrews.
I hate him for all the attacks that have wiped out our impotent rages.
For all that they've thrown at us from age to age
For being kicked, for being spit at …
I hate them for their rudeness
And above all, above all for this suspicion that never, ever subsides!
Ah! I hate them! I hate them! [Spoken:] I hate them![48]

Throughout the aria, Hahn develops Shylock's musical theme in several ways: it appears with differing tempi and instrumentation, it is fragmented into shorter sequences of chromatic motion, and it is eventually inverted and superimposed upon itself, creating a classic musical tension through contrary motion. As preserved on a recording made by Hahn's original Shylock, André Pernet (Figure 49), Shylock builds this rage to climax on one of the highest notes in the bass range (an F-sharp above middle C), held above a series of rapidly crossing chromatic lines in the orchestra. What had begun as a pronouncement against Antonio expands at the end to a grudge against all Christians, and Pernet ends the piece by literally

[48] Hahn, *Le Marchand de Venise*, 75–81; "Je le hais pour la haine que les siens ont pour les miens! / Je le hais pour la chaîne invisible que nous portons. / Et je le hais pour les pardons impossibles des trop vieux affronts! / Je le hais pour sa race heureuse. Pour sa nature généreuse / Toujours en rivalité avec notre âpreté! / Je le hais pour les terres promises que jamais nous n'atteindrons / Et pour celles qu'ils ont conquises et qu'à leurs fils ils lègueront. / Pour nos exodes en troupeaux parmi les états millénaires. / Pour nos berceaux, pour nos tombeaux, disséminés sur tant de terres étrangères! / Pour les jours nouveaux vainement attendus! / Pour les menteuses prophéties qui font nos bras toujours tendus / Vers d'insaisissables patries! / Je le hais d'aller dans la joie / Sans que jamais les apitoie le sort si douloureux de millions d'hébreux. / Je le hais pour tous les outrages qu'ont essuyé nos impuissantes rages. / Pour tout ce qu'on nous décocha d'âge en âge / De coups de pieds et de crachats. / Je les hais pour leur insolence / Et surtout, surtout, pour cette méfiance / Qui ne désarme jamais, jamais! / Ah! Je les hais, je les hais! / [parlé:] Je les hais!" All translations of lyrics from this opera are mine.

growling the phrase "Je les hais!" ("I hate them!") completing his emotional trajectory in a space beyond singing.[49]

Shylock sings his second aria, "Depouillé!" ("Stripped!"), after he has left the trial, fleeced and humiliated. Alone on stage, in front of the curtain (presumably drawn to conceal a set change), Shylock storms through his feelings of despair and his ignominious return to servitude.[50] Once again, elements from Shylock's theme appear throughout the aria, particularly the noticeable rising and falling chromatic lines. After Shylock finishes the aria, again ending with a spoken word (this time "Depouillé"), Tubal meets him and offers to follow him on his travels. Shylock refuses: "I go because, unfortunately, I must live ... to the house of a customer that I had forgotten – a shopkeeper – to lend what remains [of me]." As he utters these lines, his theme repeats itself more and more slowly until it grinds to a halt.[51] After his final words – "at a hundred percent interest" – a rapid minor-key coda completes the act. In the opera, Shylock is never seen, or heard from, again.[52]

But Hahn's Shylock was, in fact, heard from again. *Le Marchand de Venise* was revived several times in France, including a 1938 production conducted by Hahn himself, a 1947 production at the Paris Opéra-Comique, and additional Parisian performances in 1949, 1950, and 1978 (the last of which has been partially preserved in a live recording). In the United States, the work received an "American premiere," possibly of selections only, at a Carnegie Hall benefit for the New York Shakespeare Festival in April 1958. A second bare-bones "American premiere" was mounted by New York's Opera Manhattan in December 1993–January 1994; and a third "North American premiere" with full orchestral accompaniment and staging was put on by the Oregon-based Portland Opera in 1996.[53] The theatrical concept underlying this last version, which perhaps represents the high-water mark of American interest in Hahn's music, complemented the musical themes by having the entire show mounted on a stage in the shape of a six-pointed star, by costuming the Jews in

[49] A copy of this recording can be found on *Reynaldo Hahn: Recordings 1908–35* (1997; Pearl CD 1165392), track 26.

[50] Hahn, *Le Marchand de Venise*, 376–85.

[51] Hahn, *Le Marchand de Venise*, 387–88; "Je vais ... Parce qu'il faut ... malgré tout, vivre / Chez un client que j'oubliais ... un commercant, / Prêter mon reste."

[52] Ibid., 388; "A cent pour cent."

[53] "NY Shakespeare Festival Benefit." [Advertisement] *New York Times*, March 23, 1958, X8; Alan Kozinn, "Review/Opera: Lush French Rarity, Via Shakespeare," *New York Times*, January 5, 1994; Derek M. Mills, Review of Portland Opera Production of *Le Marchand de Venise*, *Opera News*, February 22, 1997, 44.

black suits and the Venetians in white suits; and by costuming Jessica at first in black pants with a white blazer, and at by the end of the show in a white dress.[54] These choices show how American interest in this opera appears to parallel contemporary views of the play as an artistic vehicle for addressing the historical issues of Jewish identity.

If Hahn indeed intended *Le Marchand de Venise* as an answer to the "Jewish Question" in 1935, his efforts went largely unnoticed. None of the contemporary opera reviews I found discussed the opera's relevance to the place of Jews in contemporary society. More typical was the reviewer for *La Revue Musicale*, who, while critical of the opera as a whole, admired Shylock's characterization. As played by Pernet, he wrote, Shylock had displayed "a character of extraordinary pathos. He completely disregards [the libretto of] Mr. Zamacoïs, he stays with Shakespeare, and this agonizing figure savages Mr. Reynaldo Hahn's dream of an operetta/opera."[55] Perhaps, as Diana Hallman noted in her account of *La Juive*'s reception a century earlier, Hahn's characterization of Shylock, and Jews more generally, came across not as a political statement but rather as a purely aesthetic construction of difference in French interwar society.[56] That presentation of difference appeared to evoke a *frisson* of pathos in an otherwise pleasant evening. In a season of more familiar operas at the Paris Opera House in 1935, *Le Marchand de Venise* may have represented another relatively successful variation on the conventions of the genre – a mildly exotic fantasy providing opportunities for the musical exploration and expression of intense human emotions.

Mario Castelnuovo-Tedesco, *Il Mercante di Venezia/The Merchant of Venice* (1956)

Unlike Pinsuti, who was not Jewish, or Hahn, whose connections to Judaism were largely determined by others, Mario Castelnuovo-Tedesco (1895–1968) openly acknowledged his Jewish identity in both his life and his work. Born in Florence, he trained at the Institute Musicale Cherubini and at the Liceo Musicale di Bologna, premiering his first opera in 1926

[54] As of April, 2015, approximately fifty minutes of video excerpts from the 1996 Portland Opera production can be found on YouTube using the search terms "Le marchand de Venise" and "R. Hahn."

[55] H. Prunières, Review of *Le Marchand de Venise*, *La Revue Musicale* 16:155 (April, 1935), 283–84; my translation. See also Gilbert Chase, "Paris," *Musical Times* 76:1107 (May, 1935), 462.

[56] Diana R. Hallman, *Opera, Liberalism, and Antisemitism in Nineteenth Century France* (New York: Cambridge University Press, 2002).

and developing a promising compositional career. Castelnuovo-Tedesco fled fascist Italy in 1939, shortly after his works were banned from public performance. He eventually settled in Los Angeles, where he composed music for Hollywood films and gained a reputation for his works for classical guitar. From 1925, when he published his series of piano pieces "Le Danze del Re David," Jewish themes figured in his creations. In the United States, he composed religious services, arrangements of Sephardic songs, and a Jewish-themed oratorio on *The Song of Songs*, among other works.

Castelnuovo-Tedesco worked extensively with Shakespeare's texts throughout his life: he set dozens of Shakespeare's songs to music in the 1920s, created musical settings of thirty-five sonnets in 1944–45, and composed overtures for eleven of Shakespeare's plays, including *The Merchant of Venice*, between 1930 and 1953. During a visit to Florence in the summer of 1954, he created libretti for his own operatic versions of *All's Well that Ends Well* and *The Merchant of Venice*.[57] At his publisher's recommendation, he started to work on the former libretto; but at the end of 1955, a friend informed him of an opera composition contest sponsored by the Davide Campari Company, the winner of which would be performed at La Scala opera house. Finding *All's Well* "too small for a big theater like La Scala," Castelnuovo-Tedesco turned instead to *The Merchant*.[58]

Rather than starting from a new set of ideas, Castelnuovo-Tedesco, pressed for time, drew from his 1933 concert overture to *The Merchant of Venice*. That fifteen-minute instrumental work began with what he later called his "Shylock theme," a musical passage that features the augmented second – a musical interval that he uses as a powerful indicator of ethnic difference (Figure 50).[59] Castelnuovo-Tedesco employs this interval twice in a rapid five-note run at the start of the theme (once going up, once going down), then adds an octave leap and a chromatic descending figure, followed by another dissonant leap downward, and a series of irregular quintuplet and septuplet runs (i.e. a five- or seven-note sequence in single beat) to complete a veritable catalog of musical indicators of otherness.

His frequent and forceful use of the theme throughout the overture, in contrast with a more conventional-sounding "theme for the Venetians,"[60]

[57] Nick Rossi, "A Tale of Two Countries: The Operas of Mario Castelnuovo-Tedesco," *Opera Quarterly* 7:3 (1990), 102. Rossi's article offers substantial additional detail about the creation of *Il Mercante di Venezia*.

[58] Mario Castelnuovo-Tedesco, *Un Vita di Musica* (Florence: Cadmo, 2005), 589–90, my translation; Rossi, "A Tale of Two Countries," 105.

[59] Castelnuovo-Tedesco, *Un Vita di Musica*, 594.

[60] Ibid.

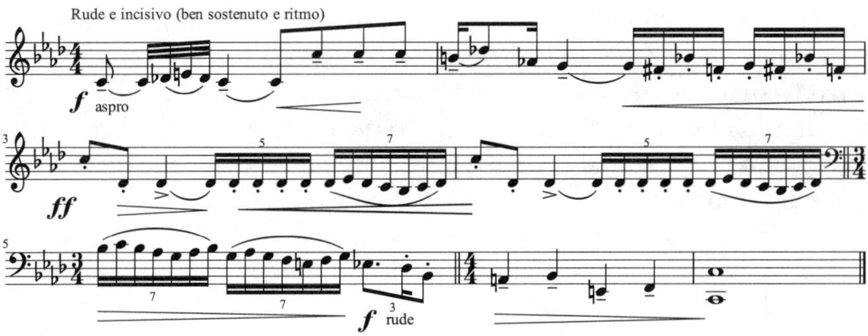

FIGURE 50 Shylock theme from the overture of Mario Castelnuovo-Tedesco's 1956 opera *Il Mercante di Venezia/The Merchant of Venice* (Milan: G. Ricordi, [1961], 1).

established Shylock as a character intrinsically and unapologetically out of step with the majority culture, maintaining his separate identity from the Venetian population around him.

The composer made a few dramaturgical changes in the play: he eliminated several of the minor characters from the libretto, based on Alfred de Vigny's 1830 French translation/adaptation of the Shakespearean original, and he credited Max Reinhardt's 1934 Venice production with his decision to transform Shylock's "My Daughter! My Ducats!" speech in Act 2, Scene 8, lines 15–17 from hearsay into one delivered directly by Shylock.[61] Despite these changes, perhaps more than any other composer, Castelnuovo-Tedesco attempted to remain as true as he could to the play's original language while still satisfying opera conventions. Although he condensed the libretto into three acts, and aimed for as few scene changes as possible, he culled his text from the play's original lines, to which he added his own Italian translation.

Musically, however, Shylock's theme controlled the work's structure: the first three and a half minutes of the 1933 overture, for example, became the overture for the new opera, while the last half of the 1933 work served, nearly note for note, to set the end of the opera's first act, which deals with Jessica's elopement, Shylock's discovery of her absence, and his subsequent rage.[62] Approximately one minute of material from

[61] Ibid., 591–92.

[62] This and all other references to the opera's content are based on the work's piano score: Mario Castelnuovo-Tedesco, *Il Mercante di Venezia/The Merchant of Venice* (Milan: G. Ricordi, [1961]).

the original overture became the opening music to Act 3, and a portion of its final section became Shylock's exit music ("Elegaico") after the trial. Castelnuovo-Tedesco created new material for the Belmont scenes in Act 2, interpolated material based on the overture to complete Acts 1 and 3, and he added the vocal parts to unify the work. While these additions all contributed to an organic whole, the opera's insistent recurrence of the Shylock theme throughout the first and third acts led some to feel Castelnuovo-Tedesco had created an uncomfortably negative interpretation of the character. In 1961 the composer defended his interest in the play, and by extension his musical portrait of the Jewish moneylender, explaining how Shylock reflected his own experience of trying to live on the fault line between Jewish and Italian worldviews:

> Many (especially amongst my own religion) believe that [*The Merchant of Venice*] is an anti-Jewish drama and were amazed that I, a Jew (having lived through the tragic period of racial persecution), would have chosen to set to music this work in which the protagonist – a Jew – comes to an unhappy end.
>
> I respond: It is precisely for this reason, because I am at the same time a Jew and an Italian! I have always thought that I could express, perhaps better than anyone else ... the double anxiety of the drama, for it is not anti-Semitic ... but rather it is a drama of the "misunderstanding" and "intolerance" of two diverse mentalities.[63]

As in previous *Merchant* operas, Castelnuovo-Tedesco set Shylock as a bass and Jessica as a lyric soprano, but he placed these characters in a world that resembled the historical Venice more than it did the imagined landscapes of operatic convention. Rather than softening or sentimentalizing the end of his opera, as did Pinsuti, or interpolating elaborate dramatic justifications of Shylock's behavior, as did Hahn, Castelnuovo-Tedesco instead stayed true to Shakespeare's hard-edged characters and plot within the stripped-down conventions of opera storytelling. As a self-identified Jew and an admirer of Shakespeare, Castelnuovo-Tedesco valued the play's tough-minded depiction of Shylock's plight, calling it "historically true and highly objective."[64] Having lived through World War II, he rejected portrayals that called for either sympathy or moral outrage in response to Shylock's treatment – two major strategies for staging the play or its operatic derivatives – in favor of objective insight into the problematics of Jewish life both in Shakespeare's time and his

[63] Castelnuovo-Tedesco, *Un Vita di Musica*, 590–91, translation by Rossi in "A Tale of Two Countries," 114–15.

[64] Castelnuovo-Tedesco, *Un Vita di Musica*, 591.

own. Jessica, for example, as Castelnuovo-Tedesco's music implies, ultimately assimilates, while her father remains an outsider.

In some ways, moreover, Castelnuovo-Tedesco sharpened his version of the opera to fit his philosophy: though keeping the trial scene mostly intact, he eliminates lines referring to Shylock's conversion to Christianity, which he considered not "appropriate to Shylock's pride or consistency."[65] And while his published score includes an obligatory final lovers' scene in Belmont, Castelnuovo-Tedesco makes it clear in his memoirs that he had wanted to end the opera with Shylock's exit after the trial.[66] Even with the lovers' final scene included, he undercuts its sentimentality with a final, fortissimo reprise of the first five notes of Shylock's theme, thereby reminding the audience to remain focused on a different story at the work's end.

The opera's performance history is curiously consistent with its tough-minded viewpoint. Although the opera won the competition for which it was entered, La Scala ultimately declined to produce it due to unexplained differences of opinion between the composer and the company. Instead, *Il Mercante di Venezia* had its only Italian performance at Florence's Maggio Musicale in May, 1961, and its sole American performance by the Pacific Coast Opera Company in Los Angeles' massive Shrine auditorium on 13 April, 1966.[67] While the score was published in 1961, the opera has existed without a voice since its one American production.

Conclusion

All four of these operas were well received in their times. Critics typically hailed these works' premieres as successes, and all enjoyed at least one subsequent performance in the short term. That most of these works then fell into obscurity tends to reflect the complexities and politics of opera production at least as much as it reflects the challenges of adapting *The Merchant of Venice* to an operatic form. Notably, these composers' engagement with anti-Semitism appears to have made the topic attractive

65 Ibid., 593.

66 Ibid., 593–94. The composer noted that: "Every time I had seen the play presented in the theater ... I had the impression that, after Shylock's exit, dramatic interest completely declines; and that the later scenes (with that annoying bickering about rings and the return to Belmont) were but a device to give the other characters a satisfying ending." Nonetheless, his wife convinced him to add the final scene so as not to stray too far from the original play.

67 Rossi, "A Tale of Two Countries," 113–16.

to contemporary companies looking to "resdiscover" challenging and relevant works. When viewed as a group, however, these operatic adaptations of Shakespeare's *The Merchant of Venice* present a deeper glimpse into the rich partnership music has held with one of Shakespeare's texts, providing valuable insights into the way each composer's musical language endowed one of Shakespeare's most controversial characters with a "Jewish" voice.

PART V

POSTSCRIPT

18

Shylock and the Arab–Israeli Conflict

Edna Nahshon

The Merchant of Venice is mostly relegated to the periphery of Israel's cultural field, as educational policy makers, presumably wishing to shield the country's youngsters from anti-Jewish stereotypes, marginalized the play within the educational system, placing *Julius Caesar*, *Macbeth*, and *King Lear* in the country's high-school English curriculum. The lack of familiarity with the actual text was comically depicted in Rafi Bukaee's 1986 Israeli film *Avanti Popolo*, which tells of two lost Egyptian soldiers who are trying to find their way home from the Sinai desert at the conclusion of the 1967 war. When the two dehydrated Egyptians meet a group of Israeli soldiers, it turns out that Haled, one of the Egyptians, is an actor who had been sent to the front shortly before he was to debut as Shylock in a production of *The Merchant of Venice*. Before he's given water he is summoned to verify his craft and proceeds to deliver Shylock's famous monologue "Hath not a Jew eyes ..." One of the Israeli soldiers exclaims, "What the hell is he talking about?," completely missing the subversive irony of the exchange. Another soldier exclaims, "He's got the roles mixed up. Give him something to drink!" The Shylock reference is used here to self-reflect on issues of Israeli/Jewish identity and on power relations between the Israeli-Jewish host society and its "other," i.e. the Arab.

Most Israelis have not read *The Merchant of Venice*, yet they are keenly aware of the derogatory uses of "Shylock," and the character's anti-Semitic baggage has led them to adopt a protective proprietorship of this archetypal character. This was particularly typical of older generations of European Jews who experienced anti-Semitic references to Shylock as collective stigmatization, and it has been enhanced by Israel's self-assumed commitment to protect Jews from attacks worldwide. Thus, for example, the obligation to safeguard the image of the Jew in the non-Jewish world was made explicit in a statement made at a press conference regarding the Habima Theater's 1954–55 repertory decisions. Meeting with journalists, the artistic director discussed the development of a new production of a Shakespeare play, which would be showcased during the troupe's upcoming European tour. Explaining that Habima's choice was between *King Lear* and *The Merchant of Venice*, he added, "If we decide to produce *The Merchant of Venice*, we'll need to put extraordinary efforts into the production, for as an Israeli theater we have a special responsibility to the world in regards to the Shylock character."[1] The theater opted to produce *King Lear*.

"Shylock" and *The Merchant of Venice* have been pressed into service by partisans of both Arabs and Jews. In 1971, the Argentinian writer, Jorge Luis Borges (1899–1986) came to Israel to receive the prestigious Jerusalem Prize. Borges, regarded by many as one of the most influential writers of the twentieth century, wrote much about Jewish topics and his stories "The Secret Miracle" (1943) and "Deutsche Requiem" (1946), penned during the war period, were amongst the earliest literary works to focus on the Holocaust. Impressed with the country's achievements and with its spectacular victory in the 1967 war, Borges wrote a poem titled "Israel." In it he hailed the new nation as "the man" who had been "condemned to be Shylock," had been "stoned, inflamed / and suffocated in lethal chambers," yet proved "an obstinate man who wants / to be immortal" and "now has returned to his battle / to the violent light of victory / beautiful like a lion at midday."[2]

While Borges celebrated Israel as the heroic resurrection of the persecuted Shylock, expressing Western civilization's monumental guilt over its treatment of European Jews, Arab culture came to see Shylock as the symbolic embodiment of the Zionist enterprise.[3] The first attempt to bring *The Merchant of Venice* to the attention of the Arab-speaking world was quite benign: a translation of the play in 1922 by Khalil Murtran (1872–1949), an important writer and translator of European drama, including *Othello*,

[1] "Habima's Plans for the Next Season" (in Hebrew), *Heruth*, September 7, 1954, 4.

[2] Jorge Luis Borges, "Israel," *Davar*, January 22, 1971. An English translation is available online: http://forward.com/culture/14781/borges-s-zionist-bent-newly-translated-poems-03025/.

[3] I wish to express my indebtedness to Professor Margaret Litvin of Boston University for helping me disentangle the history of *The Merchant of Venice* on the Arab-speaking stage, and for sharing the Arabic-language introduction with me. I am indebted to Professor Raymond Scheindlin of the Jewish Theological Seminary for reading the introduction to Mutran's text and commenting on it for me.

Macbeth, and *Hamlet*.[4] A Lebanese-Christian with deep roots in French culture, Mutran evidently based at least some of his work on French translations of *The Merchant*. His translation was prepared for a production at the Cairo Opera House where it was later restaged in 1936, during the second season of the Egyptian National Theatre, then run by Mutran himself. In his introduction to the published text of the play, Mutran did not express anti-Jewish sentiments. Indeed, in the 1920s, Egyptian literary critic Ibrahim Abdelkader el Mazini, who reviewed Mutran's translation critiqued the anti-Jewish sentiments of Shakespeare's original text.[5]

In the mid-1930s, however, allusions to Shylock took on a distinctly anti-Zionist tone. The link between the Zionist movement and Shylock was British-inspired. It was suggested by its use by opponents of the Balfour Declaration (1917), who accused the Zionists of demanding their "pound of flesh" by insisting that Britain adhere to the pledge of its official document and fulfill its obligation to facilitate the establishment in Palestine of a national home for the Jewish people. True, the "pound of flesh" phrase had been used in Britain's political discourse with relative frequency in various contexts to denote a lawful but nevertheless unreasonable recompense, but when applied to Jewish demands it projected a particularly disturbing undertone. Revisionist leader Vladimir (Ze'ev) Jabotinsky, head of the recently formed New Zionist Organisation, which was committed to free immigration and the establishment of a Jewish state, alluded to this usage when he testified on February 11, 1937 before the Peel Commission (1936–37), a British Royal Commission of Inquiry organized in response to the violent outbreak of the Arab revolt. Jabotinsky, a man-of-letters and an Anglophile, accused the British of failing to protect the Jewish community and preventing it from defending itself. In his long testimony he said:

> We are told very often: "What is meant by the Balfour Declaration promised in 1917 is clear, but since then the British people have honestly come to the conclusion that that they cannot do it." I deny it. I affirm they can; but when I am asked, when any Jew is asked: "What are the Jews going to pin us down to the promise and to say – you have promised the pound of flesh, pay us the pound of flesh?" Gentleman, here I answer you in the name of the most extreme of Zionist parties: "No!"[6]

[4] For a discussion of Mutran's Shakespeare translations see Sameh F. Hanna, "Decommercialising Shakespeare: Mutran's translation of 'Othello'," *Critical Survey* 19:3, *Arab Shakespeare* (2007) 27–54.

[5] Mutran visited Palestine in 1924 and made a direct reference to the Palestine issue in only one poem. See Khalid A. Suleiman, *Palestine and Modern Arab Poetry* (London: Zed Books, 1984), 50.

[6] "Evidence Submitted to the Palestine Royal Commission," by Mr. V. Jabotinsky, House of Lords, London, February 11, 1937, published by the New Zionist Organisation in Palestine, n.d., p. 20.

Jabotinsky's Shylock reference proved a public relations disaster. A not altogether sympathetic British press mangled and decontextualized the statement, reporting Jabotinsky as saying "You have promised us a pound of flesh; give us that pound of flesh."[7] Jabotinsky tried to explain that he was misquoted, that he meant the opposite, namely that the Zionists did not make any such demand, that what he had meant was that if the British were unable to fulfill their obligation he would not pin them to the letter of their written document but would ask them to return the mandate entrusted to them by the League of Nations.[8] His efforts at correction were of little avail. The damage had been done, and Shylock and his bond – the latter equated with the Balfour Declaration – were inducted into the imagery of the Arab–Zionist conflict. It was soon picked up by the Arab press. *Al-Liwa'*, a newspaper controlled by the staunchly anti-Zionist, future ally of Hitler, Mufti of Jerusalem, Hajj Amin al-Husseini, soon published an article titled "The Two Jews [:] Shylock and Fagin" that declared, "the world will not accept Shylock's bond and will not recognize your attempts to destroy our existence."[9] In the same vein, in March, 1939, following the failure of the London Conference organized by the British government to plan the future governance of Palestine, the popular Egyptian magazine *al-Thaqafa* printed a story titled "The Modern Shylock" in which Chaim Weizmann, who headed the Zionist delegation, was outlined as a modern incarnation of Shylock: "all he [Shylock] wanted was that pound of flesh, to cut off his enemy's body, and he will not renounce one penny of it … and that is also the position of the Zionist leaders regarding Palestine in the Twentieth century."[10]

Over the years, the Shylock trope has been invoked in the Arab media by commentators with different political agendas, ranging from leftists to Islamists. Following the 9/11 attacks, Ali Aqleh Ursan, chairman of the Arab Writers Association, was quoted by the British newspaper the *Guardian* on December 18, 2001:

> The covetous, racist, and hated Jew Shylock, who cut the [pound of] flesh from Antonio's chest with the knife of hatred, invades you with his money, his modern airplanes, his missiles, and his nuclear bombs. You must face a hard question: Do

[7] "The Palestine Commission," *Manchester Guardian*, February 13, 1937, 9.

[8] Ibid.

[9] "Iton Hamufti yotse mikeylav," *Davar*, February 14, 1937, 7.

[10] Anon., "Shaylock al-Hadith" [The Modern Shylock], *al-Thaqafa* 12 (1939), 41–44. Cited in Mark Bayer, "The Merchant of Venice, the Arab–Israeli Conflict, and the Perils of Shakespearean Appropriation," *Comparative Drama* 41 (Winter 2007): 477.

you, Christians and Muslims, wish to live, survive and fulfill your convictions? Or are you Abraham's bleating lambs on the threshold of the Jewish altar, who are led to be sent to the Hereafter?[11]

The moniker "Shylock" has been pinned on several Israeli prime ministers. The Polish-born Menahem Begin (1913–92) was particularly offended by its use during the peace talks between Egypt and Israel in 1978.[12] Begin visited Ismailia after President Anwar Sadat's historic trip to Jerusalem and at a point where the talks between the Israeli and Egyptian delegations were not going well, the semi-official Egyptian press responded by invoking anti-Semitic stereotypes, characterizing Begin as "Shylock the usurer who wanted a pound of flesh from his debtor."[13] Begin, highly sensitive to anti-Jewish slurs, was genuinely offended and demanded an Egyptian apology, which finally came, enabling the resumption of talks. In an interview with Robert McNeil, broadcast on January 25, 1978 on PBS television, Begin explained: "suddenly, during the negotiations, I am called a 'Shylock' in the Egyptian press. For three centuries, this word, 'Shylock' has been a catchword for all the anti-Semites, including the Nazis."[14]

Scholar Mahmoud Al-Shetawi explains the popularity of *The Merchant of Venice* in the Arab world as follows: first, he says, the play "has always been viewed in relation to the Arab–Jewish conflict," as "Arab writers ... see Shylock as the incarnation of Zionism"; second, because of the theme of usury, which is forbidden in Islam; and third, because "Jews are also depicted rather negatively in the Holy Quran; they are shown to be bearing grudges and hatred toward the Moslems."[15] He explains that "For many Arabs the play shows the vengeful nature of the Jew who has trapped his adversary into a legal pitfall in the hope of destroying him."

Just as Jewish writers adapted *The Merchant of Venice* to reflect their concerns, so too did Ali Ahmad Bakathir (1910–69) one of Egypt's

[11] Quoted in Linda Grant, "The Hate that Will Not Die," *Guardian* December 18, 2001. www.theguardian.com/world/2001/dec/18/september11.israel.

[12] Begin attended a Polish government high school, where he studied Latin and received a solid grounding in classical literature. He later studied Law at the University of Warsaw.

[13] "Begin Assails Cairo Press 'Hatred,'" *New York Times*, January 24, 1978, 1.

[14] For a full transcript of the interview see http://mfa.gov.il/MFA/ForeignPolicy/MFADocuments/Yearbook5/Pages/12%20Interview%20with%20Prime%20Minister%20Begin%20on%20Israel%20R.aspx.

[15] Mahmoud Shetywi, "The Merchant of Venice in Arabic," PDF posted online: *qspace.qu.edu.qa/bitstream/handle/ ... /029518-0015-fulltext.pdf? ... 3*. The spelling of the author's last name is slightly different in the two articles. For the sake of uniformity I use Al-Shetawi in the text, but use the appropriate spelling in citing each of the two essays.

leading playwrights of the 1940s and 1950s.[16] Bakathir, a strong supporter of Islam and Arab nationalism, devoted much of his work to "the Jewish problem," a theme that stood at the heart of six of his full-length plays as well as several short plays.[17] In 1944 Bakathir composed *Shylock Al-Jadeed* (The New Shylock). He explained the genesis of the play:

> It was during the year 1944, three years before *Al-Nakba* [in Arabic: the catastrophe, i.e. the establishment of the state of Israel]. This issue occupied my thoughts and I traced it anxiously either in newspapers or books. Once I read that the Zionist leader Jabotinsky had delivered speech … and hit the table with his hand saying "Give us the pound of flesh. We will never abandon the pound of flesh," indicating the homeland included in Balfour Declaration. Then I told myself, "Ah, I have found what I searched for … I will use it as the basic idea for my play." … The idea had been that neither a homeland for the Jew – nor a country – can be cut from the Arabic Palestine without shedding blood from the whole Arabic east. This was the same as the condition put by the Jew Shylock on the Venetian merchant Antonio. Shylock could never cut the pound of flesh from Antonio's flesh without shedding blood and thus killing him … Similarly, Balfour Declaration could never be fulfilled not only because it was inhuman for it meant executing the whole Arab nation instead of one person … but also because those who gave this promise do not own what they offer.[18]

Unlike the Shakespearean original, the Shylock in Bakathir's play fully dominates the play, his physical description evoking a few visual elements associated with David Ben-Gurion, then the head of the Jewish Agency and later the first prime minister of Israel. Bakathir's Shylock is the head of a Zionist organization whose objective is amassing Arab land with the help of donations from Zionist groups in Europe and America. He collaborates with the British, heads a terrorist organization, and uses the beautiful Rachel as a Zionist strumpet who serves as sexual bait to trap innocent Arab youths, leading them to sell their land so they can repay Shylock the money they had borrowed and then squandered on wooing her. The only positive Jew in the play is Abraham, a non-Zionist Jew, who

[16] Various spelling appear in English: Bā Kathīr, Ba-Kathir, Bakathir, Bakhteer, Ba-Kathir.

[17] Shetywi, "The Merchant of Venice in Arabic," 18. The full-length plays listed are *The Chosen People*, *The Lost Torah*, *God of Israel*, *The Worm and Snake*, *The Tragedy of Oedipus*, *The New Shylock*, and six of the playwright's thirteen short plays, collected under the title *Political Drama*.

[18] A. Bakhateer, *Fan Almarahia Min khal Tojarbi Alshakhia* (Cairo: Markrabat Mesr, 1958), 49. The English-language translation appears in Majed Nasser Al-tamimi and Omer Muhammad Basamad, "The Impact of Shakespeare on Ali Ahmed Bakatheer: An Analytic study of *Shylock Al-Jadeed* (*The New Shylock*)," (BA project, Hadhramout University for Science and Technology, Yemen, June, 2012), 10–11; http://www.bakatheer.com/english/The%20impact%20of%20%20Shakespeare%20on%20Ali%20Ahmed%20Bakatheer.pdf.

argues that Judaism is a religion only, that the concept of a Jewish nation is a myth, and that Jews have been historically persecuted because of their refusal to assimilate into the societies in which they live.

The heroes of the play are the Arabs, Muslim and Christian, who realize the imminent catastrophe Zionism presents and join the *mujahidin* (holy warriors) in the fight against the Jewish settlers. Bakathir devises an international tribunal that tries to find a just solution to the problem of Palestine. Shylock insists on his bond, invoking the "pound of flesh," and the British representative reminds him of the disastrous ending meted out to Shakespeare's Jew. The Zionists argue their case by bringing up their historical connection to the land and their suffering in the Holocaust, but to little avail. The judges propose to use the 1939 White Paper as a basis for a settlement, but both Jews and Arabs reject the offer.[19] A suggestion is made that Jews be given a place in Australia or Uganda, but Shylock declines, insisting that Jews are entitled by virtue of their historical connection to the land of Israel to establish their own state in Palestine. A surprise offer is suddenly announced by Faisal, a young Portia-like lawyer: the Arab League is willing to give the Zionists a chance to carry out their project, yet warns the Jews that taking up the offer would lead to their destruction. Seven years pass. The Zionist state proves a total failure, unable to survive amidst Arab opposition. The Zionists decide to dismantle it and assimilate into the Arab host society. Shylock, having seen his dream of sovereignty dissolved is brought to court humiliated and defeated. In court, the Arabs stipulate their conditions for absorbing the Jews: a ban of Zionist activities in Palestine and the criminalization of Zionism, payment of reparations to Palestinian Arabs, confiscation of all Zionist industries and properties, demolition of Tel Aviv, and the expulsion of all Zionists from the land.[20] The Jews are forced to accept these terms, and the play ends with a messenger announcing Shylock's suicide.

Post-1948 Arabic productions and adaptations of the Shakespeare original have tended to adopt the same anti-Zionist spirit. A 1964

[19] The White Paper of 1939 was a policy paper issued by the British government under Neville Chamberlain which recommended the creation of an independent Palestine governed by Palestinian Arabs and Jews in proportion to their numbers in the population by 1939. A limit of 75,000 Jewish immigrants was set for the five-year period 1940–44, consisting of a regular yearly quota of 10,000, and a supplementary quota of 25,000, spread out over the same period, to cover refugee emergencies. After this cut-off date, further immigration would depend on the permission of the Arab majority. Restrictions were also placed on the rights of Jews to buy land from Arabs. The proposal was approved by the House of Commons on May 23, 1939 by 268 votes to 179.

[20] Shetywi, "The Merchant of Venice in Arabic," 36.

production of *The Merchant of Venice*, conducted during Gamal Abdel Nasser's rule, stressed the "Arab–Jewish conflict," an approach that would later shift to an emphasis on the Israeli–Palestinian problem.[21] This was seen in Fahmi El-Kholi's post-Camp David 1978 production at Cairo University, revised and restaged in 1979–80 with an amateur cast at the Workers' Theatre at the Nasr Automobile Factory.[22] In an interview with Margaret Litvin, held in Cairo in December, 2011, El-Kholi reminisced about the production's "unbelievably warm reception" by enthused audience members some of whom came decked out with "Palestinian flags on their lapels and keffiyyehs on their heads." The production was done in modern dress. Shylock, who was wearing a black shirtdress "like an accountant or merchant," held a calculator as he was selling arms to different countries; the calculator was later used to determine "the pound of flesh," which was in fact a piece of land he will demand. The bare stage displayed two crosses, one made of olive branches topped by a Palestinian Keffiyyeh, from which droplets of blood would fall at key moments, because, El-Kholi explained, the Palestinians "were crucified on the olive branches of the peace accord." In the 1979–80 production Shylock was renamed Shylock-Yahu, referring to Benjamin Netanyahu, Israel's prime minister. Similarly, the contemporary Arab leadership was referenced when the actor playing Antonio followed Nasser's speech pattern in Act I, switching in Act II to an evocation of Sadat.

The play opened with a scene inspired by the Damascus blood libel affair (1840), when trumped up charges were made against some prominent Jews of Damascus, accusing them of murdering Father Thomas, a Catholic monk.[23] The scene began after the disappearance of a young

[21] Ibid., 10

[22] Margaret Litvin, "Fahmi Al-Kholi's Post-Camp-David 'Merchant of Venice,'" posted on December 5, 2011; http://margaretlitvin.com/category/merchant-of-venice/.

[23] The accusation was initially instigated by the newly arrived but powerful French consul, Ratti-Menton. The accused Jews were imprisoned and tortured. Several died, and one was forced to convert to Islam. The accusation led to a pogrom in which a Muslim mob attacked and pillaged the synagogue in the suburb of Jobar. Following an energetic European intervention, the nine prisoners who still remained alive of the original thirteen were released unconditionally. The abominable 1840 affair has retained some currency in the Arab world. The anti-Jewish accusations were published in the Egyptian government-controlled newspaper *Al Akhbar* in 2000 and again in 2001 in an article titled *The Last Scene in the Life of Father Toma*. In 2002, the Middle East Media Research Institute reported that some of the 1840 accusations emerged in a 1983 book *The Damascus Blood Libel (1840)* by the Syrian Minister of Defense, Mustafa Tlass. In 2007, Lebanese poet Marwan Chamoun, in an interview aired on Télé Liban, referred to the "slaughter of the priest Tomaso de Camangiano ... in 1840 ... in the presence of two rabbis in the heart of Damascus, in the home of a close friend of this priest, Daud Al-Harari, the head

Christian boy in Damascus, who was killed so his blood could be used for Passover *matza*. The gentile victims were seen hung upside down dripping blood, as a group of rabbis kneaded dough to the tune of *Hatikva*, the Israeli anthem.[24] The *matza* they ate, said El-Kholi, represented "the Arab lands from the Nile to the Euphrates." The production also featured a young woman called Palestine. Escaping her captors, the woman, dressed in a torn white dress, appealed for help from her fiancé Yasser (Arafat) and her big brother (Egypt), both of whom fail to rescue her. The 1967 defeat in the Six Day War was represented by "14 men lying around sleeping with model planes balanced on trays on their bellies; Shylock fished for these planes with a fishing rod, and when he caught one, it blew up."

El-Kholi discarded most of the Shakespearean text with the exception of parts of the Antonio–Shylock deal and the trial scene. Textual insertions included recordings of UN and Arab summit meetings, historical documents, and Sadat's pro-peace speeches. Quotes taken from Israeli politicians and the Israeli press were delivered by actors dressed as rabbis and sitting on toilets which they flushed after each one-liner. In both productions the trial scene took place at the United Nations, with the Duke representing the organization's Secretary-General. The 1979–80 stage production also included the dome of the Al-Aqsa mosque in Jerusalem, with fourteen men chained to it by ropes, coming off different sides (Litvin notes that the use of ropes is a recurrent element in El-Kholi's scenography), which El-Kholi meant to be interpreted as the Arab world's umbilical cords.

In 2007, Nehad Selaiha reviewed a new production of *The Merchant of Venice* for the Egyptian semi-governmental, English-language *Al-Ahram Weekly*.[25] The play was produced for the Egyptian National Theatre Festival and directed by Galal El-Sharqawi, then working with the Young Masrah Al-Fann Company. The production was done in the same anti-Israeli vein as its predecessors, but Selaiha was unsympathetic to this approach, faulting the director for taking the text "by the throat" and squeezing into it "a ready-made conception," by deleting parts, rewriting entire sections, and "padding up" the play with song and dance

of the Jewish community of Damascus. After he was slaughtered, his blood was collected, and the two rabbis took it." A fictional novel, *Death of a Monk*, based on the affair, was published in 2004.

[24] This is a reference to the 1840 Damascus blood libel discussed in footnote 23.

[25] For a review by Nehad Selaiha of pro-Palestinian and anti-Israel Arab theater production, including El-Kholi's, see http://weekly.ahram.org.eg/Archive/2001/526/cu2.htm.

numbers.[26] The play was chosen, she explained, with an eager eye to popular success, as "Any show that makes a show of intransigent opposition to any peace with Israel … has vast publicity potential and fat commercial value." It was done, she writes, to woo audiences and exploit Islamist sensibilities. She disliked that the production "consistently negatively stressed" the Jewishness of Shylock, who was portrayed as a thickly bearded dark-clad figure "ranting and raving and waving his clenched fists" like a parody of a nineteenth-century villain. His sung delivery of "The villainy you teach me I will execute; and it shall go hard but I will better the instruction," took place against the backdrop of the Al Aqsa mosque, an image that struck Selaiha as inadvertently ironic, as if mocking the militantly Islamist Hamas. She wrote: "To force the Arab–Israeli struggle on this play, using the ugly history of anti-Semitism in Christian Europe to bolster the Arab argument, and hauling in Al-Aqsa mosque as a rallying cry for an Islamic holy war against Jews, rather than the state of Israel, does more damage than good to the just cause of the Palestinians and their lawful rights."[27]

She concluded with the following statement:

> The production worked best when the play was left alone and the actors delivered their lines simply, without resort to forced interpretation; it was then that the play's moral complexity and deeper meaning, relevant to any age, particularly now, in the shadow of economic globalization, the alliances of the rich states, of money, power and the law, the marginalization of minority cultures and the persecution of immigrants, not to mention the recent, deplorable inner strife in Palestine, were allowed to surface and subtly intrude upon one's consciousness.[28]

While Selaiha's political views are clear, she objects to a coarsely partisan rendering of the play on the grounds that it would actually debase the cause she espouses. She assumes that if the play were "left alone … without resort to forced interpretation," the audience would be subtly influenced to see its relevance to the Palestinian cause, among other issues commonly associated with a Third World political agenda. There is no such thing, however, as a production which "leaves the play alone" and allows the actors to "deliver … their lines simply without resort to forced interpretation." At issue is really the meaning of the word "forced," or rather the degree to which an interpretation is or is perceived to be "forced." *The Merchant of Venice*, and its various spin-offs, can be subtly

[26] Nehad Selaiha, "A Cloak and Dagger Shylock"; http://weekly.ahram.org.eg/Archive/2007/852/cu1.htm.

[27] Ibid.

[28] Ibid.

or coarsely interpreted to emphasize Shylock's villainy or humanity, as is demonstrated in the contributions to this volume. In the light of these essays, the assumption that the play, or any play, has a "deeper meaning ... relevant to any age," a single universal meaning, seems unwarranted. What her comment unwittingly reveals is that all Egyptian or Arab productions and spin-offs of the play, like those in which Jewish theater artists were involved, construct the meaning of the play in the process of interpretation, even when they claim to allow the play to speak for itself.

Index